F
H36    Hellman, Aviva.
              To touch a dream.

DATE                        ISSUED TO

F
H36    Hellman, Aviva.
              To touch a dream.

## Temple Israel Library
### Minneapolis, Minn.

————

Please sign your full name on the above card.

Return books promptly to the Library or Temple Office.

Fines will be charged for overdue books or for damage or loss of same.

# To Touch A Dream

A NOVEL

## Aviva Hellman

DONALD I. FINE, INC.
NEW YORK

Library of Congress Cataloging in Publication Data
Hellman, Aviva.
To touch a dream.
I. Title.
PS3558.E4764T6 1989 813'.54 87-81423
ISBN 1-55611-055-3
Manufactured in the United States of America
10 9 8 7 6 5 4 3 2 1


DESIGNED BY IRVING PERKINS ASSOCIATES

This novel is a work of fiction. Names, characters, places and
incidents are either the product of the author's imagination or
are used fictitiously. Any resemblance to actual events, locales,
organizations or persons, living or dead, is entirely coincidental
and beyond the intent of either the author or publisher.

*In memory of my husband*
*Yehuda Hellman*

# THE DANZIGER FAMILY TREE

**MARUCIA–MAREK**

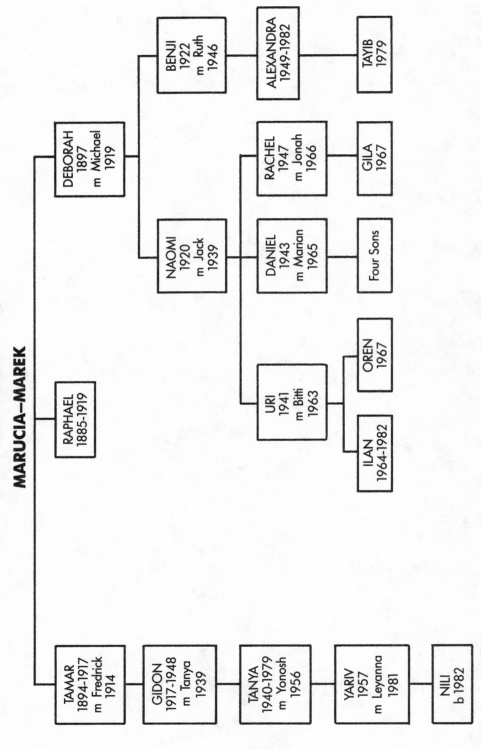

# Part I

# CHAPTER ONE

---

DEBORAH, standing on the sandy beach, looked up at Tamar and Raphael mounted on their horses. Her sister, erect and poised, was trying to hide her excitement about the pending race, with little success. Her face was flushed and her blue eyes were sparkling. She had discarded her chic riding skirt in favor of an old pair of riding pants, and the delicate riding boots were replaced by an old pair of jodhpurs. Her starched riding shirt was unbuttoned at the neck and her long blond hair was hidden beneath a worn beret. She looked like a slender young boy, rather than the elegant eighteen-year-old daughter of the illustrious Danziger family. In contrast, her brother was a picture of the perfect country gentleman. A broad-shouldered man with reddish blond hair, chiseled features and deep-set blue green eyes, he was staring down at her with concern.

"Are you sure you'll be all right?" he asked.

"Of course I will," Deborah said with exaggerated assurance. "Besides, you won't be that long."

"We're only going to ride as far as the castle and then we'll turn right back," Tamar interjected, her impatience barely disguised. "As a matter of fact, we'll never be out of your sight."

"I'll be just fine," Deborah said with greater confidence as she reached down and patted Blackie, the cocker spaniel who was nudging at her skirt.

As the figures of the riders grew smaller, the smile left her face and a look of fear crept into her eyes and she forced herself to look over at the medieval castle, which marked the finishing line of the first part of the race. A large fortress jutting out into the sea, it had always frightened her. Now she stared at it, trying to understand her fear of it. It had been part of her scenery all of her life, yet she had never been able to conquer the feeling that it was haunted. Even as she stared at it, it seemed to move and take on ominous, threatening shapes. At that particular moment it looked like a ferocious, snarling lion.

She tore her eyes away from the frightening structure and with a last glance at Raphael and Tamar, who were now mere specks in the distance, she turned her back on them and scanned the desolate coastline.

Although it was mid-afternoon in late September, the heat of the day still lingered. The blazing sun, edging its way toward the horizon, had not lost its ferocity as it shone down on the blue waters of the Mediterranean, causing a steamy mist to rise from it. Her eyes wandered across the desolate shore. The reflection of the sun on the white sand hurt her eyes and Deborah looked up at the cloudless sky. There was no hint of the rain so sorely needed in Palestine after the long dry summer. She squinted, trying to catch sight of the Haifa bay in the distance. A large steamer was anchored off shore, bobbing gently in the waters, its chimney emitting small puffs of smoke which quickly disappeared into the air. She turned her attention to the sprawling range of Mount Carmel, which seemed to rise up from the bay and stretch across the Eastern sky. The mountains looked bare and parched, relieved by an occasional orange grove, some vineyards and a few wilted olive trees. Quickly she traced the outline of the sunlit mountain peaks and shadowy valleys and tried to locate the village of Bet Enav, which was nestled in one of those darkened valleys. Finally she caught sight of the small patch of a red shingled roof with a window below its eaves. It was the attic window of the Danziger house, and seeing her home, she felt better.

Sighing contentedly, she threw one last look in the direction of Tamar and Raphael, and removing her riding boots, Deborah ran toward the water's edge. The tiny waves caressing her bare feet sent a pleasant sensation through her. Blackie, who had been romping around, came toward her, wagging his tail playfully. She picked up a stick and threw it in the direction of the Haifa bay, determined not to keep spying on Raphael, Tamar and the dreaded castle. Blackie retrieved it and Deborah continued the game for several minutes. But finally, unable to sustain her brave demeanor, she turned to look for Raphael and Tamar.

They were no longer in motion, indicating that they had reached their destination. They were obviously resting up before returning and Deborah wondered what they were talking about. A twinge of envy ran through her. She knew Raphael loved her, but she also knew that he loved Tamar more. He certainly had greater respect for Tamar. She could not fault him for that. Firstly, Tamar was three years older than she was, but that was not the only reason. Tamar was so clever, so brave, so sure of herself. She could never compete with Tamar on any level. The last thought troubled her and she shook her head angrily. She loved her sister and there were no reasons for comparisons.

Just then, Deborah saw a cloud of sand rise up around them. In spite of herself, she breathed a sigh of relief. They were on their way back. Blackie began to bark, unhappy at being neglected, and Deborah was about to lean over and pick up the stick again when she realized that Tamar and Raphael were not the only riders coming toward her. Two other riders, dressed in flowing Arab robes billowing in the wind like enormous wings, were galloping behind them. They seemed to have materialized out of nowhere, but Deborah was convinced they had come out of the monstrous, evil castle.

As the four riders drew closer, she noted that one of the strangers was a vision in white and was riding a white horse. The other was dressed in black and riding a black horse.

Paralyzed with fear, she watched as the white-clad Arab overtook both Raphael and his own riding companion and was rapidly edging toward Tamar. Terrified as she was, Deborah could not help but note that Raphael, although a brilliant horseman, was making little effort to overtake him. It made no sense. Raphael would never expose Tamar to danger, yet he seemed to be leaving his sister to fend for herself.

Deborah knew she had to warn Tamar of the danger but was at a loss as to what she could do. She wanted to raise her arms and wave them in the air, or run toward Tamar but she could do neither. Her limbs were paralyzed into immobility. Suddenly she heard a piercing scream shatter the silence around her and from the pain in her throat, she realized it was she who had cried out.

Tamar did not know what made her turn around. Raphael had always told her that in a race the winner never looked back. In a flash, she saw the two Arabs and in that brief instant, she also noted that Raphael did not seem disturbed. Regaining her equilibrium quickly, she turned her attention back to the road. She pressed her knees more firmly into her horse's ribs, lifting herself from the saddle to a near-standing position. With her face nearly touching the horse's mane, she prodded him with her riding crop. The soaring wind blew her beret off her head. Her long hair came undone and swirled madly around her face. The spray of salt water stung her eyes, blinding her to the road ahead, but none of it fazed her. She was too exhilarated. The race had taken on new purpose and she was determined to win. When she sensed the presence of a rider close behind, she refused to look back. She was in the lead and all she could think of was catching sight of Deborah at the finishing line.

Finally Deborah came into view. Triumphantly Tamar veered away from the water's edge and pulled in her reins sharply, causing the sand to rise up around her.

She was out of breath and was trying to compose herself when Deborah's ashen face appeared through the settling mist of sand. Deborah was staring past her with a look of horror on her face. Her sister's terrified expression indicated that her closest competitor was not Raphael. For the first time, Tamar felt fear. Dismounting quickly, she ran toward Deborah and put her arm around her shoulder. The physical contact calmed her and her panic abated.

"Mademoiselle, you are a truly fine horsewoman and you deserved to win this race." The man spoke French with a decidedly English accent.

Tamar, never letting go of Deborah, turned and saw a man dismount and as he did, he removed his white headdress with a grand flourish, exposing a shock of blond hair. Although deeply tanned, his skin was fair and his eyes were a startling shade of pale blue. He was an extremely handsome young man and he was staring at her with unabashed admiration. She felt the blood rush to her face.

"I believe I had an unfair advantage," she answered in French, when she felt she could speak naturally and was surprised by her self-effacing statement. It was unlike her. She had wanted to win, was determined to win. Nothing could have stopped her.

An awkward silence followed. Even Blackie, who had been jumping around and barking furiously just seconds before, grew quiet as though sensing the tension around him.

"My sister's modesty is commendable." Raphael had come to stand beside Tamar and Deborah. "And it is most considerate of you to speak French, but we also speak English." He smiled pleasantly. "I do not wish to seem rude, but if I'm not mistaken you are English, aren't you?"

The young man tore his eyes away from Tamar and looked over at Raphael. A shy smile appeared on his handsome features.

"We British are a mere channel away from France, but we'll never master that confounded, exquisite accent." He extended his hand toward Raphael. "I'm Thomas Hardwick."

"Raphael Danziger." Raphael grasped the young man's extended hand.

"Oh no!" Thomas exclaimed with obvious awe. "You're not the famous Dr. Danziger, the archeologist?"

"I don't know about the fame, but I am Dr. Danziger."

"I've been wanting to meet you since I arrived in Palestine but was told you were abroad."

"I returned from Paris early this morning."

Watching them, Deborah had the distinct impression that Raphael was ill at ease and she could not understand why. He was always comfortable with strangers.

"May I introduce my sisters?" Raphael said after a brief pause. "Tamar and Deborah Danziger."

Tamar's had regained her composure and she was sure she could handle her emotions when Thomas turned to acknowledge the introduction. But as she looked up at him, she felt helplessness. His look of naked adulation confused her. No man had ever looked at her that way. She was accustomed to being admired for her beauty, but that was not what was happening now. Thomas seemed to be etching her features into his brain, as though afraid she would vanish. She was fully aware that her look was equally intense.

The moment seemed to last forever, and it was only the neigh of the horse ridden by Thomas's companion that broke the spell.

Thomas was the first to recover. "Forgive my bad manners," he said, addressing Raphael. "May I introduce you to Prince Assad bin Sallah."

Raphael nodded respectfully.

The prince returned the nod but his imperious manner did not change. His dark eyes were veiled over, unrecognizing. No one introduced him to Tamar or Deborah.

"I've had the pleasure of dining with the prince's father, the gracious and learned Abu Assad, only a few short months ago." Raphael kept his eyes on the young prince. "A most gracious host and a good friend."

Although the prince remained aloof, Raphael's remark seemed to relieve Thomas. "Dr. Danziger, would you do me the honor of letting me call on you tomorrow? I'm stationed in Alexandria with British Intelligence, but I'm actually assigned to an archeological expedition working in this part of the world. Talking to you would be of untold benefit to our work." He caught his breath briefly. "Could I, sir?"

"I'm afraid that would be impossible," Raphael said coldly. "Tomorrow is a double holiday for my family. It is the Sabbath, and it is also my sister Tamar's birthday."

Thomas reddened with embarrassment.

"And of course Sunday would be out of the question for you," Raphael continued. "So that brings us to Monday. I would be pleased to see you at my laboratory then. You can reach it from Haifa road." He pointed toward two rows of palm trees running from the beach toward his experimental farm which stood halfway toward the main highway. "Most of my records are there and I would be happy to show you the various experiments I'm involved in. We can then discuss any archeological problems you may have."

"I'm scheduled to leave for Alexandria on Sunday," Thomas said with genuine distress.

"Well, I'm sure there will be other occasions," Raphael said graciously. "I travel to Cairo and Alexandria often. I also believe I shall be coming to England in the near future. So I'm sure we shall meet again."

Before Thomas could answer, the young prince turned his horse around and started riding away.

Thomas became flustered. "I sincerely hope so, sir," he said quickly. Then, mounting his horse, he nodded to Deborah, stared for a long moment at Tamar and with obvious reluctance followed his riding companion.

Raphael watched them, noting that they were not heading back toward the castle. Instead, they were riding north, toward Haifa.

The sun was now precariously close to the horizon and had grown into a large, orange ball, turning the blue waters bright red. A few light clouds appeared and drifted gracefully over the descending fiery ball. The melange of colors filtering through them made them look like colorful, transparent birds in flight.

The shoreline began to recede, and as the tide moved out the horses' hooves began to sink into the soft mud.

"It's almost sundown," Raphael said gruffly. "So we'd better start back before we embarrass Mama by riding through the village after the Sabbath sets in." He sounded unusually tense. Before staring off, he turned to Tamar. "Your graciousness about winning the race was proper. Mr. Hardwick may not have cared, but the young prince would never have forgiven you. He was humiliated enough when he realized he was competing against a woman." Then his manner softened. "But in truth, you did win that race."

"You would have won if Mr. Hardwick hadn't come along," Tamar whispered.

"Maybe, and maybe the prince would have won. He's one of the best horsemen I know. But why speculate? The Englishman felt you were the winner and that's really all that counts. Winning. Always winning. Defeat is for the weak."

Then pulling on his reins, he guided his horse across the sand dunes. Tamar and Deborah followed, with Blackie following close behind.

Leaving the beach, they crossed the main thoroughfare and started up the steep incline toward Bet Enav. The narrow path forced them to ride in single file, with Raphael in the lead and Tamar taking up the rear, behind Deborah. They fell into that riding pattern instinctively. It was their way of protecting their younger sister.

The mood of the three was somber, as all were involved in their own thoughts.

Raphael, feeling unusually tense, tried to absorb himself in the sights around him. The earth was dry and overgrown with weeds. The aged olive trees with gnarled trunks stood out in bald relief against the darkening sky. Large, oddly shaped sun-baked rocks lined the crooked road, which made the colorful wildflowers growing between the cracks even more startling. Their presence seemed defiant and arrogant in the midst of the otherwise desolate scenery. But to Raphael they were neither arrogant nor defiant. To him their existence and survival was proof that the land around them must have once been fertile and had much to offer. His parents had known this when they came to settle in Palestine. They were sure they could survive, grow and even thrive. And they had. But surviving involved constant vigilance and awareness of what was happening around them and it was that awareness that was now causing Raphael serious reflection.

He was deeply troubled by the appearance of the young prince and his companion. He had recently been a guest in the tent of the young prince's father. The prince had been in attendance—a great honor for him—and yet, just minutes before, he pretended to have forgotten, or preferred to ignore, that honor. Raphael was also unsettled at seeing him in the presence of a brash Englishman dressed like an Arab who claimed to be connected with British Intelligence. But Raphael was most troubled that the prince was out of his territorial realm. Like most bedouins, Abu Assad and his family lived in the southern part of Palestine and rarely ventured beyond their own borders. Raphael made a mental note to check on this strange phenomenon. Abu Assad was his friend, but in their part of the world, friendships between Arab and Jew were tenuous at best.

Deborah could not help but wonder about the looks which passed between the Englishman and her sister. She had never felt such tension between two people. It upset her. Tamar was always poised, gracious and in control, especially with strangers. Yet with Thomas Hardwick she appeared flustered and confused. Was it possible that they had fallen in love with each other? Deborah could not accept it. Tamar was going to marry David Larom. He was her steady boyfriend and everyone expected them to marry. Suddenly a new thought came to her. Was it possible that Tamar was not in love with David? Deborah felt herself blush. She had secretly been in love with David ever since she could remember, but since he was Tamar's boyfriend, she dared not even think of David except as her prospective brother-in-law. She would have sooner died than have anyone know how she felt about David. David. She allowed her thoughts to linger on him. Beautiful, sensitive, poetic David. She did love him deeply and she wondered if she would ever love anyone else. But, if Tamar was not in love with David and was not going to marry him . . . Deborah let the thought dangle, unwilling to pursue it. She decided she was being childishly romantic. She had just finished reading *Wuthering Heights* by Emily Bronte, and it had influenced her thinking. She was deeply moved by the story and since Thomas Hardwick was English, she had been swept away in her fantasy.

Tamar was barely conscious of the road. She was reliving the moment when she had first seen Thomas Hardwick. The memory alone made her flush. She tried to suppress a tremor of excitement as she recalled his eyes boring into her, but that same helpless feeling once again took hold of her. She could not even remember if she was relieved that he was not an Arab. All she knew was that suddenly nobody else existed for her. She wanted to see him again and wondered if she ever would. Raphael obviously did not want him to come to their home, otherwise he would have invited him to her birthday party. It occurred to her that Raphael had been quite rude, which was unlike him. She was tempted to ride up to him and ask him why, but decided to wait until the morning. Now he seemed tired and preoccupied. Poor Raphael, he worked so hard.

"Mama will be furious," Raphael broke the silence. He had reined in his horse and was waiting for his sisters to catch up with him. "We'll never make it before the Sabbath sets in, so we'd better ride through the vineyard and take the back road to the house." He sounded angry.

Tamar looked down at the coastline. The sun was sinking into the sea and its bright hues had faded into softer shades of pink and lavender. The sea had darkened and the dimming sun rays formed silver lanes on the water's surface, giving it the look of an exquisite Persian carpet. The gentle motions of the waves further enhanced the image.

"Isn't it the most beautiful sight in the world?" Deborah whispered in awe. "I don't believe there is any place in the world that's as beautiful." She had never been away from Palestine and to her everything surrounding them was perfect. Her sincerity was touching.

"There probably are more beautiful places," Tamar said sagely, "But I doubt if either of us would think so. And the reason is that this land is *ours.*"

"Ours," Deborah whispered. "Ours."

Raphael felt a lump come to his throat at the simple exchange. He turned and looked at his sisters. Mounted on their horses, their figures etched against the fading light, they were a study in contrast.

Tamar was a Danziger. Fair-skinned with a hint of freckles around her nose, her straight blond hair was waist length. Her ice-blue eyes, framed with unusually dark lashes, stared coldly, almost impersonally at the world. It was only when she smiled that one could see her kindness. She was also extremely restless and it worried Raphael. Deborah, in contrast, had rich, thick, chestnut-colored hair. With her heart-shaped face and unusually large, eloquent black eyes, she looked like a gypsy. Like their mother, she was petite and extremely well proportioned, and she appeared fragile.

Aside from the contrast in their looks, Raphael was struck most, at that moment, by the way in which each sister expressed her love for their land. *Ours,* voiced by Tamar, was said with sweeping assurance. Deborah's echo of that same word sounded like a prophetic prayer.

A painful knot formed in the pit of his stomach. He wondered if either knew the magnitude of the struggle which lay ahead before the land would finally be theirs. Which of them would be able to survive that struggle?

"Let's make a wish before the sun disappears completely." Tamar's voice broke into his troubled thoughts.

"I don't want to," Deborah answered watching her sister closely. "My wishes never come true."

"Well, I'm going to," Tamar said and closed her eyes.

Deborah saw a smile come to Tamar's lips and she lowered her eyes. She was sure that her sister's wish revolved around Thomas Hardwick and it bothered her. Somehow the meeting between Thomas Hardwick and her sister cast a shadow on all their lives.

The sun disappeared and it was dark.

The two girls turned their horses around and followed Raphael into the vineyard.

# CHAPTER TWO

T HE sound of rain hitting the metal shutters woke Tamar. She opened her eyes and realized it was still dark out. She wondered if the rain would spoil the plans for her outdoor birthday party and realized it did not matter. Something far more exciting had happened to her. Thomas Hardwick's image surfaced and overshadowed everything else. She smiled. That brief meeting on the beach, she felt, was a turning point in her life. He seemed to have awakened feelings in her which she had never experienced before.

She closed her eyes, hoping to recapture that moment when she first saw him. It suddenly occurred to her that Deborah had actually seen him even before she did and for the first time Tamar wondered where Thomas and his friend actually came from. The Crusaders' Castle. It had to be. Thomas and his companion must have been exploring the ancient ruin and came out just as she and Raphael started their race back to Deborah. She now understood her sister's horror-stricken look when she finally reached her. Poor Deborah. It was not only the sight of two Arabs. Deborah hated that massive black rock that was the castle, and for her to see two Arab riders come out of its depths must have confirmed her darkest, most terrifying nightmares.

Tamar smiled to herself. Unlike her sister, she loved that fortress. It represented power and endurance. Built centuries ago, it had been conquered and ruled over by countless tyrants and yet it stood defiant, arrogant and proud. In a way it symbolized the Jewish people. They too had withstood so much and continued to endure. It would last to eternity—as would her people.

Pulling the feather comforter to her chin, she snuggled beneath it and her thoughts drifted back to Thomas. From the minute she saw him dismount and bow to her, she knew that something momentous had happened to her. There was something about him which seemed to stir many dormant emotions. She was enormously attracted to him physically, but there was more—a mysterious, almost mystic quality which drew her to him. His Arab garb was strangely exciting. She was sure it was not mere whimsy. The clothes suited him, but more important, he looked comfortable in them. Although he was an Englishman, he seemed to want to blend into and understand the exotic beauty of the Middle East, with its strange customs. He wanted to become part of a people who were so different from him. The Arabs had always fascinated her, but as a woman she could do little to find out about them. Yet here was a man who obviously had the same yearning to know about these strange people and he was doing something about it. There were so many things she knew nothing about, so many people, so many customs, so many places that she wanted to explore, but until meeting Thomas, she had never thought that one could mold one's own destiny. Others had decided what her life would be. It was all preordained. She would marry David, they would have children and grow old together. They shared a dream of a homeland for their people and that bound them to each other. She paused at the last thought. *Shared a dream for a homeland.* What did it actually mean? She had been nurtured on that dream, understood that they would have to struggle to achieve it, but it was something that was going to happen in the future. It was vague and unformed, and before making a commitment to settle into a life with David and work alongside him to achieve their goal, she felt she had to understand better the meaning and the implications of that dream. Her thought lingered on David. He was her friend, she loved him as a friend, but he did not excite her. She had felt more emotion, more physical passion at the mere thought of Thomas than she had ever felt for David.

She heard Deborah sigh in her sleep and raised herself on her elbow to stare at her sister. She suspected that Deborah was in love with David, because of the way Deborah acted in his presence—different somehow from her usual self. But Deborah stood no chance with David, because Tamar's own presence dominated his existence. It seemed so unfair. Young as she was, Tamar was convinced that Deborah felt more deeply and experienced more emotions than she ever had and this bothered her. Suddenly she wanted to get away, not so much for Deborah's sake, but for her own. She wanted to know, to touch, to feel many things before she settled down.

Her thoughts returned to Thomas and she wondered if she would ever see him again. Whether she did or not, she now knew that she would not marry David. In that she was mistress of her fate. It meant defying her mother just as her mother must have defied her parents when she and her father left a comfortable life in Romania and decided to settle in Palestine. They had a dream and they set out to fulfill it. Their dream might very well be hers, but she wanted to be sure of what it was and she wanted the right to decide on how she would achieve it. She would also be defying Raphael. He wanted her to marry David. Surely he would understand her wish to see and explore before committing herself to the dream.

Dawn was beginning to seep through the slats of the closed shutters and Tamar realized it had stopped raining. Brief as it was, it had been the first rain of the season and it was a blessing. Rainfall on her birthday was a good omen.

She was suddenly sure she would see Thomas again. Somehow their paths would cross. The last thoughts filled her with excitement and she was glad to be alive.

Getting out of bed and slipping into her robe, she ran out of the room. The cold stone floor tickled the soles of her bare feet as she raced down the wide curving stairway. The grandfather clock rang out the hour just as she reached the lower landing. It was 6 A.M. She could hear Fatmi bustling around the kitchen. The aroma of the freshly ground Turkish coffee made her smile. That, more than anything, proved that Raphael was home. No one else in the house drank coffee in the morning.

Fatmi was squatting on the floor peeling potatoes, but stopped when she saw Tamar. "Why aren't you wearing your slippers?" she demanded.

"It's not really cold," Tamar said, watching Fatmi lift the heavy kettle from the kerosene burner and pour some boiling water into a Limoges teapot which was set up on a tray along with a matching teacup, saucer and delicately embroidered linen napkin. Tamar could not help but smile. Marucia Danziger had lived in Palestine for nearly thirty years, but she still insisted on European luxuries. Breakfast in bed served on delicate dishes was her way of starting her day.

"You'd better have some tea before you catch your death of cold," Fatmi said sternly.

"I think I'll have coffee this morning," Tamar said demurely.

"You may be eighteen, but your mother would not approve." Fatmi stopped and observed Tamar closely. "Of course, if you were my daughter, you'd be married by now with several children. But is it any wonder that you're not? Look at you. You're nothing but skin and bones and I can't imagine why anyone would want to marry you."

Tamar laughed and hugged the older woman. Heavy-set and dressed in her usual long, black dress with its embroidered bib, barefoot with ankle bracelets and intricate chains around her neck, she was a warm and loving woman. She had been with the Danzigers from the time they arrived in Bet Enav. She was not quite ten years old then and, although she now looked quite old, Tamar suspected that she was not yet forty.

"I will have coffee nevertheless," Tamar said as she ambled toward the window and stared at Raphael's house. A small whitewashed structure with an ornate front porch and covered with grapevines, it stood a few hundred yards away from the main house. The shutters were down and she assumed he was still asleep.

"And I'll also take Raphael's coffee to him when he wakes," Tamar announced. Then as she continued to stare out the window, she saw Raphael ride into the courtyard.

"He's here," she said excitedly. "Is his coffee ready?" She turned and saw that Fatmi was already pouring the boiling water into the *finjan*. Tamar also noted that there were two large cups beside it, indicating that Fatmi had relented and was allowing her to have coffee instead of the customary tea.

"You are as beautiful and as graceful as a deer." Raphael was waiting for her on the small vine-covered patio of his house as she made her way toward it.

"I feel beautiful." She smiled and preceded him into his living room.

Settling herself on the sofa, she started pouring the coffee, humming happily. Then, handing him the cup, she looked at him adoringly.

"I was afraid you weren't going to be back in time for my party," she whispered.

"I wouldn't have missed it for anything and you know it." He gulped his coffee and put his cup down.

"Did you have a good trip?" she asked. "I didn't get a chance to ask you yesterday."

"Exhausting. Constantinople, Berlin and Paris, in a relatively short time, can sap anyone's strength."

"I wish you wouldn't travel so much."

"So do I, but less travel hardly seems likely, especially since the Turks seem to be firming up their ties with Germany." He smiled wryly. "They're playing up my agricultural experiments as Turkish achievements in the sciences." He paused and grimaced. "I can deal with the Turks. I know them, know their corruption and double dealing, but I can't stand the Germans. There is something frightening about them. Especially now that they're trying to infiltrate this part of the world through the Young Turks. And what better way to do it than through an inexperienced group of hungry young officers? They've been in power since 1909 and in three years they've done nothing but grow weaker and crueler than their predecessors."

"It sounds ominous." Tamar said.

"Nothing to worry about right now." He sat down next to her and took her hand affectionately. "But I'll tell you one nice thing that happened while I was in Paris. I met with an American agricultural delegation and they offered me a professorship at a university in California. I turned them down, of course, at which point they offered to subsidize my experimental work at my laboratory here in Palestine."

"How wonderful!" Tamar exclaimed enthusiastically. "America! I wonder if I'll ever get a chance to go there?"

"Would you really want to go that far away from home?" Raphael was taken aback.

"Well, only for a short visit," Tamar answered, her eyes sparkling. "It must be fun to travel. America, France, Germany."

"Someday you'll get a chance to travel," Raphael said and stood up. "And now let me get your present."

"You're being here is present enough," she said sincerely.

"Not quite."

She watched him walk out of the room and, settling back on the soft embroidered pillows, she closed her eyes contentedly.

"I wish someone as lovely as you would bring *me* coffee in the morning," she heard someone say.

Her eyes flew open. David was standing in the doorway.

"When you marry Tamar, you will be in that lucky position," Raphael said as he came back into the room.

Tamar felt the blood rush to her face.

Both men saw her reaction and an uncomfortable silence followed.

"Rafi, how unworldly of you." David laughed pleasantly, breaking the tension.

"What's unworldly about it?" Raphael protested. "You obviously don't have the guts to propose and she is my sister and I know what's best for both of you."

"This is not a scientific experiment which you work out on paper and assume will work when put it into practice," David continued playfully. "As you know better than most, it often won't."

He sounded pleasant but Tamar knew him well enough to know that he was hurt.

Raphael looked from David to Tamar. "What the hell are you talking about?" he demanded.

"Why don't you leave the romance field to others," David coaxed. "You stick to science and let Tamar and me work out our problems."

"Problems?" Raphael thundered. "What problems?"

"Well," Tamar started. "I'm not sure I want to get married just yet." She looked anxiously at David.

"Come on, Rafi." David grew impatient. "I'm leaving in a few days for Paris. I'll be gone for at least a year and so many things can happen during that time."

"All the more reason to get married. Tamar would then go with you to take care of you there."

"Stop it!" Tamar said angrily. "You sound like an Arab chieftain selling off one of his daughters.[11]

"What's wrong with that?" Raphael demanded. "Arab chieftains usually have several wives and are far better equipped to choose a wife for their sons than a foolish young boy who's never been married. And that applies to choosing a husband for an innocent daughter."

"There are several things wrong with that," David interjected. "To start with, you haven't got even one wife and at the rate you're going, you'll stay married to your work and never have one. Secondly, I'm not your son and thirdly, Tamar is not your daughter."

"Thank you, David." Tamar stood up and walked over to the young man.

Her announcement about not getting married had caught him off guard and she was sorry. "But this Paris trip, does it mean you've been accepted at the Sorbonne?"

"The letter of acceptance was waiting for me when I got home yesterday. The school semester starts in October. So, actually, your party this evening can be a double celebration. Your birthday and my farewell."

"I think that's wonderful," she said sincerely. "And to start the celebration, I shall go get you a fresh cup of coffee."

The two men walked her to the door and were greeted by the sight of Mahmud, Fatmi's husband and their grandson Rafa walking toward the main house.

As always, Mahmud's hand was resting on Rafa's shoulder, guiding him gently along, since the boy was blind.

Hearing them, Mahmud stopped and he and Rafa turned and started toward them.

"Considering the number of grandchildren he and Fatmi have, it's incredible how that old man cares for that child," Raphael whispered, as the two came closer.

"It may be his feelings of guilt at not letting you take Rafa to a doctor when he was a baby and the trachoma first started," Tamar said, remembering the dreadful drama that centered on that decision—Allah's will clashing with the miracles of modern medicine. However, as Rafa's condition grew worse, Fatmi showed great courage and overruled her husband. But it was already too late. The infection had eaten into the cornea and nothing could be done. The doctor did succeed, however, in preventing the disease from disfiguring the boy's beautiful face. For that Mahmud was grateful. But Abed, Rafa's father, was furious at being defied and left his village vowing revenge against the Danzigers. When Marek Danziger was shot to death in his vineyard a year later, Abed was suspected of the crime but there was never any proof and the matter was dropped.

"*Hawaja* Raphael." Mahmud stopped a few feet away from them and bowed respectfully. "*Hawaja* David."

"*Ahalan,*" Raphael answered soberly and turning to Rafa, his face softened. "And how have you been, Rafa?"

"Well, *sahib,* well. Especially well, now that you are back."

"I'm glad you're here. I've got something for you," Raphael said and rushed back into his house.

"How are you today, Rafa?" Tamar touched the boy's arm lovingly.

He turned his blind, opaque-colored eyes in her direction and nodded seriously. Although only eight, he tried to assume the attitude of a man who was not interested in talking to women. He did however dig into a cloth bag which hung around his waist and took out his wooden flute. That was his way of saying he would play for her that evening. His musical talent was unusual and it was going to be his gift to her. She wished she could hug him but held back. It would offend him.

"I am looking forward to your playing tonight," she said instead.

"This is for you," Mahmud said suddenly and handed her a postcard. It had a picture of the Crusaders' Castle on it. She turned it around slowly.

The handwritten message was in English.

*Your eyes will shine for me into eternity. Happy Birthday.* It was signed *T.G.H.* Thomas Hardwick!

She wanted to cry out with joy, but restrained herself. "Where did you get this?" she asked Mahmud haltingly.

"Ibn Sallah rode by our village last night with a strange man, whom I have never seen before and gave it to me. He instructed me to give it to you." He was uncomfortable with the message. Raphael was the master of the house and Mahmud felt he was being disloyal.

"Who is it from?" David asked.

"Just a birthday greeting from someone we met," she said and placed the card in her pocket.

At that moment Raphael returned carrying a long thin package and, walking over to Rafa, he placed the present in the boy's hand.

For a minute Rafa fondled it suspiciously, then he started tearing at the paper. Finally unwrapped, the cold metal brought a look of bewilderment to the boy's face. Anxiously, his thin, elegant fingers ran along the object and when he realized it was a flute, his face took on a look of supreme joy. Slowly he lifted the instrument to his mouth. It emitted a strange sound but then the notes began to take form and a tune emerged.

Tamar's eyes misted and she heard David clear his throat.

"Thank you, *Hawaja* Raphael," Mahmud said solemnly.

"Will you be able to play it?" Tamar asked Rafa.

"I will play it tonight at your party," he said seriously. "On Allah's name, I swear I will."

Mahmud stooped to pick up the wrapping paper and turning the boy around, they walked away.

"Mahmud looks worried," Tamar said watching them.

"Abed was involved in a brawl with some Arabs near Beersheba and he killed one of them," David said. "He was caught and sentenced to life imprisonment in Acre."

"Justice has been done." Tamar felt relieved at the thought that Abed was no longer free. It had been seven years since her father was killed, but the fear that Abed might return to hurt Raphael was still very much alive.

"It was never proven that he killed Papa," Raphael said.

"Did you ever doubt it? No one else did." Tamar looked up at her brother. It was never proven," Raphael repeated seriously.

"Well, he's finally out of the way and I'm glad." Tamar looked back at

Mahmud and Rafa as they disappeared into the house. "What amazes me is how Mahmud and Fatmi can be the parents of such an evil human being and how such an evil man can be the father of that beautiful, angelic child."

"A bad seed can crop up in the finest fields," Raphael said.

"On this note, I shall ask your leave," David broke their serious mood. "I think I have had about all the emotion I can take for one morning." He bowed to Tamar. "I thank you for the coffee, but I must get home and accompany my father to the synagogue. I wasn't there yesterday and he was furious." Leaning down, he kissed Tamar on the cheek. "I'll see you this evening and we'll drink a toast then.

She was relieved that he was going, because she wanted to be alone with Raphael to talk about her future plans. The most difficult part had been resolved, now that he knew she was not going to marry David. Taking her brother's arm, they walked back into the house.

"Another coffee?" she asked, resettling herself on the sofa.

"I don't think so," Raphael said absently and started pacing nervously. Then spotting the present he had brought her, he picked it up almost angrily and handed it to her.

"What is it?" she asked, taking the box which was wrapped in lovely paper and tied with a big red ribbon.

"That's your birthday present," he said, but he was obviously still upset. He had had his heart set on her union with David and the change of plans disturbed him.

Tamar turned the package over in her hand. "It's so small and yet it's quite heavy," she mused as she untied the ribbon slowly. For some reason she did not want to open the leather box revealed beneath the wrapping.

"Go on, open it," Raphael urged.

Instinctively Tamar knew what the leather box contained. She held her breath as she lifted the tiny clasp and pushed up the cover. Encased in black velvet, the pearl handle was in startling contrast to the gun itself. She took it out cautiously. She was an excellent markswoman, had handled rifles, pistols and shotguns since she was quite young, yet this tiny object frightened her.

"It's not loaded," Raphael laughed uncomfortably, noting her tentativeness.

She looked up at him. "It's too beautiful to be that deadly."

"Why don't you look at it as a necessary decoration?" he answered seriously. "And hopefully, that's all it will ever be."

"Thank you, Raphael," she said but the strain in her voice was evident.

Raphael felt his heart go out to this woman-child and the brooding thoughts that had beset him the day before returned.

"Put it away now and tell me what's happening with you."

Tamar took a deep breath. "Well, now that I'm eighteen, I would like to go to Haifa and study nursing at Sonya Neeman's school."

"Do you think Deborah can take care of Mama and the house with you gone?" Raphael asked.

She was about to point out that he had suggested she marry David and move to Paris, but decided against it. "Of course she can and I'll come back every Friday. Haifa is not that far away," she said cautiously.

"Have you talked to David about it?" he asked.

Tamar smiled. In spite of what she had said earlier, Raphael was not prepared to accept her decision.

"About what?" she asked, feigning innocence.

"About being a nurse."

"Well, no," Tamar tried to keep the impatience out of her voice. "You don't seem to understand, Raphael, I'm talking about my future."

"I'm fully aware of that," Raphael nodded. "And are you really sure your future does not concern David?"

"Rafi, David and I are not going to get married. Not to each other, anyway," she said emphatically. "I thought you understood that. David understood."

"But why?"

"I'm not in love with David."

"How do you know you're not in love with David? Have you ever been in love? Are you in love with someone else?"

She lowered her eyes and pondered her answer for a minute. "I think I felt what love is when I met that young Englishman yesterday," she whispered.

Raphael stood up angrily. "Mr. Hardwick is hardly someone you can afford to be in love with, think about, dream about or even talk about."

"But why?" she was stunned.

"Because he's not one of us."

"What is that supposed to mean?"

"We're part of this little parcel of land. We belong to this land. We will work it, fight for it, reclaim it as our rightful home. Thomas Hardwick would never fit into our life, could never understand our dreams and he certainly won't fight our battles."

"How do you know that?"

"You'll have to accept what I'm saying," Raphael's voice rose. "I've traveled enough to tell you that we do not fit into other societies, certainly not the society of a Thomas Hardwick. We are not wanted by his people. We must create our own society and be proud of it."

"Do not fit into other societies?" Tamar repeated the words. "Not wanted..." Her voice trailed off. "But we *do* belong. We have always belonged."

"Tamar, you're being childish. Yes, we belong here, you belong here. And the reason we are here is so that we can finally achieve that sense of belonging, not only for ourselves, but for all other Jews. Don't pretend you don't know that Jews are not the most loved and accepted people in the world. The reason you have that wonderful sense of belonging is because you were born *here* and have never had to contend with rejection because of being Jewish. And because of the inborn pride and feeling of belonging which Papa and Mama gave us, your children will be twice as fortunate, as will all the generations following us."

She knew about the pogroms against the Jews in Eastern Europe. She had read about anti-Semitism in all parts of the world. History books were filled with the horrors Jews had suffered throughout the centuries, but that was all in books. That did not apply to her and her family.

"I know, but . . ."

"There are no buts," Raphael's voice rose. "Just forget the Thomas Hardwicks of the world. David is us. He's part of who we are and always will be. Thomas Hardwick is a stranger and nothing can change that."

Tamar had never seen him so angry. She also knew she would defy him if there were a showdown over Thomas. She had no idea whether she would see Thomas again, but her emotions were running high and she was not prepared to compromise.

"I'm sorry," Raphael's tone softened as he saw her face grow tight with determination. She was a fighter and he had touched that rebellious spirit which was so much part of her. "Why don't you let me dress so that I can go to the synagogue for the morning prayer and when I come back, maybe we can go for a walk and talk some more."

"You're going to pray?" She was incredulous.

"Well, I missed the services yesterday and since I'm away so much of the time, I don't know what's going on in the community."

Tamar raised her brow.

"There are things happening that everyone should be aware of. What better time to have a talk with the wise elders than after a good prayer?" He laughed self-consciously.

"Is something wrong?" she asked just before walking out the door.

"It's hard to say. There have been quite a few incidents with Arabs attacking Jewish villages. As I said, the Turks are in disarray and that always encourages the Arabs to go on the offensive against us." He paused. "There's something in the air which I can't quite place, but I would like everyone to be alerted to the fact that there are changes coming."

She was walking up the path to the main house when she heard Raphael run after her.

"Tamar, you forgot your gift."

She blushed as she took it from him and tried to suppress the deep sense of doom which she felt at that moment. It meant so much to him that she have the gun and she wondered why.

# CHAPTER THREE

"You're not having a good time, are you?" Avi said, and Deborah looked up at her dance partner. He was David's younger brother and her most loyal suitor, and she wished she were able to deny his accusation. But the party had been going on for quite a while and David had still not arrived. It upset her.

"I don't know why, but I feel sort of sad." She disengaged herself from his grasp. "Would you mind if we stopped dancing?"

Looking around, she wondered what could be keeping David. She was fully aware that once he arrived, he and Tamar would announce their engagement and after a long, restless night, she had accepted the inevitable. Married to Tamar, David would become part of their family and he would always be around. It would also mean that Tamar would not be taken away from them by someone like that Englishman they had met on the beach. For some reason, Deborah was still haunted by that encounter.

She turned her eyes toward the far end of the garden where Tamar and Raphael were entertaining Abu Taazi, the mayor of a nearby Arab village. He had come with several other Arab dignitaries and Deborah marvelled at the ease with which Tamar was behaving. The same feelings of envy which had taken hold of her the day before on the beach engulfed her now and she knew she was being unfair. Raphael had asked her to join them but she refused. Although she had lived with Arabs all of her life, knew most of the Arab guests who were there, had greeted them on occasions when they crossed her path, still she was uncomfortable in their company.

She was still staring at them when she realized that Tamar was moving away from the Arab's table and Raphael was heading toward her.

"Isn't David coming?" she asked running over to him.

"He'll be here a little later," Raphael assured her.

"Where is he?"

"He's bringing over a friend of mine who's just arrived from Constantinople." He patted her cheek. "Why don't you go and enjoy yourself."

She joined Tamar at their mother's table.

"Isn't it a wonderful party?" Tamar said enthusiastically.

"I guess so." Deborah stared at her sister. "What did you talk to Abu Taazi about?"

"Nothing special," Tamar shrugged. "He's a very nice man and we talked about his children, the new building that is going up in the middle of his village. Just chit-chat." Suddenly her face broke into a smile. "Oh, there's David."

Deborah turned around slowly and saw David coming out of the house. Walking alongside him was a man she assumed was her brother's friend.

"Who is that man?" Tamar asked.

"He's a friend of Raphael's from Constantinople," Deborah answered with an air of self-importance. Just seeing David made her feel better.

"How do you know?"

"Raphael told me."

Tamar observed the two men as they approached. The stranger was a tall, heavy-set man with dark hair, trimmed goatee and waxed mustache. He was dressed in the latest European fashion, except for the fez that gave away his Turkish nationality.

"Mrs. Danziger, Tamar, Deborah, I want you to meet Mr. Fredrick Davidzohn." David said formally when they reached their table.

"Mr. Davidzohn," Marucia nodded graciously, as Fredrick leaned over and kissed her hand.

Then he turned to Tamar.

"How do you do, Mr. Davidzohn," she said and put her hand out. He took it and brought it up to his lips, his eyes twinkling with pleasure. Having a man kiss her hand made her feel very grown up and worldly.

She returned the smile and noted that he was a pleasant-looking man and although his face was deeply lined, he was not as old as he appeared at first. She wondered how old he actually was.

Deborah was only vaguely aware of the introductions. She was too absorbed in David. His dark hair fell carelessly over his forehead and the suntan emphasized his strong, handsome features. His soft, dark eyes radiated humor, intelligence and compassion, but also a deep unhappiness. She wondered what had caused it and wished she could make it go away.

"Deborah." She heard her mother's voice and realized that Mr. Davidzohn was being introduced to her. She recovered quickly and smiled shyly.

"Fredrick, I'm so pleased you could come." Raphael was at their side.

The men shook hands. "I would not have missed coming to your home on this occasion," Fredrick looked back at the women. "And you are indeed a lucky man to be related to such beautiful women," he said sincerely.

"I am lucky," Raphael concurred, his face beaming.

"How about feeding our guests?" Marucia turned to Tamar and Deborah.

"Who is he?" Tamar asked again while she and Deborah were piling food onto plates. She knew most of Raphael's friends and she had never heard him mention Fredrick Davidzohn.

"Why can't you accept that he's simply a friend of Raphael's?" Deborah said impatiently. "You're always so suspicious."

"I'm going to ask David about him," Tamar said stubbornly.

"Did I hear my name mentioned?" David had come up to them.

"Why don't you take the food over to Mr. Davidzohn," Tamar suggested meaningfully to Deborah.

Deborah threw an angry look at Tamar, but realized she had to do as she was asked.

"Who is Mr. Davidzohn?" Tamar repeated her question the minute Deborah was out of earshot.

"A friend of Raphael's," David answered promptly.

"I understand that he's a friend of Raphael's, but who is he, really?"

David laughed appreciatively. "You're too clever to be a girl." Then, instead of answering, he touched her hair affectionately. "You look very lovely tonight."

She was flattered but not dissuaded from pursuing the subject of Mr. Davidzohn. She continued to look at him inquiringly.

"What can I tell you?" He relented. "Raphael has known him for years and they ran into each other in Berlin. Fredrick mentioned that he was coming to Palestine toward the end of September and Raphael invited him to your party."

"I don't believe that," she said evenly.

"Don't believe what? That Raphael and Fredrick are friends, that they met in Berlin, that Raphael invited him over?" he asked with mock seriousness.

"Oh, I'm sure they met in Berlin but Raphael hardy goes around inviting people he meets in Berlin to our parties. Besides, he would have mentioned it." She recalled Raphael's rudeness to Thomas Hardwick on the beach.

"We can't really get away with anything, can we?" He sighed in exasperation. "Well, he's German by birth but has lived in Turkey for many, many years. He's an arms dealer who is accepted by the Young Turks and is trusted by them." He took a deep breath, "He also happens to be Jewish."

"So?"

"So Raphael feels that we should cultivate him."

A slight shudder went through Tamar. Arms, rifles, guns, wars, fighting, death. She did not want to think of those things, not on this evening.

"Don't hold his profession against him," David said seriously, seeing the displeasure in her face. "We need arms. The Arabs are restless, the Turks are playing their usual game of pitting them against us and one of these days we'll have to defend ourselves."

Tamar looked over at Abu Taazi's table. Arab and Jew were sitting together, chatting amicably.

David followed her gaze.

"Don't let that scene fool you. It could turn on a button, I assure you."

"David, will there be trouble?" she asked, and the joy which she had been feeling since her party started was replaced by a deep sense of foreboding.

"What trouble?" Deborah had rejoined them.

Tamar and David looked at her blankly.

"What trouble?" Deborah repeated.

"There won't be any trouble," David said reassuringly. "There certainly can't be any for at least a year."

"Why a year?" Deborah asked.

"Well, no one would dare start anything while I'm away."

"You've been accepted at the Sorbonne!" Deborah tried to hide her dismay.

"I'm leaving in about ten days."

"And you'll be gone a whole year?" Deborah felt she was going to burst out crying but contained herself. Then at a loss for what to say next, she tore her eyes away from David and looked over at Tamar. "I think we should join Mama." And putting her arm through Tamar's and David's, the three walked toward Marucia's table.

A gentle breeze drifted through the tall eucalyptus trees that circled the garden and the colorful flowerbeds were enhanced by the flames coming from the lanterns that had been ignited when night fell. A lovely Strauss waltz came floating out to the terrace.

"Which one of the beautiful Danziger daughters will do me the honor of waltzing with me?" David asked, looking at Tamar and Deborah.

"I don't think I should. I've been a dreadful hostess and I should spend some time with Mama and her friends."

"Deborah?" David turned to the younger woman.

"I'd love it." Deborah blushed as she walked into his arms.

Tamar watched them dancing at the far end of the terrace. Deborah was dressed in an ankle-length bouffant cream colored silk skirt and tightly fitted embroidered top, which showed off her tiny waist and young, small breasts. She was looking up at David with undisguised adoration. And David, in a white shirt, black breeches and highly polished boots, was staring down at Deborah and he appeared equally taken with his young dancing partner. There was an intimacy between them which embarrassed Tamar. For some reason she resented it and she wanted to avert her eyes or turn away, but she could do neither. Was she jealous of what was happening between David and Deborah? She dismissed the thought immediately. What she was feeling was a longing for Thomas Hardwick. For a brief moment her vision blurred, and she imagined herself dancing with Thomas. She closed her eyes. The fantasy disappeared and she realized that before meeting Thomas, she could never have understood the depth of Deborah's feelings for David. Was it possible that it had all happened since yesterday? A deep sense of frustration and futility overtook her. Early that morning, she was sure she would see Thomas again. But that was wishful thinking. How would they meet? Where? When? Raphael was right. She and Thomas came from different worlds and although she had argued with her brother, she knew that even if she and Thomas did meet, they could never stand together as Deborah and David were standing, here, in her home in Bet Enav, surrounded by family and friends.

"They do make a handsome couple, don't they?" Fredrick's voice broke into her thoughts.

She looked over at him. He too was observing Deborah and David.

"Yes, they do." Tamar felt her cheeks go red. He seemed to have read her thoughts and it made her uncomfortable.

"I feel as if I know you," Fredrick said quietly.

"But we've never met." She tried to make light of his remark.

"I know you from the pictures Raphael always carries with him. Whenever we meet, he shows them to me with great pride." He smiled. "You were a lovely child and you've grown into a very beautiful woman."

"Thank you." She was genuinely flattered.

"Have you ever been to Turkey?" he asked after a brief silence.

"No. I've never been away from Palestine."

"Aren't you curious about the world outside these borders?"

"Oh yes," she said enthusiastically. "Although I don't think I could live anywhere but here." She was surprised by the last phrase, but it had come automatically.

"How would you know if you've never been anywhere else?"

"It's just a feeling." She smiled briefly.

"When Raphael next comes to Turkey, why don't you come with him?"

"That would depend on when he's going. I'm leaving for Haifa shortly to study nursing."

"You want to be a nurse?" Fredrick sounded shocked. "You mean, you actually want to work as a nurse?"

"Why not?" Tamar started defiantly but changed her tone immediately, aware she was being rude. "The truth is, I don't really know what I want to do. I know I like caring for people and when they're ill, they need that care more than ever."

A look of concern came over his face, which baffled her.

"Please don't misunderstand me." She wondered if she had offended him by not accepting his invitation. "Turkey sounds like a beautiful country," she continued feebly. The man confused her. He was probably old enough to be her father but he was talking to her as a woman, not a child. It was strangely appealing but it was also disconcerting. She had no idea how to handle the situation. To her relief, Raphael came over to them.

"I was suggesting that you bring Tamar with you on your next trip to Turkey." Fredrick turned to Raphael.

"Would you like that?" Raphael asked.

"Would you really take me along?"

"Fredrick and I have some business we're working on and I shall definitely be going there," Raphael nodded. Then, in a change of mood, he smiled and took her hand. "I'd love to have you along. You know that."

It occurred to her that Turkey was certainly further away than Haifa but the idea that Raphael was already planning a trip with Fredrick bothered her. She did not feel comfortable about Raphael's dealings with Fredrick, even though she knew little about them.

"I wonder where Rafa is?" She looked around, wanting to change the subject.

"Maybe he couldn't master the flute I brought him and is too embarrassed to come," Raphael suggested.

"He's mastered it," Tamar said with assurance. "Let me go find out what happened to him. It's awfully late and I'm worried." She hurried off, relieved to be away from Fredrick.

Both men watched her walk away.

"Who's Rafa?" Fredrick asked, never taking his eyes off Tamar's departing figure.

"The grandson of our watchman," Raphael answered absently.

"She really is lovely, you know," Fredrick said.

Raphael was startled by the statement. "She's very young," he said slowly, watching his friend closely.

"I could make her very happy." Fredrick met Raphael's gaze.

The two men stared at each other for a long moment. Raphael's mind was racing, yet none of his thoughts was conclusive. He had wanted Tamar to marry David. He was sure she would. The scene in his house that morning came back to him and he knew that it would not happen. Tamar was not a frivolous young woman. She had made up her mind and he knew that nothing would make her change it. The idea of her marrying someone like Fredrick was worth considering. Fredrick was older, he was responsible and intelligent. He was also wealthy, had stature in society and could give Tamar a good life. Young as she was, Tamar was headstrong and independent, but she was also gullible and impulsive. In a way, marriage to someone like Fredrick might be, in the long run, a better match than marriage to David.

"Abu Taazi is ready to leave." David walked over and his arrival put an end to Raphael's speculations. "And I believe he's waiting for you to say good-night."

Raphael looked around and realized that in the short time that he had been talking to Fredrick, all the guests had departed except for his Arab guests who were standing next to their table, obviously waiting for him.

"I'll only be a minute," Raphael said and hurried off.

"I am impressed with the way Danziger behaves with his Arab neighbors," Fredrick said, watching Raphael bid farewell to Abu Taazi.

"It is a tribute to him, but he's following in the tradition of his father who insisted on maintaining close ties with everyone around here," David answered. "Although it really doesn't please Mrs. Danziger. Her husband's close ties with his Arab neighbors did not stop them from killing him in cold blood when he was out inspecting his vineyards."

"I didn't know that." Fredrick sounded genuinely shocked. "Was the killer ever caught?"

"Hardly."

"Was Mr. Danziger armed?"

"It wouldn't have helped him if he were. When you're up against the rabble, you need a well-equipped army," David said pointedly.

Before Fredrick could answer, Raphael rejoined them and the three men started toward the house. Except for the sound of their footsteps on the gravel, the area was in total silence, which made the sudden explosion of gunfire all the greater.

"The vineyard!" David screamed and started running toward it.

"Could you go into the house, Fredrick, and reassure my mother and sisters?" Raphael shouted and ran after David.

"Raphael?" Marucia came running into the living room. Awakened by the shots, she had rushed down frantically. Dressed in a bathrobe, her hair braided for the night, she was ashen-faced and having a hard time breathing. "Have they hurt my son?"

"No, Mrs. Danziger." Fredrick was the first to reach her and led her to an armchair. "It came from the vineyard and he and David have gone to investigate."

Deborah seated herself on the arm of her mother's chair, stroking her hair soothingly.

The minutes ticked by and it seemed like an eternity before footsteps were heard on the terrace and then Mahmud entered the room carrying Rafa's bloodied body in his arms. Marucia let out a small cry of anguish. It was a replay of the scene of the night her husband was killed. Deborah turned her head away. Although quite young when her father was carried in by Mahmud, the memory was suddenly very vivid and very painful. Tamar stared at Mahmud and then her eyes wandered to Raphael and David and the two strangers who had followed them in. She did not know either of them but was sure they were the Jewish vigilantes who had undertaken to protect the Jewish communities and villages in the neighborhood. She was tempted to order them out of the house but restrained herself.

Fredrick walked over to Rafa, kneeled down beside him and placed his ear to the boy's chest.

"He's alive," he announced and began to examine the child to see if he was wounded.

"Who is responsible for this shooting?" Abu Taazi appeared in the doorway, his dark face contracting with rage.

"I am." One of the strangers stepped forward. Tall, with a massive red beard and mustache, he appeared to be the leader. He was shabbily dressed, his breeches worn, his boots frayed and his shirt patched. A wide bullet belt circled his waist and his rifle was slung over his shoulder. His manner was defiant and arrogant.

"Why?" Abu Taazi demanded.

"We saw someone moving about in the orchard and he had what appeared to be a knife in his hand. We were sure he was coming to do damage to the guests here."

Mahmud turned angrily and waved the brass flute Raphael had brought Rafa from France. "My grandson was coming over to play for the guests with this." He spat the words out furiously. Then focusing on the red-bearded young man, he lurched toward him.

Raphael stepped between them.

"That won't solve anything," he said quietly, placing his hand on Mahmud's arm. It was a gesture of friendship but it was also a warning that Mahmud was in the house of his employer.

"Why was he groping along in the dark?" The young man would not be intimidated.

"Because he's blind!" Raphael was having a hard time containing his fury.

"Will my boy live?" Mahmud looked around helplessly.

"Yes," Fredrick assured him. "Although he's still in shock."

"Well, we can leave now." The red-headed young man seemed satisfied.

"You're not going anywhere." David stepped forward. "You don't really believe you can shoot an innocent child, shock him senseless and walk out."

"What's your name?" Raphael's fury brimmed over.

"My name is Michael Ben Hod, *Dr.* Danziger." He emphasized Raphael's title with disdain. "And I think you know who we are and I think you should thank us. Granted that in this instance we may have been a bit rash, but if that boy was out to hurt anyone you would have been grateful to have us around."

Abu Taazi had come further into the room and stopped next to Raphael. "I believe this young man is not familiar with our customs," he said coldly.

All eyes turned to Abu Taazi.

In that instant the mood in the room changed. Arab and Jew, who a short time ago were enjoying the party together, were suddenly divided into opposite camps.

Abu Taazi felt the sudden hostility. A couple of his men started toward Michael.

"Don't you dare come near me," Michael hissed.

The men stopped and looked over at Abu Taazi.

"How badly is the boy hurt?" Abu Taazi asked.

Fredrick, who had been administering cognac to Rafa's lips, had succeeded in reviving the child. The boy sat up slowly and his blind eyes wandered aimlessly around the room. He seemed to be sniffing the air, as though trying to determine where he was.

"*Sulcha.*" Mahmud, relieved, turned to Michael. "*Sulcha,*" he whispered hoarsely.

Raphael, aware that Mahmud was demanding financial compensation for his grandson's encounter, turned to Abu Taazi. "Why don't we go to my house and discuss this like civilized men."

Abu Taazi turned on his heel and walked out of the house, followed by his men.

"I'll handle it," Raphael said coldly to Michael, "but you'd better behave yourself while I'm gone if we're going to get through this without repercussions." He looked over at David. "Why don't you come with me?"

"Mrs. Danziger," Michael started halting when the men were gone from the room. "I'm truly sorry for the trouble I've caused. I was only trying to do what I felt was my duty toward the Jewish community." His voice trailed off, aware that his words did not impress or reduce the feeling of animosity which was directed at him. "And the fact is that the boy is not even hurt . . ." he ended feebly.

"You're a very cruel young man," Marucia said coldly and stood up. Looking over at Fredrick and her daughters, she nodded and, without a glance at Michael, walked out of the room.

Michael stared after her in disbelief. "How was I to know the boy was blind and that what he was carrying in his hand was a flute?" he called after the departing figure.

"Why couldn't you check it out first?" Tamar demanded angrily.

"We can't go around checking out every filthy Arab who slinks around in the dark."

"Rafa is not a filthy Arab," Tamar shot back.

"It's only because he's blind. Otherwise that's exactly what he is." He was quiet for a minute. "And again, I'm really sorry I ruined your party."

Deborah felt sorry for him. He seemed completely sincere in his apology and she wished Tamar would stop attacking him.

"Being sorry is not good enough," Tamar said harshly. "And I hope you have to pay serious damages to Rafa."

Michael began to laugh. "Pay? Me? I barely have money to buy food, how am I to pay damages?"

"They'll make you pay," Tamar said viciously. "And they know how."

"Tamar, stop it," Deborah pleaded. The idea that someone did not have money to buy food shocked her, and she could not bear her sister's cruelty. She walked over to Michael and looked up at him. "Would you like something to eat?" she asked.

"Not in our house and not our food," Tamar said angrily.

Deborah turned to her. "That's an awful thing to say, Tamar. I can't quite imagine what it's like to be hungry, but . . ."

"I won't eat anything, thank you," Michael interrupted her. "And frankly, in your sister's place, I'd feel the same way." He looked directly at Deborah as he spoke.

Deborah, watching him, saw his face soften and the harshness disappear from his voice. He looked strangely vulnerable and it touched her.

"Would you all please calm down for a moment?" Fredrick said suddenly. He had stood by, saying nothing during the verbal exchange that was taking place. Now he moved quickly toward the front hall. Only then did everyone realize that a carriage had stopped outside the house. They heard heavy footsteps clambering up the front stoop. Loud pounding on the door followed.

Within minutes they could hear Fredrick's effusive greeting and he reappeared in the doorway with a highly decorated Turkish general and a tall, thin, blond German officer. The general was a short, heavy-set man, wearing a well-fitted army jacket, covered with numerous medals, and tight-fitting jodphurs. His boots were highly polished, and his massive leather belt held an ominous-looking the gun. He was extremely pale under the dark, trimmed beard and although he tried to appear affable, his eyes betrayed a cold cruelty.

"It was one of those little unimportant incidents of mistaken identity," Fredrick was saying, obviously referring to the shooting.

"The red-headed Robin Hood." The general's face lit up when he saw Michael. "Practicing your marksmanship again?" He laughed softly but his mirth did not reach his eyes.

"Jamal Pasha, how pleased I am to see you." Michael bowed to the man.

"What exactly happened?" The general turned back to Fredrick.

Fredrick had just finished relating the incident when Raphael walked in. Abu Taazi followed him in but stopped in the doorway.

"It's settled," Raphael announced, unaware of the presence of the newly arrived guests. When he realized they were there, he stopped and his manner changed. "General, what an honor." He walked over and extended his hand to the Turk.

"I was driving through the area with Colonel Von Hassen when we heard shots." He turned to the young German officer. "This is our illustrious scientist, Dr. Danziger, whom I've been telling you about."

Raphael nodded to the German and turned back to Jamal Pasha. "It's nothing serious, general," he said off-handedly.

"What do you mean, it's all settled?" Michael interrupted.

"What was settled, Dr. Danziger?" Jamal Pasha asked.

"Mahmud will be compensated. . . ," Raphael started.

"But I understand the boy is not hurt," Jamal Pasha said emphatically.

"Well, there was an element of pain that should be taken into consideration," Raphael smiled pleasantly.

"It was a misunderstanding and I feel that compensation is out of order," the Turk said with finality as he looked at Abu Taazi.

A flash of hate twisted Abu Taazi's features. Without a sound, he turned and walked out the door.

Raphael had a hard time controlling his annoyance at the general's interference. Jamal Pasha was the highest authority in that part of the country and he had settled the affair. Any deal previously made was now null and void. He knew it and Abu Taazi knew it.

Turning to Michael, Raphael's voice changed from that of graciousness to mild contempt. "I appreciate your efforts on our behalf, Mr. Ben Hod, but I would also appreciate it if you would not trespass on our property again."

Michael bowed, turned and walked out without a backward glance. His companion followed him.

"Gentlemen." Raphael's hostlike manner returned. "I should like you to meet my sisters."

Deborah, blushed, lowered her eyes and curtsied. Tamar, however, would not be stared down. She lowered her head briefly, but her eyes never wavered. She noted the German's smile of appreciation. She smiled pleasantly at him.

"May I offer you some refreshments?" Raphael asked when the introductions were over.

"It would be an honor, Dr. Danziger," Jamal Pasha said respectfully. "But the colonel is expected at his post in Haifa before dawn and I must deliver him, as promised." Before turning away, he looked at Fredrick again. "And as always, Mr. Davidzohn, it is a pleasure to see you. I am truly delighted that you are acquainted with Dr. Danziger. One knows a man by his friends."

An uneasy silence followed the departure of the general and the colonel.

Raphael walked over to the window and watched them drive off. Tamar and Deborah joined him and he put his arms around their shoulders. Fredrick sat down on a small divan and took out a cigarette. David threw himself into an armchair and covered his face with his hands.

"What was that all about?" David asked.

"Jamal Pasha is a practical man. He needs Raphael's help in the agricultural field and he needs my services in Turkey," Fredrick answered in a matter-of-fact voice. "And Abu Taazi, a little *muchtar* of an insignificant village in Palestine, and a simple *fallach* named Mahmud are dispensable."

"Not to mention that what he's done only heightens the bad feelings between us and the Arabs," Raphael said quietly. Then letting go of his sisters, he walked nervously around the room. "Abu Taazi will not forget this incident. He may gloss over it because he's smart, but he won't forget it. His men certainly won't. Of that you can be sure."

"God, how I hate them," David spat the words out furiously.

"They're not all that way," Fredrick said protectively. "There are some very good Turkish people."

"Where?" David would not be appeased. "I certainly haven't met any. And frankly, I'm not crazy about the Germans either, with all their refinements, culture and ethics."

"Are you speaking as a Jew or a Palestinian?" Fredrick asked.

"I'm speaking as a human being."

"How about a nightcap?" Raphael interrupted the discussion and without waiting for an answer, he walked over to a liquor cabinet and started pouring drinks.

Handing brandy to the men, he served wine to his sisters.

"Now, if you will allow me, I should like to toast Tamar and wish her much happiness." Raphael lifted his glass to her.

"May I add my sincere congratulation on this auspicious day and may I re-extend my invitation to you and pray and hope that you will come and spend some time in Constantinople as my guest," Fredrick said sincerely.

The three men downed their drinks in tribute.

Tamar lifted her glass toward David. "To a wonderful time in Paris and much success with your studies."

Deborah was about to sip her drink but as Tamar's words sank in, it dawned on her that no announcement of Tamar's engagement had been made. So much had happened that evening and it could have been an oversight, but she knew it was not. David was still free. She threw a sidelong glance at Tamar and David. They were toasting each other in true friendship. David did not seem unhappy. Tamar was glowing with happiness.

# CHAPTER
# FOUR

M ICHAEL and his companion rode their horses up the crude road toward their campsite in silence. It had grown cold and he felt a chill through his body. That's something one never got used to, he thought bitterly. That and hunger.

They had gone a distance from Bet Enav and he looked back. The village was in darkness except for the light coming from the Danziger house. Built on a small mound, it was a white, two-story structure, with long narrow windows arched at the top. It looked like a cathedral. Much as he hated the Danzigers, he could not help but admire them.

"What are you looking at?" his companion called out and came riding over.

"That house," he answered sullenly.

"Some house, all right. And some people!" the young man said. "But I must admit, that Danziger fellow is an interesting man. It's that sister, the blond one, who scares me."

Michael looked at him, puzzled.

"I've seen her out bird hunting with her brother and David Larom and I can tell you she handles a gun better than most men I know."

"Does the younger sister know how to use a gun as well?" Michael asked cautiously. He was completely captivated by Deborah and wanted to know more about her.

"Dr. Danziger believes in self-defense and if it were up to him he'd have every Jewish woman carrying some sort of weapon. I suppose he's coached both girls. The younger one can handle a gun but she doesn't seem to enjoy it. The blond one does," the boy replied. "Hey, it's freezing out and we can discuss the women when we reach the camp."

"You go along," Michael said. "I'll be there shortly."

Left alone, he continued to stare at the Danzigers' house.

He had passed it often while traveling through the countryside, but until this evening he had never been in it. It was impressive from the outside. It was overwhelming inside. No one in the part of the country where he grew up lived as grandly, as ostentatiously.

Michael was born in Metula, a tiny, poverty-stricken community in the northeastern part of Palestine. His parents, Russian emigrés, had escaped the oppressive Tzarist rule with the hope of a better life in Palestine. His mother died while giving birth to him and his father died of malaria shortly thereafter. Michael grew up knowing nothing but hunger, disease and poverty. He was raised in the rabbi's house along with their six children and as far back as he could remember he was known as the village orphan who owed his existence to charity. Warmth, affection, a feeling of belonging were alien to him. The struggle of the poor to survive precluded the exhibition of overt affection toward anyone. He was another mouth to feed and another human being to worry about. And like the others, his stomach always rumbled with hunger. But he was different than boys his age and his burnt orange hair made him stand out.

He was also a good student. The Torah and the Talmud held a fascination for him. They were documents he could assimilate, absorb and try to integrate into himself. They spoke of the dignity of man and it filled him with hope.

Sitting at the rabbi's table, he soaked up thoughts, ideas and feelings of pride, and dreams of a better way of life took form. From those books he derived a strength, a faith. They made him feel that somewhere there were rewards.

As Michael grew older, however, he began to question the rabbi's interpretations. Michael wondered about the tyranny of his religion, the authoritarian nature of the Torah, the rigidity it espoused. He even questioned the superficial dogmas. Why the need for the sidecurls he was forced to grow? Why the need for the ritual fringes he had to wear under his shirt? Why was Hebrew not the spoken language when the Torah and Bible were written in it? He suffered silently when the rabbi lashed out at him for his questions, but an anger began to form in his gut.

His bar mitzvah was the day he looked forward to. In a way, even that day set him apart. As an orphan, his call to the Torah was to take place on his twelfth birthday rather than his thirteenth. An orphan, everyone said, had to face up to manhood at a younger age. He saw it as a blessing. On the day of his bar mitzvah, he would become a man.

He chose to read the sentence from the Torah dealing with freedom and addressed himself to the Messianic ideal of a Jewish homeland, equality for Jews, the freedom which all mankind deserved. He labored over his speech and wanted to deliver it in Hebrew.

The rabbi forbade it, warned him that he would not allow him to go up to the Torah if he persisted in his foolishness. Hebrew was the holy language which would come into daily use only after the Messiah came.

On the day of his bar mitzvah, Michael watched the men go off to the synagogue with the women following after them. No one acknowledged the importance of the day. He was dumbfounded. It was not that he expected special treatment, but he had hoped for some recognition.

The rage which had been building in him spewed over. It was Saturday and the house was very quiet. His mind was in turmoil. He wanted to make some sort of statement. He needed to prove his independence, his existence, his individuality. The idea came to him like a bolt of lightning. Slowly he walked into the kitchen, opened the utensils drawer and took out the shears. Then, with trembling fingers, he cut off his sidecurls. Placing the two curls on the white Sabbath tablecloth, he stared at them. They had begun to unwind and appeared like two writhing, red, angry serpents. They too seemed to be trembling. It frightened him. He knew he had committed an unforgivable sin and a terrifying fear overtook him. Closing his eyes, he waited for the wrath of God to strike him. The minutes went by and nothing happened. He had committed an act of defiance, an ultimate act, a sacrilegious act and God had not punished him. It stunned him.

The men's section of the synagogue was crowded and no one took notice of the orphan wrapped in his prayer shawl. When his named was finally called, he walked slowly toward the Torah. Once there, with his head held high, he lowered his prayer shawl. A hush fell over the crowded room, followed by gasps of horror. Before anyone could say anything, he announced in a clear voice that his name was Michael Ben Hod. Michael, Son of Glory. He spoke Hebrew and said he would be making his speech in that language. The rabbi began to storm with rage. A debate broke out among the congregants. Some argued that the boy had a right to speak in the holy tongue, others disagreed violently. Michael listened and soon realized the nays were winning. He turned, and as everyone watched he walked out of the synagogue.

Standing in the empty, quiet street, he heard the sound of angry voices continue for a few minutes and then the hushed mumbling of the prayers took over. He felt a desperate urge to run back into the synagogue, beg forgiveness, but knew he could not do it, would not do it. The sound of prayers grew louder and suddenly he understood that he had been punished after all. He had walked out of the synagogue, walked out on the community he had grown up in and he was now alone, excluded, an outsider. The gnawing feeling that it would be his fate from that day on, came to him. He would never again belong. He would always be an outsider looking in.

He left Metula that morning and within days found refuge with some men and women who were traveling about, guarding the countryside. He looked older than his years and no one questioned him too closely about his background. Michael suspected that Reb, the black-bearded leader, saw through the deception, but Reb seemed to like him and allowed him to join the group. Reb became his mentor, his protector, his teacher.

The group was as poor as he was and they banded together to fight their poverty. They scoured the countryside for food, slept under the stars, spoke only Hebrew and dreamed of a Jewish homeland where community life, community responsibility, a life of sharing would prevail. He learned to ride a horse, fire a gun and stand up for what he believed in. He had some difficulty accepting their disregard for the Torah's teachings, but Reb put his mind at rest. They were involved in a fight for the Jewish people, a Jewish homeland, the land which their Lord had commanded them to enter and conquer and make their own. They were actively working at what the prayer books were teaching.

Ten years had gone by since his bar mitzvah. The pain and humiliation of that day had dimmed, but it had not disappeared. The need for acceptance, the need to be part of a larger community was as great as ever. How it would be done, he did not know. Money was one way, but there was little chance of him ever earning enough. The alternative was power, and political power became his goal.

He began to think about power when he first met Reb. Here was a man who could verbalize a dream and make it seem like a reality that could be achieved; who could hold his people together while offering little in creature comforts, because the dream was so real. But Reb's power was limited to a small group of men and women who had nothing else to hold on to. Having met Raphael Danziger that evening, Michael felt he finally got a glimpse of what power could be. It was not the grandeur of the house or its furnishings. It was not in the way Raphael was dressed or the things he said. It was his whole demeanor. Raphael exuded an air of confidence in the way he walked, the way he talked, in the timbre of his voice. He looked like a man who could lead people from all walks of life. Michael saw the way he spoke to Abu Taazi, his manservant and Jamal Pasha. But more revealing was the manner with which Jamal Pasha treated Raphael—with a respect he had never shown to Michael.

Michael felt that same sense of power in the Danziger women. Marucia Danziger, though frail and gray-haired, tired and frightened, dispensed authority. He disliked Tamar, but she too had that aura of leadership. Even Deborah had it, though she combined it with humanity and compassion.

Thoughts of Deborah brought him back to his own reality. He felt he could fall desperately in love with her, but it would be a hopeless love, doomed from the start. He was nothing but a poorly educated farmhand at best and she came from aristocracy. It saddened him. Already his homeland had its social classes and he was relegated to the lower rung of that ladder.

Angrily Michael turned his horse around and headed toward his camp.

Reb was sitting on the ground in front of a dwindling campfire, wrapped in his ancient thick blanket, a cigarette dangling from the corner of his mouth. He was deep in thought and Michael had a minute to observe him. In the ten years since they met, Reb had barely changed. He was probably in his early thirties but looked older. Born in Safad, Reb came from a long line of rabbis.

He left them, much as Michael did, and roamed the countryside looking for a place to settle. He finally found a spot in the southern part of Palestine and hoped to build a Jewish settlement there. His Arabic was as fluent as his Hebrew and he could pass for an Arab. His small settlement had just started taking form when marauding Arabs attacked it. It was a common occurrence and the Arab marauders expected no resistance. Reb went after them with a gun—at the time unheard of—and succeeded in killing several of them. Thus he built his reputation as a man to fear. That incident inspired him to organize the Jewish vigilantes and until this evening, Michael felt privileged to be his follower. But on this evening, Michael's feelings of inadequacy made him forget the adulation he felt for Reb.

"You look as though you've lost your best friend." Reb's deep voice jarred Michael.

"It's been a difficult evening." Michael came to sit beside the older man.

"Mistakes happen," Reb said, obviously aware of the incident with Rafa. Michael stared into the fire and said nothing.

"Met the great Raphael Danziger, have you?" Reb asked.

"Yes." Michael started slowly. "He's very arrogant and quite nasty, but he has a self-assurance, an authority, which I think people respect." A bitterness crept into his voice.

"What people?"

"Jamal Pasha, for one. He was there and although we've worked with him, done things for him, he treats us differently than he does Danziger." He paused, searching for the thought which had eluded him all evening. "The thing is, Jamal Pasha needs Raphael Danziger. He has something to offer the Turks, whereas we are being used by them. We serve a small purpose. We watch over the Jewish communities and we take the responsibility off the Turkish soldiers for whatever that's worth. But we're dispensable. Danziger is not." He looked over at Reb, who was back staring at the fire.

"Do you understand what I'm saying?" Michael asked, unsure if Reb had heard him.

"Yes, but I'm not impressed with the Danzigers of the world. They are selfish and as far as I'm concerned insincere."

"In what way?"

"They're exploiters who are out for themselves. They've grown rich since coming to Palestine and they're not prepared to share the wealth with anyone. I respect anyone who works the land and makes it come to life. Raphael's father did that. But today, who works the Danziger lands? Arabs. I doubt if Raphael Danziger knows how to use a plow, but he wouldn't dream of hiring a Jewish worker." His voice rose. "Do you know how many poor, hungry Jews live in Palestine?" he demanded.

"But most Jews know nothing about farming," Michael started feebly.

"They're not idiots. They could learn. You're a farmer. Would he hire you?

Probably not and the reason is that he feels more comfortable ordering some ignorant Arab around than someone who can read and write."

"Reb, before we start our ideological fight, we do have a mutual goal with Raphael Danziger," Michael said. "And as far as I'm concerned, the Danzigers of Palestine are as sincere about creating a Jewish homeland as we are. They're simply going about it differently."

"Meaning?"

"Raphael Danziger is in a bargaining position. We're not."

"What you're saying is, you wish you could be in Raphael Danziger's position."

"Yes, and I wish I knew how to get there. Obviously having money and an education helps."

"With all the books you read, I always thought you had enough education."

Michael winced. His education had stopped the day he left Metula. His only language was Hebrew and there were not many books translated into Hebrew.

"Of course, I could take the offer the Turks have made to us and enter their officers' school," Michael said, and the minute the words were out of his mouth, he was again the boy who had defied the rabbis back in Metula. Reb had been against any of his men taking the Turks' offer.

"I'm sure Jamal Pasha would be delighted to sponsor you." Reb's voice was low.

"Would you be angry if I did?" Michael choked the words out.

"It may just be the thing for you."

"Would you ever consider doing it?"

"Never. But then, I'm not interested in being indispensable to the Turks. I'd much rather be indispensable to my people here."

Michael covered his face with his hands. For ten years he had belonged and now he was seriously considering leaving this safe haven, these people who had accepted him, made him part of their lives. Again he would be an outsider looking in. As in Metula, he would be alone.

"I'll sleep on it." He stood up and walked quickly toward his tent.

Lying on a thin straw mat, he wondered if by entering the Turkish officers' school, he would be betraying his friends. It did not have to be. He had left Metula and the people who raised him, but he never stopped being a Jew. And the same would apply now. He would become an officer in the Turkish army but he would never stop fighting for a Jewish homeland. He might even become more effective.

Just before falling asleep, he knew he would go and he wondered if Reb would ever forgive him.

# CHAPTER
# FIVE

*January 23, 1914*

*My Dearest Child,*

*Your letter informing me that your mother is recovering was welcome news. What made the news all the more gratifying is that you are now free to accept my proposal of marriage. I have waited for this happy day for over a year and with the Lord's blessings, I shall proceed with plans to be in Palestine within the next month. Any arrangements which your family wishes to make will be acceptable.*

*Since your acceptance, I have been bought a new home. It is in Pera, has a most beautiful view of the Bosphorus and, except for your private quarters, I have had it furnished by a most tasteful decorator. You will have free hand to plan your own rooms. My Kahya is an excellent man who serves me faithfully and he has been looking for a proper hizmetkar for you. He is an Armenian but very loyal.*

*Forgive me, my dear, for rushing on, except that I cannot contain my excitement. Although I have seen you several times since that fateful day at your eighteenth birthday party, it is only now that I can tell you how much I care for you without worrying that I may be overstepping my position.*

*Please give my sincere felicitations to your dear sister Deborah and a warm hug to Raphael. Your faithful servant always,*

*Fredrick*

DEBORAH put the letter down and stared at Tamar who was trying on a traveling suit. It was the one she was planning to wear when she went off with Fredrick after their wedding.

"Why are you doing it?" Deborah asked.

"Doing what?" Tamar turned to look at her.

"Why are you marrying Fredrick?" Deborah repeated the question. "He's twice your age, he's a humorless, stiff boor and you know it."

"You just don't know him," Tamar answered vehemently but changed her

39

tone, aware that Deborah would not be put off. "He's a very kind man. He's been extremely generous to me and to all of us." She licked her lip nervously. "He's rich and he's offering me a wonderfully glamorous life. We'll travel and I'll get to see all sorts of new things. You've read the letter. I'm going to have my own rooms which I can decorate as I see fit, and my own maid."

"You could have traveled with David if you'd married him," Deborah said steadily. "You could have had your own house with David and God knows you could have decorated it yourself."

"I was not in love with David," Tamar said.

"Well, you're not going to tell me you're in love with Fredrick," Deborah said pointedly.

"It's different. There is no pretense between us. Fredrick knows how I feel and he accepts me as I am."

"David would have accepted you as you are." Deborah would not let up. The wedding was just one week away and she was troubled by it, both for Tamar's sake and for her own.

"David and I are just friends. I tell you, it's different."

"Is it different because David is in love with you?" Deborah asked, looking anxiously at her sister. Aside from her own feelings, she thought Tamar's marriage to Fredrick was a dreadful mistake and was sincere in trying to prevent it. She also had the feeling that Tamar, given a chance, would have resumed her relationship with David. Since her graduation from nursing school, Tamar had been spending a great deal of time with him. The old conspiratorial intimacy seemed to have been re-established and Deborah expected Tamar to break off her engagement to Fredrick and marry David. Suddenly it dawned on her that Tamar was going through with the marriage to avoid hurting her. But much as she loved David, Deborah knew it would be madness for Tamar to go off with someone like Fredrick just to spare her feelings.

"I don't believe David is or ever was in love with me." Tamar met her sister's eyes. "As you know, once he left for Paris, he never wrote to me directly. He wrote letters addressed to all of us and you know since he's been back he's been much more attentive to you than to me." She smiled. "And I think that's perfect. You two are far more suited to each other than he and I were." She turned away and occupied herself with her toiletries.

"But what about leaving Palestine, Bet Enav?" Deborah asked.

"I don't expect to be living in Turkey for the rest of my life. Fredrick promised me that we would move back here soon. Also, Constantinople is not that far away and I will be coming to visit." She turned back to Deborah. "Frankly, I look forward to coming back for your wedding as soon as you set the date. I wouldn't dream of missing my little sister's marriage."

"Don't patronize me, Tamar. David and I . . ." She stopped. It was true that she and David had grown closer since he had returned from Paris but marriage was never discussed.

"David and you what?" Tamar asked.

"Let's not change the subject. I think your marriage to Fredrick is a big mistake and I wish you wouldn't go through with it." She took a deep breath before continuing. "I'll accept that you're not in love with David but someday you're going to fall in love and you should wait for that day."

"Stop badgering me," Tamar shouted and walked over to the window and stared out.

It was a cold, dreary day and it matched Tamar's unhappy state of mind. Deborah's questions only confirmed her own doubts about Fredrick. Talk of marrying for love touched a raw nerve. She thought she had fallen in love with Thomas the day she met him. But as time went by with no word from him, she had put him out of her mind and had begun to accept the idea that she would never see him again.

Then she ran into him.

She was having tea with Raphael and Misha Neeman in a Haifa hotel. The lounge was a tiny European enclave in the otherwise Oriental city. It was late afternoon and a small band was playing pleasant dance music. The room was relatively empty except for some businessmen and army personnel. Misha was talking about his plans for an agricultural school for boys. The conversation bored her and her eyes wandered over the crowd. Suddenly she caught sight of a group of British officers sitting at the far corner of the room. One of them was staring at her and it took her a minute to realize it was Thomas Hardwick. The uniform had confused her but she recognized the eyes, those incredible blue eyes that had so captivated her the day they had met.

Flustered, she tried to turn her attention to the conversation at her table but she could feel her heart pounding.

"Dr. Danziger." She heard Thomas's voice and she held her breath.

Raphael looked up, puzzled.

"Dr. Danziger, you may not remember me, but we met a year ago on the beach. I'm Thomas Hardwick."

"Of course," Raphael said stiffly. "What brings you here?"

Thomas pointed to his table. "I'm here with my commanding officer and some of our men. As you may remember, we're involved in archeological work in the Middle East." He turned to Tamar. "Miss Danziger."

"Yes, you did meet my sister," Raphael said quickly. "And this is Mr. Neeman."

Misha shook hands with Thomas and an uncomfortable moment followed.

"Dr. Danziger, may I have your permission to dance with your sister?" Thomas broke the silence.

Tamar was sure that given the chance, Raphael would have said no, and anticipating the possibility, she stood up. "May I, Raphael?"

Walking into Thomas's arms was like coming home. The physical contact sent an unbearable thrill through her. She knew he felt as she did by the way he held her hand and by the pressure of his fingers around her waist. She had to suppress the urge to caress the back of his neck.

"I've dreamed of this moment since the day I saw you," he whispered, never taking his eyes off her face.

She was unable to speak.

"You don't have to say anything. I know." His voice was low and filled with emotion.

Suddenly he grew tense. "My commanding officer is furious at my behavior."

She looked around. The men from Thomas's table had stood up. She glanced over at Raphael. He was coming toward her.

"When will I see you again?" She asked frantically.

"Week from today at the Crusaders' Castle. At four."

"Tamar, I'm sorry to interrupt, but we must be going." Raphael had come up to them. She could see that he was angry.

To her great relief, the incident was never mentioned. She could not have pretended indifference if Raphael had confronted her, and was convinced that he avoided the subject, hoping it would simply disappear.

Thomas was waiting for her at the Crusaders' Castle. She had offered to help Raphael with some work at the laboratory and at one point said she wanted to ride along the shore before the sun set. She was safe in making the suggestion, since Raphael was busy and was unlikely to join her.

"Don't be long." He barely looked up from his papers when she left.

Thomas was again dressed in his white Arab robes and she walked into his arms as soon as she entered the darkened fortress.

His lips pressing down on hers were soft and moist and she responded to his kisses with a passion she had dreamed about but had given up hope of ever experiencing.

"Will you make love to me?" She was behaving wantonly but she did not care.

He pushed her away gently. "There's nothing I want more," he said hoarsely. "But it would be wrong. Not here, not now. We'll have a lifetime together. I know it."

She knew he was right and she clung to him, wanting this moment to go on forever.

Then letting go of her, Thomas removed his outer robe, spread it on the ground and, pulling her toward him.

Settling down beside him, she held on to his hands and stared at them. They were the hands of a musician. The fingers were long and elegant and the wisps of blond hair on the backs of his hands were like spun gold.

"Why do you wear these clothes?" she asked, looking up at him.

"Don't you like them?"

"I think they're beautiful and they suit you, but why do you wear them?" she repeated.

"I feel comfortable in them. They make me feel as though I'm part of the people I live with in the desert," he said, stroking her with great gentleness. "And I want the Arabs to accept me. I want them to trust me."

"Why?"

He looked startled for a moment. "I love those people and I feel I have a great deal to offer them. They possess an inner beauty which most people don't see. Someday I want the world to see them as I do." He stopped and smiled. "Why are we talking about me? I want to talk about us."

He pressed his lips to hers and within minutes their passion for each other made all thoughts disappear. Lying on the hard ground with their arms wrapped around each other, she felt his hands caressing her body. He had unbuttoned her blouse and she could feel his fingers stroking her breasts. Trembling with excitement, she reached below his loose tunic and felt his bare back. His skin was smooth and she dug her fingers into his flesh. The need for him, the overwhelming desire to belong to him, made breathing difficult.

"I love you." She did not recognize her voice. "I love you more than life itself." The words she had wanted to say from the day she met him sounded delicious.

He raised himself on his elbows, cupped her face in his hands and stared at her for a long moment.

"I love you too, my darling, and I want to marry you."

The statement sobered her. "But you hardly know me."

"I know you. I know everything about you. From the minute I saw you, I knew that I loved you, that I wanted to marry you, that I wanted to spend the rest of my life with you."

"I knew it too." She closed her eyes. It was no dream. He was there beside her and he loved her.

"How long can you stay?" he asked, kissing her earlobe.

She sat up. "Oh, my God. Raphael is waiting for me and if I don't get back, he'll come looking for me." She struggled to her feet and felt dizzy.

Thomas stood up and caught her in his arms.

"When will I see you again?" She searched his face.

"I will drop in on your brother tomorrow morning. Will you be there?"

"I go back to Haifa this evening."

"Where do you live in Haifa?"

"With the Neemans. You met Mr. Neeman the other day and his wife, Sonya, is my nursing-school teacher. She also runs a convalescent home on Mount Carmel and I live there."

"I know the house." He put his arm around her waist and led her out of the fortress. "We leave for Alexandria day after tomorrow but I shall be back. May I call on you there?"

She looked up at him. How would she explain Thomas to Sonya? How could she explain him to anyone?

"Yes," she said defiantly. "Yes," she repeated.

He walked her to her horse and once mounted, she leaned down and kissed him again.

That was the last time she saw him. As the months went by and she did not hear from him, she again forced herself to accept the hopelessness of their relationship. It was that acceptance that made it possible for her to decide to marry Fredrick. But she had not forgotten Thomas and when Deborah started talking of love, all the feelings which she was sure she had put to rest, surfaced.

"Listen, Deborah." Tamar regained her composure and turned back to face her sister. "I like Fredrick, whether you do or not. Mama likes him and so does Raphael. And there are many reasons why people marry. Aside from all the obvious things Fredrick can offer me, he's also important to us as Jews in Palestine."

"In what way?"

"He deals in arms and we need them desperately." Tamar regretted the last statement, but having said it she had to continue. "I believe Fredrick is devoted to the idea of a Jewish homeland but as his wife, I can persuade him to be even more generous." She breathed a sigh of relief. Beyond all the other excuses for marrying Fredrick, that was the one that made most sense to her.

"Good God. Next you're going to tell me that Raphael wants you to marry Fredrick for patriotic reasons," Deborah said in disgust.

"Don't be a fool. Raphael never mentioned it and I doubt that the thought ever entered his mind. I figured it out on my own and when I pressed David about it, he admitted that they did have a deal with Fredrick. I'm sure Fredrick is sincere about us, but it won't hurt if I am there to remind him of his promise."

Deborah lowered her eyes. "Is that what you and David have been talking about recently?"

"Oh, my precious sister." Tamar rushed over to Deborah. "Can't you accept the fact that David and I are simply friends?"

Deborah threw her arms around Tamar's shoulder. "I still wish you weren't going to marry Fredrick," she said through her tears.

# CHAPTER
# SIX

DEBORAH walked out of the Bet Enav post office clutching Tamar's letter. Tamar had not been back in Palestine since her marriage almost two years earlier, and Deborah was hoping that this letter would indicate when she could come for a visit.

Once outside, Deborah examined the envelope. The word *Censored* stamped in red jumped out at her and it was dated September 1, 1915. It had taken over a month to get to her but since the outbreak of the war, the mail between Turkey and Palestine had been erratic. She was about to tear the envelope open when she heard the sound of marching feet ahead of her. She looked up to see a group of young men surrounded by Turkish soldiers coming down the street. She knew at once they were the latest draftees being forced to join the Turkish army, a common sight in recent months. She moved back as they came closer and was shocked to see that one of the boys in the group was Rabbi Landau's son. Until now the Turks had respected the children of the religious leaders of the community.

The boys all looked frightened and the soldiers, bayonets drawn, looked ferocious.

They had barely passed when mothers who had been following their sons caught sight of Deborah and rushed up to her.

"Deborah, you must talk to Raphael." Mrs. Landau grabbed her arm frantically. "It's an outrage." She began to cry. "Raphael is close to Jamal Pasha and he must exert his influence. He must."

The other women picked up her plea and Deborah's heart went out to them.

"What I don't understand is why they want our boys. Our sons are not trained soldiers and I thought Turkey was winning the war," a distraught woman cried out.

"Maybe they're not winning," another screamed. "Maybe it's just propaganda."

"Not winning?" A Turkish officer had overheard the last statement and walked toward Deborah.

"Forgive us," Deborah intervened quickly. "I don't for one minute believe that anyone in Palestine, and certainly not Jews, want Turkey to lose the war," she said with great sincerity. Badly as the Turks had been behaving toward the Jewish community, everyone hoped Germany and Turkey would win the war against the British, who were allied with the French and Russians. They preferred the Germans to the Russians, many having lived through the Russian pogroms.

"Well, please explain to these ladies that it is the duty of every citizen of the Ottoman Empire to serve in its armed forces and their men are simply doing their duty."

Deborah tried to smile. "They understand it and it's just the natural concern of mothers at seeing their children leave home."

He nodded and walked away, hitting his swagger stick against his boots.

"You will talk to Raphael, won't you?" Mrs. Landau whispered.

"He's been away for several weeks," Deborah said slowly. "But as soon as he's back, I'll talk to him, I promise."

Her answer did not satisfy them, but there was little they could do about it. Turning away from her, they wove their way through the crowded street, hoping to get a last glimpse of their sons.

Deborah watched them for a moment and suddenly realized how crowded the street was. She was also conscious that she knew no one. They were all bedraggled strangers, driven by hunger into the vicinity of Bet Enav. The sight of their despair and the aura of defeat which they exuded upset her.

She turned and hurried up the road, saddened by the change that had taken place in her village since the war started. Within minutes she found herself running. She wanted to get to the sanctity and serenity of her home.

Just before pushing the garden gate open, she looked back at her beloved village. Beyond it the fields were barren, ravaged by the locust plague which had struck the country earlier that year. She suppressed a sigh of desperation. The inhabitants of Bet Enav could barely feed themselves, much less the newcomers. Friction would soon break out, she was sure of it.

Once in her garden, Deborah sank into a chair and tried to compose herself. In a relatively short time, the realities of life had come crashing down around her and she was having a hard time coping with them. One tragedy seemed to follow another and they had affected her, her family and everyone in Palestine.

Throwing her head back, she stared at the sky. Was it possible that less than two years had gone by since they all stood on the terrace, watching Tamar and Fredrick drive down the road after their wedding and disappear beyond the bend?

Deborah recalled that day so vividly. She remembered feeling sad, but that sadness was mingled with a sense of relief. Somehow Tamar's departure freed her. When David proposed to her a month later, it seemed as though it was always meant to be. The wedding took place at the end of the summer. It was a beautiful July day and the whole town participated in the event. Her mother's health had improved and she seemed happier than she had been in a long time. David had been warm and loving and when he leaned over and kissed her after the ceremony, Deborah felt that life was complete. The only thing that diminished the happiness of that day was that Tamar could not attend, since she had suffered a miscarriage and could not travel. But Deborah and David were planning a honeymoon to Turkey and Deborah looked forward to their reunion. It never happened. Within days after the wedding, the Germans declared war against the Allies. Everyone waited to see if Turkey would join the Germans or if it would remain neutral. When Turkey entered the war on the side of Germany, the honeymoon trip was canceled. Everyone hoped for an early end to the hostilities and Deborah was sure her honeymoon was merely being postponed for a while.

But it had not worked out that way. She was settling down to being David's wife when her mother suffered a fatal heart attack. Although Marucia had been ill for many years, her death was a dreadful shock to all of them. By Jewish law, the funeral had to take place within twenty-four hours of the death. So there was no way Tamar could be present. Deborah and David moved into the Danziger house and he and Raphael tried to console Deborah, be with her, fill the void Marucia's death had left, but they had work to do at the laboratory and Deborah felt completely abandoned.

Then the locust plague struck the country, devastating the land. Raphael was named director of the war against the locusts and with David as his assistant, they traveled around the country trying to teach farmers how to battle the deadly grasshopper. They were gone for weeks and she would wait impatiently for their return. But even when home, they were usually secluded in Raphael's study and Deborah felt more excluded than ever. Her offer to help them in their work was dismissed. David felt she was too young, too inexperienced, too fragile.

Everything had gone wrong and she began to suspect that her marriage was suffering. David seemed bored with her. He was kind and gentle but she felt he still saw her as Raphael and Tamar's little sister. Her longing for Tamar grew daily. She was sure Tamar would help her understand the situation.

Suddenly Deborah remembered Tamar's letter. Taking it out of her pocket, she read it quickly. Tamar was not coming. She had suffered another miscarriage and was confined to bed. Tamar's health concerned Deborah, but what troubled her most was the whole tone of the letter. As always it was strangely cheerful, filled with superficial nonsense about the weather; the parties she and Fredrick attended; Aris, her Armenian maid; the clothes she bought, the jewelry she got and other frivolous details. Deborah knew her sister well and, reading between the lines, she could tell that Tamar was unhappy. She almost got the feeling that Tamar was being held prisoner in Fredrick's home. In one letter, Tamar had humorously described how she was chaperoned by Malikian, Fredrick's valet, whenever she left the house. He even drove her to the hospital, where she had begun to work as a volunteer when the war started. The idea that her independent sister could not wander about freely was staggering to Deborah. And all references to Fredrick were guarded. He was kind, gave her many gifts, they had a beautiful home, she had a lovely wardrobe, but Fredrick insisted Tamar wear a *charshaffe* whenever she went out. Tamar in a black *charshaffe*, like a Muslim woman! Deborah shuddered at the thought and wondered if Tamar had to cover her face as well.

Putting the letter down, Deborah thought about Tamar's reasons for marrying Fredrick. She was going to have an exciting, glamorous life. Well, as far as Deborah could see, none of that seemed to be happening. She also remembered the arms Fredrick had promised the Jews of Palestine. Deborah had no idea if Fredrick had kept his promise, but even if he had, it did not justify the marriage.

It was late afternoon and Deborah looked over at their house. Her attention was drawn to the attic window and she realized the shutters and window were open. No one ever went up there and the space was used to store old clothes, furniture and books. The sun was setting, so the window was nothing but a black mass and she could not make out if anyone was there. She was still staring at it when she saw a tiny beam of light flash on and disappear. It happened so quickly that for a moment she was not sure she had seen it at all.

Rushing up the stairs, she opened the attic door.

Raphael and David were standing by the window and did not hear her come in.

"What are you doing up here?" she demanded and walked to the window and scanned the area below. The Danziger house was built on a hill and Deborah tried to see what it was Raphael and David were looking at. Suddenly she caught sight of a flashing light coming from somewhere out at sea. It blinked several times and went out.

"It's nothing," David started to pull her away from the window.

She pushed him away angrily and glared at Raphael.

"Don't involve her in this," David warned.

"David, Deborah is not a child and she has every right to know what's going on," Raphael answered vehemently.

"And even if I were a child, I'm not an idiot," Deborah cried out. "I see an open window in a room that's never used. I see a light flicker from it and now I look out to sea and notice someone out there sending signals aimed at this house. Do you really believe I would simply ignore it?"

"I told you it wouldn't work," David hissed.

"Maybe not as originally conceived, but it will have its use." Raphael said and turned to Deborah. "We've decided to help the British win the war against the Turks," he said simply. "We've contacted British Intelligence and offered them our services, which they've accepted."

"What services?"

"We're going to collect military information about Turkish army activities and transmit it to them."

"You're going to spy for the enemy?" She was stunned.

"As far as I'm concerned," Raphael said, "the Turks are our enemy. Unlike most of the Jews both here and abroad, I think the Germans and the Turks are going to lose this war. The Ottoman Empire is doomed and it's just a matter of time and their downfall would be of great benefit to us. The Turks will never help us create a Jewish state. The British promised they would. And I believe we should try to prove our loyalty to them and hope they remember their promise when the time comes."

"But if you're caught you'll be jeopardizing every Jew in the country." Deborah's mind went back to the women who had begged her to talk to Raphael about their sons.

"We won't get caught. We're a small group. Everyone involved works for me and feels as I do. They travel around the country as my emissaries, working to control the plague. It's a perfect cover for what we're doing."

"What you're doing is treason."

"It is only treason if you've switched your loyalty. I was never loyal to the Turks and I certainly owe no loyalty to the Germans," Raphael answered.

"But most of the Jews of Palestine, certainly everyone in Bet Enav, does feel a loyalty toward Turkey," she insisted. "For God's sake, Tamar is living there."

"That is precisely why our friends must not know what we're doing. In that way, their loyalty can never be questioned. If we are caught, they can honestly claim they knew nothing of this work and that's how it must be." Raphael was looking at her with concern. "Maybe David was right and we should not have confided in you."

"You said you contacted the British. How?" She ignored his last remark.

"I was picked up by a British patrol ship, which came by one night and waited for me off shore. David rowed me to it and I sailed to Alexandria. That's also the way I came back."

"And how will you get information to the British?"

"The same way I got to Alexandria. A British patrol boat will pass by when it's safe and if we signal them that we have something for them, they will send a small rowboat over to the shore and collect it."

"And you were going to do this from this window?" she asked.

"No, the work will be done from my laboratory. This window was going to be the backup. An open window means we have information. A closed window indicates we don't or that it's too dangerous to come ashore."

Deborah threw a last look at the darkening sky and turned to her brother. "How can I help?"

"Here I agree with David. I don't think you should become actively involved," Raphael said quickly. "I think it's important that you know what we're doing but you must go on as though you know nothing. Just continue to be the lady of the manor." He walked over to her and hugged her. "We must keep up appearances at all costs."

"Knowing is already an involvement," she said, disengaging herself from his embrace.

"Well, I forbid it." David spoke up for the first time.

She walked over to him and putting her hand to his cheek, she smiled sweetly. "That's silly. I'm sure I can be of help." He was treating her like a little girl and she wondered what she could do to prove to him that she had grown up.

"What are you going to call this operation?" she asked as she turned back to Raphael.

"Call it?" Raphael looked over at David. "I never thought of naming it."

David reached over for a book on a nearby shelf and opened it. "Here." He handed it to Deborah. "It's a Bible and I'm sure you can find something appropriate on this page."

She saw the words immediately. "Nili," she said excitedly. "It should be called Nili." And rushing over to Raphael she showed him the passage. "*Netzach Israel Lo Ishaker.*"

"*The eternity of Israel shall not lie.*" Raphael smiled at her. "It's perfect."

"I think I'll name my first child Nili." She grew serious and looked over at David. It was the first time she thought of having a baby. David was bound to see her differently if she gave him a child.

# CHAPTER
# SEVEN

As 1915 drew to a close, the war raged on and Germany and Turkey seemed to have the edge on most fronts. Death, hunger, disease and hopelessness prevailed. Conditions in Palestine were catastrophic, yet most Jews of Palestine continued to be loyal to the Turkish Empire. As far as they were concerned, the consequence of dissent was treason and treason was punishable by death. Nili and all who participated in its clandestine activities were in constant danger of exposure, not only by the Turks and Arabs but by their own neighbors as well. Recruiting reliable people became difficult and in desperation Raphael asked Deborah to come in and help.

Raphael's laboratory was relatively safe. It was neutral territory, since Raphael was doing work for the United States, which had not yet entered the war. Also his work on the locust plague was sanctioned by the Turkish rulers. Only the handful of people involved with Nili were aware of the secret work conducted at the laboratory in Raphael's private study on the second floor.

The Nili operation was deceptively simple. Raphael had many emissaries traveling around the country trying to control the plague. All brought their reports to Raphael. The Nili men's reports, to the untrained eye, were similar to the reports from the emissaries working on the plague. However, the Nili reports included coded military material which was sorted and evaluated by Raphael, David and David's brother Avi. Deborah, who quickly became an active member of the group in spite of David's trepidation, was the one who decoded the material and readied it for dispatch. Transmitting the information to the British was difficult. Since no set schedule for pickup could be established, someone was required to sit on the shore night after night waiting for the ship to sail by. Then, only if the coast was clear and the weather conducive would a boat row ashore for the pickup. The lookout point was beneath the Crusaders' Castle.

Deborah insisted on taking her turn in these watches. She hated them, and was grateful whenever David would join her. It also afforded time alone with him, which had grown more rare as his workload increased.

It had been a long, rainy night and Deborah and David had just finished their watch. Crawling away from the castle, they struggled up the embankment. They were drenched by the time they reached the top and Deborah, cold and tired, leaned against a water-logged wooden pole while David tried to pull the thick wet blanket over her head and shoulders.

"Maybe we should have waited a while longer," she said. "It just might clear up."

"Look around you," David answered impatiently. "That storm doesn't look as though it will ever end. Besides, it's almost dawn and Raphael is waiting for me."

She stared out at the sea. The rain was coming down in torrents and the fog sat low in the water, completely obscuring the horizon.

"It was so clear out when we got here," she murmured in frustration.

"Well, we've had a rather mild winter, so it makes sense that the end of January should bring these rains." He smiled mirthlessly. "With all our other problems, we were facing a drought if we didn't get any rain." He too looked around. "I just wish it had held off for the night. The information we now have for the British could really make a difference. Anyway, let me run down and smooth out the sand in case someone decides to search the area." He stopped and a look of concern came over his face. "You'll be all right, won't you?"

"I'll be fine," she answered. Involved as she was in their dangerous assignment, David still treated her like a child.

Before moving away, David removed his gun from his holster and placed it beside her.

"What's that for?" she asked, staring at it.

"With the Turks wandering around this area and the Arabs more belligerent than ever, you can never tell who might come by, even on a night like this."

"I could never shoot anyone," Deborah said quietly.

"You will if someone threatens your life."

"I don't think so." She thought for a moment. "Although I suppose I would if someone threatened the life of a person I loved." She reached up and touched his arm. "I would kill if someone tried to hurt you," she said softly.

"Then you understand why I want you to defend yourself. I'd hate to lose you."

She smiled gratefully and watched him slide down toward the castle. The monstrous black rock, barely visible through the fog, still frightened her, and while she did not mind any of the work involved with Nili, she dreaded crouching beneath that rock at night, waiting for the British ship to arrive. Tamar would have found it an adventure, she thought wryly. Tamar, she knew, loved that castle. Poor Tamar. She belonged in Palestine. She belonged with her family. She would have been invaluable to Nili. In her last letter Tamar wrote that she might be coming home in March, a second anniversary gift to her from Fredrick. Deborah was sure it would not happen.

"I'm back," David said and Deborah jumped with fright.

"What's the matter?" David asked.

"I didn't hear you," she whispered.

He put his arm around her. "Poor baby, you really should not be involved in this work."

"Would you have felt the same about Tamar?" She was surprised by her question.

"I don't know. I've never thought about it," David said wistfully.

"David, why didn't you marry Tamar?" she asked. More and more she was haunted by the idea that David would have been happier with Tamar.

He thought for a long moment. "The truth is she didn't want to marry me," he said. "And in a way she was right. It would not have been a good marriage." He pressed her to him. "I could never have held Tamar as I'm holding you. She would never have permitted me to take care of her or protect her." He kissed her hair. "You're my girl. A sweet, soft, gentle baby and I'm glad I married you."

David still refused to accept that she had changed, she thought sadly. He didn't see that she had grown up, that she was no longer a child. Much as she loved him, his attitude inhibited her and strained their relationship.

It was still dark when they reached the laboratory and, except for an ancient Arab watchman who had been with Raphael for many years, no one was around.

They found Raphael standing in front of a map of Palestine, pointer in hand, talking to Avi. Two extremely young men whom Deborah had never seen before were sitting on a sofa. As soon as Deborah and David walked in, Avi and his two companions left.

"What are we doing, snatching babies out of the cradle and making spies of them?" David demanded when Avi and the young men were gone.

Raphael looked up briefly, smiled and returned to the map.

"David is right," Deborah said with equal vehemence. "Who are those little boys?"

"One is named Yossi and the other is Benny. They're from the south and they're not as young as they look and they're damn good kids," Raphael said.

"But what happens if they're caught? They don't look as though they could withstand any sort of interrogation, much less any torture," Deborah cried out indignantly. Her obsession with being found out had grown.

"Deborah, get hold of yourself. Really trustworthy people are becoming more and more difficult to find. And now that the Turks have decided that the British are going to attack them from the sea, this area is swarming with their patrols." Raphael took a deep breath before continuing. "I think you should know that our neighbors in Bet Enav are becoming suspicious of us and might turn on us if they found out what we were doing."

Deborah lowered her eyes. "They do suspect something," she said.

"How do you know?" David asked.

"Well, for starters, fewer and fewer children come to play in our garden. I can also feel a chill when I go to the marketplace, or when I drop in to visit someone who's sick. They're polite but I get the feeling they want me out of their house as quickly as possible. Even Fatmi and Mahmud have commented about how the villagers are treating them."

"You should have mentioned it," Raphael said angrily.

"I wasn't sure. It was just a feeling." She became defensive.

"Damn it." David walked over and stared at the dim light of day which was struggling to penetrate the dense fog. "It would all make some sort of sense if the information we gather was getting through to the Allies. But it's been weeks, and for all we know they've decided to stop all contact with us and we're endangering ourselves and everyone around us for no reason."

"Until I hear that that is the case, we'll go on doing what we've committed ourselves to do," Raphael snapped.

"I think you should give serious consideration to my plan to get to Alexandria through the desert," David said with his back to them.

Deborah threw a frantic look at Raphael. David had spoken of this plan before and it frightened her.

"You'll do no such thing," Raphael's agitation grew. "Nili is totally dependent on four people. You, Deborah, Avi and me. At this point we can't afford to lose anyone. Is that clear? And if someone has to go, I'll try to get to Germany with Jamal Pasha's permission and somehow work my way over to the Allies and see what's going on."

"I'd much rather you'd go through Turkey," David said. "Maybe you can find out why Fredrick hasn't been sending us arms. We sure as hell could use them."

"He's not sending arms?" Deborah's heart sank. "You mean Fredrick hasn't kept his promise?"

Raphael and David both turned to her.

"How do you know about it?" Raphael asked slowly.

Deborah looked from one to the other. "That was one of the reasons Tamar had for marrying him. She felt that as his wife . . ."

"What an idiotic idea," Raphael blanched. "I wonder how she came by that notion?"

"She figured it out," David said quickly. "Fredrick was an arms merchant, she knew that. We were courting him and she put two and two together. She hounded me about it for days and I finally relented and told her the facts." He shrugged helplessly. "The rest is typical of Tamar."

"That was not the only reason she married Fredrick," Deborah came to David's defense. "She was going to marry him anyway."

"Good God, what a fool!" Raphael lost control. "My sister whoring for arms? It's insane." He started pacing around the room. "And to think that I thought this might be a good marriage for her!"

"You can't blame yourself for her marriage," David said, trying to soothe Raphael. "She wanted to get married, get away, have an exciting life."

"Well, is she?" Raphael looked over at Deborah. "I only skim through her letters. You read them. Is she happy?"

Deborah swallowed hard. "I don't know," she whispered.

"What does she say in her letters?" Raphael demanded. "How does she sound?"

"I think she's miserable." Deborah was on the verge of tears. "I think the whole thing has been some ghastly mistake and she doesn't know how to get out of it."

"Well, she's got to come home, that's all there's to it." Raphael tried to gain control of himself. "I'll write to Fredrick and tell him I want her home."

"He won't let her go," Deborah said. "As Tamar said, he may be German by birth, but he's now a total Levantine husband. She's his wife, his possession."

"We'll see about that," Raphael said through clenched teeth. "Now let's get on with things that we can do something about right now." He was back to being the scientist, but Deborah knew that he had made up his mind to bring Tamar home from Turkey.

Picking up a ruler, Raphael turned to his map and pointed toward the northern part of the country. "We know the Turks were building a railroad from Acre all the way to Gaza. Meaning that they're planning another assault on the Suez. But at the rate they were going, it didn't seem imminent. Now they've suddenly been joined by German engineers and the work has progressed so rapidly that it should be completed by the end of this month. I think the British must make every effort to blow up those tracks from the air."

"Good God," David whistled. "The end of January is ten days away."

"I'd say you have until early March," someone said and Deborah, David and Raphael swung around.

Michael Ben Hod, dressed in a Turkish officer's uniform, was leaning against the doorpost.

"How did you get in here?" Raphael demanded.

"An Arab, no matter how serious he is about his work, is hardly going to get into an argument with a Turkish officer," Michael answered looking around the room. "So, my first suggestion to you is, if you're going to run a spy ring, you should have a better security system."

"You are an insolent bastard," David hissed.

"Stop it, David," Raphael ordered, never taking his eyes off Michael. "March, you say? How do you know?"

"The station master in Acre is a friend of mine."

"Why are you telling us this?" Raphael asked.

"I think it's important for you to be accurate in what you tell the British," Michael said evenly.

"Tell the British?" Raphael did not blink.

"If Nili is going to supply incorrect information to the British, it will lose credibility."

"I'd like to kill you," David burst forth, unable to control his anger.

"How do you know about Nili? And why are you in a Turkish uniform? Are you spying on us for them?" Raphael asked.

"I don't blame you for being suspicious." Michael's tone changed. "No, I'm not spying for the Turks. I'm in uniform because I volunteered to get into Turkish military school and they've given me a commission." He paused. "But being a Turkish officer has not changed the fact that I am first of all a Jew."

"How do you know so much about Nili?" Raphael's tone took on a friendlier note.

"Not everybody distrusts me. And I make it a point to know everything that anyone does for the good of the Jews of Palestine."

"I don't believe you," David said and turned to Raphael. "You can't possibly believe that little speech."

Deborah watched Michael as this exchange took place. She had only seen him once before and that was on Tamar's eighteenth birthday. Four years had gone by since then and she was amazed at the transformation that had taken place in him. He had shaved off his beard, exposing a strong, square chin and a strangely sensuous mouth. His red hair was brushed back neatly and its rust color contrasted well with the tailored khaki army uniform. Suddenly she realized that he was looking at her and she noted that his eyes were a startling shade of green. They were the eyes of an honest man.

"I believe him." Deborah tore her eyes away from Michael.

"Thank you, Miss Danziger." He smiled and turned to Raphael. "I hope you do, too, Dr. Danziger."

"What do you want?" Raphael asked, seating himself behind his desk.

"I want to help Nili."

"Never," David said.

"I want to help fight for our Jewish homeland," Michael said more forcefully.

"How many of your friends know about us?" Raphael asked.

"Reb obviously does, but he wishes you neither success nor failure, although you can be sure he won't harm you. Then there are two or three others, but they won't turn you in either. They feel as I do. They hate the Turks and they too want the British to win. Unlike me, they won't join you, but they won't betray you."

"The stationmaster who gave you the information—is he reliable?" Raphael asked.

"He's someone we can get to work for Nili. I'm sure of it."

"When will you be seeing him next?" Raphael asked.

"I'm accompanying Jamal Pasha to Acre in a few days before we go to Constantinople."

"Get the stationmaster to commit to us and we'll have someone in touch with him from there," Raphael said, and it was clear that he had accepted Michael Ben Hod as a member of their group. "Incidentally, I would appreciate your coming by before leaving for Turkey. I may have an errand for you while you're there." Then he frowned. "March, you say? God, I hope we can get the British to blow that damn thing up before it's put into use."

"Well, if they don't, why don't we do it?" Michael asked.

"We don't believe in violence," David said.

"Spying is violence," Michael answered.

Raphael stood up quickly, sensing that David was about to explode again and walked over to Michael.

"I'm not a violent man, David," he said quietly. "But before this war is over there will be a great deal of violence and we shall not be able to avoid it."

"You can't really be serious." David's face was red with rage. "You really believe this man will be loyal to us?"

"I know the stationmaster at Acre." Raphael smiled for the first time. "We just don't have enough men to cover all the areas and contact the people who can help us." Then turning to Michael, he shook his hand and waved David to follow him out of the room.

Deborah was uncomfortable at being left alone with Michael.

"Miss Danziger," he said haltingly. "I know we meet under the strangest circumstances. And I must appear to you like some wild, ill-mannered boor. But I'm not." His voice was gentle. "Can we be friends?" he asked, extending his hand toward her.

"Of course we can," she said and put out her hand.

He shook it gratefully and smiled. "Thank you," he said and seemed reluctant to let go of her.

She withdrew her hand as gracefully as she could, fearful of offending him. "Incidentally," she said, "I'm Mrs. Larom now. But you should call me Deborah."

"Oh, I hadn't heard," he said quietly and, bowing stiffly, he left the room.

Deborah walked over to the window and watched him walk away. He was the first man who had ever treated her like a woman, not a child. It pleased her and she felt herself blush at the thought.

# CHAPTER
# EIGHT

T AMAR walked over to the window of her bedroom and stared out. The Bosphorus was breathtakingly beautiful, gleaming radiantly against the early morning sky. Yet she would have exchanged it all for a glimpse of the Mediterranean and the barren landscape she once saw from her window in Bet Enav. Just as she would have exchanged Fredrick's huge, over-furnished house for her more modest home in Palestine.

Turning away from the window she looked around the room. She had furnished it herself, as Fredrick had promised. The French style she chose blended with the Oriental architecture of the room. She had spent a great deal of time over the decor and it was unquestionably her room, her sanctuary. It was also her prison. As the last thought surfaced, she looked over at the door which led to Fredrick's room and her eyes came to rest on the doorplate, with its graceful handle and large brass key. She stared at it for a long moment. Although over two years had passed since her arrival in Turkey, the sight of any lock still frightened her and although she knew that she could walk over to it and open it by simply pushing down the handle, the feeling of being a prisoner in her own home never left her. Fredrick was her warden.

She shook her head in dismay. Her marriage to Fredrick had been a terrible mistake, and she knew it that first morning when she woke up on the ship taking them from Palestine to Turkey.

Even now the memory of it was all too vivid.

It was a beautiful sunny morning, and she was alone in the cabin. Vaguely she wondered where Fredrick was, but she was grateful for the time alone. She stared out the porthole and dwelt briefly on her wedding night. It had not been pleasant, but Fredrick had been quite gentle with her and there was little pain connected with the act of lovemaking. She assumed that what she had gone through was simply the expected ritual between husband and wife and that she could learn to live with it.

She felt at peace as she clambered out of bed and ambled around the cabin. Her thoughts turned to her family in Bet Enav. To her surprise, she did not feel the loss that was so acute the day before. She was Mrs. Fredrick David-zohn, yet she was alone with her thoughts as she would have been at home before going down for breakfast.

The thought of food made her hungry. She washed up and chose her clothes carefully. Dressed in a navy ankle-length skirt, with a matching three-quarter jacket, she scanned her image in the full-length mirror and was pleased with what she saw. She hoped Fredrick would be proud of her. She wanted him to be. She was actually excited about seeing him. She walked to the door and pushed down the handle. It was locked. She looked around for the key, assuming it was on the table. It was not. She pulled at the door again. It would not open. A panic she had never experienced before took hold of her. She thought of banging on the door to attract the attention of someone who might be passing by. Something stopped her. Fredrick might have accidentally locked the door and attracting attention to her predicament would be embarrassing. She felt faint, in need of air. Opening the porthole, she breathed deeply. In minutes her head cleared and she started pacing around the cabin. She felt trapped. Then she heard the key turn in the lock and she swung around. Fredrick, standing in the doorway, was smiling.

"You are up, my dear." His smile turned to bewilderment when he saw her expression. "What is the matter?" he asked cupping her chin in his hand and lifting her face to his.

Her impulse was to push his hand away, but she restrained herself.

"The door was locked," she whispered.

"Well, yes, my dear, I locked it." He said it as though it were the most natural thing to do.

"But why?" She tried to compose herself.

He hesitated briefly before answering. "I did not want you to be disturbed."

Their eyes met and Tamar knew he was lying. She lowered her eyes, fearful that he would see her distrust and disgust.

She was so engrossed in the memory that she jumped when she heard her bedroom door open and Fredrick walked in.

"Tamar, my dear." He came over and kissed her on the forehead. "Have you had your breakfast?" he asked, smiling warmly at her.

"Aris should be bringing it up any moment," Tamar answered, surprised at his cordiality. Since her last miscarriage, when the doctor warned her not to get pregnant for at least six months, Fredrick had been avoiding her. His sudden affectionate manner made her uncomfortable.

She turned and walked back to the window. "Have you had yours?" she asked with her back to him.

"Malikian brought up my coffee and I asked him to have my breakfast tray brought up here so we could have it together. Is that all right with you?"

"Of course." Tamar sat down in one of the armchairs, still puzzled by his behavior.

"Will you be home for dinner tonight?" she asked for lack of anything else to say.

"I'm not sure," he said. "I have a meeting with Abbas Pasha and I'll have a clearer idea of my plans after I've talked to him." He appeared uncomfortable. "In any event, we can discuss it when I come in for lunch."

"Fredrick, you know I'm going to the hospital today and I'll be there until four in the afternoon," she said patiently.

"Do you think you should be doing all that work so soon after your . . ." He stopped in confusion.

"My miscarriage?" she helped him out.

"Well, I think you should regain your strength fully before plunging back into that daily routine. Although the doctor assured me that your misfortunes have nothing to do with your work, I disagree. I believe you were run down and that's why it happened."

"I agree with the doctor. My work at the hospital had nothing to do with it," she said with confidence. Then, aware of her husband's unhappiness over her latest miscarriage, she softened her tone.

"The fact is I'm needed at the hospital. There's an awful lot of work to be done and there simply aren't enough nurses." When he did not react, she continued. "You know Fredrick, if I didn't read our newspapers which report how well we're doing at the front, I would say we were in dire trouble. There are an unbelievable number of wounded men pouring into the hospital." She paused, hoping her statement would force him to tell her what was really happening, especially in Palestine. The newspapers were vague and the news slanted.

"The war is going very well," Fredrick said firmly. "As a matter of fact we're on the offensive now and that's one of the reasons I'm so unsure about my plans for the evening. Abbas wants me to meet with some German officers to discuss some new arms deal and that could take quite a bit of time." He tried to smile. "As a matter of fact, Jamal Pasha might be joining us and we might all be having dinner together."

"And where would you have dinner?" Tamar asked, although she already knew the answer. It explained, in part, his friendly manner. If Jamal Pasha was coming to his home, Fredrick would be enormously honored and she knew it.

"I thought I'd ask them to come and have dinner with me here," he said lightly. "And I was hoping you'd help make it a truly sumptuous meal. You're so clever that way."

She bit her lip. "You want me to prepare the menu, supervise the dinner preparations, but as always, I am not to be present when the guests arrive." Her anger spilled over. "I am to stay in my room, eat dinner alone and wait until your guests leave before being permitted to come down to my own living room."

"My dinner with Abbas Pasha is a business dinner. It's an extremely important dinner for me," Fredrick said stiffly. "The army is pushing southward towards the Suez Canal and they need a whole new line of military equipment. Abbas and General Schtock are asking me to supply the arms and it could prove extremely lucrative."

In spite of herself she reacted to the news about the push toward the Suez Canal and he stopped, aware that he had said too much. When he next spoke, his voice took on a different tone.

"Tamar, I refuse to have this argument with you. We are now in Turkey and I will not have my home made into a debating society because you feel left out of my business world. Business, war business, is a man's domain everywhere, not only in Turkey."

"I hate to contradict you, but you've had your friends over on numerous occasions for social, not business, reasons and I've been excluded," she said forcefully. "Since coming to Pera, you've made me feel like some little concubine." Her voice rose and she was surprised at her audacity, but she could not stop. "What makes it all the more ridiculous is that I work with the wounded at the hospital and am accepted by the Turks there who seem delighted with my nursing abilities. But I can't sit at a table with them in my own home. Don't you see how foolish that is?"

"When we have guests who bring their wives, I am proud to have you host the party." Fredrick's voice was controlled, but he was equally angry.

"Our parties are a dreadful bore and you know it." Tamar would not be deterred. "The women sit around talking about clothes, food, their children . . ." She stopped, regretting the last words.

"I certainly can't be held responsible for that," he replied.

Tamar lowered her eyes in embarrassment. He had never openly accused her for the miscarriages.

"I'm sorry, Tamar, but you will not be able to join us for dinner tonight," Fredrick said with finality. "We are, however, invited to the Maranises' tonight. Would you like to go and represent us both? I can join you when my guests leave."

She was surprised. Fredrick did not like Rabbi Maranis.

"Would you?" he repeated.

Before Tamar could answer, there was a light tap on the door and Aris came in carrying a large breakfast tray.

"Good morning, effendi," the young woman said softly, bowing to Fredrick. She walked over to Tamar and placed the tray on a round copper table next to her chair. "Good morning, Bayan Tamar," she whispered softly and withdrew quickly from the room.

"I do wish you wouldn't allow her to call you by your first name," Fredrick said the minute Aris was gone.

"I don't see that it makes much difference," Tamar said defiantly.

"Your maid should treat you with the deference accorded to a mistress."

"What she calls me is immaterial. The fact is I look upon her as a friend."

"That's precisely what I mean. She is not your friend. She is your servant and servants in Turkey must know their place."

"She has never been disrespectful to me. If anything, I believe she is as loyal and interested in doing a good job in her service as any maid calling her mistress by whatever name," she answered quietly. They had had this discussion numerous times and she had no intention of changing her relationship with Aris. Aris was the only friend she had in Turkey and the only person she trusted. In a way, Aris reminded her of Deborah, which made her all the more precious.

"You cannot go on defying all our customs," Fredrick's voice boomed forth in rage.

"Which one are you talking about?" Tamar asked. "My wanting to be treated like a proper mistress of my own house, or my attitude toward Aris?"

Fredrick's face grew red. But whereas in the past Tamar would have been frightened by his explosive temper, now she found him almost comical.

"It seems to me that you have a very informal relationship with Malikian and you never think he's being disrespectful," Tamar continued when he did not answer.

"Malikian is a servant, has always been one and doesn't want to be anything else. Aris has had an education and she probably thinks she shouldn't be a maid."

"She's right," Tamar concurred, but her thoughts lingered briefly on Malikian. Close as she was to Aris, they never discussed Malikian. Sometimes she forgot they were father and daughter.

"Would you like some coffee?" she asked absentmindedly.

"I don't believe I have time for coffee," Fredrick said through clenched teeth and walked stiffly out of the room.

While dressing, Tamar's thoughts went back to what Fredrick had said about the push toward the Suez Canal and she wondered what effect it would have on Palestine. She knew so little of what was happening there. Deborah's letters were strangely guarded, but it was clear that things were not going well, even in Bet Enav. What troubled Tamar more was that Raphael had not come to Turkey once since her marriage. She expected that he would, if only to discuss the arms that Fredrick had promised them. The last thought upset her more than any other. She had no idea if Fredrick had kept his promise to her brother. When they were first married, she tried to broach the subject but Fredrick never gave her a direct answer. And since her last miscarriage, there was barely any dialogue between them and any mention of Palestine or her family seemed to upset him.

Suddenly she felt like a fool. Somehow she had to get away from Fredrick. She wanted to go back to Palestine and forget this unfortunate marriage.

Somehow she had to persuade Fredrick to let her go. She had tried to be an obedient and proper wife but it had not worked out. She was sure he was equally unhappy and disappointed in their union. She knew he would not agree to a divorce but he might agree to let her visit her family for a while. She would talk to him that evening, she decided. She would do what Fredrick asked of her. She would arrange the dinner, make sure it was exactly as he wished it. She would stay in her room like an obedient Turkish wife and when the guests departed, she would talk to him.

With renewed determination, she walked over to her dressing table. As she started putting things into her handbag, her eyes fell on the framed pictures of Deborah and Raphael. Her sister staring straight into the camera seemed to be smiling at her. Raphael, sitting on his favorite horse, looked powerful, elegant and self-assured. The pictures were not recent ones and Tamar wondered if they had changed since she last saw them.

She raised her eyes and stared at herself in the mirror. She knew she had changed. Her blond hair was properly coiffed, her white skin was flawless, her eyes were as clear and as blue as ever. But her expression was different. She looked older, more poised, more in keeping with the image of the wife of a prosperous Turkish businessman. At some point she had crossed the threshold marking the departure of her youth. The exuberance, the joy, the love of life which were so much part of her while growing up had vanished. Her years of marriage had taken their toll.

Unconsciously she reached over and picked up the small, framed postcard standing inconspicuously on the dressing table. It was the picture of the medieval castle in Palestine which Thomas had sent her the day of her eighteenth birthday. The loving message on the back was hidden by the matting but she knew it was there and it afforded her a happy memory, a touch of romance, a license to fantasize what might have been.

"Effendum Davidzohn." Tamar heard her name called and she looked around. Malikian was in the doorway.

"Malikian, I wish you'd knock before opening the door," she said as pleasantly as she could, although she was furious at the intrusion.

"I've been knocking for several minutes and I got concerned." Malikian, tall, erect and dignified, came into the room.

"I didn't hear you." Tamar regained her composure and focused her attention on the servant. He made her uncomfortable and she was convinced he was spying on her. Again, she wondered about how different he was from Aris.

"It's nearly eight o'clock and the carriage is waiting," he said stiffly.

Wrapping the black *charshaffe* around her shoulders, she preceded him out of the room.

"Was there any mail?" she asked, walking down the stairs.

"There is a letter for you on the console."

The letter was from Deborah. Tamar ripped the envelope open and read it quickly.

It was an unusually short letter, marked *Censored* as they all were. Deborah hoped Tamar was well. David and Raphael were working hard and she was helping them. Bet Enav had many new inhabitants. Most of the men had been drafted. Fatmi and Mahmud were well and life was continuing much as it had since the war started. It was the closing sentence that puzzled Tamar. Raphael wished to be remembered to Rabbi Maranis.

Sitting in her carriage, on the way to the hospital, Tamar tried to under-stand Deborah's last comment. She doubted that Raphael even knew the rabbi, but obviously they wanted her to contact him. The question was why. On the rare occasions that she and Fredrick were there, the rabbi showed little interest in what was happening in Palestine. He was a loyal Turkish citizen and she never suspected that his interest was any more than mere politeness. Had she misjudged him? Was he a Jew first and a Turk only by virtue of his citizenship?

She thought of changing her plans and going to the rabbi's house that evening after all. But she wanted to be home to please Fredrick and to talk with him about letting her take the trip home. She settled on the latter plan. There usually were too many people at the Maranises' gatherings and she doubted she would have a chance to speak privately with him. She would have Malikian deliver a note to the rabbi asking for an appointment tomorrow afternoon.

The carriage came to a stop and Tamar realized they had reached the hospital. As always, Malikian helped her down, assuring her that he would be waiting for her when she was through with her day's work. She was relieved to see him go.

Walking through the hospital grounds, Tamar noted that there was an unusual amount of activity around. Numerous carriages carrying the wounded kept driving up and male nurses were running around frantically, shouting at the drivers to get back to the dock and bring the next batch of wounded.

To avoid the crush, Tamar walked to a side entrance. Just as she was about to go through it, she caught sight of the prisoners' hospital. It stood at the far end of the hospital compound, and although it was hidden behind black cypress trees and thick vines, one could still see the heavily barred windows and massive steel doors. It was rumored that prisoners who had been tortured by the Turks were brought there to die. It could not be proven, since the only ones who left were in coffins. She felt a shudder go through her, and she turned quickly and ran into the hospital.

The head nurse, wearing her white uniform with the red crescent marking on her cap, was waiting for her in the nurses' quarters.

"It's a shambles this morning," she snapped at Tamar. "I don't know where we'll put all the wounded that were brought in since midnight."

"Where did they come from?" Tamar asked casually, slipping into her uniform.

"I don't know, but they're not from the north, I can tell you that. From the dust and grime, I'd say they were on the southern front."

Tamar's concern for her family grew.

The rounds were particularly grueling that morning. Following the doctor through the ward, Tamar wondered if she dared ask one of the wounded where he came from, but that would have been a breach of every rule. She was a woman and a foreigner.

"*Hemsire.*" Tamar heard one of the patients call to her. She looked toward the doctor for permission to go to the man. The doctor, busy with another patient, nodded.

She leaned over the bed and felt the man grab her arm. The gesture frightened her but before she would utter a sound, she realized the man was speaking Hebrew.

She looked at him closely. He was vaguely familiar.

"Motti Landau," he whispered, aware of her confusion. Suddenly she recognized the boy from her home village. He was Rabbi Landau's son.

"What are you doing here?" she gasped.

"Give me some water, so it looks natural for you to be talking to me." He spoke with difficulty.

Holding his head up, she put a glass to his lips.

"What are you doing here?" she asked again.

"They've drafted every man they could find," he mumbled.

"Do you know anything about my family?"

"Is everything all right?" she heard the doctor ask.

She stood up quickly, but as she did she heard Motti whisper "Maranis."

"What did he say?" The doctor asked.

"Something that sounded like maranis," she said truthfully.

"What does it mean?"

"I haven't the vaguest idea," she answered and picked up her chart.

They continued their rounds but Tamar's mind was whirling with concern and confusion. The war had obviously affected the Jews of Palestine and even Raphael's good relations with the Turks had not succeeded in sparing the young men from Bet Enav. Now she could not wait for the day to end. Much as she wanted to be in her room when Fredrick arrived home, she had to stop by the rabbi's house. Raphael had wanted her to see Maranis and now Motti was urging her to contact him.

Malikian was waiting for her when she finished work.

"You're to stop by Rabbi Maranis's house on the way home," she said as she settled down in the back of the carriage.

He turned to stare at her.

"I decided not to go there for dinner and would like to make my apologies in person."

"I would have happily delivered the message for you," he said pleasantly.

"Do as I say, Malikian," she said firmly, although her heart was pounding. She wished she could overcome her fear of him.

# CHAPTER NINE

T HE Maranises' maid opened the door and, after hesitating briefly, she asked Tamar to wait in the foyer. Tamar understood the maid's hesitation. It was unusual for a woman to come to the rabbi's house unannounced and alone and then ask to speak to the rabbi rather than his wife. The rabbi look equally surprised when he came to greet her.

"Forgive the intrusion, rabbi," she said the minute she saw him. "But it is a matter of great importance and I must talk to you."

He nodded pleasantly and ushered her into his small study. It was a musty, dimly lit room and it took a minute for her eyes to adjust to the darkness. Only then did she notice someone leaning against a bookcase at the far end of the room.

"I believe you know Michael Ben Hod," the rabbi said.

Impulsively Tamar started toward Michael but stopped when she saw him nod coldly. She regained her composure quickly, as the circumstances of their only meeting at her eighteenth birthday party came back to her. She had been so thrilled to see a familiar face, someone from home, that she had forgotten how cruelly she had behaved that night. He, obviously, had not forgotten.

"Why don't you sit down," the rabbi urged, seating himself behind his desk.

She did as she was told, never taking her eyes off Michael. It struck her that he was an extremely handsome man who exuded an animallike masculinity. She was surprised that he was dressed in an impeccably fitted Turkish uniform, indicating that he was no mere draftee but a rank above the Palestinian boys who were forced into service; and his elegance bothered her. On the occasion of their previous meeting he had said something about not having enough to eat. She also recalled that Jamal Pasha had been extremely cordial to Michael that night, and it disturbed her. What she had to say to the rabbi was hardly something a friend of Jamal Pasha should be privy to.

"Now, what seems to be so urgent, Mrs. Davidzohn?" the rabbi asked.

She hesitated, still looking at Michael.

"It's all right." Rabbi Maranis said. "You can say anything in front of Mr.

Ben Hod. As a matter of fact, I was expecting you for dinner tonight and Mr. Ben Hod was most anxious to talk to you.''

Was it possible that Raphael wanted her to contact the rabbi because Michael had a message for her? Raphael, in a way, also worked for Jamal Pasha. She had little time to pursue the thought, aware that the rabbi was waiting for her to speak.

"Well, the fact is that I won't be coming to dinner." She tore her eyes away from Michael and looked over at the rabbi.

The rabbi waited for her to continue.

"My brother sends you his regards," she continued and felt foolish. That was hardly an urgent reason to see him. "Motti Landau, the son of Rabbi Landau, is in hospital. He's hurt and he mentioned your name to me," she blurted out.

Rabbi Maranis stared at her blankly.

His attitude confused her. She was sure he would be upset. She looked over at Michael again. He was lighting a cigarette, as though he were a disinterested bystander.

"How seriously is he hurt?" the rabbi finally asked, still sounding impersonal.

"It's his legs. I believe one of them is gangrenous."

"Is he being treated properly?"

"Not properly enough," Tamar answered. "The overcrowding is unbearable and although everyone is trying, it's hardly conducive to good treatment."

"Thank you," the rabbi said almost formally.

"Can you do anything for him?" she persisted.

He looked at her questioningly.

"Should I talk to Fredrick about it?" she asked, her confusion mounting. She had no intention of talking to Fredrick about Motti and she said it for lack of anything else to say.

The rabbi lowered his eyes for a moment before answering. "Do you think you should?"

She was surprised by the question and realized that the rabbi did not trust Fredrick. Her distrust of Fredrick had grown in the last few months but she did not realize that others felt as she did.

"Rabbi Maranis, you must help Motti get out of that hospital," she whispered.

"My dear child, I don't know what I can do, but for now I think you should forget we ever had this conversation." It was said politely but she could hear the threat. Then standing up he walked over to her. "I do thank you for your concern. And now, I must leave you, but I believe Mr. Ben Hod would like a word with you." He smiled. "I'm so sorry you can't come to dinner tonight. And do remember me to your husband."

He was out of the room and Tamar found herself alone with Michael.

Now, she tried to avoid looking at him. She felt ambivalent about him being there. She disliked him, but she was pleased to see him. In a strange way he was family. They came from the same land and his presence in the rabbi's house proved that Turkish uniform or not, he was a Jew, a Jew from Palestine. In a strange way, she felt connected to him, far more than she did to anyone in Turkey.

"When did you arrive from Palestine?" she finally broke the silence.

"This morning." His impersonal manner did not change.

"Did you by any chance see my family recently?" she tried to match his tone.

"As a matter of fact I did see them just before I left, about a week ago."

"How are they?" her voice trailed upward, unable to hide her anxiety.

"Deborah is well, working hard. David is David and Rafi, as always, is preoccupied."

She was surprise at the familiarity with which he referred to her family. "How are conditions there, in the country generally and in Ben Enav specifically?" She wished he would be more friendly.

"Your brother sees to it that they have the things they need. You should know that." He smiled for the first time. "As a matter of fact, all of Bet Enav benefits from his friendship with Jamal Pasha. Although sometimes I wonder if the people in town really appreciate it."

She could not tell if he was being sarcastic. It did not matter. He seemed to be intimately aware of what was happening in her home. She needed to hear what he had to say.

"And Deborah, is she happy? Her letters lately have been rather sad."

"Yes, I think she is happy," he said thoughtfully. "Although I believe she's too intelligent not be aware that she's the compromise in her relationship with David."

"I beg your pardon?" Tamar said indignantly, but his statement made her uncomfortable.

"Well, you played God and as such you made it work for her."

"What are you talking about?" she asked coldly.

"My dear Mrs. Davidzohn, I think it's common knowledge that David was in love with you and when you left . . ." He stopped briefly and looked at her. "I suppose you must think yourself a great martyr." He paused. "I don't."

"My sister happens to be an extraordinarily beautiful girl . . ."

"Woman," Michael interrupted angrily. "A beautiful woman, Mrs. Davidzohn, something none of you seem to understand. She's not a child anymore."

Tamar was taken aback by his vehemence. Deborah a woman? She was still such a baby when she left. But what was even more staggering was the tone in which Michael spoke. This crude laborer, whose uniform did not hide his coarseness, was obviously in love with her sister. It almost amused her.

"And yes, any man could fall in love with your sister," Michael continued icily. "But David . . ."

"I really don't care for your analysis of my family's relationships." She had given him license to talk about them, now she resented what he was saying. "I believe you have a message for me." Her tone took on an imperious sound.

"Yes. Raphael wants to you know that he is very upset that you married Mr. Davidzohn because he promised to send arms to us."

She felt the blood rush to her face.

Michael, noting her reaction, became uncomfortable. He had wanted to hurt her, but now he wished he had been more gentle. "He wanted to put it in a letter, but we have to be very careful. More important, he insists that if you are unhappy in your marriage, he wants you to come home." He paused. "And if I can be of any help, don't hesitate to call on me."

"Has Fredrick sent any arms?" she found her voice with difficulty.

"As far as I know, he hasn't."

She stood up shakily. "I have to go now." She felt faint and wanted to get out of the musty little room, away from this young man who was treating her so rudely. She had to think. Fredrick had lied to her.

"Let me repeat. If you need me, you can always reach me through Rabbi Maranis," he said with great sincerity.

"How long will you be staying in the city?" she asked, coming back to the present.

"I'm here on behalf of Jamal Pasha. So it's not up to me. A week, maybe two."

"Thank you for everything," she said stiffly and rushed out of the room.

The trip back to Pera was nerve-wracking. She was going to leave Fredrick, of that there was no doubt. The only question now, was how. Losing her temper, being vindictive, angering him, would be counterproductive. She had to get him to agree to let her go home for a visit. Raphael would help her once she was there.

Entering the long driveway of their home, Tamar noted that the living room was lit up. It meant their guests had arrived. As they neared the house, she saw a large Daimler-Benz standing in front of the entranceway. The sight of the long, shiny car sent a shudder through her. It represented an autocracy which she hated.

Once in the house, she walked quickly toward the stairs when Fredrick's voice stopped her. She turned around, surprised.

He was smiling up at her, but she could see he was upset.

"My dear, I'm so glad you're here. There's been a change of plans." He walked toward her. "Do join us."

Walking into the living room, she saw only two German officers present. Abbas Pasha had obviously not shown up.

Taking her elbow, Fredrick led her toward the men. "You remember Colonel Von Hassen?"

She recognized him, even though she had only seen him once and that was at her eighteenth birthday party. She nodded and put out her hand.

He leaned over and kissed it politely. "A pleasure to see you again, madame."

"And this is General Schtock," Fredrick was saying and Tamar turned and faced a stern, rigid-looking German officer.

"General," Tamar put out her hand, almost defiantly. He shook it firmly.

"Madame," he said stiffly.

"My dear Tamar," Fredrick started slowly. "The general would like to talk to you privately."

Leaving her alone with a German officer defied every one of Fredrick's rigid rules and given his choice he never would have allowed it. She almost felt sorry for him.

"Won't you sit down, General Schtock?" Tamar said politely, seating herself in an armchair.

"I would rather stand, Madame Davidzohn."

Tamar could not imagine what the man had to say to her and to calm herself she opened a cigarette box, took a cigarette and allowed him to light it for her.

"Madame." He finally broke the silence. "I am here to ask for your help." He paused and took another sip of his brandy.

Tamar looked at him and said nothing.

"Let me put it differently." He started again. "Colonel Von Hassen feels that you might be able to help us."

Tamar put the cigarette to her lips and inhaled deeply. She refused to react. She did not like this German and wished she had not been placed in this position.

"From what he tells me, your family is extremely loyal to the Ottoman Empire and has served it well. I trust that you too share that loyalty."

Tamar still did not react.

"We have captured an Arab in the desert," he said slowly. "Or rather, we have captured a man who appears to be an Arab, although I do not believe he is."

"I'm afraid I don't quite understand." Tamar was genuinely bewildered.

"He was captured with a group of Bedouins near the Syrian border. All the others escaped before they were brought to the prisoners' barracks. He, however, was wounded and was unable to escape." He paused, letting his words sink in, before continuing. "He was dressed like them, his manners are identical to theirs, yet he is fair-skinned. His hair is light, his eyes are blue and there is something about him which makes me believe he is not who he pretends to be."

Tamar felt her throat tighten. The description could easily be of Thomas Hardwick. She dismissed the thought. Thomas was attached to an archeological expedition in the vicinity of Alexandria and that was nowhere near the Syrian border.

"Have you spoken to him?" she asked when she trusted herself to speak naturally.

"That is precisely the problem," the general said through clenched teeth. "The sounds he emits are indecipherable to us. He has cried out when in pain, but the words he speaks are incoherent." He sounded annoyed. "And I assure you, madame, my Turkish comrades can be very persuasive when they put their minds to it. Still, the man has been able to withstand all pressures." He smiled wryly, "A feat, I must admit. A real feat."

Tamar knew exactly what he meant. The Turks were noted for their methods of torture and were rarely unsuccessful in breaking even the strongest of men.

"The soldiers who captured him are convinced he is some half-breed Arab, fathered by a European soldier and a *fallahin* woman, but I don't agree. I've seen him and there is something about him that baffles me." He smiled, almost to himself. "And his stubbornness, his discipline, has piqued my curiosity." He stopped talking and seemed to be considering if he should continue. He pursed his lips and said no more.

Tamar wondered what was left unsaid. General Schtock hardly seemed like someone who would waste his time on a whim.

"General Schtock, I am flattered that you are telling me all of this, but what it is you want of me?"

"I would like you to see him," he said simply, but there was a command in his voice that irritated her. He had no right to order her about.

"But why me?"

"I have a feeling that he is on the verge of cracking. It occurred to me that seeing a beautiful European woman might break him down." His face broke into a thin smile. "You must understand, he is quite weak. The tactic just might work."

"Where is he?"

"In the prisoners' hospital in Constantinople."

Tamar put her hand to her throat. The sight of the foreboding fort appeared before her eyes and she suppressed a shudder.

"I assure you you will be perfectly safe. I shall have Colonel Von Hassen escort you to the prison and a guard will be in the cell with you at all times," he said, misunderstanding her reaction.

"I shall have to ask my husband's permission," she said slowly.

"If you will agree to go, I shall ask for you," he said and Tamar knew that he would simply order Fredrick to allow her to go.

"May I think about it?"

"I would appreciate your answer now," General Schtock said.

"Why don't you talk to my husband first," she said coldly and stood up. Then, bowing politely, she walked out of the room.

She stopped briefly before Fredrick's study but decided against going in. Instead she hurried up to her bedroom.

Too many things had happened that day and she had to digest them. But overriding all else was the discovery that Fredrick had betrayed her brother and had been leading her on about the shipment of arms. She was going to leave him and she would have to be very careful from now on. Knowing him as she did, she was sure he would sooner kill her than permit her to walk out on him.

She undressed quickly, got into bed and waited for Fredrick to come up. It seemed like an eternity before he finally knocked on her door.

"Are you awake, Tamar?" he asked softly.

"Yes," she whispered.

"Did you have a good day at work?" he sounded unusually pleasant.

Tamar was taken aback by his cordiality. She had expected him to plunge into the subject of her going to the prisoners' hospital.

"A very good day," she said cautiously and looked over at him. He had seated himself in front of the bay window and she could see the profile of his face. He was smoking his cigarette nervously.

"And did you have a pleasant chat with Rabbi Maranis?"

Malikian had obviously reported her visit. She felt herself bristle.

"And how was your day?" She decided to ignore his last question.

"Malikian tells me you got a letter from Deborah. How is she?"

There was no end to Malikian's spying on her, she thought.

"They're having a hard time, Fredrick," she said seriously. "And I feel that my going there for a visit would help." She stopped. "We could both go." She decided to risk it. "I really feel our presence would make a difference to them."

"Both of us?"

"Yes, of course. They look at you as family."

"My dear girl, I have work to do here in Turkey. We are at war and I am needed here."

"Of course you're right," she conceded. "But may I go?"

"It's out of the question," he answered with finality.

"Why?"

"You're my wife and I don't believe the trip is safe at this time."

"Is Palestine in danger?"

"I don't really know, but if it is it's a temporary situation. What I do know is that it is no place for you to be in at this time. Besides, you have a home to care for."

"Palestine is my home," her voice rose, in spite of her decision to be pleasant and docile. "It's our home. You promised me that we would eventually live there."

"Move to Palestine?" he sneered. "Me, live in Palestine?"

"But I thought it was a foregone conclusion," she said desperately.

"Tamar, I am willing to help Raphael and his friends in whatever way I can if his goals and aspirations do not conflict with mine. But that is all. Someday, I suppose, we could spend some time with your family but that would only happen when the war is over and we have won."

She was speechless. Fredrick had never spoken about Palestine that way before. But what was worse, was that he still pretended that he was helping them. The temptation to confront him was overwhelming, but she knew it would be pointless.

"You never intended to move to Palestine." She lay back, feeling more trapped than ever.

"Well, now that we've settled this nonsense," Fredrick was saying, "I want to talk about General Schtock."

She did not move, waiting for him to continue.

"You do understand that I forbid you to go."

"Did you tell that to General Schtock?" she asked icily.

"I leave that to you."

"He won't believe me," she smiled in the dark. "He knows that Turkish wives have no opinions about such things and that if I refused to go it would be because I was following your orders." She was humiliating him and she was pleased. Fredrick had betrayed her and she wanted to hurt him.

Slowly she sat up and stared at him in the dark. He was looking in her direction and she could feel his rage across the room.

"I'm afraid you will have to be the one to do it," Fredrick said calmly. "I am leaving for Germany early tomorrow morning and I will not have a chance to talk to him before I go. I shall, of course, drop the general a note to let him know my feelings, but it will be you who will have to tell him when he calls on you in the morning."

"But why?" she asked slowly. "It seems to me that you would want to please General Schtock."

"There is a conflict between the general and Abbas Pasha. Each has an opinion as to who the prisoner is and wishes to be proven right. It has become a *cause celebre* for them both and I do not wish to get caught in the middle of it. So as far as I'm concerned, you, as my wife, will not be made a pawn in this ridiculous situation. You will simply say that you cannot go and that is final." He stood up and before she could answer, he was gone from the room.

Just before falling asleep, Tamar again thought of the prisoner and wondered if he could be Thomas. And if he were? What condition would he be in and what could she possibly do to help him? The image of the prisoners' hospital loomed more ominous than ever.

# CHAPTER
# TEN

T AMAR had just finished her work and as arranged, Von Hassen was waiting for her at the side entrance of the hospital. They did not speak as they headed toward the prisoners' section. The trees and shrubbery were more densely planted than she had realized and the path was so narrow that only one person could pass through it. Soon Tamar began to notice the barbed wire with the knotted wire mesh intertwined with the vines. The wire tips looked lethal. She pulled her cloak closer to her, fearful that the fabric would catch on one of the nails. The path was badly lit, with few lanterns hanging from swaying tree branches, and Tamar got the distinct feeling that she was being watched. Escape through this path was obviously impossible. She almost smiled at the thought. Escape from whom? she wondered.

The building was larger than it had appeared from the distance and except for the massive iron door, there were no other visible openings. The high walls were also covered with clinging vines intertwined with knotted wire mesh.

There was no guard at the door, yet it swung open the minute they reached it. It confirmed her suspicion. She was being watched.

"Madame," Colonel Von Hassen spoke for the first time. "I shall not be accompanying you into the prison," he said formally. "I will be waiting for you out here."

She look up at him in surprise.

"General Schtock wants you to be alone with the prisoner. He fears the presence of anyone in uniform will frighten him."

Her surprise turned to dismay. The thought of going into a prison cell alone was unappealing.

"You will be quite safe, madame," Colonel Von Hassen said, noting her concern. "A Turkish guard will be with you." A wry smile came to his handsome, Nordic face. "Although there is little chance the prisoner could harm you."

"Have you seen him?"

Von Hassen shook his head. "But I've seen others who were subjected to Turkish questioning . . ." He did not finish the sentence.

"What can I expect to find?" she asked.

"You're a nurse, you've seen worse, I'm sure." He hesitated, as though weighing his next words carefully. "It's the mental and sexual abuse which they are put through that neutralizes them. And frankly, that's what I find so repellent."

The phrase *sexual abuse* caused the blood to rush to her face in embarrassment.

"Forgive me," the colonel said quickly, aware that he had been indelicate. "I should not have been so forward in my statement."

What struck Tamar most forcefully, as she walked through the thick, rusted metal door, was the silence. Standing in the dark, dank anteroom, she shuddered at the total lack of sound. She did not know what she had expected, but it was not this deathlike pall that surrounded her. She felt the perspiration running down her back, yet her palms were icy.

A heavy-set Turkish captain appeared and eyed her coldly. His displeasure was evident. Then he snapped his fingers and a guard rushed over, carrying a lantern. With a deprecating gesture he waved her to follow the guard.

Walking down endless steps, the silence was now accompanied by an unbearable stench of stale, damp air. It was too dark to see beyond the perimeter of the lantern's light, but at intervals she noted recesses in the grimy walls, which she assumed were doorways. The thought that behind those thick walls were living beings on the verge of death made the walk seem like a death march. She wished she had not come.

The guard stopped suddenly. A bedraggled soldier came out of the darkness to unlock one of the doors. Handing her the lantern, her guide allowed her to precede him into the cell.

She walked in slowly and look behind her to see if he had followed her in. He was already settling himself on the floor, his hand resting on his gun holster. She lifted the lantern over her head and looked around the small square room, trying to delay the moment when she would have to confront the prisoner.

Her eyes came to rest on a cot directly opposite the door. The man was lying on his back and his head was turned toward the wall. Cautiously she edged her way toward him and realized his head was swathed in bandages which covered his neck as well.

She placed the lantern on the floor and stared down at the lifeless figure. Her eyes swept over him. He was dressed in knee-length, striped prisoner's shirt and streaks of blood seeped through the thin fabric, causing the flimsy garment to cling to his emaciated body, each rib clearly visible. His legs were covered with open, seeping wounds. His feet were swollen and badly infected. She leaned closer to examine them and her mouth went dry. The prisoner had been beaten on the soles of his feet with the bastinado, a ghastly form of torture, and some of his toenails were ripped off.

She wanted to run from the room. She was foolish to come. Fredrick was right. She had been duped by the general and her own romantic fantasy and she was incapable of coping with the situation. She was about to turn away and tell the guard that she was ready to leave, when she saw the man's arm move. His hand fell limply over the edge of the cot. The festering sores, the blackened fingernails, the grime and filth did not detract from its elegance. Nor did they hide the fine gold hair on the emaciated limb. Thomas's hands had that same fine hair.

She sucked in her breath and knelt down beside the cot. Could it really be Thomas?

Picking up the lantern, she scanned the figure more closely.

"I should like to talk to you," she said in German and waited.

"I might be able to help you," she continued in French.

"I could be your only chance for freedom," she said in Arabic.

When he did not react, she wondered what more she could do. Then she saw him stir. Very slowly and with great effort, he turned his head toward her. The action was accompanied by heartrending groans of pain. After an interminably long time, he finally faced her. The bandages covered his brow down to his swollen eyes, which were mere slits over his bruised cheeks. His unkempt beard further obscured his features. He was having a hard time breathing.

"I am here to help you," she said in Hebrew but now she spoke more loudly, wanting to be overheard by the guard.

The prisoner did not react.

"Would you tell me who you are and how I can help you?" She switched to Turkish. This too was said distinctly for the benefit of the guard.

Still no reaction.

"I believe I know who you are," she whispered under her breath in English. She felt safe in doing it, since her back was to the guard. Then in a natural voice she continued. "You can trust me."

The man's swollen lids flickered and with great effort he opened his eyes. The clear, sea blue color shone through. She might not have been able to identify the features but the color of his eyes were clearly embedded in her memory.

"Thomas?" she whispered and, leaning closer to him, she undid her veil. She wondered if he would remember her. "My name is Tamar Danziger Davidzohn." She said the words clearly, in Turkish. "Why don't you tell me your name?"

A look of distrust appeared in his eyes when he saw the guard, and he began to tremble.

"I am your friend," she said reassuringly in German, her voice rising again.

He shook his head slowly and the plea in his eyes made her realize that he did not want her to identify him.

"What's your name?" She repeated the question in Arabic, hoping to convince him that she was going to play along with his determination to appear to be an Arab and that she had no intention of giving him away.

It took a moment, but finally a look of gratitude replaced the fear. He believed her.

"Who are you?" she tried to sound impatient. "Where are you from? Palestine? Aleppo? Sinai? Don't you know that Allah will punish you for betraying the sultan? Don't you care?"

She continued her questioning, switching to German, then to French and finally to English.

His eyes never left her face and suddenly she saw a tear form in the corner of his eye and slide down the side of his face.

He did remember her. She smiled encouragingly and whispered, "Thomas, trust me."

He blinked once and slowly turned his head back to the wall.

The meeting was over.

Tamar got up quickly and walked to the door. The guard had jumped up and was holding it open for her.

Except for the Turkish guard who opened the cell, no one else was around. For some reason she expected a German or Turkish officer to be there and was relieved that they were not. Obviously the Germans were depending on her loyalty and the Turks had no faith in her ability to get any information from the prisoner. She looked at the guard briefly. He, she was sure, could be bribed, but what about the others who were probably standing along the maze of stairways and corridors?

Going back up, Tamar paid closer attention to her surroundings and realized there were guards in charge of other prisoners' cells. She tried to keep count but found it impossible. All she knew was that she could not bribe them all.

Malikian, who had come to pick her up from work, was pacing impatiently outside the hospital gate. He was surprised at seeing her with Von Hassen and she ignored his look. If he guessed where she had been, he would tell Fredrick. It did not matter. She was going to leave Fredrick anyway. The new complication was how to arrange for Thomas to come with her.

Sitting beside Von Hassen, one thought dominated. Somehow she had to get Thomas transferred into the general hospital through official channels. Once he was there, she could maneuver more easily. Resting her head on the back of the carriage seat, she closed her eyes. Thomas's battered body loomed before her and she knew that time was of the essence.

She also had no idea what she could say to the general.

"We're here," she heard the colonel say, and she sat up. They had arrived at her house and she was enraged at seeing the general's car standing in the driveway.

"I shall leave you now, Madame Davidzohn," Von Hassen said, helping her out of the carriage. "And although you've had a long and difficult day, you see that the general is impatient for your comments." He sounded apologetic.

"General," Tamar entered the living room and extended her hand to him. "Please forgive me for keeping you waiting, but it's been a difficult experience and I must confess that I would have preferred to meet with you in the morning."

He shook her hand and bowed stiffly, as his eyes searched her face. He was a man of discipline, usually able to control his emotions but at that moment he was having a difficult time hiding his agitation. Taking a cigarette from the cigarette box, Tamar waited for him to light it for her. He did, but a small tic appeared on his high forehead.

She smiled inwardly. It was a test of wills and she intended to prevail.

"May I offer you a drink?" she asked pleasantly. "I should very much like a coffee." She did not wait for his answer and pulled the cord. Malikian appeared immediately.

Tamar sensed he had been standing outside the door waiting to be summoned.

"Anything for you, general?" she asked again.

He shook his head impatiently.

After ordering her coffee, Tamar turned back to him.

"Madame, it is late and I am most anxious to hear your impressions of the prisoner."

She inhaled deeply before answering. "Have you seen the man, general?" she asked, although she knew he had.

"I've seen him but the Turkish authorities refused to allow us to interrogate him."

"Well, sir, if you had been able to talk to him, you would have realized immediately that he is a German." She said it quietly and sat down on a large divan, looking unflinchingly at him.

"How can you be so sure?" He sounded angry.

"General Schtock, no man can withstand that much torture without breaking, least of all an Arab. Except, of course, if he was someone who was raised or possibly trained with true Prussian discipline."

The tic on the general's forehead became more visible.

"An interesting theory, madame," he said in a strained voice and Tamar knew she had struck a nerve.

He turned abruptly and walked toward the french doors. "Interesting," he said with his back to her. "But hardly conclusive."

"His mother tongue is German," she continued. "I spoke to him in English, French, Arabic, Hebrew and German. German was the only language he reacted to. Oh, he tried not to, I could see that. But he's very weak and I believe you were right. Seeing a European woman weakened him even further." Then throwing caution to the wind, she said, "I wonder what could possibly make a German of breeding, and I believe he is a man of breeding, join a group of Bedouins in the desert? It just doesn't make sense."

She saw his back stiffen and she held her breath, waiting for his next comment.

"Your coffee, Effendum Davidzohn." Malikian walked in and placed a tray with two cups of Turkish coffee on the serving board. "Should I pour it?"

General Schtock turned around, his eyes darkened by rage at the interruption.

"I'll do it, Malikian," she said hurriedly. "Thank you."

Schtock had regained his composure and came toward her. "You've been very helpful and I appreciate it. And I beg your forgiveness for intruding on you at this late hour."

She tried to hide her surprise at his abrupt departure. Malikian was waiting at the door to let the general out.

"If I may offer my advice as a registered nurse," she said as General Schtock was about to step into his car, "no matter who the man is, he must be attended to medically." She had a hard time keeping the urgency out of her voice. "He has been through a great deal and unless he is properly treated, he will die and his secrets will die with him."

The general bowed but made no response.

Tamar watched the car disappear down the driveway.

Back in the living room, she sat down on the divan and stared out the french doors. She felt drained, but her mind was racing. She was convinced she was right to insist that Thomas was German. Schtock would never allow a German to be abused by Turkish functionaries. He would want the full pleasure of exposing those responsible and meting out the proper punishment. She felt he believed her and if he did, he would do something about it. That was why she had made that last comment. Although he did not react to it, he had heard her. He could order Thomas moved to the general hospital. A man like Schtock would not risk the man dying before his curiosity was satisfied.

But once Thomas was in the hospital, the problem would be to get him out. For that she needed accomplices and she had none. Her frustration mounted. If only she could talk to Raphael and David. They would have known what to do, whom to talk to, how to go about arranging it all. Michael Ben Hod came to mind. Raphael had asked him to help her.

Persuading him to help her with Thomas would be a problem, but she was sure he had the means to do it. Motti had been released from the hospital rather mysteriously within hours after she saw Rabbi Maranis. And somehow she was sure that the rabbi was not the force behind that act.

She had to talk to Michael and it had to be done that night. She had no idea how to reach him except through Rabbi Maranis.

The clock chimed in the front gallery and Tamar realized it was already nine o'clock in the evening. Getting to the rabbi's house was also a problem. Respectable women never appeared alone on the street in Turkey, certainly not after dark. Having Malikian drive her was out of the question. He more than anyone had to be kept in the dark about her activities. There was bound to be a scene when Fredrick discovered her visit to the prison. Explaining a second visit to the rabbi's house, at night, would be impossible.

"Would you like some dinner?" Malikian's voice startled her.

"I don't think so," she replied wearily, turning to look at him. "I'm totally exhausted." She put her hand to her mouth, hiding a yawn. "As a matter of fact, I think I'll go to bed now. It's been a long and grueling day." She stood up and walked past him. Then, as though an afterthought, she said, "As a matter of fact, why don't you and Aris take the night off?"

"I doubt that Effendi Davidzohn would approve my leaving you alone in the house."

"I shall be asleep before you reach the front gate." She tried to smile. "If you could just lock up before you leave." And ignoring the look of suspicion in his eyes, she walked slowly up the stairs.

Once in her room, she rushed to the window and waited for father and daughter to leave. Within minutes she saw Malikian walk toward the front gate and bolt it from inside. Aris was waiting for him at the servants' entrance. He joined her, looked around to assure himself that all was in order, then, opening the gate, they walked through it and were gone from sight.

She waited a while, then wrapped the black *charshaffe* around her and covered her face with the veil. Her light blue eyes stared back at her from the mirror. They were the giveaway to her being a European, but there was little she could do about it. Quickly she walked down the stairs and headed toward the servants' gate. Opening it cautiously, she peered down the street. It was deserted.

Never having walked from Pera to Galata, Tamar had started out with great confidence but as the streets began to curve and grew narrower, an edge of fear began to rise in her. The empty streets were disconcerting. The lateness of the hour was also troubling. Arriving at the rabbi's house alone would be odd.

She was pondering how she would explain her presence to the rabbi when she caught sight of the Grand Rue Bazaar. She breathed a sigh of relief. She was nearly there.

Eyes followed her as she walked quickly through the crowded bazaar. A woman walking alone at that hour was a novelty but she ignored them as she headed toward the Jewish Quarter. Turning into the alleyway where the rabbi lived, she was suddenly enveloped in darkness and her panic returned. The houses flanking the narrow street were almost identical. She could barely make out the rabbi's house at the end of the alley. She was almost at his door when she heard the sound of footsteps behind her. Abandoning all attempts at decorum, she ran toward the house and began to pound on the door with her fists. The house was unusually quiet. She put her ear to the door. It had never occurred to her that the Maranises might not be home. Blindly she reached for the bell cord and pulled it.

Finally the bobbing light of a lantern appeared through the window over the doorway. Only then did she dare turn her head and stare down the twisted alleyway. It look deserted, but she was convinced someone was out there. She held her breath. She heard something move. Turning around, she faced the narrow passageways, daring whoever was there to come forth. What appeared to be a shadow of a man started toward her, but at that moment the door behind her opened.

"Mrs. Davidzohn, are you all right?" Rabbi Maranis lifted the lantern to her face. "You look terrified." Then, pulling her into the house, he scanned the street briefly before shutting the door. "You're alone?" He sounded incredulous.

She nodded, unable to speak.

"You came on foot from your home at this hour of the night?" He did not try to hide his dismay.

"I . . ." she started and wondered if she should ask for Mrs. Maranis. "I have to see Michael Ben Hod," she whispered.

"Why didn't you have Malikian drive you?" Rabbi Maranis asked, leading her into his study. Once there, he walked over to the window, pushed the heavy drapes aside and peered out.

"He was off doing some errands. And I had to see you tonight. It could not be put off till morning."

"Why don't you sit down and I'll get Mrs. Maranis." He was obviously uncomfortable.

"No. I must speak to Michael," she said firmly.

"I don't know where I could find him at this hour," the rabbi answered, barely hiding his irritation.

Tamar joined him at the window and looked out. The street appeared peaceful and quaint. Briefly she thought of telling him that she had been followed. She decided against it. She could have been imagining it and she would sound like a complete fool.

"Supposing you tell me what is so urgent." Rabbi Maranis changed his tone.

She licked her lips nervously. "Could you find Michael for me? It's a matter of life or death."

"Why don't you sit down and tell me about it." The rabbi seated himself behind his desk and continued to stare at her. "Maybe when you've worded your concern, you'll discover that you've exaggerated the whole matter."

She had no choice. She started slowly and as she spoke her fear for Thomas grew. Her speech began to slur and she knew she sounded almost incoherent.

"Will you help me get him out?" She asked and realized the rabbi's face had gone white, but she could not decide if it was rage or fear.

"What on earth do you expect me to do?" His voice was hoarse.

"Do?" she echoed his last word. "Well, there must be ways. Bribing the guards, talking to someone of importance in the government . . ."

"You're being ridiculous. If the Turks and the Germans are at loggerheads about this man, you must believe no guard would risk getting involved, even for a bribe."

"But if I got him into the main hospital?"

"How do you expect to do that?"

"I don't know, but if I do, will you be able to help me?"

"You overestimate yourself, madame," the rabbi said coldly. "I still don't see that I can help." He became impatient.

"You helped Motti," she ventured, and watched him closely.

The rabbi looked surprised. "Is he no longer in the hospital?"

She had caught him off guard. "No he's not," she said deliberately. "As a matter of fact, he was out of the ward within twenty-four hours after I was here and mentioned him to you."

"I know nothing about it." He swallowed hard. "Besides, if I could have helped, it would have been because he was Jewish and I would have felt it my duty to try. But I would have done it through friends, who would have understood my desire to help the son of a rabbi of Palestine."

"Only if he were a Jew?" she gasped. "I've just described a tortured human being, who is on the verge of death. Doesn't that count for anything?"

"It's getting very late and I think you'd better go home." He ignored her outburst. "But more important, I believe you should have listened to your husband when he told you not to get involved in this situation. No good can come of it. And I'm sure that when he finds out that you've disobeyed him, he will be very angry and rightly so. Now I will get you my carriage and my Kahya will see you home." He stood up and walked over to her. "And you may as well know, Mrs. Davidzohn, you're doing something that is quite dangerous to all of us. I want you to remember that."

He led her to the front gallery and before walking away he turned to her. "You're sure you weren't followed."

She hesitated briefly. "Quite sure," she lied.

"The carriage will be here shortly." The rabbi was back and standing a distance away from her, he eyed carefully.

"You do look very tired." He sounded friendlier than he had since she arrived and she was tempted to tell him she was followed, when she heard a carriage come to a halt in front of the house.

"Would you please try to get in touch with Michael?" she said hurriedly.

"I will try." He opened the door.

Malikian was standing in the doorway.

"I finished my errands earlier than I anticipated and I hoped I would catch you, effendum," he said seriously.

"Goodnight, Mrs. Davidzohn," the rabbi said coldly.

She wanted to cry out in frustration. "Please, I can explain," she started.

Maranis stepped back into the house.

"Michael," she whispered. "I must see Michael."

The door slammed shut.

She turned to Malikian. "How dare you follow me!" she hissed.

"You are far too upset for us to discuss this now, effendum."

"Don't you dare talk to me in that manner."

"I did not follow you, effendum," he said quietly.

"Then how did you know I was here?"

"Aris and I stopped by the post office on the Grande Rue, when we saw you walk by. We started after you but before we could catch up with you, I realized that you were being followed."

She paled. "By whom?"

"I sent Aris back to the house and I caught up with the culprit."

"Who was he?"

"A young boy hired by the Germans to find out if you were going to report your findings of this afternoon to the Turkish authorities."

Her knees began to buckle. "Where is he now?"

"I told him that you had to see your rabbi and that it was an innocent visit," he said pleasantly. "He accepted my explanation and will report that to General Schtock." Then taking her firmly by the arm, he guided her to the carriage. Before shutting the door, he handed her an envelope. "The post office had a telegram for you." He shut the door and took his place next to the Maranises' driver.

Tamar ripped open the envelope. "ARRIVING THURSDAY AFTER-NOON FREDRICK."

She crumpled the message in her hand. Fredrick would be back in less than twenty-four hours. Thomas was doomed.

# CHAPTER
# ELEVEN

AMAR sifted through her jewelry box. She had not realized how much she actually had. The pieces were exquisite and she was sure they were worth a great deal of money. The temptation to take them all was great. She picked out her gold bracelets, an opera-length string of pearls, an antique pin that had belonged to her grandmother, and her diamond earrings given to her by her family. The rest of the items belonged to Fredrick. Closing the box, she caught sight of the large diamond engagement ring and gold wedding band on her finger. She hoped she would not have to sell either and could return them, when she left her husband's house for good. She had to wear them until she was ready to leave.

Replacing the box in Fredrick's bedroom safe, she walked quickly back to her room.

By the time Aris arrived with the breakfast tray, Tamar had her overnight bag packed along with her jewels and her Palestinian passport. It was ready for her trip home.

"You have been up all night," Aris said looking at the bed that had not been slept in.

"Aris, I need help," Tamar said quietly.

Aris stared at her mistress, waiting for her to continue.

"I have no one in Turkey whom I can trust and you, I believe, are my friend."

"I take it as an honor that you consider me your friend," Aris answered calmly.

"I know that what I'm about to ask of you will put you in conflict with your father, but I hope you will understand that I am desperate," Tamar had difficulty with the phrase.

When Aris failed to react, Tamar continued, "I am planning to leave my husband. I don't know quite when, but I shall be leaving him soon. And since you know this city better than I do I wondered if you could arrange a place for me to stay while I make the final arrangements for my trip home?" She paused. "It's a great deal to ask and it's dangerous, I know, but you're the only friend I have here."

"I am not your only friend," Aris said quietly.

"I wish you were right, but I have spent the night trying to find someone other than you whom I could turn to. There is no one."

"You can trust my father," Aris said.

"Your father!" Tamar gasped. The idea was ludicrous. Malikian was the last person she would have turned to at this moment.

"Yes. My father," Aris repeated.

"I'm sure you mean well but please don't involve your father in this matter." She took a deep breath. "Aris, if I've asked too much of you, forget this conversation ever took place but please, please, don't mention it to him. Ever."

"I shall not mention it if you wish me not to, but you can believe me when I tell you he is your friend."

"Will you help me? Can you help me?" Tamar ignored Aris's last remark.

"I will do whatever you ask."

"Thank you." Tamar picked up her coffee cup. "And now could you tell Malikian I shall be ready to leave the house within half an hour?"

Malikian was as stiff and unresponsive as always when he came to announce her carriage was waiting.

"When do you think my husband will be home?" she asked when they neared the hospital.

"The train should be arriving at three o'clock."

"Would you fetch me at noon? I would like to be home when he arrives."

"Why don't you come to the station?"

"I'd rather be home," she said pointedly. She was sure Malikian would tell Fredrick about her exploits and she wanted to prepare for the confrontation. She had overstepped every rule Fredrick had set for her and his anger would be justified.

"As you wish," Malikian answered politely.

The chaos around the entranceway to the hospital was as great as ever. The gate was blocked by rows of stretchers waiting to get through. Tamar took her place at the end of the line. She was in no rush.

Suddenly she saw General Schtock's Daimler drive up. The chauffeur was honking his horn incessantly. Everyone scurried to the side, allowing the car to get through. It disappeared through the gate and Tamar pushed her way toward the hospital gate. Schtock's appearance at the hospital at that early hour could mean only one thing. Thomas had been transferred to the hospital.

"Why the rush?" She felt someone tug at her arm. She turned and saw Michael Ben Hod standing beside her. She almost did not recognize him. He was dressed in his Turkish uniform, but his hair was hidden under a head scarf which he had wrapped over the lower part of his face. Only his eyes were exposed.

"My God, you're here," she whispered in relief. "You're really here."

"You wanted to see me?"

"Yes I did," she looked into his eyes for a sign of friendship. There was none. "Did Rabbi Maranis tell you why?" she asked trying to compose herself.

"I was told only of your rather unusual nocturnal visit." He smiled briefly. "And it seems you were quite hysterical."

"It's an extremely urgent matter." She refused to be dragged into a confrontation.

"Urgent for whom?"

She hesitated. "I am trying to save a dying man."

"In a world where there is so much death around, is the death of one man that important?" he asked.

"I think it is."

"If that's the case, whoever it is you're trying to save must be very special. Can you tell me who he is and what makes him so important?"

"I can tell you he's important to General Schtock, which in turn has made him important to the Turks." She paused, wondering if she could trust him. She had no choice. "He is a British archeologist and is stationed in Egypt. He was on a dig in the desert and somehow he was captured by the Turks. Neither the Turks nor the Germans know who he is, even though he's been brutally tortured. But he won't be able to hold out much longer. He's bound to break."

Michael's cool demeanor seemed to crack briefly. "Where do you know him from?" he asked.

"Raphael, Deborah and I met him on the beach near Bet Enav several years ago."

"You've met him once?" Michael asked scornfully.

"Raphael and I met him again in Haifa."

"And he told you all of that in those meetings?"

"He was talking to Raphael and he explained what he was doing in Palestine. He was to meet Raphael again, but he had to get back to Egypt before they could set it up."

"You're taking an awfully big risk to save someone you barely know," Michael said.

"Michael, please stop it," she exploded. "I can't explain it any better than I have. All I know is that he must be saved."

"Something is eluding me, Madame Davidzohn." Michael's anger matched hers.

"I am asking you to help him. I have no one else to turn to. I can assure you that if Raphael were here, he'd help him."

"I wonder."

"Well, there is no way for me to prove it." Tamar lowered her eyes, remembering her conversation with Raphael concerning Thomas the morning after they met. But she had no doubts about Raphael's sentiments. She had no way of knowing where Michael's loyalties lay.

For a brief moment they stared at each other.

"Will you help me?" she asked again.

"Even if I wanted to, it would be a very complicated affair. It would involve a great deal of money, for starters." His voice took on an officious tone. "Then we'd have to find a place to hide him until we could get him out of the country. And since I understand he's been in a prison cell for a while, as a guest of Turkish inquisitors, I imagine he'll need time to recuperate. Then someone will have to travel with him at least part of the way."

"I'm a registered nurse, I can travel with him and care for him," she said quickly.

"Oh." A look of mockery came into his eyes. "How interesting."

"What else will we need?" she asked urgently, ignoring his last comment.

"Well, he'll need forged papers, so I'll have to have a complete description of what he looks like. And since I'm sure you'll not be traveling with your husband's blessings, we'll need papers for you as well."

"I have jewelry which can be sold," she said quickly. "As to what he looks like, he's fair-haired, with blue eyes. He's quite thin and about as tall as you are." She thought for a minute. "And incidentally, I have a Palestinian passport under the name of Tamar Danziger. I can travel with that."

"No, you can't. From the little I know of Mr. Fredrick Davidzohn, he'll move heaven and earth to find you. Using your maiden name would be too obvious." He stopped and thought for a minute. "What's this man's name, anyway?"

"Thomas G. Hardwick."

"What's the G stand for?"

"I don't know. Does it matter?"

"I suppose not," Michael said indifferently. "But you do understand that all of this depends on his being removed from the prison." Suddenly he noticed a disturbance behind her. "Well, part of the problem is solved," he concluded, indicating the crowd.

She looked around. A car carrying several German officers came to a screeching halt in front of the hospital gate. Colonel Von Hassen was the first to emerge from it.

"I must get going," she said quickly. "There is a German officer named Von Hassen who knows me and he'd better not see us together."

"Small world," Michael quipped. "That's the young officer who came in with Jamal Pasha the night we met."

She grew red with embarrassment, recalling their first meeting again.

"You were positively charming that evening," Michael said, obviously aware of her discomfort.

"I happened to have been worried about a young boy who is very dear to me. To our whole family," she said.

"You really have loyalties to all sorts of people. An Arab boy who might have been an Arab killer. Now its some Englishman for whom you're willing to put people in jeopardy. People who considered you their friend. People who trusted you." He paused briefly. "The question is, are you as loyal to people who really deserve it?"

"I resent that remark," she answered furiously, then she calmed down. "Oh, why bother, we simply have different attitudes toward Arabs."

"We certainly do," Michael agreed. "And you will live to regret your attitudes."

"That's beside the point," she said quickly "As for Thomas Hardwick . . ." She stopped, unable to finish the sentence.

"What about Thomas Hardwick? What is he to you? But more important, would he be as concerned for you as you are for him?"

"I'm sure he would."

"If you say so," he said and started to walk away.

"When will I see you next?" she called out.

"I'll be in touch with you." He disappeared into the crowd.

With a heavy heart Tamar pushed her way through the crowed.

"May I be of assistance?" Colonel Von Hassen had caught sight of her. "Please let me escort you to your destination."

"There's an awful lot going on around here this morning," she observed as they walked quickly toward the building.

"Well, I believe we are somehow responsible for it," Von Hassen said. "It seems your report to General Schtock impressed him and he had that wretched man brought up from the dungeon for treatment in the main building."

"I can't imagine what I said, other than report my observations." She simulated surprise. "Although I am pleased to think that he's out of that dreadful cell. He's in desperate need of proper medical care."

"The general is fully aware of that and he's asked the head nurse to have you care for him until he's well enough to be questioned by us."

She stopped walking. "That would be out of the question," she said adamantly. Then softening her tone, she looked helplessly at the young officer. "Colonel, you must inform the general that I cannot be of any further assistance in this matter. My husband did not want me to go. And frankly, I wish I hadn't. But now I must be relieved from any further involvement." She lowered her eyes, as though embarrassed to speak intimately to him. "The point is, my husband is coming home today from a trip abroad and I shall, of course, tell him of my disobedience. He will be very angry and I shan't blame him, but you must understand that I have compromised myself and the consequences could be most unpleasant."

The young colonel appeared uncomfortable and tried to smile. "I shall do my best," he promised solemnly.

Once inside the hospital. Von Hassen bowed formally to her and walked away. Tamar watched him head toward the west wing. He stopped in front of a door guarded by a Turkish soldier.

Tamar took note of the number of that door, then headed toward the nurse's room.

The tea tray was set out on the patio table. Tamar had taken special care to have all of Fredrick's favorite pastries on it. Her fear of his reaction to her activities while he was gone had grown to near frenzy. One thing was certain—whatever his reaction, she would have to leave his house. The question was when and under what circumstances. It all depended on when Michael contacted her. But if she was forced to leave her house before hearing from him, how would he find her? And would he bother to make the effort? He felt such hostility toward her. Still, he did come to meet her and she was sure Rabbi Maranis had discouraged him from doing so.

The last thought reassured her.

The sound of the carriage outside the front door jolted her. She sat up, ready for the encounter.

"Tamar, my dear." Fredrick came out to the patio and, catching sight of the spread on the table, smiled. "How gracious of you to make this such a festive homecoming." He leaned down and kissed her cheek. "I missed you," he said, looking fondly at her.

She was speechless. She tried to smile. "Did you have a nice trip?" she asked cautiously, wondering if he was playing some game with her.

"Excellent." Fredrick sat down opposite her. "As a matter of fact, it was so lucrative I bought you a lovely gift." He reached into his pocket and withdrew a long, black box and handed it to her.

She opened it slowly. It was a beautiful pearl choker with an intricate ruby clasp.

"Put it on," he urged, taking a pastry and leaning back, contentedly. "It belonged to the wife of a great sultan and I had to bargain long and hard to get it. Many people were interested in it."

"I don't deserve it," she said sincerely.

"You're a good girl, Tamar." He looked at her affectionately. "Like a child, you sometimes misbehave but on the whole I'm happy with you."

Malikian appeared on the terrace with Fredrick's raki. As always, he was the composed and proper master's valet. Yet it appeared that he had not told Fredrick about her actions. That was a surprise.

"Have you missed me, my dear?" Fredrick asked, sipping his drink.

"Fredrick, I must tell you something," she said observing Milikian out of the corner of her eye.

"Yes?" Fredrick looked vaguely interested.

"I disobeyed you." She focused her attention on Fredrick. "In spite of your instructions, I visited the prisoner General Schtock asked me to see." She threw a quick look at Malikian. He appeared unruffled.

"You went to the prison?" Fredrick put his drink down and his face grew pale.

"Yes," she said, looking directly at him.

"Milikian, you did not tell me of this," Fredrick said through clenched teeth.

"Malikian did not know," Tamar said quickly. "Colonel Von Hassen fetched me from work at the hospital."

"Malikian, will you leave us." Fredrick did not take his eyes off Tamar.

Tamar watched the servant withdraw. Her fear at being left alone with Fredrick grew, but along with the fear, she felt relief. Aris had indicated that Malikian was her friend and that she could trust him. Now she had proof. She also knew he probably had not mentoned her trip to the rabbi's house.

The blow to her head was unexpected. She turned in shock and a second slap landed on her face. She raise her hands to defend herself and felt the blood coming from her lip. Fredrick grabbed her hand away from her face and pulled the pearl choker from her neck. The small beads bounced off the tiled floor. The clasp broke and the tiny rubies looked like drops of blood on the white surface of the patio.

"You're trying to ruin me," Fredrick was screaming, hitting her this time on her ear.

"That was not why I did it." She tried to get up.

"Why then? Why?" His hand was at her throat. "Why?"

"From the general's description, I thought the man might be a Jew from Palestine." The lie came easily.

"The damned Jews from Palestine. You're all troublemakers. You, your brother and the rest of your family." He spat the words out with disgust and let go of her throat but continued to stand over her. "You want to ruin all of us who are living well. You're discontented vermin, that's what you are."

She stood up. She felt faint and held on to the edge of the table. "How dare you talk about my family that way!"

"I'll talk about them any way I please." He stepped away and eyed her for a minute. "And from here on in, you will begin to behave as a proper wife."

"I do not want to be your wife any longer," she shot back.

"Well, there is little you can do about that." His words seemed to bring him back to himself. "You are my wife. I am your husband and that is the way it is and that is the way it is going to be, for as long as you live. That is both Jewish law and Turkish law."

He was right and she knew it.

"But why would you want me as a wife?" she asked.

"Because I want sons and you will give me sons. I want two sons and until you bear those children you shall go on being my wife." The thought appealed to him. "And there will be no more hospital work. Your work will be here in this house, taking care of your body so that it will strong enough to carry my sons." He started toward her and she shrank from his touch.

"Now you will come with me to your room and you shall stay there until I decide how we continue our life together." He took her arm roughly and led her into the house.

"Will you lock me in again?" she asked disdainfully. "To keep the stewards from disturbing me, as you did on the ship?"

"How right I was to do it and how foolish I was not to continue doing it."

Tamar heard the lock turn. Her fear of being locked in had become a reality. Slowly she walked over to her dressing table and stared at herself in the mirror. Her face was swollen and the blood from her lip ran down her chin, although it had begun to congeal. A wry smile twisted her face. She would have no guilt now about leaving Fredrick.

Lying in bed with a damp cloth pressed to her face, Tamar watched the sky darken outside her room as evening turned to night. She could hear Fredrick moving about in his room. She pulled the blanket over her and wondered if he would come into her room and force himself on her. The thought made her cringe.

She fell into a fitful sleep and woke to the sound of a door opening. It took her a minute to realize Fredrick had not come into her room but was out in the hallway talking to Malikian. She slipped out of bed and struggled to her door. Her whole body ached. Pressing her ear to the keyhole she tried to hear what was being said.

"You betrayed me," Fredrick said angrily.

"No, effendi, she pleaded with me not to tell you. She wanted to be the one to do it." The servant sounded composed. "And the fact is, she did."

"Is there anything else she asked you not to tell me?"

"Effendi Davidzohn, she has spent most of her time in her room. I have been careful to watch her actions at all times."

Their voices began to fade and she realized they were walking down the stairs.

She moved to the window and caught sight of Fredrick entering his carriage.

The minute the carriage left the grounds, Tamar rang for Aris. Malikian, she knew, had a key to all the rooms in the house.

She did not have long to wait before hearing the key turn and Aris came into the room. They smiled at each other.

The two women, wrapped in black *charshaffes,* their faces covered, were indistinguishable from the other women in the old bazaar as they walked toward the Armenian quarter, where Malikian lived with his daughter.

# CHAPTER
# TWELVE

T AMAR sat on the damp earthen floor of the cave, staring at Thomas. He was lying on a straw mat. His features, lit by a small, flickering candle, were no longer swollen and the lean, good looks were as she remembered them. All her pent-up feelings for him had surfaced and she was grateful that she had been able to save him.

He had been in her care for three weeks and was resting peacefully, although at that moment his brow was wet with perspiration. She stood up and went to get a cloth.

"Tamar." She heard him call out and she rushed back to his side.

"I thought you left me," he whispered and reached out for her hand.

She stroked his hand lovingly. "Never," she said and tried to smile.

Being able to hold his hand was a great achievement. When Tamar and Aris first carried him into the cave, even though unconscious most of the time, he would cringe when anyone touched him. Now, although weak, he was on his way to physical recovery and he accepted her, wanted her near him at all times, would follow her with his eyes whenever she moved away. She felt he remembered their meetings, their love, their vows to each other, but still she had to be cautious. There were times when she would walk over to him and for no reason, he would suddenly shrink from her touch. She dared not ask why.

"How long have I been here?" His voice broke into her thoughts and she was surprised by the question. It was the first time he had shown interest in his whereabouts.

"About three weeks."

"What day is it." He started to sit up. "Or for that matter what year is it?"

She smiled. "I don't know the day. It's either the end of May or beginning of June. I know it's nineteen sixteen."

"It was February when we were captured," he said and his face grew taut at the memory. Then taking a deep breath and holding on to her hand, he stood up.

"Don't strain yourself," she warned.

"When do you think we'll be leaving here?" He let go of her and walked slowly around the cave.

"Soon," she answered, observing him carefully. He was dressed in a cotton robe tied at the waist, which emphasized his emaciated state, but he stood erect and seemed quite steady.

"I hate this place. It reminds me of that awful prison cell," he said. "What's keeping us here?"

"It won't be long now. It's really a matter of your being well enough to travel." She tried to sound convincing, since she had no idea when they would be leaving.

"Where are we anyway?"

"Somewhere on the outskirts of Constantinople." She walked over to him and led him back to his cot.

A low scratching sound caused them both to tense up. It was followed by a faint, low whistle.

"That's Aris," Tamar whispered with relief.

Thomas lay down and she ran through the darkened maze of tunnels to greet her friend. Briefly she was blinded by a shaft of sunlight pouring through the small opening to the cave usually sealed with a huge rock.

Aris stopped her. "Michael will be here shortly. He wants to talk to you."

As soon as Aris was inside, Tamar started to push the rock back into place. "Where has he been?"

"I'm not sure. Palestine, I think."

"Do you know what he wants to talk about?" Tamar asked.

"I haven't seen him. My father gave me the message."

Helping Aris unload the food from a large string bag, Tamar noted how pale and tired Aris looked.

"Anything wrong?" she asked.

"The whole city is searching for him." Aris indicated Thomas with her head. "It's getting more difficult for me to buy food. No one understands why my father and I are suddenly in need of so much."

"We've got to get out of here before we get you into trouble," Tamar said with concern. "What's holding everything up?"

"We're having a hard time selling that pearl choker. From the time I had it restrung, it's been a problem."

"Fredrick told me it belonged to some sultan and is very valuable."

"Your husband reported it stolen. No one will touch it."

Tamar looked down at her engagement ring. "Do you suppose he's got word out about this too?" She pushed her hand toward Aris.

"I don't know."

"Well, I'll give it to Michael. The obvious may have escaped Fredrick." She smiled wryly. "How could he think I stole all those beads that were strewn over the patio?" She paused. "Frankly, his faith in your father amazes me."

"We think he does suspect and is hoping my father will inadvertently lead him to you. That's one of the reasons he hasn't come here." The lines of concern on her face deepened.

"I'm so sorry I misjudged him," Tamar said.

"Don't fret about it." Aris sounded impatient.

"It's not a matter of fretting." Tamar insisted. "I was sure he was spying on me."

"Bayan Tamar, my father went to work for Effendi Davidzohn because he felt a kinship toward a man of the Jewish religion who he believed would understand the problems of the Armenian people," Aris said quietly. "Too late he realized he had made a mistake. Your husband proved more rigid than the generals in the army. More Turkish than any Moslem." Her voice grew bitter. "Mr. Davidzohn is a traitor to his people and he will live to regret it."

Tamar stared at Aris uncomprehendingly.

"The Armenian people in Turkey are being brutalized by the Turks, much as the Jews were and are by the Russians and the Poles. Worse, if possible. The Turks are trying to eliminate us from the face of the earth." Aris's face was devoid of expression.

"But does anyone know about it?" Tamar asked.

"The world knew and knows about the Jews and yet they've done nothing to help them. So even if anyone knows, it would make little difference."

"You never told me." Tamar had heard rumors about the Armenian troubles, but never thought they affected anyone she knew.

"What was I going to tell you?" Aris looked forlorn. "That my father foolishly trusted the Turks? Left my mother and me when I was ten to join their army, trusting that the Young Turks meant to accept the Armenian people as loyal Turkish citizens?"

"Why didn't he go home when he found out the truth?" Tamar felt sick.

"Home," Aris said sadly. "The Armenian people have no home."

The words spoken softly struck Tamar like a bolt of lightning. *Home. Homeland.* She had been raised with the dream of a homeland for the Jews and she thought she understood the importance of it. That was the dream she felt she could put off to be dealt with in the future. Until she heard Aris speak that simple phrase, a homeland was a vague concept. Now she suddenly understood the desperate, urgent need for it. She had wanted to go home because she was unhappy with Fredrick. She wanted to see her family, be with them, have them comfort her. Suddenly those needs were no longer important. She had to go home. She had to get there as quickly as possible. What Aris had said about the Armenians not having a home made her own dream fall into place. To make it happen she had to be there, to participate in its creation. And if she had to fight for it, she was ready to do it. She would do anything to make the dream of a homeland for the Jews a reality.

"Are you all right?" Aris asked.

Tamar looked over at her and impulsively reached out and embraced her. Aris had brought her back to reality. For the first time since leaving Palestine Tamar felt whole again and she was deeply grateful.

Thomas moaned in his sleep and both women looked over at him.

"I don't think we can stay here much longer," Tamar said. "He'll never recover fully in this place. It reminds him of the prison and he's frightened all the time. And, frankly, I can't take this darkness anymore."

"You'll stay here as long as necessary," Aris said sharply.

"Anything wrong?" Thomas, awakened by Aris voice, was struggling to get up.

"Please lie down, Thomas," Tamar said, "You'll need all your strength soon enough."

Thomas, sensing a new urgency in her voice, pushed himself up to his feet. "I'm really much stronger than you think."

"Thomas, you're much better but the soles of your feet have to be completely healed before we start traveling."

In defiance, he stamped his feet on the earthen floor. The wince of pain that crossed his face did not escape her.

"Thomas, please, I beg you, lie down."Tamar started to walk toward him when they heard a scratching noise at the cave's entrance.

"That will be Michael," Aris said and rushed out to lead him through the tunnels.

"Thomas, did you ever meet Michael Ben Hod?" Tamar asked as Aris and Michael appeared in the room.

Michael was dressed in his Turkish uniform with the abaya covering his head. He was carrying a riding whip in one hand and had a package under his arm. He looked menacing.

Thomas had grown pale at the sight of Michael. The Turkish uniform and especially the riding whip upset him.

"I don't believe we have," Thomas said slowly, getting to his feet again and putting his hand out in greeting.

"I've met you, Mr. Hardwick, but you were not in condition to remember the encounter," Michael said, ignoring the outstretched hand. "I was the one who got you out of the hospital."

Small beads of perspiration began to form on Thomas's brow. "I am most grateful to you, Mr. Ben Hod. Someday I hope I can repay you for your efforts."

"Someday maybe you will." Michael turned to Tamar. "We've got to get ready to move out of here."

"Do we have the papers and the money?" Tamar asked, furious at Michael's treatment of Thomas, but aware she could not offend him. Michael was their ticket to freedom.

"The papers were not a problem. It was selling that damned choker that proved difficult. Fortunately, I had to go to Damascus for a few days and that's where I finally got rid of it."

Tamar looked over at Thomas. He was seated on his cot, his eyes glued to Michael. He was breathing heavily and had begun to shake.

"You could try to be a little more pleasant," she said under her breath. "He's frightened enough and your behavior is not very helpful."

Michael shrugged with disinterest.

"When are we leaving?" Thomas asked.

"The sooner the better. The Turks are on a rampage in this area, looking for citizens disloyal to the empire, and these caves are often used by the local inhabitants who are trying to hide from the army." Michael dug into his jacket pocket and handed Tamar several creased pieces of paper. "These are forged identity cards for your trip to Konya."

She studied them carefully and smiled.

"Well, you do look like brother and sister," Michael said noting her expression.

"May I see them?" Thomas asked. Tamar handed them to him.

"Miss Carlotta Schluter and Mr. Hans Schluter, from Gmünd," Thomas said with amusement. "Who came up with those names?"

"And where is Gmünd?" Tamar relaxed, pleased at Thomas's reaction.

"It's in the Eifel mountains," Thomas said and handed the paper back to Michael.

Michael looked startled. "You're one of the few people who ever heard of it. Most people haven't and that's why I chose the place."

"I traveled extensively through Germany several years ago," Thomas explained. Michael's expression changed to suspicion.

"What's the plan?" Tamar asked, trying to defuse the tension between the two men.

"You'll be traveling as two German missionaries stationed in Palestine. You are in Turkey at the request of the German consul, who is concerned about the Armenian population," Michael paused as though waiting for Thomas to interrupt. But Thomas was listening attentively and Michael continued. "I will drive you part of the way but at one point you'll have to find some other means to get to Konya. Either by foot, or if you're lucky, by hitching a ride to the outskirts of the town."

"What's in Konya?" Thomas asked.

"A railroad station. A train to Palestine stops there. It's far enough from Constantinople and there is so much confusion in the army at the moment that I doubt that anyone will be looking for Mrs. Fredrick Davidzohn, or an escaped . . ." He did not finish the sentence, but the disdain was obvious.

"And then?" Thomas ignored the slight.

"Once there, you, Mr. Hardwick, will continue as a missionary and Tamar will take on the identity of Miss Tamar Danziger on her way home to visit her family." He handed her her Palestinian passport.

"Thomas cannot travel alone," Tamar started to protest.

"Don't be a fool," Michael snapped.

"Don't worry about me," Thomas said evenly. "Will it be all right for Tamar to travel alone?"

"We're trying to find someone who can accompany her. I will try to be there," Michael answered.

"Why can't we go right to Palestine as the Schluters?" Tamar asked.

"It's very uncomfortable traveling third class on these trains. Missionaries never go first class," Michael said.

"I don't care," Tamar said angrily.

"As you wish," Michael said indifferently. "But I suggest you take your passport with you, anyway. Hide it in the lining of your purse. Just in case."

"I think you should do as Mr. Ben Hod suggests," Thomas said, but his voice had grown quiet with fatigue.

"Why don't you lie down, Thomas. Rest up before we leave." Then, moving casually to the far corner of the room, she waved Michael over. "What about Aris?" she asked.

Michael's face showed emotion for the first time as he looked over at the young woman.

"It's getting her to Konya that's a problem." Michael's voice was filled with concern. "The Turks are on the lookout for every Armenian they can lay their hands on. It happens to work to your benefit. They're so obsessed with that search that two missionaries will hardly be of interest to them. But having her along would be very dangerous. Considering her concern for you, she would never agree to that."

"What do you mean?"

"This cave is an Armenian hideout, and for the last three weeks she's fought to let you and your friend stay here."

"So what happens to her after we leave?"

"Malikian will have to try to get her to Konya."

"And in Konya?"

"There we can get her papers, especially if you will go as Miss Danziger. You can say she's your maid and that your husband insists she go along."

"I can't leave her here," Tamar insisted.

"Malikian will take care of her," Michael said with finality and handed her the package he had brought along. "These are your traveling clothes." He looked at his watch. "It's almost seven o'clock and I should be back here around midnight."

"Incidentally, did you get to Palestine on your last trip?" she asked nonchalantly.

"Briefly."

"Did you see my family?"

"Yes, I did."

"How are they?" In spite of herself, her voice shook with emotion.

"Seeing you will make them all very happy," he said soberly.

Tamar escorted Michael to the mouth of the cave. Neither spoke, and Tamar tried to come to terms with her new insights. How childish she was to think that a homeland was something that would happen because she and her friends willed it! She always sensed it would involve a fight, but the magnitude of what that fight would be had somehow escaped her. Her naiveté embarrassed her.

Reaching the entranceway, Michael pushed aside the rock and the gust of fresh air made Tamar dizzy. Without thinking, she rushed out and breathed deeply, wanting to cleanse her mind of the feelings of doom that were now oppressing her.

"Get back inside, you fool," Michael pulled her back roughly.

She watched him move the stone into place and was grateful for the darkness. Leaning her head against the rocky wall, she allowed the tears that had been held back for so long to gush forth.

# CHAPTER THIRTEEN

T AMAR dozed intermittently. Giving up the idea of sleep, she sat up and stared out the window of the car Michael had found—the first she'd been in. It was a moonless night but she saw her image in the window-pane. For a brief moment she did not recognize herself. Her hair was tightly pulled back into a bun, her eyes were vacant and her face was gaunt. She looked like an old woman, a far cry from the young girl Thomas met on the beach, the one to whom he had written a poetic note of love, the one he wanted to spend his life with. The old woman staring at her could not stir that passion in any man now. Even more upsetting was that this woman in no way possessed that fiery spark so much a part of her when she, David and Raphael talked about their dreams. Those dreams Aris had re-ignited just a few hours ago. Now she wondered if she as she was today had the inner strength to go on.

She glanced at Thomas sitting beside Michael. His head was bowed and his shoulders were stooped. Could she ask him to participate in her people's struggle? Raphael's warning that Thomas was a stranger, that he would not understand their needs or fight for their cause, came back to her. The young man she met and fell in love with had the fire, the passion that was needed. Looking at Thomas she could not fathom the horror he had suffered and she felt helpless in the face of her ignorance. Would he be able to exorcise tose bitter memories? Could he ever feel again? Could he ever love again?

She was sure that, with love and care, he would recover. But if she were wrong and she had to make a choice between her love for him or love for her people, she knew without a moment's doubt that she would choose the latter.

"Aren't we supposed to be heading south?" Thomas's voice broke into her thoughts. "You're heading east."

"Yes, I am," Michael answered.

"But why?" Thomas demanded. "Konya is definitely to the south."

"I know what I'm doing," Michael snapped.

Tamar saw Thomas stiffen. His pale face flushed briefly in an effort to control his anger. She was strangely pleased by his reaction. Fear was the only emotion he had shown since she first saw him in the prison cell. And when he was not cringing with fear, he was placid, malleable, almost humble.

"Will it be much longer?" she asked.

"We'll be there shortly," Michael answered. "And if I were you, I wouldn't be in such a rush. You'll have quite a distance to go after I leave you."

He spoke in a matter-of-fact tone, but Tamar felt his hostility and it worried her. In spite of all that Michael had done for them, she did not fully trust him. She suspected that he did not trust her either. He certainly did not trust Thomas.

Michael stopped the car on a rough, cart-track road and handed Thomas a crumpled map with a detailed route for their journey to Konya.

The transfer of authority had an interesting effect on Thomas. It snapped him back to the poised, self-assured man Tamar first knew. He took the map, looked it over quickly and again questioned its validity.

"Mr. Ben Hod." His voice was crisp and authoritative. "I've dealt with maps all my life, and although I've never been in this part of the world, the route you are indicating is a much longer one and appears quite treacherous."

"You've got to avoid all villages that might have mission houses." Michael did not hide his annoyance.

"Why?" Thomas asked, still absorbed in the map.

"You're not really missionaries, you know." Michael laughed mirthlessly.

"I know my liturgy well enough," Thomas said coldly.

"Tamar doesn't," Michael snapped. "Besides, there's a great deal of unrest around the Armenian villages and you would do well not to approach any of them."

Tamar looked over at Thomas. He had a puzzled look on his face and she realized he had no knowledge of the political developments that had taken place in Turkey in recent months.

"That makes no sense at all," Thomas said angrily. "If we're here to observe the situation of the Armenian people, how could we explain our avoidance of them?"

"I assure you that no one will question why you are staying away from that human tragedy," Michael said quickly and got back into the car.

"Can you explain what that means?" Thomas would not be put off.

"Mr. Hardwick, you do what you like." Michael grew impatient. "I have given you a route and I suggest you follow it." He slammed the door of the car. "It should take you about five days to reach the outskirts of Konya. Don't enter the town until around five in the morning. There's a small café across from the station. Get your tickets and wait for the train. It stops there every other day for just a few minutes, so be sure you're close to the tracks when it arrives. If you miss it . . . ." He shrugged. "Just don't miss it." He started the motor, then turned to Thomas. "Incidentally, Mr. Hardwick, what were you doing near the Syrian border the night you were captured?" he asked.

Thomas looked confused for a moment. "Well, I suppose I won't be revealing any great military secrets at this point, but British Intelligence was told that the Turks were building a railroad from Acre to Gaza. We were going to blow it up."

Michael began to laugh. It was a strange laugh. "Didn't quite get it done, did you?"

"We were ambushed before we got there."

"Well, for whatever it's worth, the British were waiting for the attack on the Suez and succeeded in repelling it—at a great loss of life." The last words were said with bitterness. Then he drove off.

Thomas turned to Tamar the minute the car was out of sight. "Could you explain what all that Armenian talk was about?" he asked.

"I don't really know," she answered, fearful of upsetting him. In spite of his recovery, he was still quite fragile and she saw no reason to tax him.

Aware that he would get no more information from her, Thomas picked up his bag and was about to pick up Tamar's as well. She took it from him.

Following Michael's map, they found a path which led up a rocky hill. It was an arduous, uncompromising ascent and they were completely exhausted by the time they reached the top. Once there they found themselves staring down at a vast, arid, treeless plateau. The midday sun was scorching and they decided to take a rest. Thomas scanned the area below.

"There's a village down there," he called out excitedly.

She looked in the direction he was pointing to. In the distance, she saw the white domino houses, with their flat, neat roofs and the large cross atop a church, gleaming in the bright sunlight.

"You're sure it's not a mirage?" Tamar asked laughingly.

"Not if we both see it," Thomas laughed and his taut features relaxed. "And even if it is, we'll still be heading in the right direction and we'll be that much closer to our destination."

Both were aware that they were ignoring Michael's instructions, and the conspiracy brought them closer. Thomas took her arm and they hurried downhill.

The village was further away than it appeared and it was almost dark by the time they reached its outskirts. The streets were empty and as they walked toward the main square, Tamar had the distinct impression that they were being watched.

"Thomas, let's leave this place," she whispered, drawing closer to him. "There's something eerie going on and I don't want to know what it is."

"Nonsense. We've come this far. Let's see if we can find someone who might be able to help us." Thomas stopped walking and looked around. Then, with exaggerated assurance, he headed toward a small, well-kept house. Before knocking, he turned to Tamar and waved her over to his side. Haltingly, she joined him.

A man opened the door and peered at them. Dressed in a striped cotton caftan, he did not look like an Armenian. He eyed them suspiciously.

"Would you be able to help us?" Thomas began but before he could finish his sentence, the man started to close the door.

Thomas held it open forcefully and asked if there was a place where they could rest for the night.

The man hissed an obscenity at them and slammed the door shut. He had spoken Arabic and by his dialect it was clear that he was Syrian.

"I thought this was an Armenian village," Thomas mused.

"Thomas, I beg you, let's get out of here." Tamar pulled at his sleeve.

"I wonder if we should try the church."

"Let's not," she said quickly. She did not know why but she was certain they would not find anyone there.

"I'm sure they'll be friendlier than that poor, frightened man."

"Thomas, let's just follow Michael's advice and avoid situations that we might not be able to cope with."

"And what's that supposed to mean?" Thomas became more aggressive.

"I don't really know." Her hysteria was close to the surface and Thomas did not press her further.

Once out of the village, they walked aimlessly until they found a small clearing surrounded by a thick growth of fern which looked secluded and secure. They decided to spend the night there.

Thomas started a fire, and they ate their meager rations in silence. Thomas took out the map and studied it carefully.

"Well, I know we're heading in the right direction," he said finally. "And tomorrow should not be as difficult as it was today."

Tamar lay down on the hard, bare ground. Thomas lay a few feet away from her. The cold dampness crept up through the thin covering and, although exhausted, she could not sleep. She listened to the sounds of the night and soon heard Thomas's deep, mournful sighs. She longed to take him in her arms and comfort him, but feared rejection. In spite of his dependance on her, he seemed frightened of intimacy.

They started out early the next morning and tried to undo the mistakes of the day before. It soon became clear that they were hopelessly lost. Paths that seemed promising ended as abruptly as they started. Winding cart paths led into nothingness. They avoided the Armenian villages, but the ones they passed were little more than ghost towns, confirming what Aris had said. Tamar was haunted by the idea that Bet Enav could one day look like that.

That evening, still unsure as to where they were, they settled in a pleasant enclave between two hills.

Tamar pulled out the combs that kept her hair in a tight bun. Her hair now reached down to her waist. Feeling more relaxed, she braided it loosely and watched Thomas build a fire to heat some of the water poured from a thermos.

She noted that with each passing hour he gained more strength and was taking on more of the chores. His concern for her was obvious, yet they were still strangers, strangers trapped by circumstances and common purpose.

"Drink that." He handed her a tin cup of steaming tea. "And try to get some sleep. We've still got a ways to go and the rest will do you good. I'll wake you when it's time to start out."

"I'd rather you slept," she mumbled.

"As you wish." He seated himself a distance away and looked up at the sky, as though hoping the stars would give him guidance.

Tamar felt lost. At that moment in her life she belonged nowhere and to no one. She could not blame Thomas for her marriage to Fredrick. But in a way she had allowed a fantasy to replace a concrete dream and that fantasy had clouded her vision and guided her actions. Thomas was that fantasy. A tear ran down the side of her face. She did not wipe it away. It was dark and there was no one to witness her pain.

"You're crying," she heard Thomas say.

"I'm frightened." She sat up and wiped her face with her hand.

"Of what?"

"We're lost, Thomas. Hopelessly lost." The words did not only speak of their location and he seemed to sense it.

"Only temporarily," he said softly and came to sit beside her, "I've figured it all out," he said, and spreading the map down on the ground he showed her the route. She watched his fingers trace the route and in spite of herself, she reached out and touched his hand.

He did not withdraw it. Instead, she saw his hand form into a tight fist and the knuckles grow white. With her hand still resting on his, she looked up at him. In the light of the dying fire his face was ashen, but the look in his eyes held her attention. They were filled with love and desire. For a brief moment he looked as he had when she first saw him. Then he lowered his eyes.

"Thomas, whatever was or will be, I love you," she whispered and lifted his hand to her breast.

His breath came in short gasps and his body began to shake with dry sobs. She cradled his head until the sobs subsided and, lying back, she pulled him gently toward her, holding him as a mother holds a child. Soon he was asleep and she too dozed off.

When Tamar woke up, she found Thomas leaning on his elbow watching her. His face looked calm, his eyes clear. She could see his features clearly in the glowing embers of the dying fire.

He reached out and touched her hair. "You are just as I remembered you. Except that you are far more beautiful now," he whispered.

She nestled closer to him, comforted by his tenderness.

He lowered himself toward her and, lifting her face to his, he kissed her gently on the lips. "I love you too," he said quietly. "I've never stopped loving you and I believe that my love for you sustained me through my nightmare." He spoke softly, as he caressed her cheek and throat. "Through all the torture, through all the abuse and humiliation, you were there, telling me that I would survive, encouraging me to hold on to what I am, to what I was meant to be, to my manhood."

She put her hand to his lips, not wanting him to speak anymore. He pushed it away.

"You must hear me out." His voice grew hoarse, "When I heard your voice in that wretched cell, I thought I was dreaming. And when I turned and saw you I knew I was going to live, that I would somehow be saved and that I would one day be able to tell you of my love for you, and my hope that you could love me, in spite of everything."

She was too overcome by emotion to speak. She pressed her lips to his and moved closer to him. His arms encircled her, and he returned her kisses with a passion that erased all thoughts.

She felt him undo the buttons on her dress and slip it off her shoulders. Shamelessly, she pulled at his shirt and felt his smooth nakedness. His hands caressed her body and his mouth sucked at her breasts. When she felt his hardness enter her, she accepted him eagerly. Knowing that he desired and loved her as much as she desired and loved him erased all fear, all doubts, all frustrations.

The sun was beaming down on them when they awoke. Tamar was still lying in Thomas's arms and she looked up at him.

"I think we'd better start moving." Thomas touched her face lovingly and untangled himself from their embrace.

"Can't we stay here a while longer?" she asked, stretching her arms toward him. "And make love again?"

He threw his head back and his happy laughter filled the air. "You're shameless and I'd like nothing more than to make love to you again. But we'll have a whole lifetime ahead of us for that. At the moment, however, we've got to get to Konya."

They continued on their journey, now filled with greater purpose. They were no longer solitary figures who happened to be traveling together. They were lovers, heading toward a glorious future. Their happiness seemed to be contagious and the few people they met on the main road encouraged them on their way. Both were aware that they had not followed the route Michael had suggested, but they were carelessly confident, convinced that no harm could come to them. Reaching Palestine marked the beginning of a new life and they were rushing toward it.

The night before they were to reach Konya, Tamar lying contentedly in Thomas's arms listened to him talk of their future together.

"I will never be able to live away from Palestine again," she said, and waited for his reaction.

He moved away and looked at her in surprise. "I wouldn't expect you to."

"Thomas, do you know what lies ahead for the Jews in Palestine?"

He laughed softly. "Of course I do. The Jewish people must have a homeland. It must be a strong and proud land which will serve as an example to the world. But most important I want the Arabs to see it. They must be educated, must learn to understand their rights. An enlightened Jewish state would serve as a living example and urge them to create homelands for their own people." He paused to catch his breath. "I would give my life to help you make that dream a reality."

"But the Arabs are not a homogeneous people." She could not help but voice her concern. Having grown up amongst the Arabs, she knew how different they were from the Jews. "Do you really believe you can unite them?"

"Fear not, my love," he answered. "My father gave me the middle name of Gideon. I, like the biblical prophet, will choose the leaders who will not bow when drinking from the river. And it will be those leaders who will teach the masses the meaning of nationhood."

Tamar understood the allusion and smiled. "Gideon."

"Don't you see, my darling, once the Turks are defeated, the allies will help both the Jews and the Arabs make a reality of their dreams." His confidence gave credence to his convictions. Their hopes for the future intertwined, blended and formed a whole. It was bound to happen.

When they woke up in the morning, Tamar started packing their belongings. Thomas, standing on top of a small mound, called to her.

She ran happily toward him. His arm encircled her waist and she pressed closer to him.

"What's that moving down there?" he asked, pointing to a narrow twisting path in the valley below.

Tamar put her hand to her brow and squinted. "It looks like a long line of large ants scurrying about." She laughed at her own foolishness.

Suddenly a scream reached them and echoed off the rocky mountains around them. It was followed by another and yet another. As the cries grew louder, they turned into a concert of piercing, inhuman sounds.

"They're people," Tamar gasped. "The line down there is made up of people."

She started running down toward the valley. She did not know what she would do when she got there, but she was not thinking clearly. The closer she came, the louder the cries sounded, the more horrifying the sight.

She was halfway down the hill when Thomas caught up with her and held her back. They were close enough, however, to see the shuffling, scraping, creeping, groveling people, whose faces were hollow and whose eyes were vacantly staring ahead. Tamar and Thomas stood helplessly by, watching whimpering children fall to the ground, only to be snapped up by their mothers before the soldiers' whips lashed out at them and ordered them to march on.

"Thomas, we must do something," Tamar cried out helplessly.

"I'll go down and talk to the officer in charge, but you must promise me you will not move away from this spot," he said and pushed her gently down onto the grassy knoll.

She watched him briefly but her eyes returned to the horror that was unfolding before her. The line came to a stop and she realized that Thomas had caught up with the officer in charge.

She could see him pointing to the people, his arms waving in indignation. The officer's laugh reached her. Thomas grabbed the man by the arm and the officer raised his crop, ready to lash out at Thomas when a woman stepped forward and held out a bundle to Thomas. He leaned down and took it from her and Tamar realized it was a child. Thomas held it for a moment and then lifted it toward the officer. Even from the distance, Tamar could tell the child was dead.

Forgetting her promise, Tamar stood up and ran frantically toward Thomas, never stopping until she reached his side.

"Another missionary?" the officer said mockingly, looking down at her. "And a woman, yet."

She ignored the comment and looked over at Thomas, who was still holding the dead infant. Impulsively Tamar took it from him and looked around for the mother. The woman had sunk to her knees, a wild look in her eyes. Then, as though propelled by some unseen force, she started bashing her head against a rock lying beside the road. The blood splattered out, covering the rock. The woman's convulsive movements continued, even after her head was split open. Then she fell over.

"By order of the German archdiocese, I order you to stop this insanity," Thomas said threateningly.

"I do things by order of Enver Pasha, not by the order of missionaries," the captain said. "Now, if you will excuse me, I've got a deadline to meet." Turning his horse around, he headed toward the back of the line. Once there he took his gun out of its holster, fired a shot over the heads of the people and screamed out orders to his subordinates. Clubs started coming down on the backs of anyone who hesitated.

Tamar, standing next to Thomas, watched the tragic, human convoy move along, still clutching the dead infant in her arms.

# CHAPTER
# FOURTEEN

T HOMAS led Tamar to a table at the far end of the small coffeehouse and seated her next to the window, facing the railroad station. In spite of the early hour, the heat of the day was unbearable. Several men were seated around the room, sipping their thick, steaming Turkish coffee and puffing on their water pipes. They glanced at Tamar and Thomas, indignant that a woman was seated in their midst. But since she was European, they dared not voice their objections.

The Konya railroad station was a dilapidated depot, no more than a whistle stop. It adjoined the town's bazaar and consisted of a wooden platform standing on rusting metal poles. Beyond the platform were four train tracks. A similar platform stood on the opposite side of the tracks, with no rail to prevent people from crossing from one side to the other. It was hardly a station that would attract anyone who did not live in the town. Thomas and Tamar were quite conspicuous, yet no one was likely to know them.

Tamar was pale and her eyes stared unseeing into space. She had been in that state since they buried the dead infant at the side of the road the previous day. For the rest of the trip, she seemed unaware of where they were. She kept stumbling and falling, never noticing the pain even when blood appeared on her hands and knees.

"Would you like some coffee?" Thomas asked, taking her hand in his.

She shifted her eyes to him but appeared to be looking through him.

"Tamar, dear, listen to me," he said urgently. "You must get hold of yourself. I know what you're feeling, but you cannot give up now. Look." He pointed out the window. "We're in Konya and we're right on schedule. The train will be here shortly and we'll be on our way home."

"Home." She echoed the word and tried to focus on him.

"Yes, my darling. Home. Your family will be there, waiting for you. They need you and love you."

"Home," she repeated. "Will it still be there?" She sounded like a child.

"Will Deborah be there? Or will the Turks have mutilated her as they did those people on the road?"

"What are you saying?" Thomas pressed her hand in frustration.

"I don't know," she whispered. But she did know. More and more she saw her sister's face loom in place of the women who were herded and beaten by the Turkish soldiers. Deborah was all of them. Deborah was the woman who had bashed her head against the rock. Deborah was Aris.

"Deborah is safely at home with your brother and her husband," Thomas tried again. "And they will see to her safety. Your brother has influence with the Turkish government. They respect him and need him."

"I'm sure there were many Armenian men who thought they were respected and needed by the Turks," she answered dully. "But they were helpless in the face of that insanity. And if it happened to them and their families, what chance does a tiny Jewish community in Palestine have?"

"The Jewish community has powerful friends," Thomas said with assurance. "The whole British Empire will come to their aid."

"The Turks have the Germans," she answered.

"You're overestimating the Turks. They're in disarray, they're corrupt and although the Germans are a formidable army, the Turks have chosen the wrong partners." He spoke adamantly and meant what he was saying, but he could not break through her state of shock.

He hated leaving her alone, even to walk over to the bar to get them some coffee and borrow a newspaper from the owner. It was several days old, but he had not seen a newspaper in a long time and he was hungry for news of the world.

He scanned it quickly and was shocked by the reports. He understood the pro-Turkish bias; still, all reports indicated that the Allies were stymied in the desert and were suffering great losses. The Germans were advancing in Europe and the Russians appeared to be doomed. The United States was still neutral and the British and the French were carrying the burden of the Great War. A small item referred to the Armenians as the "enemies of the empire." Recalling the sight of the devastated people marching to their doom, Thomas shuddered. He wished he could show the paper to Tamar, if only to prove his point.

He threw a look in her direction. She had not touched her coffee, her manner was unchanged. He continued to read, looking for a mention of his Bedouin friends. He was shocked to realized that since Tamar had come back into his life, he had not thought of them. They were his family, his friends, they had given his life purpose.

He knew it the first time he found himself in their midst.

An only child and a sickly one, Thomas was brought up by a doting mother and a silent, stern father, who worked hard to support them. While growing up, Thomas had no friends and he assumed it was due to the fact that he did not attend school. He had no way of knowing that his parents were ostracized by their neighbors. He was six when he found out he was born out of wedlock. Many years later he discovered that his father's first wife refused to give him a divorce and that his parents had never been able to marry. The discovery came the first time he attended Sunday school and one of the boys called him a bastard. He never went back and his religious training was taken over by his father. His mother, a schoolteacher by profession, took charge of his education. The day he received his first globe of the world, he knew that one day he would leave England. He was determined to travel the world and try to find some remote place where he would be accepted and that he could call home.

His mother died when he was thirteen. His father died a year later. The pastor came by after his father was buried and announced that a relative was on his way to fetch him and that until he arrived, Thomas was to come and live at the parish.

Young as he was, he understood that the reason a relative was about to make an appearance was because of his small inheritance. The relative turned out to be his father's wife's brother. A dubious relative at best, he satisfied the pastor and Thomas was taken to Wales, where he met the woman who had never divorced his father, and discovered he had a half-brother and a half-sister. They disliked him on sight and Thomas made little effort to ingratiate himself to the family. He was sent away to boarding school. Completely lacking in social graces, he found it impossible to get on with the other boys, except for one, George Straham, who showered him with kindness. When George started making sexual overtures toward him, Thomas was stunned. The idea frightened him, but he did like the physical closeness, the caresses, the gentleness with which George fondled him. When George began to demand that they consummate their relationship, Thomas balked. They got into a fist fight. Thomas won the fight, but George labeled him a pervert. Thomas was promptly expelled.

His father's family would not take him back. They did, however, give him some money and he started traveling. Germany, France, Italy were beautiful and interesting, but did not capture him. He stayed in each country long enough to learn the language. He attended classes at various universities, where he studied history, geography, archeology and religion. He was tempted to convert to Catholicism and become a priest. He joined a Jesuit sect in Switzerland where an English student, who was connected to the British foreign office, persuaded him to go back to England.

All were impressed with Thomas's knowledge, especially his fluency in languages, and he was invited to join the foreign service. The work appealed to him and when he was asked to go on a mission to Egypt, he accepted.

He was twenty-two years old when he arrived in Alexandria and he felt as though he was born the day his ship docked.

The feeling of being truly alive came when he was sent into the desert to meet with some of the Bedouin leaders. He was greeted by the eldest son of the Grand Sharif, Prince Salim, and a friendship formed immediately. When Thomas was given his first *galabya* and the *abaya* was placed on his head, he knew he had finally found a home.

The tribesmen loved him. They looked up to him, listened to him, embraced him as a brother and, although he continued to work for British Intelligence, his loyalties were often put to the test. It was this conflict that prompted the thought of bringing the Arabs closer to the British and their way of thinking, politically.

Whenever he was in the desert, he lived with the Sallah family. The elders accepted him as their own and for the first time in his life, he was happy. He was aware that Assad, although married with children, was in love with him, as a man would love a woman. He loved him in return, but his determination not to compromise his manhood made him keep his distance. Assad respected his desire.

Thomas was an extremely attractive man and he sensed women were attracted to him. They played a small role in his life, however. He was not particularly attracted to them, although he had had several affairs, mostly to assure himself of his manhood.

When he met Tamar Danziger on the beach, all doubts about his manhood evaporated. His physical reaction to her overwhelmed him. She fulfilled every dream he had ever had. He was devastated when her brother dismissed him so rudely. As he rode away, he made a vow that he would see her again.

Their two brief meetings confirmed his feelings and he lived for the day of their reunion. She became part of his thoughts, his plans, his dreams. His future was intricately involved with her. He had no idea when he would meet her but he was convinced that even if she married another and had children, they were destined for each other.

Being captured by the Turks, tortured by them and finally raped by a Turkish officer, killed the dream. A rape under duress would not have wounded him. It was the circumstance and his reaction to it which tormented him.

He did not know how long he had been in prison but he felt that he was on the verge of breaking. One day, when lying naked on his stomach, he heard his cell door open. He waited for rough hands to pull him up. Instead, he heard the voice of a man, a gentle voice addressing him in French. He did not open his eyes and pretended to be asleep. The man's French was fluent, the tone was seductive and filled with compassion. He assured Thomas that he had come to help him. Thomas turned his head toward the wall, wondering if he could trust a Turkish officer, when he felt a cool hand stroking his hair. The hand moved down his back, touching the wounds gently, soothingly. It was the first kindness shown to him since he was captured. He continued to listen to the cajoling voice and his mind grew hazy.

He half-expected it, yet when the sexual assault came, he was caught off guard.

The pain at first was excruciating, and he made a feeble attempt to extricate himself, but he was too weak and too defeated. It would also have been futile. The Turk proved to be powerful in his determination. The last thing Thomas remembered before losing consciousness was the seducer's gleeful laugh and his mocking accusation that Thomas had allowed it to happen because he had wanted it.

The memory of the rape was so vivid Thomas started in his seat and looked around frantically. Seeing Tamar sitting opposite him calmed him. Breathing a sigh of relief, he reached over, took her hand and held it tightly.

"Tamar, I love you so much," he whispered. "Tamar, please come back." He leaned closer. "Help me, I need you so desperately."

His despair reached her. She shook her head, as though coming out of a haze. She pressed his fingers weakly and he could see her concern, but the reaction he wanted—the love and care he needed—was not there. At that moment she needed him more than he needed her and he knew it.

Still holding her hand he looked out at the square, which now was teeming with people. Hordes of men were shoving and vying for position in front of the ticket office. Most were laden with numerous boxes and crates, making their progress more difficult. Their women, wrapped in black *charshaffes,* their faces veiled, were seated on the ground a distance away, their children and assorted farm animals waiting patiently for their men to collect them.

The ticket window was open, but the line was moving slowly. Each purchase seemed to get bogged down in negotiations, endless discussions which culminated in shouting matches and occasional fist fights. Several policemen mingled with the crowd and it was their presence that prevented total chaos.

Thomas was debating whether he should try to find the officer in charge of the station to see if he could get tickets more easily when an army truck came into the square. Several Turkish soldiers jumped down and fell into an orderly line. They were dressed in full military regalia and were extremely well disciplined. Two captains inspected them critically and after a brief consultation, the soldiers broke up into two groups. One group marched briskly across the tracks and positioned themselves on the opposite platform. The remaining soldiers marched up to the near platform.

Thomas was puzzled and watched the captain march toward the far end of the station where he joined a group of high-ranking Turkish and German officers.

"I wonder what all this means," Thomas said almost to himself and stood up.

"Where are you going?" Tamar asked, looking up at him.

"I've got to get our tickets," he said, still watching the soldiers and officers.

"Can't I go with you?"

"Better not." He pointed toward the Germans and Turks. "There's something strange going on out there."

She turned her head and a look of horror came to her face.

"What's the matter?" Thomas asked.

"I know one of the Germans," she whispered, clutching Thomas's hand. "His name is Colonel Von Hassen."

"Which one is he?" Thomas asked with concern.

She pointed him out and Thomas felt her fingers dig into his hand.

"No reason to panic," he said quietly.

"He was the one who escorted me to the prison the day I first saw you." She began to shake. "He told me he had never seen you and I don't think he was lying. But he may have seen you after that."

"Well, he obviously shouldn't see us together." Thomas continued to stare at the officers.

"What are we going to do?" Tamar sounded desperate.

He was silent for a moment, then, taking out his wallet, he handed her several bills.

"I'm going to get my ticket. I shall get only one and take my place in the third-class car. As soon as I'm gone, you go out the back door. Get your Palestinian passport out and dress yourself like Mrs. Davidzohn because that is how you will be traveling. Don't come back in here, just walk around and wait until you see that I'm close enough to the ticket window. Then get in that line and buy a first-class ticket."

She started to protest, but he put his hand to her lips. "You are to do as I say."

"When will I see you again?" Her face was animated and he was relieved to see that she had come back to herself.

"Sooner than you think," he said and smiled. "Just remember that I love you. I love you more than life itself and nothing but death could keep me away from you. You must always remember that."

"Don't speak of death." She reached out and touched his face.

He leaned over and kissed her quickly on the cheek, picked up his suitcase and walked out of the coffeehouse.

Tamar watched Thomas take his place in line. He was taller than all the men around and his English appearance made him stand out. No one was paying attention to him; still, she was gripped with fear, convinced he was heading into a trap. Her impulse was to run out and beg him not to get on the train. They could continue on foot together. She was about to get up when she caught sight of Colonel Von Hassen and knew she could not risk being seen by him. Not as long as Thomas was as visible as he was at that moment.

Her mouth was dry. With trembling hands, she picked up her cup and sipped some coffee, her eyes wandering around the crowd, hoping to spot

Michael Ben Hod. He was nowhere in sight. She turned back to Thomas. He had barely moved ahead in line.

She stood up slowly and headed toward the back door. Once outside, she rummaged through her bag, took out a small compact, placed it on a jutting stone of the wall and proceeded to make up. She undid her hair and gathered it into a loose bun. Lighting a match, she allowed it to glow briefly before blowing out the flame and, using the charred edge, she outlined her eyes, as she would with kohl. Rouging her cheeks, she applied some of the color to her lips. Deftly she tied a scarf around her waist, giving the simple black dress an air of chic casualness. She looked down at her clumsy shoes, the dowdy handbag and the worn suitcases, hardly suited to the elegant Mrs. Davidzohn, but there was little she could do about it. She threw a last glance at herself in the small hand mirror, replaced it in the bag and was taking out her Palestinian passport when she heard a rustling sound behind her. She turned quickly and found Aris, dressed in a long black cotton *charshaffe*, her face covered by a veil, standing several feet away from her.

"I'm sorry I frightened you, Bayan Tamar," the young woman said and came closer. "I could not go into the café and I've been waiting for you to come out." She searched her mistress's face. "Are you well?"

"Yes. How are you?" Tamar said with relief. "How did you get here?"

"My father and I have been here since last night. We slept on the outskirts of the town and came in with the crowd heading for the station."

"Where is he?"

"He's watching over Effendi Thomas."

Tamar smiled. Malikian would see to it that no harm came to Thomas.

"Do you have papers to accompany me to Palestine?" she asked.

Aris nodded and although only her eyes were visible, Tamar could tell she too was smiling.

"You'll be safe in my house," Tamar assured her. "And my family will love you. Especially my sister." She stopped, overcome by emotion. "But we can talk about that on the train. Now I want to know what's happening in Pera. Is my husband still angry? What is he doing?"

"He's beyond anger, Bayan Tamar. He is deeply ashamed and plotting revenge. He rarely leaves the house except when he has to go out on business. No one knows that you are gone. My father was instructed to tell anyone who asks for you that you are ill and cannot be disturbed."

"Oh, my God," Tamar exclaimed, "I wonder how long he can go on doing it?" She felt uncomfortable. "And now that Malikian is gone, what is he going to do?"

"I do not know. We left his house the day the effendi left for Europe on business."

"Are you sure he went to Europe?" Tamar asked with great concern. She worried he might go to Palestine to look for her and would be waiting for her when she got there. The law, as Fredrick had said, was on his side. He could force her to return to Turkey with him.

"My father took him to the port and saw him get on the ship," Aris said with assurance.

"God, I hope you're right." She picked up her bag and put her arm around Aris's shoulder. "We'd better get going. I still haven't bought my ticket."

Aris pulled back. "I have my ticket and I shall travel in the third-class section. It would not be proper to have me sitting with you. When we reach Aleppo, it will be different. But it would be unheard of in this part of Turkey. You go ahead and buy your ticket and don't concern yourself with me until the train gets to Aleppo. Please do not look for me. I shall find you." Her manner was that of an independent woman, not a maid.

She was gone before Tamar could answer.

As soon as Aris was out of sight, Tamar walked out to the square.

The mid-morning sun was beating mercilessly down on the crowd. Voices were raised as people tried to push ahead. Tamar had no idea when the train was due to arrive, but time was obviously short.

Everyone in front of the café stared at her. She ignored them and prayed that Colonel Von Hassen would catch sight of her and come over.

"Mrs. Davidzohn?" To her great relief, she heard him call out, but she noted uncertainty in his greeting.

She turned around. "Why, Colonel Von Hassen!" she exclaimed, trying to sound both surprised and nervous. "What a surprise to see you here." She paused. "What are you doing here?"

"What are *you* doing here, madame?" His uncertainty turned to suspicion. She bit her lip and lowered her eyes.

"Your husband told me you were ill," he continued. "I tried to call on you when you stopped coming to the hospital. I was concerned."

"Indeed, I was confined to my room but not to my bed." She started slowly, her eyes still downcast. "And it was not with a fever." She looked up at him. He was staring at her coldly. "Colonel, I feel I can trust you and I would like to share my unhappy situation with you." He said nothing and she continued, trying to sound conspiratorial. "I had told you Mr. Davidzohn had forbidden me to go to that infernal prison on behalf of your general. When my husband returned from his trip, I told him." She looked at him meaningfully and her voice dropped to a whisper. "And he struck me. It was horrible. He did not stop his assault until I began to bleed. Then he locked me in my room." She wet her lips nervously. "Like you, colonel, I come from a different culture. Men do not abuse their wives in my country." She continued to stare at him. His face was flushed and he seemed confused. She was not sure he believed her, but she had succeeded in embarrassing him.

"And how did you get here?" he asked.

"My husband had to go to Europe again and the day he left, friends helped me. They suggested this train station, since it is far away from the city and they felt I would not run into anyone my husband was likely to know." She smiled briefly. "I hardly expected to meet you here."

"Which friends?" He ignored her remark and looked around.

"My husband's servant and my maid," she said urgently. "They took great risk in bringing me here, but they are Armenians and they were quite upset at how badly I had been treated."

"And you will be traveling to Palestine alone?" he asked slowly.

"I had gotten word to my brother in Palestine and he promised to come or send someone to meet me here," she said hurriedly. "That's why I'm standing here. I was told to wait by the café."

"Have you got your train ticket?"

"I feel I should stay here for a while longer. If my brother sent someone else to escort me, they would expect to find me here."

"Let me get your ticket for you." He was uncomfortable with his decision but he was a chivalrous young German officer compelled to help a woman in distress.

She threw a quick look toward Thomas. Only a peasant with his goat was ahead of him.

"I don't believe there is any great rush. I doubt that any of these people will be traveling first class." She smiled sweetly. "But what are you doing here?"

"General Schtock and Jamal Pasha have scheduled a meeting in Damascus and I've been asked to accompany the general."

"Is the general in Konya?" she asked casually.

"He's in the trainmaster's office, trying to get some decent food and water placed on the train. We drove down here, but the roads are bad and we've decided to take the train for the rest of the trip." He smiled for the first time. "If you'll allow me to mention your presence to him, I'm sure he'll be very understanding. He obviously knows nothing of what has transpired between you and your husband. And since, in a way, he is responsible for your misfortune, he will probably invite you to accompany him in his car. I assure you, it will be far more comfortable than the first-class compartment."

Her heart sank. Thomas and the general on the same train was too great a risk. "That is extremely generous, but I'd rather not."

"But why not?" Von Hassen became impatient. "Especially if no one shows up to escort you, he would be the finest chaperon you could have."

She wanted to get away from the colonel. She had to get a message to Thomas that they must not get on the train. It was much too dangerous. "Angry as I am at my husband," she said slowly. "I cannot be that disloyal to him. Traveling with the general would make my disobedience all the more humiliating to him."

"That infernal prisoner has caused humiliation to too many people," Von Hassen said bitterly. "Especially to me."

"What happened to that poor man?" She simulated mild interest, as she pretended to be searching the crowd. The farmer with the goat was arguing with the ticket vendor. Thomas would be next.

"Poor man, indeed!" Von Hassen's voice rose in anger. "He disappeared the first night he was in the hospital and although every available Turkish and German officer has been looking for him, it has been to no avail. He seems to have vanished into thin air."

"But that's ridiculous. The man I saw in that cell could not walk across a room, much less walk out of a hospital," she exclaimed.

"That's the point. In fact, the doctors felt he was even too ill to be interviewed by me."

"You've never seen him?"

"No, although I'd recognize him anywhere."

"What did the general say when he found out the man was gone?"

The colonel's face reddened with embarrassment. "I don't believe I can repeat his words in the presence of a lady." He laughed self-consciously. "But I assure you, madame, when we do find him—" His sentence was interrupted by the sound of a gunshot and they both turned to see where it had come from.

It was impossible to tell what had happened. People were running in every direction, screaming in panic. Soldiers broke ranks and rushed into the teeming mass, trying to restore order.

The colonel started running toward the stationmaster's building, pushing his way through and shouting commands in German. Tamar was close behind. His authoritative voice made people move aside, clearing a path for them.

The farmer who had preceded Thomas in line, was lying on the ground, bleeding, still holding on to his goat, while a Turkish train official was trying to pull the confused animal away. Thomas was kneeling by the wounded peasant, fending off the official. Several soldiers sided with the train conductor, while most of the farmers and would-be travelers were trying to push them back. Tamar and Von Hassen had just reached Thomas and the wounded man when a series of shots were fired. Everyone drew back, leaving Thomas and the wounded man alone. Thomas stood up slowly and faced Von Hassen. Tamar watched in horror as the colonel's hand went to his gun holster, when suddenly a man lunged at Von Hassen. For a second the German looked stunned, then he slumped to the ground, blood gushing from his mouth. A knife was sticking out of his chest. Before anyone understood what had happened, the murderer was surrounded by Turkish and German military men, but not before Tamar caught sight of the perpetrator. Malikian was being beaten with sticks and rifle butts, his clothes were ripped from his body and as he tried to defend himself, the ferocity of the soldiers grew.

As though in a dream, Tamar heard a piercing scream and saw Aris clawing her way toward her father. Soldiers grabbed her and her *charshaffe* came undone. The cross she always wore gleamed in the sunlight.

"Armenian bitch." The crowd's sentiments turned and they surged toward her, anxious to participate in the slaughter.

The loud clanking noise of the train coming into the station drowned out the sound of the frenzied crowd. Like a herd of cows, they turned away from the scene that had held them and raced toward the platform. Within seconds, the square was nearly empty except for a few soldiers standing around Malikian's mangled, lifeless body, lying on the ground. Aris was lying next to him, face down, her body crumpled and broken. Colonel's Von Hassen's body was being carried away by several German officers. Thomas was nowhere in sight.

"Here's your ticket." Michael Ben Hod was standing close to her. "Now get on that train."

"Where is Thomas?" She asked frantically.

"He's obviously got more sense than you have. He got on the train with the rest of them."

"Are you sure?"

He did not answer. Instead he pushed her toward the train, which had started to move by the time she reached it. Hands reached out and pulled her on.

# CHAPTER FIFTEEN

DEBORAH spent a sleepless night at the laboratory, feeling quite helpless. David had been arrested and she was frantic with worry about his welfare. Michael was back in Palestine, trying to get him out. Their work had gone quite well for a while, but in recent weeks the British had not been by to collect the information, and the villagers were more suspicious than ever. Now Tamar was coming home, unaware of the enormous changes that had occurred in their lives.

Deborah knew she should be home waiting for her, but she was not quite ready for the reunion. Much as she wanted her back, she resented her return at that moment and could not figure out why. She had changed. Her attitudes were different and she worried that Tamar would expect her to be the girl she was when she left after her wedding. It was not that she worried about Tamar taking over. Nili was desperately in need of loyal, fearless members willing to ignore the threat of death if caught by the Turks. Tamar would be invaluable. She was certainly not worried about how David would react to Tamar. She was secure in her relationship with her husband and whatever feelings he had for Tamar, Deborah knew she could trust him.

Her distress somehow involved Michael. Much as she loved David, her attraction to Michael unsettled her. She was sure that what she felt for Michael was not love. But she was drawn to him. He exuded a physical power that fascinated her and embarrassed her. Her attraction to him was so great that he even succeeded in replacing David in her erotic dreams. She could not understand it. He seemed oblivious to the effect he had on her. He certainly did nothing to encourage her infatuation. He was, as always, friendly and helpful, and treated her with deference. She was grateful for that. So she sought him out, talked to him, asked for his advice and listened to him with growing awe at her own reactions. Above all, he had become her friend and she felt possessive about that friendship.

When Michael came back from his first visit to Turkey and told them about

Tamar's unhappy life with Fredrick, Deborah was shocked to realize she was jealous of Tamar because of Michael's concern about her. He respected Tamar, admired her. She was jealous when Michael risked his life and returned to Turkey to accompany Tamar home. Somehow, Deborah could accept David's love of Tamar years earlier. She was not willing now to share her friendship with Michael. Tamar, she felt, would interfere with that friendship.

Deborah looked at her watch. It was seven o'clock in the morning. Tamar and Raphael had probably arrived at the house and Tamar would be wondering where she was. Reluctantly she got into the mule-drawn cart and drove up to the house.

Walking into the living room, Deborah saw Tamar pacing nervously around, smoking a cigarette. Raphael was staring out the window and the atmosphere was strained.

Tamar, hearing Deborah walk in, turned and started toward her, then stopped when she realized that Deborah was making no gesture toward her.

"What is going on here?" Tamar exploded.

Raphael turned to look at her.

"Since I got off that train in Haifa, Raphael has been treating me like some unwanted relative who has come to visit." She turned to Deborah. "You weren't even here when I came home and now you're looking at me as though I'm an intruder."

"I had work to do at the lab," Deborah started lamely.

"Now? We haven't seen each other in years!"

Deborah walked over and put her arms around Tamar. "You're imagining things. You're tired, that's all." She sounded strained.

Tamar pushed her away. "There," she said accusingly. "That tone. That's exactly how Raphael sounded from the minute we met. You're both treating me as though I were a stranger." She caught her breath briefly before continuing. "If I didn't know better, I'd say the whole village turned its back on us as we drove through." She turned to Raphael. "Some of the people we saw on that street actually seemed to be afraid of us." She stopped again and walked over to her brother. "You hardly spoke to me on the way home."

"I would not have gone all the way to Haifa to meet a stranger," Raphael tried to smile. "I thought you were tired after your long journey and needed the rest before arriving home."

"Rafi." She felt close to tears. "I have been on a train alone for nearly a week. I was terrified most of the time. I did not dare close my eyes, frightened that some filthy soldier would creep into my car and rob me, or worse. The only thing that kept me going was knowing that you were all here waiting for me. And what do I find? Deborah wasn't here. David isn't here and you're behaving so strangely." She looked around. "I know Mama is dead but that is no reason to neglect our home . . ." her voice trailed off in despair. "Look at the curtains. The rugs are worn and dirty. Everything is dusty. Where are Mama's lovely flowers? What happened to our beautiful garden? The trees look untended."

"You were never alone on that train," Raphael said quietly. "Prince Assad's men were all over that Konya station. Obviously they were there for the Englishman's sake, not yours, but they kept an eye on you as well. Some were actually on the train until you arrived at the last bridge crossing before entering Damascus."

"What happened at the crossing?" she asked, recalling the train coming to a sudden halt just before they crossed the bridge.

"Assad had his men remove the Englishman from the train at that point and they rode off with him." Tamar lowered her eyes, fearful of showing her relief and disappointment. "But I know that two or three Arabs stayed on until you got to Damascus. I believe they would have come all the way to Haifa with you if it had been necessary."

Tamar barely heard him. Now she knew why she had not seen Thomas at the Damascus train station. Before their arrival in Damascus, she dared not leave her compartment. She expected him to come looking for her. Thomas was not on the platform and was nowhere to be found. She was deeply concerned for his welfare but was convinced that once back home, he would contact her. Or she would enlist Raphael's help in finding out what happened to him.

"Are you angry with me, Raphael?" she asked, her anger spent.

"Why would I be angry with you?"

"I don't know. Because I left Fredrick?"

"Hardly. I would have killed him for hitting you," he said simply and she knew he meant it.

"Is it because I got Michael involved in helping Thomas escape?" She searched his face anxiously.

"As a humanitarian act, I believe you did the right thing."

"You did know who he was?" she asked haltingly. "You did remember our meeting him, didn't you?"

"Of course," Raphael's voice hardened. "Although, I must confess, I did not remember his name. You, I understand, did."

She felt herself blush.

Deborah was watching Tamar closely and her heart went out to her older sister. She looked so worn out, so needy. Deborah reached over and put her arms around her.

Tamar reacted to the gesture and threw her arms gratefully around Deborah's shoulders. Deborah was skeletal.

"Let me look at you," Tamar pushed her gently away, hiding her concern and confusion. "You're so thin," she said, then regretted saying it.

In truth, Deborah was more beautiful than she remembered, but she looked ill. Her eyes were ringed with dark circles, the velvety olive tone of her skin did not cover the ashen pallor and, with her dark hair pulled tightly back, her high cheekbones emphasized her sunken cheeks. But in spite of it all, she was an extraordinarily beautiful woman. Woman! The word struck and she remembered Michael's adamance about Deborah's not being a child anymore.

"Well, you're not a picture of health yourself," Deborah tried to smile. "We must fatten her up, Raphael," she continued, not taking her eyes off Tamar. "You'll take Mama's room and stay there for a few days of rest. Sleep, read and sleep again. I'll have Fatmi prepare your meals and bring them to you, just as we did for Mama." Her face grew serious. "It's good to have you home," she concluded. The phrase sounded forced.

"I may be thin," Tamar said slowly. "But I'm not sick. You, my darling, look as though you could use some rest more than I could. Now that I'm home I intend to act as though I've never been away." She looked over at Raphael. "I think you've been mistreating Deborah, working her too hard, and I won't permit it." She said it as pleasantly as she could, trying desperately to hide the hurt.

"Well, the wandering Jewess is home." Avi walked in at that moment and rushed over and kissed Tamar on the cheek. "But you do look awfully pale."

Raphael began to laugh. "You all sound ridiculous, trying to be worldly and sophisticated, when you're simply delighted to have Tamar home and are afraid to show it."

They all looked over at him.

"Well, you're all talking nonsense. Tamar's been traveling for weeks, she's tired, she's lived through hell and she should rest up." He looked over at Deborah. "And now that you've said it, Tamar, I think you're right. Deborah has been working too hard. But work has never killed anyone." He smiled at his younger sister.

There was a conspiratorial attitude between them which did not escape Tamar.

"Now, take your sister up to Mama's room, if that's the room you think she should have." Raphael was still speaking to Deborah and Tamar was conscious that Deborah had become the mistress of the house.

"You go on up," Deborah said quickly. "I just want to talk to Raphael for a minute."

As Tamar was walking out, she heard Deborah whisper something to Raphael, but could not make out what she was saying.

Tamar sensed something was going on, but she was too tired to pursue it. She closed the door gently behind her and threw herself onto the bed, feeling unwanted, miserable and confused. This was not the way she had visualized her homecoming. Rolling over on her back, she stared at the beamed ceiling. It was possible that she was imagining things. She closed her eyes and saw Deborah's haggard face. In an instant she was back in Turkey, watching the lines of women marching to their death on that far away road. They all looked like Deborah.

Tamar sat up, shaking with terror. If only Thomas were with her, she thought, she would feel better. Where was he? How would she find him? From the way Raphael had spoken of him, it hardly seemed likely that she could ask him to help her.

The light tap on the door interrupted her thoughts.

"Are you all right?" Raphael asked coming into the room. His gentle manner was reassuring. "I just thought I'd check on you and see that everything is in order," he said and started to back away. "Try to get some sleep. And when you wake up, you'll feel better."

"Raphael," she said too forcefully, making him stop and turn around. "Are you aware of what's going on in Turkey?"

"Yes."

"I don't mean the war. I meant the Armenian situation."

"Yes."

She leaned back on her pillow and stared at him. "I don't believe you can know the horror. Unless you've seen it, you cannot begin to imagine what is being done to those people."

"They are being systematically wiped out," Raphael said coldly. "The Turks have decided to eliminate them from the face of the earth. It is called genocide." He sounded like a schoolteacher.

"And no one is going to stop them?"

"What do you suggest?"

She was speechless. Her brother, whom she had always considered a humanitarian, someone who cared for his fellow man, sounded almost indifferent.

"You have influence. You know Jamal Pasha. You have friends in the German high command. I know you travel to Germany often, have the run of the countryside, all over. Here, in Syria and in Lebanon." She stopped as a new thought struck her. "Why did you *never* come to visit me in Turkey?" she asked. "You promised me you would and yet you never came."

"Enver Pasha runs that show and I don't know him." Raphael started pacing. "Jamal Pasha is very busy trying to rout the British forces in the desert. As for the Germans," he stopped pacing, "they don't give a damn." The words were spoken with unusual vehemence. Then, regaining his composure, he continued. "As for my not coming to visit you. I wanted to, but . . ." He did not finish the sentence.

"But what?"

"I've been very busy. I've taken on quite a few new workers, both Jewish and Arab. Then the locusts invaded the country. Jamal Pasha has asked me to be in charge of wiping them out and I've had my hands full."

"I don't believe those are your reasons," she said angrily. "There is something else going on which you're not telling me."

"Tamar, you're tired and imagining things." He walked toward the door. "Try to get some sleep and we'll have a long talk later."

"Raphael. The Turks are not going to stop with the Armenians," she said evenly.

"What do you mean?" He had his back to her.

"The Turks are doing what they're doing to the Armenians because they are Christians, and as Moslems they feel threatened by anyone who does not believe in Allah." She got off her bed and walked over to Raphael and forced him to look at her. "We don't believe in Allah," she said. "And there are fewer of us than of the Armenians. We will never be able to stand up to the Turks, if and when they decide to eliminate us, and you know it."

Tamar could see Raphael's eyes flash with anger. Worse, for the first time in her life, she saw hate in her brother's eyes.

"Let me give it some thought," he said and, pushing her aside almost roughly, he stalked out of the room.

Tamar got back into bed and, although deeply disturbed, she was too tired to stay awake. Her last thought before falling into a deep sleep was that David had not been there.

Tamar was awakened by the sound of voices. For a minute she did not know where she was. Within seconds, she was relieved to discover she was in her own room in Bet Enav.

Getting out of bed, she walked over to the door and opened it quietly and listened.

"I've raised most of the money, but we'll need a medical certificate," Michael was saying.

"Medical certificate?" Deborah asked and she sounded desperate.

"We're claiming David had a nervous breakdown in his youth and that he's having a relapse."

"But that's not true," Deborah protested.

"Who cares," Michael snapped. "We've got someone who is willing to ride to Haifa and get Sonya Neeman to sign the certificate." He stopped briefly. "Raphael, she will sign it, won't she?"

"Of course she will," Raphael answered quickly. "And what happens then?"

"I'll get to Beersheba and attend to the rest," Michael answered.

"Is there no other way of doing it?" Deborah pleaded.

"It's that or they'll hang him," Avi said.

Tamar was shocked. David had obviously been captured by the Turks and his life was in danger. She held back. Her family and friends were involved in something which they were keeping from her and she felt shamed by their distrust.

"Get on with it," Raphael said and Tamar heard footsteps in the hall below. The front door opened and shut.

Tamar started out of her room but stopped when she heard Michael speak again.

"How is she doing?" he asked.

"She's fast asleep," Deborah said, and a deep sigh escaped her. "But we won't be able to keep all this from her for very long."

"You can't rush it," Michael answered. "We have to give her a few days."

"You don't know my sister," Raphael spoke up and Tamar detected a note of amusement in his voice.

"I think we should wait and see if the Turks come around and make inquiries. Her husband isn't going to forgive her desertion. She has caused him great shame in the way she left him," Michael said.

"Well, we don't have to worry about Fredrick. He's been arrested and charged with supplying arms to the Jews in Palestine." Raphael chuckled bitterly. "I don't know where they got that bit of information, but he's going to spend a long time in jail if they don't hang him."

Tamar gulped. Malikian must have done it, she thought, but she had little time to delve further into that possibility. Raphael continued.

"As for the Turks, I don't care if they come. What we're doing is above board. Fredrick may have sold them arms but we help feed their army. Not to mention the work we're doing with the locusts. I have all the credentials for my men to travel around the country, signed by Jamal Pasha personally."

"David's arrest is not exactly helpful at this moment," Michael interjected.

"David should not have ventured into the desert alone. He was careless and irresponsible," Raphael answered coldly.

"Raphael, we've been working in a vacuum and that's why he did it," Deborah said angrily.

"It's water under the bridge," Raphael concluded. "Let's get David out and start all over again. As for Tamar, I think she should be told. She's got a head on her shoulders and can be of great help to us."

"We were managing quite well, I thought," Deborah said resentfully.

"Of course we were," Raphael answered quickly. "But we can use all the loyal help we can get. You know that. Someone like Tamar is a godsend."

"I think we should wait," Michael insisted. "Aside from the Turks, let's not forget the friendship between her and that Englishman. Before you know it, we'll have the Bedouins as helpmates and frankly, I could do without them."

"I wish we could get the Bedouins on our side," Raphael snapped.

"Heaven help us," Michael sneered. "With friends like that we really don't need enemies. And God knows, we've got enough of those."

"Let's not get into the Jewish-Arab conflict again." Raphael sounded tired.

"So what's the verdict?" Deborah asked.

Silence greeted her question.

Tamar, shaking with anger, slammed her bedroom door and ran down the stairs. Entering the living room, she looked from one to the other. "The verdict is that you're going to tell me exactly what's going on and include me in whatever it is you're doing."

No one spoke and the silence in the room grew heavy.

"I don't normally eavesdrop," Tamar continued through clenched teeth. "I certainly never thought I'd have to do it in my own home. But since coming into this house, the many undercurrents have reduced me to listening at keyholes." She could not contain her anger and her words poured forth with greater force. "I suppose Michael Ben Hod can be excused for his distrust. But you two?" She turned to Raphael and Deborah. "How could you think of excluding me from what is happening here?"

Still no one spoke and Tamar's anger mounted. "Why has David been arrested?"

"He's suspected of spying for the British," Michael answered.

"David spying?" Tamar almost burst out laughing. "Next you'll tell me he was doing it for money."

"No, he was doing it for Nili." Raphael spoke for the first time since she entered the room.

She knew the biblical acronym. *"Netzach Israel Lo Ishaker."*

"The eternity of Israel shall not lie," Raphael translated her Hebrew. "And that's what we've named our group. Nili."

"And what does Nili do?"

"We are spies," Raphael said simply. "Not for money but with the hope that if the Allies win the war and if we have a hand in helping achieve that victory, they will in appreciation help us redeem this land as a homeland for the Jews."

"And David got caught?" she asked.

"We've had a breakdown in communication with our British contact," Raphael said and explained their arrangement with the British ship. "However the Turks are more vigilant now and it's far more dangerous for an enemy ship to steam by. We've had these breakdowns before but this one has gone on for quite a while."

"So what happened?" Tamar asked impatiently.

"David decided to try to get to the British lines through the desert."

"Did he have any incriminating documents on him?" Tamar asked quickly.

"No, but he was close to the British lines when he was caught, and that made the Turks suspicious."

"How much money do we have to raise to get him out?" She had already assumed a role in the group.

"Five hundred gold coins."

"That's a great deal of money. Why do we have to claim he was crazy, as well?"

"The Germans are not as gullible as the Turks," Raphael answered.

"How many recruits do we have?" she asked.

"Eighteen in all."

"Who are they? I mean, other than you two, David, Avi, and Michael?" She paused over the last name, suppressing the impulse to say something derogatory.

As Tamar listened to the names of the participants, she realized she knew most of them. They were all sons and daughters of farmers like themselves, from various villages around the country and were all related to each other.

"It sounds like a family affair," she concluded. "Why haven't we got people from other walks of life working with us? How about some of the older people? Why isn't the mayor of Bet Enav involved? Are David and Avi's parents involved? How about Dr. Rosen? The rabbi? It seems to me that this is very important work and everyone should want to help."

"Forget it," Raphael said.

"What do you mean, forget it? Don't the Jews understand that the Turks must be defeated? Don't they see that this is, in its own way, the beginning of our liberation, our step toward achieving a homeland?"

"Personal courage is something you can't implant into people," Raphael said more forcefully. "What we're doing is extremely dangerous. The Turks would view our actions as treason and the penalty for treason is death by hanging. This is not a game. The stakes are very high. Empires are fighting to survive. The fate of the four-hundred-year-old Ottoman Empire is on the line and they've never been a benevolent people. Surely you must understand that they'd squash us out of existence if they thought we were trying to hurt them. The Jews of Bet Enav are frightened. By simple association, they can be accused of committing treason." His voice rose in frustration. "They are, at this point, more dangerous to us than the Turks and the Arabs. The mayor suspects something, even though he's not sure of what we're doing. But he did tell me in no uncertain terms that if we get involved in anything that might jeopardize the community, he'll turn on us. Dr. Rosen is aware, but he's keeping his distance. The rabbi? I think if I ventured into the synagogue these days, I'd be lynched." He stopped and thought for a moment. "Sonya and Misha help when we're in trouble. Obviously David's parents know, but we've purposely kept our distance from them." He paused. "The fact is that we are endangering every Jew in the country. If we're caught they would be held responsible. But I believe in what we're doing and everyone who's joined us believes as we do. We do have support from various people in different parts of the country and the numbers are growing."

"Stop pretending," Michael exploded. "The truth is that most of the communities don't want to know us. I guarantee you that they would turn us in if they felt threatened."

"My God," Tamar exclaimed. "I saw this fear in the rabbi in Turkey and I figured he was insecure because he was living outside Palestine. Now you tell me that even the Jews here are scared." She looked at Raphael. "Will it ever change? Will we ever become a people who can stand up for what we believe in without looking over our shoulder, wondering if *they* approve of us?"

"Only when we finally have a Jewish state. A homeland, in which *we* make the rules and implement them," Raphael answered.

"I think we should have some supper," Deborah interrupted. "And then I have to get down to the shore. Maybe the ship will come tonight."

"What time is it?" Tamar asked.

"Seven o'clock," Deborah answered and started toward the kitchen.

"You mean I've slept all day?"

"You were exhausted," Raphael said.

"And what have you done all day, Deborah?" Tamar asked.

"We do have a great deal of legitimate work at the laboratory, other than spying," Deborah turned back to her and tried to smile. "The lab gives us the luxury to be spies."

"After working all day at the lab, you're going to sit on the shore all night?" Tamar was incredulous.

"We have people sitting up at the station looking out to see if the ship is anywhere in sight. When and if it does come, someone must be down by the shore with the pouch."

"Suppose I go down and sit there and you get a good night's sleep," Tamar suggested.

"Tamar, you're patronizing me again," Deborah said quietly.

"I'm starved," Raphael broke in, trying to smooth over the conflict. "And after supper, I shall go down to the shore and relieve the men. Michael, you stay here and wait for Sonya's note. As for you, my lovely sisters, you will do women's work for a change. After dinner, you can start planning on how we can get some life back into this house. And see to it that you get to bed, both of you, at a decent hour."

"Let me start by helping with dinner," Tamar walked toward Deborah.

"That would be nice," Deborah said and smiled.

Just before leaving the room, Tamar turned to Raphael. "What's going to happen to Fredrick?"

Raphael shrugged.

"Mean as it sounds, I can't say that I'm sorry," she said and followed Deborah into the kichen hoping that now that they had confided in her, all would fall into place. She longed for Deborah's warmth, love and friendship.

# CHAPTER SIXTEEN

EBORAH watched Fatmi sweep up the glass from the shattered window-pane, while Mahmud boarded up the gaping hole to stop the February cold from entering the room. Stones thrown at the Danziger home had become a common occurrence, especially since David's arrest and release. His encounter with the Turks seemed to focus the townspeople's suspicions on the Danzigers. Raphael suspected the stone throwers were village children, but he could hardly accuse them, much less blame them.

Deborah looked over at the stairway leading up to the bedrooms, wondering if the noise of the shattering glass had awakened Tamar. She had been ill for several days and was forced to stay in bed. Hearing nothing, Deborah was relieved. Tamar needed the rest.

"She's had a bad night," Fatmi said, aware of Deborah's concern. "Maybe she should have stayed in Turkey with her husband. For a pregnant woman to be in the middle of so much violence is not good."

"I'm glad she's home," Deborah said in a strained voice. "We need her here and we can take care of her."

Fatmi shrugged and walked out, leaving Deborah alone with her unhappy thoughts.

The situation in Palestine had grown intolerable, especially for the Jews. Fear dominated every minute of their lives. It was now winter of 1917 and the Turks, who had expected, along with the German allies, a decisive victory within a short time after the war started, were growing both impatient and nervous. Added to their concerns, there were rumors that the Americans would join the Allies before the year's end. The Turkish rulers, always volatile, were being thrown into a panic. Their fear of being stabbed in the back reached new heights and the Jews, always considered untrustworthy foreigners, were subjected to unusual cruelties. Taxes were raised and since few had money to pay up, their livestock and meager crops were taken from them. Their groves were chopped down and used for firewood; arrests without reason, followed by days of torture and imprisonment, grew common. The sight of crippled young men returning from the front brought home the horrors the Jews were subjected to. In their state of disarray, the Turks forgot their benevolence toward the Jews of Bet Enav and the sudden change in treatment confused and frightened them. In frustration, the villagers turned their rage on the Danzigers. Raphael, who had been their savior when the war first started, was now their enemy. They were convinced that he was responsible for what was happening to them. Rumors about the Danzigers' activities ranged from the smuggling of arms or money to wild late-night parties on the beach and even witchcraft.

"Is Raphael Danziger in?" Deborah heard Rabbi Landau inquire and she rushed to the front hall. She had been so preoccupied with her thoughts that she had not heard him come in.

"I should like to speak to Raphael," he announced on seeing Deborah.

"I'm afraid he's out of the country," Deborah answered.

"Where is he?"

"I believe he's meeting with some people in Berlin," she said.

"When will he be back?"

Deborah shook her head.

He looked directly at her and she grew flustered. Rabbi Landau never looked directly at any woman.

"David, then. Is he around?" he asked.

"He's not home at the moment but I'll tell him you're looking for him." She paused. "Is there anything I can do for you?"

"It offends me to have to deliver this message to a woman, but under the circumstances . . ." He took a deep breath. "I do not know what your family is involved in. From what I hear—and I am fully aware that I have no proof—your activities might endanger all the Jews in Palestine and especially the Jews of Bet Enav. So I must warn you that if you persist in whatever it is you're doing, I shall personally see to it that you and your whole family will suffer gravely, if any harm comes to us because of you." His voice was still quiet but the threat was there and she knew he meant it.

Deborah felt a chill go through her. Being threatened by the chief rabbi of Bet Enav was serious. He was the leader of the Jewish community in the village and surrounding area, and a highly regarded, influential man.

"Are you threatening to banish us?" Tamar's voice was mocking as she walked slowly down the stairs. She was heavy with child and moved in a cumbersome manner. Her disrespect and defiance alarmed Deborah.

"I shall leave you now," Rabbi Landau addressed Deborah. "And I suggest you take my warning seriously. I do not make idle threats. As God is my witness, if driven to defend my people, I shall stop at nothing."

He hurried out without looking at Tamar.

"You could have been more pleasant," Deborah said angrily. "He is, after all, the rabbi of this community and he could hurt us badly."

"When you think that Michael and I risked our lives to save his son," she sneered. "Michael more than I, but still, the boy is alive because of us."

Deborah lowered her eyes. She did not know what Tamar was talking about, except that it was the first time that Tamar had mentioned any involvement with Michael other than his help in getting her and the Englishman out of Turkey. A shocking thought flashed through her mind. Was it possible that Tamar was carrying Michael's child? For some reason she was suddenly sure that Fredrick was not the father of Tamar's unborn child. In a way it would explain why Michael had suddenly distanced himself from the Danziger household. He had never been accepted by David or Raphael, but occasionally he would join them for a meal or stop by for a chat. Sometimes he would pick Deborah up and drive her down to the lab. She missed those trips. She missed his friendship. Now, she wondered if Tamar's pregnancy was the cause. It was a shocking idea, but Deborah knew that it was not the moral issue that was causing her shock. She felt betrayed.

"Any news?" Tamar asked.

"Raphael has been captured on the Swedish border and was turned over to the Allies," Deborah answered, barely able to look at her sister.

"How do you know?"

"David came up after his watch on the shore and told me."

"Did a ship come by?"

"No. Michael told him."

"But that's wonderful news," Tamar tried to simulate excitement. "God, Raphael is brilliant. That's exactly how he hoped it would happen. Now he won't be accused of betraying the Turks and once he gets to Alexandria, he'll see to it that our information gets transmitted with greater efficiency."

"Maybe," Deborah said dully. "But it will all take time. It's true he was caught by the Swedes, but now he has to get to Alexandria. And who knows what kind of reception he'll get there? Then he'll have to convince the British that he is not spying for the Turks, and on and on. It doesn't work as simply as you think."

"I have faith in Raphael. You wait and see, it will all work out," Tamar said with exaggerated assurance. The news was important to Nili. It was also important to her. She had given Raphael a letter for Thomas. Somehow she had to let Thomas know she was pregnant. She was fully aware that everyone thought the baby was Fredrick's and she did nothing to dispel that notion. She was thrilled with the idea of carrying Thomas's child and she knew he would be, too. Since returning home, she had gotten notes from him, delivered by Mahmud. Bedouins passing through their area would give them to Mahmud and he would bring them to her. The notes were filled with love, plans for their future and a plea that she start divorce proceedings as soon as possible so they could marry when the war was over. But there was never any return address and she had no way of contacting him.

"You'd better go have some breakfast and then we've got to get to the lab," Deborah said and ran from the room.

Tamar watched her leave. In the six months since her return, Tamar was aware that Deborah's disapproval of her never changed. At first she thought Deborah resented being replaced as the driving force behind the laboratory and Nili. But Deborah seemed happy to move into the background and take charge of their home. As days turned to weeks and months, with no change in Deborah's attitude, Tamar concluded that she was worried about David, concerned that he would again turn to Tamar as he had done in the days before she married Fredrick. It was completely unfounded. David, as always, was warm and friendly toward Tamar, and completely devoted to Deborah.

The pregnancy broke through some of her sister's coldness. When she realized Tamar was pregnant, Deborah did begin to dote on her, but it turned out to be just that—a sister doing her duty. It pained her. She missed the love, the warmth, the intimacy they had shared when they were young.

Walking over to the window, she leaned her head against one of the unbroken panes of glass. She missed Thomas. Busy as she was, he was on her mind constantly and she wished he were by her side. Missing him as she did, working endless hours for Nili and being pregnant made her nervous and short-tempered. Having him close, knowing he was safe, feeling his love would have made it all easier. Deborah was right. She should have been more tactful with the rabbi, but she had little patience for the fearful attitude of the Jews.

"There will be three more for dinner tonight." Deborah was talking to Fatmi, when Tamar entered the kitchen.

"Potato soup and bread is all we have to offer," Fatmi said. "I don't think we have enough as is."

"It'll be enough. It's food and it's hot." Deborah knew Fatmi was embarrassed by the meager table they were reduced to.

"With three more for dinner, that will make thirteen and that's bad luck." The woman tried again.

"For Jews thirteen is good luck," Deborah answered absently and looked around when she heard Tamar come in. "It's late and I think we should get started," she said, pulling on her coat.

"Of course, if we could roast the pigeons," Fatmi said, looking over at Deborah.

"Fatmi, don't even think of it," Tamar interjected sharply.

"What makes them so important? Pigeons are pigeons and they're very tasty," Fatmi said vehemently.

"You know that since Fakhri Pasha has been put in charge of this region, we're forbidden to shoot them," Tamar said quickly.

"He's crazy." Fatmi shook her head disapprovingly. "With such a shortage of food, it would be the most natural thing to let the people eat pigeons."

"Forget it," Tamar said angrily. She started to struggle into one of Raphael's old rain jackets.

"You're not dressed warmly enough for this weather," Deborah said, eying her briefly.

"I'll be fine," she answered and walked over to Fatmi, who reached under her black robe and handed Tamar the ivory-handled pistol.

"Must you?" Deborah asked, watching Tamar tuck the gun into her woolen stocking.

"Yes, I must," Tamar said, storming out.

"But why?" Deborah rushed out after her.

"Abed is out of jail and I hear he's on a mad rampage," Tamar said and climbed into the driver's seat of the mule-drawn cart.

"Good God, I thought he was in prison for life after the last murder he committed." Deborah, in great agitation, moved beside her.

"Well, Fakhri Pasha believes that having hardened criminals running around will keep us Jews on our toes," she answered bitterly.

"Who told you?" Deborah asked.

"Fatmi."

"And where is he?"

"He must be in their village. As you may have noticed, Rafa hasn't been around lately. You know how Abed feels about Rafa being around us."

"You're not going to tell me Fatmi keeps the gun so she can shoot her own son if he comes around," Deborah said derisively.

"Of course not. She keeps it for me, since she's an Arab and the Turks allow Arabs to carry arms and we're forbidden to. So if they search the house, she'll say it's hers. And when I'm out, I figure no Turk would dare search a pregnant woman."

Riding slowly through the main street of Bet Enav, they had a hard time avoiding the muddy puddles and the wooden planks that had been strewn around to help pedestrians get through. The houses looked more dilapidated than ever. Most had their shutters closed and some had their windows boarded up. The latter were the houses that had been deserted by people fearful of staying in Palestine and had gone back to their country of origin.

"Like rats leaving a sinking ship," Tamar quipped.

"Don't be unkind," Deborah said, knowing full well what Tamar was talking about. "People are scared and you've got to understand that."

They drove on in silence.

"I think we made a mistake. We should have kept the pigeons in the lab," Deborah said, suddenly.

"Raphael felt it might raise the suspicions of the Arab workers there," Tamar answered. "Those pigeons might be our last resort in getting our information to the British."

"Well, the idea of having to depend on birds is rather pathetic."

"It might all change now that Raphael is in the hands of the Allies," Tamar said.

"Oh Tamar, stop it," Deborah replied.

"Well, there is nothing else we can do. We've got information that could shorten this war, certainly in this part of the world, and it's just rotting away."

"David thinks there is something we can do," Deborah said, not looking at Tamar. "He's talking about making another trip through the desert."

"You must be joking. After all the trouble we had getting him out the last time? If he's caught again it could be fatal, both to him and to Nili."

"It's either that or the pigeons." Deborah's voice was strained.

"I'll talk to him. Is he at the lab?"

"Yes."

"What's been happening down there since I've been ill?" Tamar asked.

"We're running short of volunteers. Rabbi Landau, whether you want to admit it or not, does have power."

"Who's covering the southern part of the country? I think that's important. Fakhri Pasha is keeping a large contingency of men around here, still worrying that the British will attack from the sea, but there are generals in Turkey who are beginning to get the idea that the British will attack them from the desert. So it's important we monitor that area and see how they're doing there."

"Yossi is down there."

"That's a mistake," Tamar said impatiently. "He's too young and too inexperienced. If he gets caught, we'll all be in trouble."

"He's grown up in that part of the country, knows it well and he's a good boy," Deborah answered. "He's young, but he's trustworthy. If he gets caught, Michael will get him out. The Turks trust Michael and he has the money to bribe them."

"The Turks may trust him. I don't."

"What do you mean, you don't trust him?" Deborah said angrily.

"Oh, I trust him as a Jew. I believe he's fighting to get rid of the Turks as seriously and genuinely as we are. What I don't trust are his motives."

"Motives? Need there be any other than defeating the Turks?"

"I think he's got political aspirations," Tamar spoke slowly. "He has a concept of how to shape our homeland which is different from ours."

Deborah looked over at Tamar. "Political motives?" she asked. "I never once thought of what we're doing in political terms."

"Of course you didn't. Neither did I and I doubt that David or Avi have, or any of the people working with us." She thought for a minute. "And although I believe Raphael does think of our political future, I assure you, it's not on the same level as Michael's thinking."

"Tamar, I don't quite follow what you're saying." Deborah was genuinely bewildered.

"Well, let's just start with the way he feels about the Arabs. He'd kill everyone of them if he could. He's a man without compassion. He doesn't know what the word compromise means."

"Do you?" Deborah shot back.

Tamar was taken aback by the sharp retort, but decided to ignore it. "Why did he join Nili?" she asked and without waiting for an answer, she continued. "I know, to fight the Turks. But Reb and his friends feel about the Turks as we do. Yet he left them and came over to work with us. Why?"

Deborah did not answer.

"I'll tell you why. We in Nili have put ourselves on the line. Reb and his group are still deliberating. They'll wait and see which side wins before they actually take a stand. But when this fight is over and we win, where will Michael be?" She threw a meaningful look at Deborah. "On the side of whoever is on top. And although we may well win the battle, it will be Reb and his men who are likely to win the war. We're a minority. They look on us as bourgeois, out to exploit the workers."

"I don't care," Deborah said stubbornly. "I know you don't like Michael. I know David doesn't. As a matter of fact there are times when I actually feel David hates him, but I do trust him as a Jew and that's all that matters. Besides, he's one of the best fighters we have."

Deborah's vehemence gave Tamar a moment's pause and she wondered if Michael had made any overtures toward Deborah. She suspected his feelings for Deborah when he first mentioned her name in Rabbi Maranis's house. Since returning to Palestine, her suspicions were strengthened. Often she would catch him looking at Deborah with great tenderness and, although Deborah seemed oblivious, his longing made Tamar uncomfortable.

"Incidentally," Tamar asked, deciding to change the subject, "how did Michael find out about Raphael being captured?"

"When he was up north he saw your friend Hardwick there. He's organized . . ."

Tamar caught her breath. "Thomas Hardwick is in the north of Palestine?"

"Somewhere around the Yarmuk River." Deborah noticed Tamar's agitation.

"Why didn't David go with him?" Tamar asked, struggling to control her feelings.

"Michael wanted him to, but David prefers not to spend too much time alone with him."

"I think I should have been told about it." Tamar bit her lip in frustration. "After all, I am in charge of our agents' activities. Michael, just by going off, is out of line." She was aware that she was overreacting but could not help herself. "And if David didn't want to go, I should have gone."

"You! In your condition?"

"Michael and Thomas Hardwick don't get along. And if you knew how

Thomas feels about his Arabs, in contrast to Michael, they could come to blows."

"Michael has put those feelings aside for the duration of the war." Deborah was now watching Tamar intently. "I grant you, he still doesn't trust them but he does admit that they are rather better at sneaking around than we are. As for Michael not getting on with Hardwick, at this point his motto is 'Your enemy is my enemy.' "

"And now he's back?" Tamar was barely listening to what Deborah was saying.

"I think he might be down at the lab," Deborah answered.

They had reached the crossroads leading toward the vineyard.

"I think we'll go through the vineyard," Tamar said. "In spite of Rabbi Landau's threats, I feel the people in the village at least know us and I doubt that they would hurt us. But all those strangers who have put up huts along the path leading down to the main road—I don't trust them."

"Isn't it sad that we should be afraid of our own people?" Deborah commented.

Turning the cart toward the vineyard, Tamar reached down and, taking the gun out of her stocking, placed it on her lap.

"That's in case Abed should decide to show up," she said and tried to smile.

A wintry sun had come out as Tamar and Deborah drove into the laboratory compound. Walking up to the study, Tamar was upset that she did not know Michael was going to see Thomas. She was also deeply distressed at the strain in her relationship with Deborah.

Entering the study, she saw Michael standing at the window with his back to the door. He turned when he heard her walk in, and their eyes met.

"You saw him," she said, searching his face.

He nodded.

"How is he?"

"As always—arrogant, bossy, trying to turn his Arabs into a disciplined fighting force."

"Did he ask about me?"

"You are all he talked about."

"Did you tell him about my being pregnant?"

"Of course not. He would have jumped on that camel of his and raced down here, putting all of us in danger. You know that."

"Don't make fun of him," she said angrily.

"I'm not. As a matter of fact, I've grown to respect him."

"He does care about me, doesn't he?" she hated herself for asking, but she was lonely and needy and Michael was the only person she could mention Thomas to.

"Very much," Michael answered soberly.

"There's a ship on the horizon." David rushed into the room, followed by Deborah. He ran toward the window and put the binoculars to his eyes.

"Back at midnight, tonight," David spoke the message being transmitted. He looked around happily. "All that information finally getting into the proper hands." Then throwing himself on a small sofa, he smiled at Deborah, Tamar and Michael. "Everything will work out, you wait and see."

Michael stared out to sea. "If the weather holds out." He sounded pessimistic.

"True," David concurred. "But ship or no ship, I'm glad the four of us are here. We have to talk. Now that Raphael has turned himself over to the Allies, we must reorganize our work and our duties."

"Reorganize?" Tamar asked looking at Michael. He was still dressed in his Turkish uniform and it made her uncomfortable.

David, seeing Tamar's look, coughed self-consciously. "Tamar, when Raphael left and we did not know exactly how things were going to turn out, he did say that you, Deborah and I were to take charge if he succeeded in crossing over to the Allies. He also said that he wanted Michael to be included in our decision-making."

"How do you get away with it, Michael?" Tamar ignored David's last remark and pointed to Michael's uniform.

"It's getting more difficult all the time. But as long as I'm in this uniform, I can act as liaison between us and the Turks. And as such, you'll just have to trust me."

"Meaning?"

"I do have a pretty good relationship with my commanding officers. I've been put in charge of the Arabs scheduling all trains running between the north and the south of Palestine, which helps us. But I repeat, you'll simply have to trust me." He turned around and walked out, obviously angry. David ran out after him.

"Why do you hate him so?" Deborah asked.

"I just don't feel comfortable with him," Tamar answered.

"That's not all that's bothering you," Deborah said.

"I'm upset about how things are going," she said. "And since you've brought up the subject, I'd like to know what's troubling you and why you're behaving so strangely toward me."

"I don't know what you're talking about."

"Of course you do."

"It's all in your mind."

"Is everything all right between you and David?" Tamar decided to bring the subject out in the open.

"Everything is fine," Deborah said defiantly.

"You've been married for over two years and you're still not pregnant. Why?"

"I don't think that's any of your business."

"Don't talk that way, Deborah, it doesn't suit you," Tamar reached out for Deborah's hand.

Deborah clasped her hands behind her back, rejecting the physical contact.

"Is it something I've done or said? Just tell me what it is. You can trust me." She looked anxiously at her sister.

Deborah lowered her eyes.

Tamar dared to leap into forbidden territory. "Do you think that David is still in love with me?"

Deborah looked away and Tamar concluded that she had been correct in her assumption. Deborah was clinging to her childish fantasy and allowing it to disrupt her happiness. She was letting her life slip by, unaware of how precious time was. Tamar still ached for the months and years missed with Thomas, which could never be recaptured. And if that was the case, Tamar felt it her duty to tell Deborah the truth about Thomas. "Deborah, I am about to tell you something you must never tell anyone for as long as I live," Tamar started slowly.

"That's a strange way to put it," Deborah said quietly. "The phrase is usually 'Don't tell a soul as long as *you* live.' "

"Didn't I say that?" She fell silent, wondering how to continue.

"The baby I'm carrying is not Fredrick's child." She blurted the words out. "It is Thomas Hardwick's child."

"Oh my God!" Deborah grew pale and looked away in confusion and embarrassment. She was also relieved and hated herself for the reaction.

"And I cannot tell you how happy I am that it is," Tamar continued. The intensity with which she spoke forced Deborah to look back at her.

"Really?" she whispered.

"I'd hardly make up that story," Tamar rushed on, flustered by Deborah's reaction. "It's too important. But the fact is that I am very much in love with Thomas Hardwick. I have been since that day we met him on the beach." She paused briefly, trying to think of something that would convince Deborah of her statement. "Deborah, do you remember our standing at the top of the hill, after we met him and I made a wish?"

Deborah nodded.

"I could not formulate the wish then. I could only wish and pray that I would see him again. But if I had been more experienced, I would have wished to have him make love to me. To be able to make love to him and to have that love produce a child." Her voice grew hoarse with emotion. "And my wish came true. We have made love and I shall now have his baby."

The room was very still after Tamar finished talking.

"You've been an unfaithful wife," Deborah said, unable to think of any other response.

"As far as I'm concerned, I was unfaithful to Thomas when I married Fredrick."

"What a strange thing to say," Deborah answered, never taking her eyes off Tamar. "Do you really believe that?"

Tamar nodded and looked directly at Deborah. The younger woman stared back at her. No words were exchanged, but Tamar could see Deborah relax and she breathed a sigh of relief.

"I'd better get to work," Deborah smiled briefly. "Thank you for confiding in me. Your secret will be safe with me." She nearly ran out of the room.

Left alone, Tamar picked up the binoculars and stared out to sea. The weather had turned bad. The waves were rising again and they looked angry. Her brief feeling of exuberance at having finally confided in Deborah disappeared quickly. No ship would venture into that sea and no responsible captain would order his men into those waters.

The day passed slowly. By evening the sea looked like a gushing volcano and all were aware that their hopes for the ship's arrival might have to be put aside. As night fell, the only sound in the room came from the ticking of the clock and it almost succeeded in drowning out the sound of thunder and the torrential rain pounding against the windows. The mood of despair grew.

Tamar and Deborah, curled up on a small sofa facing the sea, were huddled under thick blankets, staring out at the fog. David was out on the small catwalk terrace of the room, straining to see if the ship would appear on the horizon.

The door to the terrace was open and a cold wind swept through the room, but they did not close David out, wanting to be apprised of any possible sighting.

"They're obviously not coming back." David came in and shut the door behind him. "It's way past midnight and there's no sight of them."

"I think I'll go and relieve the boys at the shore." Avi stuck his head through the door.

"I'll go with you," David said. "And Deborah, I think it would be a good idea if you had some hot tea ready for them when they come up. They'll be frozen." Then throwing one last look at the window. "Damn them," he whispered before leaving.

Deborah did as she was asked and Tamar walked out to the terrace. Tears of frustration were brimming over, but she dared not cry, fearful that if the tears came, she could never stop the flow.

"Get back in here," Deborah shouted angrily. "You'll catch your death of cold out there."

Tamar came back into the room, leaving the door open.

Deborah started to close it but Tamar stopped her. "I feel ill and the fresh air, cold as it is, helps."

"Why do they do this to us?" Deborah leaned against the doorpost.

"I don't know," Tamar answered wearily. "But you can't blame them for the weather changes."

"But they sailed by this morning and told us they'd be back." "Maybe they did come by and we missed them."

"With David staring out that window since early evening and the boys at the shore all watching out for them?" Deborah sounded skeptical. "We couldn't have missed them."

"Well, they might still come." Tamar sank down on the sofa. Her back had begun to ache and she tried to hide her discomfort. "It's three o'clock in the morning. It won't get light for another couple of hours."

Deborah turned to look at Tamar and realized that she was having a hard time breathing. "You're in pain, aren't you?" Deborah said sympathetically.

"I can bear it."

"Shouldn't you see Sonya again?" Deborah asked.

"What for? I saw her a couple of months ago and she assured me everything was all right. Besides, the trip to Haifa is exhausting and takes an awfully long time. The baby is due in April and I'll see her then."

"You wouldn't try to talk to Dr. Rosen, would you? He brought all of us into the world. I'm sure he'd see you."

"That's a joke," Tamar snapped. "When he sees me on the street, he turns his back on me."

Deborah sighed helplessly. In the gray pre-dawn light, she could see Tamar's face contort in pain, as though stifling a cry.

"When do you think you'll see Thomas again?" Deborah asked, although uncomfortable about mentioning his name. She was deeply embarrassed by Tamar's affair and would have preferred not to refer to Thomas. Now she hoped that talking about him would help get Tamar's mind off her discomfort.

Tamar smiled, guessing Deborah's thoughts. "I don't know."

"Will he be as happy as you are about the baby?" Deborah asked.

"Oh yes." Tamar's voice grew stronger. "When you and David have a baby, you'll understand how much it means to a couple in love when the woman is carrying their child."

"What will you call it?"

"I don't know yet."

"How about Nili?"

Tamar mulled over the idea. "No, I don't think so. It's not a boy's name, anyway."

"But if it's a girl," Deborah persisted.

"I still don't think so. It should be a name that will mean something to Thomas as well." She frowned at her words. She could not understand why she had said them and she rushed on. "If it's a boy, I'll name him Gidon. That's the Hebrew pronunciation of Gideon, Thomas's middle name. And if it's a girl, I'll wait to hear what Thomas would like."

"You really believe you'll see him before the baby is born?"

Tamar did not answer and Deborah could see the look of doubt across her sister's face.

Tamar closed her eyes. She was completely exhausted and wished she could sleep, wished she could empty her mind of all thoughts. Vaguely she heard the clatter of dishes in the next room, the sound of the wind, the rumbling thunder, the foreboding foghorns and the ticking of the clock. The latter wiped out all other sounds. She was almost asleep when Blackie began to bark.

She sat up and Deborah, her face ashen with fear, ran into the room. The barking grew louder, verging on hysteria. Tamar reached for her gun and tiptoed toward the stairway. Deborah was close behind her.

"Blackie, get up here," Tamar whispered.

The dog started up the stairs, still barking and looking back as he ran, unable to decide if he wanted to obey his mistress.

The only light in the room below came from a small oil lamp, and Tamar could see nothing. A sudden gust of cold air swept through the house. Someone had come in.

With gun in hand, Tamar started down the stairs.

"Please don't go," Deborah pleaded. "Please, Tamar, don't go."

Tamar waved her into silence and continued cautiously down, when Blackie, who had nearly reached the top of the stair, stopped, turned around and rushed down, his tail wagging. Tamar dared not move. She could hear someone shuffling around in the darkened room below and it appeared to be someone Blackie knew.

"Who's there?" she whispered, releasing the gun's safety catch.

"Tamar?"

The timbre of the voice was familiar but she could not identify it.

"Rafa," Deborah cried out and, running past Tamar, she rushed down the stairs. By the time Tamar reached the lower landing, Deborah had Rafa in her arms, laughing and crying in relief.

"Let me look at you, Rafa." Deborah pulled the boy closer to the light.

Tamar edged over to where they were standing. Rafa had grown since she had seen him last and she was struck by his maturity, but the lines of his face were as soft as ever and the dark, unseeing eyes were still filled with innocent bewilderment.

"How did you get here?" Deborah stroked the boy's wet hair.

His face tensed with fear and he lowered his head.

"Did your father bring you?" Deborah asked gently. "Is he with you?"

He started to pull away, but stopped when the sound of running footsteps were heard.

"I've got him," they heard David shouting excitedly. "I've got him."

"Who is it?" Avi's called out.

"Stop it, you bastard," David commanded angrily and then the door flew open and David, Avi and two others walked in carrying a grimy-looking man dressed in Arab garb.

They placed him on the floor, face down, holding his hands firmly behind his back. He writhed briefly and then lay motionless.

David turned him over. He was a swarthy-looking man, with dark hair and olive skin. The deep cut on his forehead was oozing blood. He lay motionless.

"Is he dead?" Deborah whispered.

"He passed out," David said, feeling the man's pulse.

Tamar knelt down beside him. "You'd better get me the medical kit and try to find some brandy. That bruise looks like someone hit him pretty hard."

Deborah came back carrying a black bag and a bottle of brandy. Tamar lifted the man's head and put the brandy bottle to his lips. He started coughing and appeared to be reviving.

"He's losing an awful lot of blood," Tamar said, trying to stem the flow, which was running down his neck onto her skirt.

"I wonder who he is." Avi leaned over and started unbuttoning the man's jacket and exposing the middy shirt of an English sailor. "Good God, he's wearing a British sailor's uniform," he exclaimed. "Although he certainly doesn't look terribly British." He started going through the man's pockets. "He has no papers on him, so we'll have to wait until he regains consciousness to find out."

"If he regains consciousness," Tamar said, pressing a cloth to the wound. The man began to moan and tried to push her hand away. Although still in a state of shock, he was obviously in pain.

"I wonder how he got here," David said. "And I wonder who hit him?"

"My father hit him." Rafa spoke for the first time and David swung around, not having noticed the boy until that moment.

"Rafa?" David gasped. "Where did you come from?"

"My father brought me from Haifa. We were walking along the beach. He stopped and told me he saw this man crawling along the edge of the water. I heard them argue and then they got into a fight. My father must have knocked him out and then he ran away."

David knelt down beside the wounded man. "Who are you?" he asked in English.

The man reacted violently and tried to sit up but was too weak and fell back into Tamar's arms.

"Did you come on the ship?" David asked.

He nodded and tried to form a word. It was too garbled to make sense.

"Was it the ship that passed by here this morning?" David demanded.

He nodded again and continued to mumble unintelligibly.

"Did you have any papers for us?" David asked.

His head bobbed up and down.

"Abed obviously has those," Avi exploded.

"Pigeons," the man gasped. "Use pigeons." He could barely breathe and then his head fell back, his eyes flew open and rolled back into his head.

Tamar felt for his pulse. There was none. She pressed her ear to his chest.

"He's dead," she said dully, closing his eyes with her hand.

"That's great," Avi remarked. "A dead British sailor is all we need right now." Then, as a new thought struck him, he turned to Rafa. "Did you say you came from Haifa?" he asked sharply.

Rafa was too terrified to answer.

"Let me handle him," David said quietly and repeated Avi's question in a gentler tone.

Rafa turned toward David and nodded.

"Well, if the man is from the ship, he must have come ashore in a dinghy . . ." David stopped. "And we'd better find it before the Turks do and it had better be before sunup."

The words were barely out of his mouth when the boys ran toward the door.

"And just do away with it when you do," David called after them. Then he busied himself with wrapping the dead man's head with a cloth.

"I hated those pigeons from the minute they arrived," Tamar hissed.

"You're right. The truth is we're obviously not being treated seriously and I resent it," David picked up her anger.

"Well, if nothing else, there is one advantage to using them," Deborah said with a sigh. "They can't talk and tell anyone who they're working for."

In spite of herself Tamar smiled. "You can find good in any disaster and I do love you for that."

"Deborah, go upstairs and close that window. We certainly don't need any British ship on our necks tonight, and you, Avi, help me get this corpse out of here."

When Deborah was gone, David and Avi started dragging the man out the front door. A pool of blood was left where he'd been lying.

With the body safely outside, David turned to shut the door and his heart sank. Tamar was on her knees, scrubbing the blood off the floor. Her head was bowed and her shoulders were shaking. He stood very still, watching her. There was an air of total defeat about her. It both moved and frightened him. In all the years he'd known her, he had never seen her cry. What made it worse was that since her return, she had become an integral part of their group. With Raphael gone, she commanded them, gave them strength, purpose and hope. She was the symbol of all that was fine and pure in Nili. A dreadful sense of foreboding overtook him. He shut the door quietly behind him, not wanting her to know that he had witnessed her breakdown.

# CHAPTER
# SEVENTEEN

MICHAEL had been away from Bet Enav for three months, and during that time his world had fallen apart. He left Bet Enav after Tamar's son was born, arriving at his Turkish headquarters only to be told that he had been relieved of his duties. He was reassigned to a desk job on the southern front. He knew that it was just a matter of time before he'd be discharged, and soon he would not be able to move about in his Turkish uniform. His future as a spy for his people looked bleak.

It was just before Passover and he wanted to join Reb and his friends for the holiday, but they wouldn't have him back. They did not even ask him to their seder. Reb would not talk to him because he felt Michael had betrayed them by joining Nili and becoming so closely associated with the Danzigers.

Alone on that Passover eve, he again wondered if God's wrath at that little boy in Metula would ever end. Going back to Bet Enav was something he didn't want to do. He could not take the personal insults Tamar directed toward him. If anything, she was further proof that he would be punished for his sacrilegious act for the rest of his life.

Now he was back, mainly because of a meeting that he had with Thomas Hardwick. A Nili member covering the Sinai got word to Michael that Hardwick was anxious to see him.

It was a strange encounter.

"You must get a message to British Intelligence for me," Thomas said as soon as they met.

Michael stared at him in amazement. "If you can't do it, why assume that I can?"

"Nili can do it," Thomas said, and for the first time he focused on Michael. "Through the pigeons."

Michael was taken aback. He was aware that Thomas knew of the work Nili was doing, but he did not realize that Thomas was that intimately acquainted with its machinations.

"British Intelligence informed me of Raphael Danziger's work and although I missed him while he was in Alexandria, I was apprised of what is going on," Thomas said, sensing Michael's bewilderment.

"What's the message?"

"I'm about to embark on a massive offensive with my men." Thomas waved toward the circle of Arabs around him. "It could mean the breakthrough the British need to end this war. I am having great difficulty in informing my superiors of my forthcoming action."

"Your men?" Michael looked around, trying to contain his laughter. "These wild-eyed, crazed Bedouins?"

"Mr. Ben Hod, spare me your sentiments about the Arabs. We are fighting on the same side, for victory. Try to remember that." He leaned closer and quickly gave Michael the details of his plan. It was a long shot and they both knew it, but Michael had to admit that it was ingenious.

"I'll do my best," Michael said and started to get up when Thomas grabbed his arm.

"How is she?" Thomas asked.

Michael hesitated before answer. "She's given birth to a son whom she named Gidon," he said, watching Thomas closely.

"Oh, my God," Thomas cried out. "And I was not with her. I was not there to comfort her." He stopped and his eyes filled with tears. "Gideon, of course." He regained control of himself. "How thoughtful of her."

The Anglicized pronunciation of *Gidon* irritated Michael, but any doubts that he may have had about who had fathered Tamar's child were gone.

"Would you tell her how happy I am? How grateful I am? How proud I feel?" Thomas was oblivious to Michael's reaction. "And tell her I shall come to her as soon as this campaign is over. It will not be long. I will be there." Then looking directly at Michael, he said, "I love her very, very much and our son carries my name and my deepest love. I will do my best to make them both very happy."

That meeting had taken place one week ago and now Michael, mounted on his horse, was looking down at the valley below and he was glad he was back. It was early morning and already he could feel the hot June sun beating on his back. It would be another scorching day.

With the sun rising behind him, he strained to see the sights below. His throat tightened with frustration at what he saw. The green carpet of the fertile land, cultivated and nurtured by the Jewish farmers, was now nothing but decaying stalks of corn and rotting vines. The eucalyptus trees, planted to dry up the marshes and make them habitable, were mere ugly stumps. The land, as far as his eyes could see, looked deserted and smelled of neglect and defeat. It had withstood an unusually ferocious winter, had a brief respite of spring, and was enduring a dry summer sun which set the muddy earth into shapeless, gaping cracks.

The sight was not unique. He had traveled from Beersheba to the upper Galilee and everywhere he saw the same desolation. And the elements were not the only cause of the devastation. The Turks were doing their share to demolish everything the Jews had struggled to create. The line of demarcation between rich and poor had vanished completely. Everyone suffered.

He was still too far from Bet Enav to see it and he wondered how they fared. He was especially worried about the Danzigers and the laboratory. As long as the United States was neutral, the laboratory compound was safe. But the Americans had declared war on Germany and Turkey, and the decision was bound to affect Nili's operations. Nili's relationship with the authorities had started to erode before Raphael left. With Raphael gone, it grew worse. Michael prayed that they would be able to withstand the tide of hostility meted out by a retreating Turkish army.

The sun was now beating down on him and Michael realized that he was dripping with perspiration. His mouth was parched and his skin began to tingle. He started toward Bet Enav.

Reaching the outskirts of the village, he saw that tents used as temporary housing for Jews who were deported by the Turks from Jaffa were more numerous than ever, and they emphasized the difficult straits they had all been reduced to in Palestine. It reminded him of Bedouin villages in the desert. It was a far cry from the glorious homeland he visualized for his people.

Fearful of the villagers, he skirted Bet Enav, but he could still see the deterioration that had taken place in the time that he had been gone. There was a feeling of hopelessness he had never experienced before. He had hoped that somehow Bet Enav would have been spared the ravages of the war, that the land around the Danziger home would still hold that old magic. He urged his horse on, impatient to catch sight of the house.

When it came into view, it stood out against the clear blue skies as it always did, but it too had lost its luster. Even the bright sunlight did not relieve the darkness that came from within. The fence around the front was broken and the path leading to the front balcony was untended. The grass bordering the walkway was yellowing.

Unwilling and unable to face the sight, he was about to turn around and go down to the lab when he heard the sound of music. He moved closer and caught sight of Deborah sitting on the stoop of the house, rocking a cradle. Rafa was sitting close to her, playing his flute. Michael felt his heart skip a beat. Deborah was still the embodiment of everything he wanted in a woman. Thin, tired, her dark hair piled carelessly on top of her head, her dress hanging limply from her thin shoulders, she was still the most desirable woman he had ever seen. He had known many women, but none compared to her. Not in beauty, not in elegance, not in kindness or sincerity. The feeling of hopelessness her presence always conjured up in him came back more forcefully. She was a Danziger and he was a poor boy with nothing to offer her.

Rafa finished playing and tilted his head toward Deborah. She laughed and patted his shoulder.

"Should I play some more?" the boy asked, clearly pleased with her reaction.

"I think you should go inside and get something cold to drink," she answered. Then, leaning over, she picked the baby up. The infant's reddish blond hair caught the rays of the sun and she snuggled her head into its softness.

Michael wanted to turn away but felt transfixed. That too was part of his fantasy. Deborah holding their child, loving it, kissing it.

"Michael," he heard her call out. "What are you doing out there?" She had caught sight of him and was waving to him. "Come here immediately."

The genuine joy in her greeting did not escape him. Was it possible? He stopped the thought. She had a great deal of love in her which she lavished on everyone. But she was David's wife. She was in love with David. Only David.

Tying his horse to the gatepost, he entered the garden and headed toward her.

"When did you get back?" she asked, cradling the baby to her bosom. There was more than just pleasure at his return. He was sure of it.

"Early this morning," he answered, striving for a tone of indifference.

She lowered her eyes in confusion. Then, turning the baby toward him, she smiled. "You haven't said hello to Gidon."

He stared at the infant. He was a beautiful baby, with large blue eyes, a peaches-and-cream complexion. He looked like both Tamar and Thomas. The thought of Thomas made Michael remember that he had a message for her from Thomas.

"Isn't he beautiful?" She looked at the child lovingly. "You haven't seen him since . . ." She stopped.

They both remembered the sad scene of the infant's *bris* three months earlier, when Rabbi Landau refused to perform one of the most sacred of God's commands.

"Sonya was a real trooper," Michael tried to laugh. "And I thought the whole ceremony was extremely civilized."

"Yes, I suppose it was," Deborah smiled wanly. "But it would have been nice if everyone from the village had been there."

"Have any of them been around?" he asked.

"No one. As a matter of fact, we can no longer drive through the village. Can you imagine, people we've known all our lives, who've known our parents, boys and girls I went to school with, jeering at us if they see us?" Her expression betrayed her dismay. "We've been pelted with rotten fruit, stones and anything else they can lay their hands on. I wouldn't risk walking through the village with Gidon." She stopped and her eyes clouded over. "I hear they call

Gidon a bastard and since the rabbi didn't officiate at the circumcision they don't consider him a Jew."

"Oh, he's a Jew, all right. His mother is Jewish and I'm sure the Lord considers him one." He reached out and touched the baby's fair skin. He withdrew his hand quickly, aware of a strange, uncontrollable dislike for the child. It puzzled him. "Thank God he doesn't look like Davidzohn," he concluded feebly.

Deborah's eyes lingered on Michael's face, trying to decide if he knew what he was saying. He returned her look without flinching.

"How are things going at the laboratory?" he asked, wanting to change the subject.

She shrugged. "Same. We thought that things would change now that America has entered the war, but so far nothing has. We send boys out to gather information. We wait for the ship to come by, which it did only once in the last three months. We recruit new people whenever we hear someone might be interested, which isn't often now that the Turks are arresting families of anyone suspected of working against the Turkish war effort." Her voice trailed off.

"And?"

"And most everyone is hungry," she concluded and tried to smile. "That's the one thing we all have in common."

"Have you heard from Raphael?"

"Occasionally word comes through. He's now in England, talking to British Intelligence there, pleading with them to listen to us. Mind you, they admit that the information we've supplied them with has been invaluable, but I think the Allies are having so much trouble in Europe that this part of the world is somehow less important."

"The work is going well?"

"I think so," she answered soberly. "The pigeons fly and occasionally we get word that our messages have been received. Other times, we can only pray that they did."

He could not bear the look of sadness that crept into her eyes.

"I'm sure they are received. The fact is that the Germans are still going strong in Europe but the Turks are retreating in this part of the world. Someone is getting the message." He was relating facts, but was not sure that what he was saying about the Nili work was true.

"Where's Madame Tamar?" he asked, wanting to change to subject. "At the lab?"

"Of course not." Deborah grew serious. "She's helping Fatmi hang up the diapers." The enmity was still there in Michael, as it was in Tamar, and Deborah could never understand or accept it. "She never leaves Gidon. When we go to the lab, we take him with us."

"When are you going down?"

"As soon as David gets here with the carriage."

Tamar came from behind the house. "Well, for heaven's sake. When did you get back?" Rafa was trailing behind her. She seemed pleased to see him, at first. Then, as though recalling an unpleasantness, her face grew cold and her eyes veiled over.

"This morning," he answered stiffly.

"Where have you been?"

"All over."

"Any success with recruiting new members?" she asked.

He shook his head.

"Then what have you been doing all this time?" Tamar demanded.

"I've been collecting information," he answered angrily.

"I've seen it and I'm not overly impressed," she said. "Does David know you're back?" Tamar's voice was edged with impatience.

"No, I came here first. I tried to avoid the main road and took the mountain route."

"What are you afraid of?" she asked suspiciously. "You're still wearing a Turkish uniform. And it's as grand as ever." She observed him closely. "I really marvel at how you succeed in always looking so elegant."

He ignored the remark, but he felt a rage rise up in him. "I have quite a few papers on me and I didn't particularly want to meet up with some Arab scum."

"Well, they're hungry too," Tamar bristled. "But that's beside the point. Do you have anything important in those papers?"

"Important enough for me to want to make sure the British get them." He was about to mention Thomas when he noticed Rafa standing on the side, listening. "Let's drop the subject," he said pointedly, nodding toward Rafa.

"For God's sake," Tamar lost her temper. "How can you be afraid of Rafa?"

"I believe that the apple doesn't fall far from the tree." He laughed bitterly. "Has Abed been around lately?"

Tamar lowered her eyes.

"I had a feeling he was," Michael said. "Black sheep have a way of coming back to the shed when they're hungry."

"He was here briefly but he left again, and I don't think he'll come back. Mahmud nearly killed him in anger this time."

"Tamar, you hold your views and I'll hold mine. That boy will be the death of all of us."

"You're irrational."

"Give me my irrationality and I'll stack it up against your rationality any day," he said dryly.

The sound of cartwheels was heard and they all looked around. David had driven the cart through the back gate.

"It's about time you got back," he addressed Michael angrily when he reached them.

"David," Michael said through clenched teeth. "We've got enough problems without you and me going at each other."

"Listen, we're in trouble," David said urgently. "I've got something that has to be delivered to British Intelligence and I need help in getting it there. I believe I know how they can break through the southern front," he whispered. "They could actually take Jerusalem without a fight."

"And Hardwick has a plan that must be followed up by a British move. He can't get through to his people and he asked me to do it for him," Michael answered excitedly.

Tamar reacted at the mention of Thomas's name.

"What are you talking about?" she asked, trying to sound calm, but her face was flushed. "What has Thomas got to do with all of this?"

"Stay out of it," Michael dismissed her with a wave of his hand. "Your friend is doing his job and we've got to do ours. With all his brilliance, he just might get his Arabs the trophies of victory, even if we're the ones who will be handing it to him."

"You see evil in everything and everyone." She was white with rage.

"I see reality, which is more than I can say for you."

"Stop it," Deborah pleaded. "We're all fighting for the same cause."

"I'm not," Michael answered coldly. "I'm fighting for the Jews."

"Thomas is fighting for human dignity for everyone," Tamar said vehemently.

"I love it," Michael sneered. "Human dignity be damned. I'm fed up with dying Jews who are remembered for having died with dignity. I'm fed up with always losing the battle, even when we're right and do our share."

"Bravo," Tamar laughed bitterly. "Now get off the speaker's podium and let's talk about what we can do on the practical level."

"We don't have many options," David said. "We must get to Alexandria."

"I won't have it." Sensing his thoughts, "You are not to try that desert route," Tamar's voice rose.

"Lower your voice," Michael ordered.

She turned to David. "Please don't even think of it."

He looked at her for a long moment. "Tamar, there is no alternative. Time is running out." He turned back to Michael.

"I'm going through that desert," David said evenly. "And this time I won't get caught."

"David, it's insane," Tamar raised her voice again. "You won't make it."

"When shall we leave?" Michael asked, looking directly at David.

"I've been working on getting an Arab guide in Beersheba. One of our own is down there, making the arrangements. He's also getting us the camels."

"I know that desert," Michael said. "We don't need an Arab guide."

"I wish you wouldn't go," Deborah said softly and her voice quavered. "I certainly don't think the two of you should go. One of you should stay here. Take Avi or any of the other boys."

"Deborah is right," Tamar agreed. "With both of you gone, it would leave Deborah and me alone—"

"Nonsense," Michael interrupted vehemently. "You are the one who actually runs Nili. Everyone knows that and they're right." He turned to David and Deborah. "Go on, tell her it's so."

Deborah was astounded. She had never seen him speak with so much passion. She simply nodded her confirmation.

"Michael is stating a fact," David said, trying not to think of Tamar crying the night they buried the English messenger. "It's your spirit that now carries Nili," he concluded firmly.

"I won't allow it," Tamar was breathing heavily. And then, losing control, she screamed, "I forbid it."

The baby began to cry, frightened by the raised voices.

Tamar calmed down immediately and taking the child from Deborah, she held him close and murmured softly in his ear.

David put his arm around Deborah. She nestled close to him, but her eyes lingered on Michael's face. Their eyes met and he turned to look at Tamar. Deborah could not tell what he was thinking. She looked up at David. He too was staring at Tamar. She turned to look at her sister.

All the anger was gone from her face. In one instant, she turned from a ferocious tyrant into a soft, warm, gentle mother.

Standing in the bright sunlight, the three were overcome by the sight of Tamar holding her son. She was magnificent. She was the embodiment of womanhood. She looked almost saintly.

It was weeks later that Michael remembered he had not given Tamar Thomas's message.

# CHAPTER
# EIGHTEEN

T HE summer passed and September was rapidly drawing to an end, but the drought persisted. Rumors were flying concerning the progress of the war, but there was little hard news of what was happening. In Europe the Allies were struggling to gain the upper hand on various battle-fronts. The United States' involvement had not yet been felt and although there was hope that their participation would soon change the stalemate, fear of failure was prevalent everywhere. It was the Great War that had taken numerous lives on all fronts. There was no end in sight.

Universal suffering, however, was no consolation to the tiny, cut-off Jewish community in Palestine. Theirs was a suffering woven into the fabric of their lives and their despair was compounded by the realization that the Promised Land was more remote than ever.

Still, that sentiment had little effect on Nili. It had none on Tamar. The work at the laboratory continued, despite all setbacks. The number of their recruits had dwindled, yet Tamar pressed on with her duties, driving her few men and herself mercilessly, convinced of victory. She could be shrill, hysterical, unreasonable, but they obeyed her. And if there was discontent, Deborah was always there to smooth the ruffled feathers. Although Deborah had her moments of doubts, she too held to the conviction that all would turn out well.

The two women spent most of their days and nights at the laboratory, abandoning any efforts to pacify their neighbors by pretending to work only in their home. They were alone most of the time but they had each other and they had Gidon.

On this September day, as dusk was setting in, Deborah stood at the window of Raphael's second-floor study at the laboratory. She stared at the empty horizon, wondering how much longer they could carry on without some signal from the British acknowledging their work. She was not given to defeatist thoughts, but there was a sadness in the air which she could not ignore.

"For a six-month-old baby, he's really extraordinary, isn't he?" Tamar's voice made Deborah turn around. Tamar had just finished breast-feeding the baby and she was staring at him adoringly.

"He's more than that," Deborah said solemnly. "There's something very special about him. I can't help wondering what his future will be like."

"His future is going to be perfect," Tamar smiled at her son. "He's got everything a child needs. A mother who worships him, an aunt who dotes on him, a homeland which he will grow up in and be proud of, and a glorious heritage."

"Does Fredrick know about the baby?" Deborah asked, pleased with her sister's state of mind.

"Fredrick is in some godforsaken prison in Turkey. And since I wanted the divorce, I wrote him and mentioned Gidon to him. He knows as well as I do that this child is not his and I thought his wounded masculine pride would force him to grant me a divorce."

"Have you heard back?"

"Our letters crossed. It seemed he divorced me before he got my letter."

"Oh, no!" Deborah burst out laughing. "Why didn't you tell me?"

"I didn't know how you'd take it," Tamar said with relief. "Considering how shocked you were when I told you Fredrick wasn't Gidon's father—"

"Who cares who the father is," Deborah interrupted and reached out to touch the baby.

"But you do understand that although Fredrick knows Gidon is not his child, legally the baby is his." Tamar grew serious.

"Meaning he could claim him if he wanted to?" Deborah asked.

"Yes. But I doubt that he will." Tamar dismissed the idea.

"He might not have if it were a girl, but a son, someone who could carry on his name, might be different."

"Such wisdom from my baby sister." Tamar laughed goodnaturedly. "But that will be in fifteen years when he's released and Thomas and I will be long since married by then, with three or four other children. I don't intend to worry about it today."

Carefully she placed the baby in a bassinet standing beside the open window. She hoped a slight breeze from the sea would lull the infant to sleep.

"Shouldn't you tell Raphael about him?" Deborah asked, not ready to end the conversation. "Much as we love Gidon, there's got to be someone with authority who knows his true identity."

"When he comes back, I probably will. But it would be foolish to write to him now." She paused. "I'm not sure Raphael would understand. It would certainly upset him and it would serve no purpose." She smiled wistfully. "At this point Gidon has Fredrick's name, whether Fredrick likes it or not, and Gidon Davidzohn is fine for now. Besides the baby has us. You and I are both young and healthy and there's nothing to worry about."

"But what about his future?"

"What about it?" Tamar grew impatient. "His life will be intertwined with mine. When Thomas and I do marry, Gidon will become Gidon Hardwick."

"Where will you live?" Deborah asked cautiously.

A look of bewilderment came into Tamar's eyes. "Here, of course." She looked confused for a moment. "What a foolish question."

"What about a cup of tea?" Deborah wanted to change the subject.

Tamar was about to answer when they heard someone come in. Both women stiffened and Tamar walked over to the bassinet.

"It's only me." Avi came lumbering up the stairs.

"You frightened us," Tamar said with relief and was about to look away when she noticed his appearance. He was disheveled, unshaven and his eyes were bloodshot.

Tamar's composure was ruffled at the sight of the ill-kempt young man.

"What happened?" she asked, trying to hide her anxiety.

Avi stared at her and said nothing.

"What happened?" she repeated. Have you had any news from David? Did he and Michael get through to the British in Alexandria?" her voice rose. "Are they all right?"

"We've heard from no one." He stopped and looked on helplessly. "Yossi has been caught by the Turks in Beersheba." His voice broke.

Tamar paled. "Yossi, I always felt, should not have been sent there, but he is a good boy and he's loyal. Besides, he's in Beersheba on David's orders."

"Wake up, Tamar," Avi snapped. "That cover won't hold. He had coded messages on him when he was caught."

"What's a coded message except a lot of gibberish that no Turk would ever begin to suspect, except to assume that it was some sort of cabalistic voodoo?" Tamar tried to keep the hysteria out of her voice.

"The Turks haven't ruled this part of the world for the last four hundred years by being stupid. A coded message in a knapsack of a Jew is very damaging," Avi answered vehemently.

Tamar bit her lip and turned her eyes toward the window.

Avi followed her look. "You still think the ship will be coming tonight?" he asked sarcastically. "Don't you ever give up?"

His defeatist attitude was contagious and Tamar could feel it taking hold of her. Since David and Michael left, Avi was her most dependable man. Other than Deborah, she had no one. For him to desert them at this point would be a disaster.

"I know they've only been by a couple of times in the last few months, but I certainly wouldn't give up hope." She felt helpless but kept her feelings in check.

Instead she busied herself with lighting a lantern and walked over to the open window. It was a moonless night. The sea was calm. It would be a perfect night for a ship to land, she thought sadly.

"We'll go on waiting on the chance they will come by." Then unable to keep her frustration from erupting, she reached over and picked up some papers which were lying on the desk. "Damn it," she hissed. "We've got all this information here and I don't know if it could shorten the war, but I know it could save lives. Many, many young lives."

"Have you sent the pigeons out with duplicate messages?" Avi asked.

"Of course I did." Tamar said impatiently. "But how do we know if they actually got through?"

Avi shrugged his shoulders. "We don't know," he said and started toward the coding room. "I'm bushed and I think I'll turn in for the night."

"I wish you wouldn't stay here tonight," Tamar had regained her composure.

"Why not?" He stopped and looked at her.

"I just don't think you should," Tamar said firmly. "Your parents have complained to Deborah that you're never home anymore and I think it would be a good idea if you spent the night with them."

Avi was taken aback. Tamar was hardly one to care about family life when the cause was at stake. He looked at Deborah.

"Your mother came by to see me the other day and she asked about you," Deborah said gently. "Your father is not feeling well and she wants you home." She sighed. "She's my mother-in-law and she spoke to me as to a stranger. Poor woman. I know she wanted to ask about David, but didn't dare. It was so sad."

Avi was shaken by the news, but tried to keep calm. "What's the matter with my father?"

"Nothing serious, but you should get home," Deborah urged.

"Yes, it has been weeks since I've been home," he said quietly. He felt torn. He looked over at Tamar, at the sleeping infant and at Deborah. They needed him, but so did his parents. With a halfhearted wave of his hand he turned and went down the stairs.

"Will Yossi be all right?" Deborah asked as soon as Avi was gone.

"God, I hope so," Tamar said. But the desperation was back.

Then impulsively she picked up the baby. "Let's go home." She said angrily. "No ship will come by tonight. And if it does, the hell with it. The pigeons were sent out and eventually the British will get the information."

"I'm scared," Deborah whispered.

"You're always scared," Tamar snapped, then regretted her tone. She softened her voice immediately. "Oh, Deborah don't be. This whole thing will be over soon. I'm convinced David and Michael are already in Alexandria. That's probably the reason the ship hasn't come by. And don't forget, Raphael is also in Alexandria and surely the three of them will get our information across." She smiled reassuringly. "The Turks are retreating and it's only a matter of time before they surrender." She was as frightened as Deborah but she dared not show it. "Just close the window so that if the ship should come by, they'll know we're not here."

Holding the baby close, Tamar walked slowly down the stairs. Blackie followed, wagging his tail halfheartedly.

Before closing the window, Deborah scanned the distant horizon. Except for the calm swells of the waves, moving gently, she saw nothing. Slamming the window shut, she rushed to catch up with Tamar.

Tamar was sitting on the passenger side of the carriage, with the sleeping infant nestled in her arms. Deborah settled into the driver's seat, took the reins and tugged at them gently.

Neither spoke, both aware of the danger surrounding them. Although the road was flanked by endless tents inhabited by refugees from the cities, everyone was either asleep or too afraid to look out. Both Deborah and Tamar were fully aware that two women with an infant, traveling alone, were easy prey for Arabs, Turks, or hungry animals roaming the countryside, but they were tired and the need to be in their own home had overwhelmed their usual caution.

As they approached the main highway, Deborah stopped to make sure there were no patrols moving about. The highway was empty. She was about to cross it, when she realized that the area was too deserted. Normally, there was little traffic on the road at that hour, but Turkish soldiers did patrol the highway and one could always hear them moving about. The total silence was disturbing.

"I wonder if the great rulers of the Ottoman Empire were scared off by the dark?" Tamar said sarcastically. She too was conscious of the stillness around them.

Having no alternative, Deborah whipped the horse into a trot, crossed the road quickly and headed for the path leading to Bet Enav. When they reached the vineyard gate, she pulled in the reins. Driving through the vineyard would be a short cut, but she hesitated. At that hour, if anyone wanted to harm them, they would be trapped. At least the open road would leave them avenues of escape.

"Let's not go through the vineyard," Tamar confirmed her doubts. "It would be different if I had my gun, but I don't."

"You mean you've stopped carrying it?" Deborah was surprised.

Tamar smiled. "Since the baby arrived, I felt it might be too compromising if for some reason someone decided to search me."

"What have you done with it."

"I hid it behind a tile over the bathtub in Raphael's house."

"I'm glad," Deborah said, guiding the horse away from the vineyard. She had always hated the idea of Tamar carrying a gun.

The incline leading up to Bet Enav seemed steeper than ever and they moved slowly. Deborah relaxed her hold on the reins and looked over at Tamar. She was slumped forward, wearily, obviously dozing. Deborah wished she could relieve her of Gidon. Small as he was, he was heavy and Tamar had been up since before dawn. She marveled at her sister's stamina. Tamar had gone back to work a week after Gidon was born, running the Nili operation and supervising everyone's activities around the country while nursing the infant and attending to him in every way. She rarely slept and ate little. Deborah felt Tamar was close to breaking, both physically and emotionally.

For no apparent reason she remembered the ride she took with Raphael and Tamar the night before Tamar's eighteenth birthday. Nothing about this night resembled that time so long ago, yet the memory persisted. Suddenly it dawned on her that Tamar would be twenty-four in the morning.

Only six years had passed, yet it seemed like an eternity. An overwhelming feeling of sadness and longing engulfed her. They were all so young, so gay, so filled with hope. She recalled the laughter, the joy, the frivolity of that party. The house was lit up, the music and dancing went on for hours, with all their neighbors, Arabs and Jews, coming by to participate in the event and paying homage to their family. That was the night Tamar met Fredrick. She also remembered that her main concern was whether David would notice her. And he had. He held her in his arms and they waltzed on the terrace. Life was so simple, almost predictable. Even then there were slight frictions but they were a family, a strong unit, who would stand together and fight together. No one had dreamed of a world conflict that would pit a whole people against her family.

Tears started streaming down her cheeks. Nothing would ever be the same again. Even if the Allies won the war, there were too many realities that would have to be faced, from within and without. Raphael would never approve of Tamar marrying Thomas. But knowing Tamar, especially now that she had Gidon, nothing would dissuade her. As for her own future? She and David would live out their lives together, but it would no longer be the simple life they had expected.

She wiped her eyes with the back of her hand. Tears, she knew, were a poor weapon against the untold dangers confronting them.

"Stop!" Tamar's low voice broke into her thoughts.

Deborah pulled in the reins.

"Look," Tamar pointed to the house.

Deborah focused her eyes on their house and realized that the shutters of the attic window were open and the window was up. They had long since discarded the use of the attic window as a signal, feeling it was too obvious and too dangerous. Other than that everything else seemed to be in order. The house was dark, the light on the front porch was on, and the front door was shut. Deborah looked over at Raphael's house. It too was dark and seemed not to have been disturbed.

Their carriage standing in a small cove, Deborah and Tamar could see the house, but they knew that anyone there could not see them.

Both women dismounted and Tamar handed the infant to Deborah.

"The wind must have blown it open," Tamar whispered. "Still, let me go up to the house and make sure everything is in order."

Quickly she climbed back onto the carriage.

Deborah started to protest.

"Don't worry," Tamar said forcefully. "Just take the baby up to the shelter and stay there until you see me close the shutters."

She kept her eyes on the house. "I won't be long."

"Let me go," Deborah pleaded. "And you stay with the baby."

"Nonsense. I'm sure it's nothing."

Deborah, holding Gidon, felt that something terrible was about to happen and she was not sure she could handle it.

"What if he gets hungry?" she asked desperately.

"He was fed a little while ago. He'll be fine." Tamar kept her eyes on the house. "And if he starts to fuss, handle him as best you can." She looked briefly at the sleeping child. "I'd rather he were hungry than dead," she said evenly. Then pulling on the reins, she was soon gone from sight.

# CHAPTER
# NINETEEN

EBORAH crawled toward the storage shelter located outside their grounds. Her father had dug out the space beneath a large rock to store wheat and other perishables in the winter. As the farm grew and more storage was needed, he dug deeper beneath the rock, so that the space was much larger than it appeared from the outside. The shelter was rarely used now, and the overgrown weeds surrounding the entranceway obscured it from view. Few remembered its existence.

Deborah had barely settled the baby on the ground when she heard Tamar cry out. The sound was followed almost immediately by a heartrending scream. It bounced off the walls around her. She looked down at Gidon. He had not stirred. She wondered if she should move him further into the cavernous space. She decided against it. The deeper you went, the colder it got.

She crawled to the mouth of the shelter and stared at the house. It was now fully lit and she could see the silhouettes of Turkish soldiers moving about the living room. Their voices reached her clearly.

"Did you really thing you could fool the Imperial Turkish army with carrier pigeons, Miss Danziger?" a Turk, speaking French, demanded angrily. "Or is it Mrs. Davidzohn?" he asked sarcastically. "Neither name will help you now." His manner of address was familiar.

"What carrier pigeons?" Tamar tried to sound incredulous, but she was having difficulty talking.

"You Jews are such fools," the Turk continued, ignoring her answer. "We've caught some stupid spy in Beersheba carrying a similar message to the one found on one of your little feathered friends. So you can stop the pretense. Now we want to know who, other than David Larom and Michael Ben Hod, is involved in this idiotic charade."

Deborah could not make out Tamar's answer.

"It's over, madame," he continued when Tamar's tortured scream subsided into a moan.

Deborah crept back into the shelter and sat down beside the sleeping infant.

She felt numb. They had been caught and Nili's work was over. Raphael was away, David and Michael were traveling through the desert and Tamar was in danger. Alone with an infant, Deborah knew she could not go on leading the diminishing group of loyal volunteers. The base was gone and she could not endanger them further. Not them and certainly not their families.

In desperate need of comfort, she picked up the sleeping infant and pulled Blackie toward her. She leaned against the wall of the shelter, hugging the child and the dog, while staring at the house and listening to Tamar's shrieks piercing the darkness.

Time got diffused and Deborah had no idea how long she had been in the shelter. From time to time the screaming would stop and she would hold her breath, hoping the torture was over. It would start again within seconds, and there seemed to be no relief to Tamar's nightmare. Finally Tamar's speech became slurred and it was clear that she would not be able to withstand the torture much longer. Deborah was sure that she would prefer death to what was happening to her at that moment.

If only Tamar had her gun, Deborah thought. If somehow Tamar could get to Raphael's house, get into his bathroom and get her gun.

The darkness grew deeper and the cold became more penetrating. Gidon stirred restlessly in her arms. He would soon be hungry and start crying. The idea made her sit up in horror. Just as she could hear every sound coming from the house, the Turks would hear the baby if he cried out. Tamar's baby! If the Turks could get hold of Gidon, Deborah thought frantically, Tamar would surely break.

Deborah felt no panic. Instead she felt extremely calm. No harm would come to Gidon. She had an obligation to Tamar, but more important, she had an obligation to this child. He was the future. She thought of Fatmi and Mahmud. He would be safe with them. The idea that she would rather have the child with their Arab servants than anyone in Bet Enav shocked her. She dismissed the thought. All she knew was that he would be safe in Ein Chod.

She looked down at Gidon. He was staring at her with his large, innocent blue eyes, gurgling happily and reaching up to touch her face. Blackie was straining to get away from her grasp. She clutched his collar more firmly, knowing he would run toward the house if she let go. Just then another piercing cry came from the house and the baby started whimpering. She had to make a choice—calming the infant or letting go of Blackie. She let go of the dog's collar and he bolted out of the shelter, barking frantically as he ran. She did not have long to wait. The sound of shots, then a feeble yelp reached her and she knew Blackie was dead. She closed her eyes. He had been given to her by Raphael when she was twelve years old.

With Gidon held close, Deborah crept out of the storage room and started toward Ein Chod. It was a difficult climb during the day and worse at night. She inched her way along the crude road, careful not to kick the loose stones which would be heard rolling down the hill. Once she looked back and noted that all the houses in the village were darkened except for theirs. She gritted her teeth in anger. Everyone in Bet Enav was aware of what was happening at the Danzigers' house, but clearly no one was going to risk his life coming to Tamar's aid. The rabbi had warned her that they would be ignored if anything happened to them and he was right.

Mahmud was waiting for her at the edge of his village. Fatmi was standing respectfully behind him. No words were exchanged as he took the baby from her. Then, Fatmi came forward and handed her a bundle. She assumed it was food. The thought of eating made her sick, but she leaned over and kissed the woman gratefully on the cheek. Fatmi nodded and patted her head.

There was no sound from the house when Deborah returned to the shelter. She looked up at the attic window. It was still open.

She lay down on the bare ground and waited. It grew colder and she wrapped her thin shawl around her shoulders, trying to control her trembling. She dared not fall asleep but she closed her eyes and listened. She could still hear Tamar's voice but by now she was incoherent.

The smell of Turkish tobacco drifted toward her and Deborah's eyes flew open. Two men, dressed in Turkish uniforms, were standing in the garden. Although they were a distance away, she could hear them clearly. She dared not move.

"The bitch," one of them said angrily. "At this rate, she's going to die and we'll still know nothing and they'll hold us responsible for her death." He spoke Arabic. An Arab, drafted by the Turks to serve in their army, he worried about the consequences. No Turkish soldier would care.

"I don't know why we just don't take her to Damascus and hang her," the other one said coldly. His accent indicated that he was Turkish. "You know, these damn Jews should be taught a lesson and what better lesson than the execution of a female traitor."

"Hanging a woman who is that good-looking would be a shame," the first man said and Deborah had the feeling he was uncomfortable with the idea.

"You feeling sorry for a dirty Jewess spy?" the Turk asked accusingly.

"Of course not. She should be hanged."

"I can't say that I felt any guilt when we hanged that idiot in Beersheba." His partner laughed triumphantly as he started back toward the house.

Deborah's heart sank. Yossi was dead. For the first time in many hours she thought of David and Michael. The Turk interrogating Tamar knew the names of David and Michael. Was Yossi the one who had informed on them? And where were David and Michael? They had been gone for six weeks. Were they dead too?

The tears brimmed over again. So much pain, so much death, and for what? They had all worked so hard, were so sincere in their efforts, were so sure of their cause. They had been so loyal to the Allies, had risked so much to help them, but somehow the British did not fully trust them. Was there no one the Jews could depend on?

A dull dawn had begun to creep into the shelter, when a shadow suddenly appeared at the entrance and Deborah stifled a cry.

"She won't be able to take much more of it." She recognized Avi's voice.

He settled himself wearily beside her and reached out for her hand.

"It's been almost eight hours since they started this insanity, and I don't think she'll be able to last much longer," he said grimly. "I hate to say it, but she'd be better off dead. No one can take that much punishment."

"She'll take it," Deborah answered through clenched teeth.

"To what end?"

"What kind of question is that?" she asked angrily. "She's doing it for you, for me, for everyone of us who worked for Nili and for her child's future. She has the misguided idea that she has an obligation to all the children who will be born in this land." She caught her breath briefly before rushing on. "And frankly, if I thought my going up there and exposing the names of every Nili member would help her, I'd do it, by God, I really would.

"Where's the baby?" Avi ignored her outburst.

"Mahmud has him."

"Mahmud? Do you feel you can trust him?"

"More than I can some other people I know," she said pointedly.

"What's that supposed to mean?"

"I don't know what I'm saying." She felt spent. "It's just that everybody in Bet Enav must know what Tamar is going through and except for you, no one seems to care." Her anger returned. "God damn it, where is Dr. Rosen? Even the Turks would allow him to come if he said he was concerned about the life of a human being." The words poured forth uncontrollably. "I'm not asking for anyone to risk their lives for us, but he's a doctor!"

"Everyone is scared," Avi said defensively.

"Come to think of it, what are you doing here?" she asked.

"My mother ordered me to leave the house when I got home last night." He lowered his eyes in embarrassment. "As you know, my father is ill. She felt my presence there could endanger them." He paused briefly, then looking directly at her, he continued. "Several of the older citizens of Ben Enav have been arrested by the Turks and are being held in a shack on the outskirts of the village. The synagogue has been desecrated and there is word that more arrests are on the way." He stopped, waited for her to react. When she did not, he continued. "By now everybody in Bet Enav knows what we've been doing and they're obviously blaming Nili for their troubles. It's going to get worse, you wait and see."

"I wonder how they found out?" she said suspiciously.

"I don't know. Someone must have talked."

"What's even more curious is how the Turks found out about us," Deborah continued.

"If it weren't so awful, it would be funny," Avi said sadly. "Remember your saying pigeons don't talk? Well, in a way, one of them did. One of the pigeons from the last batch Tamar sent out landed on Fakrhi Pasha's fence. He thought it was his and was about to feed it when he noticed the parchment attached to its claw." He paused. "When the Turks connected what they found on Yossi and what the bird had on it, they put it all together."

"Who told you about it?"

"The Arabs around here are telling it with great glee."

She edged away from him and stared. "Where did you sleep?"

"Sleep?" he asked and a grim smile appeared on his lips. "With Tamar's screaming, I doubt anyone is sleeping tonight, or will ever sleep again." The smile disappeared and was replaced by an impotent rage that consumed his emaciated face.

Tamar's screams started up again. After the lull, they sounded more horrendous than before.

"I still think she'd be better off dead" Avi said grimly.

Deborah knew Avi was right. She also knew she had to help Tamar die. Horrible as the thought was, she suddenly knew exactly what it was she must do. She had to get into the tunnel under Raphael's house where they had stored their rifles and guns. Tamar and her captors were in the living room of the main house and the windows of that room faced Raphael's bedroom. She had no idea how many soldiers were in the house, but it did not matter. Tamar could not take much more and it was Deborah's duty to help put an end to her sister's misery. She knew Tamar would have done that for her if their positions were reversed.

"I think you'd better leave now," Deborah said coldly. She had to get to Raphael's house and she did not want Avi around. Few knew about the tunnel, and at that moment, she trusted no one.

"What are you going to do?" Avi asked, looking at her suspiciously.

"I'll be all right."

"Can I do anything for you?"

She thought for a long moment. "Yes," she said finally. "I would like you to tell Dr. Rosen that he should have acted with greater compassion. It would have been the humane thing to do. And as for the rabbi and the rest of the village, they'll have to live with their consciences."

"You're being unfair," Avi started to protest. "I'm sure Dr. Rosen wants to help, wants to do something, but there is really nothing anyone can do." He spoke very slowly. "Deborah, you've got to know that even if the people in Bet Enav wanted to help Tamar, they couldn't. The Turks now know that there is a Jewish spy ring operating out of this area. Anyone associated with that operation would suffer what Tamar is suffering. And you must remember, Bet Enav feels betrayed. Every Jew there feels that you've endangered all of them. They never hid their feelings and you knew it."

"And you?" She could not resist the question.

"Deborah, I have a mother and a father. I believe that what we set out to do was important. But look at us. Yossi's been caught and will probably be hanged. Tamar is dying a dreadful death. David and Michael are gone and Raphael . . ." He paused. "Where is he anyway?"

"He's playing roulette in Monte Carlo!" she snapped. "Drinking champagne and sleeping with whores." She spat the words out disdainfully. "Go away, Avi, and salvage what you can. I mean that. But there is one other thing I will ask of you. Someday in the future, if you see me on the street, just nod to me and I'll do the same. Don't expect me to be more than mildly courteous, even if you are my brother-in-law." She sucked in her breath. "And now, just go!"

She lowered her eyes and in spite of herself, she hoped he would protest, demand to stay and take care of her as everyone had always done. Instead she heard him creep away. When she looked up, he was gone and she was alone. For the first time in her life, she had no one to turn to.

She leaned back exhausted and her hand fell on the bundle Fatmi had given her. She pulled at the string and it came undone. Instead of food, she saw an Arab dress and a *chodor* for her head and face. She smiled wanly and understood the message. Dressed as an Arab woman, she could move about more easily.

The silence around caught her attention. It was more frightening than the screaming. Was it possible that Tamar was dead? The horror of the thought was tempered by the idea that it would be a blessing. She peered out cautiously.

A Turkish officer was walking about inspecting the area.

"Okay, let's get going," he called out and Deborah saw Tamar being dragged out by four Arab soldiers followed by a second Turkish officer. Her face was swollen out of shape, her hair was caked with dried blood and her eyes were barely visible due to the swelling around them. Her ripped clothes revealed huge open gashes on her shoulders and her feet were torn from the whip lashing. Deborah stifled a cry and swallowed the vomit that rose in her throat.

With the soldiers surrounding her, Tamar stumbled toward the front gate, where they stopped and waited. How she managed to walk was beyond Deborah's comprehension, yet she did with her shoulders thrown back, almost with dignity. There was a strange smile on her disfigured face which gave her distorted features a grotesque look.

Finally an elegant Turk emerged from the house. Deborah recognized him. It was Hassan Bey, a Turkish officer who in the past used to kowtow to Raphael. Tamar had mentioned having met him while living in Turkey.

Hassan Bey walked over to the gate and, waving his arm, led the procession out of the garden.

Deborah turned to look at the house. The door was ajar and she wondered if anyone was still in there. It did not matter. She could enter Raphael's house without being seen.

As soon as the soldiers were out of sight, she crawled toward Raphael's house and, removing a wooden plank from the foyer floor, climbed down a short ladder to the hidden tunnel. In the darkness she felt her way to the rack that held the guns. Choosing the smallest handgun, she examined it quickly and was relieved to find that it was loaded. With the gun tucked into her waistband, she crawled back to the ladder and climbed out, pushing the wooden plank into place. Throwing a quick glance around Raphael's living room, she felt her heart sink. It had been ravaged. All his books, all his valuable scientific notes collected over so many years, were torn and strewn around. She turned away and rushed into Raphael's bathroom. The suit that Tamar had always planned to wear when the Allies finally entered Palestine was draped on a hanger.

Stifling a sob, Deborah pulled out the loose tile and retrieved Tamar's tiny pistol. Satisfied that it too was loaded, she replaced it and put back the tile. She wanted it there, on the off-chance that Tamar could somehow get to it. Then, cautiously she crept over to a window and looked out.

Tamar, surrounded by soldiers, was being led toward the main street of Bet Enav.

Retracing her steps, Deborah returned to the shelter and slipped into Fatmi's robe, wrapped the black veil around her head and covered her face. Only her eyes were exposed. With the pistol tucked into her belt under the loose-fitting robe, she crawled out of the shelter.

She was walking at a safe distance behind Tamar and her captors, when she realized that Mahmud and Rafa had joined her. She breathed a sigh of relief. A curious Arab and his family, following the Turks, would hardly raise suspicion.

The purpose of the walk made little sense until Deborah realized that the inhabitants of the village were being forced out of their houses to witness Tamar's degradation. Loudspeakers began blaring out the message that this was what would happen to anyone who was discovered a traitor to the Ottoman Empire.

The march continued through the village and down toward the main thoroughfare, which was now completely lined with villagers from nearby communities.

Deborah wondered how she could attract Tamar's attention. Somehow she had to let Tamar know that Gidon was safe. Knowing that would put her mind at rest. Mahmud, as though reading her thoughts, moved toward Hassan Bey and bowing, in the servile manner acceptable to a ruler, offered him a jug of water. The transaction attracted Tamar's attention. The hint of recognition was barely visible and her half-closed eyes darted toward Deborah.

Finishing his drink and handing the jug back to Mahmud, Hassan Bey signaled to have the march resumed. Suddenly Tamar began to sing. She sounded deranged and Deborah thought her sister had actually lost her mind, when the words began to connect. No one but Deborah understood what was being sung but the message was clear. "Give my love to my baby." The words were intertwined in the crazed ranting.

The march continued down the hill and Deborah hurried back to Raphael's house and crouched by the window, facing the garden, gun pointed.

By the time Tamar returned, she was no longer able to walk. Dragged by a couple of soldiers, she looked like a mutilated doll.

"We're not going to get anything else here," Hassan Bey said quietly. "Let's pack up and get her to Damascus."

"Slut!" An officer turned and spat at Tamar. The saliva ran down her cheek but she did not react.

Deborah swallowed hard. Slowly she raised the pistol, aimed it and waited for the guards to move away from Tamar long enough so that she could fire the fatal shot. She knew she would not get a second chance.

"I'm hardly a sight to show the glorious Turkish army," Tamar said and her speech was amazingly clear. "A woman beaten by big, strong, victorious soldiers. Why, they might never believe anything you tell them about me when they see me in this condition." The mockery in her voice was unmistakable.

The men moved back, uncertainty written on their faces.

"Clean her up," Hassan Bey ordered.

"That is something only a woman can do for herself." Tamar sounded indignant.

"Take her into the bathroom, but check it out first. Any possible way of escape must be avoided," Hassan Bey said impatiently.

"She couldn't walk to the front gate in her condition," one of the soldiers said and the others laughed.

"My clothes are in there," Tamar said, pointing to Raphael's house.

"Why?" The officer asked.

"I use my brother's house when he is away serving your army," Tamar answered. "You can go see for yourself. I have a suit hanging in the bathroom."

Deborah barely got into the tunnel and pulled the panel down before she heard the heavy footsteps of soldiers marching in.

She could hear the men scrambling about. Then she heard Tamar shuffle in and demand that the bathroom door be closed while she dressed. Finally the bathroom door slammed shut.

The piercing sound of the single gunshot reverberated wildly through the tunnel, and Deborah knew that Tamar was dead.

# CHAPTER TWENTY

D EBORAH was barely conscious of being helped into the crude open carriage. Fatmi handed her the baby wrapped in a black cloth. He moaned in his sleep and Deborah looked down at him almost in surprise. Tamar had always insisted that the baby be dressed in sparkling white clothing. The cruel reality of what had happened to them jolted her.

Tamar was dead. Deborah and Gidon were in danger. They were leaving Bet Enav and going to Sonya's sanitorium in Haifa for safety. The baby was dressed as an Arab infant and his blue eyes were bandaged to conceal his identity. She looked down at herself. She was still dressed in her long, black garment, her head covered by a scarf that hid the lower part of her face. Mahmud was sitting in the driver's seat with Rafa by his side. They appeared to be a typical Arab family—grandfather, daughter and two grandchildren, one blind and the other stricken with trachoma—on their way to a doctor in Haifa. Not an unreasonable sight if a Turkish soldier were to stop them.

The cart started moving and Deborah looked over at Fatmi standing a distance away. It was still dark out and she could see the older woman, her hands tightly clasped to her breast, the distress clearly written on her wrinkled face. Deborah wanted to say something that would express her feelings, but the words stuck in her throat. Instead, tears started streaming down her cheeks. They were tears of gratitude, of love, of pain at parting. Tears for all that had happened to her, to her family, to the very essence of their lives in the last two weeks.

The little wooden cart, hitched to an aging mule, creaked as it moved, the poor animal struggling wearily up the hill, away from the main road.

Deborah looked back. Fatmi had turned away and was walking quickly toward her village. She never turned around. Within seconds she disappeared into one of the mud huts. The door closed gently behind her and the village was silent.

Deborah shifted her eyes in the direction of Bet Enav. It was barely visible except for a dim light coming from the synagogue. She tried to visualize the men of the village sitting around the large wooden table, debating the catastrophe that had befallen them. She wondered if they were suffering pangs of guilt at the way they had behaved toward her family.

They all knew Tamar was dead. After the fatal shot was fired, Dr. Rosen was called in by Hassan Bey and it was he who pronounced her dead. Deborah, crouching in the tunnel below Raphael's house, could hear the soldiers dragging her sister out of the house and heard Dr. Rosen protest the treatment being accorded the dead woman. Deborah wanted to scream with anger at his sudden punctilio. Had he come by earlier, he might have prevented her sister's ghastly death. Now, when it was too late, he was showing concern.

"We didn't do it," Hassan Bey announced loudly. "You're witness to that, doctor." It was a statement, not a question.

Dr. Rosen was silent.

"I want you to sign a certificate to the effect that she committed suicide. And that, as far as we're concerned, is as good as an admission of her guilt," Hassan Bey continued. "I shall accompany you to your office, where you will write out the death certificate."

Still, Dr. Rosen was silent.

"You have little choice, Dr. Rosen. The fact is, she did take her own life." The Turk softened his voice. "So you will not be signing a false statement." He stopped briefly. "And if you refuse, I shall take her carcass with me and have my doctor write up the certificate. We shall then bury her in our fashion."

"I shall sign it," Dr. Rosen said quietly. "But I must insist that you have your men carry her to our cemetery so that she can be given a ritual burial."

In spite of herself, Deborah let out a sigh of relief. Tamar would be buried in the Bet Enav cemetery, next to their parents.

Hassan Bey gave the order. Then, "I want this area searched. We must find her sister, her son and any accomplices involved in this affair. I especially want David Larom and Michael Ben Hod. No one has seen them around for quite a while and I want them brought to me, dead or alive."

"To Caesarea?" someone asked.

There was a pause. "No, to Damascus," Hassan Bey said "There is little else for us to do in this area."

The sound of a car driving away followed his last words and Deborah could hear the soldiers scramble out of the garden, laughing and joking now that their commander was out of earshot. Their voices grew fainter and then there was silence.

Deborah pondered over Hassan Bey's last phrase. "Little to do in this area." Did it mean the Turkish army was retreating?

Still she dared not move. Crouching in the damp darkness, she stared numbly into space. Slowly the magnitude of what had happened hit her.

She did not know how long she sat there, but when she finally entered Raphael's house, it was evening. She glanced at the living room quickly, peered into his bedroom and walked slowly toward the bathroom door. It was shut and she pushed it open. In the fading dusk she could see the sparkling white metal tub with its four clawed legs. The elegant brass faucets, gleamed. The tiles, bordered in blue with a delicate, hand-painted yellow wheat stalk in the center, covered the walls and floor. They too were spotless, except for a splash of red that trailed along the floor toward her. Mesmerized by the sight, she turned and followed the trail. It grew fainter as it continued through the bedroom and even fainter as it twisted through the littered living room. It was barely visible by the time it reached the front door of the house. Only then did she relate the red path to her sister.

With trembling hands, Deborah opened the front door and ran out, ignoring the possibility that Turkish soldiers might still be around.

Once outside, she stared up at her parents' house. It looked as peaceful as ever and it was hard to equate its serenity with the dreadful events of the last few hours. Suddenly she felt lightheaded, almost gay. She had had a horrible nightmare and soon she would be inside her parents' house, which would bring her back to reality. Her family would be there, waiting for her, all standing around the dining room table, ready to sit down to supper. Impulsively she started running toward it.

She was almost at the front door when she was grabbed from behind and, a hand gagging her mouth, dragged into the hedges.

"You foolish girl," Mahmud whispered furiously. "Where do you think you're going?"

She shook herself free. "Home," she said defiantly. "Mama is waiting for me. They're all waiting for me."

"There's no one there," Mahmud whispered.

"No one?" She felt like a little girl.

"No one. But there is a baby. He's waiting for you. He needs care and you are the only one who can and should give it to him."

"Baby?" Deborah had not thought of Gidon since she handed him to Mahmud. She tried to remember when that was. It seemed to have happened in another lifetime, to someone else. "Where is he?" she asked dully. "How is he?"

"He's with Fatmi," Mahmud said angrily. "He is warm and he is fed but he needs his kin and you are the only one he has at this moment."

His tone surprised her.

"Come," he ordered. She followed obediently, relieved at being told what to do.

They were halfway up the mountain path leading to his village when Deborah stopped. Mahmud stopped too and they both looked back.

"I can't go with you," Deborah announced. "I must go back and attend to Tamar's funeral."

"You shall attend to nothing but the baby. You will see her funeral from up there," he said pointing to a jutting crag in the mountain which overlooked the Bet Enav cemetery.

"I have to be in Bet Enav," Deborah protested. "There are arrangements that have to be made. Who is going to say the prayers? Who is going to supervise everything? There should be flowers. Someone should speak up for her, explain who she was, what she did, praise her, pay tribute to her courage." She swallowed hard. "Someone must be there to cry for her."

"Someday you will be able to do it. This is not the time." He turned away angrily and continued walking.

Someday. She closed her eyes and repeated the word. "Someday."

Sitting beside Mahmud, Fatmi and Rafa, Deborah wept silently as they watched Tamar being buried. Her cries grew louder when she realized that Tamar's grave was next to the cemetery fence as prescribed by Jewish law. The rabbinate had decided that she was to be treated as a suicide victim and was not to be interred in the family plot. It was a pathetic sight, with only ten men in attendance. Other than Dr. Rosen, Deborah knew none of them. None of their friends from Bet Enav was there. None of the Nili group was present. The prayer for the dead was spoken in a muted voice. No one cried. At one point, Deborah dragged her eyes away from the ceremony and looked at the houses in the village. All the shutters were drawn. The streets were deserted.

Rafa began to play a quiet mournful tune on his flute. The music was a eulogy more eloquent than any words.

Someday, Deborah thought. Someday they would all weep for her sister. She would see to that.

"You'd better get down and huddle at the bottom of the carriage," Mahmud's voice brought Deborah back to the present. "And try to sleep. It will be a long journey."

"Are there still many Turkish soldiers in the area?" she asked.

"It's hard to tell. The Turkish army is moving north and we must not take any chances."

"What happens if the baby wakes?"

Without turning around, Mahmud handed her a small, brown bottle.

Deborah reached up and took it. Laudanum, a solution of opium in alcohol, was often used to calm the nerves. The baby signed contentedly in his sleep and Deborah realized that Fatmi had already given him some. Placing the small vial in an inner pocket of her dress, she looked over at Rafa who was sitting stiffly beside his grandfather, clutching the metal flute Raphael had given him.

She could not sleep and she watched the black night begin to brighten with a genial radiance. Raising herself slightly, Deborah peered over the side of the wagon. The sun rose slowly. It would be another scorching day, another day without relief, another day without rain. Another day with no hope.

They continued up the unpaved, twisted path. The cartwheels grew more noisy. Mahmud started lashing the donkey, who was having a hard time pulling the weight of his human cargo, and Deborah closed her eyes.

The cold edge of a bayonet, forcing her head up, woke her. An angry Turkish soldier was staring down at her.

"My daughter and my grandson," Mahmud said quietly.

"Is he blind too?" the Turk mocked.

"Allah's wish," Mahmud answered solemnly.

"Only for unworthy pigs." The soldier laughed.

"We are unworthy," Mahmud agreed readily.

"What's that?" The soldier's attention shifted from Deborah and the sleeping infant to Rafa. He was pointing at the flute.

"My grandson plays music on that."

"Play something," the soldier ordered.

Rafa obeyed and Deborah watched as the blind boy, flute against his quivering lips, tried to form a tune. Although attention had shifted from her and the baby, she felt nervous. The soldier's interest in Rafa was disquieting.

When Rafa finished playing, Mahmud got back into the driver's seat. Rafa climbed up beside him. The cart started moving, when the soldier suddenly turned and yanked the flute out of Rafa's hand. The boy reached out blindly, missed his footing and fell to the ground, still groping around, strange angry moans coming from his throat. The soldier began to laugh and started walking away. The sound of laughter identified the soldier's position and Rafa, dragging himself on the ground grabbed the soldier's foot and bit into it. The man cried out in pain and kicked the boy. Mahmud jumped down from his seat and flung himself over his grandson. The soldier laughed again but the look of hate was in his eyes. Deborah began to shake. It was her first encounter with pure, unadulterated loathing. It was a look that spoke of physical violence, even murder. The soldier could have killed Rafa at that moment.

Mahmud helped Rafa up and settled him back in the carriage. Then lashing the donkey furiously, he forced the mule to move on while he walked beside it.

Not even the sound of the grinding wheels could drown out Rafa's sobs.

Sonya's sanatorium was halfway up Mount Carmel. Anyone unfamiliar with the area would not have known it was there. An overgrown path off the main road, it appeared to be no more than a dirt road leading nowhere. Mahmud turned into it and after an unusually long ride, they came to a gravel path with colorful flowers planted along the sides. Night had fallen and small fire lanterns lit the way. Finally a large, sprawling two-storied yellow house with slanted red-tiled roof appeared. The green shutters were shut and the house itself was in total darkness. Except for a muted light hanging over the doorway, the place looked deserted. For a minute, Deborah panicked. There was no way to let anyone know she was coming and it never occurred to her that no one would be there.

As the cart came to a stop, the front door opened and Sonya appeared, followed by a young girl dressed in white. They both looked somber. Deborah realized that they had watched them approach to make sure who they were before coming out. Even the sanatorium was not without fear of the Turks. Deborah had visited Sonya and Misha many times over the years and she loved them both. Now, handing Gidon over to a white-clad young nurse, she wished she had not come. It brought back too many memories. She wanted to be home, in Bet Enav, where she could wait for David and Michael to return. It had been a mistake to leave Bet Enav. They would not know where to find her and their reunion would be delayed. Even Raphael would not know where to look for her. But most important, she wanted to be the one to tell them the sad news of Tamar's death.

"The baby is pale." The young nurse sounded scared.

"He's been given some opium," Deborah said.

"Opium!" the young woman gasped.

"It's all right," Sonya said firmly. "It won't harm him. Just let him sleep it off."

"What about food?" the nurse asked.

"He won't starve. He'll just be very hungry when he wakes, so have some warm milk ready for him." Then Sonya turned to Deborah. "And you, my young princess, are to have a bath and some tea with honey." She looked over at Mahmud and Rafa. "May I give you some food?"

Mahmud salaamed and shook his head. "We shall spend the night at the harbor and leave in the morning."

"No need to go down there. There is a room in the back of the house." She looked over at Rafa. "That child looks exhausted."

"We must leave now," Mahmud said firmly. "I shall take care of my grandson." He led Rafa to the cart.

Deborah put her hand on Sonya's arm, restraining her. She knew Mahmud's attitude toward doctors. She walked over to him.

"You must be near the house when David, Michael and Raphael come back. Since I might not be there, I want them to hear the news of Tamar from you." Her voice cracked with emotion.

He looked at her for a long time and she knew that he wanted to reach out and touch her. Instead, he turned the cart around and headed down the driveway. Deborah ran after them and, catching up with them, she hugged Rafa. "I love you and you shall have a more beautiful flute than the one they took away from you. I swear it."

He did not react. No flute would ever replace the one Raphael had given him and she knew it.

They watched the cart until it was out of sight. Taking Deborah by the hand, Sonya led her toward the house.

Sitting in the comfortable living room, covered by a light blanket, Deborah took in the room. It was a peaceful room, furnished with overstuffed armchairs and footstools. Flickering lights from small, shaded sconces cast soft shadows onto the book-lined walls. A large silver samovar filled with steaming tea stood on a small table in front of the sofa. Misha was writing at his desk. Sonya was sitting in a rocking chair, deep in thought. Prematurely white, her face was quite wrinkled and her blue eyes, although still alert, were dimmed, the lids drooping. The Neemans had been like family ever since Deborah could remember and were treated as such. But they were not family, she thought stubbornly. Her longing for Tamar, Raphael, David was overwhelming. And Michael. Yes, in a way he too had become family.

"You're a brave girl." Sonya's voice broke the silence.

"Me, brave?"

"You've been through a great deal and you've survived. That takes both courage and strength. The baby is also well. You did right by giving him to Mahmud."

"Who told you?"

"Avi."

"When was he here?"

"He got away right after leaving you."

"Where is he now?" Deborah asked, coldly.

"I believe he was heading for Beersheba. He's worried about David."

A strained silence followed.

"Deborah, I know you don't want to, but we must talk about Tamar. It's painful, but it will help if you do." She waited for her words to sink in. "What exactly happened?"

When Deborah did not answer, Sonya asked, "Is she dead?"

Deborah nodded.

"Did the Turks kill her?" She sounded clinical.

"No. She killed herself," Deborah said dully.

Sonya bowed her head and put her hand over her face. Misha walked over to his wife and stood quietly beside her.

"Where is David?" Misha asked.

"They've gone to the desert hoping to get through to the British."

"They?" Sonya looked up suspiciously.

"Michael Ben Hod was with him."

"Oh, that one," Sonya sneered.

Deborah threw her an angry look. "Why do you say it that way?"

"I don't know," Sonya retreated immediately. "It's just that somehow he's not one of us."

"One of us?" Deborah gasped. "What is that supposed to mean?"

"That was an unkind thing to say and unnecessary." Misha put a restraining hand on his wife's shoulder.

"I'm sorry. I just don't trust him." Sonya's voice trailed off in confusion.

"I do," Deborah said defiantly. "He's helped us almost from the start. Helped us valiantly and I trust him fully. We all do."

"She's right," Misha said firmly. He turned to Deborah. "When did they leave?"

"It's been quite a while now and I'm sick with worry. Is there any way we can find out where they are?"

Misha's face twisted with frustration. "Let me see what I can find out in the morning." He did not sound hopeful. "But for now, I think you've had a long difficult day and you should get some rest."

"I slept in the carriage on the way here and I don't want to sleep. I must think of some way to get to Raphael." She paused. "I wish I knew where he was," she finished helplessly.

"He'll be back soon." Misha said with authority.

"How do you know?"

"The British have finally invaded Palestine and are advancing toward Jerusalem. They're practically in control of the whole southern part of Palestine. In fact, the Turkish army is in retreat. They know it's the end and that it's just a matter of time."

"More than that." Sonya interjected. "There has been a statement by a British statesman named Balfour that commits the British to help establish a Jewish state." She paused briefly. "Nili's position about supporting the British against the Turks has been proven correct."

"How I wish Tamar had lived to hear this." Deborah bowed her head. "She wanted that victory."

"Raphael will be back and so will David and Michael." Misha tried to sound encouraging. "And sad as we all feel at Tamar's death, she did contribute to this victory. That should be some consolation."

Thoughts of the villagers of Bet Enav came back to Deborah. *Someday*—the word flashed through her mind. Someday they would all bow to Tamar's memory. The thought of their friends and neighbors, their behavior, their betrayal, seemed to energize her. "Good God, I've been cooped up in Mahmud's tent for so long, I have no idea about anything or anybody." She sat up. "What has happened to the Nili men?"

"You've had a long day and I feel you should get some rest." Sonya's voice took on a defensive note.

Deborah leaned toward her. "What are you hiding from me?" she asked impatiently.

"Nothing has been confirmed." The older woman started slowly. "Mostly it's rumors."

"Tell me." Deborah ordered.

"Two Jewish boys were hanged in Damascus."

"David? Michael?" Deborah's voice was barely audible.

"Well, as a matter of fact, we do know that one of them was Yossi. We don't know who the other one was."

"Who would know?" Deborah felt panic. "I must know."

"No one around here would know anything," Misha said.

Deborah stood up. "You did say that the Turkish army is in retreat. Doesn't that mean the roads are safe?"

"Not quite. The Turks are still very much around this area. They know they've been defeated in the Middle East, but the Germans are still fighting in Europe and the Turks haven't given up completely," Misha said.

"Can I hire a carriage?"

"When the time comes, I'll get you one," Misha said

"I want to be on the next one going to Bet Enav," Deborah said, fully composed. "Gidon and I have to get home."

"I shall decide when you go," Misha said authoritatively. Deborah was too tired to argue.

"Even when you go, you should leave the baby here," Sonya suggested. "It's too much travel for him."

Deborah looked at her with amazement. "Leave Gidon? He's all I've got. I'm all he's got. I could never leave him."

She turned quickly and left the room.

"She's not just that beautiful child anymore," Sonya said, watching Deborah leave.

"No. That is a grown woman with an iron will," Misha concurred.

# CHAPTER
# TWENTY-ONE

I T was weeks before Misha would allow Deborah to go back to Bet Enav. She was weak and exhausted and both he and Sonya felt she needed time to recover from the shock of Tamar's death. Also, word had reached them that numerous arrests had been made in Bet Enav and other villages from which Nili members were recruited. Many of the people arrested were tortured in an effort to find out who was involved in the group and what their actions consisted of. Others were detained and sent to prisons in Damascus.

Deborah felt she could cope with her neighbors and was anxious to leave, but winter set in, making the trip impossible. Torrential rains raged through the mountains, washing away all the roads surrounding the sanitarium.

The rain was a blessing to the country, but the gloomy weather plunged Deborah into even greater depression. When not attending to Gidon, she would stand at the window, staring at the raging sea far below, watching the ships moving slowly through the white foaming waters.

Waiting for news about what was happening around the country was the most difficult part of Deborah's stay with the Neemans. The occasional Arab vendor passing through would give them a glimpse into the situation around the northern part of Palestine still under Turkish domination, but they dared not press him for specifics. Certainly no one asked about the fate of the Jewish prisoners or the identity of the Jew who was hanged with Yossi in Damascus.

Deborah felt pangs of conscience about the innocent people taken prisoner by the Turks, but her concern for them was overshadowed by her feelings for the boys who did work for Nili and her desperate need to know if the second man hanged was David or Michael. She was terrified at the thought that one of them might be David. She was, however, equally upset at the idea that it might be Michael. In a way, she came to accept that she loved both of them. Loved them differently, but loved them nevertheless. She was David's wife. She wanted to spend her life with him, bear his children, grow old beside him. But she cared deeply for Michael, worried about him and prayed for his safety.

Her days and nights revolved around thoughts of David and Michael and she would try to understand what had driven them and her family to this point, where they were hunted, shunned and despised. When these thoughts came to her, she would force herself to remember her childhood, her family, their love, their hopes, their ultimate goals. A homeland, a struggle for security for their people, a haven for the displaced. It meant little in the face of the disaster she was living through.

Gidon was her only reason for going on. She had to survive for his sake. She had to carve out a future for him in Bet Enav. She had to get back. Once there, she could begin to plan their future.

It was mid-December before Deborah finally left Haifa. General Allenby had conquered the southern part of Palestine and entered Jerusalem. The Turks were in total disarray, moving northward in an effort to regroup. Their hatred for the Jews had not abated but the Nili group and the Danzigers in particular were no longer a priority. A woman traveling with a baby was not likely to attract their attention. Misha was still against her leaving, but she was adamant.

Deborah sat in the back of the covered carriage, staring at the rain-drenched countryside with a sinking heart. Swamps, which had been dried up over the years, had refilled. Small villages that had begun to thrive before the war were gone. Trees planted along the side of the road had been uprooted. Her beloved land was desolate. She turned her head away when they passed Raphael's laboratory. The structure of the building was still there, but it now appeared a lonely monument to what had once been a thriving experimental farm.

Reaching the road leading to Bet Enav, it became clear that the carriage could not maneuver the curved road. The driver left her off at the entrance to the Danziger vineyard.

With Gidon tucked under her oversized canvas raincape, Deborah entered the vineyard and started the trek toward Bet Enav on foot.

The storm grew worse and she felt the weight of the baby in her arms. Yet, as she walked, she found the familiar surroundings soothing. This small patch of land belonged to them and she would make it thrive, make it flourish again. She hastened her steps. All she wanted was to be home, where Fatmi and Mahmud would be waiting for her.

It was evening by the time she caught a glimpse of their house, outlined against the darkening skyline. A sigh of relief escaped her. She was finally home. The house was her haven. No harm could come to her once she was there. She could already feel warmth coming from the stove in the kitchen. She would hand Gidon to Fatmi and she herself would go to her room and sleep in her bed. They would be safe.

The main street of Bet Enav had been washed away by the rain and it was deserted. She could see flickering lights coming up from some of the houses, but they seemed strangely faint. It made her uncomfortable. She rushed on. As she drew closer to the house, she noted that all the upper floor windows were shuttered and the lantern that was always lit on the side of the porch was out. That was as it should be, she decided. No one knew she was coming. Still, a gnawing feeling of doubt began to rise within her. The house, although completely intact, looked abandoned.

The front gate creaked as she pushed it open. By this time completely drenched, she rushed up the front steps and pulled at the handle of the front door. It was locked. Her heart sank. The front door of the Danziger house was never locked.

It was growing dark and she was more conscious of how heavy the baby was as she raced toward the back of the house. Passing the long conservatory windows, she caught a glimpse of boarded windows. One unbroken window-pane was open.

Like the front gate, the kitchen door creaked as she pushed it open. As her eyes adjusted to the semidarkness she gasped in dismay. Shattered glass, bits of Limoges cups and saucers, overturned pots and pans, rags that had once been her mother's fine linen napkins, were scattered on the floor. The large wooden table had been hacked up, the chairs smashed.

Dazed, she picked her way through the debris and walked to the front hall. The large grandfather clock was gone. All the sconces were ripped out, leaving gaping, ugly holes in the walls. Most of the tiles had been dug up, as though the plunderers had looked for hidden treasures beneath them. She walked into the living room. It too had been stripped of most furnishings, except for a large sofa and two oversized armchairs, which were to heavy to have been moved. She could see her mother's piano still standing in the alcove of the conservatory. It looked naked without its embroidered silk covering.

A cold wind drifted through the room. She turned and started up to her mother's bedroom. She remembered noting the upstairs windows were shuttered and she hoped it would be warmer there.

In contrast to the downstairs, someone had made an effort to put the bedroom in order. Standing in the doorway, she noted that the bedspread had been thrown over the bed. An armchair had been righted, the lamp, its shade askew, rested against the wall. Even the pictures had been rehung. Whoever had tried to put the room in order had been in a great hurry to depart. She started to walk in and was stopped by a putrid odor. For a brief moment she felt faint, unable to understand what had caused the stench. It dawned on her slowly. This was the room in which Tamar had been tortured and the overpowering stench was the odor of death.

The baby began to cry and Deborah wondered if the vile smell had affected him as well. She pressed his head close to her breast, hoping to snuff it out with her own body odor. He pushed his head away and his cries grew louder. He sounded as though he were in pain. She rushed out of the room, slamming the door behind her and ran back to the living room, murmuring words of endearment into the baby's ear in an effort to calm him down. The stench followed her into the living room. Now that she was conscious of it, it seemed to be everywhere.

The baby did not stop crying and she grew worried. It was unlike Gidon to cry so helplessly, and she wondered if he were ill.

Placing Gidon on the sofa, she began singing softly to him while patting him on the small of his back. His crying turned to soft moaning and he finally fell asleep. She lay down beside him and tried to gather her thoughts. She had to reach Mahmud and Fatmi. Fatmi would know what to do. She also had to find some food for the baby and somehow heat the house. She needed some workmen to start with repairs. She tried to bridge the gap between thoughts and actions. The problems were insurmountable and she was exhausted. It was all too much and she could not do it alone. She wanted Tamar. She needed her family. She longed for the past. The tears finally came and she did not wipe them away. She had so much to cry for.

The rattling of the conservatory windows woke her. It was still raining out, but the wind had died down. She sat up and listened. Someone was tapping at the window.

She threw a look at Gidon. He was asleep. She edged toward the window, then heard a sound, like a groan of pain. Someone was lying outside the window. With great care she leaned out and stared down. It was Michael.

For one brief moment she felt unbearable joy, which was replaced immediately with fear for David. She ran to open the conservatory door.

Michael was lying near the wall of the house. He was deathly pale. As she approached him, he struggled to sit up.

She knelt down beside him. The gash in his forehead was deep and blood was dripping onto his shirt.

"Michael," she whispered, and putting her arm under his shoulder she helped him into a sitting position.

"Could you get me some water?" His voice was barely audible.

"Let me help you into the house."

"No. I can't stay here. Just give me some water and I'll be on my way." He sounded frantic.

"What are you talking about?" she asked, her voice rising.

"Speak quietly and do as I say. They're all after me."

"Who is after you? The Turks are nowhere around."

"Don't argue. I must hide."

"You're not going anywhere, certainly not in this condition or while this weather persists." She stood up. "Let me just put the baby in a safer place and I'll be back."

She reentered the house. Gidon was still asleep.

Michael was struggling to stand up when she came out. "I didn't know anyone was here. Least of all you." He was staring at her as he would a stranger.

"Michael, what's the matter with you? What happened?"

He started to move away but he was unsteady on his feet as he sat down in the mud.

"I know where you can hide," she said.

He looked up at her helplessly.

"Come." She helped him up and led him toward the storage shelter.

It was difficult getting him down the road, but once settled she bandaged his head and wiped the blood from his clothes. When the task was done and Michael was resting on the cold ground, Deborah sat down a few meters away and observed him.

Some color had come back to his cheeks but his face was drawn, his mouth tightly shut, his eye sockets appeared like sunken holes in the head of a skeleton. He was breathing steadily and she assumed he was asleep.

"David is dead." His lips seemed not to move as he spoke and for a minute she thought she imagined the words.

Michael opened his eyes. "Did you hear me? David is dead."

The blood drained from her head and she felt faint. She wanted to speak, but no words came.

"He was killed by a band of Bedouins."

"Where?"

"I don't know exactly where. We were on our camels, moving toward the British lines, when they came swooping down on us."

Deborah could not relate to what he was saying. David, her love, her husband, the man she was going to spend the rest of her life with, was no more. She would never see him again. Her mind rejected the idea.

"David is dead." She mouthed the words, as though she were speaking a foreign tongue. "David is dead." She repeated slowly and suddenly the full impact of what the words meant struck her. For a minute her head felt light. A soft laughter gurgled up in her throat which turned into a stifled scream. She felt herself sinking into an abyss and she lowered herself to the ground. Her body began to shake uncontrollably.

When she could cry no more, she sat up and leaned her head against the wall and stared at the ceiling.

"Deborah, I am sorry to be the one to bring you this terrible news." His voice was low and hoarse with emotion. "And you've got to believe me when I say I wish it were me instead of him. He had so much to live for. He was so brilliant, so full of life. He was a leader of men and should not have died so young. He was needed. Not only by you, but by the whole Jewish community." His voice broke. "I wish it were me, I swear, I wish it were me."

"Michael, stop!" she muttered and looked over at him. His face came into focus slowly. "How did you escape?"

"They hit him first and he fell, then they hit me. I must have fainted and they probably assumed I was dead. When I woke, which could not have been more than minutes later, David was gone."

"How do you know it was only minutes?" She was suddenly fully alert and knew she sounded like an interrogator. She regretted her tone but she could not help herself.

"The dust from the Bedouins' horses could still be seen in the distance and I saw a small boy limping away from where we were attacked. He had David's shoes strapped around his neck."

Deborah listened carefully and tried to visualize the scene he was describing.

"You do believe me, don't you?" he asked and he sounded desperate.

"And what happened then?" she continued, ignoring his question.

"I must have passed out again and when I next woke, some Allied soldiers were carrying me to their van." His eyes met hers. "You do believe me, don't you?" he repeated, sounding frantic.

"Is that head wound the one they gave you?" she asked, not quite ready to give him an answer.

"The British doctors tended that. As soon as I could travel again, I joined the troops who were heading toward Beersheba. But they were moving too slowly, so I took a shortcut through the villages and realized the Turks were on a mad rampage. I thought I'd find refuge with my old friends . . ." His face grew flushed, "They would not help me. They said the Turks were looking for David and me and they were not willing to endanger their position. I didn't blame them. But when I told them about David, they actually turned on me and accused me of killing him. We got into a fight and Reb, of all people, hit me with the butt of his gun. I barely escaped their vengeance." A wry, sad smile crossed his lips. "I don't believe I ever ran as fast. It was as though my fury and humiliation gave me wings."

Deborah never took her eyes off him as he spoke. Reb had been one of Michael's closest friends before he joined Nili.

"What made them think you killed David?"

"Apparently everyone does," he said slowly. "Avi, as I understand it, is also looking for me."

"Good God! Why would anybody accuse you of killing David?" she found herself screaming "Why?"

"God only knows. Mass hysteria? Rage at Nili and the feeling that we're to blame for the way the Turks treated the Jews? They have to vent their anger on somebody. I'm the outsider, remember? And it seems that everyone knew David and I didn't get along."

She looked down at Michael. He was holding his head in his hands and his shoulders were heaving with quiet sobs. Her heart went out to him and she knew without a doubt that he had not killed David. Michael was not a killer.

"Do you believe me?" she heard Michael ask again.

"Yes, I do," she said, and she meant it. "And now I think you should come into the house and get a good night's sleep."

"That would be stupid. If word got out that I was around, every man, woman and child would come after me. They're out for blood." He stopped. "And frankly, I don't think you have any business being here either."

"I'm going back to the house," she said feeling completely drained. "Gidon is alone and he wasn't feeling well. I'll come by later with some food." She started toward the opening of the shelter.

"Where is Tamar?" Michael asked.

She stopped, horrified at the thought that he did not know.

"She's dead," she said with her back to him. She heard him gasp and turned around. He was looking at her and the expression on his face was grotesque, his eyes were glassy and his arms were raised over his head, as though surrendering to an enemy. His shoulders began to shake and she wondered if he were going to burst out crying.

"How?" he whispered.

"The Turks found out about Nili."

"Tamar, David, Nili, all dead." He shook his head in bewilderment. *"The eternity of Israel shall not lie* is a lie after all."

The phrase shook her. "The eternity of Israel does *not* lie," she screamed. "Don't you ever say that again. Ever."

She ran out of the shelter and did not stop until she reached the steps leading to the house. Before entering, she took a deep breath, trying to control her hysteria and looked up at the darkened sky. "God," she whispered helplessly. "God, please help us."

Michael was gone when Deborah came back to the shelter the next morning. Carrying Gidon in her arms, she had rushed over as soon as the baby woke. She needed to reassure him that she believed him.

Walking out of the shelter, she looked down the rain-drenched road. He was nowhere in sight and her heart went out to him. He was more alone than she was. He had no one. Not the Nili people and not even his own comrades.

In the days that followed Michael's departure, Deborah tried to make a life for herself and Gidon. It was an impossible task, made all the more difficult by the treatment accorded her by the villagers. They simply ignored her. It was as though she did not exist. She walked through the sparsely filled stalls in the market place, carrying Gidon in one arm and struggling with a string bag in the other. No one came forward to offer help. If a child whom she had taught in school smiled at her or tried to approach her, the mother would pull him away angrily, whispering words of reprimand. She pretended she did not care, but she cared deeply. These women had been her friends. Now they had each other and she had no one.

In her loneliness, she clung to the hope that David was not dead. Raphael's letter from London put all doubts of David's death to rest. It also confirmed her belief that Michael had told her the truth. Raphael had contacted the soldiers who had found Michael unconscious in the desert. He was badly hurt and near death and although they found no trace of David, it was clearly established that the Bedouins had been there.

Only then was she was able to start mourning David's death. She sank into deep melancholy, convinced that death was stalking her, circling about her with a ferocity and determination that she was powerless to fight. Where it would strike next, she did not know, but she waited for it almost impatiently. Her greatest fear was for Gidon, that he too would be taken from her. She guarded him like a tigress watching over her cub.

With a heavy heart, Deborah started putting the house in order. Within days after her return, Fatmi appeared and resumed working around the house. As in the past, she worked from early morning until late at night, saying little except what related to household chores. Mahmud, however, was nowhere around and Deborah gathered that he and Rafa had not returned after taking her and Gidon to Haifa. When Deborah pressed her for answers as to his whereabouts, the woman shook her head sadly, indicating she did not know, or she would raise her eyes to the skies, assuring her that Allah was watching over her husband and grandson and she had complete faith that He would take care of them.

Deborah worked long hours and it did not bother her. What she could not bear or escape from was the stench coming from her mother's room. It seemed to engulf the whole house, and much as she tried to air the room, the odor would not go away. It followed her wherever she went, even when shopping in the village. It more than anything kept alive the horror of what had happened to them.

As spring approached, Deborah planted some vegetables with Fatmi's help and Fatmi brought bits of food from the Arab villages for Gidon. He was all Deborah lived for. His survival motivated every one of her actions.

The war in Europe continued through the winter and spring, but the number of Turkish soldiers dwindled. The fear of them, though, was as great as ever, felt in every passerby. People walked around like ghosts, shoulders hunched, eyes downcast, their faces averted as if ashamed of their impotence. The village of Bet Enav was shrouded in sadness. It seemed to be dying, fading from existence, and there was no relief in sight.

The community was so completely spent that when Michael finally returned, they did not react. He walked through the main street of Bet Enav and no one took notice.

Deborah accepted his return without questions. He stayed in the shed behind the house and helped as best he could. The land had to be tended and he tried to recruit workers from the local inhabitants. But as much as they needed the work, the farmers from Bet Enav refused to work for Deborah. In desperation she was forced to hire Arab workers. It went against everything Michael ever believed in.

"It's wrong," he cried out the day Deborah made the suggestion.

"Wrong?"

"Morally, ethically, ideologically. We as Jews should not be employing Arabs to work our lands."

"Why?" She felt completely confused. "It's not that I don't want to hire Jews. But they won't work for me."

"Deborah, I don't know the answer. All I know is that if we are to build a Jewish homeland, it must be worked and cultivated by Jews. That's what Reb and his men are talking about. That's where the Danzigers and most of the Jews in Palestine differ."

"I've never met your Reb," Deborah said angrily. "But it seems to me that he's hardly someone you'd want to quote. If his behavior toward you when you needed help is any indication of his morality, spare me his teachings."

"Don't be so quick to judge him," Michael said. "In retrospect, his anger at me may have been justified. He wasn't judging me for David's death. He did not feel that I betrayed him when I joined the Turkish army. He felt I betrayed our cause when I joined Nili, that I became too much like the Danzigers." He paused briefly. "And here I am, doing exactly what Raphael Danziger would have done."

"And what would Reb do in my place?" Deborah asked feeling hurt.

"I don't know what he'd do. That's the difference between him and me. That's what makes him a leader."

"Well, we've got to survive and Arabs will be hired," she said defiantly.

Michael did hire the Arabs and that turned the indifference of the village to raging anger. Suddenly everyone was up in arms. They came storming to the house, demanding vengeance for David's death. Stones were constantly thrown at them and so they rarely left the house.

Spending all her time alone with Michael, Deborah's feelings started coming back. She fought them, but she was too lonely, too confused, too needy, to ignore his presence. He was always correct in his behavior toward her but occasionally she would find him staring at her with deep concern when he thought she did not notice. He would rush to help her carry a heavy pail or move a clumsy piece of wood. He even helped out with Gidon. She sensed his feelings about the baby, but he was quite tender with him and she was grateful. They rarely spoke. Nili was never mentioned. David was never mentioned, nor was Tamar. But Deborah knew that both Tamar and David were with them at all times and would always be. In a way, both she and Michael needed the ghosts and clung to their memory.

In April 1918, Gidon was one year old and Deborah suggested they take the child to the beach where Tamar and Thomas first met. On the way down, they tried to avoid the crowded streets, but someone saw them and started chanting "Murderer." A stone was thrown in their direction which missed Deborah by a hair. Michael grabbed Gidon from her arms and sped toward the house with Deborah following close behind.

Gidon was crying hysterically by the time they reached the house. Michael handed her the boy and stormed off. Deborah looked after Gidon, trying to calm the child. When Fatmi came out, Deborah handed Gidon to her and walked slowly toward Michael's shed. She found him throwing his meager belongings into a sack. His face was clouded over with anger.

"I've got to leave here," he said when she walked in. "They'll never stop accusing me of David's death and you shouldn't have to take it."

"Oh, stop this nonsense," she said. "You have nowhere to go and you know it."

He ignored her and continued packing. She walked over to him and grabbed a garment from his hand. He pulled away from her with great force and she lost her balance. He reached out to her and suddenly she was in his arms and his lips were pressing down on hers. She clung to him and she felt his tongue push into her mouth and she bit it hungrily. She felt ravenous with desire. She could feel him tearing at her clothes and she willingly slipped out of her dress.

She felt his hardness against her and she sank to the ground, pushing her lower body toward him. He was passionate in his lovemaking and she accepted him with every part of her being. Nothing mattered except that Michael was inside her. Their desire wiped out every cruel reality that they had lived through. When she finally felt his wetness between her legs, she pressed him closer, wanting to drink in every bit of his being. Finally spent, Michael buried his head in her shoulder. The sound of their breathing was the only one heard in the shed. Deborah came back to herself slowly, as a dreadful thought surfaced. She had made love to her husband's murderer.

"I didn't do it," Michael whispered, as though reading her mind.

"Oh, Michael, I know you didn't," she said, throwing her arms protectively around his shoulders.

"But for one minute, it did cross your mind," he whispered in despair.

She pushed his face away from hers and stared at him. "I did think it but I swear to you I believe you are innocent. I know you're innocent."

She sensed that he did not believe her and she wanted desperately to prove her sincerity.

"Michael, will you marry me?" she said and was surprised at her question but not displeased.

"Oh, my God," he murmured. "Oh, my God."

"I can think of worse things happening to you." She tried to mock him, but she was hurt and puzzled by his attitude. "You don't have to, you know."

"I want to marry you." He could barely say the words and he leaned over and kissed her tenderly on the lips.

"I would like to have Raphael at the wedding," she said, stroking his cheek. "Would you mind if we waited until he returned?"

"No." He continued kissing her forehead and fondling her hair. "There is one request I must also make."

She looked up at him, smiling.

"You must give up Gidon."

"To whom?" she laughed, convinced he was joking.

"To his father."

"Fredrick?" She remembered suspecting once that Michael knew the true identity of Gidon's father, but pretended she did not.

"Thomas Hardwick," he said soberly.

She withdrew from his embrace and pushed herself to the corner of the shed, holding her knees to her chest.

"I shall never give him up," she said. "He's mine now. He's all I've got."

Michael stared at her and said nothing.

"Besides, why would Thomas Hardwick want him? Does he even know he exists?"

"He knows all about Gidon. As a matter of fact, the last time I saw him, just before David and I set out for the desert, I told him about the baby. He nearly jumped out of his skin with joy. He wanted to rush down and see Tamar and his son, but he was committed to a military operation that could not be put off." He pressed his hands to his brow. "I was going to tell Tamar about Thomas the minute I came back. Remember? You were playing with the baby and she came out. But she went at me with her sarcasm, her innuendos and accusations. Then David came by . . ." He stopped. "Oh, it all became too much and events took over."

"Poor Tamar. If only you knew how she lived for the day that she could show Gidon to his father." She began to cry.

"So you see, Thomas would be thrilled to have their child. I swear to you, he would."

"Never," she mumbled through her tears. "Never."

"But someday you will have children of your own."

"I might, but even if I do, I shall always look upon him as my first born."

The subject of marriage was never mentioned again.

Michael left shortly thereafter. Although she missed him, she knew that she could never give up Tamar's baby.

In October 1818 the Ottoman Empire signed an armistice agreement. Germany surrendered to the Allies one month later. The bloodiest war fought by modern man had ended. The victorious Allies occupied the whole of Palestine and although there was jubilation throughout the country, the one concrete victory for the Jews was the Balfour Declaration, which promised them a homeland. Their eyes turned to the British Empire for help in achieving that goal.

Bet Enav emptied out. The remaining community was too exhausted to feel the full joy of victory. The land had been neglected for too long and remained barren as it had been during the last years of the war.

Deborah too, was depleted, but she persevered. She had lost everything and everyone but somehow she managed to pick up the pieces of her former life. Arabs continued to work the land, and she watched over Gidon. He was the only human being she cared about except for Raphael. She waited for her brother's return, hopeful that he would bring them some joy and give her strength to continue.

And then Michael returned.

She was out in the field that day when she saw him walk toward her.

He stopped a few paces away from her. "May I stay?" he asked.

She nodded. She was happy he was back.

He looked around at the small progress she had made. "You're doing well for a woman alone."

"I have help from my Arab neighbors."

He did not react. "How is Gidon?" he asked instead.

"Extraordinary," she said with motherly pride.

"Deborah, I'm sorry to tell you, but you'll have to give him up."

She started to laugh, except that something in his tone made the sound stick in her throat.

"It's out of the question." She got the words out with difficulty.

"Abed has vowed to kill him."

"Abed? Rafa's father?"

"An eye for an eye," Michael said soberly. "Rafa was murdered by a Turk when Mahmud was driving back from Haifa. Apparently you had an encounter with him and Rafa hurt him. He was waiting for them on the return trip. By then he also realized who you were, so it was double vengeance. He shot Rafa and took Mahmud prisoner."

Deborah felt the circle of death grow tighter around her.

"Where is Mahmud now?" she whispered.

"I found him in one of the Turkish prison camps up North and I brought him back to his village. He's a broken man. Aside from witnessing Rafa's death, he was badly tortured by the Turks."

"Will he be all right?"

"He'll never be the same again, but to his credit, he never told the Turks the truth about your identity."

"Oh, the poor man." The pain was almost unbearable.

"But all of that is beside the point. Abed somehow got wind of Rafa's death and he's determined to kill Gidon. He's always hated the Danzigers and he feels justified in his plan."

"Gidon," Deborah screamed and started running toward the house. Death was staring down at her. Death was still following her around. It had not completed its work.

*Part II*

# CHAPTER
# TWENTY-TWO

T HOMAS Hardwick loosened his tie and sat back in the worn, upholstered armchair at the Fast Hotel, the most prestigious in Jerusalem.
He sipped his drink slowly as his eyes wandered around the room
aimlessly. He had had too many drinks and he was having a hard time focusing
on specific objects.

"Your move," Owen Cartwright said, looking up from the chessboard
placed between them.

Thomas was roused from his reverie. He had forgotten the chess game he
had been involved in.

"Forgive me, old chap, but I'm tired and I can't concentrate."

"You're a sore loser," Cartwright chided. "Why, I expect that within three
moves it'll be checkmate and you know it."

Thomas smiled wryly. "I concede."

"Did you know it, or are you pretending to be a good sport?"

Thomas sat up, stared at the board for a moment and moved a pawn.

"What an utterly ridiculous move!" Cartwright was annoyed.

"Ridiculous? Not at all. You just didn't expect it." He took another sip of
his drink. "The trouble with you, Owen, is that you tend to underestimate
your opponent. You're smart, smarter than most, but not all."

"Meaning you're smarter than I am?"

"Yes, as a matter of fact, I am smarter than you are. But you're shrewder."
He stared at the handsome man sitting opposite him. Maj. Owen Cartwright
was the best that British Intelligence had produced, an excellent combination
of poise and breeding; well-informed with an uncanny ability to gather information and apply it properly, as well as improperly, when necessary. He was
like a chameleon who could blend into any situation and make it work for him.
His talents were not lost on his superiors, and his career in British Intelligence
was bright. But he was flawed. Just beneath the shock of black hair, brown eyes,
and pencil-thin mustache was a weak mouth. The heavy, protruding lower lip
spoiled the image of British manhood.

"Shrewder?" Owen coaxed Thomas, who had obviously lost his train of thought.

"And being shrewder, you'll go much further than I will."

"Balderdash. Shrewdness has nothing to do with it. The trouble with you is you're a sentimental fool," Owen Cartwright said angrily. "Here you are, the man responsible for one of the most brilliant feats of the war in this area. You manipulated your Arabs into capturing one of the most vital strongholds, which probably hastened the end of this war. Some would even credit you with the toppling of the four-hundred-year rule of the Ottoman Empire. Yet you're sitting here eating your innards out because blood had to be shed." His impatience mingled with envy was hardly disguised.

"I didn't manipulate, Owen, and they're not *my* Arabs. It's thoughts like that which make it impossible for me to go on. You and the likes of you have totally misunderstood my feelings and attitudes. You keep looking for the divisiveness amongst them. I've tried to find a unifying point to which they could all rally." He was pale with anger. "It's the likes of you who will keep the whole Arab world in a state of subjugation to the whims of outsiders."

"Take it easy, Thomas," Owen said soothingly. "I was actually giving you a compliment. And the truth is that your campaign was brilliant and frankly, bloody as it was, the Turks got what was coming to them."

"Stop it," Thomas hissed through clenched teeth. "Stop it, you damn fool. No one deserves to die the way those men died. No one, do you hear?"

In spite of his firm tone, he seemed to shrink as he spoke. Putting his hand over his eyes, he appeared to want to hide from the words of his companion. "It was a bloody massacre," he continued hoarsely. The vision of beheaded men, limbless corpses mutilated beyond recognition, with protruding eyes unable to disguise their agony as the end came, appeared before him.

"So why did you do it?" Owen egged him on, knowing full well that Thomas's failure earlier in the year to blow up a railway crossing in Palestine had forced him to push his men to that final battle.

"For England." Thomas regained his composure and looked down at the chessboard. "Your move."

They played on in silence, although Owen grew more tense as he began to lose.

"Have you walked around Jerusalem since we've entered the city?" Owen asked suddenly.

"I went to some of the mosques. Quite beautiful, I must say. The churches are in a dreadful state of disrepair, though."

"How about the Jewish quarter? You must have gone there." The sarcasm was evident.

"Yes, as a matter of fact. Bloody shame to have people living in such poverty."

"The Arabs don't have it much better," Cartwright said with annoyance.

"I was not comparing," Thomas answered.

"Do you really believe the Jews deserve more than the Arabs?"

"Not for a minute. I believe both have a right to better living conditions. The only thing is that the Jews here have a dream. They have a goal. They know what they want. The Arabs don't. And a people with an unrequited dream are probably more aware of their condition."

"Nonsense. The Jews don't belong here. They should go back where they came from."

"Where's that?" Thomas asked. "To some Polish town where they're unwanted, hounded, abused, their women and children . . ."

"They're trespassers here." Owen would not let him finish.

"Read your Bible, Cartwright."

Owen Cartwright stared at Thomas for a long minute. "You baffle me. You organize the Arabs, try to infuse a sense of pride in them and then you turn around and say that another people should usurp their land because of some biblical fairy tales."

"Obviously there are people in England who don't see them as biblical fairy tales," Thomas said dryly.

"That Balfour should be put up against the wall and shot," Owen snapped. "It certainly has put a dreadful thorn in all the plans that had been worked out with the various Arab leaders."

"Leaders!" Thomas laughed briefly. "I love my desert companions, love them dearly, but you could hardly refer to them as leaders, men who can sit down and say they are speaking for a whole people." He stopped and stared at Owen for a long moment. "But as I said, it fits in with your plans. It leaves lots of room for maneuvering. You thrive on Arab disunity. I loathe it."

Owen Cartwright sucked in his breath in an effort to control himself. "So what happens now?"

"I don't know." Thomas raised his hand to the passing waiter, indicating he wanted another drink. "And frankly, at this point, I don't care. I've asked Allenby to sign my transfer order. I'm going back to England, settle down for a while and write."

"And leave all your loved ones here to wander through the desert on their own?" Now the sarcasm was blatant, almost insulting. "And I'm not just talking about the masses, I'm talking about individuals."

Thomas's eyes blazed for a moment but before he could reply, the waiter came over with the drink. Thomas downed it in one gulp.

"For someone who had taken up most of the Moslem habits, I thought you'd given up alcohol." Cartwright was gloating and made no effort to hide it.

Thomas's face broke into a smile. "That's what I meant before, Owen. You're obvious, too obvious. You're delighted I'm going. You'll have a field day with the masses once I'm gone. As for the individuals, they're my friends and will stay my friends." He stared at his empty glass. "As for my drinking, I did stop for a while. And even now I wouldn't drink in their presence, but there are times when alcohol comes in handy. It helps diffuse reality."

Suddenly he doubled over and his hand gripped the arms of his chair. He had consumed his drinks too quickly and for a minute he blacked out.

Cartwright stood up and, coming around, leaned over Thomas. "Anything wrong?"

At that moment, Michael was standing in the doorway to the small bar. He scanned the room looking for Thomas. He recognized Owen Cartwright, who was leaning over someone and he was about to look away when the crouching man sat up. Michael was shocked at the change that had taken place in Thomas. He had not seen him in two years, but he did not appear to be the arrogant camel-rider in his flowing white robes who had led the Arabs through victorious battles. Instead, he saw an emaciated man whose hair was thinning and growing gray. His shoulders were stooped and his loose jacket was unpressed. Michael thought of the strange trip he had taken with Tamar and Thomas, when he had helped them leave Turkey. He had hated Thomas then, resented Tamar's devotion to him, was jealous of him for having Tamar's love. Since that time, he had grown to understand Thomas, had even begun to respect him. He was especially moved when they last met and he told him about Gidon. The pure, unadulterated joy, the love that came through when asking about his son embarrassed Michael. The great Thomas Hardwick, on the eve of one of his most important campaigns, stood blubbering about his baby. Still Michael resented him, resented his politics, and secretly envied the Arabs for having someone like Thomas on their side.

As these thoughts crossed Michael's mind, he saw Owen Cartwright return to his seat and he could not help but marvel at the contrast between these two British officers. Thomas Hardwick had achieved fame and glory on the battlefield as well as in the diplomatic arena, whereas Owen Cartwright, although known for victories on the battlefield, was a failure in the diplomatic area. Looking at them now, Thomas seemed like the loser while Owen appeared the winner.

Aware that he could no longer put off the encounter, Michael walked toward their table and Thomas caught sight of him.

"Why, Mr. Ben Hod." Thomas stood up quickly.

As they shook hands, Thomas searched Michael's face anxiously, but Michael's expression remained impassive. Thomas then turned and introduced him to Owen.

Owen pretended not to see Michael's outstretched hand and looked around for the waiter. He barely acknowledged the introduction.

Annoyed, Thomas stared down at the chessboard. Then, as though it were an afterthought, he reached over and moved one of the pieces.

"Checkmate," he said quietly and, standing up he took Michael by the arm, and moved toward the terrace of the hotel.

"Would you like a drink?" Thomas asked.

"No, thank you." Michael walked briskly toward the railing of the terrace and stared at the wall surrounding the old part of Jerusalem. He knew the sight well, but its beauty never ceased to fill him with awe.

It was dusk and the air was filled with the sounds of a day coming to an end. Church bells and chimes could be heard in the distance and were transmitted by the soft breeze which fluttered over the tops of the ancient buildings below the terrace of the hotel. It had rained earlier, and the air was clear. A strange lavender mist hovered over the area, causing the large, crude stones to glisten.

"It's that confounded color that staggers me every time," Thomas murmured, obviously overcome by the sight. "I can never decide if it's the setting sun that gives it that strange hue or the color of the stone."

"Probably a combination of both," Michael answered.

They stood silently next to each other.

"Was it as brutal as I've heard?" Thomas broke the silence and Michael understood that his thoughts were in Bet Enav.

"From what I understand, no human being could have stood it as long as she did without breaking," Michael answered.

"May her soul rest in peace," Thomas whispered.

"It will be a while before that happens. A good number of people will have to repent before she ever rests."

"How is her family?" Thomas asked haltingly.

"Well, you know Raphael was killed in a plane crash over the channel."

"Yes, we got word of his death a few days ago."

"The timing seems rather bizarre, wouldn't you say?"

"Bizarre?"

"To die while being flown to the peace conference in a British plane to plead our cause before the international community?" Michael's voice rose slightly.

"The pilot was killed as well," Thomas said evenly.

"Indeed." Michael looked over at his companion for the first time. "I suppose that proves it was an accident."

"I should say so."

Michael grimaced. The answer did not satisfy him.

"And how is Mrs. Larom?" Thomas decided to ignore Michael's statement.

"Considering she's lost the three most important people in her life, she's bearing up remarkably well."

"Three?"

"Her sister, her husband and now her brother."

"Oh, the poor girl." Thomas was genuinely distressed. "Is there anything I can do for her? Where is she?"

"She's here in Jerusalem with the baby."

Thomas's impersonal façade broke. "How is he?" he asked softly.

"He's a robust, healthy, happy child who is far too pampered by his aunt, but that can't be helped."

"Can I see them?"

"More than that. She has come to give you the baby, if you'll have him."

Thomas gasped. "Would she really give him up?"

"She has little choice. Someone wants that baby dead. In fact, she would have come sooner. But traveling was dangerous even though the armistice has been signed. The Turks are not taking their defeat graciously and every so often they forget that they are no longer the great Ottoman Empire. The Arabs, in all the confusion, believe they are now running the show and are behaving accordingly."

The bitterness in Michael's voice did not escape Thomas, but his excitement about seeing his son overshadowed everything.

"When can I see him?"

"She has offered to bring him here at your convenience. The point is, she has certain conditions, which she will discuss with you."

"Of course," Thomas answered quickly. "I will need some time to work it out." He stopped and his voice grew soft. "What does he look like?"

Michael's face cracked into a twisted smile. "There is no doubt as to who his parents are."

"Where are they staying?" Thomas was trying to hide his concern. Living conditions in the Jewish quarter of Jerusalem were terrible. Diphtheria and other infectious diseases were rampant among the inhabitants there, and though he had tried to convince the British medical staff to tend to them, his efforts were rebuffed. The thought that his son might be exposed to disease upset him.

"Don't worry, your son is staying with friends of Deborah's outside the walled city," Michael answered through clenched teeth. "Fatmi, the Danzigers' maid, is with them and I can assure you that he's being properly cared for." He threw a sideways look at Thomas. "Like all Englishmen, you believe that only the western world knows how to care for their own. We, in our primitive way, do quite well, you know."

"I did not mean to offend," Thomas replied quickly. "Frankly, I think it's quite remarkable how the Jewish quarter does manage, in spite of everything, especially with their young."

"We have a stake in our youth," Michael answered simply.

"When will I be able to see them?"

"She's here for the sole purpose of seeing you and will wait to hear from you."

"I shall have my driver pick her up at one o'clock tomorrow."

Michael scribbled Deborah's address down on a piece of paper and handed it to Thomas. "I'll tell her to expect your driver," he said.

When Deborah first appeared in the restaurant, Thomas did not recognize her. Along with everyone else in the room, he turned to stare at the extraordinarily beautiful, elegant woman who was standing in the doorway. Dressed in a simple black walking suit with only a hint of white lace at the collar, her dark hair pulled tightly back into a bun, her large, deep-set eyes coolly scanning the room, she looked like a biblical vision come to life. Her expression was stony until she caught sight of Thomas. Recognition caused her to smile and her features softened. Thomas stood up and rushed toward her. It was Tamar's smile.

Leading her to his table at the far corner of the room, they passed Owen Cartwright's table. Thomas would have happily ignored him, except that Owen stood up, blocking their way.

"Thomas, you simply cannot monopolize this enchanting young woman. I insist on an introduction."

Introductions were made all around Cartwright's table and Deborah, although maintaining her aloof demeanor, could not help but note the care with which the major listened to her name. It was as though he were inscribing it into a file to be referred to at some later date. For some reason, she felt that he was not interested in her as a woman but rather as a point of information.

"You've made quite an impression on all of my comrades," Thomas smiled at her.

"Especially on your friend, Major Cartwright."

Thomas threw a quick look at Owen. He was watching them closely.

"Yes, especially on Cartwright."

The waiter came over and they placed their orders.

"You're not eating very much," Thomas said, handing the menu back to the waiter.

"Frankly, we've gotten used to eating quite little and I find it difficult to eat large quantities at one sitting."

"Has it been that bad?"

She nodded. "But we've managed and things will now return to normal. I've succeeded in recruiting men to work the fields, and as soon as possible I hope to have the farm in working condition. The vineyards and orange groves will take longer."

They continued with inconsequential subjects until coffee was served and finally Thomas asked about his son.

"We call him Gidon. That's the Hebrew pronunciation," Deborah said pleasantly. "Although I expect he will be called Gideon when he goes to live with you." She sounded sad but accepting.

"I think it would be wise not to make him feel like a stranger in any way. Don't you agree?"

"Of course." She lowered her eyes, fearful of showing her disappointment. "Now I do hope you don't mind if I become a bit personal." She took a deep breath. "I believe my sister would be pleased that you have agreed to undertake his guardianship. I also believe she trusted you to bring him up in a manner which would not conflict with who he is."

"I shall bring him up as best I can to be an honest, intelligent, understanding, compassionate human being." He stopped for a long moment. "And although I will not insist on a specific religious affiliation and will teach the values of all religions, I do believe it would be wise for him to belong to the Church of England. Obviously, as he grows older, I shall most assuredly give him choices."

Deborah mulled over the statement. She had given the subject of religion a great deal of thought and although what Thomas was saying was not to her liking, she could see the value of the suggestion.

"Will you tell him about his mother?"

"When the time comes."

"Will you tell him about who you are, who you were in relationship to her?"

"Probably not," Thomas said slowly. "It would confuse him." He paused before continuing. "I shall tell him I adopted him. He will call me uncle, which will be for the best. Being introduced as my son could stigmatize him. Labels would be attached to him that can be very cruel and humiliating. I should like to spare him that pain. Certainly it should be so until he is grown and can begin to understand what went on, what the circumstances were that brought him into the world."

"Who will care for him?"

"The best nanny I can find. I already have an excellent housekeeper. As soon as he is old enough, I shall see to it that he has the finest tutors. I have done nothing but think about his future since seeing Mr. Ben Hod yesterday, and I can assure you, the boy will want for nothing if I can help it."

"And who will care for him while you're here?"

"I've asked for a discharge. General Allenby was very understanding and will make all the necessary applications on my behalf. It should not take very long."

"But who will care for Gidon while you're here in Jerusalem?" Deborah persisted, aware that he was not answering her question. "He's not yet two years old and he must be watched constantly." Her voice broke with emotion.

"I've already talked to the nuns at the convent in Bethlehem," he said quickly.

"Oh." Deborah's voice was barely audible.

"They are extremely kind and caring," Thomas assured her.

She smiled. "I've never met a nun."

"You're more than welcome to come with us when I bring Gideon to the convent."

The use of the plural pronoun and the Anglicized name made her wince. Already Gidon had become a part of Thomas Hardwick's world.

"Does anyone else know about him, other than General Allenby?" she asked.

"No one. And it will remain so."

A strained silence followed before Deborah spoke again.

"Major Hardwick, I don't know if you are aware that now that my whole family is gone, Gidon and I are the sole heirs to my father's properties. They are hardly worth anything at the moment, but with time they will again be quite valuable and I wish Gidon to have his share."

Thomas's features hardened but his tone was still cordial. "I think that is most generous of you, Mrs. Larom, but I believe that once he is put in my care, there should be no contact between us. He will be brought up in England and I do not feel he should be burdened with knowing he has had any special connection to this land." He sucked in his breath before continuing. "If his mother were alive, it would be different, but unfortunately for all of us, she is gone and he should not be encumbered with . . ." He stopped, groping for the proper word.

"His Jewish heritage." Deborah finished the sentence for him.

"It is a fine heritage," Thomas said quickly. "But he will be English, and life as my ward will be difficult enough. It would only be a further complication." His voice had risen in spite of himself. "I know how difficult it is when you don't feel you fully belong, when you're forced by circumstances beyond your control to be an outcast, an outsider." He leaned forward and placed his hand over hers. "Believe me, Mrs. Larom, I am speaking from experience. Let him be my nephew, adopted during the war from some orphanage in the Middle East."

"But you did say that someday you'd tell him about us." She sounded like a little girl.

"Years from now, when he's a grown man, when he is mature enough to cope with the knowledge."

"But if he has this property here, why should he not benefit from it?"

"Why don't we discuss it some time in the future?" Thomas said with finality. "Trust me to take care of him in every way. Involving him with inheritances and financial arrangements would only cause trouble."

"But what if something happens to you," she asked without embarrassment.

Thomas was taken aback. Her manner had changed. The sweetness was gone.

"I can't imagine anything happening to me in the conceivable future. Hopefully by the time I'm dead, Gideon will be a grown man who can make his own decisions about his life."

She laughed bitterly. "Tamar said that not long before she died. She said it the day she was caught by the Turks." She was completely transported back to that day when they sat in Raphael's laboratory discussing Gidon's future. Her lips began to quiver. "She died the next day."

Thomas, clearly shaken by her words, cleared his throat.

"I have come to understand the suddenness of death," Deborah continued coldly. "There has been so much of it around me and I must apologize for being so blunt."

"I understand," Thomas said, "And please believe me when I say I'm truly sorry. Tamar meant everything to me. I would give anything if I could bring her back. I wanted to marry her, be a proper father to our child, but that was obviously not meant to be. I do hope to live to the age where I can give Gideon the best of everything that life has to offer. But I understand your concerns. I shall give instructions to my solicitor that you be notified and that you get full custody of the boy in the event of my death."

"To be fully in charge of him?" she pressed the point.

"To be fully in charge of him," he consented.

Satisfied, Deborah dug into her bag and produced a photograph which she handed Thomas.

A beaming, blond infant stared up at Thomas. He was so engrossed by the image that he did not notice that Owen Cartwright was standing next to their table.

"Family pictures?" Owen asked, peering down at the picture.

"Mrs. Larom's nephew," Thomas said, handing the picture back to Deborah.

Owen intercepted the movement and took the picture out of Thomas's hand. "Lovely-looking little chap." He scrutinized the photograph for a few seconds. "Very fair. Isn't that unusual?"

"Unusual?" Deborah asked pointedly. "I hardly find it unusual that many Englishmen have dark hair, brown eyes and swarthy complexions." She turned to look at the remaining British officers in the room. "Very few of the men here seem unusual to me."

Owen blushed. "I'm sorry. It's just that you are so different from him."

Thomas tore the picture out of Cartwright's hand. "And now, if you'll excuse us, we have some rather important business to discuss."

"What a dreadful man." Deborah watched as Cartwright left the room.

"Yes, he is. Worse, he's a dangerous man, because he is petty."

"How will you explain the baby to someone like him?" she asked, still staring at the doorway through which Owen Cartwright had left.

Thomas shrugged. "He's hardly a friend and I doubt that he will be coming back to England in the near future. He's aiming to conquer the whole Arab world." He chuckled with bitterness. "It should keep him quite busy."

Michael was waiting for Deborah when she emerged from the hotel. She was deathly pale but succeeded in carrying herself with dignity. He wished he could help her, but there was little anyone could do. She had just agreed to give up an intrinsic part of who she was. It was like a final death to her family and she would need to have time to mourn yet again.

# CHAPTER TWENTY-THREE

## 1927

I T was early afternoon on Friday. Lunch was over and Deborah stood on their balcony and stared out at the tree-lined street. It was a lovely boulevard in the best section of Tel Aviv and she and Michael had lived there for seven of their eight years of marriage. The house, situated in the wealthiest section of the newly created city, was similar to the ones across the street. Most were built in the Bauhaus style, introduced by the European Jews who had come to settle in Palestine. White and sparklingly clean, none was taller than two floors and each had a pleasant garden whose trees were still young. The flowers and grass still lacked the look of lushness that only time could achieve. Deborah missed Bet Enav. She missed the open spaces, the patina which her village had acquired through the years.

Built as a suburb of the overcrowded port city of Jaffa, Tel Aviv was inhabited by well-to-do merchants and bankers who, like the Danzigers had done many years earlier, had come to Palestine to live in a Jewish environment. The barren sand dunes of the Mediterranean were slowly acquiring the air of a cosmopolitan city. Streets were paved, houses went up, schools and synagogues were built, theaters and lecture halls were being planned. The shoreline was dotted with small cafés, where ladies spent their mornings while their children swam in the sea, or where couples went in the evening to listen to music and spend a few hours with their friends. As in every growing city, the demarcation line between the haves and have-nots was already starting to form. Surrounding the luxurious enclave where the rich lived were small, quickly constructed houses flanking narrow unpaved streets. These huts, shacks and tents were inhabited by people who came to work for the ones who could afford to pay them.

City life was not what Deborah had visualized for herself and her family when she and Michael got married. They returned from Jerusalem to Bet Enav right after their wedding, intending to settle in the Danziger house. It became immediately clear that they would not be able to live there.

Memories of the past were difficult, but it was the attitude of the villagers that drove them away. The citizens of Bet Enav refused to accept them. They could not forgive the Danzigers for their Nili work. Deborah alone might have overcome that hostility, but being Mrs. Michael Ben Hod made life in Bet Enav impossible. David's mysterious death had made him a martyr. His death as a Nili operative was blamed on Michael. It was Michael, the villagers thought, who led David astray and that he killed him in a fit of jealousy.

It was Deborah who chose Tel Aviv as the place to establish and create that new life for them once there.

In a way, she had adjusted to their life and had even learned to enjoy it. Michael did not. She was used to luxuries. Their home in Bet Enav had been a luxurious, spacious house. Michael had always lived in tents and abandoned shacks. He often slept in open fields without benefit of any shelter. For him to have the modern facilities that make up a home was embarrassing.

The Danzigers' home had been a cultural center and a meeting place for the village of Bet Enav, and Deborah quickly succeeded in making their home in Tel Aviv a social salon where her friends congregated for musical recitals, dinner parties and serious political discourse. At first Michael, whose political views were radically different from those of their new friends and neighbors, resented them. With time, he came to understand them and although the ideological arguments went on till late hours at night, he learned to accept them as they did him. Deborah was aware that he was unhappy at not having any of his old friends around and she would have gladly invited them to her home, but they still shunned him because of his association with Nili, even after all these years. All she could do was hope that one day he would stop looking back and accept their new life.

Deborah was so absorbed in her thoughts that it took her a minute to realize that the street had grown quiet. Fewer cars drove by. Carts and carriages were gone, children were called in for their afternoon naps and she realized that Sabbath eve was setting in.

Reentering the living room, she glanced around. It was spacious and comfortable, furnished much as their home had been in Bet Enav. The small baby grand piano dominated. Her eyes came to rest on the pictures sitting on it. Photographs of Tamar, their parents, David and Raphael, were all framed in black. Smiling photographs of her two children, Naomi and Benji, on the beach with Michael. Gidon, as an infant, lying on a furry rug. She bit her lip at the sight of the blond, chubby child. It was taken on his first birthday and now he was ten years old. Quickly she looked away and her gaze fell on the picture of herself and Michael on their wedding day. Picking it up, she stared at it. They were a handsome couple but they did not look happy. They were two lonely people who had no one but each other.

With feelings of nostalgia and sadness, Deborah headed toward her bedroom. Passing her children's room, she stopped and opened the door quietly. They jumped back into bed when they heard her enter and pretended to be asleep.

She smiled and, walking over to Naomi's bed, she leaned down, kissed her on the cheek and tucked in her blanket.

"Not another sound until Tova comes in to get you up." Deborah reached down and smoothed out the girl's curly red hair.

Naomi sighed happily and snuggled under the covers. "Can I whisper?" she asked.

"Very quietly so you don't wake Benji." Deborah turned to look at her son, lying in his bed on the other side of the room.

"I'm not sleeping yet," Benji announced, sitting up.

Deborah walked over to him. "It's Friday and if you want to have Sabbath supper with Abba and me, you must nap."

He looked at her seriously. "Can I go to the beach with him and Naomi before supper?"

"No, you can't," Naomi stated angrily. "It's my turn."

"No fighting," Deborah said firmly. "I'll take you for a walk and get you some ice cream while they're gone."

The boy lay back, put his hands behind his head and stared up at the ceiling.

Deborah looked down at her son. He was an attractive five-year-old boy with brown hair, dark brown eyes, but he appeared discontent in spite of all the love she showered on him and the unreserved adoration of his father. She could sense a rage in him waiting to explode, and it puzzled and upset her. It also caused her feelings of guilt. From the day he was born she silently compared him to Gidon as an infant. They were very different, not only in appearance, but in temperament. As an infant, Gidon was a happy, outgoing baby who radiated love. Benji, from the time he was born, was cranky, seemed dissatisfied and closed-in. Often Deborah wondered if the reason was that she had given more of herself to Gidon, because she was all he had. Or was it possible that she doted so on Gidon because he was Tamar's son? These thoughts would disturb her. She loved Benji but he had to share that love with his sister, his father and, yes, with Gidon. Gidon was still very much part of her thoughts.

Before leaving the room, Deborah threw a last look at her daughter. A year older than Benji, she favored Michael with her red hair, large green eyes, high forehead, light, pencil-thin eyebrows and deep dimples on each side of her mouth. Only her expression was different from her father's. Her small, heart-shaped face belonged to a happy little girl who looked out on the world with trust and love.

Naomi was going to be Deborah's Nili. As the day of birth grew closer, she began to hesitate. The idea of Nili was still too painful and brought back too many sad memories. The name seemed too weighty for a little girl to have to live up to. Someday there would be a Nili in her family. But not yet.

Her bedroom was in semidarkness as she entered and lay down beside Michael. Fridays were unique, since it was the one afternoon that Michael came home for lunch and then took a nap.

She looked over at him. He seemed to be asleep, but his body was taut. He worked hard and she was looking forward to their annual trip to Europe, right after Passover. He always seemed to relax when they were away and by the time they came back, he was rejuvenated.

Feeling drowsy, she closed her eyes, then felt Michael pull her to him. After all their years of marriage, she was still thrilled when he desired her. She pressed herself to him and her body went limp as she gave herself to him, willingly and with the passion she had the first time he made love to her.

"I thought you were asleep," she whispered when they were both spent from lovemaking.

Michael stared down at her and stroked her cheek with the back of his hand. With her head resting on the pillow, her thick, lush hair framing her face, she was more beautiful now than she was when they married. He worshipped her. He wished he could put his thoughts into words. He wanted desperately to tell her how he felt, but he dared not. She had given him life and he wished he could tell her how grateful he was. Being married to her, making love to her, feeling her kindness and warmth, wiped away some of the pain of rejection by the people he had known in his youth. The words would not come. She was his wife, but he was convinced that David was the man she carried in her heart. Even more painful was his feeling that she still doubted his story about David, despite her assurances. There had to be doubt. He could never explain, even to himself, how he had survived that Bedouin attack. After all these years, he still rode out to the desert to try to find some trace, some relic, some sign, that would verify his story. He kept trying to find the Bedouins who might know about the attack. The little limping boy, grown up, could possibly set the record straight. The silence of the desert, the undisturbed dunes, yielded nothing. Until he could prove to Deborah that he had told the truth, he would never dare speak of love to her.

The last thought made him turn away from her, fearful that she might see his pain. Deborah was taken aback by the sudden gesture. For a moment, Michael looked as though he wanted to talk to her. She had rested in his arms waiting, as she always did, for him to speak, to tell her his feelings, to voice his thoughts. She watched his expression change, his lips grow thin holding back.

When he turned away, she felt cheated and stared up at the ceiling helplessly. At moments like this, the presence of Tamar loomed larger than life. Neither she nor Michael had ever said they loved each other and although she did love Michael, she could not bring herself to say it. Instead she rested her hand gently on his back and dozed off.

The muted sound of the shofar announcing that the Sabbath had begun woke her. The work week was over. Deborah could hear Tova, their maid, tending to the children.

"Will you come with us to the beach?" Michael had also been awakened by the children's cries.

"I don't think so." She sat up and stretched lazily. "There are still some things I want to attend to before the guests arrive."

"I will have to go out after supper."

"But Michael, it's Friday."

"I won't be long."

"Where are you going?" She was surprised by her question. She never pried.

He turned and stared at her. "If you must know, I'm meeting with Reb."

"With Reb? Why?"

"He's starting a weekly magazine and he's asked me to help him."

Deborah lowered her eyes. She objected to his being used by the people who had betrayed him and were now willing to take from him what they could—time, talent, perhaps money.

"But why would you want to work with those people?"

"Deborah, the people are not the issue. It's their ideology I care about. Besides, I've been outside the mainstream for too long and I'd like to become part of their movement again. You and your friends are fine people, but their thoughts are foreign to me. I believe in what Reb and his followers believe in and I want to fight for their cause, because it is my cause."

"But they don't really want you and you know it." She was being blunt but she did not want him to be hurt.

"I know what I'm doing," he answered cryptically. He paused briefly before continuing. "Incidentally, I've hired Jewish workers to harvest the fields in Bet Enav."

She was stunned. "What about the Arab workers who've been so loyal to us through the years?" she asked. "Can we afford Jewish workers?"

He bristled. "You asked me to manage your properties and I believe I've done it quite well. I know we can afford it. But most important, I have always felt uncomfortable with Arab workers. I don't trust them. Something is brewing which I don't understand, and I don't want them around."

"What about Mahmud?" she asked.

"He's still going to be the watchman but he's really too old to do any of the heavy work."

"I'd like to go up to Bet Enav with you next time you go," she said evenly. "I miss it."

She was surprised by her words. She did miss it, but she had never admitted that to Michael.

Michael's face tightened. He was about to answer when Naomi and Benji rushed into the room and pounced on the bed. He gathered both children into his arms and his face softened into a smile.

"May I go to the beach with you and Naomi?" Benji asked, obviously choosing to forget his conversation with his mother.

Michael looked over at Naomi. Her eyes were brimming over with tears. "If you want it, Abba," she choked the words out.

"No, it isn't fair," Michael said quickly.

"But I want to go with you," Benji insisted.

"Let him come," Naomi said quietly. "I don't really mind."

"Benji, you and I will have a lovely time," Deborah said firmly. "And now, both of you go and get ready."

The children scrambled out of the room and Michael jumped out of bed and pulled on his robe. In the brief moment before he covered himself, Deborah caught sight of his naked body.

"You're a handsome man, Michael," she said softly.

He looked over at her. "And you're a very beautiful woman."

She was aware that the conversation about Bet Enav had been forgotten and in a way she was relieved.

# CHAPTER
# TWENTY-FOUR

GIDEON was sitting on the grass, listening intently to his tutor and having a hard time containing his anger. Mr. Stewart was discussing the defeats the British had endured during the first years of the war between Germany and the Allies. Defeat in battle always upset him, especially ones he was sure could have been avoided if only the Allies had been better informed about the enemy's position.

"Gideon, are you following what I'm reading?" Mr. Stewart asked, seeing the boy grow restless.

"I'm trying, sir," the boy said. "But I'd be most grateful if we could go to another subject."

"I don't believe we should," Mr. Stewart said firmly. "It's part of the history of that period and your uncle would like you to be aware of it."

"But where was Uncle Thomas when these battles were taking place?" Gideon asked indignantly. "If he had been there, I'm sure he would have foreseen the disaster."

"He was involved in the planning of the desert campaign, which he felt would turn the tide for the Allies."

Gideon mulled over the tutor's remarks. They made sense, since he was fully aware of his uncle's work with the desert Arabs and his efforts to mobilize them to fight on the side of the British. Still, he was not satisfied. So many futile deaths, deaths his uncle could have prevented.

It was an unusually balmy day for April and although such days were rare in the English countryside, Gideon was too preoccupied to appreciate it. He lay back and looked at the clear sky. His eyes clouded over, as though he were trying to forget the horrors of what his tutor had been talking about.

Mr. Stewart, watching him, could not help but feel that, although Gideon was only ten years old, his expression, especially around his eyes, seemed to belong to someone much older. Gideon's compassion and understanding were far beyond his years.

"Gideon, please try to concentrate on what I'm reading," Mr. Stewart said sternly.

"Of course, sir." Gideon continued staring at the sky. As much as he respected Mr. Stewart, Gideon resolved to discuss the Great War with his uncle. Uncle Thomas would surely explain it all to him.

The tutor continued to read out loud, but Gideon was distracted by the sight of a butterfly circling around him. Rolling over on his side, he rested his head on his palm and watched the creature settle on a large, colorful flower. The butterfly was yellow and the black and red markings on its wings seemed painted on with delicate brush strokes. How he loved beautiful things. He wondered if Mr. Stewart would understand his feelings and decided he would not. He wished he could talk to someone about his fascination with the esthetic things of life rather than war, death, winning and losing battles and the need to save the British Empire. In a way he was ashamed of his love for the frivolous. Even when studying the Bible, whether the Old Testament, the New Testament or the Koran, he was far more impressed with the ethics that religions had to offer. He saw a great deal of beauty in religious themes and wished that all the negative commands starting with "Thou shalt not" could be done away with. He would have liked to talk to his uncle about his thoughts, but he knew that his uncle, much as he loved him, wanted other things from him. Justice, fairness, order and law, were what Thomas Hardwick thought important in a young boy's education.

It was at moments like this one that Gideon wished he had a friend, someone who would listen to him. The thought upset him. He was being unfair to his uncle. The fact was that he did have friends. Mr. Stewart was his friend and so was his uncle. There were also the boys he saw at church. And some of their neighbors had children, whom he played with when their parents came to visit. He closed his eyes, aware that he was not being honest. That was not what he truly wanted or needed. He wanted to be loved by a sweet, gentle woman who would cuddle him and understand his deeper needs. He had Mrs. McGregor, who'd been his nanny since he was an infant, but she did not fill the void. He wanted a mother's love. He wanted a mother and he did not have one. He did not know who she was and he dared not ask about her. In all the years he had lived with his uncle, she was never mentioned. Instinctively, he knew that he must not bring up the subject.

His mother, he was convinced, was gentle and beautiful. Some nights, just before falling asleep, a vision would come to him. He was very young and he was lying in the arms of a woman who was holding him with loving care and was kissing him with great tenderness. The vision was enhanced by a lovely scent and he could hear her voice. It was melodious and filled with tenderness. It was not a clear picture, however. It was shrouded in darkness and hard as he tried to bring it into focus, his mind would close up and he would fall asleep.

By morning the scene had evaporated and he had to assume it had all been a dream.

Mrs. McGregor was certainly not the lady of his dreams. Maj. Thomas Hardwick was elegant, aloof and very conscious of his position. He would have only been involved with a woman of the "right" background.

Knowing and associating with the "right" people was something Thomas often spoke about. Gideon was not quite sure what he meant. The Arabs who came to the house were certainly not socially acceptable. Still, Thomas must have considered them acceptable, because he seemed more alive, more vibrant, happier when his Arab friends came. So why weren't they considered "right" people?

Gideon sighed deeply. He wished he could understand his uncle better and wondered if the day would come when he could talk to him about these thoughts. Much as he loved his uncle, he could never bring himself to confide in him. His uncle loved him, cared for him and saw that he lacked for nothing. Thomas Hardwick, a bachelor, a warhero and a scholar, had adopted a tiny, helpless infant he had found while fighting in the desert. Everyone who knew the story commended the major for his generosity. He treated the boy like a son and shared everything he had with him. Still, there was a void in Gideon which longed to be filled.

The butterfly's wings came together and within seconds it rose and was gone from sight. Its disappearance deepened the emptiness within Gideon. He envied its freedom. It came from a cocoon and had no obligations toward anyone. The thought surfaced slowly. Butterflies evolved out of a cocoon but people did not. Suddenly Gideon had an overwhelming need to know who he was and where he came from. It was not the first time he had the urge to find out about himself. Secretly he suspected he really was Thomas Hardwick's son. They looked alike and there was a bond between them deeper than that of man and adoptee. He was having dinner with Thomas that night and he would press him to find out.

He sat up slowly. He had avoided asking Thomas these questions for fear of hurting him and he was amazed by his determination. Then he remembered that it was his tenth birthday and that was probably the reason why he felt so strongly about the subject. Somehow he had to convince Thomas that he could confide in him and that once Gideon knew the truth, he would never divulge it to anyone.

"Mr. Stewart," Gideon interrupted the droning voice of his tutor. "Do you know anything about my adoption?"

Mr. Stewart looked up, startled.

"I'm ten years old today and I wonder where the records are that indicate my date of birth."

"Surely your uncle could answer that better than I can," Mr. Steward said.

Suddenly Gideon felt very tired.

"Could we possibly stop now, sir?" Gideon implored. "I'm having dinner with my uncle and I would like to rest up before the meal."

He needed to be alone. The dinner that evening was very important. He felt he had a right to know the truth, and he wanted to decide how best to confront Thomas.

"Well, it's almost tea-time and I suppose it would be all right if we did let up a little earlier today." Mr. Stewart stood up. You have been working hard." He smiled warmly at the boy, tousled his hair affectionately. "I don't know if I've ever told you this, Gideon, but you do have an exceptional mind and it is a joy for me to spend my time with you."

"Thank you, sir," Gideon answered and started collecting his books.

"I believe Mrs. McGregor has tea waiting for us in the kitchen," Mr. Stewart said as they walked toward the large house.

"I shan't be having tea with you today. Uncle Thomas and I are having an early dinner."

They reached the back terrace and Mr. Stewart started walking toward the servant's entrance but stopped when he realized that Gideon was not following him.

"I'll go around the front," Gideon announced. He knew Thomas was working in his study and it occurred to him that if the door was open, he might go in and spend some time with him before dinner.

"Make sure you don't disturb the major. You know how strict he is about his work hours," Mr. Stewart warned.

Gideon walked along the neat path trying to contain his excitement. Uncle Thomas disapproved of overt exuberance.

He was just rounding the corner when he saw Colonel Cartwright's command car standing in front of the house. He wanted to cry out in protest. Tonight was to be his night alone with Thomas. This evening was crucially important to him. What made it even worse was that he hated Colonel Cartwright. He also knew that Thomas did not care for him. He never understood why the man ever came to their home. Gideon was aware that the two man had fought in the Egyptian campaign, but whenever they were together, the atmosphere was tense. They were extremely polite to each other but the undercurrent of hostility was evident. He wondered if Cartwright would be staying for dinner.

With a heavy heart, Gideon continued toward the front door when he saw Colonel Cartwright's driver leaning over Thomas's motorcycle. The man was unaware that he was being observed and was fiddling with the cycle.

"Get away from that!" Gideon ordered furiously. "You have no business with that machine. It is a highly valuable piece of equipment and my uncle would be furious if he knew you were anywhere near it."

"Sorry, lad, didn't mean no harm, I was just curious."

"Just stay away from it," Gideon said again and entered the house, slamming the door after him.

Thomas heard the front door shut and raised his hand toward his guest. He turned quickly to the library door.

"Come in, Gideon, and say hello to Colonel Cartwright." He reached over and gently pulled the boy into the room.

"You have grown since I saw you last," Cartwright said cheerfully after they shook hands.

Gideon moved quickly to stand by Thomas's side and said nothing.

"Studying hard, boy?" Cartwright continued in the same affable manner.

"Yes, sir."

"It must get pretty lonely up here, when all boys your age are off to public school." He turned to Thomas. "Why don't you send him off to . . ."

"He's being tutored at home at the moment," Thomas interrupted. "But we're thinking about it. Maybe next year."

"A lad should have companions his own age." Cartwright would not be put off.

"I have friends, sir." Gideon felt the need to defend his uncle. "There are several boys at church and they come over here and I go to visit them."

"Church? Indeed." Cartwright smiled. To Gideon it seemed like a sneer.

"Very well, Gideon," Thomas said pleasantly, "You run up and get ready for dinner. Mrs. McGregor has cooked all our favorite dishes and I expect we'll have a feast."

Gideon looked gratefully at his uncle, bowed politely to the colonel and rushed out of the room.

"Handsome little fellow," Cartwright said the minute the boy had gone.

"And quite brilliant as well," Thomas said with pride.

"Well, if we don't sound like a proud parent," Owen Cartwright said sarcastically. "Does he resemble his mother? I don't believe I ever met the lady, but I always assumed she was sort of dark and swarthy. You know what I mean, like her sister."

"She was extremely fair and quite beautiful," Thomas answered, keeping the shock out of his voice. He had not realized that Owen had any idea about Tamar. "And yes, he does resemble her. Would you care for a drink, Owen?" Thomas wanted to put an end to the conversation about Tamar and Gideon. He was trying to absorb the fact that Owen was aware of Gideon's background. Owen had seen the boy several times over the years but had never given any indication that he doubted the adoption story.

"A scotch will do nicely," Cartwright bowed politely. He knew he had made his point and was satisfied.

"What brings you to this part of the country?" Thomas asked, handing the drink to his guest. "Isn't it rather out of your domain?"

"I had a meeting in Brighton and thought I'd stop by on the way," he spoke slowly, "And since we all know that you've become a recluse and are always in, I thought I'd chance it."

"I'm just finishing my manuscript, but it's taken me quite a while and I do prefer not to socialize when I'm working on a book."

"I say, I do hope I'm not disturbing you," Cartwright said with exaggerated concern.

"I hear you might be off to Cairo shortly." Thomas decided to stop the game Cartwright was playing and find out the real reason for his visit. Normally Cartwright would never drop by without announcing his arrival. His presence was disturbing.

If Cartwright was surprised at the abrupt change of subject, he pretended not to notice. "Recluse or not, you do seem to be up on what's happening in London." When Thomas did not react, he continued. "Well, as you know, I've been waiting for this assignment for quite a while."

"Director of the Arab bureau in Cairo is something worth waiting for," Thomas conceded.

"Bet you would have taken it like a shot, given the chance."

"Another drink, Owen?" Thomas asked.

Cartwright shook his head and Thomas went over to the bar to refill his own glass.

"If you'd give up that confounded boy, I'm sure you could have had it." For the first time Cartwright sounded unsure of himself.

"Owen, you do press on, don't you?" Thomas's voice was icy. "So I'll set your mind at rest. I was offered the assignment and I turned it down."

"Were they ready to have you take the boy with you?"

"As a matter of fact, they were. The only reason I turned them down was that I don't feel he is ready to cope with that part of the world just yet."

"I don't believe you," Owen shot back, all pretense of cordiality gone.

"Don't believe what?" Thomas asked.

"That you were offered the post. And if you were, that you turned it down."

"Is that why you came down here?"

A light tap on the door brought the conversation to an abrupt end.

"Come in," Thomas called out. When Gideon entered, Thomas grew flustered, wondering if the boy had heard what had been discussed in the room.

"Mrs. McGregor said that dinner is ready," Gideon said quietly.

"Thank you, my boy," Thomas said brightly. Turning to Cartwright, he shrugged in resignation. "Sorry, Owen, but Mrs. McGregor rules the house."

"Of course." Cartwright stood up. "I do hope I haven't inconvenienced you with this brief visit."

"Not at all. And I sincerely hope you got the information you came for."

"Oh, I know I did." He bowed to Thomas and tousled Gideon's hair as he passed him. "And you, my lad, must ask your uncle to send you off to school."

Gideon smiled politely, relieved to see him leave.

"Go into the dining room," Thomas winked at Gideon. From the expression of relief on his face, Thomas gathered that the boy had not overheard the conversation but was simply upset at the idea of having to dine with Cartwright.

Thomas watched Cartwright's car drive off and stared at the empty driveway long after it was gone. He was not pleased with Cartwright's visit. Although he had spoken the truth about turning down the Cairo post, he was sure Cartwright did not believe him. Was he trying to ascertain that Thomas would not change his mind? Is that why he brought up Gideon and let it be known that he knew about Tamar? He was disturbed that Owen had that information at hand. Owen had always hated him, and even after all these years he continued to compete with him. Now he wondered if Owen could use what he knew about Gideon to harm the boy. Gideon had to be protected at all cost. Maybe the time had come to send him away to school. He was ten years old and until now, he had not been troubled by Thomas's relationship with his men friends. How much longer could he go on without the boy becoming aware of and perhaps resenting these relationships?

Thomas leaned his head against the doorpost. It only Tamar had not died his life would have been so different.

Troubled and depressed, Thomas entered the dining room and seated himself at the head of the table.

Gideon sensed Thomas's mood and knew that the conversation he had planned to have with him might have to be postponed.

Mrs. McGregor served their dinner and they ate in silence.

"Would you like to go off to school?" Thomas asked suddenly.

Gideon's heart sank. He often wondered why he had not been sent to public school, but he assumed that his uncle wanted him near him and he was happy that he was wanted.

"Not unless you want me to go, sir," Gideon answered politely.

"I prefer having you here." Thomas smiled for the first time since they sat down and his mood seemed to improve.

"Did I tell you that Kalil is coming to stay with us for a while?" Thomas said after a minute. "I believe he will be staying for quite a long time."

Gideon kept his eyes on his plate. Kalil was his uncle's newest friend and whenever he was around, Thomas seemed genuinely happy. He was the handsomest man Gideon had ever seen and was extremely gracious and kind, but Gideon hated having him stay in the house. Gideon was aware that Kalil felt the same about him, and although he tried to ingratiate himself with the man, it did little good.

"Is that why you asked if I want to go away to school?" Gideon asked slowly.

"Heavens, no." Thomas was sincerely shocked.

"Uncle Thomas, do you love me?" The words came unexpectedly.

"More than you'll ever know, child." Thomas nodded and an unbearable sadness came over his face. "More than you'll ever know."

"I don't believe I'm your nephew," Gideon continued impulsively.

"Oh? And who do you think you are?"

"Your son."

"Would that make you happy?"

"Oh, sir, more than anything in the world."

Thomas stared at the boy for a long time. He had known the day would come when he would have to tell Gideon about Tamar, Deborah, Nili and the whole sad saga, but he had not expected it to happen so soon. He wanted to do justice to the woman who had given birth to the child, justice to her family and to her people.

Getting up from his chair, he walked over to Gideon and placed his hand on his shoulder.

"I believe you mean it," he said solemnly.

Gideon held his breath waiting for Thomas to continue.

"It is a long and wonderful story and I want to tell it to you," Thomas said quietly. "But I must think about it carefully so that you will understand and appreciate it." Then cupping the boy's chin in his hand, he looked directly at him and continued. "Let me go out for a while and when I come back, I shall come up to your room and tell you exactly what happened. But for now, I will say one thing which you must always remember. Your heritage is one of the finest a man could have and no matter what, you must be proud of it, carry it with honor and always, always fight for it."

"May I come with you?" Gideon pleaded. "I won't ask any questions, I promise. It's just . . ." He did not know why, but he wanted to be with Thomas.

"No, not tonight," Thomas said firmly. Then he was gone.

Gideon heard the heavy front door slam shut. He was badly shaken by the impulsive physical contact between his uncle and himself. It was both thrilling and frightening. Above all, he was now sure that Thomas was his father. But who was his mother? He thought of a faded photograph of a woman on horseback he had once seen in Thomas's wallet. It was years back and when he asked about her, Thomas became flustered. Gideon never saw that picture again. He tried to conjure up the woman's face, but it was all so long ago.

He heard the motorcycle start up, when he suddenly remembered Cartwright's driver toying with it. He jumped from his seat and ran out of the room. By the time he opened the front door, Thomas was racing out the front gate. He called out to him, but the sound of the motor was too loud. He could hear the motorcycle speeding down the road. He walked back into the house. He was being foolish. No one was a better cyclist than Thomas Hardwick.

Gideon lay in bed waiting for Thomas. He strained to hear the sound of the motorbike, but only silence greeted him. The hours went by and he grew drowsy. Finally sleep came, restless, unhappy sleep disturbed by strange and frightening dreams.

He woke to the sound of loud voices and he knew as though he had been told that something had happened to Thomas. Mrs. McGregor walked in and stood next to his bed. She looked strange. She was wearing a bathrobe, her long braids were hanging down out from her nightcap and her eyes were darting around wildly, tears streaming down her ancient cheeks.

Major Hardwick was dead. He had skidded on a wet curve in the road and was killed instantly. A dreadful, freak accident.

Gideon stopped listening. His uncle was dead but he knew it was not an accident. He remembered Cartwright's last words as he left the house. Thomas had asked him if he had got what he came for and Cartwright had assured him that he had. Of course he had, Gideon thought helplessly. He had come to kill Thomas and he had succeeded.

The funeral was well attended and was done with great pageantry. Many wreaths were placed at the freshly dug grave and the minister spoke at great length about the honorable and courageous Maj. Thomas Hardwick. Gideon could not concentrate. He looked at the members of Parliament, ambassadors, military men, generals, admirals and air force personnel. None impressed him. He saw Kalil standing with several other Arab chieftains, all dressed in their ceremonial robes. Kalil was looking at him with contempt and Gideon again wondered why the man disliked him so. If anything, Kalil should have been his friend. In fact, Kalil was the one person who might have been able to tell him who he was, where he came from and, above all, who his mother was.

Gideon continued to stare at the huge crowd when he caught sight of a woman staring back at him. She was very beautiful, with dark hair and extraordinary dark eyes. She was dressed in black and wore an elegant hat. He wondered who she was. He had never seen her before. She looked foreign, which made her presence all the more mysterious. She did not flinch when his eyes met hers. It occurred to him that nobody had ever looked at him with such concern. He wondered if she was sorry for him and he resented it. He did not want anyone to feel that way about him. He turned his eyes to her escort and realized it was Charles Waxman, Thomas's barrister. Gideon looked at her again. Her eyes were still glued to his face and her expression had not changed.

When the funeral service ended, everyone came over to pay their condolences. Gideon shook everyone's hand but paid little attention to what they were saying. When Cartwright came over, Gideon turned away and found himself facing Mr. Waxman and the beautiful lady.

"Gideon," Mr. Waxman said soberly, "I want you to meet your aunt, Deborah Ben Hod."

# CHAPTER
# TWENTY-FIVE

G IDEON watched Deborah out of the corner of his eye. She was staring into the distance and he could see tears form in her eyes. He followed her gaze and wondered what caused her to be so emotional. Their ship, the *Ranjitata,* was anchored off the shore of Palestine, but the morning mist obscured the view of the shoreline.

He looked back at her. She seemed to have forgotten his presence and for a minute he was frightened. In the month since Thomas died she had become his protector, his guardian, his sole connection to the world. He could not have survived without her.

As soon as the funeral was over, she took charge. They had gone to London to stay with some friends of hers who lived in Mayfair. He was surrounded by numerous people who went out of their way to be kind to him. They were very different from anyone he had ever met before and it took him a while to get used to them. The reserve and restrain that Thomas had insisted on was far from the exuberance, the excitement, the changing moods of the people he now encountered. They kissed and hugged each other, and argued at dinner, sometimes so heatedly that Gideon feared violence would erupt. Then suddenly the argument would be over and everyone would be laughing and having another coffee. Although they spoke English, he understood little of what they were saying.

Deborah was the one who fascinated him most during those debates. Her face would become flushed, her dark eyes would glow like embers, and she would press her point with ferocious intensity. Fight, if necessary, she would say with great passion. A homeland was worth fighting for if there was no alternative. Promises were made and had to be kept, she would insist and if they were not, then the Jews of Palestine had a right to claim what was theirs, even with physical force. Once she referred to Nili, and although Gideon had no idea who that was, he looked over at her. She was very pale and her eyes were blazing, He tried to visualize this gentle, loving woman using physical force and, to his surprise, he could. She appeared to be someone who would fight to the death to achieve what she felt to be her right. That was the kind of passion Gideon felt Thomas had possessed.

But much as he enjoyed being in the company of all these strange people, he looked forward to the time spent alone with Deborah. She exuded kindness. She took him everywhere, showered him with gifts and told him endless stories about his family.

*His family!* It was an exciting idea. The fact that Thomas was his father came as no surprise. That his mother was a heroine, a magnificent, powerful woman, excited him, both for himself but mainly for Thomas. Thomas deserved to be loved by such a woman. On the other hand, the idea that there were cousins and an uncle frightened him. He was content with knowing who his parents were and having Deborah as an aunt. The idea of having to share her with others made him nervous.

At night, when sleep would not come, he would turn on his light and study the pictures of this new family.

The one he looked at most often was that of his mother. Tall and proud, she was standing next to her horse, a serious expression on her face. He found her very beautiful. Her stance reminded him of Thomas's demeanor and Gidon understood why he loved her.

The other pictures were of Deborah's family.

Naomi was a pretty, happy-looking girl with curly hair, large eyes and a sweet smile. Benji was small and angry-looking. He scowled into the camera, his mouth set, his eyes squinting. Gideon did not like him. Michael, however, disturbed him most. He was standing next to a horse, obviously on a farm, his face stern, his eyes staring beyond the camera. Gideon saw that he was extremely good-looking and he felt jealous of him. That was Deborah's husband and he probably demanded all of her time and attention. It was the fourth picture that bothered him most. It was the one taken of the whole Ben Hod family and they were all huddled together. Gideon wondered if he could ever fit into such a tightly knit group.

That was the reason he kept his physical distance from Deborah. He wanted to be with her, be as close to her as possible, but he would move away whenever she tried to embrace him. He wanted to avoid the rejection that was bound to occur once she was back with her family.

"Look, Gideon," he heard Deborah call out excitedly. "You can see the land."

The mist had lifted and the shoreline was visible.

"That, on the right, is the Jaffa port. And to the left is Tel Aviv." The latter name was said with reverence.

Gideon surveyed the scene she was pointing to. Jaffa was a familiar name to him. It was referred to in the Bible, both old and new but it had none of the majesty which he had expected. It reminded him of fishing villages in Italy which he once visited with Thomas. He turned his attention to Tel Aviv, and saw a wide strip of white sand with small white houses built quite close to the shoreline. It was, however, no different from any resort town in the South of France. Jaffa and Tel Aviv appeared as one huge city from the distance.

"Tel Aviv is a new city." Deborah was saying excitedly. "It was started as a suburb of Jaffa. It's the first all-Jewish city in the world and it's growing rapidly. It's quite European in every way and yet it's right here on the Mediterranean, so we have the benefit of both worlds." Her pride was touching and she appeared happier than she had been in England. In a burst of enthusiasm, she put her arm around his shoulders and hugged him. "You'll love it. You'll love it as much as we do. You'll become part of it, help build it, help make it strong and beautiful. It's ours, all ours and we're so proud of it."

Gideon did not move away from her embrace. For a minute he was carried away by her excitement, but when she uttered her last words, he felt himself stiffen. *Ours.* He was being given an identity, he was being told he belonged, told that he was needed and wanted and, although it was something he dreamed of all of his life, he suddenly resented it. He was not being given any choice. He was, after all, Thomas's son. He was brought up as an English boy and expected to grow up as an English gentleman. Now he was being told he belonged to the Jewish people and that Palestine was his homeland. He had studied the Old Testament and it did appear that the Jews were destined to live in Palestine. But Thomas had told him the Jews in Palestine were a small, poor community, barely able to eke out a living. How could they hope to reclaim it? And what about the Arabs? Those gentle shepherds, where would they go?

Nothing he was seeing matched his preconceived notions. It dawned on him that Deborah was not poor. She was Jewish, lived in Palestine, yet appeared no different than any lady in England. But then, Kalil and all of Thomas's other Arab friends hardly looked like shepherds who tended sheep. If anything, they were far more lavish in manner and dress than anyone he had ever met in England.

"Mrs. Ben Hod, Master Hardwick." A ship's stewart had come up to them. "The captain wishes to have you accompany him to shore in his launch."

The chaos that greeted them when they reached the lower deck was staggering. Passengers who had traveled on the lower decks wearing shabby winter clothes, inspite of the balmy weather, were rushing about nervously. In contrast to the passengers, the porters were nearly naked, barefoot, dripped perspiration and smelled of garlic. They were running about, carrying crates and bags strapped to their backs or balanced on their heads, screaming angrily. Gideon was fascinated by the porters and realized they were speaking Arabic. That these grimy people were Arabs shocked him. Hardly did they match the image he had of them. They certainly had no relationship to the princely image created by Kalil. Gideon's distress deepened.

The captain arrived and escorted them down to the waiting launch ahead of everyone. The similarity to the tranquil, sleepy Italian ports he knew vanished the minute the launch cleared the slippery moss-covered rocks and was tied to the pier. Jaffa was filthier than any port Gideon had ever seen. As pathetic as the porters were on the ship, here misery abounded. Blind men, maimed children, women crouching next to buildings, breasts exposed and feeding infants, were everywhere. Youngsters—beggars—tugged at Deborah's skirt, their hands outstretched. Open sewer holes were oozing dirty, oily water and the stench of fish mingled with spices and sweets filled the air.

Were these the people whom Thomas admired, fought for, hoped to revive into a vibrant, proud force? Something was seriously amiss and Gideon felt lost. He wanted to be back in England. He wanted to talk to Thomas. Thomas would surely explain it all to him.

"There they are," he heard Deborah cry out joyfully and Gideon found himself facing his new family.

Deborah stooped down and kissed the children who clung to her. Finally disengaging herself from them, she straightened up and embraced Michael and he put his arms around her waist and held her for a long moment. Gideon watched from the side. Deborah was suddenly different. She was laughing gaily, but she was not the same Deborah he knew in London. He felt abandoned.

"He looks silly," Benji announced, staring at Gideon, who was dressed in a navy Eton jacket, gray trousers, white shirt and a tie.

"That's an unkind thing to say to your cousin," Deborah whispered in Hebrew, aware that Gideon did not understand it.

Benji would not be put off. "Why is he dressed that way?"

"I think he's very handsome," Naomi said seriously and walked shyly over and kissed Gideon on the cheek.

Gideon felt himself blush and hoped he would not burst out crying. He had avoided physical contact with his aunt, instinctively aware that he was unable to cope with a woman's affection. Having a young girl come over and kiss him unbalanced him. He did not know how to react.

"This is your cousin Naomi," Deborah said and Gideon put his hand out. The little girl giggled, took his hand and shook it.

"Your cousin Benjamin." Deborah indicated the young boy.

Gideon put his hand out but Benji hid his face in Deborah's skirt.

"And this is your uncle Michael," she said.

Gideon looked up and was taken aback by the look on the man's face. His expression was stony. The man did not like him and made no effort to hide it.

"And this is Gidon."

The pronunciation of his name shocked him. Deborah had never called him that while they were in England. *Gidon!* He felt his identity being taken away from him. He wanted to cry out in protest but dared not. He bit his lip, trying to control the impulse.

"It's the way we pronounce it in Hebrew," Michael spoke for the first time. The voice was deep, yet lacked warmth.

The pier noises were deafening and Gideon, unable to think of what was expected of him, turned to look at the people around him. "Are they all Arabs?" He asked.

"Why, yes." Deborah looked around, seeing the scene through Gideon's eyes. "It's different in Tel Aviv," she assured him.

The luggage was loaded onto a small railway cart. The Ben Hods and Gideon took their places in the front cars of the miniature railway. It traveled slowly through the narrow streets of Jaffa and the Oriental flavor of the city made Gideon uncomfortable. The houses built along side the tracks were in a state of disrepair. The whole street looked black with soot. The washlines did little to enhance the scenery. Women dressed in long black dresses, their faces covered, coins dangling from their ears, with large baskets balanced on their heads, walked along the tracks. Men mounted on donkeys walking on the tracks disregarded the small train, making its progress interminable. Cats and stray dogs skipped ahead of the train so close to the front engine that Gideon feared they would be run over. The cavernous shops lining the path were filled with ugly raw meat dangling from huge metal hooks. Vegetables and sweets glued together with honey were covered with flies. The smells of garbage mingled with animal excrement drying in the hot sun. Gideon was afraid he would be sick. He held his breath, praying the trip would end.

The train finally came to a stop in a large square, which was relatively clean. What caught Gideon's attention was a large tower with a clock installed at the top. He looked at his watch. The clock accurately recorded the time. It was the first civilized thing he had seen since getting off the ship.

A car was waiting for them when they got off the train.

The trip to Tel Aviv was quite short and Gideon marveled at the rapid change in scenery. Suddenly the streets, many still unpaved, widened. The houses were pleasant and looked habitable. Some were flanked by small, colorful gardens and finally they arrived at a wide, tree-lined street that formed an island between the houses on each side. The houses appeared to be individual villas. They were large, mostly whitewashed with dark green shutters on the windows. Many were hidden behind hedges and trees.

Michael drove into one of the driveways and parked the car in a garage at the back of the house.

Gideon was stunned. Nothing of what Thomas had told him was proving to be true. He did not know what he expected, but the spaciousness, the furnishings, the overall feeling was gracious and elegant.

Settled in Michael's study, Gideon observed the room. The large desk was made of heavy, dark oak. The two brown leather chairs looked comfortable, the Oriental rug was plush, and the leather sofa was covered with needlepoint pillows. He walked over to the bookcases. The shelves were nearly sagging with the weight of the books and they were all in Hebrew.

What was he doing here, he wondered. He would never be able to adjust to these strange surroundings. He loved Deborah, he felt warmly toward Naomi, but Michael and Benji were strangers who did not want him here. He could hear Deborah and Michael talking in the living room. He did not understand what they were saying, but the conversation sounded hostile. He lay down on the small leather sofa and covered his face with his hands. He was in an alien land and he wanted to go home, to England.

"It won't work," Michael glared at Deborah. "He's a product of another world, a foreign world, a hostile world."

"He's only a child," Deborah answered angrily. "He's an orphan and we're the only family he has."

"He's Thomas Hardwick's son."

"He's also Tamar's son," Deborah shot back.

"That has long since been erased from his being."

"I disagree. I've spoken to him. Thomas has given him a wealth of knowledge. He may not have told him he was Jewish, but he certainly educated him to know a great deal about us."

"I'm sure Mr. Waxman in London could have made some other arrangement for him. Sent him off to boarding school or something."

"He suggested it but I wouldn't hear of it. He's Tamar's son and my flesh and blood. I feel about him as I do about my own children and I want him here. He's an extraordinary child. Bright, kind, gentle, and at this moment he is confused and lost."

"Benji hated him," Michael said viciously.

"That attitude must have come from you," she answered bitterly.

"I never discussed it with him."

"You don't have to. He feels what you feel, reacts as you react, emulates you in every way." She spoke more forcefully than she meant to and was aware of her own hostility toward her son. It troubled her. She turned to stare out the window, feeling confused.

"Michael, let's stop fighting." She was tired from the long journey, drained from the emotion of being reunited with Gideon. From the minute she saw him at the funeral, she knew she had never stopped loving him and hoping the day would come when she could reclaim him.

"We can try it for a while," Michael gave in. "If it doesn't work out, we'll send him to that new agricultural school Misha is heading. I hear they've got a very good program there."

"It will work out," she said with greater assurance than she felt at that moment. Then, walking over to her husband, she put her hand to his cheek. "Did you miss me?" she asked softly.

"The house is very empty when you're not here," he conceded.

He was obviously pleased she was back and Deborah wondered why he was so frightened of showing his feeling toward her. Was it David, Tamar, their different backgrounds? So much time had elapsed since those days. Gideon's presence obviously brought it all back.

# CHAPTER
# TWENTY-SIX

EBORAH read the letter carefully. Misha urgently wanted her to come to the agricultural school. She had suspected for several months that Gidon was not adjusting to this school either, but she had hoped that Misha would somehow be able to cope with the boy. Misha was a superior educator, his experimental methods of teaching were highly praised, and he liked Gidon. More important, Gidon seemed to like him. But like all the other arrangements she had made for him since bringing him from England nearly two years earlier, this one too seemed to be failing.

At first she had enrolled him at the Gymnasium Tel Aviv. In spite of his unquestionable intelligence, he was turned down since he spoke no Hebrew. A private tutor gave up after a brief try. Gidon was uncooperative. She next tried special classes with other foreign students. He learned to speak Hebrew, but refused to learn to read or write. Deborah suspected that he had mastered both but would not admit to it. Next was an all-boys religious school. It was a disaster. He argued with the teacher, referring constantly to the New Testament, which infuriated the faculty. Deborah was told to remove him. Except for Naomi, he made no friends and spent his time reading books in English or going for long walks. Occasionally when he returned he seemed composed, but Deborah was convinced he had been crying. His morose mood had its effect on everyone. Benji picked on him, made fun of his manners and made his life miserable. Michael started spending longer periods of time in Bet Enav and when in Tel Aviv, he would come home late, explaining that he was working on Reb's magazine. Michael continued to argue that Gidon should be sent away to boarding school. Deborah, fearful that her marriage was coming apart, was pleased when Misha offered to take the boy.

Now, if this latest effort also failed, she worried that Michael might prevail and Gidon would have to be sent back to England. The thought of another separation from him was unbearable. Difficult and disruptive as he was to her life, her love for him was greater than ever. In him she saw the continuity of the Danziger family.

Misha was visibly upset when he met her at the school's gate. They exchanged pleasantries as he led her through the winding, tree-lined path toward the administration building. It was a long walk and they stopped to rest under a large oak tree.

"I'm sorry, Deborah," Misha spoke quietly. "It just won't work out." He waited a minute for his words to sink in. "He doesn't fit in and the worst part is, he won't even try."

"But what has he done?" Deborah asked in frustration.

"It's not anything specific," Misha answered. "The truth is, he's brilliant in every subject and he's wasting his time here." He sounded uncomfortable.

Deborah raised her brow. "That's a silly excuse and you know it."

"You're right—it's an excuse. But the fact is that he's causing me a great deal of trouble. He's different from the other boys and he won't make any effort to conform. His manners are impeccable, which is admirable, and I only wish our boys were like him. But they're not. They're boys, working the fields, romping about, involved in childish pranks, and Gidon makes them uncomfortable. He doesn't say anything, but they feel embarrassed in his presence. He's superior in all physical activities. He's a wrestler and a boxer, but he's too aggressive and has hurt others when they are up against him." He paused and looked around before continuing, his voice lowered. "As you know, we train the boys in defensive tactics. We're trying to teach them to use firearms. Well, apparently Gidon has been hunting with his father, so he knows all about guns." He paused briefly. "There is one more thing. There are times I feel his inner pent-up rage and I fear for him. He's downright militant and, frankly, some of the boys are afraid of him."

"Afraid of Gidon?" She was flabbergasted. "He's as gentle as a lamb. I know he's unhappy and I can't really blame him. He was uprooted so suddenly. You must remember that he loved Thomas dearly. The man gave him so much." She caught her breath in despair. "With me he's as helpful as can be, he's respectful and I know he's trying to adjust to this new life."

"That's all part of it," Misha shook his head sadly. "He has no understanding as to who we are. He doesn't understand our conflict with the Arabs and he makes his views known. Our boys have seen their fathers in their struggle with Arabs and are fully aware of the troubles we've had with them. They know there is always the danger of further uprisings, of an outbreak of violence. To have Gidon lecture them about the Arabs his father knew and loved is a bit hard for them to take. And that's when his anger surfaces." Misha looked at Deborah with compassion. "I'm sorry, Deborah," he said sincerely.

"What am I going to do?" she asked, aware that there was no point in arguing. Gidon had failed again and would be coming home.

"As I said, he's scholastically brilliant. He's actually quite ready for the gymnasium. He speaks, reads and writes Hebrew and he's also gifted in languages. He has a smattering of French and Arabic. Latin would probably interest him. You could try the boarding school in Haifa. They have quite a few Anglo-Saxon children there and that just might work out."

"When do you want him to leave?" she asked.

"When the summer vacation starts. He can stay until then. Take him to Bet Enav for a couple of months. He can help Michael in the fields and ride horses on the beach. He'll like that, and you can break the news to him over the summer."

"He doesn't know he's not coming back?"

"Of course he knows, but he doesn't really care. That's what I'm trying to tell you—he doesn't seem to care about anything."

"Where is he now?" she asked.

Taking her by the arm, Misha guided her toward a group of boys standing in a semicircle around a tractor while a teacher explained the mechanics of it.

She caught sight of Gidon immediately. Although dressed like the others in khaki shorts, blue shirt and sandals, he stood out. He was taller than most, his face was tanned and his blond hair, in need of a cut, was brushed down neatly. His young arms and long legs were equally brown and already his shoulders had broadened. Like the others, he was listening intently but he was, as Misha had said, an outsider.

All her love and devotion had not erased his sense of loss. It tore her apart.

Deborah left the school with a heavy heart. Michael would be angry at this news, but worse, he would be upset at the idea of spending the summer at Bet Enav. The rare Sabbath, the short holiday when the children were out of school and they went there were filled with tension, both from within and without. She did not understand Michael's behavior. He was constantly fighting with the children, anxious about their activities, demanding of their time. At first she thought it was fear of Abed, but Mahmud and Fatmi assured her that Abed had taken his wife and children and moved to Syria. He had apparently gotten into trouble with the law again, and the British were slightly more conscientious in dealing with troublemakers. She concluded that the past was still haunting Michael and the truth was that their neighbors in Bet Enav were still quite hostile to him. She suspected Michael was concerned that the children would learn about the circumstances of David's death. She girded herself for the scene she knew would occur, but she was determined to prevail. In the two years that Gidon had been in Palestine, they had been to Bet Enav only a couple of times and it would do him good but it was also something she now wanted for herself. Since Gidon's return, the old feelings of longing for the house of her youth had begun to surface and she felt she was ready to reach back to the past.

The first few days in Bet Enav were tense, but as the weeks went by, they settled into a pleasant, lazy routine. Revisiting old sites with Gidon, retelling stories of the past and seeing it all again through his eyes was thrilling. Even

Michael began to enjoy their stay and Deborah felt closer to him than she had in many years.

In the middle of the fifth week of their stay, Deborah spent the morning sightseeing with all three children, then drove back to the house for lunch. They stopped at the village market and some childhood friends greeted them as they would have years back. Someone invited Benji to play with their child and he went off happily. Deborah bought some vegetables and cheese and was looking forward to spending some time alone with Michael.

He was not yet home and left a message that he had some work to do and would be home later.

After lunch, Gidon and Naomi took off on their horses for a ride on the beach. Deborah hesitated when they asked if they could go. It was a beautiful day, so it seemed unfair to refuse them.

She stood by the gate and watched them trotting down the main street, laughing happily. Some of the villagers waved to them and Deborah's heart swelled with joy.

She started toward the house and stopped to admire it.

Over the years, Deborah had it restored it to its former beauty, and this summer she was finally strong enough emotionally to enjoy it. She felt that Gidon's presence had a great deal to do with it. It was as though she had been in a deep sleep since she gave him up and now he was back and she had begun to mend.

Yes, she thought with satisfaction, the time had come to reclaim her position in Bet Enav. This summer proved that the past had been forgotten, the anger and recriminations had subsided. She remembered Mahmud's prediction that someday she would be able to pay homage to her family, to Tamar. She wondered if that day were at hand. She turned and looked toward the cemetery. It lay on the outskirts of the village and she could not see it, but Tamar's lonely grave, placed near the fence, stood out vividly in her mind. She decided she would move it closer to their parents' resting place, an honorable plot in the center of the graveyard. The legend of Tamar was becoming part of the folklore of the community and it seemed like a good time to approach the village council about it.

The idea excited her and as she walked briskly toward the front door, she decided to go into Raphael's old house. She rarely went there, but suddenly she wanted to be in it and allow herself the luxury of remembering.

Standing in the doorway, Deborah felt transported back in time. Fatmi and Mahmud had cared for it as though Raphael were still alive and would be coming back. The pictures were all reframed and rehung. The furniture had been restored, the carved wood panels on the wall were replaced, the rugs cleaned and hung in their original location. The books had been rebound and were neatly arranged on the shelves. Even the fabrics had been duplicated on the upholstered pieces, as well as the curtains and pillows, so that the atmosphere of the past engulfed her. She had supervised the project of restoration, but this was the first time that she allowed herself the luxury of seeing it.

Slowly she walked around the room, touching the various objects that had meant so much to her brother. She ran her hand across the paneled walls and paused when her fingers touched a secret panel which in the past held Raphael's hunting rifle. The panel blended so completely into the wall that even the Turks had missed it when they ransacked the house. Now, so many years later, it held Michael's rifle, which he was hiding from the British, as Raphael had hidden his rifle from the Turks. She removed her hand quickly from the spot. The memory jarred her and she refused to be swept up by sad memories. Instead, she walked over to the sofa and lay down on the colorful cover, her head sinking into the softness of the pillows. The feelings of nostalgia were stronger than ever. Closing her eyes, she realized that although the pain and longing for the past were still there, they were bearable. As she drifted into sleep, she felt Raphael's presence. He was talking and his voice was gentle. Then she heard Tamar's happy laughter and her mother was playing a Chopin Etude on the piano. Her father was setting in his rocking chair, holding a young, happy Deborah in his arms, rocking in rhythm with the music.

Gidon looked back and saw Deborah move out of sight. He and Naomi had reached the crossroad. Turning left would lead them to the beach. Turning right would take them to the mountains where Mahmud's village lay.

"Let's go up there," Gidon said.

Naomi hesitated. Her father had forbidden them to ride into the areas where the Arabs lived.

"My father will be angry."

"He doesn't have to know we did it." Gidon sounded impatient. "Besides, who could want to harm us up there?" Then he smiled. "And you know I'd take care of you. I always will."

They guided their horses up the crude paths heading toward the hazy, blue mountain ridge. Soon the path disappeared and they moved along a huge rock quarry rising steeply on either side. It had recently been blasted and the white stones looked raw, their jagged edges jutting out like daggers. It was an untraveled area and occasionally small stones slid down, followed by larger ones. Naomi was frightened. She wanted to turn back but Gidon forged ahead.

Leaving the quarry, they continued through wild brush which made riding difficult. Naomi was relieved when they finally reached a flat plateau and Gidon brought his horse to a stop. It had been a difficult ride and it took her a moment to catch her breath. Only then did she look back at the area they had covered.

"Look, Gidon," she called out excitedly.

He turned. "At what?"

"Look at our beautiful land." Her voice was filled with awe.

"What's beautiful about it?" Gidon asked, staring at the scorched, sun-baked, barren earth relieved only by a few ancient olive trees, colorless cactus plants and drying weeds.

"Not here, silly," she laughed. "Look down there." She pointed to the land closer to the shoreline.

She was pointing to orange groves, vineyards, green grazing land, fields of yellow wheat, and areas covered with colorful flowers. Gidon saw roads inter-twined with the farming land and houses with their red shingled roofs dotting the landscape. The demarcation line was too distinct to ignore. It did not seem possible that anything as alive and vibrant as the land far below could be so close the area where they stood.

"Believe it or not, that place down there was once like this." Her arm swept up the mountain. "Until my grandfather and his friends bought it and cul-tivated it. Before Uncle Raphael helped make it beautiful." She scanned the distance. "Look down there, you can still see the trees he planted next to his laboratory." Her eyes glistened. "His laboratory stood next to a swamp and he had it dried up and built a whole experimental farm on it. You should read some of the things he wrote."

"Your grandfather was my grandfather," Gidon said slowly. He mulled the words over as he spoke. Deborah had told him all those stories, but hearing them from Naomi and seeing the land from this vantage point made it seem more real. He had a grandfather and an uncle who had done all that. The thought appealed to him.

"Of course he was, silly. And your mother, she helped too. She's a great heroine, you know. She really loved this land. She died for it," she concluded seriously.

"Yes, I know she did." Gidon dismounted, knelt down and picked up a handful of dusty sand. "And who does this belong to?"

"I don't know," Naomi said. "Probably nobody."

"Did all that down there really look like this?" he asked, letting the sand filter through his fingers.

"Ask my mother if you don't believe me," Naomi said angrily.

"I believe you," he said quietly and looked up the mountain. It looked more barren than ever. In the distance, he saw a young Arab boy walking slowly between the rocks, leading a flock of sheep. Further up, they could see a cluster of black tents and some mud huts huddled together with splashes of the bright blue paint smeared on them. That would be Mahmud's village. Mahmud and Fatmi were very kind to him but he had never been invited to their village. He wondered why.

"Can we go to Mahmud's house?" Gidon asked.

"Of course not," Naomi said indignantly.

"Why not?"

"I don't know," she answered and turned her horse around. "I want to go home." She was visibly upset. "I don't like it up here." She kicked her horse and started down.

Gidon watched her, feeling confused. *Home.* The word sounded hollow. He rushed to catch up with her.

"Can't we ride for a while longer?" he asked. "It's still light out."

She smiled and appeared to relax. "Of course we can, but let's ride down rather than up and I'll show you another beautiful sight."

They headed southward and reached a pleasant cove from which they could see the coastline. Sweeping up from the shore, the terrain was covered with a green blanket of trees and fields of colorful flowers.

Gidon was moved by the sight. He scanned the area and a small hill caught his eye. It was surrounded by a brick wall but some shingle-topped houses were visible above it.

"What's that place there?" He pointed to the hill.

"That's a famous Roman amphitheater. I've never been there, but they say that after all these centuries it's still intact."

"I don't mean the amphitheater. I'm talking about that wall and those houses on that hill next to it."

"That's Tel Ada, a tiny new settlement. They only have eight houses and they've built that wall for protection."

"From whom?"

"Thieves, I guess," Naomi answered.

The idea fascinated Gidon. "A wall? Do they have a gate?"

"Obviously they do and they lock it every night," Naomi said seriously.

Gidon began to laughed. "Do they really expect a wall to keep out someone who wants to rob them?"

Naomi shrugged her shoulders.

"Let's ride over there," Gidon suggested. "It doesn't look very far away."

Naomi hesitated. The day was coming to an end and the long shadows of the mountains stretched down into the valley. "It will be dark by the time we get there," she said. "We'll be here all summer. We can do it another day."

Deborah was awakened by the sound of Gidon and Naomi's laughter. She got up quickly, realizing she had slept through the afternoon and that dusk was setting in. She walked over to the window. They were heading toward the stables and she was about to call out to them when she saw something move in the small pine forest bordering the stable. She stepped into the shadow, never taking her eyes off the cluster of trees. Whoever was there was moving furtively, trying to avoid being seen. She looked back at the children. They disappeared into the stable. She breathed a momentary sigh of relief. They would stay there for a while, tending the horses after the long ride. She thought of going to the stable when she saw Fatmi come out of the kitchen and begin to remove the laundry from the clothesline.

Deborah turned her eyes back to the pine trees and it occurred to her that the shadows of the oncoming dusk had played tricks on her vision. Still she waited, never taking her eyes off the small forest.

Fatmi finished her work and headed back toward the kitchen. She was barely out of sight when the leaves rustled again.

Someone was lurking among those trees. Deborah's heart began to beat furiously and she could feel the perspiration run down her back. Slowly she groped along the paneled wall and pushed aside the panel that held Michael's hunting rifle.

She was feeling for the rifle when she realized there was more than one stored there. She peered into the darkened hiding place and was stunned to see several rifles standing side by side. On the small shelf at the top was a handgun and some bullets. She grabbed it and a fistful of bullets and turned back to the window. She had not handled any firearms in years but the urgency of the moment brought back all that Raphael had taught her. She loaded the gun quickly.

With gun aimed in the direction of the pines, she waited. She had no idea who was there or why. She was, however, convinced that whoever it was wanted to harm her children. Memories of waiting to catch sight of Tamar, to try to kill her to put her out of her misery, clouded her vision. She shook her head, desperate to clear her mind and concentrate on the small clump of trees that held danger.

Deborah could hear the children talking in the stable. Then Naomi came out and ran toward the house. At that moment, a rifle butt appeared from between the trees. Deborah released the safety catch of her gun and was about to fire when she realized the muzzle of the rifle did not follow Naomi but was aimed in the direction of the stable. Whoever was manning the rifle was obviously waiting for Gidon.

Deborah threw a look at the main house. Naomi was nowhere in sight. The garden was empty.

The moments ticked by slowly and finally Gidon came out of the stable.

Shots were fired and a man's body toppled out from between the trees and fell to the ground.

Gidon, dazed by the burst of gunfire, saw a man lying face-down near the pine forest, a smoking rifle beside him. He looked around and saw Deborah standing on the stoop of Raphael's house. She was ashen and was holding a pistol in her hand.

Michael, Naomi, Fatmi and Tova came running from various directions.

Michael knelt down beside the silent form, lying on the ground. "It's Abed and he's dead." Then looking up, he saw Deborah standing beside him, staring down at Abed. Her eyes were glazed and she was holding a pistol in her hand.

"He wanted to kill Gidon," she whispered, never taking her eyes off the dead man.

Michael stood up and put his arm around her shoulders.

Deborah looked up at him, a puzzled look on her face. Then, as the horror of what she had done reached her, she began to tremble and the gun fell from her hand.

"You had no choice," Michael said gently. She was in shock and he was frightened for her. "You've got to remember that. You had no choice."

"Is he the reason you didn't want us to come up here all these years?" she asked dully.

Michael nodded. "It has been ten years and it began to seem foolish. Also Mahmud felt it was safe."

The garden began to fill up with workers from the fields and several pass-ersby who had heard the shots.

Fatmi was on her knees next to her son, wailing mournfully.

Everyone stood about, looking helplessly at the bereaved mother. The wailing grew louder and Fatmi started pounding her breast.

Deborah disengaged herself from Michael's embrace and walked over to her. She moved in a daze, instinctively trying to help someone who was hurting deeply. She helped Fatmi up and held her close. The older woman stared at Deborah briefly, then with sudden composure said, "It was Allah's wish." And pulling away from Deborah, she walked toward the kitchen.

"There will be an investigation and reprisals," one of the workmen said.

"There will be no investigation or reprisals," Mahmud appeared from be-hind the stable, a rifle strapped to his shoulder. "I did what I had to do. My son was about to kill an innocent child in cold blood. I had no choice."

"What are you saying?" Deborah asked, showing emotion for the first time.

"I killed him," Mahmud reiterated.

"No, you didn't. I did," Deborah screamed. "Two shots were fired. One from my gun and one from his."

"There were three shots," Mahmud said with authority. "Now I must go to my village and tell them what has happened."

"Please, Mahmud, don't do this to yourself. Think of your family," Deborah pleaded. She started toward Mahmud, but Michael restrained her.

"Gidon, how many shots were fired?" Michael turned to the boy.

Gidon looked at Deborah. She was very pale and appeared frightened. His heart went out to her.

"Gidon, I asked you a question."

"Three," he answered solemnly.

Deborah screamed, then she lost control and broke down, sobbing.

Michael held her close and let the tears flow. She needed the release from the nightmare she had just lived through.

The crowd that had gathered stood watching the difficult scene. Michael searched their faces, trying to evaluate their reaction. He could not read their thoughts.

"Why don't you remove the body," he said gruffly.

Several men rushed forward, picked up the body and carried it off. Michael, Deborah, Gidon, Tova and Naomi watched in silence. Within minutes the crowd dispersed, leaving the stricken family alone.

"Why did he want to kill me?" Gidon was the first to speak.

"To avenge his son, Rafa. He thought you were the cause of Rafa's death," Michael answered.

"Was I?"

"No."

"Did he know that?"

"Of course he did. But he wanted to kill a Jew. He's always wanted to kill a Jew."

"And I was the Jew?" Gidon asked slowly.

"You were your mother's son, Gidon. He knew you only as Tamar's son," Michael's manner was strangely gentle.

"What will happen now?" Gidon asked.

"I don't know," Michael sighed. "But I'm sure this will not be the end of the matter."

"But Deborah did it to save me," Gidon whispered. "It was justified."

Michael looked at him sharply. The boy had just contradicted his earlier statement about the number of shots fired. "Everyone will be told it was Mahmud who killed his son. That could be tragic. Tragic, because his friends will say he did it to save a Jewish child. That they will never forgive and they will look for vengeance."

"Is this Arab justice?" Gidon felt sick.

"Unfortunately, this is Arab justice," Michael nodded, watching Gidon closely.

"Michael, I can't let it happen." Deborah had regained her composure. "Mahmud could never defend himself and I believe I can."

"It's a little more complicated since Gidon verified Mahmud's claim and there are witnesses to his statement," Michael said wearily.

"I don't care. A lie from a child to save his aunt is very understandable. Unbelievably honorable, in fact." Her voice cracked with emotion.

"Let's wait till morning and see what happens," Michael conceded. "I'll try to talk to Mahmud. He's a wise old man and he does love this family. What I don't know is how his friends will react. Although if he sticks to his story, the British authorities will probably intervene and mete out their punishment. What I do know is, we will be made to suffer for this death." He lowered his eyes and caught sight of the gun on the ground. Deborah too was staring at it. Michael started to say something but changed his mind, leaned down to pick up the gun, and without a word walked slowly toward Raphael's house.

"Tova, take the children into the house," Deborah said and rushed after Michael.

She found him cleaning the gun she had just fired. He did it expertly and she was reminded of the young Michael from their Nili days, authoritative and self-assured, whom she found so attractive and who so confused her in that attraction. She pushed the memory aside. "What are all those rifles doing there?" She waved her arm at the opening in the wall. "You're permitted only one hunting rifle by the British."

"You had no business finding them."

"No business finding them? Michael, I do live here. This is our home and I have a right to know what we have on this property."

"Knowing could be dangerous," Michael said seriously.

"We've lived through dangerous times before."

"We were much younger then."

"Michael, what is going on? I must know."

"We're in danger and we're trying to get people to learn how to protect themselves."

"Is it a problem?"

"We're disorganized," he sighed and stared at the small arsenal. "I so wish we had more of these and could teach more people to use them."

"Are the people in Bet Enav aware?" she asked.

"At long last your wonderful fellow farmers are ready to concede that we are in danger. They wouldn't agree when we told them about the Turks, but somehow they've accepted the fact that the Arabs might not be the most reliable friends in the world, even under British rule."

"Don't make fun of them," Deborah said wearily.

"I'm not making fun of them, but I wonder how dependable they're going to be after this little incident with Abed?"

"I'm sure they'll side with us."

"If they do, it will be because of you."

Deborah could hear the old anger, the old resentment. She walked over to him and placed her head on his shoulder. Haltingly he put his arm around her waist and kissed her hair. She turned to him and pressed her body to his.

Gidon, staring through the window, saw Deborah and Michael in their embrace. Then he saw Michael lower his head toward Deborah and kiss her on the lips.

He averted his eyes in confusion.

# CHAPTER TWENTY-SEVEN

GIDON could not sleep. Too many things had happened, too many emotions had surfaced and he could not put them out of his mind. It started while he was out riding with Naomi. Her complete sense of belonging to the land of Palestine, her references to her family and her home, the innocence with which she included him as a matter of course touched him but it also disturbed him. He wanted to believe her, but he did not feel it. Now someone wanted to kill him just because he was a Jew. It was too much for him to cope with on his own. The aunt he met in London two years ago was someone he could have talked to. Now he felt shy with her. In Palestine she was Naomi and Benji's mother and Michael's wife.

The shades were down and the room was in darkness. Gidon got out of bed quietly and ran down to the kitchen and out the back door. Daylight was breaking but it was still too early for anyone to be up. Crouching, he edged toward the back gate and started down a road which led toward the open fields. Once out in the field, he began to run.

He did not know how long he had been running, but finally out of breath, he stopped and found himself near the Bet Enav cemetery. He had never been there and it occurred to him that he had never thought of it.

The front gate was shut. He scaled the stone wall with ease. Even in the dim light of morning, he was stunned by the beauty of the place. The ground was covered with flowers. The trees were carefully trimmed. Many stones were exquisitely carved, with pretty flower arrangements placed on them. The serenity of the place soothed him. Walking around the small cemetery, he found his grandparents' graves without difficulty. They were prominently situated and placed next to each other, each with laudatory quotes inscribed on the stones. He expected his mother's grave to be beside them. It was not. Puzzled, he continued his search with growing frustration, when he finally stumbled upon it. Sitting at the far end of the cemetery, it was pressed up against the fence.

Gidon sank down to his knees and placed his body against the stone.

Suddenly all the pent-up emotion surfaced. His whole body to began to shake and he felt the tears run down his cheeks.

He must have fallen sleep, because he next felt a hand shaking him. He looked up, dazed.

"What are you doing here?" Someone was standing over him and gripping his shoulder.

He blinked to clear his vision and found himself staring at a small, olive-skinned man with long sidecurls and a yarmulke. Beneath a scraggly beard was his pointed chin. The beard plus his slanted eyes made him look like an ancient Chinese figurine.

Gidon started to get up, but the little man held him down. Small and wiry as he was, he had a powerful grip.

"No, you don't," he said slowly. "First you tell me what you're doing here."

"I came to visit my mother's grave," Gidon said, trying to extricate himself from the firm hold.

The man threw a look at the gravestone and let go of Gidon's arm, a look of astonishment transforming his peculiar features.

"You're Tamar Danziger's boy, aren't you?"

Gidon nodded.

"Come," he said urgently and pulled Gidon up. "Come quickly."

Gidon followed him out of the cemetery and they headed toward a small shack standing a few feet away from the entrance.

When they reached the doorway of the shack, the man pushed the door open and waved Gidon in.

Gidon hesitated. "I should be getting home."

"You're not going anywhere alone," the man said sternly.

"Who are you?" Gidon asked, getting angry.

"My name is Nechemya and I'm the caretaker of the cemetery," he announced with pride. "And you will do as I say."

What struck Gidon as he walked into the small front room of the shack was its cleanliness. A large wooden table stood in the center, covered with a white cloth, surrounded by numerous chairs. None were matching, but they were neatly placed. The stone floor was bare and in the far corner stood a large ancient stove with steaming vats. Rusting pails placed on the window sills held planted flowers, giving the room a strangely festive mood. The poverty was evident and the only thing of value were the two silver candlesticks arranged on the table. Gidon remembered it was Friday.

"Sit," Nechemya commanded, pulling one chair away from the table. He then lit a kerosene burner and placed a water kettle on it.

"My family will be worried about me," Gidon started again.

"Your family *is* worried about you. They're running around the whole area, looking for you."

Gidon got up quickly. "All the more reason that I get back there."

"I will take you when I'm ready."

"But why not now?"

Before Nechemya could answer, the front door opened and a youngster who resembled Nechemya entered the room. Like Nehemya, he was small and dark and wore a yarmulke, but had no side curls. He looked no older than Gidon, but a sparse dark fuzz had already begun to grow on his upper lip.

"My son, Tuvia," Nechemya announced, handing Gidon a glass of tea. "Drink that," he commanded and turned back to his son. "Is it as bad as it sounds?"

"Worse," Tuvia answered.

Nechemya nodded thoughtfully. "I'll be back in a few minutes and until then, see to it that the boy doesn't leave here."

Tuvia settled himself on the floor next to a window and seemed to be staring out.

Gidon, feeling trapped, tried to judge the distance between where he sat and the front door. Convinced that Tuvia was too preoccupied to notice, he jumped toward it. Tuvia lunged across the room and easily pushed Gidon down to the floor. Gidon was stunned at the boy's agility and power.

"That was stupid," Tuvia said quietly.

"It certainly was," Gidon conceded and smiled sheepishly.

Tuvia smiled back and put his hand out. Gidon shook it firmly. "Where did you learn to tackle that way?" Gidon asked with admiration.

"Where did you learn to fall so gracefully?" Tuvia had not answered his question.

In the silence that followed, Gidon looked around the room and his eyes came to rest on a large piece of cardboard with the motto "In blood and flame Judea fell/In blood and flame Judea will rise." It was scrawled in a childish handwriting.

"What's that?" he asked pointing to the sign.

"It speaks the truth. It was said by a leader who knows that only a land fought for can truly be called a people's homeland. To make Palestine a Jewish homeland, we shall have to fight for it."

Gidon had heard the sentiment before but this was the first time he fully understood it.

"But the Arabs think Palestine belongs to them," he said.

"The British promised us this land," Tuvia answered innocently.

Gidon mulled over the statement. According to Thomas, the British had promised Palestine to the Arabs. Could they have promised the same land to both people?

Tuvia continued, "This land is big enough for both of our people. And if the Arabs do not agree to our being here, we will fight them."

"But you can't just chase a people away from their homes," Gidon said tentatively. "The British may have promised the Jews a homeland in Palestine, but what about justice?"

"Justice is spoken of in the Bible," Nechemya had come back into the room. "Nili is our justice."

Gidon raised his brow. He knew its meaning, but could not apply it.

"The eternity of Israel shall not lie," Nechemya continued. "The prophet Samuel said it to King Saul when the Jews appeared to be doomed. And we prevailed then and we will prevail now." He stopped briefly and when he next spoke his voice was reverent. "The British may be all-mighty, but we have the Almighty on our side. The eternity shall not lie."

*The eternity of Israel shall not lie.* Thomas could not argue with that sentiment. He was a religious man; surely he would have understood what Nechemya was saying. Gidon felt comfortable with the idea.

Gidon wanted to continue the conversation but Nechemya opened the front door.

"We must go now," Nechemya said.

They did not walk through the village. Instead, Nehemya led Gidon through the fields. Nechemya was crouching and indicated that Gidon do likewise. He also noted that Nechemya kept looking about anxiously.

The sun was up and Gidon figured it was mid-morning, yet the day was strangely silent, particularly for a Friday, a short working day. Most farmers were out early in an effort to complete their work before the Sabbath. There were no sounds coming from the village, either. Suddenly, Nechemya grabbed him and pushed him to the ground. Someone was moving about in the bushes. They lay very still. Lying with his face pressed to the damp earth, Gidon smelled smoke. He lifted his head and looked back. A black cloud of soot rose from the valley, beyond the groves.

Nechemya rose and started walking again. Gidon followed.

"Why are we taking this road?" Gidon asked, unable to contain himself any longer. Nechemya silenced him with a wave of this hand.

When they entered the Ben Hod garden, Gidon spotted Deborah.

Naomi was clinging to her and crying. Tova, standing close beside them, was clutching Benji's shoulders. Deborah was looking about anxiously. When she heard the back gate open, she turned and with a cry of relief ran toward them.

Gidon could feel her body shaking with emotion. "Where have you been?" she kept mumbling as she searched his face anxiously. "Oh, my precious child, I thought . . ." She was too choked up to continue.

Naomi too ran to him, and Tova began scolding him in her strange accent. Tense as the moment was, Gidon wanted to laugh.

"What happened?" he asked, trying to disengage himself from his aunt's embrace.

"Where were you?" Michael came running through the front gate. His face was filled with concern, his eyes were bloodshot and for a minute Gidon thought Michael was going to strike him. As Michael came closer, Gidon had the impulse to start running when, to his surprise, Michael put his arm around his shoulder and embraced him.

"I went for a walk." Gidon stared up at Michael. None of it made any sense.

"One hell of a day to do it in," Michael did not let go of his shoulder.

"Please tell me what happened," Gidon exploded. He was pleased with their concern, but could not bear the suspense.

"Mahmud was found murdered and his body was placed on the steps of the synagogue with the words *Jew Lover* smeared on the floor beside him," Michael said.

Gidon felt sick. "Why?"

"That too is considered Arab justice," Michael answered, and there was deep sadness in his voice.

"Tell him about the massacres," Benji cried out. "Tell him."

Gidon looked from Michael to Deborah and back to Michael.

"There's been a terrible bloodbath in several towns and villages around the country." Michael spoke with difficulty.

"Who?" Gidon blurted out. "Why?"

"Arabs around the country have gone on a rampage, killing Jewish men, women and children."

"Everybody is dead in Tel Ada." Naomi began to cry again. "The wall, the gate—remember, Gidon? Well, you were right, it didn't protect them."

"Was there no one to defend them?" Gidon could not quite comprehend what was being said. "Can't Jews defend themselves?"

"Defend with what?" Michael sounded tired and defeated. "With guns the British won't let us have?"

Gidon stiffened. "Where were the British?" he asked.

"The British came too late, as usual."

"Michael," Deborah spoke sternly, "Please don't."

"You're right," he conceded. "But remember, you were the one who trusted the Arabs. Not me." His words were directed at Deborah.

"We'll talk about it later." Deborah refused to get drawn into the argument.

Gidon screamed, "I don't understand anything. Please, I don't understand." He was suddenly terrified.

Michael gripped his shoulder. "It's all right, Gidon," he said. "It's bloodletting, which the Arabs seem to have a need for," he continued. "It's like the biblical seven-year cycle." He cleared his throat. "Now let's go into the house."

With his arms around the children and Tova and Deborah following, they started toward the house. Suddenly a car screeched to a halt at the front gate and a British officer followed by two soldiers came running up the driveway.

"Mr. Ben Hod?" The officer looked toward Michael.

"Yes, I'm Michael Ben Hod." Michael stepped forward.

"My name is Captain Reston and by order of His Majesty's armed services, I've been ordered to search these premises."

"Search for what?" Michael asked.

"Guns."

"Guns?" Michael seemed to relax and moved closer to the captain.

The latter, an attractive young Englishman, held his ground, but a look of uncertainty came over his face.

"Yes, we've had a report about a shooting which took place on these ground yesterday. A native boy was shot dead and now we hear his father was found murdered on the steps of your synagogue in Bet Enav."

"Indeed," Michael nodded seriously. "Did the report mention who killed the boy and the reasons for this death? And furthermore, did the report also indicate that there was a message written next to his father's body when it was found?"

"Quite," the young officer snapped. "But all of that is immaterial. Shots were fired on these grounds. Three shots, we're told. Meaning that someone here possesses firearms. That, sir, is against the law."

"And the law must be upheld at all costs." Michael's tone matched the officer's.

"Quite right." Captain Reston nodded. "Now for the guns."

Michael smiled pleasantly. "I do have a hunting rifle and I have a permit for it."

"I'd like to see it, as well as the permit, and I must insist that my men be allowed to search the premises."

"Who authorized this search?" Michael asked, his manner still cordial.

"Colonel Owen Cartwright."

"Colonel Cartwright?" Gidon cried out involuntarily.

The captain looked around, startled. "Beg your pardon?"

"I seem to have read his name in a history book," Gidon said quickly. "Is that possible, sir?"

"Who are you?" the captain asked, confused by the boy's English accent.

"He's my nephew," Deborah spoke for the first time.

"What's your name?" the officer asked. "And I'd like the boy to speak for himself."

Gidon hesitated briefly. "My name is Gidon Danziger," he answered calmly.

A small smile appeared on Michael's lips.

"Captain Reston, you may search the grounds if you like. But I can help you out by simply showing you my hunting rifle, as well as the permit." He pointed toward Raphael's house. "It's in there, in the bedroom cupboard."

"You go into that house and search it," Captain Reston spoke to his men. "I'll stay here and keep an eye on things."

The minutes dragged by and the tension mounted. They could hear the soldiers in Raphael's house slamming cupboards and drawers shut.

Deborah, holding her children, was rigid with fear. Small beads of perspiration began to form on her upper lip. Gidon held his breath and his muscles tensed with nervousness. Michael, however, was looking about calmly, a disinterested expression on his face.

It seemed like an eternity before a soldier came out, carrying Michael's rifle.

"Sir." He handed the rifle to the captain. "It was in the cupboard as he indicated and there are no other firearms in that house."

"You're more than welcome to search the main house as well," Michael said graciously. "And the rest of the grounds."

The captain lost his composure. "I don't believe that will be necessary at this time. But you do understand, sir, that there will be an investigation concerning these two shocking murders."

"Captain Reston," Michael sucked in his breath and his voice grew icy. "I assume you heard about the massacres that have taken place in various Jewish quarters around the country."

"Shocking, indeed," the young officer's tone was properly serious. "His Majesty's government has sent its condolences to the bereaved families. And the prime minister has sent a stern letter of protest to the mufti of Jerusalem. But the laws of the mandate must be upheld. No individual has the right to possess armaments. That is the law."

He saluted Michael in proper military fashion, bowed to Deborah and marched away carrying Michael's rifle, followed by his men.

"He took your rifle, Michael," Gidon cried out the minute the men were out of sight.

"Poor bastard," Michael sneered. "In his simple mind, he's following orders." He put his hand to his brow and rubbed it briefly. "He probably feels like a hero."

With his arms around Gidon, Naomi and Benji, he led them toward the house.

Overwrought as she was, Deborah was moved by the sight of Gidon being included in Michael's embrace. She was deeply grateful for his concern for the boy.

Walking slowly behind him, she wondered if it was possible that all the tragic events of the last twenty-four hours would form a bond between Gidon and her husband. Gidon had stated his identity with pride. He had announced that he was a Jew and a Danziger.

# CHAPTER
# TWENTY-EIGHT

As Michael had said, the bloodletting had taken place and the country returned to a state of calm. For a time speeches were made, protests were launched, the government gave lip service to both the Jewish and Arab communities, promising that efforts were under way to right the wrong that had been done. No one pinpointed what the wrong had been. No one bothered to discover or understand what the issues were.

In Palestine, the divisions within the Jewish community grew more distinct. Fight for your right to exist, said the militants. Negotiate for your right to exist, said the mainstream leadership. Both tried to recruit segments of the population to their side.

The divisiveness was also felt within the Ben Hod household. Deborah, who tried to avoid discussing politics with Michael, found herself in direct opposition to everything he said.

"We've been betrayed," she said one evening at supper. They were still in Bet Enav, in spite of the atmosphere of fear that still lingered over the area.

"I wouldn't rush to conclusions," Michael answered, surprised by her statement.

"Rush to conclusions?" Deborah exclaimed "All these people murdered in cold blood. Families in Hebron, Safad and other small communities, bludgeoned to death by Arab fanatics while the British stand by doing nothing? That's jumping to conclusions?"

"What do you suggest we do?" he asked.

"Defend ourselves."

"Violence will only breed more violence. The British government has an obligation toward us and I'm sure they intend to keep it."

"You weren't always so quick to reject armed resistance," Deborah stared at him. "I remember when you first came to us at Nili. You joined us because we were actively doing something to help defeat the Turks. You were willing to put your life on the line then. We certainly would have fought the Turks physically if we could have."

"The British are not the Turks," Michael said coldly. "We had no one to talk to in Turkey. We have friends in England and among the various other European countries. I put my faith in them. They promised to help us attain a homeland and I believe they will."

"We're almost into nineteen thirty. It's twelve years since the war ended and what do we have to show for it?" Deborah demanded.

"We are doing everything we can," Michael assured her.

"When you say *we*, whom do you mean?" Deborah asked, and there was a hint of sarcasm in her voice. She was fully aware that Michael had been trying to reclaim his position of confidence with his old friends and she suspected that his efforts had not yet borne fruit.

"We?" Michael said slowly. "We are the majority of the Jewish people in Palestine, led by people like Reb who are going to go on negotiating, talking, placating, doing everything to avoid violence."

Gidon listened to his aunt and uncle arguing and agreed with Deborah but dared not voice his views. Michael had been extremely kind to him since the shooting of Mahmud and he was pleased to be included in his uncle's good graces.

"I'm going up to Safad tomorrow," Michael suddenly announced. "And I'd like to take Gidon with me."

Deborah's head shot up. "Is that wise?" she asked.

"Gidon should see the country, not only from the comforts of Tel Aviv and Bet Enav, but the whole land," Michael said and smiled at Gidon.

"I want to go too," Benji cried out indignantly.

"No," Deborah said too sharply. She did not know what condition the city of Safad was in after the dreadful killings that had taken place there. She doubted that Gidon was old enough to witness it. She was sure Benji was not. But she had rejected her son's request too sharply and she knew it. "You're still too young, Benji," she softened her voice. "Another time, maybe."

"I want to go, I want to go, I want to go," Benji screamed and ran out of the room. Michael followed him.

"May I be excused?" Gidon asked. He wanted to get to Nechemya's house. Tuvia was waiting for him and he had much to discuss with him.

"Of course you can," Deborah said, still preoccupied with her attitude toward Benji. Vaguely she was conscious of Tova and Naomi clearing the table as she tried to understand her feelings toward her son. He was a difficult child, but not as difficult as Gidon. Yet, she could cope with Gidon. She felt a deep bond with Gidon, a far deeper bond with him than with her own son.

Gidon, sitting with Tuvia and Nechemya in the amphitheater outside Bet Enav, related the conversation that had taken place at the dinner table.

"Your uncle is naive," Nechemya smiled his sad smile. "But he'll learn. They all will. There will be lots more blood spilled, Jewish blood, before he and his friends will come around and know that we must not be shy of spilling blood to claim our rights."

Gidon crept into his room late that night, fearful of waking Benji. Nechemya was right and he agreed with him. Instinctively he knew that he should try to keep his friendship with Nechemya and Tuvia from Michael.

Returning to Tel Aviv, Deborah was pleased by the enthusiasm with which Gidon entered the gymnasium. The relationship between Michael and Gidon had grown quite solid and if she noted Benji's discontent over his father's attention to Gidon, she felt that Michael's love for Benji would not suffer. Gidon needed the attention.

The early 1930s saw Tel Aviv develop from a sleepy, seaside village to a full-fledged cultural center. People from Europe, the United States and England gravitated to it. Most came because they wanted to come. Others came because of rumbles of anti-Semitism in Europe, especially Germany. New settlements and villages were built. The kibbutz, a communal way of life, was proving a serious movement, attracting many of the young. It was a difficult way of life, but it was fulfilling and constructive. Every achievement was hailed by the whole Jewish population with festivities and pride. Each group of newcomers brought with them a part of their past culture and each made its mark. Tel Aviv became a small melting pot. Houses, shops, streets, small parks, museums, cinemas as well as theaters, flourished. Concerts, with prominent musicians performing, came from all over the world. Magazines and newspapers were published and although the politicians argued about the need for a Jewish state, most assumed that someday it would happen. Until then they were in Palestine, they were Jews and by being there, they made it a Jewish homeland. Traditions were adhered to. Everyone worked six days a week and rested on the Sabbath. The Sabbath had a holiness about it that was felt by all. Buses stopped running. Shops were closed. Parents spent the day with their children, walking along the beach or sipping cold drinks in small cafés along the shore. It was a relatively peaceful community, with little or no crime except the occasional bloodletting by Arabs. Most of the land inhabited by Jews barely had a police force, since none was needed. The people trusted the British, for the most part. There were setbacks. There were unpleasant declarations from London aimed against Jews, but the overall mood was optimistic.

As Tel Aviv grew and flourished, so did the social status of the Ben Hods. Michael was pleased for Deborah, but he was much too involved in the politics of the country to participate in the activities that preoccupied her. He was inching his way back into the graces of the friends he had abandoned when joining Nili, although an air of mistrust toward him still existed. His marriage to Deborah Danziger did not help. It never ceased to amaze him that someone as intelligent and perceptive as Deborah would be unaware of the poverty that existed around them. Most of his friends were struggling to eke out an existence and the lavishness he lived in disturbed him. Yet it was his financial independence that enabled him to give so much of his time to public works and he suspected that his old friends, in a way, took advantage of him. Money was what his party needed and he was able to supply it when a difficult situation arose. He was fully aware that Reb had never forgiven him for his affiliation with the Danzigers and that the offer to write for the magazine was to a great extent dependent on the fact that he did not ask to be paid for his contributions. Still, the idea of a homeland for the Jews, where communal life would prevail, was his goal as much as it was Reb's and that was the motivation for all his actions.

The occasional flare-ups at home over Deborah's political views or his basic dislike of her friends were difficult for him. That was to be expected when one considered the vast difference in social, financial and political matters that existed between husband and wife. Gidon's presence did not help. He more than anyone churned up the secret conflict that still existed in Michael. In the dark recesses of his mind, he was torn between his secret loyalties to the Nili activism and his own party's determination to move the country into a peaceful transition to statehood. Gidon was the reincarnation of Tamar in Michael's eyes. The boy was showing that same blind dedication, that fanatic heroism that Tamar displayed in defying the Turks. Just as Michael had always been intimidated by Tamar's haughty, superior manner toward him, Gidon, although only a child and trying hard to ingratiate himself, also intimidated Michael. Much as he loved Deborah and his children, Gidon seemed to dominate their home and made Michael feel like an intruder in his own house. He began to spend much more time with Reb and his old cronies.

Deborah was fully aware that she and Michael were drifting apart and it pained her greatly. For a while after they returned from Bet Enav, she had hoped that the closeness that they had during their summer would continue. She even began to hope for another child, for her Nili. Michael would not hear of it. They had three children, he stated firmly, and Deborah modified her disappointment with the idea that Michael finally considered Gidon a son.

Gidon joined the boy scouts and appeared to be as serious about his after-school activities as he was about his school work. More and more he resembled Tamar. Often Tamar's image would replace Gidon's physical presence and Deborah would feel a chill go through her. At those moments her love for Gidon would overwhelm her and she prayed for his well being. She wanted him to grow to an old age and derive the happiness from life that had not been granted to Tamar. Deborah hoped he would fall in love. A strong, loving, dedicated wife, she felt, would help him settle down.

Naomi was a joy. A petite, cuddly redhead with freckles, she went through an awkward period during her early teens. But unlike other girls, Naomi did not seem to mind it. She was a tomboy and preferred shorts and simple blouses to the dresses that Deborah had sewn for her. As she grew older, the flaming red hair became a deep shade of amber. The long, thick braids were cut into a short, curly bob, the freckles on her nose multiplied and her green eyes never lost their wondrous look of hope and merriment. She lived for the time they spent in Bet Enav. She spoke often of joining a group of youngsters and starting a kibbutz in the northern part of the country. Michael was pleased with her ambition. Deborah, although proud, was fearful. Starting a new settlement in an isolated part of the country was fraught with problems and danger. The British government was adamant in its refusal to allow the immigration of Jews to Palestine or the establishment of new Jewish settlements in Palestine. On these two issues, the whole Ben Hod family was in agreement. Immigration and settling the land were essential and any and all means had to be applied to achieve both.

Benji continued to worry Deborah. He was an attractive youngster but more belligerent than ever, with a dreadful temper that he did not even try to control. He was extremely jealous of Gidon and took pleasure in hurting him. Often he made remarks about Gidon being an orphan who was living off the family without contributing to his upkeep. Deborah tried to explain to Benji that Gidon was not a charity case but an equal partner in the family. It had no effect.

He withdrew into himself and spent his time scheming and plottind business ventures. He had an uncanny business sense that amazed Michael and embarrassed Deborah. She found it more and more difficult to relate to her son. He seemed equally pleased to separate himself from her.

Still Deborah was happy with her life. Her household was running smoothly. Tova managed the household and gave Deborah the freedom to spend her time doing her charity work, watching her children grow and going to Europe in the spring.

At first all of them went, but in a relatively short time she found herself going on her yearly trips by herself and Deborah knew that her children had grown up. It was the first time she felt old. She was not yet forty, yet she felt like a lonely old lady.

It was only in Bet Enav that Deborah felt a sense of family unity. Somehow she had succeeded in making the house in Bet Enav their home.

The first sign of political friction came when Reb was murdered on the beach in Tel Aviv. The man charged with the crime belonged to a political party in opposition to Reb's. The whole country went into mourning. There were few murders in Palestine. Political murders were almost unheard of. Michael was shattered. The newspapers were filled with descriptions of the murder. The assailant was convicted in the press before formal charges were issued. Michael's editorial in the magazine called for the death penalty.

Gidon, aside from feeling the man charged with the crime was innocent, accused Michael of unfair bias. Angry words were exchanged and the mood in the house grew tense. When the accused man was released for lack of sufficient evidence, a near break occurred between Michael and Gidon. On the surface it was a family argument, yet it ran deep. Deborah was uncomfortable with the issue, especially since she agreed with Gidon. The incident troubled and surprised her. Gidon had never voiced a political opinion. His adamance worried her. She began to watch him more carefully. He was fifteen and was a good, polite and obedient boy and she trusted him. But whereas in the past she accepted his comings and goings, she now worried and was uncertain about his activities. There was nothing concrete about her concern, and she wondered if Michael too was concerned. She dared not ask. And although the atmosphere in their home returned to its peaceful routine but the closeness that had existed since that first summer in Bet Enav seemed to be coming apart.

It was Benji who snapped the fragile cord of unity.

"I saw Gidon wearing the brown shirt of a soldier today," Benji announced one day, almost casually but the malice was there.

The family was having a rare supper together and Deborah saw Michael go white with rage.

"Brown shirt?" Michael exploded. "Hitler and Mussolini's thugs wear brown shirts," he raged. "No member of this family should be caught dead in one of those."

Gidon did not flinch. "Brown, blue or white-and-blue. We're all Jews. We all fight for the same cause."

"We fight as a last resort!" Michael screamed, completely losing control. "We negotiate. We discuss. We behave in a civilized manner. We prepare ourselves for a possible fight, but our aim is to avoid fighting. And when we fight, it is only to defend ourselves."

"Like we defended the people in Tel Ada? In Hebron? In Safad? We fight only when we are threatened? Well, we are threatened, every day of our lives," Gidon answered calmly.

"Who's threatening you today?"

"No one is doing it openly, but it's brewing all around us. The only chance we have of winning is to be strong and unafraid."

The gulf between them widened. Gidon was Tamar and Thomas's son and in him, Deborah saw their passion. She knew that, like his parents, he would not be swayed. Michael, still a forceful, dedicated man with a desperate need to prevail, had met his match in his own home.

The subject of the brown shirt and its implications was never again mentioned, but the relationship between Gidon and Michael changed. Michael no longer trusted the boy. The beneficiary of the falling-out was Benji. Michael turned his full attention to his son. Deborah was more conflicted than ever. Benji needed his father's love, but what Michael was giving their son was not what the boy needed. He simply indulged him. Benji was a selfish young man, greedy and arrogant. On the rare occasions when she pointed these failings out, Michael defended him vehemently. More and more Benji was given responsibilities dealing with the properties in Bet Enav. The latter concerned her and it occurred to her that she should start taking greater interest in her business affairs, but events happening around her made her put off doing anything concrete.

The shifting alliances in the household did not seem to affect Gidon in any way. He continued to excel in school and his behavior at home was exemplary. If he was party to any protests against the British, who were trying to appease the Arabs by suppressing the Jewish community, he did so with great discretion.

Still, Deborah waited. She did not know what it was she was waiting for, except that she dared not leave her family alone. The house was now shrouded in a strange silence. Mundane subjects were discussed, but there was an absence of talk about the future. In a strange way, she related the atmosphere in her home to the one that existed in the country. There were undercurrents of unrest, although they rarely surfaced.

As Gidon's graduation from the gymnasium grew close, Michael again suggested that Gidon go off to England to continue his education. He mentioned it to Deborah almost as an afterthought, but she knew he very much wanted Gidon out of their home.

"Discuss it with him," she suggested.

"There's no discussion possible with him," Michael said impatiently. "He's off in some never-never land of fantasy."

"I find him easy to talk to," Deborah continued in a matter-of-fact tone. "Besides, I don't want him to go."

Michael looked at her for a long moment. "Someday you'll have to let him go."

She was taken aback by his tone. He's still jealous, she thought. Like Benji, Michael was jealous of Gidon and she was both indignant and embarrassed. Embarrassed because she knew that Michael had a right to be jealous. And indignant because she had suddenly been confronted with a truth she had been hiding from.

"He's Tamar's son, Deborah, not yours," Michael continued. "You've tried to ignore that fact but you must face it. Benji is your son and there are times I feel you forget that fact. You're wrapped up in the past, in Nili, in Tamar, in what was. In a way, you've never become your own person. All of them, and Tamar in particular, seem to haunt you. Gidon to you is the past reborn."

"She haunts you, too," Deborah blurted the words out.

Michael appeared stunned by her words and was about to answer when Gidon walked in.

"Am I intruding?" he asked.

"I'll get you some breakfast." Deborah wanted to get away. She and Michael had always avoided discussing the past. Certainly Tamar's name had rarely been mentioned and having her presence surface disturbed her.

Her hands shook as she carried a tray back into the breakfast room.

"Political science at the University of Jerusalem?" Michael was saying as she walked in. "It's the most ridiculous thing I've ever heard." He was still seated, but he was leaning forward as though ready for a fight.

"What's ridiculous about it?" Gidon asked.

"What will that prepare you for? Someday you will have to earn a living, you know."

"I could become a teacher," Gidon answered.

"You'll never teach," Michael sneered. "You're too arrogant."

Deborah was shocked by what Michael was saying. Gidon had the makings of an excellent teacher. But more than that, he was a wealthy young man in his own right and there was no need for him to be concerned at this point about how to earn a living. Besides, he was young. They were a close-knit family who would care for each other if the need ever arose.

"I don't have to stand here and be insulted," Gidon said stiffly. "I may be arrogant, but I'll figure out a way of making a living, Michael. I assure you."

He was angrier than she had ever seen him when he walked out of the room.

"That was unfair," Deborah said the minute Gidon was gone. "He would make an excellent teacher. He is very talented in many areas, and extremely resourceful. He has some money from his father. There is no need for him to rush into anything."

"He's never worked a day in his life," Michael snapped. "Wealthy or poor, a man has to work for a living."

"And I'm sure he will," Deborah said. Then after a long pause, she continued. "Michael, half of what we have belongs to him."

"It belongs to you, Naomi and Benji."

Deborah paled. "Michael, I've asked you in the past to help me draw up papers giving Gidon what is his. You've always been too busy. I was busy and never got it done. Now I insist."

"By all means," Michael said coldly. "You don't need me for that. Go to any lawyer and have it done. But I suggest you think carefully about what you're doing. Gidon is a confused young man. He'll waste it, and in wasting what is his, he'll waste what belongs to Naomi and Benji as well."

"It can be divided up properly," Deborah argued.

"Hardly," Michael said. "What will you divide? The quarry? The houses? The farm? It's agricultural land. Orange groves, vineyards, olive fields. And Gidon wouldn't know an orange tree from a grapevine or an olive branch. So think carefully before you do anything that will harm your children."

The subject did not come up again and events caused Deborah to keep putting off the formal writing of her will.

Gidon's graduation from the gymnasium coincided with the outbreak of hostilities in Jaffa. The senseless killings started with Arabs rioting against their Jewish neighbors. Within days the disturbances spread throughout the country. The British government stood by, doing little to stem the violence.

Deborah was beside herself with worry. Gidon's behavior became erratic. Naomi was completely immersed in her plans to join a kibbutz. Benji was at Misha's agricultural school, but it was surrounded by Arab villages and she worried about his safety. Michael was rarely home. Only when they were all in their rooms would she finally fall into an exhausted sleep.

The tension in the country mounted as did the tensions in the Ben Hod household. As summer passed, the Arabs, incited by rumors, were now on a religious rampage, led by the mufti of Jerusalem. Traveling on the roads was more dangerous than ever. When the British government, in a further effort to appease the Arabs, issued the vicious "White Paper" forbidding further immigration of Jews to Palestine and suggesting a shocking partition of the country, the whole Jewish community was up in arms.

That White Paper was a serious departure from British policy toward the Jewish population and contradicted its basic promise to the Jews. With Hitler's power solidifying in Europe, many Jews wanted to leave Germany. Suddenly the gates of Palestine were closed to them. The partition plan was an even greater stab in the back, since it left the Jews with only a small sliver of land. The British were reneging on every promise they had made to the Jews.

The latest British action brought an uneasy truce to the Ben Hod family. They had all congregated for a holiday reunion at Bet Enav and Deborah was worried that Michael and Gidon would not get on.

Gidon arrived from Jerusalem, where violent protests had been organized against the British. Deborah was sure he had a hand in those actions, although she had no proof of it. Naomi came with a friend and they spent their time planning their trip to the United States to recruit youngsters to come and help them build their new settlement. The White Paper seemed not to affect her at all. Benji ignored it, as though it had not happened. Michael had come from Tel Aviv after numerous days of debate about how to deal with the new situation. The declaration by the British was a serious blow to Michael's party, which had become a provisional government of the Jews while awaiting the creation of the Jewish State.

To Deborah's utter amazement, Michael spent a great deal of time with Gidon. For that brief period, they had a common enemy—the British mandate. Michael and Gidon were not in agreement as to how to deal with the new situation, but they were Jews who would fight together if a fight were to occur. It was one of the happiest times for Deborah and one of the last times Michael and Gidon would present a united front.

The turmoil in Palestine continued. In 1939, talk of war against Germany was rampant and still the Arabs continued their vendetta. Almost daily a killing was reported, or an act of sabotage was discovered. When a retaliatory measure was expedited, the Arabs, indignant at the Jews' audacity, would commit an even more violent act of brutality. The British stood by, seemingly helpless, guided by the Colonel Cartwrights of the world.

But even in the midst of the almost daily terror, a brutal mutilation of a family in Bet Enav sent a shudder of revulsion through the country. The bodies of the victims disappeared and only the blood on the walls of their house gave evidence to the monstrous crime.

Sitting in Raphael's house, where Gidon stayed when in Bet Enav, Deborah waited. It was a hot summer night and Deborah had the windows open and was staring at the mountains in the distance. In the past the sight would have calmed her. On this night, she was too overwrought. Something dreadful was about to happen, although she had no idea what it was.

It was past midnight when he finally came in. Even in the dim light she could see the dark, ugly bloodstains on his clothes. Standing in the open doorway, he did not seem surprised to see her. He was extremely calm. She could not decide which frightened her more, the bloodied clothing or his strange, detached mood.

Without a word, she took the clothes from him, walked into Raphael's bathroom and washed away the blood. As the water turned red and splashed onto the white tiles, she remembered the sight of Tamar's blood drying on the floor so many years back. When she walked back into the living room, Gidon was fast asleep.

Michael arrived early the next morning. He looked old and tired.

"Whoever avenged the death of that family cannot be faulted," Michael said. "But it should have been organized under the auspices of a governing committee. We can defend our actions if they're carried out properly. As it is, we'll be subjected to a cruel investigation, difficult searches, abuses by the British that will be hard to counter."

"What happened?" Deborah asked.

"A caravan of mules was shot dead and their owner was killed in cold blood."

"Hardly in cold blood, I'd say," Gidon appeared in the doorway. "A father, mother and two innocent children wiped out for no reason—that's murder in cold blood."

"Don't split hairs, Gidon," Michael thundered. "You know what I mean."

"Was the owner of the mules possibly involved in the murder of that family?" Gidon asked.

"We don't know and that's the point. We know where the killers came from and once found we would have dealt with them."

"Where was he from, the Arab who was killed?" Gidon looked mildly interested.

"He was heading toward the village we suspect the murderers came from," Michael conceded. He looked up at Gidon. "Why?"

"Just a thought. It might be that whoever committed this act of revenge might have known what he or she was doing."

"Does anyone know who did it?" Deborah wanted the dialogue between them to stop.

"No," Michael answered, never taking his eyes off Gidon. "We do know that whoever did it must have been bloodied. The mules were shot, but a bayonet was also used." He paused briefly before continuing. "I've been asked to investigate this part of the country. Frankly, I thought it might be Tuvia."

"Tuvia!" Gidon laughed. "You are well organized, aren't you? He's become one of your fellow travelers recently. Haven't you heard?"

"I've heard, but I don't have to believe," Michael said. "Are you two no longer friends?"

"He's my brother," Gidon answered simply. "He always will be."

Michael decided to change the subject. "What are you doing here, anyway?"

"Me? It's my summer vacation. Naomi is leaving for the United States and I'd like to spend time with her before she goes." He stood up, bowed graciously and left the room.

Deborah studied Michael's face. He was staring at the door through which Gidon had gone.

"I don't trust him, Deborah," he said through clenched teeth.

Her heart fell. "You never really did."

"That's beside the point. What's worse is that everyone I'm involved in with doesn't trust him. It's making my position very difficult."

"Is that what you're worried about—your position? Why don't you worry about Gidon?"

"It's taken me a long time to regain the confidence of my friends. I refuse to have it jeopardized by him. Oh, Deborah we're fighting an enemy greater than the Turks now and I want to participate in that fight. And this time I want to be with my friends."

"This time we're all fighting for the same cause," she said, but she felt deeply conflicted. Michael was her husband and she wanted his happiness. But Michael had her, the children, his friends. Gidon had no one. Her conflict reminded her of the time she had sided with Michael against Raphael, David and Tamar. Then, Michael had been the outsider; now Gidon was.

"Yes, we're fighting for the same cause. But it's the likes of him who damage us with wild grandstanding."

"What are you saying!" she asked, frightened by his tone.

"I'm not sure," he answered and stood up. "Where is Naomi?"

"I'll go find her," Deborah got up quickly. She had forgotten that Gidon's clothes were on the clothesline and they were clearly visible from the kitchen windows.

Michael followed her into the kitchen.

Naomi was standing there at the ironing board, pressing some clothes. A pile of clean laundry stood beside her, waiting to be ironed. Deborah caught sight of Gidon's shirt and trousers at the bottom of the pile.

Deborah felt faint. Naomi knew. Who else? Gidon was smart, but so was Michael.

The investigation intensified as both the British and the Jews searched for the killer. Gidon was questioned but Tuvia supplied him with an alibi. The British were satisfied. Michael was not, and Deborah knew she had to get Gidon out of the country.

"War is imminent," Michael shouted when she said she would be accompanying Naomi as far as Cherbourg and then stay on in Europe for a couple of weeks.

"I promised Naomi I'd go with her part of the way. Besides, I'm not going to Germany," Deborah answered pleasantly. "I'll go to Switzerland. I'm tired, I haven't had a trip in quite a while and the war hasn't broken out yet. Chamberlain is negotiating with Hitler and the reports are encouraging."

"You're mad. A woman alone, even in Switzerland, at this time."

"Gidon can come with me," Deborah said carefully. "Naomi would love that."

She prevailed and was relieved when Gidon agreed to join her.

# CHAPTER
# TWENTY-NINE

A FTER two hectic weeks in Paris, Deborah decided on a week's vacation in Switzerland. The inn she and Gidon checked into was nearly empty, since rumors of the impending war were louder than ever. It seemed like a perfect respite before returning to Palestine.

Deborah retired to her room when they arrived and Gidon felt abandoned.

From the minute they had landed in Europe, Deborah had seen to it that he was never alone. She filled their days with endless activities, stayed with him until the early hours of the morning and was there to have breakfast with him when he woke. Gidon was grateful, since it gave him little time to himself and even less time to think. But he knew the time would come when he would have to come to terms with what he had done.

It was early afternoon in August and the sky was crystal blue, with small fluffs of clouds drifting aimlessly toward the snow-capped mountains of the Swiss Alps. The air of serenity made Gidon feel as though he were on the periphery of eternity. It seemed uncanny that just beyond these mountains there was a real world, a world terrified of war and trying to survive, hoping to see another day, another week, another month of peace.

Standing at the edge of a cliff, Gidon took in the sights around him. He followed the slow movements of the clouds, stared at the snow-capped mountain tops and then looked down at the valley below. A huge blanket of green, lush forests stretched over endless acres and the sight gave him pleasure mingled with sadness. He remembered standing with Naomi on Mount Carmel and recalled her pride in their little patch of land, with its meager greenery—greenery achieved through hard, back-breaking work. He had forgotten that most countries did not suffer a lack of water. In Palestine they had to struggle to make every inch of land fertile. It seemed so unfair. Switzerland was inhabited by so many different nationalities who lived peacefully, protected by their mountains. Palestine, flat and exposed, was in constant turmoil, surrounded by nothing but hostility and the constant threat of terror, having to fight not only the elements but hostile neighbors as well.

He forced his mind away from these unhappy thoughts and tried to immerse himself in the pastoral scene, but his brain resisted the effort. Slowly his mind moved back to the recent past and the events that had taken place in his life just before their departure for Europe. He could feel his muscles tense up. He could not pretend that all was well, that he was satisfied with himself. He had to face up to what he had done, who he was and how he wanted to live his life. The choices were narrowed down. There was Michael's way or his way.

Trapped by his solitary state, he tried to think back to the point where his life changed.

Ten years earlier, right after the attempt on his life by Abed and the massacres of 1929, Michael had started traveling to the towns and villages where the slaughters had taken place. For reasons Gidon could not understand, he was invited to go along and felt he'd seen the depths of hell in the twisting, narrow alleyways in Safad, where terror mingled with blood that clung to the walls. The memory of children clinging to terrified mothers and men walking around mournfully, all trying to clean up the horror, stayed with him long after they left the city and returned to Bet Enav. Gidon remembered being angry at Deborah for letting him go, but he would have been angrier if she had prevailed, for he would not have witnessed the cruelty and irrationality of the Arab rage. He felt deep compassion for these helpless people and felt a great love for Michael, who walked among the defeated inhabitants of the community, giving them hope. Gidon, young and impressionable, felt unbearable frustration. Michael's controlled anger puzzled him.

"We must do something," Gidon cried out one day. "We can't just come by and comfort them. We must see to it that they never have to live through this kind of nightmare again."

"We will," Michael assured him. "We will, but we'll do it in an orderly manner. We'll do it legally. There is a world out there that knows justice."

"Justice?" Gidon remembered asking. "Justice? Who are the judges? Owen Cartwright?"

"Do you know him?" Michael had asked.

Gidon did not answer.

"I guess you do," Michael observed him closely. "And you don't like him, do you?"

"I hate him," Gidon choked the words out. "He is evil. I know he is."

"In time, evil gets its own reward." Michael seemed not to want to continue the conversation.

But Gidon was twelve and did not have the patience to wait for the judges of the world to prevail. It was Tuvia who introduced him to the idea that one could rush into the future.

Through Tuvia, Gidon met a group of youngsters in Bet Enav who felt as he did.

The group consisted of boys and girls from different walks of life, all dedicated to the idea that the Jews can and should fight for their rights. They accepted him without question. They were the first people who gave him the feeling that he was wanted. Better, that he was needed.

A clandestine group, they met haphazardly in different locations around Bet Enav and he soon became one of their influential members. It was an honor when Tuvia finally introduced him to Amit, one of their leaders. It was Amit who explained to Gidon the essential difference between what the Michael Ben Hods were hoping to achieve and the manner in which Amit's group hoped to achieve it. The goals were identical. The method was different.

The meeting with Amit was a turning point in Gidon's life. Sitting opposite him on the steps of the ancient Roman amphitheater, Tuvia's favorite hiding place, Gidon watched Amit. A young man in his twenties, he was short, muscular, with unusually large, powerful hands which he kept running through his dark, curly hair when trying to make a point. His dark eyes, rimmed with thick, curly lashes, did not waver as they stared at Gidon with unabashed interest. He appeared older than his years except when he smiled. It was a warm smile and the serious look would be replaced by a boyish, almost carefree manner. He reminded Gidon of someone, but he could not think of who it was.

Most of what Amit said at first was banal and Gidon was not impressed. Like Misha Neeman at the agricultural school, he related the history of the Jews, their plight, their defeats, their struggle, their helplessness. Suddenly Amit mentioned Raphael's name.

"You know, of course, Gidon, it was your uncle Raphael who is the intellec- tual father of our thinking." Amit directed the statement to him.

"But Raphael was very pro-British," Gidon protested.

"He used what was at hand," Amit answered. "They were the alternative to the Turks. And much as I hate the British, I know and he knew that the Turks were capable of slaughtering us as they slaughtered the Armenians. He was safe in assuming that the British weren't. At least not blatantly. It was the right choice for the times. But the situation has changed."

"Can we physically chase the British out of here?" Gidon asked.

"Let's put it this way. We can make them uncomfortable," Amit answered.

It was with Amit's approval and encouragement that Gidon joined the boy scouts when he returned to Tel Aviv. He was bored with most of their activities. Learning to tie rope knots, march in an orderly fashion, salute properly and listen to lectures about the plight of the Jewish people through the ages seemed irrelevant in face of the enormity of overthrowing a foreign ruler from the land. It was not that they were not serious. Everyone was conscious of the perils that lay ahead, but to Gidon it seemed that all was done in slow motion, in an amateurish manner.

More and more he understood the difference between Michael and himself. Michael and his friends focused on defending the Jews against the Arabs.

Gidon agreed with Amit. It was the British who were suppressing the Jewish community in Palestine. The British, he felt, were demanding fair play from the Jews while allowing the Arabs to run wild.

Although Gidon was uncomfortable with his scout friends, he continued to go to their meetings in Tel Aviv during the school year and waited impatiently for their visits to Bet Enav.

Gidon was on his path, achieving his goals, until Benji mentioned the brown shirt. Michael's fury upset Gidon. He enjoyed his relationship with Michael, respected him on many levels, especially now that he knew about Michael's past, knew about David's death and the distrust the Jewish leadership had had of him. Secretly, Gidon had hoped that one day he could persuade Michael to join Amit's faction. It was not an unreasonable idea. Michael had been an active member of Nili and it was possible that he would see the value of an open fight against the British. Michael's reaction to Benji's revelation put an end to that dream.

Gidon, however, had made his choice and, in spite of Michael's displeasure, he continued his friendship with Tuvia and followed the dictates of Amit. Theirs was not an organized group and Gidon discovered that one of its rules was anonymity. He knew few of the members other than the kids he met in Bet Enav. He knew none of the leaders other than Amit.

When the British mandate government began to suppress the Jewish community, Gidon and his friends were vocal in their opposition. They carried out acts of sabotage against the British. They blew up a train depot. They destroyed official buildings. They even stole ammunition from various British installations. They had never killed anyone knowingly. They were disruptive, no more.

When, in 1936, the Arabs started rioting against the Jews, a change occurred. For the first time Gidon found himself involved in a debate about an assassination. The idea frightened him but he understood the need for such an action. Tuvia balked. He fought the plan and when he failed to dissuade the action, he left the group. Tuvia's departure and subsequent enlistment with the mainstream fighters in Palestine upset Gidon. But by then he was deeply committed and refused to follow. Their friendship, however, held. Gidon knew he could always count on Tuvia and Tuvia could depend on him.

Amit was partially responsible for Gidon going to study in Jerusalem. He was needed in that part of the country and he was there when word came about the murder of the family near Bet Enav. Amit contacted him the day the news broke and asked him if they could meet to discuss retaliation. Gidon was flattered.

"We know who did it," Amit said, sipping a coffee in an outdoor café in Jerusalem. "We've checked it out and there's no doubt."

Gidon did not react.

"Some think we should eliminate the whole village," Amit continued.

"That's not justice. That's mass murder," Gidon said slowly.

"What do you suggest?"

"Can we pinpoint the actual killer?"

"We know. There were five of them."

"I'd go for the five killers if we actually knew who they are."

"We need volunteers."

They looked at each other for a long moment. Gidon thought of the walls that did not protect the villagers of Tel Ada.

"I'll do it," Gidon said quietly. "The British certainly aren't going to do anything about it and my uncle's friends will debate the subject for weeks and then do nothing."

Gidon did not regret killing the Arab. The man was guilty of the brutal murder of a whole family. When Gidon stopped him on that dark, isolated road, the Arab was dressed in the murdered man's clothes and had the woman's jewelry in his pocket. Determined as he was, Gidon was still nervous about what he had undertaken to do. Then the man began to plead. The pleading, the miserable bargaining for his life, enraged him. It was clear that the man would have given up his children, his wife, his village in exchange for his life. He had killed for personal gain and was willing to give it all up so that he could go on living and perhaps commit another purposeless murder.

Even now, what troubled Gidon was the killing of the animals. It was an act of madness that he could not explain. He suffered in their death. It shook his confidence in what he was involved in and he was desperate to find a rationale which would make it possible for him to live with what he had done.

An unbearable feeling of despair rose up in his chest as he tried to wipe away the sight of death and bloodshed. But his mind seemed riveted to the scene. He felt helpless.

"I'm sorry," he cried out to the wilderness. "I'm not a murderer. I don't want to be one."

The echo coming back at him shook him. He looked around. For a minute he did not remember where he was. Mountains towered over him and he turned and saw the abyss below. It looked inviting. He abruptly turned away.

A girl seemed to appear from nowhere. She was surrounded by tall blades of grass reaching up to her waist. She had a colorful scarf covering her head, but the long, blond hair streamed down her back and touched the tip of the grass. She was looking at him. Her eyes were blue, her skin white, her cheeks rosy, her mouth full and sensuous. She was only a few feet away from him and she appeared to be as startled at seeing him as he was at the sight of her.

He started toward her. She turned to run and tripped. Gidon reached down and helped her up. Her hand was cold.

"Please forgive me," he said and was surprised at the breathlessness in his voice. "I didn't mean to frighten you."

"You are not a frightening-looking man," she answered slowly and smiled.

Her accent was foreign and he could not place it. He did not let go of her hand and she made no effort to withdraw it.

Deborah, bathed and refreshed, came into the small hotel sitting room. Evening was approaching and the room was warm and friendly. Although still summer, the fireplace had been lit, giving the place an extra feeling of intimacy. Pouring herself a cup of tea from the teapot standing on the sideboard, she picked up a newspaper and seated herself in front of a large picture window facing the mountains. The front-page headlines were ominous. They predicted war, although Chamberlain was still trying to appease the Germans. England was pessimistic. France was mobilizing. The Italians were wavering. The Poles were frightened. All countries bordering Germany were nervous. The United States was withholding comment. Deborah scanned the paper for word of events in Palestine. If anything had happened there since she left, it apparently was not worth reporting at this time.

She leaned back in her chair and watched the shadows of the mountains grow long as darkness began to envelop them. She felt content. She had received a letter from Michael while in Paris, telling her that he and Benji were both in Bet Enav and would be there until she returned. She was glad to know where they were. It was different with Naomi. She had cabled that she had arrived safely in New York, but Deborah had never been there and could not visualize her daughter's whereabouts. She wished Naomi had not gone to the United States and it dawned on her that Michael had been in favor of Naomi's travel plans but upset by Deborah's trip to Europe with Gidon. She wondered why. Was it possible that America was safe even if war came? Her thoughts returned to Naomi. It had been only three weeks since she had parted from her, but she already missed her. Naomi's trip was the first step toward their inevitable separation. Once back in Palestine, Naomi would go off and settle in some far-off place in the Galilee, cut off from everyone, struggling to survive. There was no way of stopping her. Deborah smiled inwardly. That's what her own parents had done. And now, Bet Enav was a thriving, flourishing community with many other villages around it. That was the hope. That was the dream Naomi and her friends had. Sweet, gentle Naomi, now very much her own person. Deborah remembered how they'd argued about her travel wardrobe.

"Mother," Naomi had said patiently, as she packed a couple of sweaters and skirts in a knapsack. "I'm going to recruit people to come and live a frugal life in a kibbutz."

"But must they think you're poor and needy? Must you look like a beggar?"

"Materially we *are* going to be poor and needy." Naomi hid her annoyance but Deborah heard it clearly and it troubled her.

"Then why would they come?" Deborah asked.

"What we're offering is so much more than pretty clothes," Naomi answered seriously. "And if I have to explain that, then I'll know that I'm talking to the wrong people. What I'm talking about is values."

"Are my values so different from yours?"

Naomi took a long time to answer. "Yes, they are," she said simply.

Deborah was disturbed by what her daughter had said. She had always thought Naomi a happy girl, pleased with her life.

"They're different, mother, but I thank you for all you've given me. And in a way, it's what you've given me that makes it possible for me to choose the way I now want to live." Then Naomi rushed over to her and flung her arms around her neck.

More than ever, Deborah saw Naomi as the link that held their warring family together. The last thought made her uncomfortable and she reached over for her teacup.

It was growing dark out and Deborah looked down at her watch. She wondered where Gidon was. She was not worried and it amused her. In Palestine, she would have been frantic.

A group entered the room and Deborah turned to look at them. They appeared to be students who had been out hiking. She listened to their chatter and realized they were Polish. There were five of them and they were very gay. A tall, heavy-set man with graying hair followed them in and they congregated around him. After a minute they all dispersed and Deborah could see them through the picture window, running out toward the foot of the mountain.

"Forgive me, madame," the man came over to her. "We are here on a brief vacation from Warsaw and one of our girls is missing. You have not by chance seen a blond girl in the past hour or so?"

His voice was deep, his manner cordial, almost military, and she could see that in spite of the graying hair he was quite young. She turned to face him. Their eyes met and he seemed taken aback by her look.

"No, I haven't. I've been down here for about half an hour and no one has been by. I'm sure she's all right," Deborah said reassuringly. "It was a lovely day and she probably wandered off to take in the sights on her own."

"I do hope so." He smiled for the first time. "Every group has that one soul who wants to be independent. Basha is the one in this group."

"I have a nephew like that. He too has a need to be alone."

"I'm Captain Yanosh Barlovsky." He clicked his heels and put his hand out formally. "Polish cavalry." He was studying her face carefully.

"Deborah Ben Hod." She shook his hand.

"Ben Hod?" His brow wrinkled. "Palestine?"

"How did you know?"

"I'm Jewish, madame and I studied Hebrew when I was a boy and my grandfather was still alive. I don't know what the words mean, but they sound like words in Hebrew."

"Son of glory." Deborah felt herself blush and was glad the room was in semidarkness. In all the years of marriage to Michael, she had never thought of another man or how another man might see her as a woman. The men she met were husbands of her friends or professional men she dealt with on a daily basis. She was shocked to realize she was attracted to this Yanosh Barlovsky. She was also aware that he was much younger than she was.

"I think I shall go for a walk." She felt flustered and wanted to be away from this man.

She nearly collided with Gidon as she stepped out the front door. He put his arm around her shoulder and kissed her cheek. He seemed happier than she had ever seen him.

"You do know, don't you, that I love you?" He smiled at her.

It was the first time that Gidon had ever said these words to her and she reached up and touched his cheek. "I love you, Gidon. I love you very much. Thank you for telling me that you love me too."

Gidon was unusually talkative during dinner. He chatted and laughed easily. Deborah had never seen him so animated. She tried to concentrate on what he was saying but her eyes kept wandering toward the door that led into the dining room. She was fully aware that she was hoping to see Yanosh Barlovsky.

He came into the room with his youngsters while she and Gidon were having their coffee. Yanosh nodded to her. She nodded back and turned quickly to Gidon. She felt like a fool.

Gidon was staring at the group with unabashed interest. He seemed to have forgotten she was there. Deborah turned back to them, trying to discover who had captured his attention.

"She's very pretty," Deborah said seriously. The blond girl had not been part of the group that had come in to the small sitting room earlier in the day. "Who is she?"

Gidon's face reddened. "Her name is Basha and she's a student at the University of Warsaw." He looked down at his plate. "I think she's beautiful."

"What are they doing here with Poland on the verge of war?"

"The top five students of the class always go to some conference at the end of the year. The faculty felt they ought to continue the ritual. The older man is their chaperon."

"Does she speak English?" Deborah asked.

"I understand her," Gidon said sheepishly.

With dinner over, Gidon excused himself. Deborah watched him walk out the gate with the young girl. He was laughing and Deborah was pleased. The girl obviously made him happy.

"May I join you, madame?" Yanosh was standing by her table and she realized the dining room had emptied out.

She nodded and as he sat down she noticed the same uncertain, almost awed look on his face which she had detected when they first met. His eyes seemed to bore into her.

"You embarrass me, captain," she blurted out in spite of herself. "You're looking at me as though I reminded you of someone."

"No," he laughed self-consciously. "No, you remind me of no one. You are, however, the most fascinating woman I have ever seen."

Flustered, she stood up, ready to go up to her room.

"Will you have an after-dinner drink with me?" he asked, leading her toward the sitting room.

She watched him walk to the bar and order the drinks. He was a big man but carried himself gracefully. He was a very attractive man. Despite his youth, she found him sophisticated, knowledgeable, stimulating to talk to and be with. He seemed eager to talk about himself and his background fascinated her.

He was third-generation Polish; his grandfather was a rabbi, his father a psychiatrist and he was going to be a history professor. His mother was a teacher and he had two sisters, both married to Christian Polish men. His family practiced Judaism until his grandfather died. He had had a bar mitzvah because of his grandfather. After the old man's death, the family continued the traditions for a while, but their lives were too full of the here and now and they had little time for religion. His loyalty was to Poland. He loved Poland.

"But you are Jewish," Deborah insisted.

"Of course I am and proud of it," he said seriously. "I'm concerned for the Jewish people. I try to keep up with what's happening in Palestine but you know how it is, we have so much going on at home." He took her hand in his. "I would, however, love to hear about your life there."

Deborah had never known anyone who wasn't deeply involved in the events taking place in her small country and she happily answered all his questions. It made it easier for her to put aside her feeling of physical attraction for him. It kept surfacing, but she was deeply conscious of her age as well as his. She was nearly forty and figured he was in his mid-twenties.

It was nearly dawn when Yanosh walked her back to her room. He kissed her hand and held it. "Thank you," he said seriously and walked away.

In the morning, flowers were delivered to her room on her breakfast tray. Deborah realized that no man had ever sent her flowers before.

They had lunch together and walked down to the small village at the bottom of the hill. In contrast to the evening before, Yanosh was quiet and she felt his eyes on her when he thought she was not looking. Gentle, caring eyes, filled with emotion. She felt very young.

He had prepared a picnic basket when she came down the next morning. They spent a glorious day walking along flowery paths, drinking wine with their lunch and talking about themselves. There was no world beyond the Swiss Alps. There was no Palestine, no Poland, no Germany. No wars. When he said he loved her, she believed him. She felt as if no man had ever told her he loved her. Yanosh loved her! He did not know her sister and in a way,

Deborah would not have felt threatened if he had. Yanosh truly loved her.

In spite of her great desire for him, she could not be physically unfaithful to Michael. Yanosh understood her feelings and did not press her. They spent endless hours together and late at night, he would take her up to her room, kiss her hand and walk away.

When he proposed marriage, she was shocked.

"Ten years from now, I'll be an old lady and you'll be in your prime," she laughed. The thought of leaving Michael had never entered her mind. She could not visualize life without Michael. It made no sense.

"You'll never grow old," he said seriously. "And I shall love you as I do now until the day I die."

"Yanosh, I must tell you that aside from being married, I live in Palestine. It is my home, it is my life."

He hesitated. "Poland is my home," he answered.

For the rest of the week, they clung to each other. She had accepted their relationship as an interlude in her life. Yanosh did not. He continued to plead with her to come to Poland. "Give it a chance," he urged. "It's a beautiful country. You'll love it and it will love you."

His words were beyond her comprehension. Not his proposal, but the idea that he as a Jew could think of Poland as his home.

"Palestine is the only home for Jews," she kept insisting. "You can live anywhere, but your roots must be in Palestine."

He would kiss her with great tenderness and their conversation would come to an end. He loved her and wanted to share his life with her. He was sure he would prevail.

As the week drew to an end, Deborah was surprised to discover that she was faltering. The idea of not being with Yanosh, not having him close, not being able to reach out and touch him, frightened her. In less than a week, she actually began to think of going to Poland.

She saw little of Gidon that week and much as she enjoyed his company, she was grateful that he was not around. For that brief time, Yanosh was all she thought about, all she cared about.

The night before their departure, Deborah lay awake, trying to understand her feelings. There was no question that she was deeply in love with Yanosh. She also loved Michael. He was her husband, but he was also Palestine. That more than anything bound them together. She knew she could not survive away from her home. And Michael was part of that home.

She had begun to doze off and was wondering why she did not go to live with Yanosh. She had wanted to and wondered if she would regret it in later years, when she heard a knock on her door. She sat up, hoping it was Yanosh. It was Gidon.

"War has been declared," he whispered hoarsely.

Her first impulse was to run from the room and look for Yanosh.

"We've got to get to the Geneva train station," Gidon continued.

"What happened?" She got out of bed and pulled on her robe.

"It's not quite clear. It seems that Germany has invaded Poland. But the reports are muddled. It may be just a rumor, but damn it, I want to get back home as quickly as possible."

She looked for Yanosh when paying the hotel bill. He was nowhere in sight. She dared not ask about him with Gidon standing by.

They took the ski lift down to the train station. It was very crowded. Where the people came from was not clear. Yanosh and his group were not there. They barely got on the train. Deborah felt numb and was grateful that Gidon had taken charge of the arrangements. Where was Yanosh? If only she could have said goodbye to him. Would she ever see him again? He was an officer in the Polish army and from the news coming through, it seemed that Poland was doomed.

Once in Geneva, she gave up hope of seeing him and tried to concentrate on what Gidon was saying.

"We must get to Trieste," Gidon explained. "It's the only way for us to catch a ship to Haifa."

"Trieste? But Italy is allied with Germany."

"Not yet," Gidon assured her. "Besides, we're probably safer there than most, since we're Palestinians with passports and visas and money to pay for the trip."

She looked around the station. The air was thick with fear. Unlike Gidon and herself who were tanned from their vacation, everyone appeared to be in a state of desperation.

The conductor called out the last warning before departure. Gidon helped Deborah onto the train. He stayed on the platform.

"I will not be going with you in the train," he said, handing her a small suitcase.

"But why?" she gasped.

The train whistle blew. The noise around was deafening.

"There's no room on this train," he screamed over the din. "And with the Swiss, you don't argue. But I will meet you in Trieste."

The train lurched and started moving slowly. He ran along the side. "Don't worry," he called out, keeping pace with the slow-moving train. "The boat for Palestine is due to sail in a week and I will be on it." The train began to pick up speed. "I'll be there. I promise."

A burst of steam obliterated him from view briefly. The train was moving more quickly. She caught sight of him waving to her, then he disappeared.

Deborah sat by the window and stared, unseeing, at the landscape rushing by. Her heart ached for Yanosh and Gidon. She wondered if she'd ever see either of them again. With the train going full speed, the sights changed rapidly but over each lovely scene, Yanosh and Gidon's faces appeared, masking the view. Hard as she tried to close her mind to what was happening around her, the tension of the passengers kept penetrating her pain. Even as it grew dark out, the passengers on the train did not seem to relax. The heat was stifling and the hysteria around her mounted. Mothers clung to their children, who looked confused and lost. Men looked around furtively, frightened, clutching papers in their hands, anxious to show them to any official who passed by. Old people stared ahead as if they had traveled this route before. They never looked out the window. Deborah could not react to their misery. She kept thinking of what might have been.

Reaching Trieste, Deborah was told that the announcement of war had been a false alarm. That war would break out was clear. The question was if it would happen in a day, a week or a month.

The week in Trieste was a nightmare. Although in a first-class hotel, Deborah's room was small and uncomfortable. She spent her days checking train schedules from Geneva and then would try to be at the station when it arrived. Gidon was on none of them. Evenings, she ate dinner alone and walked along the pier, staring at the sea, wondering when the ship taking them to Palestine would arrive and if Gidon would be there before it departed. The city grew more crowded as droves of people kept arriving. The train station was difficult to enter. She had her tickets for the ship, but passing the travel offices in the city, she could see the frantic demand for passage. People were waving money, jewelry and other valuables at the ticket officer, to no avail.

The day of departure arrived and Gidon had not yet come. She thought of postponing her departure, but knew it would be foolish. She had succeeded in contacting Michael by telegram and told him the date of her arrival. He answered promptly, telling her he would be waiting for her at the pier.

Standing on the deck, Deborah searched the crowd coming up the gangplank. It was too crowded for her to make out any individual.

"Deborah." She heard her name and turned.

Gidon was standing beside her, holding Basha's hand in his.

"Deborah," he said, "I want you to meet my wife."

# Part III

# CHAPTER
# THIRTY

## 1940

B ASHA walked around the room, trying to straighten it up before Deborah, Michael, Naomi and her bridegroom arrived from Haifa. Heavy with child, she moved awkwardly and was breathing hard.

"Basha, darling," Gidon pleaded. "The house is in perfect order. It always is. Why are you running yourself ragged?"

"I can't help it." She threw herself on the sofa and buried her head in her hands. "Every time Deborah and Michael come here, I feel they're inspecting Raphael's house to see if I haven't infected it, contaminated it or done something sacrilegious to it."

Gidon walked over to her and lifted her face to his. It was stained with tears. "Oh Basha, I know Michael makes you nervous. But you know Deborah loves you and she's very supportive."

"I know," she whispered, taking his hand and pressing her lips to it. "I love you so much, Gidon, and I want so to have Michael accept me."

"Michael is difficult, but since he discovered you're pregnant, he's really been trying."

"I guess he has," she conceded. "But then there's Benji. He's so unpleasant. He makes me feel like an intruder."

"Well, Benji has many problems, none of which have anything to do with you."

"He's furious that we're going to have a baby, you know."

"Yes, I'm aware of it. He's worried about the inheritance. He sees it getting smaller and smaller. Now with Naomi married, he's quite frantic."

"But Naomi is going to live on a kibbutz. Surely he doesn't think she'll be wanting anything from him."

"Well, neither do we, yet he's behaving as thought we're having the baby to spite him."

Basha stood up. "Gidon, I know you hate it when I mention it, but the truth is that he makes it sound as though you're working for him."

"Well, I am at this point," Gidon said indifferently. "He's running the farms, the vineyards, the groves. I'm employed by the family to run the quarries and for that I'm being paid."

"That doesn't make sense," Basha said patiently. "You own half of everything and it seems to me that he's getting a much bigger slice of the profits."

"Basha, we've had this conversation before and I really hate going through it again. I don't know what profits there are and I really don't care. Benji works very hard and seems to be doing a fine job at it. Michael trusts him completely and Deborah seems to. As for me, I get a salary for what I do. We live rent-free in this lovely house, so I imagine I make out all right." He put his arms around her waist and pressed her to him. "And I have you, which he doesn't."

"When the baby comes, we won't be able to go on living here. It's too small for us and a child."

He nodded thoughtfully. "That's true, but we have some time to figure out what to do." He knew that what she was saying had nothing to do with the space. Basha did not care for Bet Enav. She was a city girl and the quiet of the village bothered her.

"Time goes by quickly," she whispered, resting her head on his shoulder.

"All right. I promise to talk to Deborah about finding us a place in Tel Aviv before the baby comes."

She smiled up at him. "Thank you, Gidon."

The sound of a motor car coming up the road made them draw apart and walk, hand in hand, toward the front door.

Naomi and her young American husband, Jack Stern, stepped out of the car just as Gidon and Basha appeared on the small patio.

Naomi caught sight of Gidon and rushed toward him. He pulled her into his arms and held her for a long moment. Then pushing her away, he stared at her with unabashed adoration.

"God, I've missed you," she whispered, studying his face carefully. Then her face broke into a smile. Gidon appeared calmer, more composed, more relaxed. He seemed happy.

"No more than I've missed you," he answered and kissed her on the cheek. Then, still holding her shoulder, he turned toward Basha. "And this beautiful woman standing in the doorway is my wife, Basha." The pride was unmistakable.

"I knew he'd marry a beauty." Naomi walked quickly over to Basha. "And he didn't disappoint me." She put her hand out, then changing her mind she threw her arms around Basha's shoulders and kissed her warmly on the cheek.

Basha was moved and a hint of a tear trickled down her cheek.

As unobtrusively as possible, Naomi put her hand to Basha's face, wiped the tear away and smiled warmly at her. "I'm so glad Gidon is married to you," she said with great sincerity. Then turning around, she pointed to Jack. "And that is your new cousin, Jack Stern, my husband."

Gidon walked over to Jack and clasped his hand warmly.

"You don't know how lucky you are, Jack," he said, searching the young man's face seriously.

"I feel very lucky," Jack said with embarrassment. A shy, gangly man, he seemed overwhelmed.

Michael put his arm around Jack's shoulder and led him toward the house. "We're not as formidable as we look." He smiled reasuringly at the Jack. "But forgive a father's prejudice, you are indeed lucky to have someone like Naomi. She's a rare human being."

The conversation around the dinner table that evening revolved around the planned move to the kibbutz.

"Because it took us forever to get here," Naomi said, "We've got to postpone it until late spring."

"I'd say June would be a better time," Michael said.

"Why so late?" Naomi asked.

"You're going up north and you may as well do it when the ground is solid. You don't want to have to trek through mud. Besides, it will give all of you a chance to start planting vegetables and maybe a few fruit trees, so that by the time you get there, you'll be ahead of the game."

"The baby will be born by then," Basha interjected shyly, "and it would mean that I could also help."

"That's if the baby is actually going to be born in May," Deborah laughed softly.

"He'll be here by then," Gidon said with assurance.

"Oh, for the prophet in his own time," Naomi said with mock scorn. "Never mind predicting the date. You go one better. You know it's going to be a son."

"Actually, I won't mind a daughter," he laughed and put his hand over Basha's. "Especially if she looks like her mother."

"There you go again," Naomi laughed. "She could look like you, you know."

"I wouldn't mind that," Basha said.

"Anyway, whether Basha comes along or not, I'll be there," Gidon announced.

"We will all be there," Michael said emphatically.

"I wouldn't miss it for the world," Deborah concurred.

Jack sat quietly, listening to the family banter and wishing he could fade from sight. He had fallen in love with a pretty, red-headed girl from Palestine and wanted to share his life with her. She seemed straightforward and appeared to be the epitome of a pioneer's daughter from humble origins who toiled the land and struggled to survive in the country known as Palestine. Her dreams of forming a kibbutz blended with his and they married quickly. But from the minute he saw Deborah and Michael waiting for them at the pier, he felt like a fool.

Deborah Ben Hod was one of the most elegant women he had ever seen. Although it was a mild February day, she wore an exquisitely tailored coat made of cashmere. Her small black hat and leather bag and gloves were unmistakably expensive. Even Michael, who was much less formal, was wearing a fine blazer and his gray trousers were made of expensive wool flannel. He wore no tie, yet he still looked elegant. Seeing them, Jack thought of the two dilapidated suitcases filled with his mother's old clothes for "the poor relatives." Entering the driveway to their country house in Bet Enav caused him further embarrassment. Once in the house itself, he could think of nothing but how to get rid of the baggage he had brought along. Throughout the trip, Naomi had asked him what the suitcases contained and he had assured her it would be a welcome surprise for her family. She accepted his explanation and did not pry. Although he now understood that the Ben Hods were not average Palestinians, he still felt like a fool.

"You're awfully quiet, Mr. Stern," Naomi broke into his thoughts. "Don't you like us?"

He smiled sheepishly. "Like you? I'm overwhelmed," he said sincerely.

"You'll get over it," Gidon assured him. "They seem overwhelming but they're really simple people deep down."

Everyone at the table was aware that Gidon had excluded himself from the family.

"Meaning you're not simple people deep down?" Naomi decided to confront the issue.

Gidon smiled. "I didn't mean it that way."

"As a matter of fact, he doesn't think he's simple." Benji spoke for the first time since they sat down.

"Benji, don't," Deborah snapped.

"I'm sorry," he said and sounded sincere in his apology.

"Well, I'm exhausted." Naomi stood up. "Would you all excuse me?"

Jack stood up as well. "Thank you." He looked at everyone around the table, then, impulsively he leaned down and kissed Deborah on the cheek. "I thought I was lucky to have Naomi as a wife. I didn't know how lucky I'd be with my mother-in-law."

"Before you go," Deborah said, "I have an announcement to make."

They all looked at her, expectantly.

"I'm having Tamar's grave moved to a special plot in the cemetery." She paused, waiting for her words to sink in. Then with great emotion, she continued. "I've dreamt of this for so long."

Michael was looking at her intently. He knew how desperately she had wanted it and he wondered if she had finally reached the point where she could put Tamar to rest.

Naomi rushed over and kissed her mother. Benji smiled at her shyly. Gidon walked over and pressed her shoulder.

"Thank you Deborah," he whispered.

Michael saw her look up at Gidon adoringly. Reburying Tamar was an important step, Michael thought, but Tamar would linger on in Deborah's life as long as she loved Gidon. Her love for Tamar's son was too engrossing, too deeply embedded. Sometimes he wondered if she did not love Gidon more than she did her own children. He felt a small shudder go through him.

Within minutes after Naomi and Jack's departure, Gidon and Basha excused themselves, leaving Deborah, Michael and Benji at the table.

"That was quite an accomplishment," Michael said soberly. "And I'm proud of you."

She blushed and nodded. "It's long overdue." She cleared her throat. "Anyway, we're all here and it seems like a good and proper time for it, before everyone wanders off to start their new lives."

"It won't be long now," Michael concurred. "Naomi going off to a kibbutz is only the beginning. And I must say, I think she's made a fine choice. Jack seems like a reliable sort."

"I'm relieved," Deborah said. "I was worried about an American boy coming to Palestine to live in a new kibbutz. But he looks like an intelligent young man, a solid person, and I think it will work out. They certainly seem to be devoted to each other."

"You may be relieved. I'm thrilled," Benji announced. "I thought we'd get another parasite who needed to be supported."

"Benji, you've got to stop this nonsense. You're not supporting anyone." Deborah's voice shook with anger.

"Benji has a point, Deborah," Michael interceded. "Gidon's working hard but he's not really pulling his weight. Benji is far more involved and is devoting much more time to everything." He could see Deborah bristle and he tried to pacify her. "I will admit that since he married that girl, he's certainly calmed down and changed for the better." Deborah resented the slighting way he referred to Basha.

"He's more than changed, Michael. He's a different person. He takes his work seriously and is practically a homebody," Deborah said pointedly.

"I guess so," Michael conceded. "As a matter of fact, he's been very inventive with the illegal immigrants coming down from Lebanon." He smiled. "Some of our people actually look to him for advice about how to get through the British barriers."

"His appearance helps," Benji said disparagingly. "He looks more British than most of the officers he meets."

Deborah ignored her son's remark. She was far more interested in what Michael was saying. It was true that since Gidon married Basha, he seemed to have settled down. Her fears that he would again plunge into political work with the country's radicals seemed not to have come true. She still watched for hints of his past behavior and still worried when he was gone from the house for any length of time. Now Michael had explained Gidon's strange absences. She breathed a sigh of relief.

"I have to go out to the shed. We're expecting a calf," Benji announced and, standing up, he smiled at his father and walked out.

Michael looked over at Deborah. She had taken a cigarette and was waiting for him to light it for her. He obliged quickly and lit one for himself. Her smoking did not bother him. What puzzled him was that she had suddenly taken up the habit.

She had changed since her trip to Switzerland six months earlier. He had noticed something about her the minute he saw her disembark the crowded ship from Trieste.

It had been a rough trip, and all the passengers were bedraggled and hysterical. The British control officers, in turn, were rude, almost brutal, while examining their papers. Deborah, erect and elegant, appeared unruffled. When asked for her papers, she handed them to the officer almost disdainfully. The man reacted to her haughty manner, but she did not flinch and he finally smiled, almost apologetically, as he stamped her passport. Michael saw her stand by as Gidon and a blond companion went through the same procedure. Although he was too far away to hear the exchange, he could see Deborah intercede and within minutes they walked through the gate and came toward him.

He had waited impatiently for her return. He always missed her when she was away, but this last separation was more difficult since he had come to terms with his past and was anxious to share new revelations with her. He was now an important and accepted member of the Jewish establishment, involved in policy-making relating to Palestine. It gave him license to try to forget his humble past. He had accepted the idea that proving his innocence in David's death was probably impossible, and the time had come to put that tragic incident behind him. Although it would always haunt him, he no longer feared it would keep him from performing for his country to the best of his abilities or showing his deep love and admiration for his wife. He had no doubt Deborah believed him innocent. To prove her trust, she had agreed to marry him. Yet even after all their years together, he still needed her reassurance. He also wanted her love. More important, he wanted to tell her of his love for her. He wanted to take her in his arms and hold her close and beg her to forgive him for all the lonely years which he now realized she must have lived since they got married. He wanted to start a new life with his wife.

But that day at the pier, when she came to stand beside him, he felt strangely inhibited. She was genuinely pleased to see him, was obviously thrilled to be home, but she was removed, almost aloof. There was an air of independence about her that he never noticed before. In an instant, he was thrown back into his solitude, his feelings of insecurity returned and he closed up.

"Michael, this is Basha, Gidon's wife." Deborah, always sensitive to his feelings, seemed not to have noticed anything this time. He tore his eyes away from Deborah and looked over at the young woman. The tall, slender girl with large blue eyes sent a chill through him. He disliked her on sight and had a hard time hiding his feelings. Indifferent to his mood minutes before, Deborah was now alert and sensing his attitude. She put a protective arm around the girl and said pointedly, "Michael, aren't you going to welcome the bride?" She pushed Basha gently toward him.

He complied with a halfhearted kiss and felt the girl withdraw from him as though defending herself from his hostility. He moved back, annoyed at Deborah's insistence.

No one spoke on the trip back to Bet Enav.

Once in their room, Deborah was furious.

"That was totally unnecessary. She's a lonely, frightened girl in a strange land, and you were downright unkind."

"I'm sorry, I just didn't like her. There's something about her that bothers me. I don't know." He hesitated, trying to understand his feelings. "She's just not one of us."

"That's what you said about Gidon when you first met him."

"I wasn't wrong then and I feel I'm not wrong now." He watched Deborah closely. She was sitting by the window, staring out. "Who is she, anyway?" he asked slowly.

She turned to him, her eyes flashing with anger. Her beauty was dazzling and he wished they could stop arguing. He wanted to make love to her. He wanted to talk about himself. He wanted to talk about their life together and what he hoped their life would be like in the future.

"She's a history student from the University of Warsaw who happened to be in Switzerland on vacation with some other students." Deborah turned back to the window. "Gidon fell in love with her and she with him and from what I gather, they contacted her family in Poland, who were thrilled at the idea of their daughter being spared the horrors of war. She and Gidon are very much in love with each other. You can see it in the way they look at each other, in the way they touch each other, in the way they talk to each other. It's quite beautiful."

Michael heard reproach in her voice and his heart sank. That love, that affection, was what she had wanted from him and now that he was ready to give it to her, she seemed to have moved away from him.

He walked over to her and looked to see what she was staring at. Gidon and Basha were standing in the garden. He had his arm around her shoulder.

"Where will they live?" Michael asked.

"In Raphael's house," Deborah answered, never taking her eyes off the young couple. It was a statement, one he knew he could not dispute.

"That's a mistake," he said.

"Mistake or not, the house is empty and Gidon has been using it for years.

It's his home in a way, and he should have the right to bring his bride to it."

"I shall always see it as Raphael's house," Michael said.

"Gidon is his nephew and I'm sure Raphael would be pleased to have Tamar's son using it."

Michael threw a sidelong glance at her. Tamar and Gidon. It crossed his mind that Deborah would not be as generous with Raphael's house if it were for Benji and his bride. He gritted his teeth.

"Shouldn't you discuss it with Benji and Naomi?"

"Benji is still a child. He has a beautiful room in this house and I'm sure that once he's married, he'll build a house for himself, either on these grounds or elsewhere. As for Naomi, even if she weren't planning on going to a kibbutz, I know she'd want Gidon to live there."

It was settled. Deborah had settled it.

He made love to her that night and again noted a change in her. She had always desired him, as he desired her, but that night there was a demand on her part which had not been there in the past. Long after she fell asleep, Michael lay beside her, puzzled by this beautiful woman who had been his wife for so many years and who was suddenly different in a way he could not explain. The possibility that she had met someone in Europe, may even have had an affair, frightened him.

In the months that followed her return, her assurance, her newfound sense of self was evident in everything she did. From being a docile, pleasant, warm housewife, she somehow became a worthy partner. It pleased him, even if it did bring him into conflict with her more often. It also deepened his love for her, though he felt more isolated than ever.

"I don't like what Benji is doing," Deborah was saying and Michael, so engrossed in his thoughts, looked around and realized they were in their dining room and Deborah was talking to him.

"What is he doing?" he asked in genuine confusion.

"He's too young to be in charge of the whole estate. He's not yet twenty and he acts as though he were the sole owner of everything."

"I supervise what he does." Michael held his temper, knowing Deborah was again going to demand rights for Gidon. "He never makes a serious decision without consulting me. He certainly never signs anything without my approval."

"I know that, but you're away a great deal of the time. I think it would be a good idea if he would consult with me when you're away."

"Tell him," Michael snapped.

"I will, but you'll have to back me up." She took a deep breath. "I also think Gidon should be earning more money."

"For what?"

"He works hard, Michael. In a way he works harder than Benji. And now that he's married and is about to be a father, he has responsibilities that Benji doesn't have."

"That's out of the question," Michael said firmly. "I don't know how long this war is going to last and I don't know how the citrus industry will fare in the coming season. We certainly won't be able to export our fruit to Europe with the war on, and that could cut into the profits."

"I've thought of that. We can start producing marmalades and jam," Deborah answered without hesitation.

Michael began to laugh. "You're wonderful, Deborah. Completely and utterly wonderful."

"Well, what do you think?"

"I think it's brilliant." He stood up and came around to where she sat. Putting his hand under her chin, he looked at her. "You're not only very beautiful, you're also smart."

"Thank you." She smiled. "Will you talk to Benji? His anger still frightens me."

He leaned down and kissed her forehead, tenderly. "Of course I will."

Deborah lowered her eyes quickly. She could not react to Michael's touch as she would have before meeting Yanosh. She wanted to, but in the months since she'd come back from Switzerland, thoughts of Yanosh, never far from her mind, were suddenly very much alive.

She needed him. She wanted him. He had given her so much, but in a strange way he had also taken her away from Michael. It seemed unfair. She knew Michael had been trying to come toward her. She sensed it the minute she saw him at the pier in Haifa when they disembarked. She pretended not to notice, but she knew him too well. He was anxious to talk to her and from the way he looked at her, she was sure that what he had to say was important. But that day, she could not have listened. Much as she cared about Michael, Yanosh was still too fresh in her mind. Since then she had succeeded in resuming her relationship with Michael. Habit, more than anything, helped. But there were days when she reached into the dark recesses of her mind and relived the time spent with Yanosh. Knowing him as briefly as she did, she knew he loved her and that knowledge sustained her. Even if she never saw him again, the memory of his being would never leave her. She could not even bring herself to talk to Basha about Yanosh. She had no idea if Gidon and Basha were aware of her relationship with him, but she knew that mentioning his name would bring him alive and she did not want to disrupt her life with Michael. Somehow she had to separate the two men and the only way to do it was to keep Yanosh to herself.

Deborah forced herself to look up at Michael. He was still standing beside her and he looked lost.

"I'm exhausted," she whispered. "Shall we go to bed?"

At least that part of their relationship had not suffered. Michael was still enormously attractive to her and she could give herself to him without guilt.

# CHAPTER
# THIRTY-ONE

*I*N spite of Michael's feeling that summer was the best time to go up north to the new kibbutz, by mid-April of 1940 the British were cracking down on all new Jewish settlements and there was no way of postponing the move.

The need to establish roots, take possession of what was theirs, populate deserted areas and force the British to meet their commitments reached a frenzied pitch. Small settlements were established in various parts of the country, but the upper Galilee, a strategic area for the promised Jewish homeland, was relatively barren. Naomi's group was determined to build their future home there in spite of the dangers.

A desolate, windy mountain top, long deserted and uncared-for, hardly seemed a likely home on which youngsters could build a thriving community. The courageousness of the action caught the imagination of the whole country. As the day of moving grew closer, the air around the country and especially the Ben Hod family was electric. Everyone helped. Even Gidon and Benji, rarely in agreement about anything, were brought together in this venture. They made numerous trips together to the area. Under the guise of transporting fruit and vegetables to Haifa for export, they actually transported building equipment hidden beneath the innocent-looking cargo. Gidon's appearance and manner were invaluable. It was easy for him to befriend the soldiers on patrol between Bet Enav and the northern part of the country. Often he and Benji would stop on the highway, take out a picnic basket and open a bottle of wine and invite British soldiers to join them. Sometimes a bottle of brandy would be the lure, or a bottle of scotch. Michael, for his part, was in charge of the security arrangements in the area, while Deborah collected clothing, bedding and various household items needed for daily living. Basha, only weeks away from giving birth, insisted on working along with everyone. It was no easy task for her, since the overgrown path that led up to the intended kibbutz was too narrow and twisted to accommodate a car. They would have to leave the car on the road miles below and climb on foot to the designated spot carrying packs on their backs. Basha proved to be the perfect cover on these trips, since the British patrol, seeing her condition, would wave them on with good cheer.

Deborah was fascinated by her dedication. Basha's need to prove she was part of the family was touching.

The scheduled day arrived and everyone felt the sense of excitement and unity of purpose. Except for Benji and Deborah, everyone was already in the area where construction was to start that night. With Benji driving, they started out just as dusk was settling in.

Sitting in the car beside Benji, Deborah felt a warm kinship toward her son.

"You do drive well," she said and reached out to press his shoulder affectionately.

"I enjoy it." Benji looked at his mother. "This whole thing is a marvelous adventure, when you come right down to it."

"I hope it all goes smoothly." She turned her eyes to the empty road ahead. It was growing dark and although there were no other cars in sight, they both knew that there was a great deal of covert movement taking place around them.

"Why shouldn't it?" Benji tried for nonchalance. "I'm simply driving my mother to visit friends in Safad. It's the most natural thing in the world."

"Well, not quite when you consider that we've got enough food in the trunk to feed an army. We can hardly say that all that food is for me."

"You only eat kosher and you insist on bringing your own groceries." Deborah laughed. "And I eat like a pig."

"We can always say you have a tapeworm." Benji too laughed.

As the dusk settled, Benji put on his headlights and they picked up the evening mist that rose from the road. As they approached the city, the road widened and the houses tucked into the side of the mountains came into view.

"I hope Basha is all right," Deborah said. "She's been living with Naomi and Jack in a tent for the last couple of weeks and I can't help but worry how she's feeling. Can you imagine her going into labor suddenly?"

"Mother, you don't seem to understand the magnitude of what is happening today. This new settlement has grabbed the imagination of the whole population. Everyone from all walks of life wants to be involved. There are more doctors and nurses around that area today than there are in the rest of the country."

"I know that." Deborah nodded but was not pacified.

They entered the city and to their surprise, the streets were unusually crowded. Traffic was backed up to the point where they were forced to slow down and finally stop because of the congestion.

"I wonder what's happening." Benji stuck his head out the window.

"Could be an accident." Deborah tried to see beyond the mass of people, horse carts, trucks, bicycles, donkeys and camels.

"No." Benji's voice was tight. "There's a road block and a British patrol ahead. They're checking everyone's papers."

The British sergeant peered into the car. "Car license, ownership papers and identity cards."

Benji handed over the papers and Deborah dug into her bag for her identity card.

"What have you got in the trunk?" The sergeant asked, searching their faces.

"I'm spending Passover with relatives in Safad." Deborah said quickly, "and I'm bringing the food for the seder."

"Open up," he ordered.

Benji started to get out of the car.

"What seems to be the problem?" Gidon appeared from nowhere.

He was dressed in a British uniform with gold captain bars on his shirt.

"These people are heading to Safad ostensibly to celebrate Passover with relatives and I don't like the looks of it."

Gidon leaned over and looked at Deborah. "Why Mrs. Ben Hod," he smiled broadly. "How are you?"

"Well, thank you," she answered pleasantly.

"When is Passover, anyway?" he asked.

"A week from today."

"And how are Mr. Ben Hod and the family?"

"Everyone is quite well. They're all in Safad waiting for us."

"How nice." He turned to the soldier. "I know these people, sergeant. And I don't know how long you've been in the country, but Passover is one of their more important holidays. Let them pass."

"Is anything unusual going on?" Deborah could not resist asking.

"Oh, you know how it is, Mrs. Ben Hod. There's another boat trying to land. And this time some bloody fools tried to shoot their way into the harbor. In fact there was a gun battle and several British soldiers were hurt." He shrugged his shoulders in mock exasperation. "It would seem to me that our policy on immigration is quite clear, yet these people keep coming." He smiled, bowed his head and waved them on.

Deborah looked back nervously. She saw Gidon salute the sergeant and amble away in a leisurely manner.

"I hope he'll be all right," she whispered.

"I wonder what he was doing here?" Benji mused. Then, as an afterthought, he continued. "It must have been some battle to bring out such heavy reinforcements. I wonder who did it?"

"Did what?" Deborah asked.

"Started shooting and wounding British soldiers."

"Whoever did it has my vote," Deborah said firmly. "The whole idea of not letting those poor people into the country when no one else will have them is so unreasonable."

"I know that," Benji answered quickly. "But you don't start shooting. That's going too far, and I bet it was done by those fanatic hooligans who believe they must keep up the pressure on the British, even now that we're all fighting the Germans."

*Fanatic hooligans,* Deborah thought bitterly. That's what the Danzigers were considered years back when they were trying to defeat the Turks. They too fought the oppressors of the Jewish people in Palestine. Now the British were repeating the actions of the Turks: their senseless intimidation; their outrageous rulings against the Jews; their continuous stifling of any constructive efforts to make a home for themselves and a home for the Jews who were fleeing Europe and the Nazis. What made it all the more obscene was that the British expected the Jews to help them in their war effort, expected them to be loyal citizens of the mandate. Deborah did not approve of violence, but it did no harm to let the British know that the Jews would not forget their claim.

As these thoughts crossed her mind, she too wondered if Gidon had been involved in the shooting. If she were younger, or if Raphael, David, Tamar were around, they would have been involved and she was sure she would not have been as filled with trepidation as she was now for Gidon.

She threw a sidelong look at her son. His face was set, his eyes narrowed, his lips pressed together. He did not suspect Gidon. He was convinced of Gidon's guilt. Unhappily, she turned her attention back to the road. They were out of the city and driving along the highway again. It too was crowded with British armored trucks and soldiers.

The sun started setting as they reached a crossroad. Benji turned away from the main road and brought the car to a stop in a cove that could not be seen from the highway.

Turning off the ignition, he looked around.

"If I didn't know better, I'd say there was nothing extraordinary going on around here." He smiled and seemed to relax.

Deborah got out of the car. A few ancient olive trees stood nearby. Red poppies and other colorful flowers livened up the drab soil. A short distance away there were several wooden huts surrounding a half-built stone structure; a playground with swings and slides stood next to it. It was a small, poor village, one of the few the British had authorized several years back. The inhabitants had high hopes for it when they first started building it, but the funding promised by the mandate was abruptly cut and, with the Arabs constantly sniping at the villagers, many were forced to leave. The few that stayed were still struggling to make it a home. She turned to look at the mountain. It was shrouded in darkness and it too looked deserted. Nothing moved and she was about to turn away, when she saw them.

Moving along an undefined snakelike path, one could catch a glimmer of light briefly followed by darkness. Then it would reappear and she knew it was the convoy of people moving furtively to the top of the mountain. Anyone unaware of the project would never have known they were there.

"You're to go to the village." Benji pointed to the cluster of wooden huts. "And stay there," he ordered.

She was deeply offended and started to protest.

"Mother, it's all been arranged and everyone has a job to do. You've been assigned to help prepare breakfast. We should be finished with building the fences and the guardposts as well as the watchtower by that time and we'll all be starved."

Being relegated to the position of preparing food for the new settlers rather than taking part in the actual constructing of the kibbutz rankled throughout the night. Memories of the times when she was an intricate part of every facet of every detail kept cropping up, and Deborah had a hard time ignoring the pain. Life had passed by so quickly. One day she was a young, vibrant woman—and now?

She looked up the mountain again. The lights flickered less frequently and finally there was complete darkness as the convoy disappeared behind a curve in the road.

In spite of her unhappiness, she took charge the minute she entered the small compound of fifteen small huts, a large schoolroom, a playground and an auditorium attached to a kitchen. She assigned various women to different chores, some to take care of the children, others to tend to supper preparation to make it appear like a regular evening in the settlement if a British patrol should happen by. Everyone followed her instructions, grateful for her organizational abilities, but tension was high. Naomi came by during the night and commended Deborah for her ingenuity. Instead of being flattered, Deborah felt patronized. At one point Michael appeared with several other men. They were on horseback and she could tell that they were all armed, although the guns and rifles were carefully hidden. From the look on Michael's face, she knew they expected trouble. Some British patrol cars stopped by, asking for water, but it was clearly a ploy. They knew something was going on and were checking out the area.

It was long past midnight and Deborah, feeling exhausted, left the kitchen and sat on a rock, her eyes glued to the mountaintop. It stared back at her, barren, desolate, lonely. That was where her daughter would be living, she thought, and proud as she was of her, she felt sad. Naomi was carving out a difficult life for herself. Difficult and dangerous. Deborah shifted her gaze to the far-off distance. She could not see it, but she knew the Syrian border was within view in daylight. High as Naomi's settlement would be and tall as her mountain was, the Syrian border sat above them. Someday her grandchildren would be playing in their yards within range of hostile eyes, and possibly guns.

As though affirming her gloomy thoughts, the darkness grew thicker as it always did just before dawn, and her feelings of sorrow deepened.

"Okay, it's time to go." Benji, leading a caravan of mules, came toward her.

"Are they finished?" she asked.

"All done. Fence up, watchtower with projector in place, tents sitting cozily around it and guards posted, daring anyone to come and disturb the peace."

Deborah along with the other women walked slowly behind the mules, who were loaded with food. Except for the shuffling of footsteps and an occasional neigh from a mule, there was no sound around. As they drew closer to their destination, a projector light passed slowly over their heads. Finally the top of the watchtower came into view and then the campsite.

In one night, the foundation of a new settlement had been established. Deborah wiped the tears from her cheeks. No one would dare tear it down.

A triumphant cheer greeted them and the gate was flung open. Within minutes, everyone was involved in their first meal. The faces of men, women and children could be seen in the early morning light, shining with pride of achievement. The only discordant note was the projector, circling silently, searching the distance.

Deborah saw Naomi leaning contentedly against Jack. Michael was talking to Gidon, who was now dressed in civilian clothes. Benji joined them. They were laughing. Several youngsters were playing hide-and-seek, while older people sat around in a leisurely fashion, eating and chatting. Basha was no-where around. Deborah was about to go over to Gidon and ask where she was when a hush fell over the area. She realized the projector had stopped moving and was focused on a group of British soldiers, guns in readiness, standing outside the front gate.

"You won't get away with it," an officer shouted angrily. "We won't have it. There are specific orders about setting up new settlements without permits." He kicked the front gate, which crumbled all too easily and, followed by his soldiers, marched into the camp.

Michael walked over and blocked their progress.

The officer pushed past Michael and continued toward the water tower. His men, guns ready, followed cautiously. In the silence a click of a rifle lock being unlatched was clearly heard. The officer stopped and searched the crowd with his eyes, trying to decide where the noise had come from.

"Don't start with any rough work, gentlemen. We outnumber you, both in men and guns. And we have the law on our side," he said, his hand going to his gun holster.

"You may have the men and the guns and your unlawful pronouncements, but we have the will and the moral right on our side," Michael answered.

The officer ignored him. "Start tearing down the fences."

The soldiers spread out in several directions, rifle butts in readiness for demolition.

"I warn you, sir," Michael hissed and the threat in his voice frightened Deborah. He was standing a few feet away from her and she could see his eyes blazing.

The officer took his gun out of his holster and faced Michael. Unflinching, Michael walked toward him.

They came face to face. Michael towered over the Englishman but the officer had a gun aimed at Michael.

The sound of an infant's cry broke through the silence and everyone turned in its direction.

"What the hell," the Englishman started.

"It's a girl. A beautiful little girl." A young woman came running out of one of the tents, her face wet with tears. "Gidon, Basha has had the baby."

"*Mazal tov!*" someone cried out in jubilation.

Everyone started running toward the tent with Gidon leading the way.

"Baby?" the Englishman gasped.

"Sorry, old fellow," Michael smiled at him. "Sometimes we simply need a miracle. And sometimes, a miracle actually happens." He reached over to a table and picked up a bottle of wine. "Will you join us in a toast?"

Sheepishly, the officer took the glass, raised it to his lips and was about to take a sip when he suddenly doubled over and fell to the ground, blood spurting from his mouth.

A blast of gunfire from the water tower stunned everyone to silence.

"Get down, everyone." Orders came from the tower. "The Arabs are closing in and they're aiming for a fight."

When the battle was over, two settlers and one Englishman were dead. Beyond the fence lay several Arab corpses. The dust from the retreating Arabs settled slowly.

The new settlement was inaugurated with the birth of a little girl and the death of three men.

Basha was rushed to the hospital in a nearby town. She was recovering from the birth when Deborah and Michael arrived. Standing outside the nursery window, Deborah observed the infant.

"I thought Naomi was the most beautiful baby I'd every seen, but I must tell you, this baby is quite outstanding," Michael whispered as though fearful of disturbing her sleep.

"Is she Nili?" Deborah asked and held her breath, waiting for his answer.

"No," he said after a long moment. "Maybe Tamar, but not Nili."

"She does look like Tamar, doesn't she?" Deborah said slowly, looking at the blond hair, tiny features and the small chin. She glanced briefly at Michael. Was he aware of the similarity and was that what caused his obvious enchantment with the infant? She smiled inwardly. It would have hurt her deeply in the past. Now she was touched that he might feel that way. In fact, she was pleased. This baby might draw him closer to Gidon and Basha.

"Well, it's really not our decision, it is?" she said as she started toward Basha's room.

Basha was lying in a room with four other women, but her bed was hidden behind a curtain. Gidon was sitting next to the bed, holding his wife's hand. They were staring at each other, oblivious to their surroundings. Deborah felt like an intruder. Gidon stood up the minute they pulled the curtain away.

Deborah hugged Basha and Michael leaned over and kissed the new mother. Then he shook Gidon's hand solemnly.

Deborah was pleased. There was warm feeling among them all. She prayed it was the beginning of a new truce, if not a complete peace.

"Have you chosen a name?" Michael asked gruffly.

"Deborah?" Gidon deferred to her. Like the rest of the family, he knew of Deborah's dream of having a child named Nili.

"What do you think?" She avoided an answer. Lovely as the baby was, she knew that she should not be named Nili.

"Michael suggests Tamar," she said, when she realized they were still waiting for her answer.

Gidon looked over at Basha.

"Would you mind if we called her Tanya?" she asked. "It's my mother's name."

"Oh, Basha," Deborah tried to hide her shock. "We don't name children after living people."

Basha bit her lip and her face reddened with embarrassment. "I know. I'm sorry," she whispered. "But . . ." she stammered. "I would like to call her Tanya, anyway."

Deborah felt sorry for her. Basha missed her parents desperately. She had written numerous letters to her family since arriving in Palestine and had received no reply to any of them. Since the fall of Poland, she was frantic with worry and it was only the pregnancy that seemed to protect her from the horror of the possible death of her parents. Her wanting to name her baby after her mother was her way of accepting the dreadful possibility of her mother's death. It was a sad thought but Deborah felt that no one had the right to interfere in Basha's decision.

"It's not a religious law," Michael said haltingly. "It's only a superstition, and if that's what you want to name her, then we now have a small, beautiful Tanya in the family."

"Tanya Danziger," Gidon said the name, testing it for its sound.

"You'll have to go through the legal procedure eventually," Michael said sternly. "I know you call yourselves Danziger, but the fact is, you're still registered as Davidzohn."

"You're right," Gidon agreed quickly. "I should do it and I will."

Naomi and Jack came in, followed by Benji. The settlement's gift to the newborn baby was the decision to name the place after her.

"Tel Tanya," Deborah said in awe.

Tamar's granddaughter, she felt, was a link to the future. The Danziger heritage was being carried on.

# CHAPTER
# THIRTY-TWO

G IDON did not rush to enlist. For him to join the British army was a difficult decision. His contempt for the British was greater than ever. Being related to Michael made him even more aware of the odious double standard practiced by the mandate government against the Jews. The British had no qualms about asking for the help of the Jews in their war effort, but they never gave them credit for their contributions because they feared antagonizing the Arabs.

Gidon was deeply involved in bringing illegal immigrants into Palestine. Like the British who were fighting fascist tyranny in Europe, Gidon felt that he was fighting another kind of tyranny—that of the British mandatory administration's laws which forbade the saving of Jews from the Nazis. Basha too got involved in helping the rescue operation. Her knowledge of Polish and German was a great asset once the refugees were ashore and needed someone to talk to them, calm them, help them disperse and disappear before they were discovered by the British. Her dedication and zeal matched his and it brought them even closer.

The work was dangerous and frustrating. The illegal ships kept coming and all were turned away. Seeing decrepit barges reaching the shores of Palestine returned to sea, began to wear him down. He raged at the British, but soon his fury turned on the Jewish leadership as well, for they continued to try to negotiate, cajole, even beg the British for a change in their attitude, rather than use force. Everyone was aware of the duplicity of the mandate government and Gidon was certain the British would not dare go on with their hideous game if the organized Jewish leadership took a forceful stand. He knew he was right, and offered as evidence the Arabs who ran from Tel Tanya that first night the kibbutz was established when they faced Jewish defiance. The new settlers had used the few guns in their possession and it worked.

As the mandate decrees against Jewish immigration grew more absurd, Gidon stood by helplessly, watching the pathetic refugees unable to land on the one shore in the world that was willing to accept them. He could not contain his need to avenge them. More and more his thoughts turned to Amit and his friends, wondering where they were and what they were doing.

He was on assignment in Haifa, acting as an observer for what promised to be a difficult confrontation between the refugees and the British, when he ran into his friend.

A ship had arrived in Haifa harbor and the British, having forbidden the refugees to disembark, ordered the ship to sail to an island in the Indian Ocean. Since the ship was too battered to undertake the voyage, the refugees were to be transferred to another vessel. Gidon was sitting on the balcony of the Panorama Hotel on Mount Carmel, waiting for the arrival of the replacement ship. Intervention would occur when the actual transfer took place.

Gidon looked comfortable and very much in place sitting on the terrace of the hotel, watching British officers sipping their Sunday afternoon cocktails, when he saw Amit standing in the doorway. Spotting Gidon, he came over to his table and without a word sat down opposite him. He looked older than Gidon remembered. His body was taut and his hands shook as he lit a cigarette. It was unlike him. Amit's cool demeanor was his trademark.

"Drink?" Gidon asked.

"Hardly," Amit shook his head. "I'm too wound up as it is."

A strange statement, Gidon thought, from someone who never spoke about personal feelings.

"Anything I can do?" Gidon asked.

"My mother and sisters are on that ship."

Gidon gulped. He had never though of Amit as having a family.

"Where are they coming from?"

"Poland."

"Are you Polish?"

"I was born in Bulgaria."

"When did you come here?"

"When I was thirteen. My family moved to Poland at that point. I did not want a bar mitzvah and asked for a trip to Palestine instead."

"And you never went back?"

"No."

"Why?"

"Have you ever been to Poland?" Before Gidon could answer, he continued. "I hated it. Hated the way the Jews lived there, hated the way the Poles treated them."

"Where is your father?"

"He died shortly after I left."

"Do you have any other relatives there?"

"Uncles, aunts, cousins, but I don't know where they are. All I know is that I've been trying to get my mother and sisters to come here and when I finally got the certificates, it was too late."

He lit a second cigarette before he crushed the one he had just finished.

"Will there be trouble?" Gidon asked.

"There always is."

"Can I help?" Gidon asked.

"Where are you staying?"

"We have friends who run a sanitarium on Mount Carmel." He took out a piece of paper and scribbled Sonya and Misha's address down.

"Will they mind if I bring them my family?" Amit asked.

Gidon smiled. "They take in people so often, it's almost routine."

He was handing the paper over to Amit when the area suddenly lit up. The explosion which followed was deafening.

Everyone ran to the edge of the terrace. Several British officers took out their binoculars and one could hear them gasp with horror as they passed the glasses to others. Gidon's turn came and as he focused, a feeling of nausea rose in his throat at the sight that greeted him. The ship he had been watching had blown up. Mutilated bodies, severed heads and limbs were floating in the darkening waters. Those still alive made frantic gestures with their hands, feebly splashing in the water around them. The cries issuing from gaping mouths were quickly stifled as they were sucked into the oily sea. Numbed, Gidon lowered the binoculars and looked around for Amit. He was gone.

The British High Command admitted that the people on the boat had blown themselves up rather than go off to an unknown exile. There was, however, no apology from His Majesty's government. The White Paper forbidding Jewish immigration to Palestine was the law passed by His Majesty's government, and it had to be adhered to.

Within days, Gidon received a request from Amit to write a proclamation in English charging the High Commissioner of Palestine with murder. He did it willingly and the next day Gidon's text, along with a photograph of the High Commissioner and a hangman's noose dangling next to his image, appeared on posters around the country.

For several weeks there were retaliatory actions against the British. Army installations were bombed, British Intelligence offices in Haifa, Tel Aviv and Jerusalem were ransacked, and there were some British casualties. For once, the usual outrage of the public against such actions was muted. The activists had scored a tacit victory.

Gidon was convinced Amit's organization was responsible for these retaliatory acts and he wanted to be part of that group again. When he got word that Amit wanted to see him, he went willingly.

The meeting took place in the Roman amphitheater outside Bet Enav. Walking toward it, Gidon looked over at Tel Ada. It had been resurrected, but it now looked like a fortress. A solid wall around it held a high water tower and a searchlight that surveyed the surrounding terrain.

"I wanted to meet with you," Amit started slowly, "because I feel that the time has come for you to make a commitment."

"Commitment?"

"You're either with us or you're with them."

Gidon did not answer. He had killed for Amit's organization and had suffered horrible guilt over that incident. Was he ready to make the commitment now with all it entailed?

"Before you answer, I think you should talk to someone who can explain things more clearly than I can," Amit said, noting Gidon's hesitation.

"Who?"

"Gidon." He heard his name called and looked around to see who was calling him. He saw no one.

"I know how you have suffered after killing the Arab several years ago," the voice continued and Gidon's eyes searched the ruins surrounding him. Whoever spoke obviously knew him and was answering his unspoken thoughts.

"You felt like a murderer. What do you think the British are doing to the Jews who are trying to land in Palestine? That is blatant murder of innocent people. But obviously murder is all in the eye of the beholder. You were at Tel Tanya when the Arabs came to murder the settlers the first night they were there. The line that defines who is the murderer and who is the victim has grown very thin. Somehow it has become acceptable for us to be the victims. But no one likes victims, so they've labeled us intruders on their stage of history. What they've forgotten is that *we* have created that stage." A deep silence followed the speaker's last words.

Gidon was confused. He knew the voice but could not place it. He looked over the valley spread out before him. Tel Ada came into view again. He remembered the first time he saw it. He was with Naomi. He next knew of its existence when he was being led home by Nechemya. Nechemya! That was who the voice belonged to. Sweet, gentle Nechemya, the caretaker of the cemetery, who first told him the deeper meaning of Nili.

Then he saw him. He was sitting amidst the rocks, a small smile playing on his thin lips. As he came closer, Gidon saw that he had grown gray, his beard was thinner and even more scraggly than it had been.

"I don't think we can debate murder in a world that thinks so little of human life." Nechemya seated himself next to Gidon. "There is a whole world out there fighting a common fascist enemy. That is not murder. But, as always, we are in the position of having to fight two fascist regimes, the Nazis and the British. The British want our help in overpowering the Nazis, hoping we'll forget our own goals and dreams. Hoping that we will be so grateful to die for this cause, we will forget ours. They'll promise us anything now. But the British are known to have short memories. Therefore, even as we fight beside them, we must not let them think we will forget. Because as soon as this war is over, they'll turn on us again."

Gidon was mesmerized. Nechemya was voicing his own thoughts. Those were his feelings and now this wise father was assuring him that he had a right to feel anger, a right to want to avenge the wrongs that were done to his people, a right to fight for what he believed in. Yes, a right to kill for what he knew was injustice.

"You've been doing an admirable job helping to bring in the illegal immigrants into the country," Nechemya said, looking at him closely. "And we can use your talents on our side."

"Why can't we join forces with the others?" Gidon asked, haltingly.

"Join forces with bleeding hearts who believe that in helping the British today we will be rewarded tomorrow?" He laughed bitterly. "No. They do what they think they should and we do what we know we must. Mark my words, before this thing is over, before we allow ourselves to be eliminated from the world, they will join us."

"What would you like me to do?" Gidon asked.

"Pledge yourself to our cause," Nechemya answered. "Think about what I have said and make your decision according to your conscience." He put his hand out and Gidon took it gratefully. Nechemya's thin fingers were icy. For a moment Gidon felt as though he were touching death.

"Where is Tuvia?" Gidon called out when Nechemya started to walk away.

Nechemya stopped and without turning around he said quietly. "He was killed in Syria on a mission for British Intelligence."

"When?" Gidon was flabbergasted. "I hadn't heard about it."

"No one has. The British use us but never acknowledge us. Not in life and not in death."

He was gone before Gidon recovered from the shock.

"We think you should join the British army," Amit spoke up and Gidon was startled. He had forgotten Amit was there.

"But why?" Gidon was shocked.

"We need recruits. Trained men and women who will be able to fight the British when this war is over. We can't make contacts here with everyone looking over our shoulder. We have men in the army but we need leaders who will keep our cause alive. You can do that. Besides, we need arms. Guns, rifles, explosives, anything we can lay our hands on. You can help there too." He paused briefly, letting his words sink in. "We have some very influential friends in Cairo and Alexandria who will help. If you decide to enlist, let me know and I'll give you their addresses." He spoke with the old passion but his voice had lost its timbre. The zeal of youth had turned to a murderous rage.

Still, Gidon held off, aware that Basha was against it. She was lonely and frightened when he was not with her. She was also terrified of a German victory.

"We all are," Gidon kept assuring her. "But we can't afford to lose, so we'll fight them and we'll win."

"You don't know them," she shook her head. "I do."

"Well, we're not the only ones trying to defeat them." Gidon became impatient. "All of Europe is fighting them."

"But most of them are not Jews," she cried out impatiently. "They're Poles, Romanians, Hungarians, Bulgarians, they're Christians."

Gidon was taken aback by her outburst, but he could not argue. She was right, of course, but he had never equated the plight of the European people as being different from the plight of the European Jews.

"And if you join the army and you're captured . . ." She could not finish the sentence. Instead she burst out crying and it was a scene he could not cope with. He promised not to do anything rash.

He was very much in love with her and he worshipped his daughter. In a way, it was Tanya who caused him the most hesitation. Basha would not go to the Ben Hods if he was away and he wanted Tanya to be part of their life.

It was the obvious delight of the Arabs at the reported success of the Germans that finally tipped the scales. The Germans, commanded by Rommel, were advancing toward the borders of Palestine. They had infiltrated Syria and Lebanon. Gidon realized that he had little choice.

His enlistment coincided with the United States' declaration of war on the Axis powers, after the attack on Pearl Harbor on December 7, 1941.

# CHAPTER
# THIRTY-THREE

EBORAH put the last pile of winter clothes into the drawer, sprinkled camphor flakes over them and closed the drawer firmly. Turning around, she caught sight of a pair of winter socks that had rolled under the bed. She stooped to pick it up and caught sight of the doll Tanya had misplaced the day before. Picking it up, she stared at it and a strange longing for the past came over her. Why was it that the past remembered always seemed happier, more exciting, she wondered. Her past had been exciting. It had been filled with turmoil, adventure, happiness, sadness, tragedy and triumph. But was it not all in preparation for a time when she could enjoy peace and tranquility, a time when she could sit back and appreciate what had been and look forward to a hopeful future? She felt her mind balk. Something was missing and what it was eluded her. Somehow that lovely transition had not materialized and instead she felt her life was over. Whatever the future held for her, it could in no way compete with what had been.

In the three years since Naomi and Jack had settled in Tel Tanya, Deborah felt life slipping away. The feeling of being useless came back more frequently and she simply felt old, unwanted and unneeded.

She looked down at the small, battered doll. There was no longer place for dolls in her house. This doll belonged to Tanya, who was visiting them for a few days. The room she was in had once belonged to Naomi and Benji and it had been a children's haven. She remembered the care with which she chose their cribs, then youth beds and finally regular-sized ones. The yellow baby chiffonniers went when the desks were brought in. The shelves sagging with toys were transformed into bookshelves. Nothing remained of those colorful days. Now the room was drab and bare. It contained two cots and a crib, with a wooden chest of drawers. The crib had been for Tanya when she was an infant. It remained even after Gidon and Basha moved to their own apartment in Tel Aviv. It would accommodate Uri, Jack and Naomi's son, when he came to the city. This room which once held so much promise, which once was filled with dreams of an exciting future, appeared empty and forlorn.

The late afternoon sun began to fade and Deborah became aware of the silence around her. It should have been soothing but it did not bring her contentment. There was a time when she longed for a brief period of quiet, was grateful for a few minutes of tranquility before the children came rushing in. No one would be disturbing her today. Not even little Tanya.

Still holding the doll, she walked over to the window. Tanya, a tow-haired child with skimpy braids tied with ribbons, was sitting in the sandbox, making mud pies. She was hard at work, her small face strained in concentration. Only three years old, she was the most self-sufficient child Deborah had ever known. Well-mannered and extremely disciplined, she did not seem unhappy, but as far as Deborah was concerned, there was a lack of childish spontaneity about her. Like Gidon had been, she was different from other children. Basha seemed to want that emphasized, dressing the child in starched white dresses and frilly pinafores, while other children romped around in playsuits and shorts. Small as she was, Tanya personified loneliness. She did have joy in her, but it only came to life when she was with Gidon or Michael. Then a happy little girl would emerge and that mystical quality which she exuded from the minute she was born would burst forth.

At that moment, as though aware she was being observed, Tanya looked up. Seeing Deborah, she smiled shyly, waved and then, in her fastidious fashion, she put her toys in order, shook the sand from her hands and came toward Deborah.

"Look what I found." Deborah handed her the doll.

Tanya's smile broadened. "You are the most wonderful grandmother and I love you very much." She leaned against Deborah and rested her head against her leg.

"What would you like to do this afternoon?" Deborah asked, lifting the child's face to hers.

"Isn't Mommy coming back today?" Her expression grew serious again.

"Even if she is, she can wash up and rest if we're not here."

"I want to wait for her," Tanya said. "She's been gone a long time."

Deborah was taken aback. She too felt that way. An unusually conscientious mother who never allowed anyone else to care for her child, Basha suddenly announced that she wanted to leave Tanya at the Ben Hods' for several days. In the months since Gidon had joined the British army, they had seen her rarely, which was curious. Tanya missed her father and it made little sense to heighten his absence by having her mother away.

Deborah wondered where Basha was going but dared not ask. Basha knew almost no one in Palestine except Naomi and Jack. If she were going to visit them, she surely would have taken Tanya. Aware that the relationship between Basha and Gidon was strained because of his decision to enlist, Deborah decided that Basha simply wanted to be alone to sort out her thoughts. That was understandable since Gidon's enlistment was puzzling to everyone. His loathing for the British was greater than ever, which made the decision all the more bizarre.

"Will Daddy be coming home soon?" Tanya asked.

"I hope so." Deborah picked the child up and hugged her. "But Grandpa Michael will be home early today because you're here and he loves being with you."

Tanya nodded solemnly. "I miss my Daddy," she whispered.

"Why don't we go into my room and I'll fix your hair and then we'll go out."

They nearly collided with Tova, who was entering the room. She had a concerned look on her face.

"Anything wrong?" Deborah asked. Tova was a cheerful, easygoing person, and for her to look worried was out of character.

"There is someone here to see you," she said.

"Who?"

"I don't know. He's dressed in a uniform and although he speaks Hebrew, he has a heavy accent." She paused. "He reminds me of the Polish officers in Kraków." She shuddered at the memory.

Deborah pressed Tanya's hand involuntarily. Somehow she was sure it was Yanosh. She had not thought of him in a long time yet the idea that it might be he made her nervous.

"Did you get his name?" she asked.

"No. He's a big man with very nice manners, but there is something about him that made me uncomfortable."

"I'll go out and meet him in a minute." Turning to Tanya, she tried to keep calm. "Let Tova dress you and comb your hair and in a little while we'll go out and buy something nice for dessert." She leaned down and kissed the child.

The minute Tova and Tanya left, Deborah rushed to her room and seated herself at her dressing table. The late afternoon light was dim and she lit a lamp and raised it to the mirror. Staring back at her was a well-groomed, attractive woman, but a woman past forty whose eyes did not sparkle as they used to, whose skin was not as firm around the chin, whose lines on the forehead were a little deeper. She put her hand to her face, trying to smooth it out, make it appear younger. The gesture embarrassed her. She was being foolish and she knew it. She was not sure the man was Yanosh and if it were, it had been years since they last saw each other and he was bound to see the change. She stood up and examined her figure carefully. She had gained some weight but she was still slender and her tiny waist had not thickened. She contemplated changing her dress but decided against it.

With a pretended air of assurance, she walked into the living room.

He was standing with his back to her, looking at the photographs sitting on the piano. She watched him for a brief moment. He was thinner than she remembered and yes, his stance in the well-cut uniform was military. His hair was completely white.

He turned slowly, aware of her presence and smiled. "How beautiful you are," he said simply.

She walked over to him and he put his arms around her and kissed her. For a minute she forgot where she was and she responded to his embrace. Then, moving away, she bit her lip and stared at him, fear and embarrassment creeping into her eyes.

"I'm mad. Completely mad," she whispered.

"I've missed you so desperately." He did not take his eyes off her.

"When did you get to Palestine?" she asked when she felt she could speak naturally. And before he could answer, she rushed on nervously, "How did you get here? Are you well? Did you suffer much when the Germans entered Poland?" The questions poured forth, nervously.

"I'm fine, Deborah. I'm even better now that I'm here talking to you." He started toward her.

"No, please don't," she pleaded. "Tell me, tell me everything from the minute I last saw you. When we left Geneva I was so worried. And then never a word. I had no way of finding out where you were. And now you're here." She stopped and caught her breath. "How did you get here?"

"It's a very long and complicated story. I'm here with General Anders. He organized the Free French Polish army in exile and I joined him the minute I could."

"Where were you?"

"In Siberia."

"Siberia?" Deborah paled. "How long were you there?"

"A while. It was not as bad as it sounds. I'll tell you about it some other time. Now, I'd just like to sit here and look at you."

"Oh, please do sit." She became flustered. "And I'll get you some tea. Or would you like a drink?"

"I want nothing." He seated himself in a large armchair. "Just sit with me." His eyes were boring into her and she wanted to reach over and touch him.

"How long will you be staying?" she asked.

"I'm going to ask for a release from the general, now that I'm here."

"We're speaking Hebrew." Deborah was stunned. "Where did you learn to speak Hebrew?"

"From a very old lady and her grandchild in Russia before I was captured."

"Captured by the Russians?"

"Well, actually I turned myself in. It was a strange experience. The Polish army was badly trounced, as you know, early on. I was with my men in a forest and there was nothing but snow around us. There was a terrible explosion and I was knocked unconscious. When I woke, I was alone. I must have been thrown by the bomb. I don't know how long I walked and suddenly I saw a little house on the outskirts of a village. I was frozen and I walked up to it and knocked. An old lady answered the door and stared at me blankly. I barely noticed her. On the table behind her, I saw two lit candles and a memorial candle burning in a glass. I knew immediately it was Yom Kippur. How I knew I can't tell you, but I knew."

He was completely transported to the past and Deborah did not dare interrupt.

"I said shalom in Hebrew, which was one of the few Hebrew words I knew and she reached out and pulled me into the house." His eyes cleared and he looked directly at Deborah. "I thought of you at that moment and remembered your saying that Jews can look only at Palestine as their home. I stayed at her house for nearly two months, hidden in the attic. Her son was off to war and her grandson was staying with her. He was thirteen and studying for his bar mitzvah. Some ancient man came by daily to teach him his portion of the Torah and Hebrew. I sat in on those sessions. It was like some miracle. Everything I had ever learned as a child came back to me."

"What made you give yourself up?"

"The Russians were becoming suspicious and I knew I was endangering the old lady, so I left and turned myself in." He looked at her seriously. "I turned myself in as a Jew, not a Polish officer."

"And then?"

"I was sent to Siberia and by then, I was hungry for my roots and I found many *landsmen* there. Jews who, like your parents, had a longing for their homeland, but who had not had the foresight to come here when your parents did." He smiled sadly. "My parents never even thought of coming here."

"How are they?"

"They're dead. In fact, I believe my whole family perished."

Just then Tanya, neatly combed and dressed in a freshly ironed organdy pinafore, appeared in the doorway next to Tova.

"And who is this little angel?" Yanosh cried out.

"That's Tanya." Deborah stood up quickly and rushed toward the child. "Come, little one, and say hello to Uncle Yanosh."

Tanya put her hand out and looked up at him. "Are you really my uncle?"

Yanosh swooped Tanya up in his arms and cradled her. "I certainly want to be your uncle." He kissed her tenderly on the cheek.

To Deborah's surprise, Tanya rested her head on his shoulder and smiled contentedly at Deborah.

Suddenly, Deborah knew where Basha had gone. She had gone to meet General Anders for information about her parents.

"Yanosh, you don't happen to know anything about Basha's parents?" she asked excitedly.

"Basha's parents?" He seem shocked by her question. "Basha Juzelski?"

"Well, you know Basha and my nephew Gidon got married even before we boarded the train to Trieste," she started and stopped. Yanosh was staring at her in disbelief.

"Married?" he asked in a strained voice.

"Why, yes." Deborah's mouth went dry. "Didn't you know?" she asked, trying to compose herself. "They fell in love and when word of war came, they called her parents and asked for their consent, which as far as I know was given."

"Well, I knew she stayed behind, although I was not told why. She was a headstrong girl and when she made up her mind, nothing could dissuade her." He paused and Deborah could see that he too had lost his composure. "When we said goodbye, she asked me to see her parents when I got back to Warsaw and give them her love. Nothing more."

"Did you seem them?"

"I had to report to my commander before I could do anything else. It was several days before I got to their house. They were gone by the time I arrived. No one knew where they went. I was sent to the front within hours." He pushed the child gently away from him and scrutinized her carefully. "Yes, now I see the resemblance," he said quietly.

"Can Uncle Yanosh come with us when we go buy the cake for Mommy?" Tanya asked, her head still resting on Yanosh's shoulder.

"Of course he can," Deborah replied and took the child from his arms. "But I think you'd better have Tova give you a sweater, it's getting chilly out."

Tanya skipped out of the room.

"You're shocked by the news," Deborah said the minute they were alone. "May I ask why?"

"It is a shock. What I mean is, I could see they were attracted to each other. But marriage." He stopped again, obviously searching for a plausible explanation for his confusion. "She comes from a very strict family and it seems strange that they would let her marry someone they did not know."

"Gidon's a very fine young man," Deborah said defensively. "His pedigree, I assure you, is excellent." She could not keep the sarcasm out of her voice. "If anything, I think we could claim the same prerogative. We knew nothing about her, yet we accepted her." She took a deep breath. "They are very much in love, have a very happy marriage and as you can see, an adorable little girl."

"I meant no offense." Yanosh had come back to himself and his voice softened. "I did not mean it in any disparaging way. Certainly not toward your family. As I recall, and it is a very vague recollection, your nephew seemed like a most appealing and well-mannered young man. I'm sure that Basha's parents would have been pleased with her choice."

They stared at each other, both at a loss for words.

"Anybody home?" Michael's voice could be heard from the front vestibule.

"Grandpa Michael!" they heard Tanya cry out joyfully, then a loud happy greeting and finally Michael, carrying Tanya in his arms, walked into the living room.

He stopped at the sight of Yanosh.

"Michael, this is Yanosh Barlovsky. Someone I met in Europe a few years back."

The men shook hands.

"As a matter of fact, we met on that last trip, the one Gidon and I took to Switzerland. Captain Barlovsky was the gentleman who chaperoned Basha's group, and as a matter of fact, Captain Barlovsky knew her parents," Deborah rushed on.

"A pleasure, sir," Michael said. "And I must admit that I am rather relieved to know that Basha has some point of reference other than our nephew's love for her." He smiled. "Do sit down." And still holding Tanya, he seated himself on a settee and placed the child on his lap. "Would you like a coffee, a drink, a schnapps?"

"I think I would like some cold water." Yanosh was watching Michael carefully.

"When did you arrive in Palestine?" Michael asked, meeting Yanosh's gaze.

"A week ago. I came with General Anders's troops."

"Where are you stationed?"

"In Haifa."

"How long will you be staying in Palestine?"

"For good, I hope. I don't know the general's plans, although I believe he will keep a portion of his men in the country."

"But you will stay on, no matter what."

"Yes, as a civilian. I want to settle in Palestine."

Michael raised his brow. "Won't that be a problem? As I understand it, all Polish officers are subject to Anders's orders and if he should decide to transfer you, can you disobey? His agreement with the Allies is very strict on that matter."

Yanosh smiled. "I believe I can work it out."

"Interesting." Michael nodded. "Were you involved with us before the war?"

"Involved?"

"In any of our Zionist movements."

"No, I wasn't," Yanosh answered quickly. "I came to realize who we are as a people when I met the Nazis and other anti-Semitic groups after the war started." His face hardened. "The senseless brutality toward us as a people exceeds the imagination."

Michael lowered his eyes. "We have heard, but it is so monstrous that it is hard to imagine, much less believe."

"What is it that we don't believe?" Deborah asked. She had been following the conversation but its meaning eluded her.

"The mass murders, the death camps, the torture, the burning of living men, women and children." Yanosh's voice lacked emotion but his eyes were filled with unbearable pain, as though reliving some sort of hell.

"Where?" she asked.

"Please, let's not talk about it now," Yanosh said soberly. "It is still so fresh."

Michael coughed self-consciously. "I'm sorry. I did not realize you actually witnessed it." He turned to Deborah. "I believe our guest has asked for some water. And I would like some tea." He turned back to Yanosh. "Would you join us for supper?"

Yanosh looked over at Deborah.

"It would be our pleasure, Captain Barlovsky."

"Only if you call me Yanosh."

The meal was pleasant. Michael chatted with Yanosh while Deborah helped Tova serve. She caught smatterings of the conversation but she was preoccupied with thoughts of Yanosh. How strange to have him sitting at her table talking with her husband. He had once asked her to marry him. He had begged her to go back to Poland with him. She had almost agreed to go.

"Mommy," Tanya cried out, jumping up from her seat and running to the door. All eyes turned to find Basha standing in the doorway. She was staring at Yanosh and her face was ashen.

"Basha, dear, you look as if you've seen a ghost." Deborah walked over to the young woman and led her in.

"Yanosh," Basha whispered the name and tears started streaming down her cheeks. "Yanosh," she repeated and placed her hand on his face. "You're safe."

"Yes, I'm safe." He searched her face for a long moment. "And so are you."

Basha lowered her eyes. Then almost inaudibly she asked, "My father, mother, are they all right?"

"I don't know. They were gone by the time I went to their house."

"Where?"

"I don't know. No one knew."

She withdrew her hand self-consciously and turned to look at Deborah and Michael.

"Forgive me. This is a shock. If you don't mind, I am tired and I think I'll take Tanya home."

"I want to stay, Mommy. I want to stay here, Mommy. Please let me stay."

"No," Basha said firmly. "We're going home."

"I have my car and driver outside," Yanosh offered. "We could drive you home."

"No," Basha began to tremble. "No. I want to go home alone with my daughter."

She turned and nearly ran from the room, clutching Tanya's hand.

Michael, Deborah and Yanosh stared after her.

"I'm sure she did not mean to be rude. It must have been the shock of seeing someone from home. She's usually so controlled," Deborah said, barely able to hide her confusion. She did not understand the exchange between Basha and Yanosh, although there was something between them beyond the teacher-student relationship, beyond the kinship of country.

They resumed the meal, but the strain was evident. Deborah tried to entertain Yanosh, with little success. Yanosh was as helpful as he could be, but he too was uncomfortable.

Michael said nothing, absorbed in his thoughts. The scene that had just taken place upset him. He did not know what caused Basha's hysteria, but as Deborah explained, the presence of someone from her home probably upset her. What troubled him was Deborah's reaction. Yanosh was no mere acquaintance. This man meant something to his wife. He remembered the change in her after her arrival from Switzerland, just after the war broke out. He suspected she might have met someone during that vacation. He dismissed the thought then. Now, watching Yanosh and Deborah, he knew he had been wrong to do so. Yanosh Barlovsky was the man responsible for the change in Deborah. He must have meant a great deal to her and his reappearance confused her.

The meal over, Deborah and Michael walked Yanosh to the door.

"I would very much like you to meet some of the Jewish leadership and possibly give them a report about conditions in Europe. It's important that we have as many facts as possible, since we have few eyewitness reports at this time," Michael said.

"It would mean a great deal to me to share this information with people who might be able to do something. As I said, the tragedy is far greater than anyone knows."

"I shall look forward to hearing from you." Michael and Yanosh shook hands.

"If we can be of any help to you in settling down here once you're a civilian again, please don't hesitate to call on us," Deborah said politely.

He took her hand and kissed it. She blinked, trying to suppress her memories.

Then he was gone, and in spite of the doubts that had come to her during the evening, Deborah hoped she would see him again.

"I wonder if he's trustworthy," Michael was saying, and Deborah was shocked.

"Of course he is," she said adamantly.

"What makes you so sure? General Anders has brought an awful lot of Poles with him, and we believe they're not all innocent, defeated soldiers longing for their motherland."

"I would stake my life on his character." Her voice was icy.

"Really?" he said. "Well, we'll see." Then over his shoulder, he said, "But you'll have to trust me, if at any point I say he's not."

"Michael." Deborah rushed after him. "What do you mean by trustworthy?"

"Well, the reports and rumors about atrocities being perpetrated on Jews in Europe are mind-boggling and still not conclusive. Having someone who actually witnessed them, someone we could depend on to tell us the facts, would be important." He entered the living room and Deborah was close behind him. "I wonder if he is the one."

"What is this about atrocities?" she asked impatiently. "War is atrocious, we all know that, but you keep implying something more sinister."

"It is." He poured himself a brandy and gulped it down.

Deborah watched him. He rarely drank and she was surprised at the rapidity with which he downed the drink.

"But no one else seems to know about it. I mean the public. I haven't heard a word from anyone and there's nothing in the papers," she insisted.

"For now it's best that way."

"Michael, you're treating me like an imbecile and I resent it."

He turned slowly and faced her. "Deborah, there are times that the public at large should be protected from knowing too much, for its own good." He took a deep breath. "For now, I'd like to stop this conversation."

"No!" she shouted. The tension of the day's events had taken its toll. "What are you talking about?"

"The Jews of Europe are being exterminated by the hundreds of thousands. Millions are dead and millions more will die before this bloody war ends. Are you satisfied?"

She gasped. "And you don't think the public in Palestine should know about it?"

"What exactly can the public do except get hysterical and lose its head?" He was white with frustration. "Practically everyone living here has relatives in Europe. It would cause panic that would be impossible to control." He stopped and tried to calm himself. "So for now it's best we say nothing. Certainly not until we have all the facts. Maybe then we can figure out what, if anything, we can do about it. I assure you, we are at a loss about how to deal with this nightmare. Sharing it at this point with a mass of distraught and frustrated people will not help."

Unable to sleep, Deborah lay beside Michael. She knew he too was awake and she was sorry she had forced him to expose a secret that must be torturing him. She reached over and took his hand. He pressed it gratefully.

# CHAPTER
# THIRTY-FOUR

B ASHA opened the letter with trembling fingers. It had been hand-delivered by a man who did not identify himself. The handwriting was not Gidon's, and before taking the letter out of the envelope she looked at the sender's name again. It was dated January 8, 1945 and it had taken two weeks to reach her.

*Dear Madame,*

*I hasten to tell you that Gidon is alive. He has, however, deserted the army and is absent without leave. I know this to be a fact since he left me a note telling me he was going to do so.*

*It is all incomprehensible to me, since he has fought heroically in battles and has gotten the medal of honor for his efforts. I do not know if you are aware that at one point he asked to be transferred into the Intelligence Corps and was attached to a unit that preceded the troops into occupied territories. It was then that I noted a change in him.*

*The shock of what the Germans and their collaborators in occupied countries did to the Jews was something few of the men, Jewish and Gentile, were able to take. Many of the brave Jewish soldiers succumbed to emotional breakdowns and although Gidon kept his wits about him longer than the others, the stench of death obviously took its toll on him as well.*

*I am a friend of Gidon's. You must believe that. In fact I love him as a brother and I am worried about what he might do. His rage at the Germans and their lackeys is shared by all decent people around the world. His feelings, however, toward the Nazis are almost bland in comparison to his feelings toward the British.*

*I am a correspondent for British Reuters, but am Irish by birth, and as such I can sympathize with his sentiments. But in view of the shocking experiences he has recently lived through, I fear for him.*

*What concerns me most is that he may try to enter Palestine illegally and be caught in the attempt. I do not know in what way you can help. Hopefully, through contacts you have in Palestine, you will be able to locate him and persuade him not to do anything rash.*

*If I can be of any service to you, you can reach me at the address on the envelope and I shall be awaiting word from you.*

*This letter is being hand-delivered, since I do not want to risk the censors intercepting it. I would be grateful if you would use similar caution when writing to me.*

*Most sincerely,*

Cornelius Sullivan

"Who was that?" Deborah came into the room and stopped when she saw Basha's expression. "What happened?"

Basha handed her the letter and Deborah read it quickly. "Who delivered it?" she asked.

"I don't know. Some man just handed it to me and left."

"I didn't hear a car drive up. Was he in uniform?"

"I didn't pay attention." Basha began to tremble.

Deborah walked over to her and tried to put her arm around her shoulder, but Basha pulled away and ran from the room. The bathroom door slammed shut. She walked over to the window and stared out. Tanya and Uri were playing in the garden and Naomi was holding her second child, Daniel, born ten days earlier. They were ten wonderful days when the whole family got together in the house in Bet Enav, to attend his *bris*. It was like the old days, when the whole village came to call and wish the newborn luck. Missing from that happy gathering was Gidon. Everyone felt his absence and spoke of him with great affection.

She looked down at the letter she was holding.

Poor Basha. Aside from her concern for Gidon, she had to be reminded again of the terrors they had been hearing and reading about in recent days. Deborah had no relatives in Europe, and yet she was horrified at the news of the exterminations. For Basha, whose parents were there, the reports were sheer hell. She had not heard from them and it was becoming clear that they were victims of the slaughter, along with all the other Jews of Poland.

"What does this man mean when he says I might be able to persuade him from doing something foolish?" Basha asked.

Deborah had not heard her reenter the room.

"What greater foolishness can he do than desert from the army when the war is nearly over?" Basha continued.

Basha, Deborah realized, knew nothing of Gidon's past associations and activities. Obviously Mr. Sullivan did and was worried that Gidon would rejoin his former friends, who were involved in violent acts against the British in Palestine. Yet he had changed since marrying Basha. He appeared to want acceptance from Michael, acceptance from the establishment. He still hated the British and their capricious mandatory policies, but he fought them within the framework of the Jewish resistance and followed the rules set down by the leaders of the community.

"Well, he says what he means," Deborah started slowly. "He's concerned that Gidon will get caught trying to enter the country. For that he could be severely punished. He might even have to go to prison. It certainly would leave an ugly mark on his record."

"Will Michael be able to help?" Basha asked.

"Possibly, but frankly, I think Yanosh is the one to talk to," Deborah said haltingly.

Basha shook her head furiously. "No, not Yanosh," she said firmly.

"He had influence with the Jewish Agency and he has contacts abroad."

"No," Basha repeated. "If Michael can't help, I'll go to General Anders."

Deborah lowered her eyes. She loved Basha like a daughter, yet there were so many things she did not understand about her. She trusted her, but her reliance on General Anders and his men concerned her. It certainly troubled Michael. She forced the thought aside. Basha had proven her loyalty to Palestine. She was risking her safety at that very moment by storing illegal arms in her little flat in Tel Aviv. She also knew of the arms that were hidden in Raphael's house, although Michael never told her the code words to use in case of a search by the British. Michael's distrust of Basha was due to her relationship with General Anders and his officers. Not all had proven their loyalty to the Jewish cause. Still, if the British were to search the premises and discover the arms, it would be Basha who would be charged with illegal possession.

Most baffling to Deborah was Basha's attitude toward Yanosh. He had become a member of their household. He was loving and kind to every member of the family and they all loved him. He was adored by Tanya and he worshipped the child. Basha avoided him. Deborah got the feeling that Yanosh was equally relieved not to invite them over together.

"Will you speak to Michael?" Basha asked.

"Obviously I will." Deborah's answer was drowned out by the sound of Michael's car coming into the driveway. She looked out and saw Michael step out of his car and open his arms wide to hug the children. Deborah's eyes misted. Michael, who could show no overt love for her, worshipped his grandchildren. And to Deborah's relief, he looked on Tanya as one of them. She watched as Naomi walked over to him and placed the infant in his arms. Naomi looked like a child herself. She certainly did not look as though she had recently given birth to a child.

The mood at the supper table was tense and Deborah noted that Michael was distracted. As soon as the meal was over, Basha took Tanya and Uri off to be bathed and put to bed in Raphael's house. It had become, for the moment, the children's house, with only Naomi sleeping there. Basha slept in Naomi's old room in the big house.

"What's bothering her?" Michael asked.

"Never mind that. What is bothering *you?*"

"The usual nonsense. It's just a very busy time. As a matter of fact, I've got to get to Haifa this evening. I came home only to see the children." His tone was in sharp contrast to his agitated state.

"You're involved in this monstrosity called the 'season', aren't you?" Deborah said cautiously.

"Well, someone's got to stop these terrorists from going on with their senseless acts of violence against the British," he answered, and stood up. "We're not doing that well with the British, and to have these lunatics blowing up bridges, buildings and railroad stations isn't helping."

"I don't think you've got a right to call them lunatics," she said through clenched teeth.

"You know what I mean." He tried to soften his tone. The war is nearly over and we want a bargaining chip. We've helped the Allies. We fought beside them. We've proven our loyalty. The Arabs have behaved outrageously and the British aren't blind. These terrorist acts are harming us at this point."

"I think it's horrible." Naomi spoke up for the first time. "I don't know that I believe in assassinations, but damn it, we've been passive for so long. And if what we've been reading in the papers about European Jewry is only half-true, I think our passivity may be partially to blame. It certainly hasn't helped."

"You think we're traitors to our own people, don't you?" Michael turned on his daughter furiously. "Go on, say it."

"Yes. I think you're doing an evil thing to people who have the same goals you have, except they believe their method might be more effective. And frankly, at this point, I think they're right."

Michael paled. "They're behaving like senseless killers and their methods are antagonizing the British."

"Antagonizing the British!" Naomi exclaimed with mock horror. "Has anybody thought of how the British have antagonized us? Tel Tanya was searched the other day and they found fifteen worn-out rifles and a few rounds of ammunition. Jack was arrested along with several other men. They were released after a couple of days, but the children saw their fathers being treated like criminals. And why did we have these rifles? To protect ourselves from the Arabs who are flaunting their disloyalty to the Allies while attacking us."

"When the war is won, we'll be the ones to benefit. Not the Arabs," Michael stormed.

"Michael, we trusted the British once, remember?" Deborah had regained her composure. "We fought with them, helped them, sacrificed so much and where did it get us?"

"Things have changed. There is a world out there and someone is bound to listen to reason."

"Please, Michael, don't be party to this traitorous act," Deborah pleaded.

He looked at her closely. "I have to do what I think is right and the only thing you can be thankful for is that Gidon is in the army and not involved with them anymore. Because I'd turn him in in a minute."

"I know you would," Deborah lowered her eyes. Where *was* Gidon?

"I've got to go now," Michael said, and walked out of the room.

"What's going on?" Naomi asked, noting her mother's strange reaction to her father's statement about Gidon. Without a word, Deborah fished Cornelius's letter out of her pocket and handed it to her.

"Oh, my God," the younger woman said bitterly. "I wonder where he is?"

"Probably trying to get home. And I was going to ask your father to help find him."

"How about Yanosh?" Naomi asked. "I'm sure he'd help."

"Basha won't hear of it," Deborah said. "I don't understand why."

"I suppose he reminds her of her family and it upsets her."

"No. It's something else."

"Have you asked him about it?"

"He's evasive when I mention it. I think Basha makes him uncomfortable, although I believe he would help Gidon."

"Why don't you talk to him? Yanosh would do anything in the world for you."

"Nonsense." Deborah felt herself blush.

"He's crazy about you. Everybody knows that," Naomi started and stopped. She had said it innocently, but she suddenly realized she had hit a raw nerve. Yanosh and her mother . . . their relationship had always seemed strange. There was an undercurrent of feelings between them whenever they were together. Occasionally, she had wondered about it, but dismissed it as fantasy. Now her mother's reaction caught her off guard and she felt uncomfortable.

"Well, I think you should talk to him. And the sooner the better," Naomi said quickly. She walked over to Deborah and put her arms around her. "I adore you, mother." She kissed her on the cheek and ran out of the room.

Deborah smiled to herself. *He's crazy about you. Everybody knows that,* Naomi had said. Yes, they were still very attached to each other, although time had mellowed her feelings for him. She knew she still meant a great deal to him and occasionally, when she would find herself alone with him, he would declare his love for her. It made her feel young and desirable. There were times she wished she could tell someone of her romantic adventure with Yanosh. Naomi would be horrified at the idea of her mother falling in love with anyone, especially a younger man.

She put the thought aside and wondered how she would word her request to Yanosh. She was sure he would do all he could for her. But this was not for her, it was for Gidon. Would Yanosh betray her? Betray Gidon? The thought upset her. Already she was condemning Gidon. In spite of his exemplary behavior since marrying Basha, Deborah felt he had not changed.

With Tanya and Uri bathed and in bed, Basha read the children a story and turned off the light. Naomi came in and they exchanged a sad look.

Basha felt trapped. She wished she could have talked to Michael, but she knew how he felt about it and she could not win him over. If only Gidon were home! She missed him so desperately. He was the only thing that made life worthwhile. Now he was wandering somewhere in Europe or the Middle East.

She looked around and the walls of the house appeared to be closing in on her. It was very quiet. She felt lonelier than she had in many years and suddenly she wanted to get away. Throwing a sweater over her shoulder, she ran out of the house.

"Basha?" She heard her name called and saw Deborah holding a lantern, walking toward her.

Without a word they headed down the main street. The townspeople had turned in for the night, but the peaceful atmosphere did little to comfort the two women when were walking quickly, as though heading toward a specific destination. Who they approached the crossroad Deborah turned toward the vineyards. Basha followed.

"Tell me about Gidon, when he was small," Basha broke the silence. "Tell me about Tamar. What was she like? Not just the legend, but the woman, the girl, your sister."

Deborah began slowly, recalling every detail, every nuance, in her effort to do justice to Tamar. She spoke most knowingly about the night her sister was tortured.

"We drove up to the house and had reached a cove and . . ." She stopped and looked around. "We were standing just a few feet away from where we are now," she whispered in awe. "Come, I'll show you." Rushing ahead, she arrived at the spot where she and Tamar had parted that night, twenty-eight years earlier. "I stopped the carriage and realized the window of the attic of our house was open." She pointed toward the house, which was barely visible. "There were no trees then, so we could see the house clearly. Tamar decided to go up to the house alone and told me to care for the baby while she went to investigate." She caught her breath, reliving the memory. "I offered to go, telling her she had a baby to care for. She wouldn't hear of it. She ordered me to stay and take care of Gidon. I was terrified, and when I asked what I should do if he got hungry, she said, 'I'd rather he were hungry than dead.'" As she said the words, she gasped. "Good God, she must have felt that she was going to her death. She knew and she wanted to save the baby and save me."

Basha stared at Deborah. In the soft light coming from the flickering lantern, she could see her trembling.

"She was such a powerful woman. Her strength carried all of us. We survived because of her," Deborah whispered.

"You're a pretty strong woman yourself, Deborah," Basha touched her shoulder. "This whole family is surviving because of your strength. You must know that."

"Let me show you where Gidon and I hid, when Tamar left us." Deborah seemed not to hear what Basha had said as she went off toward the storage shelter.

She had not been near the place in years and it was a shorter distance than she remembered. The entrance was overgrown with tall weeds. She stopped when she realized that some of the weeds were trampled, as though someone had stepped on them or pushed them aside. As far as she knew, no one ever came there. Feeling for Basha's hand, holding the lantern over her head, she led the way.

Gidon, naked to the waist, was standing in the middle of the cave. He looked up when he heard movement and, realizing who they were, he allowed a small smile to come to his lips. He was as handsome as ever, but even in the dim light, Deborah noted that he was covered with brown dirt. His trousers were equally grimy.

"Gidon," Basha screamed and ran to him. He put his hand up, holding her off. His hand had that same muddy substance on it and Deborah realized it was dried blood.

"I don't want you to dirty yourself," he said hoarsely, his eyes devouring his wife's face with longing. "How I prayed for this moment." Then, unable to control himself, he pulled her toward him and kissed her passionately on the lips. His bloody hands encircled her waist, leaving dark patches on her sweater.

Deborah averted her eyes and they fell on the shirt lying at Gidon's feet. It too was drenched with blood.

"Oh, Gidon," she whispered. "What have you done?"

Gidon, still holding Basha close, looked up at Deborah and followed the direction of her eyes.

"No, Deborah," he said softly. "That is not Arab blood. It is the blood of my friend Nechemya, killed by the British, who were led to his door by Michael and his men."

Basha turned slowly and stared at Deborah. The look of doubt was still on Deborah's face. Basha looked back at Gidon. *Arab blood?* she thought. *What Arab blood?*

"Basha, go and get Gidon some fresh clothes and bring them here," Deborah said. "And you, Gidon, give me that shirt and those trousers. I'll have to burn them." She stopped and looked at Basha. The young woman was looking at Gidon with a puzzled look on her face and Deborah knew that this was not the time to explain Gidon's past. "Go," she ordered.

Gidon brushed his lips against Basha's cheek and pushed her gently toward the cave entrance.

"What happened?" Deborah asked the minute Basha was gone.

"What happened?" Gidon repeated her words and sat down wearily. "I left the army. It got to be too much. War—killing, maiming, destroying—is something you get used to. Seeing helpless women and children reduced to masses of bones piled up on top of each other, still groaning and gasping for air as their life was ebbing away, was more than I could take." He shuddered at the memory. "What made it even worse was that I knew that many of them could have been saved if the British had not forbidden these people to come to Palestine. It made it all the more unbearable. So I left. I deserted."

"Where did you go?"

"To Lebanon. I sneaked into Palestine from the north."

"And then?"

"I got to Haifa. No easy feat to get there without being caught by the British. I wanted to see my friend Amit and find out what had been happening. Nechemya was there, as well. Amit was telling me about the latest craze called the 'season' when the place was suddenly surrounded by British armored cars and a loudspeaker called for Amit and anyone with him to come out with hands up. We made a break for it out the back way. There was a car waiting for us. Apparently Nechemya thought something like this might happen. We drove down back roads to the beach. We thought we had eluded them, but they caught up with us and began to fire. They got Nechemya in the head. He fell into my arms and this is his blood." He pointed to his pants. "He died just as we reached the turn to Bet Enav. Amit ordered me out. I jumped out while the car was still moving and he and the driver continued with the body in the back seat. I hope the British will end up with nothing more than a corpse."

"Nechemya," Deborah whispered. "I've known him all my life." A bitter taste gurgled up in her throat. She regained her composure with difficulty. "And you came up here through the vineyard?" she asked.

He nodded.

"The earth is damp. There will be footprints."

"No. I took one of the railcarts and rode most of the way. My footprints only go up to where the rail tracks start. And when I got to the end of the line I pulled the switch, which sent the cart back to the starting point."

She breathed a sigh of relief. "As soon as Basha is back, you'll go up to the house, the big house, and you'll spend the night in Naomi's room with Basha."

"Where is Michael?"

"He's out and I doubt that he'll be back tonight."

"Why can't Basha and I use Raphael's house? I want to see Tanya."

"Naomi has given birth to a baby boy. She, the baby, Tanya and Uri are asleep there. Let them rest until morning. You spend the night with your wife."

Only then did she go over to him. Placing her hands on each side of his face, she looked into his eyes. "Thank God you're safe, my dearest child." Then she rested her head against his shoulder. His arms encircled her waist.

The flame in the small compartment under the bath tank shot up as Deborah placed Gidon's shirt and trousers into it. She poked them gently with the metal spoon and watched the fire devour the bloodied clothing. In a few minutes there would be no evidence.

The grandfather clock struck midnight as Deborah walked into her bedroom and closed the door behind her. Undressing slowly, she picked up her hairbrush and walked over to the window. The fog had grown thicker and the rain was coming down more heavily. Any footprints that Gidon might have left would be washed away, she thought with relief. And there was no trace of his having been near the house. In the morning, he would be off to Tel Aviv, and Basha and Tanya would leave shortly thereafter. Once there, Gidon would probably contact his friends and they would shelter him.

She began to relax and was about to turn away from the window when she saw Michael's car turn into the driveway. Heartsick, she ran out of her room, nearly colliding with Basha, who came running toward her.

"Wait until Michael comes into the bedroom. Then get Gidon up to the attic. Let him go alone and you get back into bed," Deborah ordered and raced back to her own room. Shutting the door behind her, she climbed quickly into bed.

When Michael came in, she was absorbed in a book and pretended surprise at seeing him.

"I didn't hear you drive up," she said.

"I didn't expect you to be awake." Michael threw himself into a small chair and put his hand over his face.

"You look as though you've had quite a time."

"It wasn't one of our more glorious actions." He did not look at her as he spoke. Instead he got up, undressed and climbed in beside her.

She looked over at him. He was staring at the ceiling.

"What happened?"

He took a long time before he answered. Finally, he turned to her and their eyes met.

"The British killed one of them," he said angrily.

"How many did you want them to kill?" she asked ironically.

"I did not want them to kill anyone. I only wanted them to catch them, imprison them, keep them out of harm's way."

"Was there more than one?"

"We thought there were two and a driver, but it turns out there were three. One is dead and the other is unconscious. Another jumped out of the car at the crossroad and ran into the grove. I don't know what happened to him. I didn't stay around to find out."

"Sounds like a motion picture," she said sarcastically. Much as she wanted to end the conversation, she needed information. "Have they searched the grove?"

"It's pretty dark out there and the rain isn't helping. We saw some muddy tracks leading to our vineyards, but they were unclear and then they stopped. We'll have to wait till morning."

"You've done enough damage by fingering these people. Leave it at that. Let the British do their own dirty work."

"They're Jews and we feel responsible for everything the Jews do in this country."

Neither spoke, pretending sleep. Deborah dozed off as dawn was breaking.

A loudspeaker calling out orders woke her. She sat up, dazed, and listened.

"It is five A.M. and a curfew has been put on the village of Bet Enav. His Majesty's forces will make a house-to-house search. No one is to leave his home until further notice. The village is completely surrounded, so that anyone trying to escape will be shot on sight."

"Your friends have come to visit," Deborah said, climbing quickly out of bed and pulling on her robe. "I'd better get Basha and then go over and get Naomi and the children."

"I'll get the children." Michael was already dressed and was racing out of the room.

Basha was standing by her window, staring out, when Deborah came in.

"You'd better dress and come down for breakfast," she said.

"What are we going to do?" Basha did not move away from the window.

"I don't know yet. Michael is working with them. Maybe we'll be spared a search."

"We've got to get Gidon out of here," Basha said frantically.

"Hardly a good suggestion under the circumstances," Deborah answered angrily. She walked casually toward the window and looked out. "It will be a while before they get to this house. For now, let's behave as though everything were in order." She looked over at Basha. Although she had dark circles under her eyes, her beauty was still startling. Her blond hair falling to her waist gave her a look of innocence. She had barely changed since the first time Deborah had seen her in the Swiss Alps. Had she not married Gidon, she would have been with her family. The thought shook her. *And where was that?*

Tova was hovering over the breakfast table. Tanya was sitting on Michael's lap, Naomi was feeding Daniel, and Uri was standing at the window.

"Uri, come to the table," Deborah called to him.

He shook his head.

"But why not?" she asked.

"Not until they go away," he answered without turning around.

"That could take hours."

"I don't care. I won't take a bite until they go away."

"Leave him," Naomi said quietly. "Since Jack was arrested he has grown to hate the British, and we've decided to ignore it rather than make an issue of it."

"Next he'll go on a hunger strike," Deborah said and looked over at

Michael. He pretended not to have heard her as he sipped his coffee. Tanya sat contentedly in his lap, her head on his shoulder.

They spent a long time over breakfast, hoping the sight of a family sitting peacefully around a table would put the British off. The tension grew unbearable. Michael and Deborah kept looking at each other. They were nervous for their family but they were also concerned about the rest of the village. Most of the people had changed over the years. Their reticence over Nili's activities had reversed itself and the majority of the inhabitants of Bet Enav had grown militant. As a result all the houses stored illegal arms in their yards, basements and attics.

The children grew restless and Uri was finally persuaded to have some food, with the promise that he could then go out and play. Naomi tended the baby. Michael, Basha and Deborah sat on the stoop of the front porch, watching the children.

Several times Deborah caught Basha looking up at the attic window. It was shuttered and when she finally caught Basha's eye, Deborah shook her head, warning her to stop bringing attention to that part of the house. Basha got up nervously and walked away.

It had stopped raining but the weather was grim. Time passed slowly. At twelve noon, a truck loaded with soldiers arrived at the front gate.

Michael stood up and walked toward the captain.

"I'm Michael Ben Hod and I've been working closely with your commanders in the area," he said firmly. "I hope you have been alerted to that fact."

"I have, sir," the young officer assured him, "but we are searching for a member of a gang of murderers and although I'm sure you would not be knowingly hiding him, he might have slipped into your house. It is my duty to search through it." He looked over at Raphael's house. "Who lives there?"

Before Michael could answer, Basha came running out, smiling. "Officer, oh how wonderful that you've come. I began to worry that you would overlook us." She came closer to him, her smile broader and her manner flirtatious.

The officer stiffened.

"Come with me," she urged, charmingly. "I must show you something wonderful and then you will understand my pleasure at your arrival."

The captain waved to two of his soldiers to follow him. They all disappeared into Raphael's house.

Michael turned to Deborah. His face was white with rage. "The bitch," he whispered. "Couldn't even wait for them to search the place. She'll just hand the arms over to them. They're looking for a killer, but needless to say, they'd love to find arms in the process."

Deborah was speechless. Could she have misjudged Basha to that extent? Or was giving away the arms to the British her way of preventing the soldiers from searching the main house? It was an unfair trade, Deborah thought angrily. It was putting all of them in jeopardy if the arms were found.

Defiantly she strode over to Raphael's house. The door was open and she found the soldiers standing around Daniel's crib. Naomi was lying in bed, looking pale, frightened and bewildered.

"Isn't he adorable?" Basha was saying. "But the problem is that we don't have any milk for him." She lowered her voice. "It was a very difficult birth and his mother is too ill to feed him, so we need milk. We get it from the farmer who has his shed outside the village." She looked up appealingly. "We've not been able to leave the house because of the curfew, but now that you are here, you will take me there, won't you? For the milk?"

The captain looked confused. He turned to his men. They were staring at him blankly.

"All right," he relented. "You come with us."

Michael saw everyone come out of Raphael's house, smiling. Deborah looked relieved.

"Basha has persuaded the captain to take her to Mr. Tinokot's farm for Daniel's milk," she said, emphasizing the farmer's name. "I don't know if you are aware of it, Michael, but Mr. Tinokot has generously given us milk for the baby, in view of Naomi's condition. In fact, Mr. Tinokot has been very considerate under the circumstances, especially since everyone knows how stingy he can be."

She repeated the name, hoping Basha would understand that *tinokot* was the code word for arms and hoping she would be able to transmit to the villagers, as she drove through with the soldiers, that all was under control, at least as far as the arms were concerned. Basha, she knew, was aware that the farmer's name was Moshe and that he was never referred to by his last name. *Tinokot* in Hebrew meant babies, a symbolic reference to the arms the Jews had succeeded in collecting.

Deborah and Michael ran to the front gate and watched Basha drive away with the soldiers. They could see the villagers standing in their doorways, looking distrustfully at the passing car. Basha was laughing gaily, bubbling over with gratitude and then with happy exuberance she began to wave to the people, calling out the message about going to Mr. Tinokot's for milk.

Deborah sighed with relief when she saw the villagers waving back to Basha. They had understood the message.

By the time Basha and her escorts returned, the British envoy was behind schedule and the captain decided to skip the search of the Ben Hod home. Basha jumped off the truck and the captain ordered two of the men to carry the milk cans into the kitchen.

"Won't you come in and have some coffee?" she asked.

"It would be our pleasure," Deborah said pleasantly.

"No, we must press on," the captain said, then bowed to her. "We're glad we could be of help."

Turning on his heel, he walked out of the yard and got in beside the driver. The loudspeaker announced the end of the curfew as it drove down the main road. Soon the truck was out of sight and the sounds from the loudspeaker died away.

Basha's exuberance faded the minute the truck drove off and was replaced by a look of exhaustion. Deborah threw her arms around her.

"I'm going to Tel Aviv," Michael said gruffly. "I've got to report this whole affair to headquarters." He paused and looked at Basha. "Thank you. It was very clever the way you handled the situation."

"I'd like to go to Tel Aviv as well," she said wearily. "Can Tanya and I join you?"

"Of course," Michael said formally.

She went to look for Tanya.

"When will you be back?" Deborah asked Michael.

"I'm not sure."

She started toward the house.

"When will you be coming to Tel Aviv?" he called after her.

"Within a few days," she answered without turning around.

"Let me know and I'll come pick you up."

"That won't be necessary. I'll manage."

She had to get Gidon to Tel Aviv and Michael was not the one to help her.

"If that's what you want."

"Yes, I would prefer that."

"Oh, stop it!" Michael's voice rose. "What was I to think?" He mimicked Basha's voice. " 'Come with me into the house, I've got something to show you. I've been waiting for you.' "

"I don't give a damn what you thought. You could have been a little more gracious when you realized how wrong you were."

He lowered his eyes. "I am sorry. I've become so suspicious of everyone and everything."

"Michael, this is as close as I've come to hating you," Deborah hissed.

Basha came back with Tanya, ready for the journey.

"Basha, that was brave of you and I'm grateful for all of us," he spoke with great sincerity.

Basha looked up at the attic window. "I did it for my family," she said simply and climbed into the car.

# CHAPTER
# THIRTY-FIVE

THE Second World War came to an end and the world breathed a sigh of relief. The free world had prevailed and rejoiced at the defeat of fascist tyranny. Although the guns were silenced in Europe, they continued to be heard in Palestine and their din grew louder with every passing day. The mandate government continued its vicious rulings against Jewish immigration, against the right of Jews to defend themselves, against the right of Jews to live as a free people in their own land. Still, the provisional Jewish government in Palestine continued to hope and went on negotiating with Britain. Michael Ben Hod, like the rest of them, turned his attention to the postwar British government, certain that they would change their attitudes. It was just a matter of time.

"Wait for the Labor government to be elected," Michael said with assurance. "They have always repudiated the Conservatives in England. Once Labor is in power, the change will come."

Deborah listened quietly and said nothing. She had long since grown to distrust the British and doubted that their policy toward Palestine and the Jews would change.

The enormity of the tragedy of European Jews seeped in slowly at first. Most inhabitants of Palestine had relatives in Europe and for a while held a glimmer of hope that a miracle had saved them. But that hope soon faded too and the country went into deep mourning. The behavior of the British only emphasized their vulnerability and the Jewish leaders, hard as they tried, could not ignore what was taking place among the people. Restraint was becoming more difficult. When the Labor Party swept into power in England and the attitude toward Palestine grew even more hostile, the Jewish leadership faced a serious dilemma. Abiding by the law, showing good will and discipline, was beginning to wear thin. It was getting the Jews nowhere.

For Michael Ben Hod the conflict was even greater. His dream of seeing a Jewish state come into being without bloodshed was rapidly eroding and he was having a hard time keeping his aversion to physical action in check. He tried to persuade his colleagues to be patient but he knew he was waging a losing battle. Slowly he withdrew from both his friends and his relatives.

For Gidon, who had surfaced as soon as the war ended, nothing changed. Although he chose not to be smug, he knew the British and was not surprised by their behavior. He had spent the last months of the war in hiding, working closely with Amit and his friends. Their actions against the British became more furious with each passing day. To Michael's demands about where he had been since deserting the army, Gidon answered candidly. He had spent some time with Naomi and Jack in Tel Tanya and then had gone to Haifa and stayed with Misha and Sonya at their sanitarium. Michael felt betrayed by his daughter as well as by his old friend Misha and he cut off contact with both. Gidon was forbidden to enter the Ben Hod house.

Deborah's heart ached for Michael. She saw his growing isolation and although he still seemed to be an active member of the Jewish governing power, she began to feel that he was becoming an outsider again. She missed her family and longed for them to be together again. Divergent as their views were, they were a family and all had the same dream.

Ironically it was Benji's wedding that brought them together. What made it even stranger was that Benji was the one who wanted the whole family be invited and insisted on inviting Gidon as well.

The ceremony was set for the end of summer. His bride was named Ruth. She was a charming, unassuming, well-spoken girl and extremely pretty. Small in build, she had dark curly hair, tiny features, a well-shaped mouth and a pleasant smile. Born in Palestine to a middle-class family from a village in the south, she seemed an ideal wife for Benji. She adored him and his brash manner softened when he was in her presence. He wanted a big, elaborate wedding, and the idea embarrassed Deborah. It was less than a year since the war had ended and no one could avoid the sight of hunger and misery among those immigrants who had succeeded in arriving in Palestine. Still, the idea of having her whole family around her made Deborah go along with Benji's wishes.

Traveling around the country had grown dangerous, as Arabs now routinely ambushed passenger cars. So the wedding took place in the Ben Hods' home in Tel Aviv. Deborah was delighted to discover that Naomi was pregnant again. Her pleasure, however, was tempered with concern. Safety around Tel Tanya was more precarious than ever, with the British claiming an inability to restrain their Arab friends.

"Three children are an awful responsibility at this time," she ventured.

"Mother, having a baby shouldn't depend on conditions. We want a big family. At the rate we're going, internal immigration may be our only solution," Naomi answered.

Gidon was pleased with the invitation. He too missed Deborah and Michael, both for himself and his small family, but as the day grew closer, he suspected he would not make it. His group had planned an action against the headquarters of British Intelligence. His job was to make a telephone call and warn everyone to get out of the building. His British accent was invaluable on such occasions. The call had to be made from a mobile truck so it could not be traced, and the hour that the call was to be made coincided with the time the wedding was to begin. He arrived at the ceremony late and was quite tense by the time he got there.

A traditional ceremony took place as prescribed by Jewish law. Deborah scanned the faces of the guests and a feeling of supreme happiness engulfed her. The mixture of people was a tribute to her and Michael. They had come a long way from the days when they were ostracized, looked down on, made to feel like traitors. Listening to the rabbi intone the marriage vows, she recalled Tamar's wedding to Fredrick. Not since then had anyone in her family been married in this grand a manner, and she was glad her son was so honored.

With a feeling of pride, she looked at Naomi and Jack, who were holding their two sons, and her eyes wandered to Gidon and Basha, with little Tanya standing between them. Basha was staring intently at the couple under the canopy, a bewildered look on her face. Suddenly the young woman winced with surprise and Deborah realized that she had been so engrossed in Basha that she had missed Benji stomping on and breaking the glass placed under his foot, which marked the end of the ceremony.

She had little time to ponder Basha's reaction, as she was surrounded by well-wishers. Then the musicians started playing and Tova, leading a procession of caterers, marched out with platters of food and refreshments. The pleasant hum of conversation, along with the music, was soothing and Deborah walked around greeting her guests.

She was in the middle of a conversation with Jack when she caught sight of Yanosh talking to Basha at the far corner of the garden. They were having a heated debate, but she could not hear what they were saying. Basha was flushed and was shaking her head furiously, and Yanosh looked threatening. When he put his hand on her arm, Basha wrenched it from him, as though she'd been burned by a lit torch, and started to walk away. Yanosh restrained her. Deborah, fearful of a scene, walked quickly over to them.

"You two don't look as though you're having the best of times," she said pleasantly.

They both looked at her and their manner changed abruptly.

"Is anything wrong?"

Basha threw a look at Yanosh.

"Basha wants to go to Poland and I feel it is too soon for her to face what has taken place there," Yanosh answered.

Deborah was surprised by his statement. The fact was that Basha had not mentioned going back to Poland since the war ended and Deborah had wondered about it.

"I agree with Yanosh," Deborah said. "It's too soon."

Basha lowered her eyes. "Well, if you say so." She agreed too quickly, Deborah thought.

Gidon joined them. "You all look too serious for this festive occasion."

"Well, you look happy," Deborah said.

"Yes, I am happy. Benji has just asked me to go back to work in the quarries."

"I think it's a dreadful idea," Michael said. He had been standing a few feet away and had overheard Gidon's last remark.

"Michael, I think it's a perfect idea," Deborah intervened. As far as Deborah knew, Gidon had not worked since returning to Tel Aviv when the war ended, and it left him with too much free time.

Michael ignored her. "What do you think, Yanosh?"

"We are in desperate need of gravel for construction and the British are very stingy with their dynamite when we need it to blow up a quarry." He looked at Gidon. "Actually, it seems to me that Gidon, having worked so closely with them in the past, might be able to be quite convincing in letting us have it."

"I don't approve." Michael stormed off. Deborah watched him approach Benji and the two walked into the house.

"There goes my career," Gidon laughed and taking Basha's hand, invited her to dance.

"Yanosh, talk to Michael," Deborah said when they were left alone. "It's a wonderful opportunity for Gidon to get back into a routine." She looked over at him. He was staring down at her with love and affection. As always it pleased her.

"Why is Michael against Gidon working the quarries?" she asked, determined to continue talking about Gidon.

"He's afraid Gidon will walk away with some of the dynamite for his terrorist friends," Yanosh answered simply.

Deborah gasped. "And you aren't?"

"Benji will make a deal with Gidon. Some dynamite for his group and some for us. We've talked about it. Obviously Gidon agreed and I trust Gidon to keep his word."

"You trust him?"

"I trust anyone who fights for our rights. I disapprove only of Jews being killed," Yanosh said firmly.

"Why isn't Michael aware of any of this?" she asked, tentatively.

"Michael is having a hard time accepting the fact that we must cooperate with terrorist groups. I don't know why he's so resistant. As I understand it, he was very militant years ago."

Poor Michael. Feelings of tenderness for him swept over her. He was again out of step with the people he had courted and seemed to have won over. Again, he was on the outside looking in. She was tempted to excuse herself and follow him into the house. She was all he had. They had lived through so much together. They were bound by so many memories, good and bad. Theirs was an intimacy of a shared life. She knew his soul.

Tova walked over, interrupting her thoughts. She handed Yanosh an envelope, which he tore open and read quickly. Then, taking out a cigarette and some matches, he lit a match, put the flame to the note and the envelope, and proceeded to light his cigarette from the burning paper. The blackened ashes fell to the ground and Yanosh ground them into the earth, looking around as he did with a cool, composed air.

"Uncle Yanosh." Tanya, followed by Uri and Daniel, came running toward them, leaving Deborah to wonder at the scene she had just witnessed. "You haven't given me a kiss and I want to kiss you," the little girl squealed.

Yanosh picked her up and she put her lips to his. "I love you, Uncle Yanosh." She laughed merrily. "I love you almost as much as I love Daddy and Grandpa Michael."

"That is an honor," he answered and hugged her to him.

Tanya's laughter pealed forth and her little face reminded Deborah of Tamar. It was not just her coloring—the straight blond hair falling on her shoulders, the green-blue eyes, too eloquent in one so young, the almost transparent complexion. It was her manner, her whole demeanor. The thin, little body, the long legs, the proud posture. It was also her spontaneous warmth with family compared to her reserved shyness with strangers. She was Tamar reborn, except for her propensity for tears. Tamar had never cried, not even as a child. Did Michael see the resemblance between Tamar and Tanya and did that account for his devotion to the child? She missed Tamar almost every day of her life. Why shouldn't he?

"I don't kiss anybody," Uri's voice reached her.

"Well, you're going to be kissed by your grandmother whether you like it or not." Deborah leaned down and kissed both Uri and Daniel.

The blast of a siren, followed by a garbled announcement over a bullhorn, broke into the gaiety.

"I wonder what this is about," Yanosh said and, placing Tanya down, he raced into the house. Deborah followed him.

The guests dispersed within minutes and the family, along with Sonya, Misha and Yanosh, gathered around the radio.

A clipped, cold voice announced the bombing of the King David Hotel in Jerusalem, which housed British Intelligence. Dozens of people were killed and wounded, among them quite a few Jews.

"No one has yet claimed responsibility for this dastardly act. But wholesale murder of our soldiers who are trying to keep peace in the region will be avenged. Mark my words," the announcer's droned on ominously. "English blood will be avenged."

"And so will Jewish blood." Gidon stood up. "I didn't hear them announce their latest manner of transferring refugees from their ships to British transports in cages and returning them to Germany. These fine keepers of the peace who have given orders to fire at the ones who protest."

"Is that true?" Michael turned to Yanosh.

"Yes, it is," Yanosh nodded. "They even invited the foreign press to witness their actions. You see, they're so twisted in their thinking that they've come to believe that illegal refugees are the invention of a Zionist plot and should be sent home. They pay no attention to the fact than the refugees do not have a home to go to." He paused. "But that does not justify the killing of Jews at the King David." His last words were directed at Gidon. "One would think that some warning would have been given to the occupants of the hotel," he concluded.

Gidon met his gaze. "I'm sure a warning was given," he said quietly. "The Brits probably chose to ignore it."

The brief exchange made a chill run down Deborah's spine.

"A curfew has been ordered for six o'clock." The voice on the radio broke into the silence that followed Gidon's words. "It will last until further notice."

Michael walked over and turned off the radio. "We're no better than they are," he said with his back to everyone in the room. "We've adopted their barbaric methods and now we're actually trying to outdo them." Then turning around slowly, he looked at Gidon.

The panic in Deborah grew. Gidon was at the wedding, she wanted to cry out, so he could not have been involved. But Gidon had been late in coming and he had looked flustered when he arrived.

"In a state of war it is impossible to fight ruthlessness with consideration, guile with sincerity." Misha spoke for the first time, diverting attention from Gidon. "And make no mistake, we are in a state of war. How did the Allies behave, as the world war was coming to an end? They bombed Germany indiscriminately, flattening their cities. What did the United States do? They dropped an atom bomb on Japan. They needed decisive victories and that was the only way to achieve them."

"And violence begets violence, begets violence," Michael's voice trembled as he spoke. "Will it ever end?"

"When we win." Yanosh stood up. "And now I must leave if I am to get home before the curfew goes into effect." He turned to Misha. "My quarters are rather small, but I could put you up if the Ben Hods have room for Sonya."

"Of course," Deborah said quickly. She glanced over at Sonya.

"Misha, you and Sonya can stay with us," Gidon intervened nervously.

While Misha was talking, Gidon had suddenly realized that Misha belonged to his organization. The views he had expressed were views his group believed in, lived by. Yanosh, with all of his benevolence toward the extremists, was still very much part of the establishment. If he found out who Misha was, it could be uncomfortable.

Misha smiled at Gidon. "I think we'd be imposing."

As soon as they were gone, Gidon walked over to Basha. "Well, in that case, I think we'll be on our way." He stopped. "Unless you'd like to stay here with Tanya."

"No. I'll go with you."

Everyone retired as soon as Gidon and Basha left except for Michael, who insisted on staying up and listening to the radio for further news.

Early the next morning, a house-to-house search was made and most of the Jewish leadership was arrested. Michael went with the officers who had come for him and Deborah spent her time nervously waiting for word from him. She tried calling Gidon, but all phone lines had been disconnected. The curfew was in full force and no one was allowed out.

By mid-afternoon, exhausted with worry, Deborah was still sitting by the window waiting and listening to the latest reports on the radio.

"Four terrorists have been captured." The announcement came just as she saw Michael walk through the front gate. The sight of her husband caused her to blank out the sound of the speaker. Michael was walking slowly and he looked like a defeated old man.

"Is everything all right?" she asked when he came in.

"I don't know. They asked me a few questions and released me." He seemed offended by the ease with which he was allowed to go.

"Were there many people there?" she asked, hoping to find out if Gidon and Yanosh were arrested as well.

"No one of importance," he answered bitterly.

"Gidon?" She could not hold back. "Yanosh? Misha?"

"No. They were all probably forewarned and got out before the search." Then, without looking at her, he left the room.

Deborah knew he was right. The note given Yanosh at the wedding must have been a warning. Michael was obviously not important enough to be told. Her concern for Gidon mounted.

The curfew lasted six days. In spite of it, the cycle of violence continued with greater ferocity and the whole country lapsed into a state of depression.

When the curfew was lifted, Michael began to spend most of his time in Bet Enav.

# CHAPTER
# THIRTY-SIX

BASHA was sitting on the bed brushing her hair, staring aimlessly out the window. It had been a wonderful day, since Gidon had spent it with her. Usually he was out of the house before she woke, and sometimes he would not come home until late at night, if at all. But this day he was there in the morning when she woke and insisted she stay in bed while he gave Tanya breakfast and took the child to school.

As evening approached, she felt sad. She missed the Christmas festivities. She missed the Polish countryside, usually blanketed with snow at this time of year, and the fireplaces that were lit in every room of their house. There was the excitement of going to the city to shop for gifts and the singing in the street, with complete strangers smiling and greeting each other. All these years later, she remembered the aroma of the special dishes prepared by the maid, which they ate by candlelight in the large dining room, with all the relatives sitting around. It seemed to have happened so long ago, yet it was all so vivid.

A sigh escaped her and she looked around her bedroom. It was small and shabby. The rug was worn, the spread on her bed a hand-me-down from some relative of Gidon's, and the curtains were frayed. But that was not what was depressing her. At that particular moment, it was the gray December weather. It never really changed. It was winter but it was a dull, chilly day that would probably be replaced the next morning by lusterless, wintry sunshine. She even missed the changes in weather that Warsaw offered. She missed her home.

"How do I look?" Gidon asked as he entered the room. For a minute his physical beauty dazzled her. Then it struck her. He was dressed in his crisp British officer's uniform.

"Why are you wearing that uniform?" she asked.

He was examining himself in the full-length mirror. "I'll bet no one could guess that I am not a proper English officer."

She was about to repeat her question when she saw that he was extremely pale and that his lips were pressed into a thin line. He would not answer her question. "Why shouldn't you look like one," she ventured. "You were one."

"I was an officer in the Jewish Brigade attached to the British army," he said emphatically.

"It was still the British army." She did not take her eyes off him.

"Well, for one night, I guess I can forego my principles." He continued looking at himself in the mirror. Suddenly his face lit up with excitement. "That's it," he called out triumphantly. "My medal. That would be the perfect touch." He rushed over to his desk and started rummaging through the drawers. "If only I knew where I put that piece of junk."

"I have it." Basha got up and walked over to the dresser. "And it's not a piece of junk. Few Jewish Brigade soldiers were given the Victoria Cross for bravery on the battlefield."

She opened the drawer and removed her jewelry case. The medal was lying on top of her marriage license, Tanya's birth certificate and her Polish passport. There were other documents and pictures beneath them, but it was the cross tangled in its chain resting in the corner that caught her attention. The sight of it unsettled her and it took her a minute to regain her composure. Only then did she take the medal out, slam the box shut and hand it to Gidon.

"What do you have in the box?" Gidon asked. "Diamonds from a lover?"

"Not quite," she answered, pulling her sweater tightly around her.

"You're cold," Gidon said with concern. "Why don't you put the stove in here?"

"I have it in Tanya's room."

"Let me buy you one for this room."

"We can't afford it and it's not necessary," she answered almost angrily. "This cold weather doesn't last very long and I'm used to it. Tanya is not."

"Why don't you pin it on for me?" He handed the medal back to her.

She did as he asked and then she was in his arms and his head was buried in her shoulder. She kissed his hair and, lifting his head, she kissed his eyes, his cheeks and then his mouth. He responded with great passion.

"Make love to me," she whispered. "Please, darling, make love to me."

"You're a harlot," he laughed, pushing her away gently. "Besides, you seem to have forgotten that Tanya and Uri are in the next room." Then his expression changed and he looked at his watch, walked over to the window and scanned the street below.

"Waiting for someone?"

"Yes, I'm being picked up but they're not here yet." He checked his watch again. "And they're late."

"Will you be back tonight?"

"Basha." He turned back to her. "You know better than to ask. I have to go out and I'll be back as soon as I can." He tried to sound impersonal, but standing in the middle of the room, she looked lost and frightened and extremely young. She had barely changed since that first time he saw her on the Swiss mountaintop. And the expression of bewilderment in her large, innocent eyes was almost identical to the one she had when he walked over to her and introduced himself.

He wanted her at that moment as much as he ever had, but there were passions in him that far exceeded his desire to make love to her.

"Let's go in and see the children." He took her hand and together they walked into Tanya's room.

Tanya and Uri were playing jacks on the floor and did not hear Basha and Gidon walk in. The room was warm and strands of Tanya's reddish blond hair were glued to her forehead. Her cheeks were flushed and she was biting her full lower lip in childlike concentration.

"Who's winning?" Gidon asked.

Both children looked up. "You look funny, Daddy." Tanya said and her eyes began to twinkle. "Are you going to a masquerade party?"

"That's a British lieutenant's uniform," Uri said.

"That's very clever of you, Uri," Gidon said approvingly. "How did you know?"

"In the kibbutz we know these things," the boy answered. "And I know them better than all the other kids." He continued to examine Gidon carefully. "But I want to be a general. That's much more important."

"You probably will be one." Gidon winked at him and patted his head affectionately.

"Are you going out?" Tanya stood up and pressed up against her father possessively.

"Just for a little while."

"Can I sleep at Grandma Deborah's house?" She looked over at her mother, leaning closer to Gidon. "Or can Uri sleep here, maybe?"

"No," Basha said before Gidon could speak.

Tanya's eyes began to brim over with tears.

"But I'll tell you what." Basha softened her voice. "You can sleep in my bed tonight."

Gidon raised his brow in surprise. That was unlike Basha. She was a strict disciplinarian and did not approve of such pampering. It had been so since Tanya was born and he had tried to talk to her and get her to change her attitude. He had described his own craving for a mother's love and warmth when he was a child, how much it would have meant to him, but somehow he could never get her to understand that need. Her offer to have Tanya in their bed made him realize the depth of her loneliness when he was away.

"Why don't you all sleep at Grandma Deborah's house?" he suggested.

"I would rather not," Basha said quickly. She did not know when Gidon would be back and she wanted to be there when he came in.

"Is Grandma Deborah really your grandma?" Uri asked Tanya. He was standing close to her and although she was seven and he was a year younger, he was much taller.

"Of course she is," Tanya said indignantly.

"Not quite," Gidon said quickly. "Tanya's grandmother was called Tamar and she died many, many years ago."

"Was she very old?" Uri demanded.

"No," Gidon answered.

"Then why did she die?"

"It was a terrible accident." Gidon began to feel quite helpless under the boy's interrogative manner.

"Well, where is your other grandmother?" Uri would not let up.

Tanya's eyes grew wide with confusion and she looked over at her mother.

"We don't know." Basha tried to speak naturally, but her voice shook.

"But my grandmother Tamar was a heroine." Tanya regained her equilibrium. "And she was very, very beautiful and I look like her."

"Who told you that?" Basha asked sharply.

"Grandpa Michael and Grandma Deborah," Tanya answered innocently.

"I have a grandpa in America, too." Uri would not be outdone and then, as though sensing the awkward mood, he changed his tone. "I guess it's right that you should call Grandma Deborah grandma since we're cousins," he concluded.

"I believe he's going to be a diplomat." Gidon laughed with relief. Then he looked at his watch again and walked over to the window.

An old, dilapidated Mercedes taxi was standing at the corner, its parking lights flashing. Gidon gritted his teeth. He had told Zak to get a car, any car he could find, but the one standing there did not look as if it could get them to Jerusalem.

He turned back to the room. "You behave yourselves while I'm gone and be very good to Mommy." He kissed Tanya on the head. "And when I come back, I'll take you both out for an ice cream soda."

Walking over to Basha, he wrapped his arm around her shoulders and as they walked out of the children's room, she could feel his tension.

Once in the living room Basha moved away from him.

"I wish they'd stop feeding Tanya that stuff about heroism," Basha said. "Why force her to live up to legends?"

"But Tamar is a legend," Gidon became defensive. "And frankly, I think Tanya does look like Tamar."

She swallowed hard before speaking. "Gidon, where are you going?" she asked.

He took a deep breath. "Okay, if you insist. I've got a date with Colonel Cartwright in Jerusalem. I called him and he was pleased to hear from me."

"Why do you want to see him?"

"Several reasons," Gidon said, slipping into his military overcoat and placing his army hat and swagger stick under his arm. "For starters, I would like to tell him that I agree with him that the partition plan for Palestine is a disaster. And that the Security Council resolution approving the plan last month was a big mistake. He should like that. I'll suggest that they either give the whole country to the Arabs or to the Jews. Then they can fight it out and may the best group win.

"Secondly, I think I might be able to persuade him that hanging the four terrorists, as he likes to call them, is a mistake." His expression changed and Basha saw the pain in his face. "That's why he's here, you know. They've left the decision to him."

"Gidon, you're being absurd."

"Not at all. I can speak with great authority and explain to him that commuting the sentence would show Britain's great humanitarian side. As far as he's concerned, I am a loyal British subject who fought for the empire and who's looking out for my people." A bitter laugh escaped from his throat. "The only thing he doesn't know is that what he considers my people and what I consider my people are two rather different things."

"Gidon, you are bound to come away with nothing but disappointment." Basha threw herself onto a small loveseat, trying to appear indifferent, but her heart was pounding with fear. She knew Gidon was lying but she dared not confront him. She looked around the room anxiously and her eyes came to rest on the wall clock. "The curfew starts at eight tonight and it's nearly six now. You'll never make it back in time."

"My darling, you do underestimate me. When I spoke to Cartwright and mentioned the curfew, he couldn't have been more cooperative. You see, he is so anxious to see me, he arranged for a pass so that I can leave whenever it's convenient." He walked over and kissed her lightly on the cheek. "After all, he's terribly anxious to see what Thomas Hardwick has spawned." His smile broadened. "And I'm looking forward to the meeting."

"Is he aware that you deserted from the army?" She did not want him to go and was trying to detain him.

"Now, why would I mention that to him?" Gidon laughed. "There is no record of Gideon Hardwick deserting. There is no record of a Gideon Hardwick ever being in the army. The deserter was one Gidon Davidzohn and you know I refer to myself as Gidon Danziger."

"Gidon, must you go?" she asked. "The struggle is nearly over. The partition plan has been agreed to by the Security Council and now it's only a matter of time before the United Nations will recognize the state. Please, darling, don't go. I beg you, don't go to Jerusalem tonight."

A cold smile appeared on his lips. "The Arabs haven't accepted the partition plan. Do you really believe they'll accept a Jewish state?"

"But the world will be on our side. They'll help make it happen."

He leaned down and searched her face. "I know how frightened you are and I understand your feelings. But I have to go." Then, almost roughly, he pulled her up and cradled her head in his arms. "Do you have any idea how much I love you?"

"Do you know how much I love you?" Her voice muffled against his shoulder, as she clung to him. "Oh, God, Gidon, if you only knew! If you only knew how much I need you. If you only knew how much I long for the day when I won't have to share you with a cause!"

"Someday it will happen, but you must believe that until then, I am yours to the best of my ability." He closed his eyes and was grateful that she could not see his pain. "I love you very much and that you must believe. But before I can give myself to you and Tanya, I have things I must do. Otherwise I shall be only half a man. Can you understand that?" He could not control the plea that came into his voice. "But never, never doubt that I love you, Basha. Never. No matter what happens, I love you."

She wanted to hold on to him, forbid him to go, but knew it was useless. Whatever it was that drove him was stronger than his love for her or hers for him.

He turned from her and was gone. She heard his footsteps racing down the stairs. The sense of foreboding which had been with her for too long was more acute than ever.

The clock rang out the hour of six, and the evening loomed ahead, long and lonely.

For a brief moment she thought of taking up Gidon's suggestion and going to stay with Deborah for the night. Deborah always made her feel better. She dismissed the idea. Gidon might need her when he got back and although he had suggested it and probably meant it, she would not risk being away from their home. Besides, Deborah was bound to wonder why she had come and she would begin to worry.

She felt chilled and walked quickly into Tanya's room.

The children looked up briefly when she came in, then went back at their game.

Settling herself in an old straw chair, she tried to calm her fears. She could not understand why she was so troubled this evening. She had lived through so many evenings like it. Sometimes he would be gone for days and when he finally did come home, he would go to their room and sleep for many hours. She would sit by the bed and watch him as he twisted and turned, occasionally moaning in despair as though reliving some nightmare. She should have gotten used to the worry and fear. Yet, for some unknown reason, when he walked into their bedroom dressed in that uniform, the fear started and had grown into sheer panic. Somehow she was sure this night was different.

For the first time she wondered why Gidon had stayed home that day. He had never done it before. She started reconstructing the events of the day.

When he returned from taking Tanya to school, he brought a tray with two cups of coffee, a fresh roll and a flower next to it. They ate in silence and then they made love. Wonderful, passionate, tender love. They whispered, although they were alone in the house, as they had done when they were first married, and they laughed at silly jokes. Gidon seemed particularly mellow and she brought up the subject of having another child. Always, in the past, when she spoke of wanting another child, he was against it. That morning, he promised they would have more children. Then they slept for a while and when they woke, they drank some wine. Gidon reminisced about Thomas, his childhood in England and Thomas's funeral. She remembered that he also mentioned Owen Cartwright. She remembered being vaguely surprised, because he hated Cartwright. The mere mention of the name could make his features twist with rage. Yet he had spoken the name almost casually. His mood, however, changed after that.

Col. Owen Cartwright was the clue.

She had no idea why Gidon hated the man but she sensed a meeting between them would end badly. The feeling of panic returned and she could barely breathe. If only she had someone to talk to. Deborah. She could talk to Deborah. Maybe she could explain Gidon's loathing for Cartwright.

She tried not to run out of Tanya's room, so as not to frighten the children.

Once in her bedroom she picked up the phone, but replaced it immediately. What if Michael answered? He had mellowed toward her since the milk incident in Bet Enav, but circumstances had changed for her and now she could not accept his offer of friendship.

A tear rolled down her cheek. Would it ever end? Would the lonely nights of worrying about Gidon ever cease?

"Basha?" She heard Deborah's voice. She sat up and, wiping her eyes, walked out to greet her.

"You look tired, Basha," she said with concern.

"I am, sort of." Basha led the way into the living room.

Deborah followed and looked around. "Gidon gone out?" she asked casually.

"He was all dressed up in a uniform," Uri announced proudly.

"Really?" Deborah sat down on the sofa and held out her arms for the children to come sit beside her. "When do you think he'll be back?" She directed her question to Basha.

"Not late, I'm sure," Basha answered. "Would you like a cup of tea?"

"I don't think so," Deborah said, aware that Basha was trying to change the subject. "Children," she said cheerfully, "why don't you go in and collect Uri's things? Grandpa Michael is waiting for us to light the Hanukkah candles and Tova has supper almost ready."

Tanya looked meaningfully at Basha and followed Uri out.

"Basha, I would like to suggest that Tanya sleep at our house tonight,"

Deborah said. "And before you object, think about it for a minute."

The two women looked at each other without speaking. Both had known other nights when Gidon was away and the fears that those absences caused. Since the arrest of his friend Amit, their tension had grown worse. On one occasion, Basha had even called to ask her to come over and help care for Gidon. That night she was grateful that Michael was spending most of his time in Bet Enav. Basha would never have shared Gidon's troubles with her if Michael were around. And he would never have let the incident pass.

"I would be happy to have you come and stay as well, but I know that is out of the question. But believe me, Basha, although Tanya is only seven years old, she can sense things, even if she doesn't actually witness them." She paused. "Uri's reaction to the uniform is not a good one, either."

"Why do you say that?"

"I don't know, but I think I won't have him stay in Tel Aviv. I know he was looking forward to spending the rest of the holiday with us, but I think I'll have Benji arrange to drive him back to the kibbutz first thing in the morning."

"That's not fair," Basha protested. "We're both imagining things."

"Maybe." Deborah said thoughtfully, "But I still don't think Tanya should be here when Gidon comes in."

She's as frightened as I am, Basha thought. She too feels that this night is different from the others.

"What I do want you to do is call me the minute he arrives. I don't care what time of night." Deborah said urgently. "And if he's not here by the time curfew is over at six in the morning, Uri goes home."

The gleeful sound of the children going off with Deborah rang in Basha's ears as she reentered her bedroom and lay down on her bed. The room was dark and she closed her eyes but knew that sleep would not come.

# CHAPTER
# THIRTY-SEVEN

G IDON looked up at the windows of his apartment and then rushed toward the car waiting at the end of the street.

"Are you ready?" A voice called out and Gidon saw Zak sitting calmly in the driver's seat, smoking a cigarette.

"Where did you get this heap?" Gidon asked, hitting the roof of the car.

"Gidon, it has four wheels, a motor and will get us to Jerusalem." The young man flipped his cigarette out the window and started the motor.

"Just take me to the King David." Gidon settled into the back seat. "And once you drop me off, you're to turn around and drive right back to Tel-Aviv. Is that clear?"

Zak eyed then briefly in the rear view mirror and without a word drove off.

Despite the destruction of one of the hotel's wings, the doorman was dressed in livery, pretending that nothing was amiss. He bowed low as he noticed the English officer get out of the car, and if he was surprised at the condition of the dilapidated vehicle, he did not show it. Once in the lobby of the hotel, Gidon walked swiftly over to the large balcony facing the old city of Jerusalem and was promptly led to a seat. An enormous black waiter, dressed in African garb, came over and presented him with a menu.

"Scotch straight with a glass of soda on the side," Gidon said in his perfect British accent.

"At your service, *sahib*," the man replied and left immediately.

"Well, hello there." Cornelius Sullivan slipped into the seat opposite him and put his hand out in greeting. As arranged, Gidon took the key from his palm and smiled. "Haven't seen you since . . . ?"

"Naples," Gidon helped him out.

"Right. How have you been?"

"Just fine. How about a drink?" Gidon waved to the waiter and ordered another scotch and soda.

The drinks arrived and both men toasted each other silently. Cornelius took out his cigarette case, handed a cigarette to Gidon and leaned closer, lighting it for him.

"It's the Pilgrim Hotel, which is not far from the nightclub," he whispered. "Room Seven-twelve." He settled back and lit his own cigarette in a leisurely manner.

"Pilgrim Hotel?" Gidon answered, surprised by the choice.

"It's close to the bathhouse and close to the bus stop."

Gidon too leaned back and tried to relax.

"When did you get here?" Gidon asked conversationally.

"Right after the bombing of this grand hotel." Cornelius looked up at the mass of stones that had been pushed aside. "It's making headlines all over the world. With so many Jews killed, it's really making waves."

"I understand there was a warning call to tell everyone to get out," Gidon said.

"Obviously no one believed anyone would try to bomb the main offices of British Intelligence."

"Messy affair," Gidon agreed.

"And what are your plans for the evening?"

"Haven't quite decided yet," he answered and looked around. Satisfied that no one was paying any attention to them, he again leaned toward Cornelius. "What's the bus schedule from Jerusalem to Bethlehem after midnight?"

"Erratic, at best. Your best bet is one at five A.M."

"I'll be on it."

"You can come to the hotel anytime you'd like. I'll be in all evening. I'll have fresh clothes and papers for you."

"I wish you wouldn't be there," Gidon started.

"Nonsense. I have a lovely friend who's just arrived in the country. She's from Dublin and I've known her since we were kids."

"Maria, I presume?" Gidon smiled. Cornelius always referred to his ladies as Maria.

"No, as matter of fact, her name is Bridget Donovan," he answered seriously.

"She must be very special."

"I think I'm going to marry her."

"And what happens to Maria?"

"She died under the tracks of a tank in Spain." A faraway look came to his eyes. "We were engaged when she died. And now I think I must finally bury her." He sounded sad.

"Well, all the more reason you should not be in the hotel when I get there," Gidon said emphatically.

"Bridget can only help if something goes wrong," Cornelius paused and searched Gidon's face. "I must confess, I wish it were all over."

"It won't be long now." Gidon was touched by his concern.

Cornelius got up. "I've got to run along. It was nice seeing you." The flamboyance was back when he walked away, and Gidon watched him stop to talk to some officers, who greeted him warmly. Cornelius was an enigma to him. A world-renowned photo-journalist, he knew everyone, was trusted by them, was called on to cover major world events, and had photographed most wars with total disregard for his own safety. Yet he had attached himself to the Jewish cause in Palestine and used all his contacts to help them. Gidon first met him while stationed in Cairo when he enlisted in the British army. It was Cornelius who persuaded him to become an officer and it was Cornelius who warned him about what he might expect when he arrived in Europe. He was there when Gidon landed in Salerno and marched along with the infantry, nearly getting killed in the process. After that, Gidon lost track of him, but he reappeared when they entered that first death camp in Germany. At the time, Gidon was furious when Cornelius started taking pictures of the victims. But his were the first photographs that gave the story its impact. With the war over, he appeared in Palestine and was one of Gidon's outfit's major sources of arms and medical equipment. How he did it, no one knew. Why he did it was even more of a mystery.

Gidon turned his attention to the mosques, which were visible from the hotel's balcony. They were located just beyond the ruins of the Second Temple. Dusk was giving way to a starry but moonless night and the beauty of minutes before turned into a mass of shadows, looming sad and forlorn. Gidon looked at his watch. It was seven o'clock.

He called for the check and, after paying the bill, he ambled out of the hotel and headed toward the High Commissioner's house. It was located on the Hill of Evil, so named by superstitious Arabs centuries before. It was a distance away, but he dared not take a taxi lest the driver identify him later.

The gatekeeper checked his papers and announced his arrival to the guards standing beyond the high, iron gate. They saluted him as he passed. Two more guards were waiting at the front entrance. They too checked his papers and one of them opened the door for him.

"My dear chap." Owen Cartwright was standing at the far end of the large front foyer. He started toward him. "I would have recognized you even after all these years." He shook his hand and, placing his arm around his shoulder, he led him into a beautifully decorated study. Paneled walls, bookcases, plush Oriental rugs, a huge desk with an old-fashioned lamp filled the room. The sofa was covered in dark brown leather. In front of a wood-burning fireplace were two deep, comfortable armchairs with footstools in front of each. A Christmas tree, fully decorated, stood in the corner. It conjured up the memory of the trees he and Thomas had decorated when he was a child.

"Drink?" Owen asked.

"Scotch, thank you." Gidon spoke for the first time and was relieved when he heard his voice come out naturally.

This was a moment he had dreamed about since Thomas's funeral. He wanted to walk over and strangle Cartwright's flabby, aging neck then and there.

"You look so much like Thomas." Owen handed him his drink. "Although, I hope you don't mind my saying so, you are better-looking. That must come from your mother's side of the family." He laughed politely. "I never met her, but I'm told she was quite beautiful, for a native."

Gidon's fingers began to twitch. "Yes, she was, sir."

"I'm delighted to see that you've served your country during the war." Owen was observing him closely. "Captain, were you? Where did you serve?"

Gidon related the story of his service, omitting mention of the Jewish Brigade. "And I was discharged after we liberated the camps." He sipped his drink slowly. "Ghastly sight, sir. Were you there?"

"No, my boy. My terrain is the Middle East. I'm an Oriental at heart and I figured the empire could handle the Krauts without my help."

"Of course, sir." Gidon nodded. "You're stationed . . ." He looked inquiringly at Owen.

"Cairo is my base. Wonderful city. Although I must confess, I love every one of the countries in this part of the world, except this Godforsaken one." He laughed disparagingly. "It was quite wonderful before the influx, if you know what I mean. When Thomas and I were originally here, the Jews lived in tiny enclaves and knew their place. Now it's become a nightmare. Don't you agree?"

"Well," Gidon started slowly. "As you know, I live with my aunt and her family in Tel Aviv. It's quite pleasant, in a way. Quite European, as a matter of fact."

Owen ignored the remark. "You should have been educated in England. But, I must say, she has done well by you. You're as British as any of our young men, and I'm pleased about that. I'm sure Thomas would have been pleased as well."

"Thank you, sir." Gidon succeeded in smiling pleasantly.

"Now, tell me about yourself. Tell me what I can do for you and I can assure you, I am at your disposal. That's the least I can do for my dear friend Thomas."

Gidon was about to answer when a young Arab servant boy entered the room with canapes and started serving them. Gidon recognized him. He was Omar, the youngest son of Abu Mustaffah, an Arab who lived in a small village outside Jerusalem, one of the few friendly to the Jews. No more than fourteen years old, he was a handsome lad, with dark, intelligent eyes, thick, curly black hair and a smiling mouth. When the boy came toward him, Gidon shook his head imperceptibly, indicating that the boy was not to let on that they knew each other. Omar winked at him surreptitiously.

"We shall want dinner in half an hour," Owen said as the boy started to leave the room.

Omar turned and looked uncomprehendingly at Owen.

"Oh, for heaven's sake. He doesn't understand English," Owen said impatiently. "Do you speak this confounded language? All those damn dialects. I've never been able to master any of them."

Gidon translated Owen's request and Omar left quickly.

"Beautiful boy, isn't he?" Owen stared after the departing figure. "How old would you say he is?"

"Fourteen, fifteen at most."

"Quite right," Owen said and returned his attention to Gidon. "Now, where were we?"

"Well, sir, one of the reasons I wanted to see you was very much in line with what you were suggesting. I want to go back to England."

"Excellent, my boy. Excellent. What specifically are you interested in and how can I help?"

"Foreign service, sir. Intelligence, if possible. I speak both Hebrew and Arabic, as well as German and French. I wouldn't mind being sent to any part of the world, but I believe I can be of most help in this area. Having lived here as long as I have, I think I have an understanding of it. Furthermore, I feel that what Thomas taught me has served me well in shaping my opinions."

"We're leaving here shortly, you know," Owen said slowly.

"Sir, we shall not be leaving the Middle East." Gidon succeeded in sounding indignant. "Although if you will forgive me, I believe we have made some serious mistakes in this country."

"Oh?"

"I think the partition plan is not the best solution."

Owen's brows shot up.

"I personally think the Arabs deserve the land, but obviously with the world suddenly taking an interest, the matter is complicated. But, if His Majesty's government countered with the suggestion that the Jews should have it all, the world would applaud briefly, since we both know the Arabs would overrun the country in days and that would rather solve the problem." He smiled conspiratorially. "I suspect we'd be asked to come in and help clean up the mess."

"Interesting idea. Not quite thought out, I would say, but certainly something to consider."

Gidon waited for Owen to continue.

"The Arabs, unfortunately, aren't really ready to take on these lunatics. And they are lunatics."

"Sir, to quote Thomas, what the Arabs are missing is guidance and leadership. But I'm delighted to see that people like Glubb Pasha are finally in

Transjordan, training and teaching the Transjordanian army how to fight. And with superior arms, which the Arabs have." He looked expectantly at Owen.

"Do you know the strength of the Jews?" Owen asked slowly.

"I know it well. My uncle is one of the underground leaders. It's pathetic, truly pathetic, but we're not dealing with sentiment, are we? The Jews here could never match the strength of a properly trained force, neither with manpower nor with weapons."

"Who's your uncle?"

"Michael Ben Hod."

"Oh, that one. I met him once." He strained his memory. "It was right here in Jerusalem. Thomas introduced me to him." He paused, trying to sort out his perfectly indexed mind. "Tall sort of chap. Red hair. Disliked him on sight. Michael Ben Hod. Of course. He's never lived down a murder charge, poor chap." He returned from his reverie to the present. "He's a minority in the leadership today," he concluded.

Gidon gulped. "But still very effective and with a decent following among the older members."

"What kind of weapons do they have?"

"Mainly old Czechoslovakian discards and some other stuff from equally ridiculous countries." Gidon answered with candor. Owen obviously had the information and was now testing Gidon's veracity.

"How do they get it?"

"I believe a man named Yanosh Bar Lev is in charge of acquisitions." Gidon was surprised at himself. He had not thought of it before, but suddenly he knew why Yanosh took endless trips abroad, mainly to Eastern European countries. He almost regretted his words but was confident that the information would never get beyond Owen. He was going to see to that.

"Captain Yanosh Barlovsky, if I'm not mistaken. Polish army. Imprisoned by the Russians, released to join General Anders and came to Palestine in 'forty-two or 'forty-three. Interesting sort of fellow. A Communist if I ever saw one." He smiled. "Those damn Russians are clever. They give someone like Barlovsky the right to stay on in Palestine and then one day they present him with a bill for that little favor. Poor chap, he has no idea how high the price will be."

Gidon was stunned and was having a hard time controlling his shock.

"Gidon, I've reached the position I'm in not because of my good looks. I know most everything there is to know about the players on all sides." He leaned forward. "And incidentally, you should know that I haven't found a record of a Gideon Hardwick who served in the army, either."

Gidon had been expecting it and he came back to himself quickly. "That's because I am registered as Gidon Danziger, sir. My aunt wanted that and I felt I should oblige her."

The answer seemed to satisfy Owen and he sat back. "Yes, didn't think of that." Then his eyes lit up. "Of course, your aunt married Ben Hod right after she handed you over to Thomas. And she was a Danziger from home." The faraway look, which had begun to irritate Gidon, returned. "Cursed family, unfortunately. Sister committing suicide, brother killed in a plane crash, first husband murdered in the desert. Almost like a Greek tragedy."

"Did you know Raphael Danziger?" Gidon could not resist asking.

"Not personally, but I hear he was rather egomaniacal."

"Beg pardon, sir?"

"Thinking he could get our government to repay him by giving the Jews a homeland in return for some piddling information about the Turks. Why, I heard he thought he could manipulate us as he did the Ottoman Empire."

"Did he really?" Gidon struggled for indifference.

"Well, we dealt with that one simply enough. Accidental plane crash, you know."

"The poor pilot. Did he have a family?" Gidon decided to gamble. The alcohol had made Owen verbose.

"No, we're not that callous. He had no parents, no wife, no children. Except a sister. And he was decorated posthumously by His Majesty." Then, in a change of mood, Owen smiled. "But why are we dealing with the past? Let's come back to what we were talking about. You're right, our stay here has not proven to be our most glorious period. And a grand gesture on our part at this time would help restore the polish, hmm?" He thought for a moment. "Do they really hate us as much as they say?"

"To be very candid, sir, they're quite desperate and His Majesty's Government has been rather harsh. If we are to keep a foothold here, we must appear to be giving in to their demands in unimportant areas. They can be empty gestures, but they should be gestures that will be seen as a turn in their favor, at least for now."

"Such as?" Owen had emptied his glass and stood up. "Before you answer, I would like a refill. Would you?"

"Thank you." He handed Owen his glass.

Gidon saw him fill his glass, drink it down quickly, then pour drinks into the two glasses. His excitement grew. Owen was listening to him. He wasn't sure the man actually believed what he was saying, but he was considering his words.

"Yes, you were saying." Owen sat down again and eyed him with new interest.

"You asked what gestures I thought we could make at this point." Gidon pretended to give it thought. "I certainly would not give in on immigration. That would be dangerous. The influx could be so great, so quickly, it would be impossible to stem the tide. I wouldn't let up on land reforms. I assure you the Jews have contracts of purchase of land from the Arabs ready to be signed, and before you could turn around you'd have a whole new problem of what belongs to whom and where." He stopped and seemed to be in deep thought. "I suppose the lesser of all evils is to pardon some of the prisoners you've got sitting in jail. Take those fellows who were caught for bombing the King David. There is so much anger at them from the Jews, I assure you they'd get their due from their own. Certainly save you a bundle of trouble and negative world press."

Owen shifted uncomfortably in his seat. Gidon swallowed hard, wondering if he'd overstepped his good fortune.

"I don't suppose you've heard that two of our soldiers were seized and are being held as ransom."

Gidon paled. "When?"

"Earlier today. We haven't given out the news as yet. I'm waiting for word from the High Commissioner, who chose to be away during this whole messy affair. Insisted on home leave for Christmas." He shook his head. "Dreadful affair. They've warned us that if we don't release their men, they'll execute our boys."

"Those terrorists really have no respect for law and order, have they?" Gidon said in dismay. "And I bet they'll do it too. But that's exactly what I mean, the organized Jewish community will be as indignant as you are. It proves my point."

"We cannot appear to be giving in to blackmail." Owen held his ground.

"If you don't mind my saying so, those killers will be arrested by my uncle's men the minute they're released. You'll know exactly where they are at all times. What with the Jewish need for investigations and trials, it will take quite a while for their machinery to get moving. The British soldiers will be released and then you can just pick up the killers at your convenience. But most important, the gesture will have been heard by the world."

A white-clad servant came in and announced dinner.

"Where is the boy?" Owen asked.

"What boy, sir?" the servant asked. He too was an Arab, but obviously one of the regular staff who spoke English.

"The one who served us earlier."

"He's just a temporary replacement for one of my regular staff."

"Very well. Tell him to turn down my bedsheets. I shall be retiring around midnight. And I would like him to be there when I come in, to fill my bath. The water gets cold so quickly in this house."

"If you'll forgive me, sir, the boy lives a distance from here, and after dinner he has a long way to go. I will be pleased to do these things for you."

"No reason for that," Owen snapped. "He can sleep here tonight. Save him the trip home and back in the morning."

The Arab servant, nodding, retreated. Gidon gritted his teeth. Owen was so obvious.

Dinner passed uneventfully, with Owen drinking a great deal of wine and Gidon having a hard time swallowing his food. The conversation turned back to Gidon's future and Owen made promises to write letters first thing in the morning, recommending Gideon Hardwick, son of Thomas, to a post in British Intelligence.

"You don't mind my referring to you as his son?" Owen laughed drunkenly and the glee was barely hidden.

They were back in the study and Omar was stoking the fire when they walked in.

"Not at all." Gidon laughed. "As a matter of fact I like it. I've dreamed of the day when I could take my rightful place as his heir."

"You should have been in touch with me before." Owen poured himself a brandy but his attention was focused on Omar. "Why didn't you?" He continued absently.

"I didn't want to hurt my aunt's feelings," Gidon answered, aware that Owen was no longer listening.

"Ask the boy if he's been told what to do."

Gidon turned and spoke to Omar in Arabic. "You are to nod your head when I finish talking," he said evenly. "When you are through here, you are to run out of this house and go to your father's home as quickly as possible and hide. Is that clear?"

The boy looked from Owen to Gidon. His eyes widened in surprise.

"*Aywa,* sahib," he nodded.

"He seems happy with the idea." Owen was pleased.

"I think he is." He stood up. "It's getting late and I'm sure you've got work to do before retiring."

Owen stood up as well. He was quite drunk and held on to the back of the chair for support. "Where are you headed?"

"There's a club in the old city." He smiled meaningfully. "As a matter of fact, it's quite a fascinating place." He looked directly at Owen.

"Really?" Owen tried to hide his excitement. "Would I know it?"

"I doubt it, sir." Gidon shook his head. "It's not really the kind of club that any Englishmen—or any European, for that matter—goes to. Natives know about it. Very authentic and very . . . how can I describe it? Very unusual."

"Do you go there often?"

"Whenever I get to Jerusalem and am on my own, without people who know me or my family. They wouldn't approve." He laughed self-consciously. "If you know what I mean."

"You're a chip off the old block after all, and not as stuffy, thank God." Owen burst out laughing. "I was beginning to wonder if you had a lighter side."

"So, if you'll forgive me, sir, I shall be running along. And I do want to thank you for everything you plan to do on my behalf." He sighed with satisfaction. "It really is a relief to be able to talk to someone who understands me."

"Where did you say that club was?" Owen walked him to the door.

"I don't know the address. I just know where it is."

"Would you mind if I joined you?"

"Sir?"

"I don't really have any work to do. I've given orders about the execution of the four killers." He stopped and his voice grew cold. "I agree with several of your suggestions and I shall give them consideration. But I refuse to give in to blackmail."

"I'm sure you know best." Gidon looked around for his coat, hoping to hide his dismay.

"I really would like to join you, Gideon." Owen's voice returned to its former cordiality. "If you don't mind having an older man tagging along. I enjoy new experiences."

"Why the Lions Gate?" Owen asked as they entered the car and Gidon gave the instructions to the driver. "The Jaffa Gate is so much closer."

"At this hour the Jaffa Gate is very crowded with both tourists and army men. The driver can pick us up there when we leave. By then the area should be quite deserted. Besides, the club is halfway between the two gates." Gidon sat back and looked over at Owen, who was now dressed in a dinner jacket, white dress shirt and black trousers, his trench coat flung loosely over his shoulders.

The answer seemed to satisfy Owen, who heaved a sigh of contentment. "This is certainly an unexpected pleasure." He smiled and, raising his legs onto the jumpseat, stared with pleasure at his patent leather slippers. "I have a man in Cairo who makes these for me. Aren't they marvelous? And they fit perfectly." He sounded like a frivolous woman.

Gidon suppressed a smile. Trying to look relaxed, he stared out the window. It was a clear, moonless night and as the car ascended toward the Walled City's Lions Gate, the crowds thinned out and only the lights from far away Arab villages could still be seen in the valley below.

"What time should I have the driver pick us up?" Owen asked when they reached their destination.

"Just have him drive around to the Jaffa Gate and wait." Gidon got out of the car. "For all you know, this place may not appeal to you. It's really quite unique, even for this part of the world."

Owen climbed out, unsteady from too much drinking, and leaned against the car, eyeing Gidon with interest.

"Sir?" The driver leaned his head out the car window.

"Be at the Jaffa Gate around midnight," Gidon said when Owen did not answer.

"It might be later." Owen intervened. "But you be there. And I want to be awakened at six o'clock. My first appointment is at seven." From the look of indifference on the driver's face, Gidon understood that he had often been kept waiting for his master until the early hours of the morning.

As soon as the car drove off, Gidon took off his trench coat and jacket.

"You're a handsome young man." Owen tried to sound coherent, but alcohol and desire slurred his words. "A mite too thin, but very appealing."

Gidon pretended not to notice his companion's amorous tone as he stripped himself of his khaki shirt. Underneath he wore a tight-fitting black pullover, which emphasized his broad shoulders, his strong ribcage and ta-pered waistline. Folding the discarded clothes, he placed them carefully behind a rock and turned to look at Owen, who had taken a cigarette out and was trying unsuccessfully to light it.

"If you'll allow me, sir." He walked over, took the lighter and put it carefully to the end of Owen's cigarette. In the flickering light, the older man's face was flushed as he looked directly into Gidon's eyes. His appetite made him look absurd. A vein in his forehead began to throb. It made Gidon recoil but he succeeded in mustering a smile.

"I do believe you'll like the club," he whispered and, taking Owen's arm, he led him into the Old City.

Owen's patent slippers were not meant for cobblestoned streets and Gidon tightened his grip on the man's arm as they walked quickly through the congested alleyways, trying to avoid the garbage and animal excrement strewn across their path. It was nearly eleven o'clock and the streets were quite empty, but the odor of spices, roasting lambs, perfume and urine still lingered. Shop-fronts were shuttered with iron doors and above them the worn stones of the buildings hid the deep-set grilled windows, so the occupants could neither see or be seen. A few men in *galabyas,* heads and faces covered with scarves against the cold, were standing in doorways, oblivious to their surroundings. The stench of hashish was overpowering.

Owen stopped and breathed deeply. "I love it," he whispered. "I love its authenticity. There is something pure about these people. They don't pretend. In their primitive way they make a mockery of what we call civilization."

"Quite right, sir." Gidon grew impatient. "But we'd better be getting along. The club does get crowded and I do want us to be there for the dancer. Quite extraordinary."

Reaching their destination, Gidon guided Owen into a courtyard hidden from the narrow alleyway by a tall, whitewashed wall. It was indistinguishable from the rest of the structures around. The small courtyard was bare except for an ancient olive tree whose heavy bark was gnarled with age. The highly polished heavy-arched doorway was a revelation amid the simplicity surround-ing it.

Gidon knocked gently on the door and although no sound came from within, he knew they were being observed through an invisible peephole. The door opened on silent hinges and a veiled woman bowed in greeting and waved them in.

"Master." The voice, coming from behind the veil, was a deep, masculine voice, overladen with sexual connotations. Then, in a sweeping gesture, the veil was swept away and Gidon nearly burst out laughing at Owen's expression. He let go of Owen and threw his arms around the transvestite, a heavy-set man whose cheeks were unusually smooth under the thick layer of makeup.

The host kissed him on both cheeks and pushed him away, and still holding onto his hand, he stared at him with admiration.

"Baba," Gidon disengaged himself from his host. "I want you to meet an old, old friend of mine." He moved aside and watched Owen shake hands with Baba.

"We are honored to have you, sir," Baba said with genuine respect. He had been the owner of the club for many years and could tell an important new client. "And we hope our meager home will be pleasing to you." Then, turning to Gidon, he shook his finger at him. "Being unfaithful to the Irishman, are you?" And before Gidon could answer, he looked again at Owen. "But with someone as elegant as this gentleman is, I do not blame you." He smiled, exposing three gold teeth behind the rouged lips, "But your secret is safe with me."

Gidon shifted in seeming discomfort. He and Cornelius had frequented the club in the last few weeks, making a point of being observed by Baba and pretending great attraction for each other. Baba had been so impressed with them that after their second visit he always reserved for them the same room for their amorous liaison.

"Now for a drink of greeting." Baba led them through a dark passageway, which opened into a large, smoke-filled circular room with low arched ceilings, high, thin-curtained windows, and maroon velvet-covered banquets placed around small metal tables. Candles were the only source of light and faces were blurred in the dimness.

Seated in a secluded niche, Gidon watched Owen eying the crowd. Through the smoky haze, the bodies of boys and men swayed in slow motion, and although Gidon had been privy to the sad hopelessness it represented, he could both see and feel Owen's excitement. His loathing for him was brimming over.

Baba was hovering over them and Gidon tore his eyes away from Owen.

"Champagne, Baba," he said and Baba blinked. "The finest you've got and I know you have it." He smiled knowingly.

Baba regained his composure quickly and winked at Gidon. He understood that Owen was someone special and his young patron was going to make a bundle this evening.

A tall African dressed in a flowing Turkish robe cinched by a gold-tasseled sash served the drinks along with a platter of sweets. The popping cork barely made a sound and the foaming liquid was poured into the glasses.

Owen reached over and took Gideon's hand and pressed it. Then, picking up his glass, he toasted Gidon with his eyes. Gidon clicked his glass, pretending not to notice Owen's undisguised carnality. Leaning back, but not letting go of Gidon's hand, Owen rested his head against the back of the banquette and closed his eyes. Gidon felt Owen't other hand slip under his sweater and down his back to his buttock, massaging it gently.

Gidon's hand was wet with perspiration but he dared not disengage himself from the possessive grasp. He too leaned back and tried to immerse himself in the faint music coming through the darkness. He had to hold off Owen's advances until at least midnight. That was when the concièrge at the Pilgrim Hotel was replaced by a night porter who did not know the guests. To him all European guests looked alike and since Cornelius was in his room from early evening, Gidon, posing as Cornelius, could walk past the porter without difficulty.

Suddenly the room was plunged into darkness and the music stopped playing. Owen gripped Gidon's hand but relaxed when a red spotlight lit up the center of the dance floor. Then a faint sound of cymbals and a tapping on a tambourine broke the silence. Everyone held their breath as the tapping grew louder and finally a veiled dancer appeared out of the darkness. Covered by a loose, transparent black robe, she slithered to the middle of the dance floor and started moving about, almost shyly, to the beat of the jangling metal of the instrument held high over her head. The beat grew faster, and her body picked up the tempo as her hand, tapping against the little drum, began to move more frantically. The thin robe swirled around her and her fleshy nakedness appeared fleetingly as she started circling close to the edge of the circle. Then she stopped and, throwing the tambourine into the crowd, she pulled the veil from her face. The perfection of features was breathtaking, but it was the indifference of expression that was stunning. She stood very still, waiting. The dull beat of a drum started off in the distance. The sound grew louder and the dancer started swaying her hips moving seductively under the transparent fabric, and then with a sweeping gesture she pulled off the robe, exposing a white, fleshy body with only a beaded G-string covering her pubic hair and two stars pasted over her nipples. Her legs came apart and her lower body began to move slowly, building slowly toward the belly dance. The drum lost its languid beat and grew more intense, and she lost all restraint. The red ruby lodged in her navel flashed more frantically as her lower body gyrated erotically, provoking the audience to a climax. Everyone grew restive. People began to grope indiscriminately in the darkness, while the dancer became more self-absorbed, staring down at her body as though hypnotized by the sight.

Gidon had seen the dance before, but pretended interest in an effort to avoid looking at Owen. Then he felt the older man's hand clutch his thigh. He placed his hand over his and pressed it.

"Can we have some privacy?" Owen choked the words out.

Gidon started to rise.

"Don't go." Owen sounded desperate.

Trapped in Owen's viselike grip, he raised his hand, praying Baba would notice him.

Baba rushed over. He looked over at Owen and smiled in an almost fatherly fashion. "Follow me," he whispered and picked up the champagne bottle and glasses and led them to a stairway hidden behind a stringed partition.

Once in the room, Gidon poured the remaining champagne into the glasses and turned to hand Owen his drink. In his other hand he held a small knife.

Owen, who had started toward him, stopped and the flabby fop was replaced by the officer. His hand went to the side pocket of his trouser leg.

"Don't bother, Owen," Gidon said pleasantly. "I removed it quite a while ago."

"The Danzigers are a cursed people," Owen said calmly.

"And you thought you could perpetuate the curse, did you?"

"But why?" Owen asked after a short pause.

"You know as well as I do. For Thomas, for Raphael, for my friends who will be hanged, for all of my people."

The knife slid easily through the dress shirt. Gidon moved away when the blood spurted out over his hand. He withdrew the knife and plunged it, again and again, into the dying man. He could not stop. Finally Owen fell to the floor, writhing briefly. Then he lay still. Only then did Gidon come back to himself.

When Gidon came downstairs, Baba rushed toward him. Gidon winked at him and took a roll of bills from his pocket and handed him several notes. "I'd let him sleep it off," he whispered, and slipped out of the club.

The street was deserted and Gidon walked quickly toward the Pilgrim Hotel. The porter barely looked up as he passed him. The room was on the ground floor at the end of a long corridor. Tapping gently on the door, he let himself in.

Cornelius, in shirt sleeves and slacks, was sitting in an armchair, staring out the window. A young woman wearing a robe was lying on the bed, reading. The bed was rumpled.

"Is it over?" Cornelius looked up when Gidon walked in.

"And done with." Gidon looked down at himself. He had washed his hands and except for a thin line of dried blood on the black sweater, there was no evidence of the murder.

"I'm Bridget." The girl stood up and came toward him. She was a pretty brunette with twinkling eyes.

"My pleasure." He put his hand out.

Her handshake was firm.

"Drink?" Cornelius asked, barely hiding his relief.

"No, thanks. I hate the stuff and that bastard can certainly put it away and I didn't dare refuse."

"Well, it's three A.M. and you've got two hours before the bus comes. Would you like to take a nap or something?"

"I'm exhausted, but I couldn't sleep. I'm too wound up."

"How about a game of rummy?" Bridgette asked.

"I'd love it, but I would like to change my shirt."

Bridget handed him a clean white shirt, a safari jacket and a scarf and pointed toward a door leading to the bathroom.

He had just finished dressing when he heard a loud banging on the outer door. He looked around, saw the window and started to heave himself out of it when Bridget came in, pulling her robe off and motioning for Gidon to keep quiet.

"Mr. Sullivan, sorry to bother you at this hour." A man with a British accent was talking to Cornelius. "But we're looking for a killer and someone said they thought they saw a man come into this hotel a few minutes ago." The man spoke with respect, but he sounded serious. "I hate to disturb you, but we're searching all the rooms."

"Killer?" Cornelius started laughing. "Who got killed?"

"Colonel Cartwright's driver. We found him slumped over the wheel of his car outside the Jaffa Gate. Now we're looking for Cartwright. No one seems to know where he is."

"Oh, gentlemen," Cornelius said in exasperation. "I'm here with . . ." He coughed self-consciously.

"Where is she?"

"In the bathroom, of course. She's a respectable young woman. As a matter of fact, she's my fiancée."

"Please ask her to come out."

Gidon was stepping out the window, when Bridget, naked except for a towel wrapped around her body, opened the door and stuck her head out coyly.

Gidon spent the remaining time in the bathhouse. The owner paid little attention to him as he handed him a towel and went back to his radio.

At 4:45, he walked briskly toward the bus stop. Miraculously, it arrived just as he reached the kiosk. The place was crowded with Arabs traveling to work and some British soldiers heading back to their barracks along the route. Several MPs were checking identity cards. Gidon's, in the name of Brian Donnell, a photographer from Australia sent to Palestine to photograph a day in the life of Arab workers, was in order, and he got onto the bus.

Staring blindly out the window, he reconstructed the events of the night. It had all gone according to plan. No one would identify him. Certainly not Omar. Neither would the servant who had served them dinner. The guards would give out a description of an officer named Gideon Hardwick, who was tall, fair, with blue eyes. Not an extraordinary appearance for an English officer. As for Baba? When the body was finally discovered, it would be dumped as far away from his club as possible. And Baba was hardly likely to come forward and identify it. Everything had worked as planned, except for the murder of the driver. It could have been an Arab looking to rob him. But he knew better. Zak had disobeyed him and had tried to help.

# CHAPTER
# THIRTY-EIGHT

B ASHA barely slept and was in the kitchen at five o'clock in the morning making tea when she heard the news come over the radio. The bulletin was garbled, but she heard Cartwright's name mentioned. He had ordered the execution of the four terrorists. She also heard the word *murder*, although it was unclear who had been murdered. A curfew was in place and would last until further notice. Without waiting for details, she ran out of the house.

She was stopped several times by British soldiers but was allowed to proceed when she explained that her child had slept over at her grandmother's house and that she had to see her. She arrived to find Deborah standing on the front balcony as though waiting for her.

"Was he caught?" she cried out the minute she was indoors.

"Who?" Michael was sitting next to the radio.

"Cartwright's killer?"

Deborah came into the room. "Calm down, Basha," she said urgently. "Just calm down."

"Did they catch him?" Basha demanded.

"What are you talking about?" Michael asked.

"Basha, come into the kitchen and have some tea. You're completely hysterical and you don't know what you're talking about," Deborah warned.

"I think she does," Michael interjected. "Who was caught?"

"Cartwright's killer," Basha answered in confusion.

"Cartwright is missing, not dead." Michael's eyes narrowed. "His driver is dead and they're looking for his killer but they have yet to find Cartwright."

Basha blanched. "I will have some tea, if I may."

"You may have tea, of course, but I want to know what you're so upset about." Michael walked over to her and gripped her arm.

She lowered her eyes. "Forgive me, Michael. I guess I am hysterical and for no good reason."

"Not for no good reason." He stopped and looked over at Deborah. "Where is Gidon?"

"Isn't he in Bet Enav?" Deborah asked.

"You know he's not." He turned back to Basha. "Where is Gidon?"

"He went out with some friends last night and he hasn't come back. That's why I'm so worried."

"Well, you can be sure he wasn't in Jerusalem," Deborah said calmly. "I picked the children up around six or six-thirty. And he had just left, so he couldn't be there. Curfew is at seven."

"He could have made it before curfew!" Michael snapped. "And he obviously did."

"Where are the children?" Basha turned away from him.

"They're still asleep and I think I'll let them sleep as late as possible since they won't be able to leave the house all day and maybe not for days to come," Deborah said, and turned to leave the room.

"Is anybody up?" Gidon walked in, smiling. Then, sensing the mood in the room, he walked quickly over to Basha. "Are you all right?"

"Oh, Gidon," Basha whispered. "Oh, my God."

"What's going on here?" Gidon turned to Michael.

"I wish I could order you to leave this house." Michael could barely choke the words out.

"May I ask what he's talking about?" Gidon looked from Basha to Deborah.

"Cartwright's driver has been murdered," Deborah said.

"And you think I did it?" Gidon addressed the question to Michael.

"I didn't think you did it. Now I do. Furthermore, I have a feeling that before this day is over we'll find out that Cartwright is dead, too."

"Gidon, Amit and the others are going to be executed." Basha wanted to drop the subject of Cartwright.

Gidon did not answer but he was visibly shaken by the news.

"Cartwright gave the order," Basha said pointedly.

"Where did you get the clothes you're wearing?" Michael asked, observing Gidon's rumpled safari jacket.

"Friend of mind gave them to me."

"How did you get through the curfew?" Michael continued.

Gidon did not answer.

"How did you get through, Gidon?" Michael's voice rose. "How?"

"I had my service papers with me," Gidon said offhandedly.

"You're nothing but a damn murderer." Michael spat the words out. "A cold-blooded, calculating murderer."

"And you, Michael? What are you but a cold-blooded murderer," Gidon shot back.

Michael started to speak, but the words stuck in his throat.

"You killed a man in the desert in cold blood and you dare call me a murderer? David Larom was your friend. Cartwright was my enemy. He killed my father and he so much as admitted to being involved in Raphael's murder as well. He deserved to die. Did David Larom?"

"Stop it," Deborah demanded. "The two of you, stop it." She rushed over to Michael, who had begun to tremble and was having a hard time breathing. "Get some water," she said and, taking Michael by the arm she lead him to an armchair.

Basha ran from the room and Gidon walked over to help Deborah.

"Get away from me," Michael pushed Gidon from him. "Don't come near me." He fell into the chair and covered his face with his hands.

"You shouldn't have said those awful things." Deborah looked up at Gidon. "You have no right to accuse him. David was killed by Bedouins, just as Michael had said."

"How can you be so sure?" Gidon asked. "How?"

"I know Michael. I know my husband." She stood up. "And I know you, Gidon." She continued, her voice softening. "Now go change into civilian clothes and, when tempers cool down, we'll talk further."

Basha came back with the water, handed it to Deborah and went to stand beside Gidon.

"We shall have to stay in your house until this curfew is over," Gidon said quietly. "I'm sorry."

"I know that," Deborah said. "And you will act as though nothing happened. We will be searched and we will behave as a family. But I'm afraid you will not get away with it this time, Gidon."

Left alone, Deborah held the water out to Michael. "Drink it, Michael," she said softly as she pushed his hair back from his face. "It's all right, Michael. He doesn't know what he's talking about. Rumors, gossip—they last longer than fact." She tried to smile. "I know you're innocent. I've always known you're innocent. Isn't that enough?"

He leaned back, staring at the ceiling. "If only I could prove it. God, if only there were some way I could prove it!" His cry was heartrending.

The day passed slowly. There was no news of Cartwright or any mention of his driver. The reports shifted to the details concerning the four terrorists who were to be executed and the frantic search for two British soldiers who had been taken hostage, doomed to die if the order for the execution was not reversed.

Michael spent the day in his room. The children played in the backyard and Deborah, Basha and Gidon sat by, watching them.

"I hope Uri doesn't mention anything about the uniform you wore when you went out yesterday," Deborah said, at one point.

"He's probably forgotten about it." Gidon shrugged his shoulders. "And even if he does, I was in the army, after all."

"I agree with Deborah and I hope he doesn't mention it," Basha said with concern.

The soldiers arrived at dusk. They ordered everyone into the living room and demanded identity cards. All were in order.

"Where were you yesterday?" The officer turned to Michael. "In the late afternoon, before the curfew started."

"Right here."

"Can you prove it?"

"My wife and grandchildren and I lit the Hanukkah candles," Michael sucked in his breath, furious at the indignity.

"And you are Gidon Davidzohn, right?" He examined Gidon's papers.

"Yes, sir."

"Where were you yesterday afternoon and evening?"

"I went out to get some cigarettes and coffee. Took a short stroll and returned home just before curfew started."

"Didn't want to light candles with your family?" The officer asked sarcastically.

"No. Our daughter was not home and my wife and I wanted a quiet evening to ourselves."

Deborah described her actions. Basha repeated Gidon's alibi. Tova described her evening with the family.

The soldier walked over to the children.

Basha and Deborah held their breath.

"You're name is Tanya?" He knelt down beside her. "Where were you when your Daddy went out?"

"Playing in my room," she answered, and moved toward her mother.

"With whom?"

"With me." Uri spoke up. "We were playing jacks and I beat her."

"Did you see Tanya's father go out?"

"Yes, he came in to say goodbye to us." He looked directly at the officer.

"And when did he come back?"

"I don't know. My grandmother came to get us and we slept here." His eyes narrowed. "Don't you believe my uncle when he tells you he came home before the curfew?" Uri demanded.

The major stood up, embarrassed. "Of course I do." He turned back to Michael.

"Mr. Ben Hod." His tone changed and a note of respect replaced the earlier belligerence. "Have you any theories about who might have been involved in this messy affair?"

"The same lunatics who commit all those heinous acts," he answered simply.

"Anyone specific you can think of?"

Michael hesitated. "No," he said finally.

The officer looked around. "If you don't mind, sir, I would like to search the house."

"You're more than welcome to go through it." Michael said and the old authority was back. "But if you don't mind my asking, what is it you're looking for?"

"Sir, we've got our orders."

"I understand that, but you don't expect to find us hiding the two British hostages in the attic or basement, do you?"

"Obviously not, sir, but the fact is that we're under great pressure." He paused, considering his next words before speaking. "Colonel Cartwright's body was found an hour ago. He was stabbed to death."

"Where?" Michael asked.

"In the Old City of Jerusalem. Messy affair. Very messy. Dumped like an old sack of potatoes, they say. He was dressed in civilian clothes and had no identification on him. Such indignity."

Gidon was about to speak but Basha held him back.

"May God rest his soul," she said quietly.

An awkward pause followed.

"Let me take you through the house." Michael started to lead the way out of the room.

"I don't think that will be necessary, Mr. Ben Hod. But thank you." He saluted Michael, nodded to the women and walked out.

"You were worried I was going to tell him about Gidon's uniform, weren't you?" Uri looked over at Deborah the minute they heard the front gate slam shut.

"Uniform?" She asked and smiled.

"Oh, Grandma, you are funny." He ran to her and threw his arms around her.

Deborah leaned down and kissed his head and pressed him to her. "Now you two go into the kitchen with Tova and have some juice and then we'll light the Hanukkah candles."

"So you stabbed him to death," Michael said quietly when the children left the room.

"Michael, let it be," Deborah pleaded.

"It *is* his house." Gidon stopped her and turning to Michael he continued. "We will leave your house the minute we are free to go out. But I can assure you that until then I shall keep out of your way."

"And when you do leave here, I must ask you never to come back again."

"Quite," Gidon answered and led Basha out of the room.

"I shall have to report him to the authorities." Michael turned to Deborah. "I don't condone murder. There are laws that go beyond Jews, Arabs, Englishmen or any other people. Murder is murder and I won't be a party to it."

"Michael, I won't let you," Deborah said. "You will not turn him over to the British. They'll hang him."

"They'll catch him for this one. I have a feeling he did it on his own and he will be caught. It would be better for him if I turn him in."

"No," Deborah said quietly but she was deathly pale.

"I won't be able to live with my conscience if he goes unpunished for this crime."

"But not by the British."

"Well, who else is going to judge him?"

She walked over to the window and stared out, then turned around slowly and walked over to the phone. She hesitated briefly, then picked up the receiver and dialed.

"May I speak to Yanosh Bar Lev?" While waiting for Yanosh to come on the line, she looked over at Michael and told him what happened. "I don't know if Gidon did it or not. I will, however, trust our people to judge him, rather than the British." Then she heard Yanosh's voice and as calmly as she could, she turned Gidon over to him.

# CHAPTER
# THIRTY-NINE

BASHA did not forgive the Ben Hods for turning Gidon over to the Jewish underground. They came for him the day after the curfew was over. The arrest was brutal and without warning.

Basha spent the early weeks of 1948 pleading with Yanosh to let her see Gidon and talk to him, allow her to send him food or clothing. He ignored all her requests.

Her financial state was difficult and in desperation she sent Tanya to Naomi and got a job with the French Embassy in Tel Aviv to support herself and accumulate enough money to bring Tanya home. She missed the child but more important, she had decided to go back to Poland with Tanya and was worried about Tanya's attachment to her family in Palestine, her sense of dependence and her growing feelings of belonging to the land in which she was born. Life in the kibbutz was fulfilling to any child. It was everything Tanya wanted. Family, warmth, purpose, patriotism, ideals, dreams and legends.

Deborah understood Basha's anger. She also worried about her state of mind and was deeply concerned about her lack of money. She tried speaking to Benji about an allowance for Basha and Tanya, but he would not hear of it. He was now completely in charge of all the financial dealings of the family, and the political situation had put everyone in a financial bind.

Like Basha, she could get no information from Yanosh about Gidon's whereabouts, or what the outcome of his trial had been. They saw Yanosh, as the day of decision concerning the United Nations' recognition of the Jewish state grew closer. And when he did come over, he refused to discuss Gidon.

Winter passed and the family's Passover gathering in April was a sad affair. They gathered in Tel Aviv. Naomi, Jack, Uri, Daniel and Rachel arrived without Tanya. The child was with Basha, who refused to have Tanya spend time with the Ben Hods. Sonya arrived without Misha. Misha, she explained, was busy and sent his apologies. His absence was strange. Passover was a family affair and few spent it away from their loved ones. Sonya seemed old beyond her years, very frail and strangely silent. Deborah's hope of discussing Gidon with Yanosh vanished the minute he walked in. He was pleasant, sweet, affectionate but removed.

The normal bantering and chit-chat that usually preceded the meal was dispensed with, since emotions just under the surface were too explosive.

The seder rituals were observed and Deborah noted that Michael insisted on a very formal and didactic reading of the Haggadah, so that the meal lasted until midnight. The children grew restless and what had been a festive event in the past turned into a tedious, nervewracking affair.

Naomi and Ruth were finally excused and the children were put to bed. The grownups retired to the living room and Deborah went into the kitchen to help Tova. She felt nervous and tense and wondered how Gidon was spending the evening.

Misha rushed through his Seder. Seated at Nechemya's widow's table, he said the prayers and looked at the half-dozen young men with him. His eyes came to rest on Gidon.

"Welcome back." He smiled as they were about to start the meal. "Was it difficult escaping?"

"Not really." Gidon smiled. "If I didn't know better, I'd say that some of the guards actually helped me by turning their back when I climbed that wall. And let's face it, it was the night before Passover and everyone was involved in preparations."

"Good," Misha said, and turning to the rest of the boys he continued solemnly. "As soon as the meal is over, everyone of you knows where you're to go. And remember, it's the minaret on top of the mosque that you must aim at first. That's where they've got the projector and that's where the sniping is coming from. There is only one man there and he's a crack shot. I believe we can get him. What you must be conscious of are the British soldiers. They're moving men and arms into Jaffa. What we don't know is how ready they are to start fighting us openly."

Then picking up his Haggadah, he read the final passage, ending with the vow, "Next year in Jerusalem."

All said amen and stood up.

"You're sure you're not too tired to take on this mission?" Misha turned to Gidon as everyone started leaving the house.

"I've done nothing but rest since they arrested me."

"Stop joking," Misha said seriously. "This is not going to be easy. We've got to enter Jaffa and capture it. As it stands now, every citizen in Tel Aviv is in danger."

"Don't I know it," Gidon drew his breath in. "My house is practically within sight of Jaffa."

"Meet you by the clock," Misha said before entering a car and driving off.

*The clock.* Gidon smiled. The sight of the clock that day he had arrived in Jaffa twenty years ago, was the first sign of civilization he noticed in that ugly, wretched city.

They crawled along the seashore. Gidon was in the lead, since he lived in Tel Aviv and was most familiar with the terrain. Like him, each of his men had either an old rifle or a pistol, all aimed at the minaret at the top of the mosque. The light projector went on briefly, circled the area and went out. It was followed by a burst of gunfire coming from the minaret. The aim was far off and Gidon advanced slowly, waving on the men to follow. The projector lit up again, circled, went off and was followed by another burst of gunfire. It came closer. Gidon held his hand up.

"Spread out and try to surround it from the west. I'll advance toward it and try to blow out that damn light."

They followed his orders. The gunfire from the mosque was now being answered by shots from a southwesterly direction. Gidon was pleased. It meant that some of his men had reached it from a different side. With greater assurance, he crawled forward more quickly. The light went on again and he fired directly at it. It went out but he could not decide if he had put it out or if the Arab manning it had been shot. But whoever was still there had located his presence. He waited. The light did not come on again. He moved ahead cautiously. He was within several feet of the mosque and lifted his head to see if the clock was in view. It was still too far away. He turned his attention back to his target. A burst of rapid gunfire lit up the area and Gidon saw the sniper clearly. He fired, and the man came toppling down. Gidon stood up and rushed forward when he felt a flash of pain go through his chest. The last thing he saw before falling over was the clock.

Deborah finished helping Tova with the Passover dishes and reentered the living room. Michael was gone, as was Sonya. Benji and Ruth were seated at the far end of the room, talking. Naomi, Jack and Yanosh were chatting in muted tones.

"I'd like to listen to the news." Deborah said, noting that it was 1:00 A.M.

Jack turned on the radio and the six beeps preceding the news rang out. The announcer's voice followed.

"A battle for Jaffa is raging in full force," he said and his voice was unusually tense. "Jewish fighters have stormed the beach road between Jaffa and Tel Aviv and there is fierce fighting going on. Losses are heavy on both sides. There is also an unconfirmed report that British troops are fighting alongside the Arabs and that the Jewish boys are having a difficult time penetrating the barrage of heavy machine-gun fire coming from Jaffa." His voice faded briefly. "If there are any further reports about that battle, we will interrupt the program to announce the latest developments." He continued with a description of other skirmishes around the country, but no one in the room was listening.

"The fools," Yanosh hissed. "The damn, damn fools."

Deborah turned to look at him. He was unusually pale and he was trying to light a cigarette, but his hand was shaking too violently.

"Who?" She found her voice.

"That would be Misha's group." He inhaled deeply.

"Misha?" Deborah was dumbfounded. "But I thought you and Misha worked together."

"I have great respect for him. He's brilliant and I've worked closely with him on occasion. But he's gone too far recently. This action is the proof of it. And you may as well know. Gidon has escaped and might very well be involved in this debacle."

"Gidon escaped? When? How?"

"Last night. He was very cooperative since his arrest and we had many talks that I felt were fruitful—I was hopeful he'd get a mild sentence for his crime. But when the British hanged his friends, that fanaticism in him erupted." He shook his head. "I should have realized it would happen."

"He may be a fanatic." Naomi spoke up. "But I happen to agree with what he's doing. The Arabs have been attacking us on all fronts and someone has to put a stop to it. They don't want a partition and are trying to take over what has been given to us by the world powers. Iraqi and Syrian soldiers have come into Palestine and are fighting along with the Arabs living here. And now with the British abandoning decorum and helping them openly, we've got to take a stand. We've got to hold on to what we have until the United Nations' decision." Tears of frustration and rage were streaming down her cheeks. "You're doing what you can, I know it, but it's not enough."

"She's right." Jack spoke up. "While the world is debating, we're losing ground. And as for that General Assembly decision, who knows how it will turn out? No one is sure how anyone will vote. The resolution might be defeated." He looked over at Naomi. "And as far as I'm concerned the stakes are too high and I intend to defend this land with everything I've got. I think what those guys are doing on the Jaffa–Tel Aviv road is right."

The beeping sound on the radio interrupted the discussion and the announcer, sounding even more agitated than he had before, read a bulletin.

"Losses on both sides are heavy, but our boys seem to have gained the upper hand and have entered Jaffa. Some of the dead and wounded are being brought to Tel Aviv hospitals and the families will be notified as soon as identifications are made. I repeat, our boys have gained the upper hand and have entered Jaffa. Stand by."

"Benji, go get your father," Deborah said.

"Why?"

"Do as you are told," she commanded.

Benji stormed out of the room, slamming the front door as he left.

The phone rang while the echo of the slamming door was still reverberating through the house.

Deborah watched the shroud-covered body being lowered into the grave. The rabbi intoned the prayer for the dead, followed by the mournful Kaddish delivered by Michael. She felt numb but her mind was strangely alert to minute details around her and she was captivated by Michael's trembling voice. It did not sound like him. The voice belonged to a man deeply pained by the death of a loved one. Was it possible that Michael, in his own way, loved Gidon? His voice faded and she saw some dirt falling onto the spotless white shroud. She wanted to bend down and wipe it away. Gidon was quite meticulous about his clothing. Then she realized the sand was the symbolic holy earth placed on the dead before the body was covered over. She averted her eyes as shovels began scattering sand over the silent form. It was then that she became aware of Tanya's little hand gripping hers. She looked down at the child. She too was staring as her father's body disappeared under the mounds of freshly dug earth. Deborah wanted to pick her up, take her in her arms and hide her eyes from the sight. If it had been up to her, she never would have allowed the child to be present at the funeral. It was Basha's wish and no one dared interfere. At that moment Tanya looked up at her. Her eyes were wide with wonder and silent tears were streaming down her cheeks. Deborah swallowed her own tears. Tanya dared not cry out her sorrow, knowing that Basha forbade tears. Deborah lifted her eyes and looked at Basha. With her blond hair pulled tightly back into a bun, she looked like a white porcelain sculpture. Her strong chin jutted out, her mouth was set in a tight thin line and her eyes were staring down at Gidon's body, never blinking. She appeared removed from the events taking place around her. The only sign of emotion was the movement of her jawbones, as she ground her teeth in an attempt at self-control.

The rabbi finished his prayer, the cantor sang the Shema and the mourners began to move away. Deborah threw a last look at the covered grave and saw a man she did not know place a rose on the fresh mound. He looked up and their eyes met. He quickly walked over to her.

"I am Cornelius Sullivan."

"You said you loved him like a brother." She recalled the letter of warning about Gidon's desertion from the army.

"And my brother was a true hero, ma'am. You can be proud of him. Everyone should be proud of him. He lived and died for what he believed in, without excuses and without compromise. And although too young to die, this is the way he would have chosen to go. I know that." Impulsively, he leaned down and kissed her on the cheek. "He loved you so much."

She watched him walk over to Basha, who listened attentively to what he said. A small smile appeared on her face. They shook hands and he strode out of the cemetery.

The crowd moved slowly toward the gate and Deborah walked over to Tamar's grave, a few feet away from Gidon's. She knelt down and arranged the flowers planted around the simple stone. Vaguely she wondered who tended the graveyard now that Nechemya was gone.

Nechemya. She had not thought of him in so long. She stood up and searched the graveyard, wondering where he was buried. In a remote corner, she spotted a woman sitting on the ground, leaning against a tree, its branches fanning out protectively over her.

She was old and shriveled and as Deborah came closer, she realized the woman was sitting between two gravestones, her hands resting possessively on each. Her eyes were closed and her lips were moving in silent prayer.

Deborah leaned over to see the names on the two tombstones. *Nechemya. Tuvia.* The inscriptions under each name were identical. "Died for the cause of their homeland." And the date of death.

Deborah felt chilled. *Died for the cause of their homeland.* Tamar, Raphael, David, Gidon, Nechemya, Tuvia. The sight of graveyards all over the country, filling up with men and women serving the cause of their homeland, rose before her eyes.

Michael touched her shoulder and took her arm. They walked slowly past Tamar's grave and stopped for one last look at Gidon's.

"He was too young to die," Michael said.

She looked up at him. His face was more lined than she remembered, he was completely gray and his hairline had receded. His eyes were sunken and filled with sadness. She felt a great surge of love for him. Leaning against him, they walked out of the cemetery.

# CHAPTER
# FORTY

HE Jewish underground forces joined the battle for the Jaffa–Tel Aviv road forty-eight hours after the fighting started. After several days of fierce combat, the British, sensing defeat, asked for a cease-fire. The Jewish fighters refused, at which point the British withdrew their forces from the city and the next day the Arabs of Jaffa surrendered. There was a formal signing of surrender by the Arabs conducted with pomp and ceremony. After signing their names to an agreement of terms, the warring parties shook hands and the Arab population left Jaffa.

On May 14, 1948, the British mandate rule over Palestine came to an end and the State of Israel was born. The dream seemed to have materialized. The birth of the state almost compensated for the losses and heartache that the Jewish people had borne for so long, for a homeland was established.

The celebrations lasted late into the night. Men, women and children ran through the streets, shouting their joy. Bonfires were lit along the seashore and people danced around them, congratulating themselves at their victory. The leaders who helped bring about the victory made short speeches and waved V-signs before they disappeared into their offices for serious discussions. The moment of victory was real. That joyous reality, they knew, would be short-lived. The real fight was about to begin.

The formal declaration of war by the surrounding Arab nations was announced early the next day. The Egyptian army advanced from the south. Syrian, Lebanese and Iraqi tanks swooped down from the north, and Trans-Jordan attacked from the east. The Arabs were determined to exterminate the tiny new State of Israel.

Hate was the fuel that united these disparate Arab countries. It was pitted against a poorly armed people who had nowhere to go.

Deborah was barely conscious of the events around her. The numbness that had engulfed her when Gidon was killed did not let up, although it did not affect her ability to tend to the immediate needs of her family.

She was in Tel Aviv that day in May. She heard the revelry, and tried to summon up the joy she knew she should feel, but it would not surface. The price of the dream had been too high and she was not sure she had any inner resources left. Michael stayed with her throughout the day, but at midnight the phone rang and he had to go out. When she heard the news early the next morning, she understood the hasty departure. Tel Tanya was nearly overrun by Arabs from the north. Jack was fighting for the survival of their home, trying to stave off the advancing armies in his area. Naomi, Uri, Daniel and Rachel were in primitive, hastily dug shelters and were waiting for transportation that would bring them to Tel Aviv. Benji was fighting somewhere in the suburbs of Tel Aviv. Ruth was pregnant and was staying with Deborah. Naomi and the children never left Deborah's thoughts. Even the bombing of Tel Aviv by the Egyptians did not relieve Deborah's worry about them. The news was bad and there were days when it seemed hopeless. It was Basha who finally managed the impossible. Taking Michael's car, which was too old to be requisitioned by the army, she drove off one evening and returned three days later with Naomi, Daniel and Rachel in tow. Uri refused to leave Tel Tanya.

"What do you mean you left him there?" Deborah shouted in frustration. "He's a baby, eight years old, how could you do that?"

"That is no baby. He disappeared from sight the minute he realized I had come for them," Basha answered.

"You should have forced him to come," Deborah insisted.

"He told me that he was born in Tel Tanya and would not desert it just because they were having trouble there," Naomi answered wearily.

Another trip to the north was out of the question and all Deborah could do was pray for his safety.

As the number of casualties rose, Deborah turned her house into a hospital to accommodate wounded soldiers from the Tel Aviv area. Basha, Ruth and Tova, along with a couple of volunteers, tended the men and women who were brought in, while Deborah ran around to the various military commanders she knew, hoping to find someone who would be driving up north. She found no one that would even consider taking her.

The new immigrants landing on the shores of their newfound home were mobilized and sent to battle unprepared, with few arms at their disposal. The cemeteries of Israel filled up with freshly dug graves, which, in the midst of the heroic and tragic days, turned into small gardens of Eden, tended by weeping mothers, fathers, wives and children.

Victories were hailed, defeats were mourned, but the fight continued. Cease-fires came and went. Attending funerals and visiting the homes of the families of the dead, sitting in blacked-out rooms while Egyptian planes flew over Tel Aviv, reading the newspapers and listening to the radio or waiting to hear the phone ring with news, became a way of life.

Still Deborah forbade herself to dwell on what had happened to her. For the whole period of the war, she tried not to think of Gidon. Her concern was for the living men—Michael, Benji, Jack, Uri—and Yanosh. She was concerned about his attitude toward Gidon, she was angry at his people for not joining the Jaffa battle when it first started, but her devotion to him did not diminish. He had become part of her family.

Then the final truce was declared and although the death toll of the Jewish population was enormous, the pain unbearable, and the survivors found themselves faced with a bruised, devastated, chaotic state, still it was *their* state. It was *their* homeland.

Only then did Deborah go into her bedroom, which was now emptied of cots and cribs, of wounded and dying, and lay down on her bed. The cries of anguish, suppressed for so long, wracked her body. Only then did the magnitude of Gidon's death strike her, and the enormous price her family had paid for their dream. Tamar and David had died before the British conquered Palestine and that Gidon and Raphael did not live to see the birth of the new State of Israel.

She had walked through the nightmare of the war in a state of shock. Now exhausted, she closed her eyes and her mind.

"How long has she been sleeping?" Deborah heard a voice asking and it seemed to be coming from a distance.

"She went into her room around nine o'clock last night. I came in with her tea at seven this morning but she was sound asleep and I didn't want to disturb her." Deborah recognized Tova's voice. "I've come in every hour since, and around ten I tried to force her up, but she turned restlessly and moaned, so I let her sleep."

"Well, it's nearly two in the afternoon and I think we'd better force her to wake up."

*No,* Deborah thought wearily. *No, they can't make me come back to life and face what has happened.*

"Deborah." She felt someone shaking her and a cool hand touch her brow. "You must wake up. You cannot walk out of the lives of the people who need you." The voice drifted away and she sank back into her mercifully dreamless slumber.

When she woke up, it was daylight and she looked around furtively. She was not in her room. The walls were white and stark, the window was partially open and she could see some trees outside. She tried to identify some object around her that would give her a clue as to where she was. Nothing looked familiar.

"Well, you've finally decided to join us again." A nurse was standing next to the bed, checking her pulse. Deborah stared at her suspiciously.

"I'm Hannah." The nurse smiled down at her. "And your pulse is normal. How about trying to sit up and have some tea?"

"Where am I?" she whispered.

"In Dr. Sonya's sanatorium. I can tell you that she'll be very pleased to know you've finally come around."

"How long have I been here?"

"A couple of weeks."

She struggled to sit up. Her head began to spin and she lay back helplessly.

"Don't rush it. Let me get you some tea and I'll tell the doctor to come in."

Sonya arrived within minutes and sat down at the edge of the bed.

"What happened?" Deborah asked.

"I've seen people go into shock many times, but your timing was interesting. I watched you carefully during the war and I knew you were acting strangely, but you were functioning. You continued to function throughout and then, the day it was all over, you blacked out. You just left us."

"Gidon is dead, isn't he?" Deborah said after a long pause.

Sonya's face tightened. "Yes, Gidon is dead." She said. "In a week it will be one year since he died. But Benji is alive. Michael, Jack, and everyone in your family is alive. Ruth and her little girl are in Bet Enav and they need you. So do Naomi, Jack and their children. Basha and Tanya need you and so does Michael." She stared almost angrily at her. "You are their lifeline, don't you know that? Since you've been here, they've all been wandering around in a daze."

"I'm tired, Sonya. Tired of living, tired of watching death around me, tired of having to give up the people I love. Can't you understand that?"

"I understand it better than you think," Sonya answered and suddenly Deborah realized that Sonya, usually dressed a white doctor's smock, was wearing a black dress. She scrutinized the old woman's face more carefully. She was deathly pale and wrinkled, her eyes rimmed with red. "I lost Misha."

Deborah held back the tears. "How?"

"He died just before the signing of the surrender of Jaffa. A sniper shot. Misha died on the spot."

A silence weighted by the burden of unrelieved grief descended on the room.

"Deborah," Sonya was the first to recover. "I wish I could tell you there will be no more death, but I can't. What I can tell you is that there is life around you as well. In the midst of all this misery and heartbreak, Ruth has given birth to Alexandra and she's a sweet little girl. She should not be deprived of her grandmother. Yes, you've had your share of sadness, but you've also had rewards. There is so much new, fresh young life around you and you have so much to give."

"What is it I'm supposed to do now?"

"First have a cup of tea, then start recovering from this long overdue rest that your mind demanded and that your body needed. In a few days, Michael can pick you up and take you home."

Deborah closed her eyes. Home. Bet Enav. Yes, it would be good to be home again.

Deborah was happy to be sitting next to Michael as they drove away from the sanitorium. As the car descended the mountain toward the coastal road, she marveled at the changes that had taken place in recent times. New houses were built, roads were paved and children were playing in freshly planted gardens. Michael guided the car through the hairpin turns before the road straightened and they entered the commercial district of Haifa. There had always been a marked difference between the three sections of Haifa. There were changes here since the war. But the most marked difference had occurred around the port section. The usually bustling pier was empty, as was the Arab marketplace. The small coffeeshops were shut, the houses boarded up. She had heard that the Arabs had left their homes when their leaders fled to Lebanon or Syria. Seeing it empty of its population was strangely disconcerting. The feeling persisted as they reached the coastal highway. The small mud huts, which had lined the road before the war, were gone. There were no camels, goats, donkeys or carts, which usually hindered the flow of traffic. The scenes that had been part of the landscape throughout her childhood were no more and Deborah was overtaken by a sense of nostalgia for what had been. For the first time in many months, she thought of Mahmud and Fatmi.

"What happened to Ein Chod?" she asked. "To Fatmi and her family?"

"They all left. I went up there at the very beginning of the hostilities. She and her family were getting ready to leave on the instructions of the mufti of Jerusalem. I offered her refuge in our home, suggested she come and live with us. I think she would have liked to, but she was afraid she'd be considered a traitor. One of her children assured me that they were only leaving temporarily, that the mufti had promised them victory and a glorious homecoming as soon as the Jews were defeated."

"Poor Fatmi. I wonder where she is and what her life will be like from here on in."

"God only knows. And to think she could have stayed if the Arabs had accepted the U.N. resolution. And, of course, if the British had not persisted in their determination to stay in this part of the world. The Jewish state was a fact they could not change, so they decided to goad the Arabs into doing their dirty work for them. But that is past and I did tell Fatmi she could come back to us any time. She knew I meant it and she seemed grateful."

They drove along the blue waters of the Mediterranean. Deborah put aside thoughts of the past and concentrated on the sights around her. It had been a long time since she had traveled this coastal route. The road, a main artery between Tel Aviv and the northern part of the country, had always been a busy one, but now there was a new vibrancy, a different quality to the traffic. The open trucks were filled with happy, suntanned youngsters, singing and laughing. The buses were packed with men and women who waved at them as they passed. Soldiers were standing on the side of the road, waiting for their pickup trucks, men were working on widening the narrow highway, and there were numerous new villages in what had once been sand dunes. Large fields of newly planted corn and wheat swayed gently in the sea breeze. She could not ignore the tents along the way, which still housed new immigrants, but she felt confident that they too would soon find permanent homes. That's what they had fought for and it was simply a matter of time. A new era had dawned and she was part of it. This was her home and she felt proud of her newborn land. In a way, it helped ease the pain, helped dry the tears. It almost justified the sacrifices.

She was so absorbed in what was happening around her that it took her a minute to realize that the landscape had changed from desert dunes to orange groves. When she saw the signpost indicating the direction of Bet Enav, she sat up in anticipation.

"I hope you don't mind, but I gave Benji permission to move into the big house," Michael announced as he slowed down, before making the turn.

She swung her head toward him, shocked. "I certainly do mind," she answered quickly. "I mind very much and I won't have it."

"But Deborah . . ."

"That is our house. Yours and mine and it shall remain ours until we are no more." She interrupted him, surprised at her own vehemence. "I refuse to be turned out of my home while I'm still alive."

"But the fact is that he's moved in," Michael said, stunned by her response.

"Well, we won't stop in Bet Enav now. We will drive on to Tel Aviv and you will simply tell him that he may not have the house."

"Deborah," Michael started again, "we can use Raphael's house. It's big enough for us."

"Michael, I am not just being stubborn. I will not permit my son to become a parasite, someone who feels he deserves something for nothing. I know he works hard. But think of it! At his age, working for someone other than his family—could he possibly afford to live in a house such as ours? You of all people should not want our son to be the generation of children of the rich."

"But Deborah, we have the house because you inherited it," Michael tried to argue.

"You forget. The house we moved into was a shambles, a ruin that we struggled to build up and make into a home. I grant you, we had the foundation. And I believe Benji has been given that. He has a job, a salary and he should live within his means."

"But where will they go?"

"Where did Basha and Gidon go when they left Bet Enav? They found a flat and moved into it. Benji will have to find a place that is suitable for his income and eventually he will build a house he can afford."

Michael pulled over to the side of the road. "Please, Deborah, reconsider what you're saying," Michael said seriously. "He is your son, he works hard and in a way he's supporting all of us."

"Is he now?" Deborah said slowly. "Who is he supporting? Basha and Tanya? Naomi, Jack and the children in Tel Tanya? Me? You?" She paused and mulled over her last words. "Well, we'll have to put an end to that, won't we. Especially since it's not so and you know it." Then turning away from Michael, she looked straight ahead. "Would you please drive me to Tel Aviv?"

They drove in silence for the rest of the trip. Deborah's mood changed. She had looked forward to seeing Ruth and Benji, and she was especially eager to see the new baby. She had barely spent any time with Alexandra since she was born. The consolation was that she would be seeing Tanya and Basha sooner. Much as she loved her other grandchildren, she knew that Tanya was special.

The minute they arrived in Tel Aviv, Deborah called Basha. Tanya answered the phone.

"Where is Mommy?" she asked after an effusive greeting from Tanya.

"She's out buying another suitcase."

"Suitcase?"

"Yes, we're leaving for Poland in a few days." Tanya's happy tone changed and Deborah could hear the child choking back tears.

"Why don't you come visit me." Deborah hid her shock. "Leave your Mommy a note that you're with me and have her come here she comes home."

She hung up and ran out of her room, looking for Michael.

"Did you know Basha is planning to leave for Poland?"

Michael lowered his head. "I didn't know, but I suspected that it would happen one day."

"She's taking Tanya with her and she can't do that."

"I'm afraid she can. Tanya is her child and she has every right to take her wherever she goes."

"I won't hear of it." Deborah became frantic.

"Deborah, I don't want Tanya to go, but you've got to let go. We both do." Michael spoke softly but his agony matched hers.

"Let go? What do you mean?"

"She is Tamar's grandchild, just as Gidon was Tamar's son."

The ghosts had emerged again and both she and Michael were helpless against them.

Tanya arrived with Basha in the late afternoon. The child ran to Michael and clung to him.

"Is it all right with you if I take Tanya for a drive?" Michael asked Basha, wanting to give Deborah time alone with her.

"That would be nice," Basha said after a brief pause.

Deborah seated herself in a rocker on the small back porch and Basha settled down on the stone steps leading down to the garden.

"I understand you've decided to go back to Poland," Deborah started cautiously. "It should be a very difficult task."

"I can't postpone it any longer," Basha said quietly.

"You're planning to take Tanya with you. Do you think that's wise?"

"Well, obviously." Basha seemed surprised at what Deborah was saying. "She's my daughter."

"But do you think it's the right thing to do?" Deborah tried to keep her anxiety in check. "After all, you don't really know what you'll find when you get back to Warsaw."

Basha did not reply.

"It has been almost four years since the war ended in Europe and unless you haven't told me, I believe you haven't heard from your parents." She paused and weighed her next phrase carefully. "I hate to say it, but you must assume that they have perished along with . . ." She could not finish the sentence.

"The rest of the Jews of Poland?" Basha finished the sentence for her and turned to face Deborah. "They may be dead, but they did not perish with the other Holocaust victims." Her voice was strangely lacking in emotion.

Deborah's eyes widened in wonder.

"I'm not Jewish, Deborah. My parents are Catholic and I was raised as a Catholic."

Deborah felt her lip begin to tremble and she raised her hand to her mouth, trying to stop the tremor. Her mind was whirling and she felt ill. Basha was still Basha, Jewish or Catholic. Basha was Gidon's wife. She was part of their family. They loved her. Her religion should have no effect on anything.

"I lied to Gidon, or rather I omitted telling him the truth, telling all of you the truth. I did not marry him to save my life, although now that I think of it, my parents probably thought of that when they gave their consent." Her voice still lacked emotion, but she paused as though wanting her words to sink in. "I was very much in love with Gidon. I still am and I shall always love him. But the fact is that today, with Gidon gone, I have to go back and confront my past."

"Confront your past?"

"I don't know where my parents were during the war and . . ." She stopped again, groping for words. "My father was a reserve colonel in the Polish army and I have no idea what his political affiliations were. I never paid attention to those things then." Her voice trailed off and she put her hand to her face, as though hiding from a truth that she did not want to know.

"Did Yanosh know?" Deborah asked and before Basha could react, she rushed on. "Of course he knew." She had answered her own question.

"And he was very decent about it," Basha said, "although he kept urging me to tell you the truth about my background. That was what he was saying to me at Benji's wedding. He's hounded me about it ever since."

"And he has no information about your parents either?"

"If he does, he has not told me."

They sat in grim silence, each absorbed in her own thoughts.

"Well, all the more reason why Tanya should stay with us until you find out what has actually happened." Deborah finally broke the silence.

"Deborah, you can't ask me to give up the one person in my life whom I live for, who is the product of my love for Gidon. Besides, I love this country and we will always be part of it, wherever we are."

"No. You will have a memory and it will give you comfort. What about Tanya? She was born here. She's part of this land and it's part of her. She is an Israeli. You may have dressed her in the European style, you may have insisted on certain amenities, you may have given her many wonderful mannerisms which make her appear different, but she is an Israeli child. She is a child with a rich heritage, a product of this country, its best and its worse." She spoke with great vehemence and meant what she was saying, but she also knew that she was fighting for Tamar's grandchild, for Gidon's daughter, for the Danziger family.

"She's not Jewish," Basha said evenly.

"Why don't we let her decide what she is, when she is older?"

Deborah stopped as a new thought came to her. "You say you love this country and I believe you. Has it occurred to you that you may want to come back here?"

"That's a decision I can't make now," Basha said sadly. "There is nothing I would love more than to spend the rest of my life here, but I must first find out certain facts. I must." Her voice rose in hysteria. "As I feel now, I couldn't live away from this country, ever. But—I don't know what I'll find."

"All the more reason not to take Tanya with you on this difficult journey. Why expose her to all that? She can stay with us and she can continue her schooling without interruption. She'll spend her vacations at Tel Tanya with Naomi and the children. You know how attached she is to Uri. Or she can spend her time with Benji and his kids. She adores Alexandra. In a way, I think the separation from Uri and Alexandra would be the most painful for her."

"Let me think about it."

"Why don't you talk to Yanosh, too. If he knows you're going back, he may be able to help. He has many contacts in the Eastern European countries."

"Maybe." She sounded doubtful.

That night, unable to sleep, Deborah mapped out a campaign to keep Tanya from going. First on the list was to confide in Yanosh and enlist his help, even if Basha resisted the idea. He, more than anyone, could persuade Basha to leave Tanya behind. He knew what conditions were like in Europe and she was sure he would help.

# CHAPTER
# FORTY-ONE

THE realization of what had happened to her came slowly. The first weeks after she saw her mother off, Tanya spent her time at Tel Tanya. It was the children's summer vacation and the kibbutz life, with its unstructured, carefree existence, was a novelty and a joy. The days were filled with excitement and adventure—working in the barns, feeding the chicks and collecting eggs from the coops, helping prepare the meals for the whole community, or watching over the smaller children while their parents were at work. The nights, however, were frightening. Sleeping in underground shelters was a normal existence for a child who had grown up under the gunfire of the Arabs shooting at random at the Jewish residents of the surrounding settlements. It was terrifying to Tanya, who had grown up in the relative calm of Tel Aviv. Having Uri beside her helped.

They were as close as ever, although he had changed. She noted it the minute she arrived at Tel Tanya. The boisterous boy had grown somber and thoughtful. He said little, in general, except when they were alone. And even then, he did not speak as he used to. He seemed in a hurry to grow up, join the army and teach the Arabs a lesson. He had become a loner who walked around the fields for hours, inspecting the surrounding area and acquainting himself with every nook and cranny. Tanya would walk with him, preferring his company to that of the other children, and she would see him staring at the mountains above Tel Tanya, behind which lay the Syrian border. With eyes squinted, he would map out his plan for defending his country. He always included her in his plans and gave her a role to play in that imaginary scenario. Tanya loved listening to him.

Halfway through the summer, Benji picked her and Uri up and brought them to Ben Enav. Here again, the festive mood of vacation continued. Michael and Deborah were loving, coddling and protective. Benji, Ruth and the children were back in Raphael's house, but Benji had bought a plot of land in Caesarea, a lovely seaside town a short distance away, and was building a house on the waterfront. He and Ruth were away a great deal of the time, supervising the construction, and Tanya and Uri were left almost completely in charge of Alexandra, with Tova looking on. Alexandra was considerably younger than they were, but they enjoyed having her around.

A there was Yanosh. He was the one who gave her the most comfort. When he was around, she felt she belonged. He would come into the house and swoop her up in his arms and hold her close. She would feel completely happy. When he took her for a drive to Haifa, or to visit some far-off kibbutz, she would sit beside him, feeling proud that he was her friend.

It was only when summer vacation was over and the family returned to Tel Aviv that the aura of carefree abandon faded. For the first time she realized that she would not be returning to the little flat she had shared with her mother. Worse, the reality of her parents' absence began to dawn on her.

She fell into her daily routine, seemingly undisturbed by her new circumstances. But deep inside her, the loneliness began to take its toll. Beneath the smiling, gay youngster lay a frightened, lonely, tortured child filled with fears of what might be. First her father and now her mother had deserted her. And much as she loved Deborah and Michael, they were not her parents and they could not fill the void.

At first Basha wrote almost daily. Tanya would receive her letters in batches. They were loving, caring, concerned letters, filled with hope and promise. Deborah, from the start, was apprehensive. Chatty and informative as they appeared to be, she could not help but feel that Basha was hiding a truth from Tanya and from them. Deborah had no idea what the truth was, but Basha's descriptions of her trip through Poland were very long, yet lacking in details. She traveled constantly but never seemed to arrive at her destination. There was never any specific mention of her parents. Once she mentioned that someone had seen her parents and in a few days she hoped to have further news. The news she was expecting was never referred to in subsequent letters. Then her letters started sounding confused, arriving once a week, then once every two weeks. Then, several weeks would go by with no letters at all. Deborah watched Tanya rush to the mailbox, day after day, month after month, waiting for word from her mother. The look of devastation on her face when the box was empty was heartbreaking.

A sense of foreboding overtook Deborah. It was unlike Basha to simply desert her daughter. She was too aware, too conscious of her responsibility toward her child to be simply neglectful. She was also helpless to do anything about the situation, since none of Basha's letters had a return address on them.

In desperation, Deborah asked Yanosh if he could find out Basha's whereabouts. It was weeks before he came back with the news. Basha had fallen ill and was in hospital. What her illness was remained a mystery, since the doctors would not share the information with a stranger. Deborah wrote to the doctors, imploring them to tell her what the trouble was and asking if a visit from her would help. Again, the doctors were evasive in their answers, and it was only when she announced that she was planning a trip to Warsaw that they relented and the truth came out. Basha had suffered a mental breakdown, accompanied by amnesia. It would be useless for Deborah to come, since Basha would not recognize her. Again, Tanya seemed to take the news of her mother's illness in stride and she appeared to have put Basha out of her conscious thoughts. She never mentioned Basha, never asked about her illness and never again spoke of the time when her mother would return. She began suffering strange, silent moods that would overtake her, even though she learned to hide them from family and friends. Deborah, no stranger to the suffering of the people she loved, was very much aware of the girl's inner torment and she prayed that time would somehow heal the wounds that life had inflicted on her beloved child.

The months and years rushed by and Tanya passed from childhood to adolescence with grace and poise. She slipped through the gangly awkwardness of a young girl growing into womanhood and developed into a lovely, tall, slender, gracefully striking teenager. The physical similarities between Tanya and Tamar grew more apparent, as did the differences in personalities. The determined, vivacious qualities of leadership that Tamar possessed were missing in her granddaughter. Tanya's strange moods deepened and were diagnosed as melancholia, which the doctors felt she would outgrow with time.

Like Tanya, the state was thriving—on the surface. It had absorbed nearly one million new immigrants who appeared to have settled into their new life, working and planning their future with confidence and hope. They had lived through the nightmare of war, had paid an enormous price and they had triumphed. A whole generation had grown up with the hope of achieving a dream—and it had. But slowly, reality was beginning to set in. There were food shortages and insufficient housing. The big guns had stopped firing, but terrorists from hostile neighboring countries kept infiltrating the borders of the new state, killing and maiming innocent citizens. The task of bridging the gap between diverse communities, who were deeply separated by language, education, customs and habits, was proving more complex and draining than expected. The world had watched and applauded their victory, but once the blood stopped flowing and the drama drew to a close, they turned away to attend to their own, leaving the state to struggle for its survival. That was the reality.

April for the Ben Hods was a month of anniversaries, both happy and sad. Gidon had died in April, Tanya was born in April, Tel Tanya was created in April and Passover usually fell in April. The year was 1953 and Israel was approaching its fifth anniversary as an independent state. It was also nearly four years since Basha's departure.

Tanya's thirteenth birthday fell a week before Passover and was to be celebrated in Bet Enav, followed by a dinner at Benji's house in Caesarea. The children were off for a vacation and the whole family arrived early in the afternoon. All the children from the village, whom Tanya had known since she was a small child, were invited as well, and to Deborah's delight they all came.

It was a lovely spring day and a large table was set up in the garden in Bet Enav. Due to the shortage of food in the country, the party fare was meager, but Tova did bake a cake and Naomi brought some homemade cookies, prepared by the settlers in Tel Tanya as a gift for their namesake.

Michael and Deborah settled themselves on the front porch and watched the children at play. Uri was clearly the leader, organizing the games and keeping the festivities at a high pitch. To their relief, Tanya seemed to be enjoying herself.

"Uri's certainly in control of the situation," Michael said with unabashed pride. "He reminds me of Raphael."

Deborah studied Uri for a long moment. "He certainly has Raphael's drive and singlemindedness," she agreed.

"And Tanya looks more like Tamar every day," Michael said, watching Tanya romping about in her white party dress, her hair, loosely tied into a bun, reminiscent of Tamar's hairstyle. "But let's face it, Alexandra is the real beauty. I think she's extraordinary-looking."

Deborah turned her attention to Alexandra. She was by far the most beautiful of all the children. A dark haired-little girl, she too was dressed in white party dress made of organdy, with white satin ribbons in her hair.

"She actually looks like you, you know," Michael continued thoughtfully.

Deborah felt herself blush. "That's a very flattering thing to say." She paused in embarrassment. "You know, Michael, it's been a long time since you've complimented me and I must confess, I like it."

"Well, I assume you know you're beautiful. Everyone else knows it."

She reached over and pressed his arm affectionately. "Thank you, Michael." She felt him stiffen. She withdrew her hand and looked back at the children.

Tanya was now in the middle of the group, her eyes were covered with a napkin and she was groping to catch one of her playmates. Unobtrusively, Alexandra placed herself within Tanya's grasp and Tanya caught her. She laughed triumphantly as she traced the contours of Alexandra's face and identified her. Removing the napkin from her eyes, she leaned over and kissed Alexandra. The little girl threw her arms around Tanya's neck and hugged her.

"That's what you and Tamar must have looked like when you were children."

Deborah felt transported back in time. Tanya and Alexandra could have been Tamar and herself. "They certainly seem to love each other as much as we did."

"Well, the party certainly has been a success. I haven't heard Tanya laugh with such abandon, or appear to be as happy, in a long time," Michael said soberly. "I worry about her, you know. She appears to be quite strong, but

I wonder about that strength and how long she can hold out." He turned to Deborah. "Do you think Basha will ever come back?"

The question startled her. They avoided mentioning Basha, the subject being too painful.

"The doctor in Warsaw keeps saying he's hopeful. But somehow I don't believe him. I don't really understand all he says. And frankly, after all this time . . ." She stopped and bit her lip. "It sounds to me as though he's trying to tell us that she's hopelessly insane." She looked over at her husband. "You haven't heard from him, have you?"

"No, I would have told you if I had."

"Maybe Yanosh will come back with some news," she said slowly, "He just arrived back from Europe. He knew it was Tanya's birthday and he wanted to see her. I invited him to dinner at Benji's."

"For someone as busy as he is, it's quite a sacrifice, I'm sure." Michael made no attempt to hide his sarcasm. "Not that I mind his not coming around. As far as I'm concerned, he spent far too much time with Tanya after Basha left."

"That's ridiculous," Deborah countered. "He loves her and wanted to comfort her."

Without reacting to her words, Michael continued to stare at the children, and Deborah wondered if he was jealous of Tanya's relationship with Yanosh. Out of the corner of her eye, she could see him lower his head to his chest, his eyes half-closed as though hiding an inner hurt.

"In fact, I've often wondered why he stopped coming around as often as he used to" she asked cautiously. "Did you have a fight with him?"

"Hardly. And in all fairness, he has been traveling to Europe a great deal and he's been truly busy," Michael relented, and Deborah still had the feeling that Michael was deeply resentful of Yanosh.

Dusk was settling in and the guests began to leave.

Deborah walked over to bid them farewell. She also wanted to be away from Michael's pain.

When the last guest departed, she instructed the children to go wash up and be ready for Benji when he came to fetch them for dinner.

Then turning to Michael, she said almost pleadingly, "Michael, please be civil with Yanosh, if only for Tanya's sake. She does love him."

Benji's house was built in the middle of a large garden, above the white sands of the Mediterranean shore. Set apart from other houses, it was ostentatiously big, with a carved Spanish-style front door and extra-large picture windows. It was out of place in a country where people were still living in temporary shelters, waiting to be placed into some permanent housing. From the first time she saw it, the house embarrassed Deborah and she blamed Michael for permitting their son to build it, but there was little she could do about it. In spite of her determination to take a greater interest in their business affairs, she was too busy caring for Tanya, working with the new immigrants and running her own home. Michael was in charge and he must have caved in to Benji's demands.

The interior of the house was as pretentious as the exterior. The furniture was overscaled, even for the large rooms. The upholstered pieces were covered with velvets and colorful tapestries. The wooden pieces were dark oak and the paintings, in elaborate gilded frames, were in poor taste.

Ruth, dressed in a hostess gown, greeted them at the door and was effusive in her manner. Deborah watched her as she kissed the children and led Tanya into the living room. Deborah followed them and wondered about her daughter-in-law. What had happened to the simple shy, unassuming young woman who married Benji? She still loved Benji, of that Deborah was sure, but the Ruth who was mistress of this ridiculous house was not the same girl he had married. Benji was probably responsible for the transformation. She made a mental note to discuss Benji with Michael. There was something wrong with the way Benji was living and she did not like it.

Yanosh drove up shortly after they arrived and the joy with which Tanya greeted him brought tears to Deborah's eyes. Tanya had enjoyed her party in Bet Enav, but once the children were gone, she grew silent. She was withdrawn on the trip to Caesarea. Ruth's gift of a diary bound in olive-tree wood brought a small smile to her lips but did not erase the unhappiness. Seeing Yanosh wiped away the sadness.

Deborah, sitting on one side of Yanosh at the dinner table with Tanya on his other side heard the child chatting happily about her party and her activities in general. She listened halfheartedly, wondering if Tanya would inquire about her mother. Yanosh appeared to be interested in Tanya's chatter but he was unusually subdued. Deborah looked over at Michael. He was watching Yanosh and she got the feeling that he too was waiting to see if the inevitable question would come.

To everyone relief, the question was never asked and as the meal came to an end, Uri stood up and asked if they could go out and play.

"You can play in the garden, but only in the garden," Ruth warned.

The children scrambled for the door, except for Tanya. She was staring down at her plate, deep in thought.

"Come on, lazybones." Uri came around and pulled Tanya up, almost roughly, but it was clear that he sensed her mood and was determined to cheer her up. "You and I will be a team and Alexandra, Danny and Rachel will compete against us. Okay?"

She followed him out, leaving the grownups staring after them in uncomfortable silence. All had been waiting for Tanya to ask about Basha and were awed by her restraint.

"How are things in Europe?" Michael turned to Yanosh. "I see that we've submitted a new exchange program with Russia."

"Yes, I'm glad to say they're considering it and are sending a special delegation to discuss it with us."

"Why do we need them here?" Benji asked. "A bunch of communists who want to impose a way of life on us that is foreign and stifling."

"Not necessarily," Yanosh said quietly. "Especially now that Stalin is dead, I think we can learn a great deal from the Russians and can benefit from their help."

"I'm satisfied with the United States and Western European influence. Capitalism is far more to my liking," Benji answered adamantly.

"For you that's great," Jack interceded. "But there are an awful lot of hungry and needy people here who haven't got the benefit of your resources." He did not sound resentful. It was a statement of fact.

"You're not doing too badly at Tel Tanya," Benji shot back.

"We're struggling," Jack said angrily. "We're being shot at night and day by the Syrians from the Golan Heights. Our children sleep in shelters and we are overcrowded with new immigrants in need of a place to live and food to eat."

"You'll manage," Benji said expansively. "And as for the new immigrants, they're making a lot of demands on us here in Caesarea. They're all over the place. They don't speak the language and every waiter claims to have been a banker in Europe before the war, or something equally important, and every maid pretends she was mistress of some manor back in her country. It's utterly ridiculous. Then we have the ones from the Arab countries, who are incapable of maintaining any sort of work schedule and, since they didn't have it any better where they came from, figure we owe them villas."

"Benji, stop it," Michael said sharply. "We've fought for a homeland for all Jews. That was the whole idea behind the struggle and you can't suddenly turn around and say the Jews coming here are a burden to you."

"Well, they are." Benji became defiant. "They're unskilled labor and if you must know the truth, I wish I could hire some Arabs to do my work, as I used to. At least they're cheaper."

Deborah listened and her heart ached. This was her son speaking. This was the grandson of Marek Danziger, who was brought up on a dream of a Jewish homeland. This was the young man who had fought the Arabs threatening to annihilate the Jews of Palestine, had gloried in the victory and was now angry that his life was being disrupted.

"You don't seem to have suffered much," Yanosh said casually.

"I suspect that if we had the Russians here, I would suffer," Benji countered. "I repeat, I think we should ally ourselves with the West."

"I don't know that we have to take a stand on that," Michael interrupted before Yanosh could answer. "But I do agree with Benji on one point. I don't really want to depend on Russia for my survival. Do you?"

"We have a great deal in common with the Russians, with their way of life, their music, their literature and with their ideology," Yanosh answered.

"They keep blackmailing us every time we do something they don't like," Benji said angrily.

"So will the West," Yanosh answered.

"But we can talk to the West. They listen to us. We have partners in the West. There is a large Jewish community in the Western world who can plead our case. The Jewish community in Russia has been silenced." Michael said quietly but forcefully.

"Stalin, as I said, is dead."

"Not good enough," Benji said.

"But Russia and the West are not the only allies we could look to." Yanosh spoke carefully. "There's China. Almost a billion people . . ."

"Oh, that's an interesting thought." Michael laughed. "When did you come up with that one?"

Yanosh smiled sadly. "Listen to us. We used to argue about what method to use to fight the British. Then we debated about how best to deal with the Arabs. And when the war ended, we fought to bring as many Jews as possible to the new homeland. Now our dream has come true and we're fighting about what kind of society we will create." He paused and looked around. "And in a way this is a far more serious fight, because if we can't resolve this internal fight now, we shall defeat ourselves from within. We'll be doomed."

"To survive and see a dream come true during one's lifetime can prove to be a greater burden than the fight to achieve it." Michael spoke softly and with great restraint, but he was staring at Yanosh strangely and Deborah had the feeling that the argument he was having with Yanosh had not started that evening.

"Mommy," Daniel ran in and rushed toward Naomi. "It's awfully dark out and they don't have a shelter for us to sleep in." He pressed his little body against hers. "What if the Arabs come tonight and attack us?"

Naomi picked up her son and hugged him. "Is this the dream come true?" she asked sadly, looking around her.

"How right you are," Yanosh answered. "Our dream has not yet been achieved. We are at the beginning of the struggle to make it happen."

"Father, I'd like to talk to you." Benji turned to Michael. "Could you come into my study?"

Michael hesitated briefly but stood up and followed his son out.

Naomi, Ruth and Jack walked into the living room and a maid started clearing the dishes, leaving Deborah alone with Yanosh.

"Would you walk with me on the beach?" Yanosh asked.

She was startled by the request. For some reason she did not want to go.

"I have something to tell you and I'd like us to be alone," he said.

The sound of the children playing could be heard as they walked slowly along the water's edge. It was a dark, moonless night, with only the stars blinking in the sky. Deborah was unduly conscious of how isolated Benji's house was.

"God, it's quiet out here," she murmured. "Frighteningly so."

"Basha's dead," Yanosh said.

For a minute the words did not register. Then, as the full impact of what he said struck her, Deborah felt her head begin to spin and she lost her balance. Yanosh caught her and held her to him. She did not know how long she rested in his embrace but after the first shock of the news wore off, the tears started steaming down her cheeks.

"How?" she whispered through her tears. "How and when and why, for God's sake? Why?"

"She committed suicide a week ago."

Deborah pulled away. "Suicide?"

Yanosh lowered his eyes. "She went mad when she found out that her parents collaborated with the Nazis. It took her months before anyone would even talk to her about her parents. But finally someone, somewhere told her about them. She had a nervous breakdown and was hospitalized. She never recovered. The doctors tried to help her, but they could not save her. In a way, she's better off dead. The burden was too great for her to carry."

"Did she suspect her parents while she was here?" Deborah asked.

"I think she did. That's the reason she kept questioning General Anders and other Polish officers. Although she did it subtly." He shook his head sadly. "But suspecting is one thing. Finding out was too much for her."

"But she wasn't responsible for what her parents did," Deborah cried out in desperation.

"Who knows? Guilt by association? They were her parents and she saw what happened because of the actions of people like them." He shuddered. "What a nightmare her life must have been. Loving Gidon as she did and living a lie about not being Jewish. Then Gidon dying as he did. And through it all, suspecting her parents' participation in the Holocaust, but not being sure. And finally finding out the truth."

"Did you know about her parents?" Deborah whispered.

"Yes, I knew. I've known her father since my college days. He was my professor. A brilliant man, but a diehard anti-Semite. When the Germans came, it was natural for him to join them and serve them."

"And you kept it from Basha?"

"Of course I did. That's why I avoided her. She thought I was angry with her for marrying Gidon without telling him about her religion. It did bother me, at first. But when I saw her devotion to him, how sincere she was in her love for you, your family and the country as a whole, it became so unimportant. So I decided it was better that she go on thinking I was angry with her for not confessing than having to lie to her about her parents." He paused, briefly. "She was a rare human being. I only wish I could have told her that before she died."

They clung to each other in their grief and Deborah was grateful for his closeness. She missed being held and protected. Suddenly she felt him lift her face to his and his lips brushed against her forehead, then her cheeks, then he pressed his mouth down on hers.

"I still love you, Deborah. I can't help it. After all this time, I love you as much as I did the day we met."

She pulled away.

"I'm sorry." He lowered his eyes, but did not let go of her.

"Tanya." Uri's voice broke the silence around them. "Tanya, Ruth told us not to leave the garden."

Deborah and Yanosh looked around and saw Uri running down the beach. Tanya had her back to them and was walking quickly toward Uri.

"How could you do that?" Uri came up to her. "Ruth won't ever trust us again. I promised her we'd only play in the garden." He took her hand and started running toward the house, dragging her behind him.

"Oh, my God. I wonder if she saw us?" Deborah whispered.

Yanosh let go of her. "I don't know. It's very dark out."

"We'd better go back."

They walked quickly toward the house.

"How will we break the news to her?" Yanosh asked as they mounted the steps leading to the house.

"Let's discuss it with Michael. He might have an idea as to how to do it. I'm at a total loss."

"Do you think she understands what she saw, if she did see us?"

Deborah smiled. "Oh, if she saw us kissing each other, she understood. Believe me." Her mind wandered back to the time when she was in love with David and he was in love with Tamar. She could not remember if she ever saw them embrace, but she would have known what was going on. "Yes, if she saw us, she understood."

When they reached the front gate, Yanosh stopped and held her back.

"Deborah, I'm not really sorry for what happened back there. I do love you. I shall always love you."

"Stop it, Yanosh," she said seriously. "Our love is a wonderful moment to remember. But it in no way diminishes my love for my family, or my love for my husband. And you must believe me when I tell you that I pray that someday you will meet someone and have a full and happy life with her." She tried to smile. "And I admit that I hope I'm not replaced or cut out from that life." Then, taking his hand she said more urgently, "Now, let's start worrying about Tanya. She is the one who needs us now, more than anyone else."

It was past midnight when they arrived back at Bet Enav. Naomi put the children to bed and it was only when she returned that Yanosh broke the news of Basha's death to Michael, Naomi and Jack. The shock was compounded by the news of Basha's Catholicism and her parents' collaboration with the Nazis.

"Poor Tanya," Naomi said through her tears. "To lose her father and now her mother. I wonder how she will take it?"

"She's a Danziger," Deborah said firmly. "She'll take it and with our help, our love and care, she'll overcome the grief."

"She's a thirteen-year-old child," Naomi cried out angrily. "The hell with this 'being a Danziger.' You and father have been grooming her to take Tamar's place, and she can't. She's a human being with her own feelings, her own thoughts, her own personality. 'Being a Danziger'—does that require her to be some sort of heroine? Is she supposed to live up to a legend? How long are you going to go on forcing her to be something she's not?"

Deborah was taken aback by the sudden outburst and was rendered speechless.

"That's unfair," Michael interceded quickly. "I don't think we've imposed anything on Tanya. But she is . . ." He stopped in confusion and was unable to go on.

"She's what?" Naomi burst in, her rage goaded by her deep frustration and sorrow. "Thank God you didn't call her Nili. I thank God you didn't call me Nili. Neither of us could have lived up to that. Jack and I named our daughter Rachel without discussing the name with you. We decided a long time ago that if we had a daughter we wouldn't come to you and wait for your verdict." Her face was flushed and her anger was barely controlled. "I wasn't going to stand around and wait to see if you thought our daughter was worthy of the name. As for Benji, he called his daughter Alexandra because he didn't really care what you thought."

Deborah stood up stiffly and walked to the window, hoping to hide her hurt and pain.

"That's not the way we saw it. We weren't giving out marks for worthiness," Michael said feebly. "It certainly was not our intention."

"I'm sorry," Naomi said, feeling spent. "I didn't mean to hurt you." She walked over to her mother and put her arm around her shoulder. "I'm just so shattered and I'm terribly worried about Tanya. She's very fragile, in spite of all the stiff-upper-lip attitude that Basha tried to impose on her. Basha, in a funny way, was probably more like Tamar than anyone else. She really was a tower of strength." A small, bitter laugh escaped her. "To think that she carried around her suspicions about her parents while helping us, fighting beside us, struggling to help us achieve our cause. Oh God, that poor woman. How tortured she must have been."

"I think we must decide who will break the news to Tanya," Yanosh said firmly, bringing them back to the dreadful present.

"I think my mother, father and you, Yanosh, should be here to tell her what happened. I also think we'll leave Uri here for the night. Tanya loves him and depends on him."

"Naomi is right," Michael agreed quickly. "I'll do the talking, since, in a way, I am now her formal guardian."

Secretly, Deborah felt that Yanosh would have been the better choice, but she kept her opinion to herself. It was clear that Michael was deeply shaken by Basha's death and he felt fully responsible for Tanya. In spite of the misunderstandings between them, Michael had grown to respect Basha and was probably very attached to her. If anything, the realization that she was not Jewish must have made him all the more respectful of her role in their family.

Deborah spent a restless night and by five the next morning she was down in the kitchen making breakfast, when Michael came in from the shack where he went when he needed solitude. Yanosh came in minutes later. They were drinking their coffee in silence when Tanya and Uri came in.

Uri was planning the day's activities while drinking his juice, and Tanya was strangely silent. Deborah kept throwing sidelong looks at her, wondering if she had seen the embrace on the beach. She hoped Tanya had not.

"Uncle Yanosh, did you see my Mommy while you were in Europe?" Tanya asked suddenly.

"Tanya, come over here. I want to tell you something." Michael spoke before Yanosh could answer.

Obediently, she stood up and walked over to him.

He took her hand in his and looked directly at her. She stared back at him, without flinching.

"Tanya, your mother is dead." Michael choked the words out. "She died in the hospital a few days ago. She was very ill and there was nothing the doctors could do to save her."

Tanya continued to stare at him calmly.

"Tanya, did you hear what I said?" Michael asked gently.

She nodded, never taking her eyes off his face. Her expression did not change.

Uri burst out crying and everyone turned to look at him. The shock of seeing Uri cry, rather than Tanya, confused them.

Tanya withdrew her hand from Michael and walked over to Uri, who had his face in his hands, unable to control his sobs. She placed her arms around his shoulders and put her head down on his. Her face was still expressionless.

It took every ounce of Deborah's strength not to burst out crying. She wanted to rush over and take both children in her arms, try to comfort them. She could not move.

Suddenly Uri darted away from Tanya's embrace and rushed out of the kitchen. Tanya looked lost for a moment and then she ran out after him. Deborah, Michael and Yanosh could see them running to the far end of the garden. Uri finally stopped running and threw himself on the grass. Tanya sat down next to him and started stroking his back.

"That may very well be a Danziger reaction, but it is more frightening than anything I could have imagined." Yanosh said, staring out the window.

Deborah looked over at Michael. "What should we do?"

"I think we should let the children work their grief out, on their level of understanding." He turned to Yanosh. "If you possibly can, I would appreciate your staying here for while. At some point they'll come in and look to us for guidance. Let's wait for them to give us a clue as to what they want from us."

Yanosh nodded and the three walked into the living room.

Finally, Tanya and Uri came into the living room.

"If you're driving in that direction, could you take Uri to Tel Tanya?" Tanya asked. Then, without waiting for Yanosh's answer, she turned to Deborah. "And may I go with them?"

"If you'd like," Deborah nodded. Tanya's quiet manner had become disconcerting. "As a matter of fact, you can stay there and come back with Naomi, Jack and the children for Passover."

"Oh no," Tanya said quickly. "I'll come back and sleep here." Her voice was steady, but a hint of panic was there. "I'd rather sleep here."

# CHAPTER
# FORTY-TWO

D EBORAH signed the last letter that her secretary had placed before her and started putting her desk in order. She glanced at her watch. It was two in the afternoon and as always on Friday, it was a short work day. It would give her time to get home, take a bath and rest until Michael and Tanya came home for the evening meal.

She felt good. She had recently been appointed director of the children's centers around the country which helped youngsters adjust to their new environment. The centers had flourished and multiplied and everyone felt she was responsible for their success.

Vaguely, Deborah heard a newsboy calling out the afternoon headlines and she stood up, ready to leave, when her secretary came in.

"There's been a terrible terrorist attack on the Tel Aviv–Haifa highway," the girl cried out frantically.

"Where, when?" Deborah started toward the door.

"I don't know, it was just announced on the radio."

Deborah rushed out of the building and bought a paper at the kiosk.

The black letters made her gasp in dismay. Infiltrators from Jordan had crossed into Israel and had killed several civilians at a the resort town of Netanya. That was only a short distance away from Caesarea!

She ran all the way home. Once there, she rushed over to the phone. Benji's line was busy. She hung up and dialed Michael. The phone rang and while waiting for him to answer, she looked at the paper again. The infiltrators had crossed the Tel Aviv–Haifa highway early that morning undetected and although the army, quickly alerted, chased them and succeeded in killing all the perpetrators, they had effected a serious breach of Israel; security.

She redialed Michael's number. There was no reply and she hung up. Obviously he was not home. He had recently been appointed commander of the home guard in the Bet Enav area and would be out helping restore order in the vicinity. She wondered if he would call her before starting out for Tel

Aviv. She hoped he would and she could ask him to stop in Caesarea and bring Alexandra with him.

She dialed Benji's number again. The line was still busy. It occurred to her that everyone was probably calling relatives now that the news had come out, and the chances of reaching Caesarea were slim.

She threw herself into an armchair and her eyes came to rest on the dateline of the newspaper. It was October 26, 1956.

The mythical seven years!

Michael had once said that every seven years there was bloodletting in the Middle East. Did that mean that they would be facing another war? But formal declarations of war in their part of the world were no longer necessary. The bloodletting never seemed to stop. The Arabs, in spite of their defeat in 1949, had terrorists sniping at Israel constantly. The settlements on the borders were like armed barracks instead of peaceful homes. In recent months the feyayeen activists, known as suicide units, crossing over from Jordan, had grown more fierce and frequent and were hurting the civilian population as never before.

The idea of armed conflict was too distressing. Deborah tried Benji again. Still busy. She dialed Tel Tanya. No one answered. She tried Michael again. No answer. She thought of Tanya. Friday was a short school day. She hurried toward the kitchen, hoping Tova would know where Tanya was.

"She left before I was up this morning," Tova said and looked at the wall clock. "It's only three. She's probably stopped off to talk to some friends." She tried to sound positive, but she too looked worried.

Deborah nodded and went back to the living room.

Concerned as she was for her whole family, she now concentrated on Tanya. In the three years since Basha's death, Tanya had come a long way. Still, in a crisis, Deborah wanted her close to home. She was quite fragile.

Tanya's attachment to Deborah was the only external sign of grief after Basha's death. Otherwise, nothing had changed. As in the past, she never spoke of her mother, nor did she show any curiosity about how Basha had died. She attended school, participated in her afternoon activities, continued with her lessons in piano, dance and French. The only time she displayed emotion was when Deborah was not around. If Grandma was late coming home from an appointment, Tanya would stand at the window fretting nervously, waiting for her return. She refused to fall asleep when Michael and Deborah were out for the evening. Tova would sit up with her and try to amuse her, but her concern for Deborah's welfare could not be assuaged. The melancholy states grew more severe, but the doctors assured them she would outgrow them.

For the first year, Tanya's condition limited Deborah's activities. It also had a profound affect on Michael's life. He was offered a post as ambassador to Canada, but at Deborah's insistence he turned it down.

Tanya's first independent act came when she was fifteen and started working at one of Deborah's children's centers. She was very good at what she did. She became completely involved with the deprived, displaced children and was usually elated after her visits with them. The work gave her a sense of self and Deborah hoped that she would begin to form relationships with children her own age. Until then her only companions were Michael, Deborah and Yanosh. And on the other side of the spectrum were Uri and little Alexandra. And Alexandra, as adorable as she was, was much too young to be a companion for a teenager.

Thoughts of Alexandra brought Deborah back to the present and she picked up the phone and dialed Benji's number again. It was still busy.

"Anyone home?" Deborah heard Tanya call out. Within seconds she appeared in the doorway, accompanied by Yanosh.

"Deborah, you look like a ghost. What happened?" The girl's face clouded over.

Deborah handed her the paper and looked over at Yanosh. "Did you know about it?"

He nodded and took the paper from Tanya. "Since Egypt, Syria and Jordan agreed on a Joint Arab Command, it's gotten worse. There's no doubt about it," he said grimly.

"But where was the army?" Tanya asked indignantly.

"We're only human," Yanosh answered.

"Alexandra," Tanya cried out. "Have you spoken to Benji?" She asked frantically. "Are they all right?"

"His line is busy." Deborah said.

Tanya picked up the phone and dialed. "It's still busy," she said and hung up.

"What happens now?" Deborah asked, looking over at Yanosh.

Yanosh shrugged and sat down wearily. "Maybe Michael can tell you. I really don't know."

Deborah was surprised by his answer and his manner. It struck her that she had not heard a car drive up before he and Tanya entered the house. She also realized he looked haggard and troubled. They had not seen him in quite a while and the change in him was staggering. Her eyes wandered over to Tanya. What was he doing, at that hour, with Tanya?

"Michael should be here shortly." Deborah hid her confusion and turned to Tanya. "And how was school today?" she asked conversationally.

"Deborah, you forgot. We went on a field day with my group. Yanosh was our guide and it was wonderful."

"Of course," Deborah said with relief. The youth movement Yanosh had encouraged Tanya to join had been one of the most effective antidotes to Tanya's dependence on the family. "And you enjoyed it?"

"It was wonderful. It's a new settlement of young couples near Tiberias, and Yanosh is helping establish it."

"Sounds fascinating and we'll hear all about it at dinner. Now go and get ready so that we can sit down as soon as Michael arrives."

"Can Yanosh stay?" Tanya asked.

"Of course he can, if he wants to," Deborah answered. "Now run along."

Deborah watched her leave. She was truly an unusual-looking girl, with her long legs exposed beneath her short shorts, her slim waist cinched by a coarse leather belt and her long neck graceful above the collarless white T-shirt. Her long blond braid had come undone and the fine wisps floated like a halo around her head.

"She's really a remarkably beautiful child," Deborah said with admiration.

"She's no longer a child," Yanosh said seriously. "Young woman is more like it."

"Good God, she's only sixteen years old."

"Where were you at sixteen?" Yanosh smiled.

Deborah blushed. "I thought I was a young woman, but everyone treated me like a child." Then, growing serious, she looked directly at Yanosh. "What's wrong, Yanosh? You look . . ." She did not know how to finish the question. But he was not the Yanosh she knew.

"I look what?" he asked.

"I don't really know." She stopped. "I haven't seen you in ages and I've been so busy and involved that I don't know what's going on. Where have you been? Traveling? And this settlement? It's a wonderful idea, but do you really have the time for it?"

Before he could answer, they heard a car drive up and stop in front of the house.

"That must be Michael." Deborah said with relief and was about to ask Yanosh where his car was when Michael came into the room.

"Was the road safe?" Deborah asked the minute she saw him.

"With the cow gone, the barn was properly protected," Michael said unhappily. "That road was so crowded with the military, you'd think they were going to war."

"But how could it happen?"

"Suicide squads are the latest fashion in Egypt and the Arab world. That's how it happened." He looked over at Yanosh for the first time. "What do you think?" he asked coldly.

"I don't have opinions about this sort of thing anymore."

"No, I guess you wouldn't. But I'll tell you what I think. I think we should bomb the hell out of them and teach them a lesson once and for all."

"And you probably will," Yanosh answered.

Deborah was surprised that they were talking like men from different camps.

"In any event, it's Friday and I must be running along." Yanosh turned to

Deborah. "I really do have an engagement this evening. Say goodbye to Tanya for me." He bowed formally to Michael and walked out.

"What was that all about?" Deborah asked the minute Yanosh left. "*We. You.* To listen to you two, you'd think you were enemies."

"What was he doing here?"

"Tanya's youth group went up to Tiberias. Apparently Yanosh is involved in organizing a settlement . . ." She stopped. The whole thing made no sense. "What is going on with Yanosh?" she asked.

"I don't really know," Michael answered and picked up one of Tanya's books, which the girl had dropped on a coffee table. "Well, I'll be damned. The Russian Revolution. *Das Kapital* by Karl Marx. And here is beginner's Russian. Oh, my God."

"What are you looking at?" Deborah reached out for one of the books. "What is this?" She looked up at Michael.

"Well, what did you expect? She spends all her time listening to Yanosh and you know what his politics are. He certainly does not express the views of the present government here or the aspirations of our people. In a way, I feel he's a traitor to this country."

"When did it happen?"

"I can't pinpoint the day. It happened at a meeting of our Central Committee. He presented his views, which were in total contrast to everything we stand for and have planned on. He did it cleverly and several members were actually convinced. And then he walked out—I assure you, to everyone's relief. That was that. No drum-beating, no press releases. Just the end of a career." Michael stopped briefly. "But I've always wondered about his sudden appearance on the scene, way back when. Remember? He arrived one day from Siberia and . . ." He shrugged his shoulders. "I always suspected him, but after that meeting I could swear he was a Russian agent."

"He's not a Russian agent," Deborah said furiously. "He may have different views from yours or mine for that matter, but that does not make him a traitor or a Communist. Besides, Russia is on our side."

"For how long?" Michael sneered. "We've been in existence for eight years and look at their record where we're concerned. Every time we do anything that displeases them, they threaten to break relations with us. I don't feel we can trust them in a real crisis."

"But surely you don't think Yanosh would side with them if there was a showdown?"

"I don't know. This latest terrorist act demands that we strike back. And with Nasser nationalizing the Suez Canal, I wouldn't be surprised if the British did something as well. Who knows, maybe it will be a combined effort between us and them. The Russians, I assure you, will not be pleased—certainly not with us."

"The British and us in a combined operation?" Deborah was staggered. "I just don't believe that we'd be foolhardy enough to try anything with them."

"I'm sure Yanosh would agree with you, even though you come to your conclusions from very different points of view."

"How will the United States react?" Deborah ignored his last remark.

"Foster Dulles, the secretary of state of the United States, is no friend of ours." Michael grew serious. "But at least we can discuss our situation with them. President Eisenhower is an honest man. There will be no talking to the Russians. But why go that far? The Russians are trying to get into the Middle East and they're doing it by supplying arms to the Arab world."

She could not argue the point. "I'm frightened," Deborah whispered, but she didn't know why. Was it her concern for Yanosh or her worry about the survival of her country?

"About Yanosh," she said. "I haven't seen him in a long time and he is very different. Where is he living and what is he living on?"

"I believe he has a little flat in Tel Aviv and he gives lectures around the country and writes." He stopped and looked down at the book he was holding. "But now that he's beginning to influence Tanya's thinking, I think we should stop this relationship."

*Stop the relationship.* The phrase struck Deborah and she lowered her eyes. Yanosh was a surrogate father to Tanya, she thought desperately. Tanya adored Yanosh, had loved him from the time she was a little girl. Had that childish adulation developed into an infatuation? Or love? A woman's love for a man? And Yanosh? How did he feel about Tanya? She had been so grateful to Yanosh for helping them with Tanya, that she ignored the fact that Tanya had grown up in the last three years.

Deborah felt uncomfortable with these new speculations. They made her angry. Worse, she knew she was jealous. But to be jealous of Tanya? Deborah forced the idea from her mind. She was simply overwrought and her imagination had run away with her.

"Where is Tanya, anyway?" Michael asked.

"She's dressing for dinner," Deborah said absently.

Michael picked up the paper and the events around the country came back to her.

"Michael, I want to talk to you about Benji's house."

"Oh, no. You're not going to start that nonsense again," Michael said with exasperation. "When will you begin to accept the fact that he can afford it?"

"No, no. I'm not talking about that. What I'm concerned about is that his house is so isolated. The whole area is." She indicated the paper. "Why, anyone could . . ."

"Deborah, we're all fully aware of security. I assure you that his house is well guarded by us and by the community in which he lives." He put the paper down. "As a matter of fact, I stopped by there before coming home. They're fine and Alexandra sends you and Tanya love and kisses." He smiled for the first time. "That child really is gorgeous."

"And what's happening in Tel Tanya?"

"Four men killed yesterday and they're having a service tonight. Naomi tells me that Daniel has written a musical tribute to them which is quite something. It seems that Daniel is quite a composer and pianist and the kibbutz is seriously considering sending him to the United States for a musical education."

"I haven't heard him play in quite a while," Deborah said, feeling guilty about the omission. "What about Uri?"

"He's practically a general and Jack is keeping a very careful eye on him." Talking about the children seemed to relax him. "But the one who has a real problem is Rachel."

"Rachel?"

"She's ten years old and she's engaged to Jonah." His face broke into a smile. "Her problem is, what to call her fourth child. Jonah liked Gila and she wants Dafna."

Deborah choked back the tears. She had seen the family in September when they came up to Bet Enav for the New Year celebration, but she was so preoccupied with her work, with Tanya, with preparations for the holiday meals, that she spent little time with each individual child.

"And you Michael? How are you?" she asked softly.

"I am beginning to make peace with myself," he said and picked up the paper again.

"I think I'll take a bath and rest up before supper," she said and rushed from the room.

Michael watched the door through which she went long after she was gone. His children and grandchildren had accepted him and he was grateful for that. But when it came to Deborah, whom he loved more than life itself, the barriers were still up. He was fully aware that it was he who was keeping them there, as though he had a need to go on being the little boy standing alone outside the synagogue, in Metulah. He pinned it on David Larom's death. No one remembered David Larom or how he died, but to Michael, the incident was still alive and the fact that he could never really prove his innocence ate into his soul. In a way he was convinced that it was God's way of punishing him for his misdeed that day of his bar mitzvah, so many years back.

Finished with her bath, Deborah seated herself in front of her dressing table and started creaming her face. She had been neglectful of her family and she was determined to make it up to them. She would ask Michael to drive her up to Tel Tanya and they could stop by at Benji's house on the way back. They could do it over Hanukkah, which was only a few weeks away. It would also give her time alone with Michael. He spent too much time alone in that shack of his and she actually knew very little about him these days. She winced. She did love him, and after all these years she still desired him. Yanosh was the bonus. But Michael was her husband.

She put the jar of cream down and caught sight of herself in the mirror. She leaned over and observed herself more closely.

Her robe had fallen open and before covering herself up, she glimpsed her nakedness. She was still quite slender but her small breasts were no longer firm. Still, her shoulders and neck were relatively smooth. Slowly her eyes wandered to her face. In the dim light, she looked younger than her years, except for her eyes. The deep-set, dark eyes staring at her were eyes that had seen too much pain, too much hardship, too many horrible sights and they were lusterless and wary. They were like aging lenses of a camera that had taken too many pictures and had worn out.

"Deborah." Tanya peered into the room. "May I come in?"

"Certainly," Deborah said and picking up her brush she ran it through her hair.

Tanya walked over to her and, leaning down, put her arms around Deborah and buried her head in her shoulder.

Deborah reached up to touch Tanya's hair and the girl looked up. The picture of the two of them in the mirror made her catch her breath. Staring back at her was a young, beautiful Tamar leaning over an older woman. At that moment she knew, with a certainty that astounded her, that Tanya had replaced her in Yanosh's life. She remembered telling Yanosh that she wanted him to meet someone and have a full life with her. But she had not meant Tanya.

Deborah disengaged herself from Tanya's embrace and turned away from the mirror. She had to regain her composure.

Tanya threw herself into an armchair and flung her hands up in the air, sighing contentedly.

"Have you spoken to Uri recently?" Tanya asked suddenly. "It's been ages since I've seen him."

"Michael says he's practically a general. Very involved in his military training and I'm worried sick about it. He's only fifteen."

"Uri will be fine. He's brave and smart."

Deborah smiled. "You're probably right."

"And the others?"

Deborah related what Michael had told her, ending with Michael's description of Alexandra.

"How I love that little girl," Tanya said dreamily. "Frankly, if anyone should have been named Nili, it was she. Young as she is, she's a rebel." She smiled to herself. "If I have a little girl, I hope she is like her."

"Well, that will be a while yet. You've got to graduate from school and do your army duty, and Michael and I would like you to go to university. A woman should have a career. That's important."

"Why? You didn't."

"Different times, different attitudes." Deborah stood up and walked over to her clothes closet. "But that's the future. As a matter of fact, I'm going to ask Michael to drive me up to Tel Tanya. Would you like to come along?"

"When will you be going?"

"Sometime during Hanukkah. It should be fun."

"I won't be able to join you. I'm busy."

Deborah looked around. Tanya was leaning back, staring at the ceiling. "Why not?"

"I'm going with Yanosh. He's giving a series of lectures in Tiberias."

"You're what?"

Tanya, hearing the anger, sat up. "I'm going with Yanosh—"

"I heard you." Deborah interrupted. "I heard you and it's out of the question. If you don't understand why, he certainly should." She stopped, trying to control herself. "Did he invite you to go with him?"

"Why shouldn't he?"

"Did he?"

"Oh, Deborah, stop being a prude." Tanya stood up, tall, proud and more secure than Deborah had ever seen her. "I'm going and I'm sorry you're upset, but I am going." She started toward the door, stopped and turned around. "Deborah, I'm happy. Don't take it away," she whispered and ran from the room before Deborah could answer.

Dressing quickly, Deborah rushed into the living room. Finished with relating her talk with Tanya she waited for Michael to lash out at Yanosh and his impropriety. Instead, he walked over to the radio and turned it on, saying nothing.

"You're very calm about this whole affair," she fumed.

"Well, you're overreacting."

"You mean you'd let her go?"

"Forbidding her to go is not the solution." He sounded tired.

"Well, what do you suggest?"

"I think you should talk to Yanosh. You would have a greater impact, I'm sure."

She looked at him suspiciously. "What do you mean?"

"You know what I mean." His voice softened.

His manner flustered her. Had he guessed her feelings for Yanosh? Worse, did he know? And if he did, how long had he known?

"I think it would be more appropriate if you talked to him," she said stiffly.

"I don't. He would misunderstand my motives." He looked at her for a long moment before continuing. "The fact is, I disagree with Yanosh politically, but I trust him as a man, as a human being, as a friend of this family. I'm sorry it all happened. I think Tanya is infatuated with him and it's bad for her. He's old enough to be her father. But I wouldn't suspect him of behaving improperly with her. All I can do is pray she outgrows this childish crush. And I hope he is doing everything he can to discourage it."

"You're telling me you would let her go on that trip?" She could not keep the hysteria out of her voice.

He lowered his eyes. He could not bear to see her pain. He could feel her loss and he loved her enough to want to spare her the humiliation of being usurped by a mere child, in Yanosh's affections, but he dared not let on that he knew any of what was happening to her. "Deborah, I don't want her to go. I am prepared to forbid the trip, but it won't do any good. I do expect you to talk to Yanosh. Spare me that."

# CHAPTER
# FORTY-THREE

ANYA lay on the narrow cot and listened to the breathing of the girl on the cot next to hers. The room was in darkness and she could hear the sound coming from the lake, its waves lapping gently against the shore. It was peaceful and she felt content. She wondered where Yanosh was. He had made a brilliant speech to the young audience who had come to hear him and was applauded enthusiastically when he finished.

It had been a thrilling experience for her, made all the more exciting since she was present when he announced that he was formally joining the Communist Party; that he was embarking on a new journey, which he hoped would benefit Israel and insure the country's survival. He spoke at great length about Israel's attack on the Suez Canal, understood the intention of the Israelis to stop the Egyptians from their murderous infiltrations and their constant attacks on Israel's armed forces and civilians. But he derided the government for its partnership with the French and British in that action. The British, who had treated the Jewish people so shabbily for so many years, were hardly reliable allies. He pointed out that the debate in the United States condemning Israel for its action proved that Israel could not depend solely on the Americans and that Israel must, by necessity, look to the eastern bloc of European countries for balance. He mentioned Russia specifically as a necessary ally to insure Israel's survival. The audience, aware of Russia's missile threat against Israel while the Suez Canal war was going on, became restive at his suggestion, but his brilliant oratory claimed them and Tanya felt that when he was through speaking, they understood and appreciated his views.

Tanya felt very proud of him. She felt privileged to be his friend. Although he had not told her of his decision to join the communist party, she had suspected that he was planning to doing it. And he had done it that night and she was there. She was sure he wanted her there.

She closed her eyes, hoping for sleep. Instead, the old feelings of doubt and insecurity came back. And as in the past they took control of her and she was helpless in the face of them. It had been a while since the old nightmare had recurred, but she felt certain that it would surface that night and she was frightened of it. Staring at the darkened ceiling, she found herself reliving it.

Deborah was on the beach and someone Tanya could not identify was struggling with her. She wanted to run toward Deborah and help her; instead, she turned and walked away. Then she would awaken.

Tanya broke into a cold sweat. She loved Deborah more than life itself, yet in the dream, in Deborah's moment of need, she had abandoned her. As she had done every time, Tanya closed her eyes and tried to identify the man who had been trying to harm Deborah. As always, the image eluded her.

And now she had defied Deborah and had come away with Yanosh. Would Deborah punish her and abandon her? And if she did, would Yanosh stand by her? Or would he too abandon her? She began to shake. She loved him so much, needed him so desperately. Needed to be at his side at all times. Did he feel that way about her? Sometimes she thought he did. But then there were times when he treated her like the little girl he had known since she was three.

Her fears grew. The truth was that Yanosh had not actually invited her to come along on this trip. He had spoken about it, seemed nervous and preoccupied with the event, but it was her decision to join him. She insisted and he finally gave in, although he did not seem overjoyed at the idea. Yet once they arrived at the kibbutz, he introduced her to everyone with pride, she thought, and when making his speech he did glance over at her from time to time. Then he walked her and her roommates over to their dormitory and kissed her lightly on the cheek. He had kissed the other girls, as well. There was no more intimacy in his attitude toward her than there had been toward the others.

She sat up. Was she being a silly little girl after all? The girls in the cots lining the small dormitory, were all fast asleep. She knew none of them and suddenly she was frightened. She rarely slept away from home and when she did, it was usually with Deborah's permission. This time, both Michael and Deborah had disapproved of the trip. Deborah was very upset about it and the fact that she was going with Yanosh did not seem to calm her. Perspiration began running down Tanya's back, her palms were wet and her head began to ache. The feeling of panic, which seemed to have disappeared recently, was creeping up, taking over. She covered her eyes, hoping to hide from it. She did not want to have a relapse. Not tonight. She would spoil Yanosh's celebration. The shaking grew worse and she could not control it. She threw herself back on the pillow and put her hands to her mouth, trying to stifle a cry.

"Are you all right?" The girl in the next cot asked and Tanya realized that she had cried out after all.

"I'm fine." She was breathing heavily. "I just need some fresh air."

She got out of bed, grabbed her shorts and shirt and, dressing quickly, she ran out of the dormitory.

Once outside, she stopped and wondered where to go. All the houses looked alike, except for the dining room which was still brightly lit. She ran toward it. Yanosh was probably still there. She needed to see him, know he was there, be with someone who knew her. That was the most terrifying thing of all. She needed affirmation of her being.

The dining room was almost empty except for some members of the kibbutz who were sitting around, smoking, drinking tea and debating Yanosh's speech. Some were praising it, others were not as complimentary. When they saw her, they stopped talking.

"Do you know where I could find Yanosh?" she asked from the doorway.

"I saw him walk down to the lake," someone said.

She turned and tried to figure out the direction of the water. The sound of the waves reached her and she ran toward them.

The Sea of Galilee, a calm, flat body of water, gleamed softly in the moonlight. The narrow sandy shore was deserted. She stopped and scanned the length of it. At the far end, sitting on a rock, she saw Yanosh. His head was resting on his hand and he looked like Rodin's *The Thinker.* She raced down the shore, toward him.

He did not hear her approach and she hesitated before touching his shoulder.

"Yanosh?" she whispered.

His head shot up and he looked around, dazed. Realizing who she was, he smiled and reached out to help her up the rock.

"Why aren't you asleep?" He scolded, "It's been a long day and you need your rest."

She leaned against him unself-consciously and his arm encircled her shoulder.

"I promised Deborah I'd take care of you and if you don't get your sleep, you'll be exhausted and possibly fall ill and I'll be blamed for it."

"You spoke to Deborah about taking me?" She pulled away from him. "Why?"

"She is your legal guardian and you, my little one, are still a minor." He answered quickly.

"Oh." Tanya returned to his embrace. "I guess you're right."

Yanosh looked down at the golden-haired girl resting in the crook of his arm and turned his eyes away.

He had spoken to Deborah, but it had not been a happy conversation. She had called him the day before he left and asked to meet with him. She did not say what it was she wanted to talk about and he wondered if she had found out about his decision to commit himself to the Communist Party. He had kept it secret, but there were some people who had anticipated his action and she may have heard about it. He was all geared for a lengthy explanation, which he had practiced for a long time.

It was therefore a shock when she began with the accusation that he was taking Tanya, without their permission, on this lecture tour. He had actually discouraged Tanya and assumed the matter was settled.

They were sitting in a small café on a tree-lined street, just before lunch. They were alone.

"Well, don't look so shocked," Deborah said indignantly. "Tanya told me you asked her to go."

In spite of himself, he began to laugh. "You are more beautiful when you're angry than when you're being the perfect wife, mother, grandmother and hostess."

"Well, I am a grandmother, I can't help it. Time will do it to all of us." She was nearly in tears.

He reached over and touched her cheek. "Don't cry, my darling. There's nothing to cry about. You're the most beautiful grandmother I've ever seen. And to me you'll never be older than the woman I met in the Alps." He looked at her adoringly.

"Did you ask Tanya to go with you?" she asked again, uncertainty making her voice quaver. In retrospect, she recalled that when asking Tanya if Yanosh had invited her to go, Tanya had evaded giving her a direct answer.

"No, my beloved Deborah," he said wearily. "Although she may have misinterpreted something I said to her."

Deborah relaxed visibly and a small smile appeared on her face. "I feel like a fool," she said and lowered her head. "Yanosh, I hate to say it, but I was so jealous."

He did not answer. Instead he reached over and lifted her face to his. "You will never have a reason to be jealous of any woman I happen to be with. Even a woman I fall in love with." He paused. "I'm sure you know there have been women in my life, but none have meant anything to me. Certainly none could replace that special place you have in my heart. Ever."

"But Yanosh, I do want you to meet someone you can care for." She was sincere in what she was saying, but what she could not bring herself to say was that she could not bear for the woman to be Tanya.

"Deborah, things will be happening in my life in the very near future that will puzzle and upset you." His tone changed and she studied his face carefully. "What they are matters not at the moment. You will hear about them soon enough. You are the only person I am saying this to and the reason is that I want you to trust me. I know what I'm doing and I have no choice. That you must believe."

They were silent for a while; finally Deborah asked again about Tanya and her wish to join him.

"I don't think it's a good idea that she come along," he said quietly. "Not on this trip. It's the beginning of a long journey for me and I don't really want her to be there. It could upset her."

"You'll have to be the one to tell her that. She won't believe me."

"I'll try to reach her this afternoon."

They stood up and she came close to him. He ran his fingers over her face tenderly. There was a look in his eyes of longing verging on desperation. For a minute Deborah thought he was going to say something, then he turned abruptly and walked away.

He could not reach Tanya before he left and was genuinely surprised when he saw her at the bus station. Her being there upset him and yet seeing her gave him a sense of continuity. He was severing all contacts with his past. He was turning his back on every one of the people he had grown to know, love and respect. None would ever forgive him. He had known it would happen when he made his decision.

Now seeing Tanya beside him on the lonely rock in Tiberias, staring at him with complete trust and love, saddened him yet reassured him. Deborah would surely misunderstand. Tanya, however, would always feel the same about him—his political views notwithstanding. He felt an uncanny feeling of gratitude to this woman-child. This beautiful, innocent human being.

"Yanosh, I love you." Tanya's voice interrupted his thoughts. The phrase shook him. But the voice speaking the phrase was even more upsetting. It was not a little girl speaking. It was a woman proclaiming her love for a man.

"Oh, now, little one. I love you too." He pushed her gently from him.

"No, you don't understand, Yanosh. I'm in love with you. I want to spend my life with you. I want to be by your side, always." She licked her lips with her tongue nervously. "I want to marry you. I want to have your children. I want you. I want to belong to you."

"Tanya, stop it." Yanosh stood up angrily. "Stop this nonsense immediately." He was breathing heavily and he wanted to run from her, run from what she was saying. He felt rooted to the spot.

"Stop what, Yanosh?" She stood up and coming over to him, she put her arms around his neck. "Stop what? Stop loving you? Stop wanting you?" She put her cheek against his and he felt her lips brush against his ear. "That would be like asking me to stop breathing. You came into my life when I was a little girl and you've been part of it ever since. You can't imagine how I wanted to grow up and have you waiting for me. And you did." She leaned back and smiled. "You may not have known it, but you were waiting for me." Her lips were soft and moist when she pressed them to his.

He tried to pull away, but her arms held him and slowly his arms circled her waist and he pulled her toward him. Her youthful body pressed against his and he could feel himself losing his grip on his senses. He was swept up in her love, in her warmth, in her youth, her desire. His lips touched her brows, her eyes, her cheeks, her lips, her neck. He heard her deep, joyous laugh as he pressed his head against her breasts. His lips circled the firm young nipples and he felt her body sway sensuously. Then they were lying on the hard rock, his sex pressing into her slowly, carefully, while he still held back his desire.

"I love you," she kept murmuring. "I love you. And I'll never leave you. Ever."

He made an attempt to withdraw from her, but her body held him prisoner. Her softness seemed to possess him and he lost all control.

When he came back to himself, the moon had disappeared behind a cloud and he felt as though he were coming out of a dream. He looked down at the pale, beautiful girl who was staring at him with total devotion and admiration. A beautiful young girl looking at her lover with innocence and unquestioning love.

"You do love me," she whispered. "I know it."

"How do you know it?" He barely recognized his voice.

"You kissed my forehead like a father, then my cheeks and even my eyes. But that was paternal. Then you kissed my mouth and my neck and then you kissed my body like a man in love. Thank you, Yanosh. Thank you for loving me."

"Oh, my poor, darling Tanya." He buried his head in her shoulder, overcome with shame. He had never made love to any woman with as much passion as he had just felt. Now he wondered how he could face himself. Yes, he did love Tanya. He had not realized it, but he loved her and desired her. Still he had no right to take this fragile child on the difficult journey that he had to travel. He would be ostracized by everyone for his political decision. He knew it, expected it, and alone he was prepared to live with it, because he had no choice. To impose that existence on Tanya was outrageous. But more important, he felt he had betrayed Deborah. That was something he doubted he could live with.

Withdrawing from her, he sat up and stared out at the water.

Tanya ran her hand across his back. "Yanosh, when can we get married?"

"We can't," he said without turning around.

She sat up slowly. "We can and we will."

He looked over at her. "You don't understand, Tanya. You thought my speech tonight was wonderful. Others thought so too. I'm pleased with that. But after tonight, no one from the world you come from will ever want to speak to me again, except in anger. I shall be looked upon as a traitor. I don't mind that, but I won't have you living that way. It would be hell."

"I live in my own private hell all the time," she said simply. "When I'm not with you, I may as well be dead. For a long time, having Deborah and Michael and even Uri around me helped. But Michael and Deborah have other obligations, which they've put aside for too long because of me, and Uri has his life, as well he should, and now I only feel alive when I'm with you." She paused, searching for words to convince him. "Oh, I sound selfish, but I'm not, truly not. You are alone, as I am. I feel your loneliness as you feel mine. Now you feel you've done something that will further isolate you, so you see, you need me as much as I need you."

She stood up and her lithe, youthful form outlined against the moon lit horizon made him smile with wonder and awe.

"You're like a goddess," he whispered. "You should marry a young, virile, handsome man who can worship you and give you a full and prosperous life."

She looked down at him. "You're handsomer than any man I know." Then kneeling down beside him, she pressed his head to her naked breasts. "And we will have a full and prosperous life, because we'll be together."

"Yanosh Bar Lev Makes It Official. Joins the Communist Party."

Michael glared at the newspaper and slammed it down on the desk. Then he looked up at Yanosh, who was sitting across the desk from him.

"May I ask what you're doing here?" he asked through clenched teeth. "Obviously you haven't come for my approval."

"No, obviously I haven't come for that." Yanosh looked toward the door, wondering if Deborah was about.

"If you're wondering where Deborah is, she's trying to come to terms with your latest pronouncement, added to the fact that Tanya was there with you."

"I do wish she'd come in. What I have to say concerns her too."

"Nothing you can ever say again will concern anyone in this house, I assure you. We look at you as a traitor. As long as you were preaching leftist views, everyone accepted it. To join a party, to ally yourself with a country who supports our enemies . . ." He shook his head. "I would rather Deborah be left out of this meeting." He stopped again. "Now, supposing you tell me what you want and when you leave here, please remember, you are no longer welcome in our home."

"I want to marry Tanya," Yanosh said quietly.

Michael stood up. "If you don't mind, Yanosh, I will pretend I never heard this last foolishness, although it suddenly occurs to me that you are possibly mad. That would account for your behavior." He started toward the door. "I never thought it would come to this, but I must ask you to leave."

Yanosh stood up as well. "Very well. But Tanya and I will be getting married."

Michael closed the door and leaned against it. "Why would you want to do this to a poor, confused girl? Why? She's been lost and wandering in terror through the unknown for so long and only recently has she come back to herself. Why do you want to drag her down again?"

"I can't answer that," Yanosh said. "But I believe that I am the only one who can save her from going back into the depths of despair, as you so aptly described." He waited for Michael to react.

Michael appeared to lose his self-assurance. "That's a rather arrogant statement."

"I wish it weren't so," Yanosh said sadly. "Oh, how I wish it weren't so. But I suspect that I'm right." He paused briefly. "Please, Michael, for the friendship we all shared, call Deborah in. She may understand."

While waiting for Deborah, Yanosh caught sight of Tamar's picture hanging on the wall. They were in Michael's study in Bet Enav and Yanosh realized he had never been in that room before. For a moment he thought it was a picture of Tanya, but quickly realized his mistake.

"Is that Tamar Danziger?" he asked as soon as Michael reentered the room.

Michael looked over at the picture and nodded.

"Tanya looks so much like her, I almost thought it was she."

"Yes, they do look alike, although Tanya is nothing like her." His anger seemed to have evaporated and there was a sadness tinged with loss in his statement. "For a long time we thought she was Tamar reborn, but that was not the case. Tamar was strong, sure of herself, assertive. Almost harsh in her attitude and manner."

"No, that's not Tanya. Tanya is far closer in personality to Deborah. She has Deborah's soul."

Michael turned to look at Yanosh. "Deborah's soul." He murmured. "How true. But unfortunately, she does not have her inner strength." His last words were almost muffled, since Yanosh's statement reaffirmed the deep feeling the man felt for Deborah.

Deborah entered the room and broke the strange mood which the men were in.

Yanosh explained why he was there and her face remained impassive. When he said that he felt he would be the one who could save Tanya, she lowered her eyes.

"I think it's outrageous," Michael interjected.

"Yes, it is," Deborah said quietly, "But Yanosh is probably right. As a matter of fact, I'm sure he's right."

"You'll allow it?"

"Allow?" Deborah laughed. "Our choices are to forbid this union and lose Tanya completely, or to give our consent and hope that Yanosh will be strong enough for both of them."

"Thank you, Deborah." Yanosh was looking at her with open admiration. For the first time since he'd come into their home, he felt he did not have to hide his feelings for Deborah, not even in front of Michael.

Michael walked over to the window, pretending to be absorbed in the scenery and hoping his own pain would not explode in the drama taking place around him.

"You know that Tanya is not Jewish," Deborah said suddenly.

"It really doesn't matter to me," Yanosh answered, relieved that the tacit consent had been given. "We'll fly over to Cyprus and we'll be married by a judge."

"Someone will have to break the news to her," Deborah continued. "About her not being Jewish, I mean. It will be a shock."

"I'll do that," Yanosh assured her.

She looked at him gratefully. He had taken over full responsibility for Tanya and although she felt she had lost them both, suddenly she did not begrudge them the happiness they might find in each other.

"Would you come to the wedding?" Yanosh asked haltingly.

Deborah hesitated. She was giving Yanosh up and now she was being asked to deliver his bride to him.

"It would mean a great deal to me and it would give Tanya a sense of continuity, a feeling that you were not deserting her."

"Of course I'll come." Deborah answered.

Yanosh looked over at Michael, who still had his back to them. "Michael, you wouldn't consider coming, would you?"

"No," Michael said stiffly, but his shoulders shook and Deborah walked quickly to his side.

"Michael, would it make a difference if Tanya were to convert? Would that make it easier?"

"Not unless she herself wants to," he answered. He turned around slowly and directed his attention to Yanosh. "You've really given up everything that we consider important, haven't you?" he said contemptuously. "I, for one, would have greater respect for you if you at least asked her to convert, or had given her a chance to decide. Shame on you, Yanosh. Shame. That is as low as you, as a Jew, can go." With measured steps he walked to the door and slammed it behind him.

Yanosh and Deborah stood silently by each other.

"I do love her, Deborah," he said quietly. "And although by now it may not matter, it is not at the expense of my love for you."

She looked at him for a long time. She believed him but she also knew that Tamar had somehow won out. Yanosh now loved her second to Tanya. But Yanosh and Tanya deserved happiness. Certainly, had Tamar lived, she would have wanted that for her granddaughter.

Slowly she walked out of the house and strolled around the garden. It was growing dark and she wondered where Michael was. She wanted to see him, be with him, talk to him. Be held by him.

As she came closer to his shack, she realized she had not been in it for years and was nervous about bursting in. Hesitantly she knocked on the door. Michael opened it, and with only a dim light shining behind him, he looked like a majestic old rabbi. He was preoccupied and seemed confused by her arrival.

"May I come in?" she asked, stunned by his appearance.

He moved aside and as she walked in, she felt as though she had entered a foreign land. The room had nothing but a cot, a wooden rocking chair and an ancient table laden with books and papers. The place reminded her of pictures of an ancient religious schoolroom. She looked over at him. He was very pale and his hair under the skullcap was quite long and brushed against his shirt collar and he was wrapped in a prayer shawl.

She pointed to the prayer shawl wordlessly.

He looked down and smiled. "Oh, that. I'm reaching back to the world of my youth. My heritage." He stopped and appeared embarrassed. "I don't impose it on you and the children for fear of embarrassing you and making you uncomfortable. But here I feel I can be who I really want to be. This is where I've begun to find my peace."

"We wouldn't be embarrassed," Deborah said defensively.

"Yes, you would and the children certainly would."

"Michael, I'm confused. I don't know where I've been. I don't know who I am. All I know is that I feel as though I'm waking from a long sleep." She took a deep breath. "But I want to get back, or start over, or whatever it is. I want my family around me. I want you. I love you." Her voice trailed off.

He reached over and took her in his arms. Holding her close, he closed his eyes. For the first time since they married, Deborah had said she loved him. God had begun to forgive him.

# CHAPTER
# FORTY-FOUR

T ANYA finished piling the newspapers neatly in the corner of the room, but not before her eyes caught sight of the headlines of some of them. Yanosh was still being vilified as though he had betrayed his country. Still, she noted with satisfaction, that his speeches were reprinted in full, a credit to the country's freedom of the press and an opportunity for Yanosh to state his views.

Satisfied that the desk had been cleared, she turned to look at the room to see if it could be made to look more festive for the occasion. The apartment was small and cramped, but it did have two tiny bedrooms in addition to the living room, which gave them each some privacy. Rearranging the kitchen chairs around the round dining table, she went into the kitchen for the birthday cake she had baked earlier in the day. Yanosh had promised to pick Yariv up from his first day at school and since it coincided with the child's sixth birthday, they had decided to give him a small party. As she placed the seven small candles on the cake, her hand shook. She threw her head back, trying to ward off the despair that had begun to take over that morning. It never failed. She would be fine, functioning and happy, as long as she was with Yanosh. But when he was away, she would feel the panic rise and was helpless in the face of it. He had been gone for three days and usually she went with him and one of Yanosh's assistants would babysit for them. But since it was Yariv's first day at school, she had to forego the trip. She bit her lip, trying to control the mood that was descending on her.

Carrying the cake into the living room, she put it on the table and placed three glasses and the orange juice container around the cake as well as three plates and forks. The sight of the three dishes caused her depression to deepen. It looked so meager, so wanting. Usually, Uri and Alexandra came. They were the only ones who remained loyal to her after she married Yanosh. Deborah probably would have come, but Tanya was uncomfortable with her visits, because of Michael's unbending attitude toward Yanosh. And this year Uri was abroad on a military mission and Alexandra was on a school trip somewhere in the country. So it was Yanosh, Yariv and herself. She thought back to her birthdays, the birthdays of the other children in the family, the various anniversaries and festive occasions the family celebrated over the years and her feelings of isolation and loneliness grew stronger. She was always invited, but from the start it was made clear that Yanosh was not welcome, which automatically precluded her going. She did not attend Uri's wedding, but when Ilan was born a year ago, Uri pleaded with her to come and she went, taking Yariv with her. Yanosh tactfully announced that he was giving a lecture, since Yariv balked at the idea of going without his father.

The wedding took place in Bet Enav and the whole family was there. Tanya had not seen any of them since her marriage, except for Alexandra and Uri and she realized how far she had wandered away from this close-knit clan, which had once been her whole world.

Standing on the side, she caught sight of Michael and for a minute she was shocked at how old he looked. She had not seen him in several years and he seemed frail. Although it was quite warm out, he had a shawl around his shoulders and was wearing a yarmulke. It made him look like an ancient rabbi. He had his hand on Deborah's shoulder and she appeared to be supporting him. As though aware of her glance, Michael looked in her direction. A faint smile appeared on his aged face and his eyes seemed to mist over. She had the impulse to run to him, tell him she still loved him, but she held back. It was Michael who was most responsible for making her and Yanosh outcasts and she could not forgive him for that. Her expression must have reflected her thoughts, because he lowered his eyes. Tanya forced herself to look away and watched Rachel organizing a *hora*. She was in uniform and had her arm around the waist of a tall, lanky young soldier. He had curly brown hair and his uniform hung loosely on his bony body, as though it were waiting for him to grow into it. His arm was loosely draped around Rachel's shoulder and he was smiling down at her. Tanya surmised that he must be Jonah, Rachel's love from the time she was a child. They were a beautiful couple and Tanya was genuinely happy for her. Uri came into view. He too was in uniform and his manner was that of an officer, a confident, dedicated officer, who knew what he wanted and where he was going. His wife, Bitti, was a majestically tall, blond Belgian girl who came to the kibbutz one summer, fell in love with Uri and stayed on to marry him. Daniel walked over to talk to Uri. He was living in the United States and was considered a very successful piano soloist. He had arrived for the occasion with his young bride Marian. She was a vivacious, pretty American girl and was talking animatedly to Naomi and Jack. Although only recently introduced into the family, she looked at home. Tanya looked over at Naomi and Jack. They too looked older, but behaved like newlyweds, holding hands and smiling happily at their first-born grandson, who was sleeping peacefully in a bassinette placed under a tree. Ruth, dressed in a magnificent pink linen suit, was extremely poised and elegant and Benji, standing by her side, looked distinguished.

The garden was crowded with neighbors from Bet Enav, most of whom Tanya had known since childhood. They were there with their children and their presence further emphasized the continuing reign of the original Danziger dynasty, of which she had once been a part. She was very aware that she was standing on the sidelines, feeling like an intruder. She looked down at Yariv. He was standing close to her, obviously ill at ease and looking equally alienated.

"Why are you standing alone?" Alexandra came up to Tanya and leaned over to hug Yariv. As always, she was dressed in the latest fashion, and looking very much like Jacqueline Kennedy.

"I'm enjoying the sights." Tanya tried to sound cheerful, although she wished she had not come.

"Well, you don't look it." Alexandra said meaningfully and taking Yariv by the hand she led him toward Deborah and Michael.

Michael shook Yariv's hand solemnly and they spoke for a minute, then Deborah kneeled down and spoke to him. Within minutes he was laughing. Then Deborah led him toward Raphael's house. Yariv had rebuffed everyone who had tried to engage him in conversation and yet he went willingly with Deborah. Tanya marveled at Deborah's ability to charm and for a brief moment, she resented the attraction between her son and Deborah. She knew she was being unreasonable. Yariv was, after all, very much heir to the Danziger legend. He was Tamar's great-grandson.

Her attitude toward Deborah had changed since her wedding day. She was in a state of shock when she first discovered she was not Jewish. All the feelings of not belonging, of being different from her relatives, of being an outsider, were reaffirmed. She kept thinking of running away, leaving Israel and hiding from the people who she now believed simply tolerated her and felt sorry for her. She was consumed with anger at her mother. How dare she marry Gidon and not convert, not give her child an honest and complete identity! Both Michael and Deborah assured her that it made little difference while she was growing up. But the fact that no one but Jack and Naomi were aware of her birthright, and were only brought in on the secret after her mother died, was clearly an indication that it did matter. It was Deborah who helped her live through that hell by soothing, comforting, understanding her. And Yanosh's sincere indifference to her religious affiliation finally overrode the initial shock.

She was therefore pleased that Deborah was present at her wedding. It almost overshadowed her disappointment that Michael refused to attend. But when the judge pronounced them man and wife and Yanosh kissed her and turned to Deborah, Tanya was jolted. For an instant, the sight of Deborah being kissed by Yanosh recalled her recurring nightmare of years back, of

Deborah struggling with some unknown man on a beach. It occurred to her that Deborah had not been struggling to escape from a molester, but instead was embracing him. It was an absurd idea. Deborah was an old woman. Still the image registered and lingered.

Deborah left them in Cyprus and they had a brief, glorious honeymoon on the island. When they returned to Tel Aviv and settled in Yanosh's small apartment, Deborah came by and started suggesting ways in which to make the flat more habitable. She had it all planned. There was furniture in the house in Bet Enav that would be perfect, there were drapes in a cupboard in Raphael's house that would work well. She had already ordered a set of dishes—as a gift, of course—which they could use for everyday and she would order one for special occasions. Tanya, sitting next to Yanosh, could feel him grow tense and she too resented the intrusion. Tanya expected Yanosh to object, but when she realized that he would not, she spoke up in a tone she never thought she would use when addressing Deborah, and informed her that they did not want her help or her gifts.

"But why?" Deborah looked from Yanosh to Tanya. "Why not?"

"We don't need your charity." Tanya did not falter. Instinctively she knew that she was saying what Yanosh could not.

"It's not charity, Tanya. I don't think you understand. You are a wealthy young woman and I just thought, since you're inexperienced in setting up a household, I'd help."

"I am as wealthy as my husband is, thank you." Tanya said with finality.

"Yanosh, please explain to Tanya . . ." Deborah started patiently.

"There is nothing to explain, Deborah," Yanosh said quietly. "I think she said it quite clearly and I believe she understands far better than anyone what this marriage is all about."

Deborah stood up, obviously hurt, and kissing Tanya lightly on the cheek, left with only a nod to Yanosh.

The relationship between Deborah and the Bar Levs cooled after that visit, although Tanya suspected that it was due to Michael's attitude toward Yanosh, rather than her rebuff of Deborah's offer to help. In a way she was relieved. She wanted her independence. Besides, she had Yanosh and that was all she needed and wanted. Their lives were filled with Yanosh's lectures and social obligations, mainly at the embassies of Eastern European countries. Tanya would have gladly foregone the latter, since she did not like the way the various officials treated Yanosh, especially the Russians. But they were important to Yanosh.

She was relieved of them when she discovered she was pregnant. Yanosh, however, continued to travel, leaving her home alone.

It was during those solitary periods that she began to wonder about their child. As long as she and Yanosh were around, their child would be cared for, loved, and would have a sense of belonging. But if anything should happen to either of them, whom would that child turn to? The deep unhappiness she suffered when she first learned that she was not Jewish came back to her more forcefully. Her child would be considered an outsider according to Jewish religious law. She could not discuss the matter with Yanosh. He insisted that it made no difference to him, and at the time she accepted it. But it would matter to her child, to any child born in Israel. She had no choice but to turn to Deborah.

When she called Deborah, the old intimacy was there.

Tanya insisted that Yanosh not be told of her decision. This was her personal decision and she was doing it for herself, for her child and for Yanosh. This was to be her gift to him, a gift she was sure he would cherish.

She saw a great deal of Deborah through that period. The rabbinate was suspicious of her desire to convert and it was Deborah who explained, cajoled and made her case before them. Studying the rules of Jewish law, something she had practiced as a matter of course since birth, did give new meaning to her Jewishness and Deborah was as involved in the process as Tanya was. They were like two students preparing for an examination.

It was Deborah who insisted that Michael be included in the process. Tanya was filled with trepidation. Yet the first time she reentered Deborah and Michael's house, she felt that she had come home and it confused her. Michael's joy at seeing her was all the more baffling. It was as though she had never been away. When told of her plan to convert, he put himself at her disposal. Tanya felt in awe of his patience and kindness. She had known him all of her life, but now she saw him in a new light. This man had a quality of saintliness about him. She would see him hold a book of the Torah, his eyes clouding over with love and reverence as though he were holding a precious jewel that he was thrilled to share with her.

The weeks rushed by quickly and the best of her childhood days spent with Deborah and Michael were relived. Tanya prayed that once she converted, their relationship would continue.

The day of the conversion arrived and after going to the ritual bath, Tanya and Deborah drove back to the Ben Hod home for a luncheon to celebrate.

"What time will Yanosh be there?" Tanya asked, taking it for granted that he had been asked. "I can't wait to see his expression when I tell him what I've done."

Deborah lowered her eyes. "Michael wouldn't have it," she answered, obviously uncomfortable.

"But why?" Tanya asked, convinced that now that she had converted all would be forgiven.

"My beloved child," Deborah said slowly. "I don't agree with Michael, but he feels that Yanosh's politics are damaging to Israel. I know that many families have different political views and yet they gloss over them. Michael won't. He can't. His life is wrapped up in this country and he thinks the Russians, with their support of the Arabs, encourage our destruction."

"Oh, Deborah," Tanya cried out. "People have different ways of showing their patriotism. Yes, Yanosh is a Communist, but that doesn't mean that Israel's safety, security and survival are not as important to him as they are to Michael."

"To be a Communist today, with the way the Russians are behaving toward us, is a betrayal," Deborah said firmly. "And what I've never been able to understand is when he became one. He certainly didn't sound like that when he first arrived in Palestine."

"Sound like that? What does that mean?" Tanya demanded.

Deborah looked over at Tanya in amazement. "I don't know. I guess we just never really knew his ideological leanings."

"Would that have made him less of a Jew or a patriot who was willing to fight and die for this state?"

"No, of course not. But even after the state was created, he gave no hint."

"That's not so. I'm sure that if anyone was listening, they would have heard that Yanosh believed the Marxist theories of government were the ones he felt were right for Israel."

Deborah was quiet for a long moment. What Tanya was saying had merit, but something was eluding her. "When did this ideology take form, as far as you know?"

"He told me exactly," Tanya answered with assurance. "It was while he was in Siberia that he came to understand that philosophy and he saw no conflict between being a Jew and being a Marxist."

"I can understand that, even if I don't agree with it. I believe Michael would too. But with Russia turning more and more against us, you'd think he'd separate himself from them. In fact, he became a Communist in nineteen fifty-six, when the Russians were threating us with a missile attack if we did not withdraw from Suez. That is the most baffling part of all."

"Oh, Deborah. I can't go on with this conversation," Tanya cried out and, opening the car door, she ran out, leaving Deborah more confused than ever. That last question of Deborah's was one that she had no answer to.

But the dependence on Deborah had been reactivated through her pregnancy. The baby was born prematurely and Yanosh was out of town. It was therefore Deborah who took her to the hospital, held her and comforted her through the hours of labor, waited for the birth and was there when Tanya was wheeled back into her room. When the baby was brought to her, the nurses treated Deborah as the grandmother and were duly impressed when they realized she was in a way the great-grandmother. But pleased as Tanya was to have Deborah there, she wanted her to leave before Yanosh arrived.

And then he was there and nothing else mattered. When she handed him their son and told him she had given him a Jewish child, the look of love and gratitude on his face were proof that she had given him a truly precious gift. It was the happiest moment of her life. When she looked around, Deborah was gone.

Tanya felt a tear run down her cheek. That was six years ago. And happy as she was with Yanosh and thrilled with her new son, she missed the family.

The last thought made her feel disloyal to Yanosh and she quickly wiped her eyes and went into the bedroom to get Yariv's gift.

She was just reentering the living room when she heard the doorbell ring. She looked at her watch. It was only eleven o'clock in the morning. Yariv's school would not be out until noon.

It was Alexandra, followed by two men carrying two cases of oranges, grapefruit and lemons. They placed them on the floor and left. Deborah had not forgotten, Tanya thought wistfully.

"What are you doing here? I thought you were out practicing to be a girl soldier?" Tanya said with genuine delight. "Yariv will be in heaven."

"Aren't you?" Alexandra walked over and kissed Tanya warmly. "What am I doing here, indeed. My favorite little human being is having his sixth birthday. It's his first day at school and you expect me to miss those momentous occasions?"

She placed two packages on the table and handed a third to Tanya.

"It's not my birthday," Tanya blushed.

"You deserve something for giving birth to that divine child. And I would have brought Yanosh something too, but what do you bring a man who has nothing?"

Tanya laughed and opened her gift. It was an exquisite wheat-colored cashmere sweater and an olive green silk scarf.

"I know, I shouldn't have done it." Alexandra said before Tanya could speak and sat down on the sofa.

Tanya looked at her gratefully. Alexandra was dressed in a simple navy skirt, white shirt and a navy sweater hung over her shoulders. Her beauty was breathtaking.

"So how did you get out of the army?" she asked, seating herself beside Alexandra.

"Tanya. I'm not yet in the army. This is part of the last-year curriculum in high school. We go out on field trips and learn all sorts of things."

"Such as how to kill?"

"Oh, stop it. Although I must tell you I'm one hell of a shot and I'm getting very good at handling the wireless. They might even put me into the communications corps."

"Are you definitely going into the army when you graduate?"

"Of course. We all are. We're a country at war and we have to be prepared. It's as simple as that." She caught her breath. "Even though Grandma and Grandpa want me to defer the army and go to university first."

"Well, why don't you?"

"Tamar. You know damn well that our generation is too aware of what the real threats are and I'm not going to cop out."

"And what will you do when you get out?"

"Then I'll go to university. I want to be a teacher. Teach small children. I'm good with kids. I adore being with them, watching them develop, seeing them grow up."

"So how do you combine that love for children with going into the army and learning how to kill them?"

Alexandra sat up. "Tanya. We learn how to defend ourselves. We are the ones who are being attacked. Arab terrorists kill our children. They make our children orphans, our women widows." She had grown pale with emotion. "There's been another raid on the Jordanian border last night. Arab terrorists just walk across and start shooting. At Tel Tanya the children still sleep in shelters. The Syrians are no farther away from there than Jaffa is from Tel Aviv." She stopped, remembering that Tanya's father had been killed in Jaffa. "I'm sorry. That was a bad analogy. But the fact is the Arabs started the war against us, all the way back in nineteen forty-eight. I wasn't born yet, but you were and painful as it is for me to say, your life would have been very different if not for Jaffa."

"And where do you think the children living in Jordan and Lebanon sleep, if not in shelters," Tanya retorted angrily, ignoring Alexandra's last reference. "Orphans and widows, whether Israeli or Arab, are still orphans and widows." And before Alexandra could protest, she continued. "And don't tell me they don't have the same attitude toward their children that we do. A mother losing a child, or a child growing up without a mother, has got to be the worst nightmare in the world. That I can tell you."

"Stop it," Alexandra cried out. "Please stop it. I seem to be able to take it when I talk to Yanosh. He explains it in geopolitical terms and although I don't always follow what he's saying, it sort of makes sense. But if you're going to bring it down to women and children, I will only ask you, why are the Russians arming the Arabs the way they are?"

"Because America is arming Israel and small as we are, we've already got an unbelievably powerful army."

"To defend ourselves." Alexandra repeated, "Remember that, Tanya. They attack. We defend ourselves."

"Truce." Tanya threw her hands up in the air. "Let's drop politics and tell me what happens right after you graduate. It's only a few months away and I think you have a while before you actually have to enlist."

"I graduate at the end of May and I'm going to Paris." Alexandra said, pleased at the change of subject. "Daddy offered me the world. But I want Paris. Paris in June is heavenly."

"That's wonderful. Who are you going with?"

"Irit, Amos and Arye. They're classmates of mine."

"What happened to Doron? I thought you were going steady with him?"

"He's determined to get into the air force and he's preparing for that. It's awfully tough to get into—" She was interrupted by Yariv bursting into the room, crying. He was followed by his teacher.

Tanya picked him up and tried to calm him down as she looked questioningly at the young woman standing in the doorway.

"What happened? Yanosh was going to pick Yariv up."

"There was a little misunderstanding and I thought it best to bring Yariv home. I've left a message for Yanosh."

"I'm a traitor, Mommy. They said I'm a traitor." The boy was wailing.

Tanya was taken aback. "What is he talking about?"

"I can't explain it." The young woman became flustered. "Some child apparently overheard his parents talking . . ." She paused in embarrassment.

"Thank you." Tanya said stiffly. "I believe you should be back at the school with the other children. Please explain to my husband what happened."

With the teacher gone, Tanya placed the boy down on the sofa next to Alexandra and sat down beside him, trying to comfort him.

It was the first time he noticed Alexandra and he looked up at her sheepishly. "I hit the boy who said it."

"That's not the best way to solve the problem," Alexandra said seriously.

"He pushed me first and I fell. That's how I scraped my knee."

Alexandra smiled down at the child, who was looking at her with large, bewildered eyes. The dark lashes framing the blue eyes were still wet from tears and appeared even longer than usual. Despite his fair coloring, he looked like Yanosh.

"What does traitor mean?" Yariv turned to Tanya.

Tanya grew flustered.

Alexandra intervened quickly. "Well, traitors are people who deliberately and maliciously set out to harm their homeland. People who wish to hurt their countrymen, endanger them, help in their destruction." She stopped, aware that the boy was not quite understanding her words. "Why don't we simply say that whoever accused you of being one probably doesn't know what the word means, either."

"Your father will be home shortly." Tanya said. "And I'm sure he'll be able to explain it more clearly."

"Well, I know I'm not a traitor," Yariv said seriously. "And I know that my father isn't and neither is my mother, because everything we do is to make our country a better place to live," he concluded, and disengaging himself from Alexandra's arms, he walked over to the table and stared at it.

"What are these?" He looked at the boxes.

"Presents from Alexandra." Tanya said.

He ripped the paper off. There were three books in one and a stamp album in the other.

"The album is from Uri." Alexandra said.

"Isn't Uri coming?" he asked. Then turning to Tanya. "Mommy, why don't we have big parties like Ilan had when he was born? That was a nice party."

The question gave Tanya a start. He had never mentioned that event and she was sure he had forgotten about it. She certainly had no inkling that he minded not having a big party.

"Uri is away on some military assignment," Alexandra helped out again. "And as for big parties, I must tell you, I prefer small ones. That's how you get all the attention."

"You're just saying that to make me feel better," Yariv said and sat down beside her. "Is Uri a general?" he asked, eying the album.

"He's a major in the tank corps," Alexandra said.

"I think I'll join the air force when I grow up. I want to be a pilot, a fighter pilot. That's difficult and you've got to be very smart, but I'm going to be very smart when I grow up."

Alexandra and Tanya looked at each other. As things stood at that moment, any son of Yanosh Bar Lev would hardly make it into the army, much less the air force.

"You're very smart right now and I don't think you have to decide today on what branch of the service you're going to enter," Tanya said stiffly.

"Don't you want me to go into the air force?" he asked.

Tanya was about to answer when Yanosh walked in. He looked distraught. Tanya rushed over to him, but he pushed her aside and walked over to Yariv. Kneeling down beside the boy, he took him in his arms and kissed him tenderly.

"It's all right Daddy. I know I'm not a traitor," the boy said, although Yanosh had not uttered a word. "And Alexandra said that the boy who said it probably doesn't really know what the word means, anyway."

Yanosh looked over at Alexandra. He had been so emotional when he walked in, he had not noticed her. He put his hand out and pressed her arm gratefully.

"Party time," Tanya announced, trying to gloss over the emotional scene.

As they ate and drank, Yariv and Alexandra chatted and laughed. Yanosh barely touched his cake and looked somber. Tanya watched him out of the corner of her eye. She had never seen him in that state.

"Daddy, could you tell them at school that I'm not a traitor?" Yariv said. The subject still preyed on his mind.

"I'll try, Yariv," he said and, standing up, he walked into the bedroom. Tanya followed him, leaving Alexandra and Yariv at the table.

"Yanosh," Tanya's voice came through to them. "I don't mind for us. But you can't make a child suffer. That's not fair."

"I can't do anything about it and you know it," Yanosh answered. "You know I would do anything to spare him, but I can't do it yet."

Then the door closed and Yariv turned to Alexandra, his eyes brimming with tears. "I've never heard my mother and father fight before."

"That wasn't a fight." Alexandra tried to make light of his remark.

"Yes, it was." Yariv said and, walking over to her, he climbed into her lap and rested his head against her shoulder.

Stroking Yariv's hair, Alexandra wondered about what she had heard. Yariv was right. In all the years she had been coming to the Bar Lev home, she had never seen any discord between Tanya and Yanosh. What made it all the more baffling was that Tanya seemed to think that Yanosh could change the attitude of the people in Israel toward him.

Shortly after Tanya returned to the living room Alexandra left, feeling a great sense of loss. Tanya and Yanosh were a symbol of unity and devotion to each other and to a cause. Was their cause now tearing them apart?

# Part IV

# CHAPTER
# FORTY-FIVE

1967

A LEXANDRA threw her handbag on the bed and rushed over to the french windows. Flinging them open, she stepped out onto the small grilled terrace and stared at the street below. Avenue St. Germaine never looked more exciting or more inviting. She took a deep breath and flung her arms out, trying to embrace the beauty of Paris.

Turning back to the room, she scanned it quickly. It was a far cry from the Royale Monçeau, where she always stayed with her parents when they came to Paris. But that was not what she wanted. This hotel on the Left Bank was her choice and she planned on spending a glorious month on her own.

She began to unpack when the phone rang. It was Irit. They made a date to meet at the Deux Magots at five and would then make plans for the evening.

No sooner did she hang up than the phone rang again. It was her father.

"Just wanted to make sure you arrived safely," he announced.

"I'm fine, Daddy, just fine."

"Do you have enough money?"

"I'm sure I do." She rolled her eyes to the ceiling. She adored her father, but he did stifle her so.

"If you should run short, just call Mr. Dumont in Geneva and he'll send you anything you need. Is that clear?"

"Yes, Daddy."

"You do have his number, don't you?"

"I do. I do."

"We love you."

"I love you, too."

She hung up. Money. That's all her father ever talked about. Usually she did not mind it, except that sometimes it did bother her. Their way of life bothered her. It bothered her most when she visited Tanya and Yanosh. They had so little, lived so poorly. Yet Tanya's father had been as rich as her own father; Gidon and Benji were first cousins. She was sure Yanosh would not accept money from the family, but it was Tanya's money and he could not

415

object to having his wife and son dress better or live in a nicer apartment. Yariv was always neat and clean, but his clothes were worn, almost shabby. Tanya had started working in a kindergarten to supplement their income and she was not a strong woman.

Alexandra put those thoughts aside. She was in Paris and she did not have to worry about anything except having a good time.

The café was crowded when Alexandra got there and she looked around for Irit. Standing in the doorway, she could see the admiring looks of people when they saw her. She smiled inwardly. She was dressed in a bright red leather skirt, black turtleneck sweater and black leather boots and she knew she looked good. People usually looked around when she entered a room, but that was in Tel Aviv. This was Paris! Irit called out to her and she joined her and found Amos and Arye there, too. Alexandra resented that. They all came to Paris together, but she had not planned on spending her whole vacation with Israelis. She wanted to meet French people.

The conversation at the table revolved around the political situation in Israel and Alexandra was annoyed.

"Can't we put politics aside, just for the evening?" she pleaded.

"Alexandra, we might be at war any day now," Amos said.

"We're always on the verge of war," she snapped.

"No, this time it's more serious. Nasser has ordered the U.N. troops out of Sinai. And he did it very abruptly. That's strange, even for Nasser."

"When did Nasser not behave strangely?"

Amos turned his back on her. "The hell with what she thinks. I know that if there is war, I'm going right back."

"What for?" Arye asked. "You're not in the army."

"We'll need every able-bodied man, woman and child. I'm almost eighteen and I'm sure they'll find something for me to do," Amos said.

"I guess you're right," Arye agreed quickly. "I suppose we'd all have to go back."

"I won't," Alexandra said.

"I will," Irit announced. "And you will too, Alexandra, and you know it."

"Well, maybe. But war has not yet been declared and until it is, I intend to enjoy myself." She stood up. "As a matter of fact, I think I'm going to leave all you patriots and go off on my own."

"Where are you going?" Irit asked with concern.

"I'll go over to the river and walk along there for a while and then . . ." She smiled dreamily. "Who knows, maybe I'll meet some divine Frenchman and practice my French on him."

She strode off with great confidence.

It was early evening and it was unusually cool for the beginning of June. She walked quickly and with purpose although she had no particular destination. Passing the Luxembourg Gardens, she thought of going in, but decided against it and continued toward the river. Reaching a bridge, she walked to the center of it and stopped to look down at the river. It was growing dark and the waters looked murky. She could see an ancient tugboat making its way down the river, followed by a sightseeing cruiser. The cruise boat was lit up with colorful bulbs and people were standing on the decks, laughing and singing. They looked happy. Alexandra wondered whether she would enjoy a cruise. It would be fun if she was with someone. Alone, it could prove awkward.

It dawned on her that this was the first time she was totally on her own. She had sounded sophisticated and sure of herself with her friends, but now she was uncomfortable. It was not really fun being alone. She was nearly eighteen and the fact was that she had never been alone. She was always surrounded by people. Parents, family and friends. *Friends.* She stopped to consider the word. The only friend she really had was Tanya. It was strange, since Tanya was years older than she was, yet she looked on her as her closest, dearest, most trusted friend. And she suspected that except for Uri, Tanya felt the same about her. In many ways, she felt older than Tanya, as though she had to protect her. Not that Tanya was weak. She had defied the whole family and married Yanosh. That took a great deal of strength and courage. Alexandra wondered if she would have the nerve to do what Tanya had done. If she ever did, Tanya would surely side with her. Tanya would always stand up for her, no matter what. She could tell her anything and Tanya would still be her friend. They had always had that relationship, even when she was very small. But Tanya did have a secret which she did not share with her. On Yariv's birthday, when the boy had asked Yanosh to help dispel the notion that he was not a traitor, the looks that passed between Tanya and Yanosh clearly indicated that there was something between them, something Tanya was keeping from her. They had seen each other many times since that day, but the subject was never brought up.

"I don't think a young lady should be alone on a bridge at this hour," she heard someone say.

Alexandra felt apprehensive as she turned to see who had addressed her and she found herself staring at the most handsome man she had ever seen. He was tall, his hair was black and curly, his skin was extraordinarily white and his black eyes, slightly slanted, gave him a Eurasian look. There was a hint of a smile on his lips that left her breathless. Suddenly she burst out laughing.

"Have I said something to amuse you?" he asked haltingly. His voice was soft, his manner gentle. He spoke French but he was not a native. She could not place the accent.

"No." She took a deep breath trying to stop the laughter. "I just realized that this is like a scene out of a romance magazine. Except that I'm not a rich American girl and you're not French."

"I'm afraid I do not quite follow what you're saying." He was studying her face closely.

"Well, I looked around and there you were, the handsomest man I've ever seen. That's how the story usually starts. He's tall, dark and handsome and they meet by chance, fall in love and live happily ever after."

"Do they marry?" he asked seriously.

"Not before the plot thickens and all sorts of complications have to be overcome. But in the end, they do marry and live happily ever after."

"I've never read any of those magazines," he said thoughtfully. "Are they popular?"

"Very. And the funny thing is, they all end the same way, yet women read them as if there might be a surprise ending."

"That seems rather foolish and a waste of time."

"Not really. It's fantasy and all women love fantasy."

"May I invite you for a coffee?" He seemed to have grown bored with the conversation.

She hesitated. Then she noticed the books under his arm.

"Are you a student in Paris?" She avoided answering his question.

"I'm taking some political science courses at the Sorbonne," he said, noting her interest.

"Have you been here long?"

"Too long," he smiled. "But you did not answer my question. Will you have a coffee with me?"

She looked around. Night had fallen and the few people on the bridge were oblivious to her existence. She felt anonymous and it gave her a sense of courage.

"I'd love it."

He took her arm and they started back toward the Left Bank.

"I know a nice little café on the Ile St. Louis. You will like it."

Several people greeted him when they entered the café, and in spite of herself, she was relieved that he was recognized.

He ordered their coffees and led her to the far corner of the room. Then, seating himself opposite her, he reached over, took her hand in his and smiled.

"My name is Edward. What is yours?"

"Alexandra," she answered, staring at her hand being held possessively by a stranger. She made no effort to disengage it.

"That's a good name. Have you been in Paris long?"

She shook her head. For some reason she did not want to talk. She wanted him to come and sit beside her.

As though reading her mind, he moved over to her side and put his arm around her shoulder.

A small band began playing an old-fashioned ballad and suddenly she felt shy. She could not remember ever feeling shy in the company of anyone, least of all a young man who was obviously taken with her. She leaned closer to him, pretending to be absorbed in the music. But she could barely hear the music. All she could think about was the physical presence of this man. She looked up at him and he was staring down at her. He had a puzzled expression on his face.

"What are you thinking?" she asked.

"I'm thinking of you. And you?"

She shook her head, not wanting to answer.

"You're thinking about me, aren't you?"

She lowered her eyes. She wished she could laugh as she had on the bridge. It really was very funny. It really was like those silly romantic stories. She always made fun of them, but now she was one of those heroines.

"I think I should get back to my hotel," she said and started to get up.

His arm tightened around her shoulder and she was relieved. She didn't really want to leave.

"You don't want to go," he said quietly. "You think you should, but you don't want to go."

"No, I don't want to, but I really should."

"Why?"

"Because this is ridiculous." She turned and looked directly at him. "I feel like a stupid idiot and I'm not." She stopped and caught her breath. "Do you often go about picking up girls on bridges?"

"What do you think?"

"I'm obviously not thinking, or I wouldn't be here."

"Edward." A young girl came over, interrupting their conversation. "Can you help me out with this damn chapter." She held out a book and then realizing her rudeness, she smiled apologetically at Alexandra. "Please forgive me, but he's the smartest student in the class and I have an exam tomorrow."

Edward shrugged his shoulders helplessly, took the book and scanned it quickly.

The girl sat down without being asked and stared anxiously at Edward. "You can help me, can't you?"

He leaned toward her and began explaining the passage.

Two young men came by and stood listening. Within minutes, several others joined them.

Alexandra found herself excluded and, sitting back, she observed Edward.

His French was fluent but accented and she still could not place the accent. Her first impression of his good looks had been correct, but now, with his face in motion, talking, explaining, his brow knitted, his eyes focused in concentration, the spontaneous smile exposing white, straight teeth, he was all the more appealing. The feelings of nervousness that she experienced earlier grew. She had to get out of the café. She had to get back to her Israeli friends. She had to see Irit. They knew her. They grew up together and knew the limits of what they could and could not do in each other's company. And they looked out for each other.

She had the urge to slip away, but she was unable to move. Edward had totally captivated her and she felt paralyzed. She closed her eyes, hoping to break the spell. When she opened them, he was looking at her over the heads of his friends. Silently, he was asking her to stay.

His friends left and Edward reached over and pulled her toward him. She settled in his arms, as though she belonged. She felt him kiss her hair and she could feel his fingers tracing the contours of her face. He touched her eyebrows, her eyes, her cheeks and then he touched her mouth and his fingers lingered there. She pressed her lips together, stifling the desire to kiss his hand.

She had to get hold of herself!

"Does your romantic story also say that the girl is the most beautiful girl in the world?" he asked.

"Oh, yes, most assuredly," she whispered.

"I like that, because you are the most beautiful girl I've ever seen." His fingers continued to brush her lips. "And do they really live happily ever after?"

She nodded.

"That's the part I like best. I should like us to live happily ever after."

She forced herself away from him. "Well," she said, determined to put an end to this madness she found herself involved in, "we will, if I say goodnight now and walk away. Then we can always pretend that we went through all the trials and tribulations these stories refer to and we survived them." She stood up, relieved that she was able to take a stand. Then, nodding pleasantly, she started walking away. He reached over and pulled her back.

"The trials and tribulations may be worth it," he said with what sounded like great sincerity.

"I don't want trials and tribulations. I want a simple life," she answered and, disengaging herself from his grasp, she ran out of the café.

The street was dark and she looked around for a taxi. There was none in sight. She started walking quickly toward a bridge, where she assumed she would find a taxi stand. She heard footsteps behind her and stopped to look around. Edward was walking toward her.

"My car is around the corner. I'll drive you home."

"Edward, I'd rather you didn't," she said firmly. "I'm frightened of you. I'm frightened of my reactions to you. I've never reacted to anyone as I have to you and I don't know how to handle it."

He put his hands on her shoulders and looked directly at her. "I'm as frightened of you as you are of me. Believe me."

Then she was in his arms, clinging to him, wanting to blend into his very being, become part of him. Her hands slid down his back. She wanted to touch every part of him, wanted him to fondle her. She wanted to make love to him and have him make love to her.

She did not remember climbing the stairs to his room. Once there, he guided her toward the bed, pulling her sweater over her head as they walked. She slipped out of her skirt and let it drop to the floor and leaned over to unzip her boots. When she looked up, she saw him standing in front of her, his naked sex close to her face. She kissed him hungrily. Then lifting her face to his, he leaned down and kissed her passionately, his tongue pushing her lips apart searchingly, ravenously. Throwing her arms around his body, she lay back, pulling him toward her. He lifted his body away from her and with his arms resting on each side of her head, he straddled her and slowly lowered himself to her. Shamelessly she pushed herself toward him and felt him plunge deep into her. She moaned softly as their bodies fell into a rhythmic gyration of lovemaking.

Nothing existed outside that room except the sound of their love. Her cries grew louder as their passion mounted. She wanted to open her eyes and look at her lover but dared not, fearful of losing the fantasy that surrounded her. The image of him and the feel of him inside her were sufficient to inflame the uncontrollable desire he had awakened in her. Their climax was simultaneous and long after they were both apart, she clung to him, fearful that he would withdraw from her. Only when his body finally relaxed did she dare open her eyes. His dark head was nestled against her shoulder and she could hear him whispering words of love. She touched his hair. It was wet with perspiration. She lifted her head and kissed his cheek. She could feel his desire throb in her and she held him closer.

"And they lived happily ever after," he murmured.

"Of course they did," she answered.

He raised his head and she tensed up.

"Please don't leave me," she pleaded.

"I won't," he said softly and started kissing her again. His mouth searched her body and finally his soft, moist lips circled her nipples. They hardened and she felt him grow inside her. Their passion was reignited and the fervor and ecstasy this time surpassed their previous act of love.

Time lost all meaning. They made love, fell asleep and, when they woke, made love again, their desire unabated. They cried and laughed and their intimacy and awareness of each other grew with each embrace, with each climax. They were strangers and yet they responded to each other as though they had been lovers in some different world and this night was a reunion and rebirth of that old love. Their bodies melted into each other and they lay in their wetness with joy and wonder.

Dawn was breaking and Alexandra knew she had to leave. Reluctantly she got out of bed and started dressing.

"But you can't go." Edward sat up. "We are to live happily ever after."

She laughed happily. "Who are you? I should know that, before I commit myself to living happily with you."

"Would it matter?"

She stopped and looked at him. "Not really."

"When will I see you?"

"I'm on vacation, so I'm completely free."

"I've got an exam at ten this morning. It should be over by four." Suddenly he grew serious and his brow furrowed. "I've got to see someone at five and I forgot all about it." For a minute he looked worried. "That should take some time. But there is a small nightclub close to where I will be and we can meet there about ten. Is that all right?"

She looked at her watch. It was six o'clock in the morning. "That's sixteen hours from now."

He smiled. "I know. I'll miss you too."

He took her downstairs and put her in a taxi. She stared out the back window as the car moved away. He was standing on the sidewalk, waving to her.

Once back in the hotel, she showered and got into bed, leaving instructions with the operator that she was not to be disturbed. She did not want to talk to anyone.

She woke at four in the afternoon and ordered coffee and a croissant with butter and jam. Sipping her coffee, she thought of Edward. It was like an unreal dream. A delicious, glorious dream that had come true.

At five in the afternoon she went down to find a hairdresser, had her hair shampooed and set, had a manicure and pedicure and then window-shopped, impatient for the time to pass. She bought a newspaper and returned to the hotel at seven. She had slept almost all day, yet she felt tired and she lay down on the bed and looked through the paper. Nasser had closed the Straits of Tiran to Israeli shipping. It was a declaration of war according to international law, and everyone was wondering what Israel's reaction would be. She put the paper aside, confident that the government would figure it out, and she began to plan what she would wear that evening.

The nightclub was not far from her hotel and she strolled over to it, arriving there shortly after ten. The place was crowded with students and as she moved about, looking for Edward, she heard people speaking in various languages, including Hebrew. The idea of seeing Israelis annoyed her and she lowered her head, fearful of being recognized.

"Hello, my beauty." Edward came toward her and led her to his table. She slid onto the banquette and he stood staring down at her.

"God, you are more beautiful than I remembered." Then, seating himself beside her, he put his arm around her and pulled her toward him.

The waiter came over.

"Would you like a drink?" Edward asked.

"I'm drunk without one, thank you." She took in the smoke-filled room and smiled. "A Perrier will do."

"Make that two," Edward ordered.

She pressed closer to him.

"I've missed you," he whispered.

She looked up at him. "No more than I missed you."

"I've asked some friends to join us," Edward said after a moment. "And now I wish I hadn't."

She too wished he hadn't, but said nothing. She wanted them to leave and go to his room. She wanted him to make love to her. She wanted to make love to him. That's all she had thought about all day. The idea embarrassed her.

She cleared her throat. "How was your exam?" she asked, trying to sound calm.

"Tough, but I performed brilliantly," He laughed. "What the French don't know about the Orientals could fill volumes."

"Is that what you're taking, Oriental studies?"

"Not Asian Oriental, but Middle East studies."

She was about to speak, when his friends joined them.

"Abdallah Nussiebe. Jamal and Solange Hammadi, my brother and sister-in-law, and Yussef Algoul. I want you to meet Alexandra." Edward had stood up and was introducing her.

Alexandra shook hands with the new arrivals but her throat was dry and she could not speak. Edward's people were Arabs and it dawned on her that Edward was too.

Solange seated herself next to Alexandra; the men sat opposite them.

"He closed the Straits of Tiran," Abdallah said gleefully.

"Well, it's about time," Edward answered. "If only he had the brains, he'd attack before those goddamned Israelis could get their forces down to the canal."

"He moved very quickly at getting the U.N. out, give him credit for that. And they left pronto," Yussef said.

"What will the United States do?" Jamal asked.

"Who cares?" Edward answered. "They're seven thousand miles away. And if we are properly coordinated this time, we can blast that bastard little state off the face of the earth, once and for all."

"That's a beautiful dress you're wearing." Solange was uninterested in what the men were saying and was trying to engage Alexandra in conversation.

Alexandra merely smiled but her attention was on Edward. All the gentleness she had seen the night before was gone.

"Do you really think they can be wiped away that easily?" Alexandra got the words out slowly, directing her question to Edward.

He looked over at her as though he'd forgotten she was there. Then, realizing that she had asked him a question, he smiled. "My dear Alexandra, we've waited eighteen years for this fight, preparing for this fight, getting ready for this fight, and this time we'll win."

"Wanna bet?" someone sitting at a nearby table asked and Alexandra could tell by the man's accent that he was Israeli. She slid down in her seat, grateful for the darkness around her.

One of Edward's companions swung around. "I don't bet with Zionist scum."

The Israeli stood up and so did the Arab guests at their table.

"Stop it, instantly," Edward commanded, not moving from his seat. "We're not going to have a brawl in a nightclub." The three sat down; the Israeli did not. Edward turned to him. "I won't fight you here. We'll meet on a battlefield."

The man laughed and returned to his table. Edward's face was twisted with contempt and rage.

"What will winning mean?" Alexandra asked when Edward calmed down.

"Winning?" Edward turned to her in amazement. "You have to live in that part of the world to understand the injustice that has taken place there since the Zionists arrived. They've brought us nothing but chaos and misery. They're nothing but tools of the western imperialists. They exploit my people while they live off the fat of the land. They're slaves of capitalism and they have no business in the Middle East. They're a foreign element and they should go back to where they came from. Winning will mean that we can finally reclaim our homes, our land." He was very pale and he spoke with passion, but he did not sound angry.

"They don't all want to exploit the Arabs." Alexandra was trying to remember what Yanosh had said when he spoke about the western influence on Israel, but she was too confused.

"Oh, don't say that. I know them. They're fanatics who want to become the masters of our lands and subjugate us."

She wanted to tell him he was wrong. She wanted to explain who her grandparents were, who her great-grandparents were. She wanted to tell him of the achievements of the Israelis in agriculture, in the arts, in science. She wanted to remind him that the Arabs had started the cycle of wars. She wanted to say so many things that she knew to be true, but she also knew her words would fall on deaf ears.

"Have you been there recently?" she asked.

"I wouldn't go to a place that was once my home and where today I'm considered a second-class citizen."

"Do you hate Jews?" she asked and was surprised by her question.

"No, I don't. I hate the Zionists." The color had returned to his face and he was staring at her, a puzzled look in his eyes.

"I don't feel well," she said and stood up. "If you'll forgive me, I think I'll go home."

The men stood up.

"I'll get you a cab." Edward took her elbow and led her toward the exit.

They stood on the darkened street and stared at each other.

"The story said there were trials and tribulations, but they overcame them all and they lived happily ever after." She smiled sadly. "But I don't believe our trials and tribulations can be overcome." She reached up and touched his cheek. "I could have loved you all of my life, Edward. I know it."

"And I you." Then with great sincerity he said, "I'm sorry, but I did not know you were Jewish."

"Oh, I'm Jewish, all right, but more important, I'm an Israeli."

She turned and walked quickly away, unwilling to see his reaction.

For three days, Alexandra tried to reach her father and ask him if she should come home. All telephone lines to the Middle East were busy and she could not get through. On the morning of the sixth of June the war broke out and Irit sat on Alexandra's bed, crying. Amos and Arye sat with them, watching and listening to the television commentators describe the war as reported by the Egyptians.

"Damn it, why don't they tell us what the Israelis are saying," Arye said in frustration.

"Will it be different?" Alexandra asked, feeling drained. She had not slept since walking away from Edward. Her mind was whirling with confusion. She had made love to an Arab. Worse, she thought she was in love with him. An Arab who hated what she came from, who she was, everything she stood for. And in a way, thinking of her father and the way they lived, she could not really fault Edward. She herself wondered about what her father did and the way he did it. But Yanosh was not like that and most other Israelis were not either. Certainly Naomi and Jack were not living off the fat of the land. Even Michael and Deborah, although wealthy and living well, never exploited anyone. Edward just did not know them. He was fed on propaganda and she was convinced that if she could show him who the Israelis really were, he would change his mind. Miserable as she was thinking of Edward, she was also tormented at the thought of everyone she knew who was fighting and possibly dying at that very moment on the battlefield.

Uri came to mind. She wanted to cry. Uri was a tank commander in the desert! Ilan was only a baby and if Uri was killed, he would be an orphan. Would Edward hate Ilan?

"God, I wish I were home," she cried out.

Arye and Amos left at one point, hoping to find a way to get back home and Irit and Alexandra stayed in the room and continued to stare at the television screen. They took turns sleeping, so as not to miss any late bulletins that might come through.

On the second day, when the Israelis broke their silence and the victories began to be reported, Alexandra felt elated, but to her horror and amazement, she found herself wondering where Edward was and how he was feeling.

On the morning of the sixth day, her father finally called and through tears and laughter he told her of their glorious victory and that there was no reason for her to come home.

She was relieved.

"Is everyone in the family all right and have you heard how Uri is?" she asked before she hung up.

"He's one of the great heroes of the Sinai," Benji said triumphantly. "It is reported that he and his men have captured huge tracts of land and he is being mentioned constantly on the radio."

"When you see him give him my love." She hung up, feeling proud of Uri. Proud of Israel. They were the winners. Edward was the loser. The thought confused her. She wished she could see him. Talk to him. Surely she could explain her side of the issue. Wars solved nothing. This last war should have made that clear.

"I knew we were going to win," Irit said happily.

"No, you didn't." Alexandra snapped.

"What's the matter with you? Did you think we'd lose?"

"I didn't think. But you know, there might come a day when we will lose."

"Don't you dare say that," Irit screamed. "We can't afford to lose a war, ever."

"Why not? Other countries have lost wars and survived."

"Because . . ." Irit started and stopped. "Good God, what's the matter with you? If the Arabs ever won a war against us, we'd be destroyed. They'd kill every one of us. They want to eliminate us from the face of the earth. They hate us."

"How many Arabs have you spoken to recently?"

"And how many have you spoken to?" Iris answered sarcastically.

Alexandra did not answer. Irit was right.

She turned her attention back to the television screen. Endless pairs of shoes strewn around the Sinai desert, left there by fleeing Arabs, were on display. It was a pathetic sight. The Israelis were victorious, as the announcers was saying, but they had brought about a great deal of misery to many Arabs.

As soon as the truce was declared, Alexandra set out to look for Edward. Happy and proud as she was of the incredible victory of Israel, her heart broke for Edward. He was so sure of his people, so sure of their cause, so sure of their victory. She did not know what she would say to him, but she had to see him.

She spent days at the little café they had gone to on their first date. She did not remember where he lived, but it was on the Ile St. Louis and as she remembered, his flat was a short distance away from the café.

He came in one afternoon and she barely recognized him. His cheeks were hollow and there were dark circles under his sunken eyes. He looked around aimlessly, spotted her and looked away. She got up and rushed over to him.

"Edward, I want to talk to you."

"Did you come to gloat?"

"Please have a coffee with me," she pleaded.

He sat down opposite her and waited for her to speak.

"I'm sorry . . ." she started. "I didn't know you were . . ." She stopped, embarrassed.

His face softened. "Poor Alexandra. You didn't know I was an Arab. And that of course makes all the difference in the world, doesn't it."

She bit her lip. "But it doesn't." She got the words out with difficulty.

His brow shot up in amusement.

"What I mean is, I haven't known you long, but I feel as if I have. I know you in my heart. You're a human being and I'm a human being and I believe you know who I am, in your heart." Her voice trailed off. That was not what she had meant to say. Of course it made a difference that he was an Arab, but she did not hate him and she could not believe that he hated her.

"Oh, you poor little girl. You live in your little state and you haven't the vaguest idea where I come from. You don't begin to understand what you have done to my family, my people, our home."

She lowered her eyes, unwilling to see his loathing now directed toward her.

"I was born in Jerusalem," he continued, ignoring her reaction. "I was three years old when the Israelis blew up our house and we had to leave. My father was a well-to-do lawyer and we went to Jordan first, but my father was uncomfortable there, so we moved to Beirut. He died shortly after we got there and the little money he was able to bring with him went. My mother, pregnant with my brother, had to move us into a refugee camp. That's where I grew up. In a filthy slum." He stopped and, reaching over, forced her to look at him. "Do you begin to comprehend what I'm talking about?"

She nodded uncertainly.

"And you." He waved at her disdainfully. "You live in luxury. It's written all over you. You reek of money, money stolen from lands which we were forced to leave when you decided to settle there."

She wanted to cry. She had purposely dressed in a simple pair of jeans, a white shirt and loafers, but had forgotten to remove the small diamond stud earrings Deborah had given her and without thinking had put on the expensive Patek Philippe watch her father gave her.

"You're wrong," she whispered. "I do understand, but you start from the wrong premise. What you refuse to see is that we can live together. We don't want to fight you. We would gladly share what we have with you. But you hate us so blindly, you won't listen."

"Don't do me any favors. Leave our land and get out. Just go," he hissed.

Defeated and helpless in the face of his blind prejudice, she stood up.

"I'm sorry that you refuse to listen. There is another side to this dreadful situation," she said quietly. "And the reason I came looking for you was that I wanted to tell you that you are not my enemy. You are a man I could have loved very deeply. And I believe you could have loved me, too."

"Heaven help me, you're probably right. I could have loved you, but there is an abyss between us that could never be bridged. What you represent has to be destroyed and I am committed to that destruction."

"Oh, Edward, my poor Edward. If only . . ." She could not finish the sentence, as tears began to choke her.

Quickly she turned around and walked out of the restaurant, hoping he would come after her but knowing that he would not.

# CHAPTER
# FORTY-SIX

U RI got into his jeep and revved up the motor. Several soldiers called out to him and waved as he drove off.

It was 6:00 A.M. and the drive through the desert would take him about ten hours, if he could stand the heat once the sun came up. He knew he could have waited and taken a helicopter, but there were several badly wounded boys who needed to be transferred to hospitals in Jerusalem and they had priority. Bitti had just given birth to their second child, and while it was a happy event, it was hardly a priority in the eyes of the military. Still, he was eager to see his new son.

He started whistling the tune "Jerusalem of Gold," and it occurred to him, now that Israel had recaptured the Old City of Jerusalem, that he would finally get a chance to visit it. He was not a religious person, but it felt good to know that the Jewish holy places would again be open to his people.

Furthermore, he thought with satisfaction, now that the Israelis were in control of the Golan Heights, the indiscriminate shelling from Syria to Tel Tanya would stop and his children and all the other children in Tel Tanya could start sleeping aboveground, in their own beds.

Thoughts of the Golan dampened his mood. The battles on all fronts had been fierce, but the one in the Golan Heights was the most brutal. He was involved in the Sinai campaign, but he heard the stories of Syrian soldiers, sitting in bunkers dug into the mountain, found manacled to their machine guns so that they would not desert, and who continued firing long after it was clear that they were defeated. The mere thought of having the Syrian government do that to its soldiers was horrifying. Any reasonable military officer would have had his men retreat when the Israelis succeeded in overrunning the area. But it turned out that those wretched soldiers had no choice. He felt sorry for them.

He pressed down on the gas pedal, wanting to stop thinking of the war. He was a soldier in Israel and they had been attacked and they had won against great odds. That was all that mattered. Now he wanted to get home and be cleansed of death by the sight of a newborn. His son.

The straight road with nothing but white sand surrounding him was monotonous, a scene unbroken except for the burned-out tanks and trucks left behind by the retreating Egyptian army, and the occasional Israeli army camps that were still in position at various intervals. Occasionally he saw soldiers milling about. For many of them, this was the first war they had fought in. It pained him to think that these youngsters had to witness so much misery. He had been too young to fight in the Suez Canal battle in 1956, but in the regular army he had been involved in battles with Arab infiltrators, some of which were quite bloody, and those had prepared him somewhat for this war. He shook his head, trying to snap out of the melancholy mood.

He soon lost track of time. He realized the sun had come up and the makeshift road he was driving on began to shimmer in the bright light, almost blurring his vision. He looked at his watch. It was nearly ten o'clock and he wondered where he was. Within minutes he passed a signpost with explicit directions. The Israeli army had put those up as they advanced. Losing one's way in the desert could prove fatal.

For no reason, he thought of his grandfather and David wandering through this very desert fifty years ago. The story, told in the family over the years was that they had lost their way and were attacked by Bedouins, who had killed David. The rumors that Michael murdered David in a rage, however, never died down. Uri grit his teeth in anger. His grandfather could not have killed David. Michael Ben Hod was not a killer. Uri realized that being lost and parched with thirst could drive someone mad. All people had a breaking point. But not to the point of murder. And certainly not his grandfather.

He jammed on the brakes furiously. The heat was getting to him if he could even begin to suspect his grandfather of murder. He could feel his sunglasses slip down his nose, due to the perspiration dripping from his forehead. He removed his helmet and, taking his canteen, poured some water over his head.

He started driving again, feeling great longing and love for Michael. That poor, dear, gentle man, who would die one day without ever being able to prove his innocence.

Suddenly the air was filled with strange sounds. Uri slowed down, wondering if his motor had overheated. But it was not the motor, he realized it was the sound of music and it was coming from behind a sand dune. He drove toward it. The music grew louder and he identified the piece as a Chopin Polonaise, hardly the usual music played on the army radio. It was his favorite piece and he loved it when Daniel played it. Daniel. Uri had never been able to forgive him for staying in the United States and his anger at his brother surfaced. Yes, Daniel had a kidney condition that kept him out of the army, and even though he swore he would come back if he were needed, that oath did not satisfy Uri. Israel was Daniel's home and he should not have stayed away. Naomi and Jack had explained that Daniel raised money for Israel by giving concerts abroad, but that too was not enough for Uri. Israelis should live in Israel. Even talented ones. Especially talented ones.

The music grew louder when he reached the top of the hilly mound and he found himself staring down at a sprawling army camp. The men were sitting on the ground with the sun beating down on them, facing a small improvised stage on which someone was sitting at a piano, playing. He did not have to get any closer to recognize Daniel. Uri felt his throat tighten with emotion.

There was thunderous applause when Daniel finished playing and stood up to take a bow. Daniel raised his arms, indicating he wanted to speak.

"That piece was played in honor of my brother, Uri Stern, wherever he may be."

The men surged toward Daniel and it was a while before they moved away. Only then did Uri walk up to him.

"You son of a bitch," Uri whispered hoarsely. "When did you get here?"

"I got on a plane on June sixth and believe me, it was no easy feat. But I told you I'd be back if I were needed." Daniel put his arm around Uri's shoulder and hugged him. "Did you recognize the piece I played?" he demanded.

Uri pushed him away almost roughly, always uncomfortable with overt emotion. "Does the family know you're here?" Then remembering Bitti and his newborn son. "Did you know Bitti had the baby?"

"Yes, I was there the day she gave birth. He's beautiful."

"Did Rachel have her child yet?"

Daniel's expression changed and Uri felt his heart sink.

"She had the baby on the eighth. A little girl."

A sense of doom overtook him. "Is she all right?"

"Rachel's fine and so is the baby. But Jonah is missing in action."

"Where?"

"The Golan. And Rachel, when she heard the news, went to look for him."

"What do you mean she went to look for him?"

"The baby was three days old and nothing could stop her. Dad went with her."

"That's insane. That would have been the eleventh and the fighting was still going on there."

"Look, she was out of her mind and she wouldn't listen to reason. So Dad got a car and drove her up there."

"Where are you heading when you leave here?" Uri regained some of his composure.

"Down to the Suez Canal."

"Because I'm going home."

"Go to Bet Enav. They're all there. Bitti, Ilan, the baby, Mother, Rachel and Rachel's child. There's so much work in Tel Tanya, with wounded being brought in from the Golan before being taken to hospitals, that they decided it was best the kids were out of the way. Benji drove up and brought them home."

*Home,* Uri thought with longing. Bet Enav was still their home. Deborah and Michael had seen to that. The prospect of going there was comforting.

"How is he?" Uri asked, still angry at himself for doubting his grandfather.

"Michael? He's very old and very tired, but with two new babies in the family and a circumcision to attend to, he's very involved."

"God, I love that man."

"So do I. So do all of us."

The trip had greater urgency and purpose once he left Daniel and the desert now seemed more barren. At one point, a solitary date tree caught his eye and he turned to look at it as he passed. It stood alone, without any visible means of nourishment to help it survive. The phenomenon of the desert, he mused.

Finally, the vague outline of the town of Beersheba came into view. He pressed the gas pedal down to the floor impatiently. It was already dusk and although the heat had begun to subside, he was exhausted. He also knew he could not drive all the way up to Bet Enav that night. Someone would have to help him get on a helicopter, if he wanted to get to his son's *bris.* The tops of the palm trees in Beersheba were now visible, but he could barely make them out. He blinked, hoping to clear his vision, when he realized that the jeep's motor had begun to steam. Smoke was billowing out from under the hood.

He jammed on the brakes and jumped away from the car. The hissing sound subsided slowly. The motor had been overtaxed; the radiator needed water. He stood up and was wiping the sand off his uniform when he saw a band of Arabs rushing toward him. He put his hand to his gun, but withdrew it immediately. These were Bedouins and they were not going to harm him. Not today. Not after Israel had won the war and was in control of the Sinai desert. Bedouins were survivors and one of the reasons for their survival was their ability to adjust to the changes happening around them. Egypt ruled the desert until the twelfth of June and they had lived under Egyptian rule. Now, without any qualms, they would live under Israeli rule.

"*Ahalan,* sahib," they shouted as they approached him.

There were about a dozen of them and they were all smiling.

"You need water for your car," one of them said. "We'll get it for you." Several raced off and the others walked around the jeep, examining it.

Uri sat down and put his head on his arms.

"Would you like a cigarette?" he heard someone ask and he looked up.

An ancient Bedouin, dressed in a black *galabya* and black scarf wrapped around his head, was squatting beside him, his cane planted in the dry earth, beside him.

Uri took the cigarette and the Bedouin lit it for him.

Inhaling deeply, Uri studied the man's face. He was the oldest man he'd ever seen. Wrinkled with age, his face was nevertheless majestic and his eyes were studying him with equal interest.

"You have had a rough fight," the Bedouin said quietly.

"Very rough and very painful. I have seen enough death to last me a lifetime."

"Death is frightening and one never really gets used to it."

"No, I don't believe one ever does."

"I too have seen much death," the man said thoughtfully. "It is especially frightening when you don't know where it will come from."

"One never does."

"That is true. But when you are old, you begin to expect it and you find yourself looking around for it. It is when you are young that it is bad."

Uri nodded politely, watching the men coming back with pails of water.

"I remember the first time I saw death," the old man's voice continued. "It was during the Great War and I was very young and I looked at the face of a dead man. It was frightening but I remember thinking he was very beautiful and much later I realized it was because he was a Jewish holy man."

Uri was barely listening. Bedouins were marvellous storytellers and could go on for hours. Hearing the words *Jewish holy man*, however, made him look over at the Arab.

"What made you think he was Jewish?" he asked haltingly.

"Both of them had the Star of David around their necks."

"Both?"

"There were two riders on camels and they were ambushed by some of my people who obviously wanted to rob them. My grandfather was very angry. That was his territory and he chased the killers away and we rode over to the men. They had both been shot and one was dead."

Uri did not take his eyes off the old man. The old Bedouin was talking about Michael and David. He was sure of it. He dared not speak, praying the old man would continue.

"That was the first time I saw a dead man," the old man continued, pleased by Uri's sudden interest in what he had to say. "It was a long time ago. But what I remember most was the expression on his face. He looked surprised. That's what I meant before. He was very young and he did not expect death," he concluded.

"What makes you say he was a holy man?" Uri tried to speak calmly.

"The Jewish god built a monument to him."

"A monument?"

"My grandfather decided to bury the dead man a distance away. A few years later, when we came back to that area, we found a palm tree had grown right on the spot where my grandfather buried the man."

The lonely palm tree, which Uri had seen while driving through the desert, came back to him vividly.

"What happened to the second man?" Uri asked.

"I don't know. He was still breathing although unconscious when we rode away and I suppose the English soldiers must have found him."

"Sahib, your car is ready," one of the Bedouins called to him.

Uri, shaken, stood up and walked toward the jeep.

"Did the old man tell you his favorite story?" one of the Bedouins walking beside him asked laughingly.

"He told me a story," Uri answered.

"Was it the one about the palm tree? It's a story he tells everyone he meets." The Bedouin laughed. "I think he's afraid of that tree and he made it all up so it would make sense."

Uri looked around for the old Arab. He was limping away, leaning heavily on his cane.

He remembered little of the rest of the drive to Beersheba. He had proof that Michael had not committed the murder. He also had to get someone to rope off the area of the date tree, before it was bulldozed by the army.

Leo Brodsky, the officer in charge of the southern command, listened to Uri's story and when he finished and requested that the tree be roped off, he began to laugh.

"Some old Arab told you a story and you really think that I'm going to take men away from important work and send them out to look at a tree?"

"You don't understand," Uri pleaded. "This is no ordinary tree, nor was the dead man an ordinary man." He stopped. There was no way to explain to a young officer no older than Uri that there was a time when men like David and Michael and the whole Nili group were important, were patriots, were fighters for a homeland, much as they themselves were doing now.

"No, I don't understand and there is no way you're going to convince me." Leo looked at Uri suspiciously. "Listen, Uri, I know what you've been through and you're suffering from battle fatigue. Go home, rest up. That tree, if there is such a tree, has survived, what? Fifty years? It'll survive a while longer."

"We're going to start building roads in that area," Uri said angrily. "That tree might be cut down."

"Look, for all you know, there may be no body under it. Think of it as a fable told to you by a Bedouin."

"But my grandfather was accused of killing that man. This would exonerate him once and for all."

"If anyone is still around who even remembers the incident," Leo chided.

Uri reacted to the last phrase. Except for Michael and the family, who would really care?

"I know there is a body there," Uri said defiantly. But even if there wasn't, he thought to himself, he knew that Michael Ben Hod had not killed David Larom. The limping old Bedouin was the witness.

The house was brightly lit when Uri walked through the gate of his grandparents' house. It was nearly three in the morning and he was surprised. He looked over at Raphael's house. There was a dim light coming from there, as well.

Haltingly, he walked over to Raphael's house. Bitti and the children would be in there. He pushed the door open slowly, fearful of frightening her if she were awake.

Bitti was buttoning her nightdress, having just finished feeding the baby, when she looked up and saw him. He was very tanned, but the film of powdered desert sand still clung to his hair, his face and his uniform. He had also lost a great deal of weight and the Uzi rifle, hanging over his shoulder, seemed to weigh him down. He did not look like a warrior; he looked like a boy playing at being a soldier. She had given up hope that he would be there for their second son's circumcision ceremony. Seeing him in the doorway, she wanted to shout with joy. Instead, she burst out crying.

"He's dead," she sobbed, "Jonah is dead. Blown up beyond recognition. Rachel is a widow and the baby will grow up without ever knowing her father." That was not what she had meant to say, but those had been her fears for herself and her children since the war started.

"Good God." He started and quickly looked over at the door that led into what would have been Rachel's room with her baby.

"No, she's in the big house. They're afraid to leave her alone, although she won't let anyone near her. She just holds the baby, tends to it, but won't let anybody touch her or the baby."

He walked over and, kneeling down beside her, took her in his arms and stared down at his newborn son. Bitti put her head against his and they sat together until the light of dawn started creeping through the shutters.

The circumcision ceremony at the synagogue, which should have been a joyous event, was muted. The baby's cry, which would have been greeted with gaiety in another time, was shrouded in sadness.

They returned from the service and Deborah greeted the endless guests who came to pay their respects. They stayed for only a few minutes and left.

Finally, only the family remained and Deborah, standing next to Michael, observed them with a heavy heart. Unlike other reunions, today they all looked mournful.

She looked around for Rachel.

She was sitting on the grass, staring straight ahead, her eyes glazed over. Her baby was lying on a blanket beside her, asleep. Rachel had not cried since the news came that Jonah was killed and her reserve worried Deborah. It was unlike her. She was never one to hide her feelings.

"Poor Rachel," Michael said and Deborah realized that he too was watching their widowed granddaughter. "It would help if we could have had a proper funeral for him," Michael continued. "It would have given her a feeling that she had said a proper goodbye to him." He shook his head. "What a terrible way to die. Blown up, with only his dog-tag to identify who he was."

Deborah and Michael now saw Uri walk over to Rachel. She stared up at him briefly and then looked away. He seated himself beside her and took her hand wordlessly. She did not withdraw from him and Deborah hoped that he might somehow reach her.

"We've named the baby Oren," Uri said and waited for Rachel to react. Deborah strained to hear the answer. Rachel had refused to name the baby until Jonah came home and when the news of his death reached them, she was silent and no one dared ask her what the baby would be called.

"That's a nice name," Rachel answered, not looking at Uri.

"What will you call her?" he asked, indicating her sleeping infant.

Rachel turned to him almost in surprise. "Gila, of course."

Alexandra joined Uri and Rachel and sat staring at the baby. She had cut short her trip to Paris and arrived a couple of days earlier. She'd been gone two weeks rather than a month, which surprised Deborah. When she arrived she was unaware of Jonah's death, of Bitti's and Rachel's having given birth. She just showed up in Bet Enav and set out to help with the children. This pampered little girl washed diapers, helped Tova with the meals, took charge of Ilan, who was quite a handful with no one able to pay much attention to him. She was pale and wan, with all the laughter gone out of her. Deborah wanted to talk to her, listen to her, but there was so much to do, so many people to care for.

"May I join you?" Yanosh was standing beside them. He put his hand out to Michael and the older man shook it and their eyes met. It was the first time the two men had been in each other's company since the day Michael ordered him out of their house, almost ten years earlier.

Deborah was surprised to see him, yet it seemed almost natural for him to be there. Tragedy such as they had suffered wiped away all differences in families. And he was, after all, family. She had seen little of him over the years and she realized he had grown old. It was not just the years which had changed him. There was a sadness in his manner that had not been there before. He was years younger than Michael, yet he looked almost as old.

She looked around for Tanya and Yariv. Tanya was talking to Naomi and Yariv was seated next to Alexandra.

Yes, they were a family. No matter what happened, they would always be a family.

The afternoon sun began to fade and everyone moved into the house. Deborah started to help Michael up.

"No, you go. I'll be in in a while." He waved her away.

She hesitated. She hated leaving him alone. Then Uri walked over.

"Was it very bad, Uri?" Michael asked as soon as Deborah was gone.

"Yes. It was," he answered, watching his grandmother disappear into the house. Seating himself beside his grandfather, he put his arm around his shoulder. "But I did find out that the story you told about David Larom's death is true."

He saw the old man stiffen. "It's unimportant now, Uri," he said in a low voice. "It happened fifty years ago. Why bring it up now?"

"I met the limping boy whom you described."

Michael disengaged himself from Uri and looked at him suspiciously.

"More important, he told me where David is buried."

"I've searched that desert so many times." Michael was trying desperately to speak naturally, but his voice began to waver. "That desert buries its secrets, year after year, with a fine layer of sand. And with time that sand becomes more solid than any metal vault built by man. There is no way he could tell you where David is buried."

"A tree, a date tree, grows on the very spot. I saw the tree. It stands alone in the middle of the desert and it caught my eye as I drove through. The old man said it marks the spot where David was buried. And I believe him."

A sad smile appeared on Michael's face. "A date tree," he muttered. "Of course. We always carried dried dates in our pockets. It helped slake the thirst."

"So I'm right. David is buried there," Uri cried out with satisfaction. "I wanted to have the area roped off, in case they bulldoze the tree when they start building the roads in that area. But the army can't spare the men."

Michael nodded in agreement. "They are right. That tree has survived fifty years and it can hold its own for a while longer, I assure you."

"Are you pleased, Grandpa?" Uri looked over at his grandfather. He was old and wrinkled but his eyes were very much alive.

"Very pleased, because discovering that tree as you did, when you did, reaffirms my faith in who we are and what we are fighting for. To me it represents the triumph of justice. I represents truth. It restates that eternity of Israel which shall not lie. It's Nili."

Then standing up, he put his arm around Uri's shoulder and together they walked into the house.

# CHAPTER
# FORTY-SEVEN

A LEXANDRA left Paris the day after she saw Edward and arrived home to the aftermath of war. It was not Edward or their affair which troubled and confused her. It was what he had said when she last saw him. She discounted the bitterness in his voice, but she could not forget his description of his people.

Sitting on the plane, she was deeply troubled and it was not until the Israeli coastline appeared on the horizon that she was able to wipe Edward out of her mind. As the plane descended toward Lod Airport, she began to feel better. She was a loyal child of Israel and she would do anything to help her country survive and flourish. Edward faded into oblivion.

She arrived knowing nothing of the horror which had befallen her family and found herself in the midst of the unbearable suffering of the people she loved. She had little time to ponder her own state of mind, as she plunged into helping her family recover from the tragedies which had struck them.

It fell to her and Deborah to bring a sense of coherence into the nightmare of their shattered lives. She was eighteen and her grandmother was nearly seventy, two women separated by many years, trying to mend the tattered center.

It was a difficult and grueling job. Deborah spent her time at Bet Enav caring for Michael, whose health was precarious, and her great-grandchildren, who out of necessity stayed with her. Alexandra spent her time with her family in Tel Tanya.

She concentrated on Rachel. The young widow was inconsolable and kept insisting she wanted to go up to the Golan and search for some remnant of Jonah—a watch, a key chain, an I.D. bracelet, anything that might have been overlooked when the army collected his remains. The area was still blocked to civilians because of possible undiscovered land mines. Uri finally got a permit and the three of them drove up. To Alexandra's surprise, Rachel was not alone in her search. An older man, a young soldier in uniform, a woman holding a young child were there as well, sifting through the rubble. They too were accompanied by soldiers, who watched over them with a sad compassion.

Sitting next to Uri, Alexandra watched Rachel in her futile search and for the first time since her return, she thought of Edward. Again it was not the man who came to mind, it was his description of the suffering of his people. Misery and heartbreak, she realized, did not discriminate. Everyone involved in war suffered.

"She's leaving Tel Tanya, you know." Uri's words caught Alexandra by surprise.

"Who, Rachel? Where will she go?" Alexandra was shocked. Rachel was so involved in reliving the past, Alexandra doubted that she ever thought of the future. "She hardly looks capable of caring for herself, much less caring for a child alone."

"She's thinking of settling in Beersheba."

"But why?"

"Tel Tanya is stifling her and it holds too many memories. And she feels there is more she can do outside of Tel Tanya."

"What will she do?"

"She wants to care for children of working widows," Uri answered. "You see, Rachel has accepted her fate and is going to move on with her life while helping other young widows to get on with theirs."

Alexandra realized Rachel had given a great deal of thought to her future. It also struck her that a new category of work had opened up to the women of Israel—caring for widows with young children.

Suddenly Tanya's statements about orphans and widows came back to her and Alexandra knew that she would not join the army. It was a shocking thought but she was convinced that she could not be part of a machinery that helped kill, that there had to be a different way to solve their conflicts.

"Are your parents aware of her decision?" Alexandra asked.

"No, but I'm sure they'll understand."

"They'll miss her and especially little Gila."

"They'll miss us all. Bitti and I are also leaving Tel Tanya," he continued, with a trace of nostalgia in his voice. "We're planning on starting a new settlement further north."

"Good God, where? In Lebanon? Tel Tanya is as close to the border as you can get," Alexandra exclaimed.

"Not quite. Let Lebanon remain Lebanese. No, several of us guys are being given a tract of land by the government and we're planning on building a moshav. The kibbutz concept is great, but we feel we would like to develop a piece of land along with people our age, communal but with a certain individuality for each family. I want my boys to grow up with a sense of pride in possession. I want them to know what they're fighting for."

"It's land that was captured in this last war, isn't it?" She tried not to sound accusatory.

His face tightened. "It's Israel and we're going to be the guardians of that border." He looked at her strangely for a moment, then his features relaxed. "Wait until you get out of the army, get married and have a couple of kids, then you'll understand what I'm talking about." He tousled her hair.

"Uri, I wish you'd stop treating me like some spoiled little child. I don't have to join the army or get married and have kids to question what is happening around us."

"What do you think is happening?" He looked at her in surprise. "We're fighting for our survival. That's where it starts and that's where it ends. Borders are important. That's not a debatable subject."

"Oh, Uri, all I want is peace, for all of us."

"Amen," he answered soberly.

Everyone had plans, all knew where they were going and Alexandra realized she was floundering. Since her trip to Paris she had lost her center, was no longer that girl who knew exactly who she was, where she was going, what her future would be like. And she could speak to no one about her inner turmoil. Neither to her family nor to her friends. The latter were involved in preparations for their army service and she was avoiding them, fearful of being asked about her future plans.

Tanya and Yanosh were her only hope and she could not wait for the day she could go to Tel Aviv and speak to them. Somehow, she was sure she could confide in them. Certainly, she could confide in Yanosh.

Her hopes were dashed the minute she saw them. They were the first people she had seen since returning to Israel who looked defeated. It stunned her. Their home appeared even more shabby than she remembered and Yanosh seemed to be seriously ill. He had lost a great deal of weight, was very tense and was obviously in pain. He was delighted to see her, but had an article to write and left her with Tanya shortly after she arrived. Tanya was visibly worried about him, but refused to discuss the matter with Alexandra. She pretended that nothing was amiss and insisted on talking about Alexandra's trip to Paris.

"It's a very different existence than the one we have here," Alexandra started slowly. "I think we Israelis tend to isolate ourselves from the opinions of the world."

Tanya sighed. "They don't have our problems."

"But our problems won't be solved by wars," Alexandra ventured haltingly.

Tanya looked at her in surprise.

"I've taken your advice and I'm not going into the army." It was the first time she had spoken the thought out loud and it frightened her.

"What brought that on? You were such a patriot the last time we spoke," Tanya said. The look of confusion on her face was blatant.

"I thought you'd be pleased."

"Oh God," Tanya cried out in anguish. "Yes, and I'm still against wars and killing. But . . ."

"But what?"

"We are so isolated and we're surrounded by so many who want our destruction." She caught herself and tried to smile. "How will you get out of going?"

Alexandra was taken aback by what Tanya was saying. "I'm going to go to the university. That will give me an automatic postponement until I graduate. Then I'll see."

"What will you study?"

"I told you, I want to be a teacher."

"I wish you could talk to Yanosh," Tanya said, obviously upset. "Have you told anyone else about your plans? Uri?"

"Heaven forbid. I think he'd never talk to me again."

"Your parents? Deborah, Michael?"

Alexandra shook her head. Something had happened to Tanya and it troubled Alexandra. "Do you think I should join the army and put off plans for the university?" she asked.

"No, no," Tanya said hurriedly. "You'll make a wonderful teacher and we need teachers more than we need women soldiers. But Alexandra, don't do anything foolish, anything that you will regret. Remember who we are, where we come from and above all, remember we have an obligation to this land, to its people, to its survival."

Alexandra left Tanya's house with a heavy heart. She was sure she would find an ally in Tanya. She even thought she could tell her about Edward. And then she realized there was nothing to say about Edward, except that she had had an affair with an Arab.

She continued with her chores in Bet Enav, and drove up to see where Uri and Bitti planned to live. She spent more time with Rachel and watched the country recover slowly from the war. Still, a gnawing feeling of doubt, a sense that something was wrong, would not leave her.

And then she began to feel a change in the mood of the people around her. Suddenly she noted that an arrogance had crept into their behavior. Her friends, her relatives, strangers from every walk of life, mostly modest, unassuming people, became boastful braggarts. That was a new phenomenon and it jarred her.

"Why is this happening?" she asked Michael one day as they walked up a mountain path leading to a small village nestled in the hills overlooking Bet Enav. "What has caused this sudden burst of chauvinism, this attitude of the victor gloating over the vanquished?"

"My dear Alexandra," Michael put his arm around her shoulder. "Our history is that of a people who throughout the centuries had right on their side, and yet we were always the losers. At which point the world bowed its head in compassion and felt sorry for us. As recently as the Second World War, the free world felt our pain and probably wondered why, with right on our side, we went so quietly to the gas chambers of Europe. Again, right was on our side, but we lost half our people to that evil tyrant. And here, for the first time in modern history, we have fought a just war and won. So is it any wonder that, after all these centuries of defeat, we are proud of our victory? We defeated six Arab nations in 1948, but that was a war fought in desperation. The Six Day War was our first real victory as a nation. Right had triumphed at last. And it did something else. It has united us in a way that no other war could have."

He looked down at her. "So, my dear child, are we not allowed to show our pride? Yes, we are being arrogant. I've noticed that and it saddens me, but I understand it." He paused briefly. "Be tolerant. We have had a great victory and our people should be allowed to revel in it." He stopped walking and looked down to the shoreline. "We've done so much with our land. I remember a time when the sea seemed so close, you felt you could reach out and touch it. Between where we are standing and the coastline, there was nothing but rocks and weeds. And look at it today. Groves, houses, trees. Yes, we have so much to be proud of."

She looked up at him. He was very old and although slightly stooped, he was still tall and proud and the handsome features were still chiseled, the blue eyes still clear. His hair had turned white, but his beard was streaked with a reddish tint, reminiscent of his youthful flaming red hair.

"Grandpa, I love you so much," she cried out with great emotion.

He smiled down at her. "My God, but you do remind me of your grandmother when she was your age." And placing his hand on her shoulder, again, they continued their ascent.

Reaching the village, Alexandra marvelled at the extraordinary transformation of what had once been an Arab shantytown. She remembered coming there with Uri and Tanya when she was quite small. The houses were dilapidated and the mud huts were nothing but piles of red dirt. Now there were roads, a small playground, a park and picturesque houses surrounded by landscaped gardens.

They entered a small coffeehouse and everyone greeted Michael as a long-lost friend. They were led to a table next to a large window overlooking the terrain below. It was a beautiful sight and she understood what Michael had been saying, but she was still troubled.

"But what about the Arabs, the innocent Arabs who were uprooted with nowhere to go?" she asked.

Before Michael could answer, a waiter came over to take their order. He was a young man, wearing army fatigues, but one of the sleeves was armless.

"Alexandra, the Arabs started this war," Michael said soberly, watching the waiter walk away. "Just as they started the war in nineteen forty-eight, which turned out to be our War of Independence." He observed her for brief moment. "I saw you looking around at all the new houses here, and you are probably wondering what happened to the Arabs who lived here. Well, let me give you a history of this village. I knew just about every Arab living in it, before the 'forty-eight war. We had a couple working for us, Mahmud and Fatmi, who came from this village. They had worked for your great-grandfather and great-grandmother as well. Mahmud died tragically long before 'forty-eight, but when this area was captured by our men, I came up here and begged Fatmi to stay. She wanted to, but was afraid. Her children insisted they leave, having been promised a glorious victory and a triumphant return by their leaders. She left with her whole family and God only knows where they are now."

"Would we have let her keep her house?" Alexandra asked.

"Others who have stayed have thrived." He pointed to a village at the foot of the hill, which could be seen from where they were sitting. "You see that village? They were Arabs who did not run from us in 'forty-eight and they are living with us peacefully. It's a thriving community alongside us. But that is not the point. The fact is that we have taken in more than two million Jews, all forced out of their homes in Europe by the Nazis and their sympathizers. We took them in, people who had little in common with us except our religion, and even that was something they had forgotten. They've integrated and are proud Israelis today.

"The Arabs who left here have a great deal in common with the rest of the Arab world. They speak the same language, they pray to the same God, they have the same customs and values. Let the Arab world learn from us. Let them take their brethren in, as we did." He stopped and thought for a minute. "The fact is, my dear, if the Arab world wishes to go on fighting our existence and losing those battles, they cannot then come and demand justice from us. Let them demand justice from their own people. And let me tell you something else. Every time they attack us, they harden our resolve and make us less generous. Fatmi could have stayed in 'forty-eight. I would have fought for her right to stay then. I don't know if I would today. Somehow I could not justify it to Rachel, or Uri, or that young waiter who served us."

She was silent. What her grandfather was saying had merit and she could not find the argument to dispute it. She tried to recall Edward's arguments, but they were diffused. Still, somewhere deep inside her, she felt there was an injustice being done to innocent people, and all of Michael's explanations did not make it right.

She moved through her days cloaked in sadness, suffering her doubts in silence and feeling the noose of confusion grow tighter around her. The date of her recruitment grew closer and in spite of all that her grandfather had said, her decision not to join the army had not changed.

Spending time with her parents strengthened her decision. She tried to see as little of them as possible, but she had stayed with them when she first returned from Paris and knew immediately that she could never live with them again. The grandeur, the luxury, the false values of her parents' life, were intolerable to her. She knew she was seeing them through Edward's eyes, but she had begun to resent them even before meeting Edward. Knowing him only enhanced her awareness of the emptiness of their lives, the waste, the futility. Her involvement with the family put off the inevitable confrontation that she knew was bound to come.

It happened the day she received her enlistment letter. She was having tea with her mother and father in their garden, when her father handed her a letter from the army recruiting office.

"When do you have to report?" Ruth asked.

"I'm not going," she answered quietly.

"You're *what?*" Ruth gasped. "What are you talking about?"

"I'm asking for a scholastic deferment. I've decided to get a degree at the university before joining. I've applied to Jerusalem University starting next semester. I'll enter the army when I graduate."

"When did you become a scholar?" Benji laughed good-naturedly.

"This minute. Yesterday. What difference does it make? Everyone goes to the university at some point. It's either before the army or after." Alexandra tried for nonchalance.

"Oh, Alexandra, stop talking nonsense." Benji took a bite of his pie. "I expect you'll be married long before you finish your army duties. Somehow I don't think university life is really your style."

Alexandra swallowed hard. "Not my style? What is this future you've mapped out for me? I don't want to get married. I do have a mind, you know, and feelings and opinions."

"University is a four-year commitment," Ruth said quietly, looking nervously at her husband.

"I'm in no rush."

"I never doubted your intelligence." Benji started slowly. "But that's beside the point. As far as I'm concerned, you're going into the army." His voice grew firmer. "And furthermore, you do understand that I will not support this idiotic notion."

"I don't need your money. Grandma will be happy to help me."

"We're a family with a certain background, we have a responsibility toward the community. I just won't have it. It's something I could never explain to our friends, to the family, to anyone." Benji had grown red with indignation. "One thing we've all prided ourselves on is our patriotism."

"Your patriotism is there only for what you can get out of it," she answered, equally angry. "Nothing you do is for the good of anything but your own financial gain, and you know it."

"You enjoyed the fruits of that financial gain!" Benji shouted hysterically and stormed into the house.

"You should not have said that," Ruth said quietly.

"He deserved it," Alexandra answered, nevertheless feeling contrite.

"He's your father and he's having many problems."

Alexandra looked at her mother. Her pretty, frivolous, cheerful mother suddenly looked tired. "What are they?" she asked.

"You would not understand and you certainly would not be sympathetic."

"Try me."

Ruth started to speak but changed her mind. "I think I'll go see how he is," she said and walked away.

It was past ten when Alexandra arrived in Bet Enav. The children had long since gone to bed and Michael had retired as well. Deborah was sitting in a rocking chair on the front porch.

Alexandra threw herself into a hammock and related what had happened at her father's house.

Deborah sat quietly, listening. She did not doubt the girl's sincerity. What she wondered was what had brought about this change in her.

"Are you angry with me for my decision?" Alexandra finally asked.

"No, of course not. I trust you and I'm sure you have your reasons for wanting to take this direction."

Alexandra sat back and looked at her grandmother. She was still a very beautiful woman. Her white hair was pulled back into a loose bun and held by a tortoiseshell comb. In the dim light of the porch lantern, no wrinkles were visible on her face. For no reason, the biblical story of the prophetess Deborah came to Alexandra. She too had been sure of her actions. But as she grew older, did she begin to doubt her youthful deeds? Did her grandmother have any doubts? Any regrets? She had seen so much suffering throughout her life. She had suffered hunger, had been frightened and lonely, had been widowed and then married Michael in defiance of everyone and stood by him. She had nursed her sick, had watched loved ones die, had stood by their graves, weeping with anguish. She had been the pillar of strength for the whole family for so long. Was she that secure in who she was? Did she think it was worth it? Alexandra dared not ask, fearful of the answer and not quite sure what she wanted the answer to be.

# CHAPTER
# FORTY-EIGHT

As Alexandra suspected, Benji did not carry out his threat; he agreed to support her while she went to the university. She got a small rooftop apartment with a huge planted terrace from which one could view the Old City, the Judaean mountains and on clear days, the Jordanian coastline.

Everyone in the family was amused by her decision except for Michael. He was genuinely delighted. She was the first of his offspring to attend college. Naomi had married and gone to a kibbutz. Benji went into the family business, Tanya and Rachel had married soon after graduating from high school, and Uri had chosen the military as a career.

"You're not only beautiful," Michael said the day before she left for Jerusalem. "You've got a head on your shoulders."

It was the first time that someone had acknowledged her as a person, rather than a pretty, fun-loving dilettante. She was grateful and was determined not to disappoint her grandfather.

She registered for a degree in Liberal Arts, majoring in Middle Eastern studies and languages, including Arabic. Someday Arab children might join Israeli kids at school, and knowing Arabic would help.

Like all Israeli children born after 1948, Alexandra had never been to the Old City. She had glimpsed it from the balcony of the King David Hotel, and its domes, church spires, minarets and ancient stones were hauntingly beautiful. Often she felt that she could reach out and touch them, but the closeness was deceptive. It was a foreign land, enemy territory, and the valley separating her from it was an abyss that could not be crossed. She had once walked over to a barbed-wire fence separating the Jewish section of Jerusalem from the Old City, hoping to get a glimpse of the Wailing Wall. An Arab soldier sitting in a makeshift hut waved his rifle at her menacingly, and she hurried away.

She fell in love with it all the first time she was able to walk through it. It was everything she imagined and more. She spent her free time walking through the winding streets, mesmerized by the varied cultures cramped so close together and yet so different from each other.

It was the Jewish quarter that puzzled and fascinated her most. Surrounded by Arabs, it overlooked the Wailing Wall. Most of the houses were ancient and dilapidated. Although it was being refurbished, she wondered why any Jew would want to live there. Yet they did. They even sent their children to school here, to be taught their Talmud and Torah. She would see them in early morning on her way to the university and would watch them, sometimes after sunset, walking home after a long day of study. They looked tired but alert and secure in the knowledge of who they were and where they were. They were home. Both the eastern and western parts of Jerusalem were theirs and would stay theirs, because their God so deemed it in the Bible.

Arab children and Jewish children were living side by side, and the difference was staggering.

Her grandfather's words began to wear thin. The Arabs in the Old City of Jerusalem had stayed, but they were not being treated as equals. Her pain for the people who were defeated was fed by the memory of Edward's description of the toll the wars had taken.

Jerusalem, however, being the seductive and mysterious city that it was, swept her up and consumed every part of her. Her schoolwork was stimulating and compelling. Her small apartment became the social center where students met, argued, talked, listened to music and enjoyed their youth. Politics seeped through their conversations and basically everyone agreed: if the Arabs wanted to live with Israel in peace, all would be well.

She was finishing her second year when she met Ami Tzur, a highly decorated air force pilot, and if she still had doubts as to where she belonged, they vanished completely. He personified the best of Israel.

Handsome, secure, intelligent, dedicated to the Israeli air force, he had fought brilliantly during the Six Day War and his future in the air force was secure. He was brought as a guest to her flat one Friday evening.

It was a lovely spring evening and they all drove down to Jericho. She was attracted to him and he seemed equally taken with her. She was not surprised to hear her phone ringing as soon as she returned to her flat and opened the door. He was calling from a phone booth and asked if he could come up for a drink.

Sitting on her terrace, she watched him staring at the Old City, which was lit up like a tiny jewel among the ancient ruins. Ami had curly brown hair, deep-set blue eyes and a strong face with high cheekbones. His features were finely etched except for his mouth, which was full. The corners turned up in what seemed to be a smile. He had taken his jacket off and was lounging comfortably in an armchair. She wondered if she wanted to have an affair with him.

"God, I would die for this city," he murmured, his eyes focused on the sight below them.

The phrase upset her. "Why not live for this city?" she asked.

He came back to himself and smiled. "It's just an expression. Of course I want to live. I want all of us to live to be happy, old people."

"You sound as though that's some sort of luxury."

"For us it is."

"Where do you live?" She wanted to change the subject.

She discovered that he grew up only a few miles from her home in Caesarea and within minutes they were embroiled in gossip about mutual friends and relatives.

The hours passed and the sun was beginning to rise and still they talked. He grew more appealing with each hour and she wished she had the nerve to ask him to go to bed with her. Not promiscuous, she had had a couple of affairs since coming to Jerusalem and they were fun but not serious. They were not meant to be. Ami, she thought, was different.

When he left with only a peck on the cheek, she was puzzled.

They started seeing each other regularly. He would come to Jerusalem on weekends and they would go out to dinner, a movie or a concert. Always, he came up for a nightcap and would leave, kissing her affectionately on the cheek.

Her summer vacation was coming up and she was scheduled to go back to Bet Enav. Michael had had a mild stroke and Deborah asked if she could come and stay with them.

She was packing when Ami arrived, and she was irritable. She felt rejected and it infuriated her.

"I suppose I won't be seeing you for a while," she snapped as she continued putting her things into the suitcase. "Unless you come to Bet Enav. My grandfather is quite ill and I won't be able to travel about."

"What's the matter with you?"

She stopped what she was doing and turned to him. "I don't understand what it is you want of me," she started angrily.

"Want of you?" He began to laugh. "I want to be with you always."

She swallowed hard. "Your actions certainly would mislead anyone. I would say you weren't particularly attracted to me."

"Why, because I didn't push you into bed the first time we met?" he asked quietly. "From the minute I saw you, I decided you were the girl I wanted to marry and spend my life with."

"Marry?" she whispered. That was not what she had been thinking about.

"Is that so strange? I'm very much in love with you and I just wanted to be sure that you felt that way about me before we got involved and have this end up as just an affair. I can have affairs anytime. So can you. Marriage is forever and it has to be something we're both sure of."

For no apparent reason, Edward came to mind. She had not thought of him in a long time and it surprised her.

"I think I can love you, Ami," she said seriously. "But I think being physically compatible is equally important." She walked over to him and kissed him on the lips.

Ami was a gentle lover, considerate and loving and although there was none of the passion that existed between her and Edward, she felt comfortable with him. They satisfied each other and when they lay on her bed after their lovemaking, she felt content. When she whispered, "I love you," she meant it.

By the time she left for Bet Enav, she wanted to marry Ami and she knew they would be happy.

"Ami Tzur." Michael was delighted. "I knew his grandfather. A wonderful man. What a pity he died. He would have been as delighted as I am that our grandchildren are going to be joined in marriage."

Deborah was equally pleased. Benji and Ruth were overjoyed and Uri was thrilled.

"I first met him in Sinai," he beamed. "He's a superior pilot and given a chance, I bet he'll be offered the job of commander of the air force. What a great guy! What a perfect union this is going to be!"

Alexandra was at peace with herself. This was as it should be. This was where she belonged. She was back in the fold and she was happy.

# CHAPTER
# FORTY-NINE

ALEXANDRA returned to Jerusalem for her third year at the university, anxious to complete her last two years in one. Ami wanted them to get married as soon as possible, and the wedding was planned for the day after her graduation. She was happy, content and in love. For some inexplicable reason, Edward kept cropping up in her thoughts and it annoyed her. He was a tiny episode which she would always cherish, but Ami was her life.

Ami was stationed in Elat, but they saw each other every weekend. Life should have been perfect, except that suddenly she realized she had avoided joining the army, only to be deeply involved with it now through Ami. The army was his life. She lived through every action taken by the Israeli air force. A bombing in Lebanon to squash a terrorist training camp, an air raid against a refugee camp on the outskirts of Beirut, where a nest of Al Fatah men were harbored, an attack on a missile site in Syria or in the Sinai would send a chill of terror through her as she wondered if Ami was involved. When a plane was shot down over enemy territory and the pilot was reported to have bailed out, she rushed home and waited to hear if it was Ami. After that, the ringing of the phone would send her into a frenzy.

She now devoured the newspaper reports. Old doubts returned. Was there no other way to solve the never-ending wars? Was killing and maiming the only way? She had no clear idea how one stopped the circle of violence from escalating, but she was more convinced than ever that the killing had to stop; only then would a rational solution be found. She began to fantasize a meeting between Ami and Edward. If only they could meet, talk to each other, explain their positions, she was sure they could arrive at a solution that would satisfy them both. They were sensible young men with their whole lives ahead of them. Neither wanted to die.

She began to take an interest in student meetings that dealt with social as well as political issues. Not having any political affiliations, she spent her time listening and observing her fellow students in a way she had not done before. They were highly political and all had either served in the army or were planning to as soon as they graduated from the university. The views were diverse. Quite a few of them thought of entering politics. None had her optimism. On the rare occasion when she voiced her opinions, they seemed to move away from her. She even tried to talk to some of the Arab students. She found them friendly but aloof, as they were to the other Jewish students. She could not decide if it was fear or distrust that made them turn from her. Sometimes she'd wander through the Arab quarters, hoping to run into them. When she did, they were cordial, even invited her to have a coffee, but she was never invited to their homes.

Her state of uncertainty grew, as did her concern for Ami. It all came to a head after a vicious Arab terrorist attack on a schoolhouse in the northern part of the country. It was a harrowing experience and the whole country watched the events on television. The trapped children were screaming, the army surrounded the area and sharpshooters were stationed on rooftops. Loudspeakers were warning the terrorists to give up or face the consequences. Gunfire could be heard coming from within the schoolhouse. Finally the army stormed the building and the terrorists tried to escape as the children came running out of the building. The terrorists were running toward the mountains when several planes appeared, swooped down and shot the infiltrators dead. The television cameras briefly scanned the dead bodies before returning to the children, who were crying in their mothers' arms.

Alexandra felt numb. Everyone had behaved heroically, yet she knew she did not want Ami involved. She was afraid for her future husband. Somehow she had to convince him that she could not live with his career.

She broached the subject one evening after having dinner with some of Ami's friends who lived in the Jewish section of the Old City.

Hillel and Sarah's house was one of the newly renovated ones that Alexandra had passed several times while exploring the area. It did not look as though it were habitable. It stood in a narrow alley behind a solid iron gate that slid open easily. She and Ami entered a small stone courtyard. The aroma of Sabbath cooking was everywhere and everything was peaceful.

The first sight that greeted them as they entered the apartment was that of the Wailing Wall, clearly visible through the arched windows. It was illuminated and breathtakingly beautiful.

"Now that's the way to live," Ami said, walking over to the window. "Would you like me to get us a flat in this area?" he asked, turning to her.

She did not answer. He seemed serious and the question upset her.

To Alexandra's surprise, their hosts turned out to be Orthodox Jews. Hillel, an army doctor, was a tall, dark, bespectacled young man with an impish smile that seemed to say there was no problem that could not be solved. Sarah, a charming young woman, was simply dressed. She wore a scarf around her head, was quite tall, thin, with elegant posture. What struck Alexandra most about her was the air of serenity in her carriage.

It was a pleasant evening. Conversation flowed during dinner. When it was over, Sarah fussed in the kitchen and Hillel regaled Alexandra and Ami with stories about his soldiers, talked about his family who lived in an Orthodox village near Tel Aviv, and spoke about the future.

"Where will you live after the baby is born?" Alexandra asked, feeling relaxed and happy.

"Right here. We're hoping to buy this flat."

"But you're surrounded by Arabs and they don't seem terribly friendly. And for children . . ."

"If the Arabs don't like us, let them move. I don't mind them," Hillel answered and although still smiling, a rigidity had come into his voice. "This is my home. This is ours. Just read the Bible."

She did not want to argue, but she found herself asking about the future of the Jews in that part of the city. Her questions irritated Hillel. He answered every one of her doubts by quoting biblical tracts she had never heard of but assumed existed. She could not counter Hillel's arguments and she looked to Ami for help. He had an amused smile on his face. Sarah joined them and although she did not take part in the conversation, it was clear that she was in accord with her husband. For the first time in many months, Alexandra felt like an outsider again.

When they left, Hillel was still gracious and charming, but his manner toward Alexandra had changed. She was convinced he felt sorry for her. She did not blame him. She felt sorry for herself.

"Ami, I can't take it," she said after they had walked for a few minutes.

"Can't take what?" he asked absently.

"Your being in the regular army and my worrying about you every time you go into action."

"Look at that," he said, pointing to a new archeological dig that was underway, close to the Wailing Wall. He seemed not to have heard her.

"You're not listening to me." She stopped walking.

"I heard you." He put his arm around her shoulder. "And I'm glad you worry about me. That means you love me." He started leading her closer to the site of the dig.

"It's because I love you and want to spend my life with you that I won't have you flying around, shooting and getting shot at. I want to have your children, I want them to have a father and my nerves will not hold out if you stay in the air force."

He pushed her away and stared at her. "I don't believe it." He started to smile, but it froze on his lips when he realized she was serious. "You can't possibly mean what you're saying. It's my life, my career, and what I do is important. What I do is to guarantee that you and our children will live and survive."

"At whose expense? Some pathetic refugee who's helpless in the face of your bombs?"

"That refugee is sitting where he or she is, waiting to come and take your place, right here. Can you understand that?" He waved his arm and pointed to the area around them. "This place, this magnificent area, which we've cleaned up, nurtured, cared for as never before. And now, having lost it—in a war, mind you—they want it back. But that's not all they want. They want Haifa, Jaffa and while they're at it, why not Tel Aviv?"

She looked around. "Can't we share it? We lived with the Arabs in Jerusalem before the state was created."

"We were willing to. But they weren't. They went to war in 'forty-eight and were in charge of this part of Jerusalem for nineteen years. And during that time they tried to destroy every semblance of what was Jewish and had been for centuries. They made pigsties out of our synagogues, demolished our cemeteries, and they wouldn't even allow us to pray at the Wall, our only holy shrine." He had grown very serious. "We got it back in nineteen sixty-seven and we'll never give it up again." He took a deep breath, trying to compose himself. "So why don't you stop talking nonsense."

"But they hate us. You can see it in their eyes when you walk through the walled part of the city."

"That's their problem. Not ours."

"Ami, I know all of that, but I beg you to stop flying. Get some other job in the air force. I'm terrified for you, for us. Please." She began to cry. "If anything happens to you, I'd be lost. I know it."

He kissed her and held her close. "You're just new to the game. It isn't as bad as you think. And I'll take care of myself. I too have a great deal at stake."

It was hopeless. A life of daily concern for the welfare of the man who was to be her husband loomed up before her. And for no reason, she thought of Rachel.

For weeks after that evening, Rachel's image would not leave her. When the call finally came, she knew she had been expecting it.

"Miss Ben Hod," the voice said and her heart sank.

"Ami?" she asked dully.

"He was flying back . . ."

"Is he dead?" she screamed.

"We don't know. He was in a dogfight with some Syrian planes that were trying to infiltrate our airspace. It's not clear what happened, but his plane exploded over the sea. There is a possibility that he succeeded in bailing out before the crash. A couple of the men in that flight formation said they thought they saw someone bail out of Ami's plane."

She felt an icy chill overcome her body. It spread through her and numbed her brain.

"Are you there? Are you all right?" the man asked. "Would you like me to send someone over to be with you?"

"I'm fine," she answered and hung up.

As she walked out to the terrace, one thought overrode all others. Unlike Rachel, there would be no place for her to sift through in the hopes of finding a remnant of her lost love.

By evening, Deborah had arrived with Tanya. Rachel arrived late that night. Her mother and father came, but her father had to leave early. Ruth remained. Naomi came, Bitti came and Alexandra watched them perform their roles, each doing her bit, as in a well-rehearsed Greek tragedy. Tanya, her eyes swollen from crying, was serving coffee. Rachel, pale, worn-out and drained, was preparing the food. Ruth was occupied with some household chore and Bitti was manning the phone. Deborah, austere, almost rigid in manner, sat with Alexandra, holding her hand. Her face was devoid of expression but her grip was firm. Alexandra clung to her, trying to absorb some of that strength.

"How much longer can we take this?" Alexandra whispered. "Not just waiting to hear about Ami, but a whole nation sitting on the edge of this mad volcano, waiting for it to erupt?"

"Until our enemies come to understand that we are not afraid of their heat," Deborah answered. "People do not leave their homes because of a fire, a storm, an earthquake or volcano. They simply learn to build stronger homes on more solid foundations. This is our home."

"It's a cursed home," Alexandra said and lowered her eyes.

"I don't agree," Deborah answered without flinching. "I think our home is blessed."

On the evening of the second day, Ami was found, badly hurt but alive. After seeing him in the hospital, swathed in bandages, except for his eyes which were smiling sheepishly at her, Alexandra felt relieved. She hoped that now he might have to give up flying.

Ami had injured his spine but the doctors assured them that he would recover completely. His fighter pilot days, however, were over. Alexandria hid her euphoria.

The price turned out to be too great.

Ami was assigned to train young flying cadets and his inner rage and frustration changed him. He became impossible to be with. It happened soon after he started working with his students. The self-assured, charming, considerate Ami turned into a distracted, indifferent, ill-tempered, angry man. More distressing, he had once been a kind man, filled with love and compassion. Now he appeared to be fighting some internal battle with the same vengeance that he used when firing at the enemy. And, irrational as it was, he blamed Alexandra for the accident.

"You wished this on me," he shouted one evening after a party, where he had had too much brandy. "You put a curse on me."

He apologized the next day, but she knew he had meant it. Still she hoped that after they were married and had a child, he would calm down. Soon, however, she realized that he was not rushing to get married. He did not want to break off their relationship, but he had no desire to change the status quo.

His new attitude about getting married suited her well. She was deeply involved in her final exams and she was satisfied to wait and see how their relationship would evolve. Sometimes he would come home late and she never questioned his whereabouts. And in the evening when they were both home, they would sit on their terrace like an old married couple, with Ami talking about his students. They were his life.

One such evening Ami was unusually tense.

"Anything wrong?" she asked, conversationally.

"I had to ground a cadet."

She mumbled her sympathy, wondering why it upset him so.

"He would have made a damn good pilot, too."

"So why ground him?"

"It's regulations. They go through the whole course, which is grueling. They are put through hell on so many levels, not to mention the fortune it costs to train them. Then comes the big day. They go up with only an instructor for what is their last flight before they go solo." He shook his head. "He was great. Perfect. A-One. I was sitting next to him and he was ready to take off and I asked the question." He stopped and leaned on the bannister of the balcony, staring blankly into space.

"What's the question?" she asked.

He turned to look at her. "I asked him what he was thinking of at that moment. And he said he was thinking of his mother." He pounded his fist against the rail. "*Idiot.* His mother was the *last* thing he should be thinking about."

"Good God, why?"

"There is something soft about that, Alexandra. We can't afford to have a pilot who will go soft on us, do you understand?" His voice rose in fury. "Do you understand what I'm saying?"

She stared at him in horror. "I understand and I think you do too."

Robots, she thought. That's what they were looking for. Ami would want his children to be robots.

What saddened her most was that at that moment she loved him more than she had since the time they met. It was the Ami who was hurting for his cadet whom she could have married. But, having exposed that man, Ami could never marry her.

They stayed together through her graduation and then announced to their respective families that they were separating.

They were made of the same cloth, but the cloth had worn thin.

Her predestined fate had been shattered and she did not know where to turn, had no one to talk to, cry to, be consoled by.

Alexandra was debating whether to leave Jerusalem when Yanosh was suddenly rushed to the Hadassah Hospital in Jerusalem. Alexandra had seen him rarely, since Tanya had begun to discourage visitors to their home in Tel Aviv. But once in the hospital the secret was out. He had cancer and it was in an advanced stage. Except for Tanya and Yariv, no visitors were allowed, although when Alexandra asked, Tanya made her the one exception. She began to spend time in his hospital room and for the first time since returning from Paris, she felt that she might be able to talk to him about her doubts.

When Deborah arrived in Jerusalem, Tanya asked Alexandra if she could stay with Yanosh, and Alexandra was pleased. She sat in a small chair next to the bed and watched him. He was extremely frail, his pallor more ashen than ever, his body thin and emaciated. But when he opened his eyes, she could see that his mind was as alert as ever.

It was growing dark and the large hospital windows facing the Judaean mountains were aglow with orange light from the fading sun. Alexandra wondered if she should trouble Yanosh with her problems.

"You're sad, Alexandra." Yanosh reached over and took her hand.

He had been watching her closely. She was still very beautiful. Her lush auburn hair, cut short, fell limply over her forehead. Her large, expressive eyes were like burning coals, but there were dark shadows beneath them, as though she had not slept in days. Her skin appeared lifeless. Her clothes, slacks and a boy's shirt, hung loosely on her thin frame. He could feel her suffering and wondered what had caused it.

"You're a very different girl from the one who used to come to our house and babysit for Yariv," he said quietly. "Something happened to you and I wonder if you want to tell me about it." He smiled encouragingly at her. "I believe you can trust me."

"I know I can trust you. I'm having a problem trusting myself," she answered.

He did not react and waited for her to continue.

"I don't like who we are as a people. I don't like what we have become," she started slowly. "I say that, knowing our history. I know how much we've suffered. I am fully aware that the Arabs around us cry for our destruction. But I can't help but feel that they too have a legitimate argument. More important, I don't believe they all want to destroy us. I think there are many Arabs who would live with us in peace, if given a chance. And it seems to me that in our state of euphoria over our victory in the Six Day War, we have forgotten, or have chosen to ignore, the misery that we have inflicted on the innocent Arab civilians." She was out of breath and was trying to control her emotions. "Somewhere there must be a meeting of minds, a common ground that would satisfy both the Jews and the Arabs."

"I hear you're not going to marry Ami."

She shook her head, wondering if he had heard any of what she said.

"Is there someone else?" Yanosh asked.

"No. I had an affair a long time ago with an Arab, but this has nothing to do with him. It's the things he said that have stayed with me. Listening to him I realized how much suffering we have inflicted on his people and how callously we're behaving."

"Who was he?"

"His name was Edward Hammadi."

"Abu Tayib."

"Who?"

"Edward Hammadi is better known as Abu Tayib."

Alexandra gasped. "Do you know him?"

"No, I don't know him personally, but I know of him. Everyone in Israeli Intelligence knows of him."

She held her breath.

"He's very militant. A leader among the young lions of their cause. He is a true anti-Semite, a true hater of Jews, committed to our total destruction."

"Oh no!" Alexandra protested. "He hates the Zionists, not the Jews. He told me. He feels that the Zionists are the agents of Western capitalism and that is what he hates. I'm sure of it."

"Are you also aware of recent articles he wrote in which he places all the evils of the world on the Jews? He claims that we are a people who are almost completely literate and that makes us dangerous. He backs up his claim by citing that we are the people who produced Jesus, Freud and Einstein—all, as far as he's concerned, a menace to world order."

Alexandra stared at Yanosh in disbelief. "But that can't be. He told me specifically that he did not hate Jews." Alexandra felt frantic. "And since then his distinction has been repeated by every Arab leader when they discuss the situation in the Middle East."

"He and they are spouting a Russian Communist line because it serves their purpose."

"But Yanosh, you are a Communist."

"I am a Jew first and yes, I believe in the Marxist philosophy. But there is a great difference between Marxism and Stalinist Communism. Unfortunately, many people confuse the two and the Arabs are playing on that confusion." His face twisted into a strange grimace. "I confused the two once, and I paid dearly for that mistake."

"I don't understand what you're saying."

"At one point, while I was in Siberia, my sympathies for Marxist ideology led the Russians to believe that I was one of them. They misunderstood where my loyalties lay."

"But you weren't a Communist when you arrived in Palestine," Alexandra said.

"No. I was a Jew who came to Palestine to fight for a Jewish homeland. That superseded all other ideologies and that is something the Russians never understood."

"So why did you join the Communist Party?"

"That's a long story and it does not really matter. What you must understand is that one cannot embrace one's enemy no matter how beguiling he may seem. And Edward Hammadi and his friends are Stalinists and they are our enemies. They hate Jews and they hate Israel. The Arabs who claim they love you as a Jew but not as a Zionist, may accept you but they will demand your full loyalty and if you discover for whatever reason that you cannot give it to them, they will destroy you, not as a Zionist, but as a Jew."

"I shall never stop being a Jew or an Israeli and I have no problems with my loyalties. But I think we've lost sight of our original goals. We're feeding each other on images that have nothing to do with reality. We've stopped questioning our actions and are being asked to follow blindly whatever course is set for us. And we're inflicting a great deal of pain and suffering on innocent people. I feel I have a responsibility toward these people, that I must help them. That it's my duty to help them."

"And how do you intend to do that?" Yanosh asked quietly.

"Well, for starters, I want to know what is true and what is not. I cannot believe that we have a right to kill and maim innocent people."

"Absolute truth does not exist when you're fighting for survival."

"I cannot accept that. And somehow I have to find it out for myself."

"How?"

"By talking to them. Being with them, listening to them. And I don't mean from a podium, where everyone spouts theories. I'm talking about people. People like me, who are not political."

"Alexandra, listen carefully. For the Arabs there are no half measures. If they think they have your sympathy, they will expect your loyalty as well. And at one point, you will discover that you will have to pay a very high price for thinking you can divide your loyalties. A price higher than you can afford. I know. I paid a very high price for thinking the Russians were my friends."

"Why are you telling me this?" Alexandra asked slowly, recalling the conversation between Tanya and Yanosh at Yariv's sixth birthday. Somewhere there was a connection between what Yanosh was saying now and their argument then.

"The price I paid has hurt our family badly and I don't want you to hurt them as well. Especially Michael. At this late stage of his life, he has finally regained his self-esteem. Whether he admits it or not, the fact that he has been exonerated of the murder of David Larom has meant a great deal to him. Don't do anything to hurt him."

She reached out and touched his hand. She did not understand what Yanosh was saying, but whatever he had done was out of his loyalty to Israel and it had broken him. Was there justice in that? Did Israel have a right to demand such loyalty from anyone?

Tanya and Deborah entered the room at that moment, erasing all questions from Alexandra's mind.

"You two look like conspirators," Tanya said as she turned on a light and walked over to Yanosh.

"You're tired, Yanosh," Deborah ventured, noting Yanosh's difficulty in breathing.

"No, I'm not tired. As a matter of fact, Alexandra and I were having a most interesting conversation." He tried to smile as his eyes wandered around the room, resting briefly on each of the women. "How fortunate I am to have all three of you here." Then turning to Deborah, he addressed her with great intimacy. "I am grateful to you Deborah, for many things, but most of all I'm grateful to you for being the first person to tell me about how important being Jewish is and speaking to me of our dreams as a people. I thank you and I have always loved you for that." He turned to Alexandra. "And you have given me a chance to express my undying loyalty to my people." Turning to Tanya, he reached for her hand and held it. "As for you, my beloved wife, you gave me, in your pure and innocent love, the most precious gift when you converted, so that our son could be born a Jew. And now, I have just one more request from you. I want Yariv to say Kaddish for me when I die. He may not understand the request, but he is a good and obedient boy and he will abide by my wish. And I would like you to ask Michael to help him come to understand the full meaning of that prayer."

He's dying, Deborah thought. Her beloved Yanosh was dying and there was nothing she could do to save him. She looked up at Tanya. She had her hand on Yanosh's brow and was stroking it gently. She also knew that Yanosh's life was ebbing away and she was trying to keep contact with him for as long as possible. Deborah turned to look at Alexandra. She was standing by the window, her back to the room, and her shoulders were shaking with sobs.

Yanosh died that night.

Yariv stood at his father's grave, intoning the Kaddish, clinging to Michael's hand. His voice was filled with pain and bewilderment. Everyone understood the confusion as he spoke the words. Yanosh had not seemed like someone who would have wanted Kaddish said for him.

# CHAPTER
# FIFTY

A LEXANDRA sat up with a start. She was wet with perspiration and she looked around cautiously. It was dark out and it took her a minute to realize she was in her room in Bet Enav.

She lay back, aware that the nightmare had awakened her again. It was a recurring one that varied little each time. Always she was confined in a coffin, her eyes bound, her mouth gagged and her wrists shackled in iron chains. She was very cold and she could not breathe. Then the lid of the coffin would fly open, and she could feel someone unshackle her wrists and undo the bandage over her eyes, but by the time her sight would clear, her savior would be gone. She was never able to identify who had set her free. Then she would wake up.

She ran her fingers over her wrists. They were smooth and unbruised and she felt like a fool.

She understood the dream was her reality. She was shackled to her family, to her country, to the traditions in which she had been brought up. She had served her time in the army after her breakup with Ami and she was now staying with Deborah and Michael, watching her grandfather's health deteriorate. Was it any wonder that her life had turned into a living nightmare?

Getting out of bed, she threw on a pair of slacks and a shirt and went down to the kitchen. Tanya was already there, making coffee.

"I hope Uri gets here soon so we can go see the house and come back quickly," Tanya said, handing her a cup. "I hate leaving Deborah alone with Michael for any length of time."

"You really think you want to move to that desolate little fishing village?" Alexandra asked, sipping her coffee.

"It's beautiful. Wait 'till you see it. It's quite primitive and the beach is heavenly."

"I've been there and it is primitive," Alexandra said. "And what about Yariv? He's nearly fifteen and he'll have no friends."

Tanya's face tightened. "He has no friends in Tel Aviv either."

"What is it?" Alexandra asked, unable to hold back. "What is the terrible secret that Yanosh kept and that has brought so much unhappiness into your lives?''

Tanya reached out and took Alexandra's hand. "Don't concern yourself over it. Each person has a duty to himself and Yanosh did what he did because he felt he had to." Her face broke out into a smile. "I'm not trying to be mysterious, except that after Yanosh's death, I explained his feelings to Yariv and now it's Yariv's decision as to whether he wants them made known or not."

"And what did Yariv say?"

"Yariv is an intelligent boy. He loved his father and does not want to make apologies for him, especially since he feels people will think he is doing it for himself. That he's trying to make his own life easier. Someday, when he feels he's proven himself, he'll talk about it."

"Good God. Everyone is a martyr," Alexandra exploded. "You and Yanosh carried a burden that caused you so much unhappiness and now Yariv is being made to do the same."

"Stop it, Alexandra," Tanya said sharply. "We're not martyrs. We're people trying to survive. We set our goals and do what we can to achieve them." Then looking more closely at Alexandra, she softened her voice. "What's troubling you? You're as taut as a wire."

"I don't know," Alexandra answered. "I'm really floundering. I've done everything that's expected of me. Gotten my degree, served in the army and now I don't know where I'm heading."

"At twenty-three, I don't think you've got to have it all so clearly laid out."

"That would probably apply to most girls, but in this family we seem to be dedicated to causes. Whether we like it or not, we've been fed on our heroic ancestry and we're expected to be bigger than life. And I'm just not."

"Didn't you meet anyone in the army that you liked? I was sure you would."

"I almost got engaged twice while I was soldiering, but the men I got involved with were all army men and that life is not for me."

"In the army, I suspect that soldiers are what you meet."

"These men were 'My country, right or wrong.' The dedicated ones." She shrugged. "Those seem to be the type I attract. That's what Ami was and I couldn't take it."

"You didn't like being in the army, did you?"

"No."

"Frankly, I was surprised when you enlisted," Tanya said slowly. "I could have sworn you didn't want to go into the army."

"I didn't."

A strained silence followed Alexandra's last remark.

"What happened to the girl who gave me that big patriotic speech, way back then, about having to serve your country?"

"She obviously got wiped away with time," Alexandra answered. "Besides, things have changed. That need to be alert, on guard against our enemies, real and imagined, has gone by the wayside. And the whole idea of making girls serve in the army is sort of silly." Her face grew flushed. "Look around you. We've grown so arrogant, so sure of ourselves. No one would dare go to war against us."

Tanya winced. "Don't say the word so lightly. 'War' means that my son will have to fight."

"I'm sorry," Alexandra said quickly. "I didn't mean it that way. It's just that it seems to me we've achieved what we wanted. Grandpa and Grandma's generation, and even Naomi and my father's generation, were struggling for something concrete. We're the generation that is left to fulfill that dream and I'm damned if I know what I'm supposed to do."

"You don't have to *do* anything." Tanya was looking at her strangely. "You live in Israel and that, in it's own way, is enough. You build a home, you watch the country grow and become a nation like all others. Eventually you marry, have children and watch them grow up. That's what Deborah did, that's what I'm doing. That's what women around the world do. You're a teacher. Put it to use."

"Well, I've got two jobs waiting for me. One is in Jerusalem starting in September this year. The other is in Haifa starting in January 'seventy-four."

"I'd love it if you were in Haifa. You'd be close to me." She stopped and observed Alexandra for a moment. "Look, right now Michael is our concern and when he's . . ." The pause was imperceptible, "When he's all better, take a vacation. You're tired and that too can cloud your thoughts."

Alexandra caught Tanya's hesitation. They both knew that Michael would not get better, that he was dying, and the idea was very painful. But to Alexandra, Michael's death would be a release. She did not know what she wanted to do, but Yanosh had warned her not to hurt Michael and what she could not say to Tanya was that, somewhere in the back of her mind, she was thinking of leaving Israel. It was only a vague notion, but she would not dream of doing it as long as Michael was alive.

"You're right," Alexandra agreed. "As soon as Michael is better, I'll take a vacation."

Tova walked in at that moment and to Alexandra's relief, the conversation came to an end.

Without a word, Tova started preparing Deborah and Michael's morning tea. She appeared exhausted and the younger women exchanged understanding looks. Tova had been with the family for so many years that she had become a part of it. She celebrated with them, she suffered with them and she felt their pain. Michael was gravely ill and Tova was hurting like the rest of them.

"Funny how habits don't change," Alexandra said, watching Tova laying out the linen napkins on a tray and placing the Limoges cups and teapot on it. "I understand Grandma's mother always had her tea in bed before she came down in the morning."

"She deserves it more than anyone I know," Tanya said angrily.

"I agree," Alexandra said quickly and, getting up, she took the tray from Tova. "Let me take it up to them." Uri came in just as she was leaving the kitchen.

Alexandra walked up the stairs, tapped gently on her grandparents' door and pushed it open slowly. Deborah was fully dressed and was sitting on Michael's bed. She looked up when Alexandra walked in and put her finger to her lips. Alexandra tiptoed over to the bed. Her grandfather was still asleep.

"Just put the tray down and I'll take my tea and drink it downstairs," Deborah whispered. "He's had a restless night and I don't want to disturb him."

"You're an unprincipled woman," Uri said good-naturedly, when he saw his grandmother walk into the kitchen. "After all these years, you suddenly leave your husband to have his breakfast alone." Then, noting her expression, he came over and put his arm around her. "How is he this morning?"

Deborah leaned against him. "Poor Michael. He's tired from the struggle to stay alive and yet he so wants to go on living."

"Would you like us to stay?" Tanya asked.

"No, you go along. I have some things to attend to."

The children left and Deborah looked up at the clock. It was eight in the morning and she had promised Michael she would go to his shack that morning. She walked into the kitchen and instructed Tova to go up and sit with Michael while she was out.

If Tova was surprised by Deborah's request, she didn't show it. Deborah had rarely left the house in the past few months, fearful that Michael would need her while she was gone.

Deborah walked quickly toward Michael's shack. That was what he had asked her to do when he was able to catch his breath during the night. His words were almost inaudible, but he indicated that he had left her a letter. She promised she would read it first thing in the morning.

The sight that greeted her when she entered the shack saddened her. All of Michael's precious books were covered with dust, and cobwebs had begun to form in the corners of the desk. The mattress on his cot was bare and the pillows wilted. Small and unpretentious as it was, Michael had always kept this room neat and clean. She had neglected the place and she saw her neglect as an omen. She had accepted that he would never go back there, live there, work there, pray there again.

The letter Michael had spoken of lay folded on top of a thick ledger on the center of the desk. It was only one page long and it was his last will and testament.

She read it quickly. He had little to leave, it said, since all was in his wife's name and any properties he bought or any improvements he made during his time as overseer were automatically hers. He wanted all of his religious books to go to the Bet Enav library. The few precious mementos he collected over the years were listed and every grandchild and great-grandchild was to receive one. There was also a Bible for each with a dedication and a special psalm marked which he felt would benefit the recipient. The final paragraph was directed to her personally.

*And my dear Deborah.*

*I have no material properties to leave you, I simply return this estate, which I oversaw, to your capable hands. I know you will run it as fairly, efficiently and intelligently as you did our home. It is all in order, except that you will have to deal with Benji. I have been too lenient with him and I regret it. Somehow it was beyond my power to refuse him anything all these years. I related to his anger, his loneliness, his inability to communicate his feelings. He reminded me of myself when I stood outside looking in and thought that money and power would fill the need. I was fortunate to have you. Benji has made some bad mistakes and, too soon, you will be confronted with them. I should have listened to you years ago, when you wanted to divide the property between yourself and Gidon. I was greedy then. Not for myself but for my son. Now this division becomes much more complex. How I wish I could spare you this agony. But I trust your judgment. Mine was colored by emotion.*

*The ledger beneath this letter is a complete financial report of all my dealings, as well as Benji's, relating to your properties, and I trust your wisdom and sense of fair play in dealing with him.*

*All my love forever,*

Michael

She felt the tears on her cheeks. The one thought that stayed with her was that he felt he had nothing to leave her. He had given her so much, and although she'd tried to tell him of her devotion to him, her words always fell short. Did he know it? Did he know how much she cared?

Putting the letter in her pocket, she sat down and scanned the ledger. She had not realized how extensive their holdings were, nor did she realize their value. Michael had handled their affairs brilliantly and she was a very wealthy woman. Tanya, of course, had fifty percent of the property and Naomi and Benji, also heirs, would share in the other fifty. Neither Tanya nor Naomi had been advanced any money. Benji had. Michael had, indeed, indulged their son and Benji's expenditures were staggering. He owed the estate a great deal of money. And according to Michael, Benji would soon be coming to her for help. She felt torn. She could, without difficulty, forgive his debt to her, but she would not cancel out what he owed Tanya. Poor Tanya, since marrying Yanosh, had lived a frugal life.

With the ledger under her arm, she walked home, praying that Michael would be up and that she could talk to him. She did not know how she would deal with Benji. She never did know. She had been afraid of his rages when he was young and that fear had not abated. She wondered if he felt her fear. After all these years she still felt guilty about not spending enough time with him while he was growing up. But the others had needed her more. Especially Gidon. And Benji did have Michael, as none of the others had. Benji was nearly fifty years old, yet he was still Michael's little boy. Now Michael was dying and Benji felt abandoned. In a way, Michael had inadvertently stunted Benji, made it impossible for him to grow up. Would Benji have been a different kind of person had he lost his father at a younger age? Was there a right age for one to lose a parent? She had lost her father when she was eight. Was that better, had it made her stronger?

Troubled by her thoughts, Deborah pushed open the gate to the house and saw Benji's car standing in the driveway. For a brief moment she was pleased, but the pleasure evaporated quickly. He had not been to see Michael in several days and she wondered if he was there for some other reason. She hesitated before entering the house. She was tempted to go up to Michael before meeting with Benji. She needed his strength and support. She glanced up at their bedroom window. The shades were still drawn, indicating that Michael was still asleep. She had to face Benji alone. Soon she would have to face life alone. She shuddered at the thought.

Benji turned toward her when she came in, although he did not come toward her. She sat down and observed him. He was a handsome man who was aging well. The graying temples gave him an air of distinction and his face was relatively unlined, which made him look younger than his years. Only his eyes, still a deep, velvety blue, were the eyes of an older man. Her heart went out to him.

"Where is everyone?"

"Your father is asleep. Uri, Tanya and Alexandra drove down to look at Tanya's new house."

"Why would she want to live in that godforsaken fishing village?" he asked. "I've seen the house and it's a dump."

"It's all she thinks she can afford and she likes the seashore."

"Oh, well." Benji started pacing.

"Why don't you sit down, Benji?" Deborah suggested. "You always pace when you're upset and it makes me nervous."

"Well, I am very upset." He sat down opposite her and clasped his hands together so tightly that his knuckles went white. "How is Michael feeling?" he asked.

"He's dying, Benji." She had not used the word before and it echoed in her ears. She could not imagine why she had said it.

"That's nonsense." Benji went pale and he wet his lips with the tip of his tongue. "What does the doctor say?"

She did not answer.

"What does the doctor say?" his voice rose.

"Don't shout," Deborah said evenly.

"I'm sorry. It's just a terrible thing to say." He stopped. "Can I see him, talk to him?"

"About what?" she asked, but before he could answer Tova came rushing in.

"Deborah, Michael wants you." Tova was standing in the doorway, tears streaming down her face.

Deborah looked from Tova to Benji and suddenly he looked like a needy, frightened child. He had never really grown up.

She walked over to him and took his hand. "Come," she said gently. She was losing her husband, which was deeply painful, but Benji was losing his father. How sad, she thought, as they walked up the stairs, that this tragic loss would make it possible for him to finally become a man.

Alexandra stepped over the debris and a small stone wall that separated the house from the shore. She settled on a moss-covered rock and looked out at the calm, blue waters of she Mediterranean. It was early May and the air was clear. She could see the bay of Haifa. Small sailboats were gliding silently through the waters. A large steamer was anchored off shore. The smokestacks of the oil refineries were emitting thin white clouds which blended into the air and disappeared. She looked southward. At an adjoining beach, children were splashing in the water, their cries muted by the breeze. Her eyes came to rest on the Crusaders' fortress jutting out into the waters. It stood proud and majestic. It had been part of her scenery since childhood and she loved it. She had gone there years back, with Uri and Tanya, and Uri told them its history. She had never been inside, but had imagined its interior. She had planned to go there and explore it when she grew up, but somehow she never did. She contented herself now with the idea that it would always be there and that someday she would spend time there.

Her thoughts went back to her conversation with Tanya. Why was she so restless? She had everything any girl could want. She was young, she knew she was pretty, she had no financial problems. She loved her family and they loved her. No one was pressing her to make any decisions.

She turned to look at Tanya's house. It stood alone and looked forlorn. She could never live in such seclusion, she thought. Yet Tanya seemed to be looking forward to living there.

Tanya and Uri appeared from behind the house. Tanya was chatting excitedly. She sounded happier than she had since the day Yanosh died.

Alexandra envied her. Tanya was thirty-two years old, but she looked younger than her years. She was still extremely thin and graceful and with her blond hair pulled back into a loose ponytail, she could have been mistaken for a carefree teenager. Alexandra wondered if she would ever marry again. She doubted it. Short as it was, her life with Yanosh had been a fulfilling one and she would probably devote her time to caring for Yariv and helping him grow to manhood. Suddenly she understood Tanya's desire to move to the area. Tanya was at peace with herself.

"Alexandra, we're ready to go back," she heard Uri calling.

She stood up quickly and, losing her balance, skidded on the jagged, slippery rocks.

"What happened?" Uri rushed toward her and helped her up.

"I don't know," she said and she started trembling. "I'm terribly cold."

"Cold?" Tanya put her hand to Alexandra's temple.

"I'm frightened and I don't know why." But she did know. She looked from Uri to Tanya. "We'd better get back to Bet Enav."

"Grandpa," Uri cried out and started running toward his car. Tanya followed close behind.

Alexandra was rooted to the spot. Her limbs were strangely heavy and she could not move. She raised her eyes to the hills of Bet Enav. She knew her grandfather was dead. She also knew that his death had freed her and she hated herself for the thought. Slowly she raised her hands and stared at her wrists. They were bruised.

# CHAPTER
# FIFTY-ONE

A LEXANDRA arrived in Paris in the middle of June.
In the end she did not know why she was leaving Israel. Even as
she prepared to leave, she was not fully convinced that she would not
return. Her actions, rather than her plans, dictated her decision. They took
shape as she went from one relative to the other to bid them farewell. Jack and
Naomi, living under the shadow of the occasional firing of Katyushas from
Lebanon, were building for the future. Uri and Bitti, settled in their new home,
were full of plans for their future. Ilan and Oren, blond, blue-eyed boys, were
growing into handsome youngsters, playful and precocious. Rachel, in Beersheba, was surrounded by a half-dozen children, all growing up without fathers, as though that were the norm. Gila was a happy little girl who giggled
and cried as any child anywhere in the world would. Tanya was settled in her
new home on the beach. She seemed happy, she still missed Yanosh, but was
involved with Yariv, who was suffering the awkwardness of adolescence. Only
Benji and Ruth were at a loss as to what their future held. After Michael's
death, Benji had suffered serious financial setbacks and he was forced to
declare bankruptcy. Rumor had it that Deborah had refused to help him out.
The big house in Caesarea was nearly empty of furniture, and the house was
being viewed by prospective buyers. It saddened her. Her pompous father and
her frilly mother looked old and lost. They had no idea where they would go,
once the house was sold. Alexandra felt sorry for them and she did not know
why Deborah had not helped them out, but she trusted Deborah. She would
come through when the time was right. The Danzigers, in the end, always took
care of their own.

Still, the full realization that she was leaving her home, possibly for good,
came to her only when the plane took off and she did not look back at the
disappearing shoreline.

From the minute Alexandra arrived in Paris, she felt calmer than she had
in a long time. She knew no one and no one knew her. On occasions when

strangers would sit down beside her in a café, she would listen graciously to their chatter. They were not concerned with politics, injustice, terrorists, territories or wars. They were concerned with the moment, with being charming, seductive and making an impression. And she loved it.

Occasionally she would wander into small Left Bank clubs, where students from all countries were discussing their views with great seriousness. But none were belligerent. Serious and intense, these young people were going to save the world with slogans and theories, not guns and bullets. She avoided going into cafés that were known to be frequented by Arabs or Israelis, but when she did find herself in one of them, she would listen to the accusations they flung at each other. Both sides sounded outrageous. What did amaze her was that the Arabs who voiced their vociferous loathing of Israel, though excessive, were strangely convincing. But the Israelis countering the attacks sounded equally convincing, except when the subject of the refugees came up. They existed and the Arabs kept talking about them, but it seemed that no one was willing to do anything about them.

She behaved like a tourist. She contacted none of her family's friends and associated only with foreigners, mainly Americans, who were a happy group determined to have a good time. She went on organized tours with them and dated several American men whom she found thoroughly refreshing. Their only political concern was that their President Nixon was involved in some scandal involving tapes. She tried to understand why they took this incident so seriously; to her, anything that did not involve life or death seemed soluble. They were delighted to have her as a companion, since she spoke French and most of them did not. They assumed she was a young woman from Switzerland on vacation.

June and July passed pleasantly and since she had already decided that she would not take the teaching job in Jerusalem in September, she gave herself until at least January to make up her mind about her future. She was running out of money and knew if she wanted to stay on she'd have to get a job. Without a work permit, it would be a problem. She thought she might get work as an au pair, possibly with an American family. That would mean a trip to the United States, which could be fun. She had met an attractive American man named Steve, and he too was pressing her to come.

Stephen Larimore III was from Texas, his family was in oil and he was on his way back from Saudi Arabia. He was a big man physically and was extremely affable. She enjoyed the ease with which he approached life.

"Solid home, plenty of food, nice healthy children, those are the things we dream about. And having money is important. Lots of money." He laughed happily. "But you shouldn't get greedy."

"When does enough money become greed?" she asked. They were sitting in Maxim's and it was Steve's last night in Paris.

"The Saudis are getting greedy," he answered, serious for the first time since she met him.

"What are they like?"

"Who knows? They never really socialize with you. You do business with them and let me tell you, they're damned shrewd and that could be dangerous for us, since they feel exploited by us."

"But the oil is theirs," she said.

"Yes, that's true, but they're so primitive." He looked over at her. "Have you ever been there?"

She shook her head.

"Well, don't go. Now, if you're interested in the Middle East, go to Beirut. You know, Lebanon. Except that it too is changing."

"In what way?"

"Well, they've got all those refugees there and they're growing very visible."

"Growing visible?"

"Acting up. Showing their discontent. They've been there for an awfully long time and Israel, as far as I can see, is not about to take them back."

"What are the refugees like?" she asked.

"How would I know?" He began to laugh. "They're a mess. You can see them on the way to the airport. They have this slum that they live in. They have a lot of children who scream a lot and the older ones complain all the time."

"But you've never met a refugee, have you?" She was surprised at her own question.

"Hardly. I've got my own problems. And frankly, even in Texas we've got slums. I hate to admit it, but slums exist everywhere. In the Middle East they're called refugee camps. But I think that's political gibberish. Trying to make a point."

Alexandra leaned back and sipped her drink. She wondered if anyone had ever met a refugee. Everybody talked about them, but who were they? What did they think about? What did they want? She knew what the Arab leaders said they wanted, but leaders did not always voice the opinions of their people.

Suddenly she became aware of a woman sitting across the room, staring at her intently. Then the woman got up and came toward her.

"I know you from somewhere," she said.

Alexandra could not place her.

"Solange Hammadi." The woman smiled uncertainly.

Alexandra froze. Solange Hammadi was related to Edward, she had forgotten how.

"Alexandra," she said slowly. "Edward introduced me to you several years back."

"Of course," Solange said and relaxed. "I hate it when I forget a face, particularly if my brother-in-law is involved."

"Steve Larimore, Solange Hammadi," Alexandra said, praying Solange would go away.

"Pleased to meet you." He smiled. "Hammadi? Are you Egyptian?"

"No, Lebanese."

"Isn't that funny, we were just talking about Lebanon." Steve laughed good-naturedly. "Have you been here in Paris long?"

Solange grew flustered. "I really shouldn't stay." She looked over at her friends. "I'm here with some guests from Syria and I should get back to them."

"Nonsense. Why don't you all join us?" Steve said expansively.

Solange hesitated, but Steve became insistent. "I've just been to Saudi Arabia and I'd love to talk to some people from Syria."

"How could I forget you?" Solange said to Alexandra when they were seated. "You were the loveliest little thing. Even Edward remembers you. In fact, I've never seen him so taken with any girl as he was with you. And if I remember correctly, you walked out on him and we were all flabbergasted. No one walks out on Edward."

"Did he tell you why I walked out?" Alexandra asked cautiously. For some reason, Alexandra suspected that he did not.

"No, but he was furious. Why did you walk out on him, anyway?"

Alexandra was relieved from having to answer by the waiter, who interrupted to take their order.

"And your husband, how is he?" Alexandra asked, wanting to change the subject.

"He's in Beirut with Edward." Solange sighed and lowered her voice. "Thank God I didn't have to join them. I just can't take all that upheaval they're going through. You never know where the next bomb is going to fall. So he's there and I'm here and I just hope that Edward doesn't persuade him to stay. And if he does, I'll simply have to ask Jamie for a divorce."

"But aren't you needed in Beirut?" Alexandra asked.

"That's what Edward keeps saying. He expects Jamie and me to stay there all the time, while he gets to go back and forth. Frankly, we both prefer Paris." She smiled at Alexandra. "You know, I remember what you wore the night we met. Your dress was beautiful." Now she was trying to change the subject and Alexandra let it pass. "Clothes," Solange continued. "I love chic clothes. That's one of the reasons I love being here. Thank heaven Jamie's mother loves clothes too, so Edward can't become too upset with me when I shop. I do wish she could come and live here. She's elegant and knows about good living, but Edward makes all of us feel guilty about that. When he's around, we have to sit on the floor and wear sacks, or we're considered traitors."

Alexandra remembered distinctly Edward telling her he had grown up in a refugee camp. Every detail of her evening with him came back to her.

"You sound very close to your mother-in-law," Alexandra said.

"Oh, I adore her and she loves me. Which is very unusual. She says I'm the daughter she never had. And she means it."

"Do you have children?" Alexandra asked, not knowing what else to say.

"What would I do with children?" Solange asked laughingly.

"Does Edward?"

"Hardly. He's not married and he's such a prude. Besides, he's quite fanatic. He wants his children to be born in Palestine."

"And what do you do with yourself all day?" Alexandra asked, not really interested in the answer. Instead she tried to conjure up Edward's image. He was the handsomest man she had ever met.

"Well, thank God the season is just beginning, so I'm involved in several charity functions. When it's a charity, even Edward understands I have to look well."

"Edward sounds like he's running your whole life," Alexandra ventured slowly.

"Well, it's practically so. But I think Jamie is getting fed up too. He has a mind of his own and he really doesn't agree with Edward on the basic approach to the refugee problem. He's much more . . ." She paused. "He doesn't think you have to live in poverty to help the refugees. I do hope he succeeds in breaking away from Edward."

"Do you see Edward that often?"

"Whenever he comes to Paris." She started giggling. "Oh, I wish I had known you were here, I would have surprised him by inviting you over. That would have been a scene." The thought appealed to her. "Would you like me to tell him you're here when I see him next?"

"No," Alexandra said quickly. "What I mean is, I don't really know where I'll be living or how much longer I'll be here. I'm running out of money and if I stay I'll need a job."

"What kind of job?"

"Tutor, nursemaid, au pair, something like that." She regretted her openness, aware that Solange's expression changed. Solange obviously had little use for anyone who did not have money, and although she seemed on the surface a silly chatterbox, Alexandra sensed she was very shrewd. "My family wants me to come home, get married and settle down. Or they'll cut off my allowance," Alexandra hurried to explain.

"Well, I know someone who's looking for a girl Friday. He's a Lebanese newspaperman, needs a sort of housekeeper-secretary." She stopped briefly. "You do speak Arabic, don't you?"

"Of course."

"The only problem is"—she leaned closer again—"I'm not sure what he is."

"What do you mean?"

"He may be Jewish." She looked around furtively. "But if he is, I'm sure he'd deny it. And in spite of it, everybody trusts him, which means he's totally untrustworthy." She laughed merrily. "I heard Edward say that."

"Where do I find him?"

Alexandra took out a pad and pencil and got the phone number.

"Well, you two look like you've had a wonderful reunion," Steve said, and Alexandra looked around in surprise. She had forgotten he was there. Seeing Solange made the past and Edward suddenly come alive and it troubled her. To her relief, Steve stood up and after hearty goodbyes and promises to be in touch, they left.

The man's name was Tufik Mazzari and his house was close to the Luxembourg Gardens on the Left Bank of Paris. A pleasant, middle-aged man, he was looking for someone who could do simple secretarial work and look after his children.

"It's actually an easy job, except that I go to Lebanon constantly and I need someone here to stay with my children when I'm away."

"How old are your children?" she asked politely.

"Twelve and fourteen and they've very good, except that they miss Beirut."

She wanted to ask why he did not take them home, but he supplied the answer.

"Unfortunately people like us, it will soon not be safe there."

She waited for him to continue, baffled by the phrase "for people like us."

"You are a close friend of Solange Hammadi?" he asked.

"Not really. I knew her brother-in-law briefly, years ago, and I ran into her in a restaurant the other night."

"Edward Hammadi?"

She nodded.

"If you will forgive me," he said after a moment, "I can usually place accents, but I don't recognize yours."

"I am from Israel, Mr. Mazzari."

He nodded slowly. "How do you know Hammadi?"

"When I met him I didn't know he was an Arab and unlike you, he did not question my accent and did not realize I was Israeli."

"Your French is excellent."

"Swiss summer camps and private tutors."

"And you're looking for work as an au pair?"

"Mr. Mazzari, I left Israel quite recently. I will not take money from my family and I am looking for work, but I do not have a work permit. Au pair is all I can do and even that is illegal." She started to get up.

"No, no." He waved her to sit. "I am Jewish. My wife was not. I have not lived as a Jew for many years, but what is going on in Lebanon now concerns me. I also think I would like to give my children a taste of my heritage, which is almost impossible in Beirut today."

"Then why didn't you take your children to Israel?"

"I am trying to get them away from hostilities, not bring them into another war zone."

A cold shudder ran down her back. "Will there be other wars?"

"There will be many other wars." He nodded his head thoughtfully. "They come every six or seven years." He smiled wryly. "Let's see. This is 1973-so we're just about due." He sounded almost clinical. To her, war was very personal. Little Yariv's life would be at stake.

"There is one other thing. Are you free to travel if the need should arise?" he asked.

"Travel?"

"My mother lives in Beirut. At the moment she is too ill to travel, or I would have brought her to Paris. In September, her housekeeper goes on vacation and I will need someone to take over while she's gone."

Alexandra smiled in spite of herself. "I would do it happily. But I have an Israeli passport, and I believe that would be rather difficult."

"I can attend to that. I am well connected and can probably get you one that would be acceptable." He looked at her for a minute. "Greek? Italian? Maybe Swiss?"

She laughed. "I'll take the Swiss one, if it's that easy."

"Even Swiss is easy these days," he said sadly. "In spite of our internal conflicts, the Lebanese currency is still strong." He studied her closely. "What name would you like to use?"

She mulled it over. "I've tried Benneau and it works, since it's close to Ben Hod."

"Alexandra Benneau." He mulled the name over. "Can I count on you? You won't change your mind?"

She nodded and smiled inwardly. Because of Edward's sister-in-law, she might get to Lebanon. The idea was too outrageous.

# CHAPTER
# FIFTY-TWO

T HE job proved to be pleasant. The children were rarely around, the
secretarial work simple and she soon understood that the main reason
she was hired was to accompany Mazzari to Beirut. Few young women
would be willing to go there, with the news growing more ominous daily. She
only hoped her passport and visa would arrive by the time they were ready
to leave.

Working for Mazzari brought Israel and the problems of the Middle East
back into her life. She wasn't sure what he did, but newspapers from all over
the world arrived at his house and although every corner of the universe was
having its problems, Alexandra automatically focused on the news from home.
She had been living in a dream world as a tourist out to enjoy herself. But the
reality of Israel was as harsh as ever.

The terrorist attacks appeared to be growing. The retaliatory attacks were
as ferocious as ever. She condoned neither and being privy to newspapers that
were not all sympathetic to Israel, she was now confronted with a very different
picture of her country. Israel, the reports claimed, was the cause of the conflict.
The Arabs wanted peace and all they wanted was what had been stolen from
them by the Zionists. Israel was the aggressor and any terrorist act was justified.
She was stunned to discover newspaper articles that referred to towns and
villages she knew well as property that belonged to named Arab individuals.

Alexandra could not understand why none of the articles gave the history
of how the wars started, who started them and how brutal each war had been.
It seemed the facts were not relevant when newspaper editors were trying to
make their point. She tried to remember what Yanosh had told her on his
deathbed. The Russians and their followers were enemies of Israel and would
do everything to dismantle the state. She did not doubt Yanosh, but old
doubts returned and new ones were born.

The trip to Lebanon, which had started out almost casually, took on new
meaning. She did not expect to solve any problems, but she desperately
wanted a perspective and insight to help her in mapping out her future as a

Jew and an Israeli, no matter where she decided to live. The thought was both frightening and thrilling.

Solange called a couple of times after Alexandra went to work for Mazzari, but she told the cook to say she was out. Solange Hammadi was a silly lady and Alexandra did not trust her. Neither did Tufik Mazzari. She had the distinct impression he was afraid of the Hammadis, especially of Edward, and preferred her not to be in contact with them.

"Jamie and Solange are hungry and their hunger is easily fed," he said on one occasion when Solange called and Alexandra did not accept her call. "Edward's hungry too, but no one can satisfy his hunger."

She was curious about his statement, but he did not elaborate.

August was coming to an end and Alexandra grew impatient. The Mazzari children were in summer camp and Mazzari was in Beirut. Paris was nearly empty of Parisians and she found herself wandering around aimlessly, trying to decide what she would do if Mazzari did not get her the passport and visa. She missed her family and friends, yet she was not yet ready to go back. She had a running correspondence with Tanya, who kept her informed about all that was going on in the family, and Alexandra did not feel she was missing anything. Deborah was staying with Tanya. Uri's boys were spending time in Bet Enav. Yariv had gone down to Beersheba to visit Rachel, and at fifteen he was madly in love with a Moroccan girl named Leyanna, whose father was a big shot on the political scene. Tanya also described the Arab terrorist attacks, the tensions on the borders, the new Jewish settlements that were going up in the occupied territories. And the fear of the future. The letters were a running commentary about life in Israel, which Alexandra was trying to move away from but was still bound to in every way.

At one point she even tried wording her thoughts to Tanya in a letter. It was a long letter, explaining her need to get away and admitting her confusion. It was rambling and had no point of view, no conviction. She kept repeating that she wanted peace, that she loved Israel, loved her people, but there was something that was going on in Israel that she could not accept. She emphasized that her feelings were not motivated by politics. Politics and politicians were the culprits and she wanted no part of their activities and conclusions. She ended the letter by saying she did not know when she would return but knew that when she found herself, found some peace within herself, she hoped to go back to Israel. She begged her not to have anyone try to find her. She needed time alone. Rereading the letter embarrassed her, and she never mailed it.

But most disconcerting was that since meeting Solange, she found herself thinking about Edward. He became an obsession. It had been six years since she'd seen him and although she had not thought of him in a long time, now she was genuinely curious. When Solange called at the end of August, she accepted the call.

"Edward's in town," she said, and Alexandra detected a note of malice in the woman's voice. "Do you want to see him?"

She was about to ask if he wanted to see her, but it did not matter. Yes, she did want to see him. It was crucial for her to see him. In a way, Edward was the one who had started her on the path of confusion.

"Yes," she said. "Where?"

"There's a café in Montparnasse. Nobody's ever heard of it, so write down the address and give it to the taxi driver. He'll find it. And when you get there, just sit and wait. Edward will come."

"At what time?"

"Ten o'clock this evening."

Alexandra dressed with great care. She wanted their meeting to be reminiscent of their first encounter, not their last one. She did not want him to see her confusion. She observed herself in the mirror. She looked well and it pleased her. She moved away and took in her overall appearance. She had on a simple black dress that was gathered below her breasts and then draped softly to mid-knee. The bateau neckline exposed her smooth neck and set off her small, dimpled chin. She had on sheer black stockings, black high-heeled pumps, which made her look taller than her petite size. Other than her diamond earrings, she wore no jewelry. She added some rouge to her cheeks and put a touch of lip gloss to her lips. Then, as an afterthought, she ringed her eyes with black pencil to add mystery to her face. She looked like an Arabian Nights princess and the thought made her smile. She was not looking to seduce Edward, but she wanted him to like her. She also hoped they could be friends.

With the address tucked into her bag, she threw on her wool cape and rushed out of the house.

While waiting for a taxi on the boulevard, she got the feeling she was being watched. She looked around but saw no one who appeared suspicious. It was nearly 9:30 and people were rushing about, heading toward their various destinations, and no one was paying attention to her. There were no available taxis and she began to walk to another intersection. The feeling that she was being followed persisted. At one point a small Peugeot stopped and the driver offered her a lift. She smiled her thanks but continued walking. She reached a bridge and waited for a light to change before crossing. Several people stood beside her, also waiting. Someone pushed up against her and she stared up, annoyed. The man apologized and asked if he could buy her a drink. She turned away and ran across and hurried along the river side of the road, wondering if she should try to catch a bus. She looked at the paper in her hand. The address meant nothing to her. She recrossed the avenue and started looking for a phone. She waited outside the booth while a woman finished her conversation, came out, apologized for taking so long and walked off. Alexandra dialed information, misdialed, hung up, and dialed again. The number rang and she leaned against the wall of the booth, staring out. Someone was standing a few feet away, under a street light, staring at her. She hung up without waiting for an answer and ran from the booth. She was sure she had seen the man before, but could not remember where. Just then a taxi stopped in front of her, left a passenger off, and she jumped in. Handing the taxi driver the address, she sat back and looked out the rear window. The man was trying to hail a taxi, but was having no luck.

The restaurant was small and dilapidated. It was also empty. She found a seat near a window facing an abandoned little park. She ordered a coffee and stared out at the neglected garden.

"Solange told me you were in Paris." She heard Edward speak and she swung around.

He had barely changed. He was as handsome as she remembered. The broad forehead, the finely arched brows, the same gentle face, the jet black eyes, warm and filled with compassion. Except for his mouth. It was set into a thin, grim line.

"You look as if you've seen a ghost, yet you knew I was in Paris," he said.

She nodded, unable to speak.

"I understand you wanted to see me," he said.

She nodded again.

"Why?"

"I'm not sure." That was not what she had meant to say, but his presence flustered her.

"That's a waste of time. So if you'll forgive me, I'm busy." He started to walk away.

"Please don't go," she whispered. "I really do want to talk to you. It's important to me."

He hesitated briefly, looked around, then sat down opposite her and took out a cigarette.

"Do you smoke?" he asked.

"I don't want one, thank you."

He lit it and looked expectantly at her. When she continued staring at him, he grew impatient. "Well, what's so important?"

"Recently I've thought a great deal about you." She felt like a fool.

His expression did not change.

"Did you ever think of me?" she asked, and felt even more foolish.

"Yes. Often."

"Do you hate me?"

"No." He inhaled deeply and watched her through the smoke. "The truth is, I believe I love you. I told you when we met that I did. I've never said it to any other woman and I don't think I ever will." He shrugged. "But you probably expected that from the hero of your little fantasy." His lips parted slightly. "Unfortunately, fantasy is all I can afford."

"But why?"

"Because my reality is so grim and I must escape occasionally—into fantasy," he said, looking directly at her.

She tried desperately to think of something to say, but her mind had gone blank.

"So now if you'll forgive me." He started to get up.

She reached out and touched his arm. The physical contact sent a strange sensation through her. She had forgotten what physical desire was. He stared down at her hand holding onto his sleeve but did not shake himself free and she knew that he was reacting to her touch.

"What's the matter?" she said.

"Nothing." He looked around him and peered through the window.

Still clutching his arm she too looked out "Is there someone out there?" she asked and was surprised by her question.

He turned to her and a strange expression came to his face. "I don't think so. Unless . . ."

"Unless what?"

"What is it you want of me?" He shook his arm free of her and he was suddenly angry.

"I want to go home with you." She was shocked by her statement, but did not regret it.

"Is this some part of a plot? Has someone put you up to this? Aren't you afraid of what might happen to you?"

"Plot? Put me up to it? Something happen to me?" She repeated his words slowly. "What could possibly happen to me? It's been six years since I've seen you and . . ." She did not know how to complete the sentence.

He began to laugh. It was a mirthless, angry laugh.

"Why are you laughing?" she cried out. "What have I said that's so funny?"

He grew serious instantly. "In a bad movie, you wouldn't be convincing. I really gave your people more credit than that."

"What are you talking about?"

"If they've asked you to whore for them, you're doing a lousy job." He stopped. "Or is it that you simply want to be made love to by a passionate Arab?" he concluded mockingly.

She ignored the insult. "I don't know what you're talking about."

"Stop it," he snapped. "Just stop it. Stop looking so innocent, so vulnerable, so needy. It won't work."

"You don't believe me." She lowered her eyes in embarrassment. What he was saying made no sense at all.

"Oh, you poor, naive girl," she heard him say. For the first time he sounded like the Edward she remembered. She looked up at him.

"Obviously you're not prepared to tackle this ridiculous assignment." He sounded sad. "Did you really think that by seducing me you could help your cause?"

"Oh, my God," she whispered, understanding for the first time what he was implying. "You think I've been sent here to spy on you?"

"Well, why else would you be alone in Paris, looking for me?"

"I didn't come to Paris to look for you." She regained her composure quickly. "The truth is that you grew dim in my memory. But I never forgot what you told me the last time I saw you. In spite of what you said, I don't believe you hate my people. I certainly don't. I love them, and I think I could love your people too. My heart breaks for them and I want to do something to help them. More important, I want the truth. I want to find out for myself who my people are and who you are. I believe we can live together without killing each other."

"You have been fed so many lies about us since the day you were born, that if truth hit you in the face you wouldn't recognize it," he said angrily.

"And you're that sure that what you know to be the truth is right?" she countered.

"Yes," he hissed. "My truth is that my home has been taken away from me and I shall fight to the death to get it back. My people and I want peace and yours want war. That is my truth."

She was taken aback by his fury but maintained her calm. "Well, you may be sure of what your truth is. I am willing to discover it for myself. You may not believe me, but I am filled with doubts about what we are doing and that's one of the reasons I left Israel."

He was staring at her strangely, and at that moment the waiter came over and whispered into Edward's ear.

"I've got a telephone call." He said and she watched him walk away.

He looked the same but he was different from the young man she met six years earlier. She was glad she had come. Whatever her doubts were, they had nothing to do with Edward.

He was gone for quite a while and she grew restless. When he came back, his face was grim. He lit a cigarette and she could see his hand shake.

"You didn't tell me you were working for Mazzari." His lips barely moved as he spoke.

"You didn't ask, and since I got the job through Solange, I assumed you knew."

His eyes narrowed, "Have you seen her since you started working there?"

"No. But she called the other day and said I should meet you here."

"She comes off like a fool, but she's not, you know," he said slowly. "Does she see Mazzari?"

"I don't know, but I doubt it. He isn't very fond of her."

"Affection would not be the reason Solange would see someone like him."

"I take care of his mail, his house and, when he's away, his children. I know nothing about his social life."

"Did he put you up to this?"

"Put me up to what?"

"Did he ask you to see me?"

"He isn't in Paris and has no idea that I would be seeing you."

"But he knows you know me."

"Yes."

"He's a spy for the Zionists, you know."

"If he is, I don't know it. He told me he writes for some newspapers."

"He sells information to anyone who buys his lies, but he works for the Zionists."

"Edward, how can I prove to you that I am here because I want to be here." Suddenly she was angry. "I did not come to Paris to look for you. I came to Paris because I did not feel comfortable in Israel. After meeting Solange accidentally, I admit I wanted to see you. Don't ask me why." She took a deep breath. "I wish there was some way I could prove to you that what I am saying is true."

"I was convinced you were lying, when I first saw you. Now I'm completely confused." Then he started to list her actions from the minute she left Mazzari's house until she got to the café they were in.

"Good God, *you* had me followed." She gasped. She looked around for her cape. "I think I'd better go."

"Wait," he said coldly. "I'll have you driven to your little Zionist employer."

She turned slowly and stared at him. "You poor man," she said. "Some day you'll regret this evening."

"Zionist whore," she heard him mutter as she walked out the door.

Alexandra felt strangely calm the days following her meeting with Edward. His behavior that night seemed to relieve her of her fantasy. She was looking forward to going to Lebanon and was ready to discover her own truth about what she was about and where she belonged. She would be there only a short while, but the trip was important to her.

Mazzari came back a few days later and brought her a passport. They were to leave in early September. She told him immediately about her meeting with Edward. Somehow she felt he should be aware of it.

"Yes, I know," he said simply.

Stunned, she sat silently for a long time. "Am I still being followed?" she finally asked.

"No. The Mossad thought you would lead them to Hammadi. But he's very shrewd and he was ready for them."

"But how? Why?" She started.

"Solange Hammadi."

Alexandra paled. "Who's side is she on?"

"The one that pays the most."

"Did she set it up?"

"Maybe."

"Does Edward know this?"

"Everybody knows it." He shrugged. "But she's not a problem anymore. She was shot dead a few hours after you left Edward."

"Who?" She started and then unable to listen, she put her hands to her ears. "I don't want to hear anymore. It's too terrible." She stood up. "If you'll excuse me, Mr. Mazzari, I should like to go to my room."

Just before leaving for Beirut, Alexandra wrote one more letter to Tanya. She said she was going on a trip and would be in touch. She left no forwarding address.

# CHAPTER
# FIFTY-THREE

I T was raining the night Alexandra boarded the Air France flight to Beirut. She was alone. Tufik Mazzari had left two days earlier.

She was tired by the time she got on the plane and slept during most of the journey.

The captain's voice, announcing their imminent landing at Beirut Airport, awakened her and she peered out the window. She saw a strip of brightly lit hotels lining the coastline, with the sprawling city behind them, and a high mountain range reminiscent of Haifa.

The lights in the cabin were turned on and the steward opened the plane's doors. The humid heat rushed in, bringing the familiar odor and sounds of the Middle East. Alexandra took a deep breath and leaned her head back, trying to stop the tears that began streaming down her cheeks. She had not realized how much she missed the textures of that part of the world. Her world. She was a daughter of the Middle East.

Stepping out of the plane, she was surprised at the size of the airport. It was a simple one-story structure, not unlike the Tel Aviv airport. The weather was balmy. The sky was a wondrous midnight blue, and millions of tiny stars were made brighter by the full moon. It appeared to be welcoming her.

It was past midnight but the terminal was humming with life. People were rushing about, shouting, arguing and haggling in various languages. She noted that most were dressed in European fashions. She also noted an inordinate number of uniformed guards, with rifles slung over their shoulders, scanning the crowd. They made her uncomfortable.

"Miss Benneau?" A strange-looking man addressed her. "Mr. Mazzari is waiting for you just outside the terminal in a black Mercedes." The man spoke in fluent French. "If you will give me your stub, I will find your bags and bring them along."

He took her passport and indicated that she was to follow him. He walked with great authority, without waiting on any line. Officials stamped her documents with barely a glance at them.

Tufik Mazzari kissed her hand respectfully and helped her into the car. It was a polite gesture, but she noted a change in him. He looked as he did in Paris, but his manner was that of an Oriental man—protective, patronizing, almost condescending. He was like a chameleon and it amused her. He was, after all, a Levantine.

The gentleman who had met her arrived with her bags and got in behind the wheel. As the car started off, Mazzari looked out the back window and smiled.

"Don't drive too quickly, George." His tone was humorous. "Let them catch up with us."

"Tufik, don't make fun. This is serious," George said angrily.

"Not at all. We have nothing to hide. Mlle. Benneau is a legitimate Swiss citizen, the relative of friends of mine in Geneva, and she has been kind enough to help me with my mother until our housekeeper comes back from vacation. If we become evasive, they will think we have something to hide."

"Who exactly is following us?" Alexandra asked nervously.

"It's very hard to tell these days. The people from the Lebanese Securité, for one. Habbash's people, Arafat's people, I don't know. I don't think they themselves know who they are supposed to report to."

Leaving the airport, they drove a short distance, and, reaching a cul de sac bordering on a pine forest, they turned into a darkened highway. She was only vaguely aware of the surroundings when she saw a fence running along the road. Beyond it, she could see the outline of dilapidated wooden huts and numerous tents that appeared to be crammed together. There were dimly lit light poles meant to serve as streetlights for narrow, dark roads. The place was shrouded in silence, except for an occasional cry of an infant, or the yelping of a dog. Other than those noises, the place seemed empty of inhabitants. Dimly lit as it was, the smell of misery rose from it, like a heavy, mildewed blanket.

The fence seemed to stretch for miles, interrupted only by gaps, next to which stood men, their heads covered with checkered scarves, rifles strapped to their shoulders. Some were chatting, others were squatting on the ground playing cards, their rifles jammed into the earth beside them. Several of them turned their heads as the car passed and Alexandra saw that they were very young men.

"That's a refugee camp, isn't it?" she asked, staring out the window.

"It's not a camp," George snapped. "What you're looking at is nothing but a filthy slum, and the only reason for that fence is so the children do not run out into the road."

"You mean the people living there can leave it whenever they want?"

"Nobody is keeping them there but their own leaders." He was breathing heavily, obviously angered by her implied question. "We never had slums like this before they came here."

"How did they get here?" she asked with pretended innocence.

"It goes back quite a few years. At first we took them in as guests and treated them as such. Slowly their numbers grew. And since then, every time they encounter a misfortune, they flock to these areas. Between that and their unbelievable birthrate, the slums have grown and grown. And when Jordan expelled them, it's become a total nightmare."

"George, calm down," Tufik ordered.

"Why should I? Lebanon is a sovereign state, the gem of the Middle East. We have our laws, which are there to keep order in our country. Now, we're suddenly negotiating with their leaders for our rights to exist. Hussein just massacred them and ordered the ones he didn't kill to leave. It's not very democratic, but he certainly got rid of them."

"George, stop it," Tufik said more forcefully.

George complied but pressed the gas pedal down, obviously trying to get away from the area.

Alexandra leaned back and stared out the window. They finally turned off the highway and drove through a brightly lit avenue. Although it was late, the cafés were quite crowded, the shops well lit, and the displays in the windows elegant. As they maneuvered through the heavy traffic, she caught sight of several movie marquees advertising the latest American, French and Italian films. The billboards crowding the rooftops advertised the best of European products. Then, turning off the main thoroughfare, they drove into a quieter area and she could see they were approaching an elegant residential area. The car stopped in front of a whitewashed cement wall topped by wrought-iron grillwork. The iron gate was locked.

George jumped out and pushed the gate open. The short, graveled driveway was well cared for. A clust of pine trees caught her attention and she sat up. This could have been the driveway in Bet Enav, she thought. It troubled her. She dismissed the thought and concentrated on the house.

"Your bags will be taken up to your room," Mazzari said. "Sleep well and I shall see you at breakfast. After that I'll introduce you to my mother."

Her room was large and comfortable. Done in a shade of old rose, the walls and furnishings blended pleasantly. It could have been her room in Caesarea, she thought wryly.

She walked out to the balcony. The mountains were bewitching. The night was slowly coming to an end, and behind the peaks the sun had begun to rise. She sat down in a large wicker chair to watch the brightness edge its way slowly to the crests. It was a new day and the Middle East was waking up. Thoughts of sleep were far from her mind. She was a daughter of this part of the world and she felt strangely close to her home in Israel.

Mrs. Mazzari was a very old woman. She lay in a huge, canopied bed, covered with a heavy comforter in spite of the warm weather. Her voice was low and the expression in her eyes clearly indicated that she was in great pain. Alexandra felt that she was filled with fear and she could not shake the feeling that the old woman's fear went beyond her fear of death.

Tufik Mazzari left after one week, assuring Alexandra that Mrs. Dansur, the housekeeper, would be back in a few weeks and then she could come back to Paris.

While waiting for Mrs. Dansur's return, Alexandra began to plan her speech to Mr. Mazzari in case she decided to stay on for a while. It helped that he knew she was an Israeli and that he was Jewish. He might even help her stay. Mrs. Mazzari began to plead with Alexandra not to leave her alone in Beirut.

"But Mrs. Dansur has been with you for a long time and I understand she is very devoted to you."

"She is devoted, but working for me is dangerous for her and I suspect that she will not be coming back."

"Why?"

"I am Jewish, she is a Christian and she does not feel safe in this house."

"But Jews have nothing to fear in Lebanon."

Mrs. Mazzari smiled feebly. "That was so before. Now Jews have everything to fear in Lebanon."

"From whom?"

"From everyone. The leaders of the refugees hate the Christians, but they hate us more."

"I think you're wrong. They are angry with Israel, but not with the Jews."

Mrs. Mazzari looked at her sadly. "That is rhetoric which is sold to the world by the Arabs. It sounds good, but that is not their true sentiment, I assure you."

Yanosh's warnings came back to Alexandra but she shook them away. These people were of a different generation. Things had changed.

Mrs. Mazzari was right about her housekeeper. Mrs. Dansur did not return. Her note was filled with apologies, but her family forbade her to return to Beirut.

Mazzari returned within days after Mrs. Dansur's resignation. George had been trying to find a replacement, but to no avail. Mazzari was equally unsuccessful and he was greatly relieved when Alexandra offered to stay on.

"Just until she's well enough to travel," he said firmly. "Then you'll both come back to Paris."

Other than an old gardener, a laundress and a part-time maid, George was Alexandra's only companion.

It was he who took her on short drives while Mrs. Mazzari slept and was watched by the gardener or the part-time maid.

Often as not, she and George would shop, have coffee in some elegant outdoor café, and drive around. She got a full view of cosmopolitan West

Beirut, from its elegant streets, luxurious hotels, lovely beaches, impressive embassy buildings and the American University, to the markets full of round baskets piled high with vegetables and fruits. Tattered street urchins dodged in and out of the throngs of people, which included hatless, sleeveless, stockingless European women wearing makeup, walking poodles on leashes, and battling with the vendors in two languages, beside their Arab sisters who were swathed from head to toe in thick black cloaks, some with veils over their faces. The city abounded in luxury but the proximity of the camps to all this affluence never ceased to bother her. Nobody seemed care about the refugees.

Aware of George's feelings about them, she hesitated to ask him to drive her toward the airport.

"You're fascinated by that ghastly slum, aren't you?" He mocked her. "Why? It's terribly depressing."

"I don't know. Maybe I need an antidote to all this luxury." She tried to make light of her request.

He swung the car around and headed toward the area inhabited by the refugees.

They drove along the wide highway, passing numerous cars, and quite a few were streamlined, chauffeur-driven limousines. The occupants were usually black-veiled women who peered out their windows as their cars raced toward the airport. Then traffic suddenly slowed and finally came to a halt. It seemed to take forever, but finally the cars started moving again and the cause of the traffic jam was made clear—a stubborn donkey, who had refused to budge from the middle of the road. Alexandra began to giggle at the incongruity: the whole modern machinery of the advanced world put on hold because of a mule.

George glanced at her with annoyance.

She grew grimly sober as the fence along the side of the road appeared ahead of them.

George drove slowly past the area.

Her wildest imagination could not have conjured up the misery that now in daylight could be seen through the mass of tangled wire fence. What had appeared a sleepy slum the night she arrived was now pulsating with life: screaming men and women; laughing children; blaring music; vendors hawking their goods; women squatting in the middle of a street doing their laundry, their faces covered with veils, their bracelets gleaming in the suffocating heat as they worked. Boys, brown as earth, disheveled and in tatters, were chasing a football amid the squalor. A nondescript dog whose bones were visible through his colorless fur walked aimlessly, trying to keep himself from being trampled underfoot, and several goats were scurrying over open sewers as if in search of something. The filth was everywhere. And above the din, the sound from the minaret could be heard, calling the people to worship.

Alexandra felt sick and turned her head away.

"Had enough?" George asked and, without waiting for an answer, he pressed his foot down on the gas pedal and raced ahead.

"I don't understand any of this," she whispered. "Why would anyone live there?"

"Don't ask me," George asked soberly. "As far as I'm concerned, these wretched people should have been relocated years ago."

She recalled the exchange between George and Tufik the night she arrived. The refugees were polluting his beautiful country.

"Listen, Alexandra. You're from Switzerland, I'm a Christian Maronite. Would your government tolerate this mess? Even if you had a good portion of Moslems living in your country, would you allow them to impose their co-religionists on you? You don't have to answer. We in Lebanon feel that there are enough countries around here who should have taken them long ago and given them a home." He took a deep breath. "What baffles me is that their leadership uses them as a bargaining chip with us, mind you, with us, as if we're to blame for their problems."

"What about Israel? Shouldn't Israel do something?"

"My dear girl, the people in charge of this show don't want to share anything with anyone. They want the Jews out of that country. Soon they will demand that we Christians get out of Lebanon. That's their way. And that's why my church always supported a Jewish state. We are a minority in this part of the world and we felt that the Jews could be our partners."

"But isn't Israel responsible for their being here?" she asked haltingly.

"Well, that's an interesting question. Do you think Israel does not have a right to exist?"

She bit her lip in confusion. That was not what she meant. She did not want to get into that debate. "What's going to happen to these people?"

"God only knows. Most of them don't even know where their homes were. Oh, some of the older ones remember, but the little ones who speak of their olive trees somewhere in Jaffa, or wherever, are being fed on some idiotic fantasy. And to what end?"

"It's their home."

"They've never seen it. And as far as I'm concerned, my country is now at stake because of them. This can lead to a civil war, and then heaven help us. I certainly won't fight for them to stay here. In fact, I'll fight to kick them out."

She did not answer. She understood what he was saying, but like her grandfather's explanation, it left too many unanswered questions.

In mid-September, Mazzari returned and stayed a few days. He looked troubled and was unusually attentive to her, as though he were begging her forgiveness and pleading for patience. Before leaving, he arranged for her to have a car so that she would not be solely dependent on George. He promised to be back in early October. Alexandra grew impatient. She had a reason for coming to Beirut. She wanted to go into a camp, wanted to talk to the people, find out who they were, what they thought, what they felt. She could hardly ask George to help her, and Mazzari was much too busy with his mother's welfare to be bothered.

By late September, Alexandra grew edgy. Something was happening in the city and she did not understand what it was. There was an air of excitement and anticipation that she had not sensed before. The women in the market-place in their black embroidered dresses seemed to be chattering in louder voices. There were more young men, their heads wrapped in the checkered scarves worn mainly by Arab refugees, out on the streets. They too were noisy and boisterous, which was unlike them. And as always, the streets were filled with uniformed men, their rifles slung over their shoulders, scowling at the crowd. But whereas in the past they simply stood around looking bored, they now seemed to be waiting for someone to start a fight so that they could begin shooting.

She called George and although she tried to sound calm, he sensed her anxiety.

"Let me get some of my men to stay at the house until Mazzari comes. He should be here by next Friday at the latest and we'll work something out."

"Have you heard from him?" He had not called her in several days, which was unlike him.

"No. But next Saturday is a very important Jewish holiday and he always spends it with his mother."

"Holiday?" she asked with genuine surprise.

"It's the Day of Atonement, which the Jewish people take very seriously," George explained.

She hung up, feeling miserable. If next Saturday was Yom Kippur, then today was Rosh Hashanah and she had not realized it. She had no idea why she wanted to cry, yet she did. In spite of all her efforts to cut herself off from the past, it was still part of her.

The guard was posted outside the Mazzari house, and Alexandra waited impatiently for her employer's arrival. She was not worried for herself. She was concerned for Mrs. Mazzari. For some reason she was convinced the woman should not be in Beirut.

Mazzari was delayed and could not come until Sunday after Yom Kippur. He did call, however, and made her promise to light the candles with his mother.

On Friday evening, as the sun was setting, Alexandra, holding Mrs. Mazzari's frail hand, watched the old woman light the candles. Then, closing her eyes, Mrs. Mazzari said a silent prayer and lit the memorial candle, as Jewish women around the world did in memory of a loved one who had died. In Israel almost every house lit one on the eve of this holiday. At that moment Alexandra thought of going home. Hard as she tried to drown out her longing for Israel and her family, it was there.

She placed the memorial candle, which would burn for twenty-four hours, on the dresser so that Mrs. Mazzari could see it when she awoke.

At noon, with Mrs. Mazzari fed and bathed and ready for her afternoon nap, Alexandra decided to drive into town. She needed time to herself. Also, the burning candle was conjuring up too many memories and she wanted to get away from what it recalled.

It was five in the afternoon when Alexandra was rounding the last bend in the road leading up to the Mazzari house when she noticed a bright light coming from that direction. She floored the gas pedal, her heart pounding. Then she saw the house being devoured by flames. She slammed on the brakes and, getting out of the car, she raced up the small incline. Police cars and fire engines were everywhere.

"Where do you think you're going?" a fireman shouted at her.

She ignored him and pushed her way into the burning house.

The lower gallery was filled with smoke, and flames were shooting up around her. She started up the marble stairway. The wooden bannister was burning. She got to the second-floor landing. Fire was coming from Mrs. Mazzari's room. She ran into her own room and got into the old woman's room through the terrace entrance. It was enveloped in flames and she could see Mrs. Mazzari sitting up in bed, her eyes staring blankly into space. The four wooden bed posts were on fire and the bedding was being consumed by the flames. She tried to reach the bed when a huge beam came crashing down and the ceiling caved in.

The last thing Alexandra remembered before she passed out was Mrs. Mazzari's terrified look. Then she felt someone dragging her out onto the terrace.

# CHAPTER
# FIFTY-FOUR

THE phone rang at six o'clock in the morning. Uri picked it up quickly before it could wake Bitti and the children. He listened intently, his brow wrinkling in concentration, his eyes blazing with anger.

"I'll be there." He replaced the receiver.

"What's going on?" Yariv asked.

Uri stared at him, shook his head and walked out of the kitchen.

Yariv poured himself a second cup of coffee and looked out the window. The house, standing at the edge of the village, faced north, and the Hermon mountains were clearly visible. It was a lovely sight, but his thoughts were on Uri's phone call. It was strange to have anyone call at that hour, particularly on Yom Kippur.

Ilan walked in rubbing the sleep from his eyes. A tall fair-headed boy, he was dressed in warm pajamas. Mumbling good morning he opened the refrigerator door.

Uri came back into the kitchen. He was now dressed in uniform and was fastening his gun holster to his belt.

"Where are you going?" Yariv asked.

Before he could answer, Bitti, struggling to get into her robe, came running in.

"What's going on?" She looked from Uri to Yariv to Ilan.

"I've got to go out and I want you to stay inside this house until you hear from me," he barked. "Is that clear?"

"Wait a minute," Bitti started.

"Shut up, all of you," Uri ordered angrily. "Just do as you're told. Stay indoors, and if I don't call I'll have someone call for me and whatever they tell you to do, you do it."

He started out and stopped. "Yariv, walk me to the car." And then turning around, he looked at Bitti. "I'm sorry. I'm very tense, but I beg you, just accept what I'm saying."

"What are you saying?"

"I'm not sure." Then, impulsively, he gathered Bitti and Ilan to him and held them. "Take care of yourself." He whispered and walked out the door. Yariv followed him out.

"I've got to report to headquarters in Haifa and I'm leaving you in charge. Don't do anything foolish." He paused. "Just stay close to Bitti and the kids." Then, in the same impulsive manner with which he hugged Bitti and Ilan, he pulled Yariv toward him. Releasing him almost roughly, he opened the car door cautiously, looked around and, releasing the brakes, put the gear shift into neutral. He then walked to the back of the car. "Now, help me push the car toward the edge of the incline."

"What . . .?" Yariv started and stopped, seeing Uri's determined look.

"I don't want to offend anyone's religious sensibilities. It is Yom Kippur, after all."

Together they pushed the car and before Yariv could say anything, Uri jumped into the driver's seat, popping the clutch, and glided down a path—an indirect route to the main road—leading to Haifa.

Through his rearview mirror, Uri could see Yariv with the small, white houses of Ginat-Or behind him. Yariv had a baffled expression on his face. Uri put his hand out the side window and waved to him. Yariv waved back.

Ginat-Or. *Garden of Light.* That was what they had named their settlement when they arrived five years earlier. Soon it would be in darkness. The thought shook him and he forced his mind back to the present.

"Get to headquarters in Haifa as soon as possible." He had recognized Boaz's voice at the other end of the line. Boaz was the commander of the northern sector of the country and the urgency with which he spoke was frightening. Boaz was not given to hysterics. "And do it as unobtrusively as possible." And he hung up.

Uri knew something was going to break. He had discussed it with Boaz a week ago when they last met in Haifa. The massing of Syrian troops on the border as winter was setting in was very unusual. Rumor had it that the Egyptians were doing the same, which made it all the more serious.

Was it possible that there was going to be a war? A surprise attack? And how much of a surprise could it be if he, a commander of a reserve armored brigade in the Galilee, was aware of what was going on?

Oren. He had not said goodbye to his youngest son. For a minute he was tempted to turn the car around and drive back.

"God damn that Kissinger," he muttered. "Don't be the aggressors" was what he kept telling the Israelis. "Don't be the aggressors, be damned," Uri repeated angrily. Ghetto mentality, that's what it was. Be the nice guy. You may be dead, your family may be dead, but history will say you were the good guy.

The main highway came into view and Uri maneuvered the car toward it.

The road was empty. Nothing moved. Even though much of the population was not Orthodox, on Yom Kippur every citizen obeyed the religious laws of the holy day. Although that was not the reason he pushed the car out of the driveway. He did not want his neighbors to know that he was leaving, nor did he want to upset Yariv. Since Yanosh's death, Yariv had spent a great deal of time with him and Uri was glad he was there. He felt he could count on him in an emergency. Young as he was he could handle a gun, even a machine gun, and was a superb mechanic. He could even drive a tank, if the need arose. Uri shook his head angrily. He was letting his imagination run away with itself. The boy was only fifteen and could hardly be held responsible if anything serious happened. Now he wished he had talked to one of his neighbors before leaving. Their village was so close to the Syrian border. He tried to calm down. Maybe he was making too much of Boaz's call.

The situation was worse than he had imagined. All unit commanders were gathered at headquarters. All looked grim and there was a sense of helplessness in the air.

Uri listened to the intelligence reports. The Syrians were poised for a three-pronged attack and the number of tanks in their possession, as well as the number of the latest Russian models, was staggering. It was clear that the Israeli army was not prepared to defend itself against such an all-out attack.

Questions were asked and answers were given. The regular army was on alert. There was time to start a general mobilization.

Oren. He had not said goodbye to Oren.

"What are we waiting for?" Uri finally asked.

Boaz shrugged. "We have a prime minister, a minister of defense and a chief of staff," he answered cryptically.

"What about the civilians living so close to the border? Can't we at least evacuate them?"

Boaz threw him an angry look. That was an ongoing debate between them. When he and Bitti decided to move, Uri had asked to be transferred to the northern sector. Boaz thought it unwise.

"That's like asking a surgeon to operate on his own child, Uri," Boaz had said. "You know the Sinai, you know that terrain. Stick with it."

But he had insisted and Boaz finally relented. Now he wondered if he had done the right thing. Always when he went into battle, he was tense and nervous, but his mind was clear, his goals were defined. Now his thoughts were clouded. This time the stakes seemed higher than ever.

Finally they were given their instructions. Uri was told to head directly to his post in the upper region of the Galilee. It was close to home, but he knew he did not have a minute to spare.

Driving through Haifa, he could see that the usual Yom Kippur silence had been broken. Cars were pouring onto the highway from every side road.

Trucks were picking up men standing on the road, waiting to be taken to their units. Armored cars were whizzing by crazily. A few camouflaged tanks were lumbering toward the northern part of the country.

Arriving in Safad, the holy city of the mystics, Uri saw people still carrying their prayer books and wearing their prayer shawls leaving their synagogues, grim-faced and walking purposefully. The Israeli civilian army was being mobilized.

It was Deborah's first Yom Kippur since Michael's death, and she decided to spend it with Tanya in her new house. In spite of the doctor's instructions, Deborah decided to fast. Tanya, out of sympathy and respect for her, fasted too.

"It'll do you good," Deborah assured her as they sat on Tanya's little porch, facing the sea. The house turned out to be very pretty and its remote location provided a strangely peaceful serenity. It was always quiet there, but the texture of the silence was more pervasive because of the holiday.

Around noon, Deborah felt faint and Tanya insisted she have some tea. She led her into the small living room and ordered her to lie down while she went to heat the water.

Deborah looked around the room and her eyes came to rest on a photograph of two young women. At first she thought the women were Tamar and herself in a photo taken years ago. Reaching into her pocket, she took out her reading glasses and leaned over to examine the photograph more closely. To her surprise, it was a picture of Tanya and Alexandra, taken in the garden of Bet Enav at some family gathering. Both girls were smiling into the camera.

"She was very beautiful," Deborah heard Tanya say and she turned to look at her. She had not heard her come in.

"Was?" Deborah blanched. "Is she dead?"

"Good God, no. Certainly not the last time I heard."

"When was the last time?"

"Well, I haven't heard from her directly, other than the letter which I showed you. But Uri told me that at one point Israeli Intelligence picked up her trail in Paris. She was working as a secretary for some Lebanese newspaperman." Tanya paused, wondering if she wanted to share all that she knew with Deborah.

"Don't play games with me." Deborah guessed Tanya's thoughts.

"I'm not playing games, but it's all so painful." She sighed. "The fact is, Alexandra seems to have become involved with some Arab and the Israelis followed her around for a while. But for whatever reason, they lost interest in her and the last Uri heard was that she went to Beirut to take care of her employer's mother. No one has heard from her since."

Deborah removed her glasses and pressed her fingers to her eyes.

"Uri considers her dead," Tanya continued tonelessly. "He said that if he were religious, he would have spent seven days mourning over her."

"That would have been a dreadful thing to do," Deborah said angrily. "Alexandra is not dead. She is lost. She is hurting and obviously deeply confused." She stopped and thought for a minute. "I wonder which one of us has caused so much bitterness in her to have driven her to this action."

"Alexandra does not hate anyone," Tanya protested. "Unless it's herself." Her voice trailed off in confusion at what she had said. She had spent endless days trying to figure out why Alexandra had left them and could come up with no answers.

"She was the most loving young girl. Why would she hate herself?" Deborah asked.

"Different generation, different values," Tanya answered thoughtfully. "What you accepted as the norm—fighting, killing and being killed, struggling to survive against a constant threat of annihilation, may have worn her down."

"It hasn't affected our young people," Deborah shot back angrily. "If anything, our children learned to cherish life because they know they may have to fight for it." She paused. "Alexandra is searching for something and when she finds it, she'll be back. Deep down she is us. She is a Danziger."

"Being a Danziger has a great deal of merit. It can also be a burden," Tanya answered quietly. Then, remembering Deborah's tea, which she was still carrying on a tray, she put it down and poured it. "Drink this, it will make you feel better."

"Maybe you should pull the shade down so we don't offend any of the neighbors," Deborah suggested.

"What neighbors?" Tanya laughed and was relieved to get away from discussing Alexandra's tragic life. Although not certain, Tanya felt that Alexandra's life was indeed a tragic one.

"Did Yanosh fast on Yom Kippur?" Deborah asked suddenly.

Tanya looked up in surprise and nodded her head.

"I thought so," Deborah said thoughtfully. "Can you tell me who he really was?"

Tanya thought for a long time and then taking Deborah's hand in hers, she said simply.

"Yanosh was a devoted and loyal Jew. A true patriot of Israel. In a way he was the spy who went out into the cold." She sucked in her breath before continuing. "He asked a Russian commissar in Siberia to arrange for him to stay on in Palestine after General Anders left. He was naive and it seemed like such a small favor. It was granted, and years later they threatened him with exposure if he did not give them the information about Israel that they wanted."

"Good God, was he working for them from the time he arrived here?" Deborah was astounded.

"Of course not. He wasn't a Communist. He was someone who was respected by the Russians as well as our own people and everything he did was with the full knowledge and approval of our government. Remember, Deborah, for a long time the Russians were on our side." Her face grew taut. "It was when they turned against us and Yanosh was no longer willing or able to exchange information with the Russians that they turned on him. And the only way he felt he could neutralize himself was to become a card-carrying Communist. From that moment on, no one trusted him and he lived out his life as one of the loneliest and saddest men in the world."

"Did you know it when you wanted to convert?"

"Not then. Yanosh played the game all the way. Pretending indifference to Judaism was part of the image." She smiled. "My conversion was an honest act of faith and complete trust in Yanosh. He told me the truth after Yariv was born."

"He could have confided in me. He could even have told Michael about it. Why didn't he?"

"He was a Marxist. He expressed his views openly long before he joined the Communist Party. He made no secret that he felt that Israel should adopt Marxist ideology. Think of it. If the Russians had announced suddenly that Yanosh Bar Lev was a Russian agent, would you have believed that he was not spying for them? Certainly Michael would not have believed it and you know it."

Michael's distrust of Yanosh, from the first time they met, came back to Deborah. Tanya was right.

"And you were the only one who knew?"

"No one," Tanya said. Then taking a deep breath, "Now I want to ask you a question."

Deborah looked at her, knowing what the question would be, but waited for her to speak.

"Were you in love with Yanosh?"

"Yes, I was. I fell in love with him many years ago. Long before you were born. Even before your father married your mother."

"And?"

"There was no *and,*" Deborah said. "I was Michael's wife, I was a mother and then a grandmother and he became part of my family."

"Did he love you?"

"I think so. But not the way he loved you. Of that you can be sure."

"Thank you for telling me. If anything, I feel more honored that Yanosh loved me, having known you first."

It was at that moment that the sirens went off.

The two women looked at each other. Without a word, Tanya walked over to the radio and turned it on.

Classical music floated through the room, interrupted by coded massages and the music resumed as soon as the announcer stopped talking. No explanation was given as to what was taking place.

"We're at war," Deborah said quietly. "I think we should go to Bet Enav immediately. Not that there is anything we can do there, but at least we have a phone there and we can find out what's going on."

"I've got to stay here and wait for Yariv." Tanya's voice was tinged with hysteria. "I wonder where it started?"

"Wherever it started, he won't be heading back here. The roads will be jammed with soldiers heading for their units. If he does come, it will be with Bitti and the children and they'll come to Bet Enav."

"I can't leave here." Tanya was trying to control herself but was having a hard time doing it. "On the off chance that he does, I want to be here."

"Sitting here without a phone, just waiting, seems insane." Deborah tried to sound reasonable in the face of Tanya's rising hysteria.

"No." Tanya shouted. "I want Yariv, I want him home. I want him with me. Something terrible is going to happen to him and I want to be here, I have to be here. He will expect me to be here." She was running about the room, shouting uncontrollably.

Deborah grabbed hold of her and slapped her across the face.

Tanya sobered up immediately and stared at Deborah.

"Now, come." Deborah ordered.

Tanya drove but even before reaching the main highway, they saw children standing on the side of the road, paintbrushes dripping blue paint in hand, to smear the headlights of cars. Israel was at war and everyone knew his duty. By nightfall, the black out would be complete.

Traffic along the highway was moving quickly and in an orderly fashion. "Whoever started this war was a fool." Deborah said. "On any other holiday these roads would have been jammed with holiday travelers. As it is, Yom Kippur is the one holiday where we stay close to our homes and families."

Edging her way across the highway, Tanya turned into the road leading to Bet Enav. A man wearing his prayer shawl was cuddling his son in his arms and the boy, his rifle tucked under his arms, was clinging to his father. Tears were streaming down their faces.

"Is this the dream?" Tanya asked, staring straight ahead. "Is this the dream that your grandparents, parents, Tamar, Raphael, David, my father and Jonah had?" Her voice rose with each name. "Is it?"

"Yes. But establishing a Jewish state was only the beginning of that dream," Deborah said quietly. "The dream did not end with the creation of the state. Dreams are the foundation of our reality. And we must never stop dreaming because dreams give us hope. But to keep the dream alive, we must nurture it, love it and care for it, or else it will vanish." She stopped and looked into the distance. "Creating a Jewish state gave us a glimpse of our mercurial dream, but we have not yet touched it." She looked over at Tanya. "So we must continue to dream and now we must dream of peace."

By the time the siren was heard in Ginat-Or, it was too late to evacuate the civilians and Bitti, Ilan and Oren, with Yariv close behind, were rushing into the bunkerlike shelter. The village was so close to the Purple Line, the cease-fire line created after the Six Day War, that the shelter was more military than civilian in structure.

Bitti was calm, settling Ilan and Oren down with crayons and toys when she saw Yariv edge his way toward the exit.

"Where do you think you're going?" she demanded.

"Uri has a rifle and some hand grenades in the shed," Yariv answered.

"Well, that's where they're going to stay," she snapped.

A couple of soldiers came down and looked around.

"What's happening?" Yariv asked.

"The Syrians have broken through our lines a few miles up the road," one of them whispered so he would not be overheard by the mothers and children. "And the colonel was wondering how many of you were here and if there was any way to get you all into a truck and get you out of this area."

"No way," Yariv whispered back. "What are you going to do?"

"We've been ordered to pull back."

"The hell you will," Yariv shot back. "And leave everyone here to be slaughtered?"

"Of course not. Several of us will stay around and hope the reserves get here," the young soldier answered. "It just would have been easier if there weren't so many women and children in here."

Yariv looked at the crowded shelter. Bitti was preparing some food. Ilan was absorbed in his drawing. Oren was playing with another youngster.

The soldiers walked out and Yariv followed them. They slammed the metal door shut and stood staring at each other helplessly.

"Is it very bad?" Yariv asked.

"It's a complete massacre," one of the soldiers said. "The Syrians seem to have thousands of tanks and armored vehicles coming at us and we've got fifty tanks, most of which have been knocked out. And unless we get reinforcements soon, we'll all be dead."

"Where are those tanks?" Yariv asked.

He pointed to a small hill up north.

"Let's go."

Yariv started running in the direction the soldier had pointed to. Bodies of dead and wounded were lying all over. The moaning of the wounded was sickening. Yariv spotted a young lieutenant and some soldiers working furiously to repair the damaged tanks and joined them.

Within minutes one of the tanks was ready to move.

The lieutenant jumped into it and ordered two of his men to come with him.

"And the minute you have another one repaired, follow me," he ordered the remaining men, and then looked over at Yariv. "And you, get into the third one when it's fixed and join us. We'll have to go on repairing tanks as we wear these out."

The tank lumbered up the hill and soon machine guns could be heard as they reached the enemy lines.

For the next twenty hours the lieutenant along with his small force including Yariv forged ahead, removing the bodies of those who had been killed from tanks. The repair team darted in and out of Syrian columns, often forced to exchange their damaged tank for an abandoned one found along the road. They succeeded in creating the impression of being a much larger force than they actually were. Their incredible bravery paid off. The Syrians, taken by surprise at what looked to be a major Israeli offensive, were brought to a standstill for a brief time. But it was enough time to give the Israelis a chance to mobilize the reserve and move them up to the front line.

Uri, with about a hundred tanks against a Syrian force of almost five hundred tanks, managed to hold his ground. For four days and three nights the battle raged without letup. The fighting was brutal, but the Israelis continued their advance. They were fighting on their own land for their very survival. The Syrians retreated in disarray, leaving their fallen comrades lying on the killing ground. That area came to be known as the Valley of the Tears, tears for all who had died there.

Uri came back to Ginat-Or one week after the fighting started and was told that Bitti and the children along with all the other civilians had been evacuated. Ginat-Or lay in ruins; his house was nothing but a deep hole in the ground.

Devastated as he was, he knew he would come back and rebuild his home. Getting into his jeep, he headed for Bet Enav. Bitti would be there, of that he was sure.

# CHAPTER FIFTY-FIVE

T HE heat in the small room was oppressive. The blades of the overhead fan barely moved and the small floor fan, although whirling furiously, succeeded only in stirring up the unbearable humidity.

Edward, sitting opposite Abu Shara, tried to control his impatience with the older man who was in charge of the refugee camp on the outskirts of Sidon in southern Lebanon. Edward disliked him and felt he was too old to be running that particular camp, but his efforts to remove Abu Shara had proved futile. That failure troubled him. Edward had recently been put in charge of all military operations against Israel to be carried out within Israel's borders. Abu Shara's camp was the ideal launching site for the work but Abu Shara was not cooperating with the plan.

"Now, let's get this straight," Edward said. "I want to start training our children as early as possible. The earlier they learn to defend themselves, the better chance they will have of surviving."

"Ten-year-old children should not have to be enlisted into a fighting unit," Abu Shara said. He spoke softly but his tone was firm.

"Ten? I was fighting at eight. Fighting for our cause is what keeps our spirit alive, our goals clear. Frankly, one of the few things I buy from the Catholic Church is that stuff about 'give me a child until he's seven.' Yes, seven is not too early to start teaching them what our battle is all about."

"I run this camp, Edward."

"Well, maybe you've been running it too long," he snapped.

A small window faced the Mediterranean and Edward tried to absorb himself in the view of calm, blue waters. He looked toward the horizon and followed it southward. The same horizon stretched across Palestine. The same sea bordered Palestine. Whenever Edward came to Sidon, his sense of frustration would overwhelm him. Palestine was so close and yet it was so far from his grasp.

He was so engrossed in his thoughts that when the figure of a woman crossed his sight of vision, he barely took notice of her. As she disappeared from view, it occurred to him who she was: Alexandra. The memory of her jarred him.

He stood up and walked over to the window. The woman was heading toward the sea and had her back to him, but even in the loose-fitting black dress, he had recognized her distinctive walk. The memory of Alexandra walking away from him in Paris after he discovered she was an Israeli came back to him vividly. Head held high, shoulders thrown back, her feet seemed not to be touching the ground.

He started and turned to face Abu Shara, who had also noticed the woman. "What the hell is she doing here?" Edward asked.

"Do you know her?"

"I think I do. The question is, do you?"

"Of course I do. That's Ali, our sainted Ali." There was no sarcasm in the remark.

"I think what I said about you being here too long has suddenly been confirmed. You've lost contact with reality and you don't know what you're doing."

Abu Shara took the pipe out of his mouth and started refilling it calmly.

"You don't know who she is, do you?" Edward said slowly.

"She's Alexandra Ben Hod. She's an Israeli girl, born in Bet Enav in nineteen forty-nine. She's the granddaughter of Michael and Deborah Ben Hod, the latter being a descendant of the Danziger family." He smiled. "I knew her great-uncle, Raphael Danziger. My grandmother worked for him. Brilliant man . . ."

"So what is she doing here?"

"She takes care of the children, the mothers, the wounded, and she's one of the gentlest, sweetest, most sincere people I've ever met."

Edward became impatient. "She's a plant, a spy for the Israelis, and you've got her sitting in the middle of this camp. I think you're senile."

"Edward," Abu Shara's head shot up and his eyes blazed. "You may be a great fighter for our cause, but you're overstepping yourself. That girl was found by Lila shortly after Sadat's fiasco, which she would call the Yom Kippur War. She was badly burned in a fire she thinks she caused. Her employer was killed in that blaze. It was Tufik Mazzari's mother."

"Did she cause it?"

"Hardly. On the day the war started, our kids were exuberant. As you remember, it looked as if we were finally going to win and be able to go home. Many of our men fought valiantly in the hills and mountains alongside the Syrians, but the younger boys in Beirut went on a rampage. Mrs. Mazzari was one of their victims."

"How did you get involved with Alexandra?"

"Someone brought her to the hospital. It was overcrowded and she was simply dumped there. She had no identification on her and the firemen probably thought she was the Mazzari maid. No one paid any attention to her, except Selma.''

"Who is Selma?"

"A little orphan girl who was badly hurt on that same day and she was lying next to Ali in the hospital. They brought each other back to life. I think the sight of a thirteen-year-old clinging to a helpless, burnt-out human being was what touched Lila.''

Edward seemed annoyed by the last phrase.

"Yes, Lila does have feelings," Abu Shara answered Edward's reaction.

"She took pity on them and brought them to us. Ali was still in terrible shape physically. Aside from the burns, the smoke affected her sight, so her eyes were bandaged and she was in shock. It was months before we could get her to say anything, and then all she kept mumbling was that she was not a murderess. I was skeptical, so I started an investigation. It didn't take me long to find out who she was. As soon as she was well enough physically, she began to help Lila.''

"That's a very touching story," Edward said derisively. "Why didn't she leave when she came to her senses?"

"Without letting on that I knew anything about her, I asked her if she wanted to rejoin her family." He shrugged his shoulders. "She said that she had no family and wanted to stay. And she was really a great help, especially with the children. She has an unbelievable way with them and they adore her. I kept her in the Tel El Zaater area under surveillance for two years. I may be old, but I'm not a fool. She's completely trustworthy." A sad expression came into his eyes. "She's been with us now for four years and the truth is that I suspect that no one in her family gives a damn about her anymore."

"And no one has questioned her identity?" Edward asked.

"That's not unusual. Many of us prefer to bury the horrors of the past."

"How can you be so sure of her loyalty to us?"

"If you saw her running around gathering up the children and getting them into the shelters when those bastard Zionists come swooping in for the kill, saw how desperate she is to make sure that everyone is safe and then watched her stand at the doorway of the shelter staring at the approaching planes while they pour down their venomous fire at us, you'd know her sincerity. She just stands there, defying them to kill her. She's been hurt a couple of times, but that hasn't stopped her. She's always out there, standing guard."

"She's probably signaling those damned planes and guiding them," Edward shouted in frustration.

"If you were right and they knew she was here, I assure you they wouldn't be bombing us as they have been. As for her signaling them, unfortunately, they know exactly what they want and where it is. They don't need some woman as a guide."

Edward started pacing nervously.

"Well, even if you're right, I wouldn't let her near our children," he said defiantly. "What can she possibly say to them that tells of our struggle?"

"She speaks of a homeland with the same longing that every Arab does. She does not differentiate between a Jewish homeland and an Arab homeland. Homeland has no other meaning to her than the longing for a place to call one's own. When she describes a town, a village, a house, an olive tree, she does not identify it as Jewish or Arab. The children respond to her sincerity."

"You're a fool," Edward said in disgust.

"No, I'm not. And you need not worry. We have the Lilas and men like yourself who add the adjectives that inflame the children."

"Who's woman is she?" Edward asked suddenly.

"No one's. She lives with Lila and spends all her time working around the camp. Although every boy and man has tried to seduce her, I assure you. And the truth is, everyone is a little in love with her." He stopped and a smile appeared on his weathered face.

"And so are you, you old goat," Edward said, but his tone softened.

"Yes. I probably am in love with her, but not in the way you mean. I'm in love with her purity, her innocence, her faith. She honestly believes that humanity will someday settle its conflicts with love and mutual understanding. She is the only woman I've ever known whose inner beauty matches her external beauty."

Edward sauntered back to the window. He could see Alexandra sitting on the white sand, her back to the camp, staring out to sea. She had removed the scarf and her hair fell to her waist. It was still dark and lush and he felt a knot of pain grip his chest. The sight of the young girl standing on a bridge in Paris, the memory of her beauty when she turned to look at him, the image of her face flushed with desire, staring up at him after they had made love, sent a strange sensation through him. He also recalled their last meeting. He had hated her that night, hoped never to see her again. That night she was the embodiment of evil. She belonged to a people who wanted his destruction and he wished she were dead. Now, watching her on the beach, he knew he still cared. After all the years that had elapsed, he was still in love with her.

"How do you know her?" Abu Shara's voice broke into his thoughts.

"Are you really convinced of her loyalty?" Edward ignored the question and continued staring out the window.

"I'm an old man and I've been at this game too long to be fooled," Abu Shara answered, but something in Edward's voice troubled him.

When Edward turned to him, Abu Shara was taken aback. For the first time since he had known him, he saw a flicker of humanity in his eyes. He lowered his own. Yes, he thought, Ali may prove to be dangerous after all.

Alexandra opened her eyes and the miracle of sight still thrilled her. She looked around the room. Small, neat, with a window facing the sea. A small bouquet of flowers sat in a water glass, and the colorful flowers made her heart sing with joy. She could see.

It had been nearly four years since the day when she tried to open her eyes and was greeting by nothing but darkness. Her eyes were bandaged and when she tried to lift her hand up to remove the bandage, the pain was too excruciating. She had no idea where she was. The last thing she remembered was the burning beam falling in Mrs. Mazzari's room. The memory of the old woman's terrified face, combined with the conviction that she was responsible for Mrs. Mazzari's death, made Alexandra wish she could fall back into unconsciousness. If only she had not left that burning candle on the dresser!

When next she woke, it was the stench that struck her. Excrement, garbage and decay, mingled with hospital-like antiseptic odors, filled her nostrils. Her eyes were still bandaged and she moved her fingers, trying to identify her surroundings. Rough textured fabric similar to her army blanket gave no clue as to her whereabouts. She was even more conscious of her own physical pain. She had no desire to relieve the pain. She deserved it. She had killed Mrs. Mazzari and she deserved to suffer. She again fell into her deep slumber.

Waking, sleeping, waking again, she got used to the noise and the odors and she tried to speak. No sound came. It was then she felt someone touching her. The sensation of panic died quickly when a hand took hold of hers and she realized it was a small hand, the hand of a child. It seemed to be asking for protection. The hand lingered in hers. And it was that little hand that became her contact with reality. Whoever was caring for her kissed her. It was that gesture that brought back feelings. She felt grateful. She felt love. The sleep following that kiss was the most peaceful she had had since the first time she woke up in this unfamiliar location. Death with a kiss, she thought. Maybe it was time to die. The thought did not frighten her.

Time lost all meaning and then one day strong arms lifted her from where she was lying. She was terrified, but the reassuring little hand never let go of hers. She was carried a distance and she could hear a great deal of screaming and then she realized she was breathing fresh air. She had no idea where she was being taken. The small hand was her only comfort.

Alexandra gave herself up to being cared for. She still had no idea where she was or who was caring for her. The only sounds that reached her were those of children laughing and playing.

Her recovery was slow, but when the bandages were finally removed, she found herself looking at a man, a young woman and a child. Abu Shara, Lila and Selma. They became her family.

That had taken place three years earlier and Alexandra still marvelled at her good fortune, was still grateful for her sight and for being alive.

"Are you up?" Alexandra heard Lila come into the room and she looked up at the woman. Lila, with her usual angry scowl, was carrying two cups of coffee.

"Want some?"

Alexandra sat up and stretched lazily. "You shouldn't have bothered."

"No bother," Lila said gruffly and handed her the cup. "You deserve a rest. That was a lovely wedding you arranged for Selma and we all thank you for it. Even Abu Shara was touched."

"She deserved it," Alexandra answered, sipping her coffee. "When you consider how far she's come in the last three years. How hard she's worked to become a productive human being around this camp. That terrified little waif, grown into lovely womanhood, falling in love and, more importantly, willing to accept love. I think that's quite an achievement and I'm proud of her."

"You had an awful lot to do with it," Lila said. "Now the question is, when will you be ready for all that?"

"I have all the love I need from the children and the people around me," Alexandra said lightly.

"Well, you'd better get ready to accept some more love. We're expecting a huge number of new refugees coming to Sidon. And the question is whether we move or make do with this new place."

"Let's not move," Alexandra implored. "It's been relatively quiet in the last few weeks. No raids from them." She nodded southward, towards the Israeli border. "And on the whole, everything is actually running quite smoothly." The idea of moving upset her. They had moved so often in the last four years and the outskirts of Sidon had begun to feel like home.

"There is talk about moving us up closer to the Syrian border," Lila said indifferently. She had spent most of her life in camps and moving meant little to her.

Alexandra's brows shot up in surprise. "The Syrian border? I think the Syrians hate us as much as the Israelis do."

"Nobody likes the refugees," Lila snapped. "But, no one hates us as much as those Zionist pigs."

Alexandra lowered her eyes. That was one of the first lessons she learned when she was well enough to realize where she was. At first she thought she was simply living in a slum area. The full realization that she was living in a refugee camp came to her only when they began to move toward the Israeli border, and the bombing started. Cruel, senseless bombing by Israeli planes. These, she recalled, were the "retaliatory attacks," which the Israelis claimed were essential to wipe out the terrorists. But the people she was living with were not terrorists. They were helpless, frightened creatures who had nowhere to go. The articles that had so upset her in Paris took on new meaning. The Israelis *were* responsible for the refugees being where they were, living the way they were. She even began to accept that most of the terrorist acts committed by the Arabs were their only way of continuing to make their claim. Every refugee wanted to go home—to the home which the Israelis had taken from

them. And as the bombs fell on these helpless refugees, she began to understand the hate that Lila and the rest of the people felt toward the Zionists.
Soon she too began to share that feeling.

"I'm going into Sidon," Lila's voice brought Alexandra back to the present.
"Want to come?"

"I don't think so. Later I'll go down to the beach."

"You and your beach," Lila laughed. "It's nothing but sand and water."

# CHAPTER FIFTY-SIX

LEXANDRA stared at the Crusaders' Castle jutting out into the sea of the Sidon bay. The castle is what she usually looked at when she came to the beach. It reminded her of the one in Caesarea. It had taken her a long time to be able to look at it and not feel the longing for her home. In recent months, she had even begun to think of Tanya and her little house, wondering if Tanya, too, might be sitting on her beach and gazing at the castle in Caesarea.

It was pleasant thinking of Tanya. Although Alexandra was sure she would never see her or her family again, she now occasionally allowed herself to think of them. The scene she recalled most often was of the day she, Tanya and Uri had gone to see Tanya's new house. She envied Tanya for having the inner strength to live in that isolated spot and be content with her existence. Living among the homeless, working with them, caring for them, Alexandra felt she was close to reaching that peaceful state. How she wished she could share her thoughts with Tanya. Sweet, gentle Tanya, she was sure, would be happy for her.

She lowered her head into her hands. She had chosen her path and followed it, but somewhere deep inside there was a void.

"Alexandra." She froze. No one had called her that since she had come to her first camp in Beirut.

She could hear someone coming toward her and she did not turn around, trying to identify the voice. It came to her slowly. It was Edward. Her heart began to beat wildly and she could not decide if it was caused by fear of being exposed or the thought of seeing him.

He came to sit beside her and took her hand. She let it rest in his without looking at him. When he touched her hair, she began to tremble.

"You're as beautiful as ever," he whispered. "More beautiful, in fact."

She turned to face him. He had grown a beard but in spite of it, she could see his cheeks were gaunt. He was in his early thirties but his temples had already begun to gray and the lines around his mouth had grown more distinct.

His eyes, however, were as gentle as she remembered them on their first meeting.

She put her hand to his cheek.

"Your romantic fairy tale just might have a happy ending," he smiled. "You have overcome the trials and tribulations for both of us, and you are here."

She disengaged herself from him and lay back on the warm sand, staring up at the sky. A sliver of moon appeared overhead and she cleared her eyes. She felt his lips on her forehead and then he kissed her on the mouth. She did not respond. His kisses grew more amorous and she turned toward him. It felt good to be held, to be touched, to be desired. She had forgotten what it was like. She gave herself over to fantasy. She was with Edward and they were on the beach in Caesarea. The Crusaders' Castle was close by, protecting them. She was Tanya and Edward was Yanosh. She was home and she was completely happy.

Spent and still filled with desire, she lay beside him, cradled in his arms. She could feel his hand caressing her body with great tenderness and she drew closer, wanting to stay with him forever.

Edward stayed in the camp for one week. It was a glorious week in some ways and a disturbing one in others. She saw little of him during the day. He spent most of his time by the shore, surrounded by his men, their rifles clearly visible. No one was allowed near that area when they were there. When not working at the shore, he went about making basic changes in the children's programs. No longer were they to be allowed to draw, mold plaster, dance and sing. Even the little ones were required to learn to march in formation, obey orders on command and handle wooden guns and rifles. The older boys and girls were taught to use real weapons. Alexandra was deeply troubled but felt she had no right to interfere. These were his children, his people, and he knew what was best for them. Vaguely she recalled Yanosh telling her that Edward was Abu Tayib and that he was a fanatic leader of his people, but she was convinced that Yanosh had confused him with someone else. Edward could hardly be a mad terrorist. He was too young to be that important. And when he came to her at the end of the day, he was her gentle, passionate lover. All her doubts about him disappeared.

On the sixth day, she woke up to find Edward gone. Convinced he had left the camp, she got out of bed, dressed and walked out of the room they had shared. It was dark out and she wanted to cry. Until Edward's arrival, her life had seemed full and rewarding. Now she felt empty and the future loomed lonely and pointless. More than ever she knew she had to share her life with someone. She wanted a family, children and a home of her own. She thought of Tanya, Bitti, Rachel, all women who had married, had children, had homes. They looked forward to their future. She had none. Her mind turned to Deborah. Deborah was the epitome of womanhood, a true matriarch of her family. She belonged to them and they belonged to her. She knew who she was and where she belonged. Had Alexandra forfeited her right to be a woman like Deborah and the others? No answer came. For the first time since coming to live with the refugees, she thought of leaving.

The beach was empty, and as she started walking toward the water's edge, she heard voices. Urgent, whispering voices. She strained to hear what they were saying, but they were too far away. Crouching behind a pile of stones, she held her breath, then saw some men stepping out of a rubber dinghy. With quick, decisive motions, they deflated the little craft and started packing it away. Daylight was rapidly enveloping the area, and she saw that they were dressed in diving suits. They started running in the direction of the camp. Israelis. That was her first thought and she wondered how she could give a warning without being detected. Then she recognized Edward. He was urging the men to hurry and he sounded angry. They disappeared quickly, then Edward, scanning the area briefly, followed his men. He was soon out of sight.

The scene baffled her; she could think of no logical explanation for this expedition. She raced back to her room. Edward would be looking for her and wonder where she had been.

She had little time to ponder the event, since Edward announced he was leaving the next day and insisted she spend the day with him. They went hiking in the mountains, had a picnic and relived the memory of their first meeting. They chose to ignore the intervening ten years. It was Paris 1967, not Sidon 1977. They were in love and as the romance story predicted, they were going to live happily ever after.

"Will I ever see you again?" she asked as the day was coming to an end.

"I would like you to have my child," he said quietly.

She looked at him with amazement. She remembered distinctly someone telling her that Edward wanted his son to be born in Palestine. The idea thrilled her. The child of Edward Hammadi and Alexandra Ben Hod might be the one to bridge the gap of hate between their people.

Edward left early the next day.

The weeks following his departure were hectic. The new influx of refugees arrived at Abu Shara's camp and violence broke out in the surrounding areas. Alexandra gathered that internal conflicts had begun to flare up between various Arab factions vying for political control over the refugees. These conflicts had always existed but since 1975, when the civil war broke out in Lebanon, they grew more severe. And now, three years after the fighting in Beirut, simple rhetoric was no longer acceptable. Physical violence became the way to make the point.

Often during the night Alexandra could hear rockets and mortars exploding around them. The use of heavy armaments connoted something far more serious, and she wondered where it all came from. The idea that all this equipment was stored within their area troubled her. The possibility that the Israelis were actually aiming at military arsenals when bombing the camps crossed her mind, but she dismissed it quickly. The thought was outrageous. Abu Shara cared too deeply for his people to permit them to be exposed to such danger. Still, she felt uncomfortable. Things were changing quickly and she felt lost and confused. She wanted Edward. She felt safe with him.

When she discovered she was pregnant, her first reaction was of unimaginable joy. But as the reality took form and with Edward away, she began to have doubts. They had avoided discussing the reality of their lives, but now it was a matter of a child's life and future. Their child would be a product of their two worlds, but their worlds were growing further and further apart. More important, their child would be born into the misery of a refugee camp. Her heart went out to the refugees. She identified with them, lived as they did, helped where she could. But she had chosen to do so. She was not sure she had the right to impose that life on their child.

While she was desperate to see him, she also dreaded his arrival. When he finally showed up, she was paralyzed with a fear born of indecision.

She watched him hug the children and shake hands with the older people, but she could tell that he was searching for her. When he caught sight of her, his smile made all doubts disappear and she ran to him.

He swooped her up into his arms and was about to kiss her when a camera flashed and a frightening silence fell over everyone. Edward let go of her and looked around to see who had taken the picture. Spotting a boy holding a camera, Edward grabbed it out of the terrified child's hand and throwing it to the ground, he stamped it repeatedly, crushing it out of existence. Then, with the same uncontrollable rage, he turned on the boy, but at that moment, Abu Shara intervened. Edward stormed off without a backward glance. The crowd dispersed and Alexandra feeling dazed walked over to her room.

Lila was sitting on the bed, waiting for her.

"That boy deserved it," Lila said. "There are no photographs of Abu Tayib anywhere, and there must not be any. We have few leaders like him and we must not endanger him."

"He looked as though he was going to hit the poor boy," Alexandra murmured, almost to herself.

"We must learn the rules early in life," Lila answered.

Edward left the camp suddenly, without saying goodbye and Alexandra never got the chance to tell him she was pregnant. Her doubts about having the child outweighed her anger. Was this the man she wanted to be the father of her child?

In desperation she turned to Abu Shara. His office was in one of the few stone structures in the camp. It looked like an abandoned church and was located at the edge of the camp. When she walked in, he suggested she close the door behind her. She sensed that he had been expecting her.

"You're pregnant, aren't you?" he said quietly, watching her as she settled down opposite him.

She looked at him in surprise.

"I can recognize death at a glance, but I can also recognize a woman who is carrying a new life within her," he answered her unworded question.

"I don't know what to do. Edward frightened me when he smashed that camera." She looked around nervously. "There is so much I don't understand about him and I wonder if it would be right for me to have this child."

Abu Shara did not react.

"What kind of life can we give a child?" Alexandra asked.

"The life of a proud Arab whose father is a dedicated man, fighting for justice for his people and whose mother is a gentle, kind and saintly woman."

"I'm not an Arab," she said slowly and waited for his reaction.

"I know that."

"You know?" she whispered.

"I know all about you, Ali. In fact, I knew your great-grandfather, your grandfather and your grandmother." He smiled at her dumbfounded expression. "My grandmother was nursemaid to your grandmother when your great-grandmother was too ill to care for her as an infant."

Alexandra could not find her voice. She continued to stare at him.

"In fact I saw your grandfather on the last day I spent in my home. It was in nineteen forty-eight. He came to our village to talk to my grandmother." A faraway look came into his eyes. "My grandmother was a very brave woman. We were evacuating our homes, running away from the Zionist onslaught, when your grandfather came to our village. We were forming the caravan, trying to clear the area, when we saw him coming. I was eighteen years old and all able-bodied young men were in particular danger. My friends and I were at great risk by still being there. I begged my grandmother to hide, frightened by what could happen to her if she were caught. She waved me away and stood waiting for him to come over to her."

"What did he say to her?" Alexandra asked curiously, recalling all too vividly Michael's story of his conversation with this woman.

"I don't know. I was not within earshot, but having seen the horrors of what the Zionists did to the Arabs in Jaffa, I could only thank him for sparing her life. I was sure he would kill her."

"Horrors of what the Zionists did in Jaffa?" Alexandra felt her mouth go dry. "What horrors?"

"It was before the Zionists announced the creation of the State. I was in Jaffa and they started shelling us from Tel Aviv. For days the bombs fell, killing thousands of innocent men, women, and children. We were completely helpless. The British were helping the Zionists and they had all the ammunition and weapons needed to continue their treacherous attack. We began to evacuate the women and children in boats, to take them to Gaza. Many drowned, since the boats were too small to carry all the people. Then, in a mass force, with tanks and heavy artillery, they stormed Jaffa, killing at random, raping, looting. They simply overran us."

Alexandra stood up shakily and walked over to the window. The sincerity with which Abu Shara had told his story made it sound plausible. What the Arabs said always sounded plausible, and she had accepted much of it. But his version of the events in Jaffa was so different from Michael's and she could not doubt Michael.

"I know the lies the Zionists have told the world. But believe me. I was there," Abu Shara continued.

She was about to say that she also knew people who were there, and who knew what happened, but she kept her silence. She was not there. Abu Shara claimed he was. Truth, she kept thinking—what was the truth?

"Does Edward know my background?" she asked without turning around.

"Yes, but it does not matter to him. He loves you very much."

"Does anyone else?"

"No. There's no reason for them to know." He paused. "I know Edward will want you to meet his mother and I'm sure she'll approve of you. Then, once you've converted, no one need ever know. You are one of us in every way and becoming a Moslem woman will be very simple for you."

She turned slowly and faced him. "I won't convert," she said, surprised by the conviction in her statement. At that moment she remembered Yanosh's words about paying a price for loyalty if you embrace your enemy. But Abu Shara was not the enemy. And surely Edward would not ask that of her.

"Why not?" Abu Shara sounded surprised.

"I don't think it would matter to Edward."

"What about the child?"

"I don't know what our child will grow up to be, but I don't think we should label him or her at this point." She avoided giving him an answer.

"But Edward can't marry a Jew."

It was the first time she heard the word *Jew* since coming to live with the refugees. Zionists, Israelis—they were the enemy. Jews were never mentioned. Like the rest of the world, Jews were the victims of Zionist propaganda. She also knew that the reason she had not answered Abu Shara's question directly was that she wanted to avoid using the word. It shocked her. She was no longer an Israeli; she was a Jew.

"Edward has nothing against Jews. He told me so and I believe him. It's the Zionists who are his enemy."

"That's true and it's a feeling I share, a feeling we all share. But when it comes to marriage and children . . ." He hesitated.

"What makes one Jewish?" she asked and almost laughed at the ridiculous question. "It's an age-old question and I don't expect you to give me an answer. I certainly no longer know what it means to be Jewish. I'm just a human being." She did not take her eyes off his face. "I believe that is how we can bridge the abyss between our people. Religious labels have brought too many disasters on all of us." When he did not react, she walked over to his desk. "Or am I wrong? Are you really fighting a religious war?" Still he did not answer and she continued. "I don't believe you are, and I believe Edward feels as I do. I *must* believe that." Her voice rose with emotion.

"Ours is not a religious war," Abu Shara said firmly. "We are fighting for peace. You know that. You've lived with us long enough to know that our only aim is to get our homes back. Then there will be peace."

"But so many lives have been lost in the name of God and peace," Alexandra said sadly.

Abu Shara lowered his eyes.

"You've changed since he came into your life," he said after a moment.

"In what way?" she asked, although she knew. Because of Edward, she had begun to feel alive. She loved Edward. But she also felt anger, compassion, desire and hope, emotions that had all been dormant for too long. She now wanted—needed—to rejoin the living. And her greatest hope was that if loving Edward could bring these changes into her life, his loving her would help him grow and become the man she knew him to be. The gentle, kind, understanding person she had met in Paris. She certainly wanted to try.

When she left Abu Shara's office, she knew she was going to have Edward's child. That was the hope. That was the future.

# CHAPTER
# FIFTY-SEVEN

Y ARIV stood with several other soldiers on the highway leading from Tel
Aviv to Haifa, waiting for a lift. It was Friday afternoon. He was heading
home for the Sabbath, but he wanted to stop off and see Deborah first.
He was facing a serious decision. Having graduated from high school early
and spent a couple of years at the university, he was finally inducted into the
army. Like all the other recruits, he was tested and, early that morning, he was
informed that he had been accepted into the air force training school. It was
something he had dreamed about ever since he was a child, but now he was
not sure he wanted it. Much had changed in Israel since 1973. New situations
had arisen that had to be addressed. He was seriously thinking of going to law
school and then going into politics. Somehow the old need to prove himself
had diminished.

Much as he adored and respected his mother, she could not be objective
about this decision, whereas Deborah, he felt, would be. The generations that
separated them brought them closer together in a way. He understood what
the Danzigers had been fighting for, and after all these years the purity of that
dream was something he wanted to make a reality. Deborah was a highly
intelligent woman. But more important, she had lived the history of Israel and
would be far more likely to understand his dilemma.

The line moved slowly and finally Yariv was at the head of it. A car came
to a stop a few feet ahead of him.

"Place for just one," the man called out.

Yariv opened the door.

"How far are you going?" the man asked.

"The turn to Bet Enav."

"Jump in. I'm going all the way to Haifa."

Yariv settled down, counting his blessings. It was not often you found
someone who was going beyond your destination. For a moment he thought
of skipping the visit to Deborah and going directly home, but he knew he
couldn't. He had to talk to Deborah.

"Yariv?" He heard his name and he looked around.

"Leyanna!" he cried out with delight. "God, you've grown up."

"So have you. But that does happen when you don't see someone for four years."

He could not take his eyes off her. She was beautiful at fifteen, but she was ravishing now. "Where are you heading?"

"Haifa. My father is making a speech there tonight. Want to come?"

He hesitated. "I'd like to. But I've got to stop off in Bet Enav and see my great-grandmother. Then, on Fridays, I always try to have dinner with my mother." He turned to the driver. "Would you mind if I sat in the back?"

The man chuckled. "Go right ahead."

Sitting beside her Yariv looked at her more closely. The man-tailored khaki shirt, open at the neck, did not detract from her extraordinary femininity.

"You're in the army. I didn't realize you were in uniform, which shows you how observant I am." He laughed self-consciously, staring at her with unabashed admiration.

"So are you," she laughed happily, flattered by his gaze.

"How much longer do you have?" he asked.

"A year."

"Where are you stationed?"

"Near Jerusalem."

"And then?"

"Well, I graduated from high school and I'll probably go on to study law. And you? When do you get out?"

He hesitated.

"You're planning on staying in the army?" Leyanna said, misunderstanding his silence.

"Good God, no. It's just . . ." He stopped, embarrassed. "It's just that I've been accepted in the air force training program and I don't know if I really want that. It's five long years out of one's life."

"What does your mother say?"

"I just found out about it. But knowing her, she won't say anything. She's too smart to give me advice, unless she knows what it is I want to hear."

"Well, I think you should go into the air force," the driver joined the conversation.

Both Leyanna and Yariv tried not to laugh.

"Why?" Yariv asked.

"It's a great honor, and you can best serve the country that way."

"Have you talked to anyone else about it?" Leyanna asked.

"Well, I can sort of predict what each one would say. My cousin Uri will be pleased and demand that I go into the tank corps. Jack and Naomi will argue among themselves, with Jack saying no way and Naomi saying go." He stopped. "They're Uri's parents in the kibbutz. My uncle Benji and his wife, Ruth, will say they have to think about it. Rachel—you remember Rachel, I met you when I was staying in her house in Beersheba—she'd be for it. Although her husband . . ." He looked over at her. "Did you know she married again and has two children?"

"No. Who is he?"

"A doctor, Eli something or other. Nice guy."

"And what would he say?" The driver refused to stay out of the conversation.

"God only knows. He's only been in the family for three years and he has a minority vote."

Everyone laughed.

"And your great-grandmother?"

"That I don't know. That's why I want to stop by and talk to her."

"Great-grandmother. That's quite something. How old is she?" The driver, now completely involved, nodded his head respectfully.

"About eighty, and she's really wise. I think she's the most wonderful woman that ever was."

"What's her name?" the driver asked.

"Deborah Ben Hod."

"No! God, I remember her," the driver said excitedly. "I never met her, but she's a legend. Her family is. The Danzigers, right?"

Yariv felt himself blush. "Actually, Tamar Danziger was my real great-grandmother."

Leyanna, seeing Yariv's reaction, took his hand and pressed it.

The driver turned around briefly. "That's a family to belong to. Well, I can't wait to get home and tell my wife who was in my car today. What's your name?"

"Yariv Bar Lev."

"An honor, my boy. A real honor." Then turning back to the road, he looked at Leyanna through his rearview mirror. "Do you know who Tamar Danziger was? Have you ever heard of Danzigers?"

"We grew up on the legend of Nili," she said quietly.

Yariv was no longer listening. All he could think about was Leyanna's hand in his. He picked it up and a small smile spread over his face. "Won't your father object?" He held her hand up.

"Oh, come on, Yariv. He found us kissing when we were fifteen, so obviously he was furious then."

"And what do you think, Leyanna?" Yariv lowered his voice. "About my going into the air force."

"I think I'll stick with your mother. It's something you have to decide."

A strained silence followed and Yariv had to check the impulse to bring Leyanna's hand to his lips.

"Would you have time to stop by and have a cup of tea with my grandmother?" he asked. "I'm sure she'd love to meet you."

"I wish I could, but I promised my father and mother that I would not be late. It's Friday and although we're not religious, we do eat dinner together. Then I want to hear him speak."

"What's his speech about?"

"The Camp David peace talks."

"Oh."

"In a way, I'm relieved you're not able to come, because I think you'll disagree with everything he says and it will upset you." She tried to smile. "At fifteen you had quite definite views. Or have you changed them since then and come to your senses?"

"I think the peace process is a great move in the direction we have to go. I can't imagine anyone disagreeing with that," Yariv answered.

To Yariv's relief and sorrow, he could see they were approaching the Bet Enav turn off. He wanted to continue talking to Leyanna.

"Could you stop at my mother's house tomorrow afternoon on your way back from Haifa?" he asked her.

"I'd love to. Where does she live?"

"Coming from Haifa, you get off on the turn before Caesarea and walk down the path until you get to the beach. You can't miss it. Hers is the only house there."

"I know that house. It's beautiful. Your mother lives there? I've often wondered about the place. There is something marvelously haunting about it."

Yariv stepped out of the car and Leyanna leaned out the window. "Five o'clock. I'll be there."

He watched the car disappear and started up the road to Deborah's house.

Deborah saw Yariv walk up the driveway. He looked like Yanosh but had Gidon's coloring and bearing—tall, blond, erect and proud. Tanya had done a good job in bringing him up. Yanosh would have been proud of him.

She headed toward the front door, wondering why he had come to see her. A problem he felt only an old lady could solve, she mused to herself. It felt good. Old as she was, the family still came to her.

Yariv, serious and concerned, looked at Deborah after he finished explaining his dilemma. "I'm just not a military man," he said haltingly. "And now that we're probably going to have peace on the Egyptian border, I think they can spare me, don't you? And bombing refugee camps, for whatever legitimate reason, is not quite my scene."

"They can spare you anyway, Yariv, if you have any doubts about going into the air force, and you know it."

He nodded.

"Then what is it?" she asked after a minute. "What's the problem? Just say you're not interested and do what Uri suggests. He thinks you're a born tank corpsman and heaven knows you proved yourself in the Yom Kippur War."

"That was the heroism of innocence." Yariv smiled sheepishly.

"Maybe," Deborah said. "And maybe it was a strong desire to survive." Still, he looked unhappy.

"Grandma the question I want to ask is not whether I should go into the air force or not. The question goes back to my father. If I go into the air force, I will be doing it for him. I will be saying to the world I am Yariv Bar Lev, son of Yanosh Bar Lev, a man who was maligned, misunderstood, shamed and shunned, and now I want you to listen to what I have to say about him." He looked at her sheepishly. "Somehow, going into the air force for that reason doesn't make sense."

Deborah lowered her eyes and waited for him to continue.

"I know you know. My mother never mentioned that she told you, but I knew in my heart that you knew about my father and that was fine with me. Now I must decide how important that is in the scheme of my life, my mother's life and my father's memory. I know who my father was and suddenly I don't care to prove anything to anyone else. You and my mother loved him and most people who knew him respected him, in spite of everything." He stopped. "I don't want to go into the air force," he concluded.

"Then you've answered your own question, and nothing more need be said."

He rushed over to her and threw his arms around her neck. "You are the greatest Grandma anyone could have. Ever."

She walked him to the front gate. "Any other problems?" she asked affectionately.

"I think I'm in love."

"That's a problem which I will not be able to help you solve. Who is she?"

"Yoram Azriel's daughter, Leyanna."

"The problem grows bigger," Deborah said seriously. "Azriel. I like most of what he has to say, but you probably don't."

"You're right. If it were up to him, he'd thank Sadat for his visit to Jerusalem and that would be that."

"That's an oversimplification of Mr. Azriel, but I know what you mean." She kissed him on the cheek and watched him walk away. For the next three years Yariv would be in the army and she prayed that no war would break out during his term of duty. Since 1973 things had been relatively calm, and now with Sadat's bid for peace with Israel, she hoped the calm would prevail.

In a way it was all falling into place. The children were growing up, all with their views, proud of who they were and what they thought.

She found Tova in the dining room, placing the Sabbath candles in their holders and Deborah looked for the memorial candle. It too was there. There was no reason to light it that evening, but she always kept it there. Yearly memorials for her dead came around too often. To date she had never lit a candle for Alexandra, although many in the family considered her dead. She still hoped that her granddaughter was alive and well and would some day come home. She suppressed a sigh. Alexandra, lost, and Daniel, blinded, were the casualties of the 1973 war. Each war had taken its toll on the family. Each war had a drop of Danziger blood shed for the survival of Israel.

Tanya's house looked festive. She had a large table set on her terrace overlooking the water and the garden around the house was in full bloom. Rachel and Eli came early to help with the preparations and Tanya could see Gila playing with her new sister and brother on the beach. At twelve, Gila already had that special gift with children which she inherited from her mother.

She looked over at the table. Everything was in order and she hoped Yariv would be pleased. It was a party in his honor on his graduation as an officer from the tank corps, but Tanya knew it was also the day Yariv would propose to Leyanna, who had become the focal point of his life.

She knew it that day, three years earlier, when he told her the girl was coming to tea. When she first met Leyanna, her resemblance to Alexandra shook her.

She liked Leyanna and, as her visits grew more frequent, Tanya watched her son grow into manhood. She wasn't entirely happy with the idea of Yariv marrying Leyanna. Not because she disapproved of the girl. On the contrary. Leyanna was a wonderful girl. But Yariv had had a difficult life. He had grown up in conflict with his peers and only recently did he come to terms with who he was. To marry someone like Leyanna, whose approach to life was so different from his, could tear him apart again. Yariv would not discard his political beliefs for love, nor would Leyanna. Tanya had been seventeen when she married Yanosh and had no serious opinions about politics, no political philosophy. When she took on Yanosh's philosophy, she happened to have understood it and agreed with it. But Leyanna and Yariv were of a different generation. Their political views were formed and became entrenched at a young age and it would take a world-shattering experience to make them change. Yariv was too much in love to think about that. Whereas Leyanna, Tanya suspected, although equally in love, was aware of those deeply rooted differences. Tanya hoped her son would not suffer too much when presented with the choice. Her heart ached for him, and there was no way she could prevent that from happening.

The guests began to arrive. The small house grew crowded and noisy, but the atmosphere was happy. There was a tense moment when Yoram and Batel Azriel arrived with Leyanna, and Tanya threw a pleading look at Naomi to make sure that Jack did not say anything to spoil the occasion. Uri, Bitti, Ilan and Oren came. Finally Daniel and Marian arrived with their four boys having just arrived from abroad to honor Yariv.

Everyone sat around the table and the clinking of glasses and the hum of conversation was pleasant. As the meal was drawing to an end, Gila and Oren took Daniel's boys and Rachel's two children down to the beach, leaving the grownups to finish the meal in peace.

"Silence, everybody." Uri stood up and cleared his throat dramatically. "This is a momentous occasion in our family's history and I insist on making a toast."

"I wish you wouldn't," Yariv said, looking at Leyanna. He wanted the meal to be over. He wanted to take her for a long walk on the beach and tell her how much he loved her and present her with an engagement ring. It did not matter. Leyanna had promised to spend the night at his mother's house and the evening was still young.

"I still outrank you, young man," Uri said and laughed. "The air force's loss was the tank corps' gain," Uri started seriously. "I wasn't consulted but I'm proud that when given the choice, Yariv chose the tank corps. So now, to our new Lieutenant Yariv Bar Lev, who, having graduated first in his class, should be well on his way to being chief of staff of the Israeli defense forces by the time he's thirty. Nothing else will do." He lifted his glass to Yariv, as did everyone else at the table. Then, losing the pompous manner, "I'm so proud of you." He was no longer the officer. He was the loving relative.

Tanya got up and walked over to her son. "How wonderful and how right," she whispered, overcome with emotion. "Now go kiss Deborah."

"You don't have to tell me to do that. I would anyway," he answered and walked quickly over to her.

"How's the political scene moving?" Jack turned to Yoram Azriel.

"Must we?" Rachel asked and looked over at her husband. "Eli, ask them not to start. Tell them as a doctor that politics is bad for the digestion."

"I don't think it is," he laughed. "As a matter of fact, what's an Israeli party without a good debate?"

"This debate could end in a declaration of war," Naomi whispered under her breath.

"Such wars we can cope with," Eli assured her and turned to Azriel. "I hear you're planning a new settlement in the territories."

"It's way past planning. We've started to build it."

Yariv turned when he heard Azriel's statement. His eyes darted over to Leyanna. She looked calmly back at him.

"Great," Jack said. "And now the army will have to go in and drag you away. Are you a member of Parliament yet?"

"Whose army?" Mrs. Azriel asked innocently. A small, heavy-set woman, she had a round, small face with large brown eyes.

"Our army," Jack said pleasantly, but the edge of irritation was already there.

"I'm a pretty heavy lady and my girlfriends are equally well endowed," she said seriously. "And our soldiers would look foolish physically dragging us off the land."

"I'm not so sure the army would interfere," Uri said.

"But why should you do it?" Jack's voice rose, unable to contain his anger. "We've signed a peace treaty with Egypt. Why antagonize?"

"Who's antagonizing? We paid a high price for that peace and Sadat got what he wanted. We gave him the whole Sinai and the oil fields. Our borders have shrunk and we have to build new defenses and there is nothing more secure and sacred than a green belt."

"Green belt, my foot," Jack stormed. "Tanks and the army will have to defend you."

"Not so. We'll plant our trees, build our houses, grow our vegetables and make that barren hilltop green. That's going to be our defense."

"Why there?" Jack cried out in frustration.

"What exactly do you mean, *there?* It's part of Israel, just as Jaffa, Haifa and Tel Aviv are. At the moment, of course, it's a mountaintop that the Arabs have always claimed is cursed, so it stands barren. They wouldn't go near it. I can't help it if the Bedouins have always considered the valley a more fertile place to live than a mountaintop."

"But why now?" Naomi intervened.

"My dear Naomi. I've meant to ask why you and Jack and the whole country rushed to a mountaintop in the Galilee in nineteen forty to put up a settlement? It was against British mandate law. Everything was against you, but you did it. Why?"

"That was nineteen forty. Things were different then. We were facing a partition of the land. We had to take a stand, define our borders, tell the world what land we felt was crucial to our survival," Naomi countered, although as she spoke her voice faltered. Her arguments was playing into Azriel's hand.

"I believe you've just answered Jack's question. We have to take a stand. We feel that that area is crucial to our survival. Unfortunately, as you did then, we in nineteen seventy-nine have to define our borders. More important, we have to defend our borders. The arguments you made then are valid now. The only difference is that we've paid with the lives of so many boys to get to where we are. I will defend your border anytime and I think you should offer to do the same for me."

"It's a different world," Jack began to shout.

"Yes, the Arabs are more hostile and we have terrorists to contend with," Azriel countered. "The Egyptians got what they wanted. The rest of the Arab world wants all of Israel. And frankly, I don't care what they say to the world. Their acts of terrorism prove what they really think. I don't trust them. They'll say anything, but they'll never stop thinking of how to destroy us."

As the argument escalated, Yariv walked slowly toward Leyanna. She stood up and together they walked toward the beach. The voices followed them until only the echo of the anger could be heard.

"You didn't tell me," he said, throwing himself down on the sand.

"No, I didn't." She sat down beside him.

"Why?"

"You were on your final maneuvers, you were nervous and I didn't want to upset you."

"Will you be living there with them?"

"Probably, when I'm not at school."

"Is that where you want to live?"

"Not necessarily. But as long as I'm a single woman who lives with her parents, where would you expect me to live?"

"But after you're married?"

"Depends whom I marry. If it's someone who lives there, I'll live there. If he lives in Safad, I'll live . . ."

"Stop it," Yariv said angrily. "You know what I mean. I want to marry you, but I won't live there. I won't ever set foot in that place."

"Then I think you'll have to marry someone else. Because I'll live with my husband where he wants to live, but I won't marry someone who will not come and visit my family." She stood up.

He pulled her down and held her close. "I love you so much, Leyanna. I want you. I want to marry you, I want us to spend our life together. But I can't be torn apart by this basic difference in our attitudes. It would kill me."

"Why, Yariv? Why? Didn't we fight and die for that land? When does a land begin to belong to a people? When some politicians sit around a table thousands of miles away and decide it's so?"

"I didn't make the rules. All I know is that if your father persists in settling on lands whose sovereignty has not yet been determined, it will bring about another war."

She took a deep breath. "Oh, Yariv, we're such a small country and we're so vulnerable."

Yariv put his head in his hands.

"Yariv, I believe that what my father is doing is right. I believe that we have a right to settle in land that belongs to us today and was given to us thousands of years ago." She stood up again. "I think I'd better catch my parents before they leave. I told them I was spending the night here, but now I don't think I will."

"Please stay," he begged.

She sat down and stared silently at the setting sun.

Yariv looked at her. Her face was set with determination and he knew it was hopeless. He wanted to cry. He felt as he had the day his father died. Like then, he felt he'd suffered a terrible loss that could never be replaced. His love for Leyanna seemed to be the reward for his patience, for his resolve, a compensation for all the loneliness of his young life. And now she was slipping away from him, not because he did not love her enough or because she did not love him. Their country was demanding another sacrifice.

He lay back on the sand and pulled her toward him. He knew he would not give her the ring, but for that moment they were together and he contented himself with holding her close.

It was dark when they returned to the house. Tanya had put everything away and was listening to music and staring into space. She looked up when they walked in. From their expressions she understood what had happened.

"I'll just take Leyanna to the bus," Yariv said. "Would you like to come?"

"No. I'm tired. It's been a hectic day. You run along and I'll have some coffee ready when you come back." She put her arms out to Leyanna, who went toward her and kissed her.

"It was a wonderful day. A day we will all remember," Leyanna said, but she sounded miserable.

With the children gone, Tanya threw her head back and closed her eyes. Life, she felt, had rewarded her and she was grateful. Now she wished for some reward for her son. She prayed that he would someday find happiness. He deserved it.

Her thoughts drifted to Yanosh. He would have been proud of his son, but would he have persuaded him to behave differently with Leyanna?

Hearing footsteps on the terrace, she sat up.

"Yariv?" She called out, surprised that he would be back so soon. He must have forgotten something, she decided and, standing up, she walked toward the door. A creature dressed in a black wet suit was coming toward her. Before she could cry out, she was grabbed from behind.

# CHAPTER
# FIFTY-EIGHT

E DWARD was overjoyed at the news of Alexandra's pregnancy and within
days she left Abu Shara's camp and the life she had known for most of
the time she had been in Lebanon.

She moved to Edward's small apartment at the edge of the Shatilla camp,
south of Beirut. Actually, his home was no more than a separate shed bordering a pine forest, beyond which was the road leading to the airport. Books
lined the walls and he had a stereo, which was quite a luxury. The only other
personal touches were two photographs. One was of Edward's father, a handsome man wearing rimless spectacles. He was dressed in a three-piece business
suit, with a gold watch on a chain dangling from his vest pocket and a fez
perched on his head. The other was of a very young boy aiming a machine
gun directly into the lens. It was Edward as a child and she wished it were not
there. She learned to ignore it and went about making their home a happy
place. She was very much in love with Edward, as he was with her, and she
spent her time dreaming about their child.

Edward forbade her to work while pregnant. With all the rhetoric about
liberty for his people, he was a middle-class Levantine man, overprotective and
jealous of her time. The latter worried her. Often she would find him staring
at her and she got the feeling he wanted to control her thoughts as well. Yet
he never spoke of marriage or her need to convert. Getting married did not
seem important at that moment. She assumed that at some point, before she
had the baby, the issue would be resolved.

She spent her days wandering around the camp. The area was much larger
than any of the other camps she had been in, and it had the same air of misery,
helplessness and hopelessness. There was, however, a sense of permanence
here that did not exist in Sidon. Although everyone was free to move in and
out of the area, fear dominated their lives. Many worked in Beirut, but they
all rushed back when darkness descended, looking to be close to their own.
Like all the other camps she had lived in, this too was a slum filled with
unwanted foreigners who were fearful of any stranger. The fear however was

not only of strangers. They feared the Israelis, they feared the Christians in Lebanon and they feared their leaders. Leaders who demanded loyalty for conflicting causes, and who gave little in return for that loyalty.

The realization that even the so-called leadership did not care about the refugees shook Alexandra. It reaffirmed what she already knew. Nobody cared about the refugees.

Staring out the window of her room, she would watch the sleek cars drive by, heading toward the Beirut airport, and she recalled her feelings as she drove by that stretch of road with Mazzari and George. The feeling she remembered most vividly was that of caring. Her heart went out to these slum dwellers. The people driving by now barely threw a glance in their direction. It was as though the camp and the people living in it did not exist.

More and more she thought of her family in Israel. One thing that existed both in her family and in Israel was the concern for each other. Their daily lives were filled with many problems, but they cared.

It was her loneliness and desperate need to belong and be cared for that made her want to marry Edward.

She waited for the right moment to broach the subject. He was away a great deal of the time and usually he was very tense when he came back. She kept putting it off, not wanting to upset him further. In that he was like Ami. Ami too used to be overwrought after a flying mission. In a way she realized she was repeating the life she had with Ami, the life she hadn't wanted. The difference was that she knew what Ami did! She had no idea what Edward was involved in. She began to scan through the camp's newspapers and listen to the radio in an effort to find a link between Edward's absences and the events occurring in the Middle East. Neither were helpful. They reported numerous victories achieved by the various Arab fighters, but none gave names or mentioned places where these feats of victory took place. Occasionally she would find a page of a French newspaper wrapped around her groceries and she would read it avidly in the hope of finding another point of view. The newspapers were usually days, sometimes weeks old, and none shed any light on what Edward might be involved in. She thought of going into Beirut proper and buying a current paper or magazine, but she was only weeks away from delivering the baby and decided to put it off until after the birth. She was sure that once the baby came, all would change.

Going to Beirut, however, became imperative, when she saw a photograph of Daniel in one of the foreign papers. The caption beneath it read: "Blind pianist gives concert in Carnegie Hall after years of absence."

She studied the picture carefully. It made no sense. Daniel blind? How? When? An accident? An explosion? The idea made her shudder. She recalled that Daniel had entertained the Israeli soldiers during the Six Day War. Was it possible that he had been wounded in the nineteen seventy-three war?

"Do you know who he is?" she asked when Edward was next at home.

"I've never seen him before in my life." Edward threw the paper aside. "Why?"

"He looks like a cousin of mine," she said nervously. "And I wondered how it happened. He is a very talented musician."

She saw his back stiffen. "Well, he could have been blinded in a car accident, someone might have tried to mug him, who knows."

"He might have been in Israel in nineteen seventy-three. Playing for the troops," she said haltingly.

"Then he deserved what he got."

"He was not a soldier. He was entertaining the men."

"You mean those murderous killers."

"If he was there, he was an innocent bystander."

"So are all my people who are constantly bombed by the Zionists. Those children you cared for in the camps. Those widows, orphans—all those homeless human beings were innocent bystanders."

"If it is Daniel, he lives in the United States. And if he was in Israel, it was because he chose to be there. The people here did not have a choice."

"And you? Why are you here?" he asked and he was staring at her strangely.

"Now it's because of you. Because I think I was trying to relieve the pain of suffering people," she answered feebly.

"That's a little girl's romantic excuse. You're a woman now and you can't go on hiding behind silly clichés. Sooner or later you'll have to make a commitment, one way or the other. You can't live with us and not make it to us."

She was stunned. "I'm here with you because I love you. *That* is my commitment." She caught her breath. "You said you loved me, that you wanted me to have your child, but you haven't made any commitment to *me*."

He stood up and started pacing.

"Alexandra, I made a vow, many years back, that my children would be born in Palestine. My wanting you to have my child was an enormous compromise on my part. I did it because I loved you, and yes, I want to marry you. But I cannot marry you unless you convert. I would ask that of any woman I married who was not a Moslem. I thought you understood that and hoped that you would offer to do it long before now. It must be your decision. That is when I will believe you have made a full commitment to me, to my people, to my cause."

She lowered her eyes. That was the price, she thought. Yanosh was right. She had not believed it when Abu Shara said it, back in Sidon, because she did not think Edward would ask it of her. Now Edward was asking and she knew that the price was too high.

"Is it too much for a man to want his child to know who he is and what he's fighting for?" His voice was edged with impatience.

"I would like our child to be someone who sees the world not only through the viewfinder of a gun."

"How do you think the Israelis see the world?"

"When they're eighteen, they go into the army. Until then they go to school, study, play, have fun and they live with hope for a better future."

He came over to her and took her in his arms. "We will give our child a future. A wonderful, peaceful future in my home. I can even tell you where it is." He leaned over and picked up his father's picture. "Recognize the house behind him?"

She looked at the picture carefully. She had never done so before. Suddenly she realized she knew the house well. She had friends living in it.

He didn't wait for her answer. "It's in Jerusalem—Talbiye, to be exact. I was born in it and my son will grow up in it."

He was holding her close and she dared not move.

"The Zionists must come to understand that we will live with them in peace, but only if they give us back our homes that they stole from us." He took a deep breath. "All my people pray for peace. You've lived with us for so many years. Do those poor refugees want war? Just give us back our homes and they can live with us peacefully, just as we did before the creation of their state."

Alexandra was speechless. Like Abu Shara's words, what Edward was saying had a ring of truth to it.

She felt his lips on hers and she clung to him. She could not understand why she was fighting him. She had given up her identity a long time ago and today she was nothing except the woman who was going to bear Edward's child. Still, she felt an inner resistance.

The conversation was left unresolved and Alexandra understood that the decision was now left to her. But late that night she remembered Daniel's picture in the paper. She would have to find out on her own. First thing in the morning she would go into Beirut, stop off at the French or Swiss Embassy and ask them about Daniel Stern. He was, after all, an internationally known pianist.

Early the next morning, as soon as Edward left the house, she started to get ready to go into Beirut. She even thought of contacting George. She wondered where she would find him.

She walked briskly out the door. It was a bright, sunny day and even the small alleyway outside her house looked festive. She turned right, stopped and could not decide what the shortest route was. She turned left and had gone a few steps, when she froze with fear. She had been a fool. She could not leave the neighborhood, much less leave the camp.

Racing back to her house, she remembered her conversation with George that first night she arrived in Lebanon. She asked about the fence they saw as they passed the camp. He assured her it was there only to protect the children from racing out onto the highway. And in a way he was right. There was no fence around Shatilla and people could come and go as they pleased, but no one did. The invisible fence that surrounded the refugees was thicker than any man-made wall and far more formidable. It was a fence of fear.

In all the years that she had lived in the camps, she believed she was only a spectator, a visitor who could leave whenever she wanted. But one could not be just a spectator to the misery of others. Misery was too powerful. It sucked at one's very being and now she, who had come to Beirut to find out what the refugees wanted, what they thought, what they dreamed of, was one of them, living in a camp outside Beirut, infected by a powerful disease called fear.

She rarely left their rooms after that. The baby was due any day and when Edward mentioned that they were going to meet his mother, she agreed without further arguments.

As she dressed for the date, she stared at herself in the mirror. She did not recognize the image there. She had ceased to exist. No one would know there had ever been an Alexandra Ben Hod. She wanted to cry out in protest. That was not what she had wanted. When she left Israel she felt lost and was looking for an identity. She thought she had found it the day she woke up in Abu Shara's camp. While there, a sense of self began to emerge and by the time she met Edward on that Sidon beach, she thought she was ready to embrace life. With all her trepidations about having a baby, she hoped her child would be a bridge to the future. To *her* future. Secretly she had even begun to fantasize that some day she would return to Israel and introduce her family to Edward Hammadi and Alexandra Ben Hod's child. Their child would be the proof that there was a way to live with their Arab neighbors. That was her dream of the future and she held on to it until she came to Shatilla.

Waiting for the car that was to pick them up, Alexandra wondered what Mrs. Hammadi was like. Solange had said Mrs. Hammadi was a very elegant woman. It hardly seemed likely. But then again, where was Mrs. Hammadi? Where did she live? Where was Jamie? Edward never mentioned his brother.

"Will Jamal be at your mother's house?"

"He'd better not be," Edward snapped.

"Why?"

"Simply stated, he's betrayed our movement."

"Oh?"

"He's working with the people who will eventually sell the Arab cause down the river. He's joined the forces that are benefiting from the chaos we're living in and amassing fortunes at our expense. And when they're rich enough and powerful enough, they'll betray us all." His voice was thick with hate.

She was about to speak again, when she caught sight of his face. He looked angry and it made her nervous.

An armored car came for them and aside from the driver, there were two bodyguards sitting in it. One sat next to the driver and one sat with her and Edward in the back. Both were heavily armed and kept their eyes glued to the road as they sped through the city. But as fast as they drove, Alexandra was stunned by the sights of Beirut. It was almost unrecognizable.

Most of the elegant hotels lining the shore had been reduced to a heap of rubble, overgrown by weeds and covered with debris. Few buildings remained intact and the ones that were still standing were pockmarked with bullet holes or were charred beyond recognition. Yet amidst the ruins, there were still shops filled with goods, people walking about, cafés with customers talking and laughing while sipping their drinks. Children were running about, selling lemonade, their rifles on their shoulders. The destruction went on for miles, yet life seemed to go on despite it. The contrasts were staggering.

They were stopped several times by young men pointing their guns into the car, demanding identification.

Alexandra could feel Edward grow more tense every time they were con-fronted, but to her surprise and relief, he said nothing. Finally the car turned toward the coast and they drove down a small, relatively well-paved path. Within a short time, they reached a high stone wall and stopped at a gate. The four guards who came toward them looked ferocious.

Edward stepped out of the car, as did the two bodyguards. An argument ensued. Finally, Edward got back into the car but his guards did not. The gate opened and they drove through. The house at the end of the driveway, although small, looked like an Italian villa.

A maid opened the door and led them through a spacious living room furnished with modern furniture. There were fresh flowers in large vases and Alexandra saw several paintings that looked very expensive. But what caught her attention were three framed pictures standing on a small table. One was of Edward, in full military uniform, the other was of Jamie, wearing a tuxedo and the third was of Solange in an elegant evening gown. Solange's statement that night in the nightclub came back to her: "Edward thinks you have to wear a sack to prove your patriotism. Jamie and I think differently." Poor Edward, she thought. How difficult it must be for him to see his mother living in all this splendor.

Mrs. Hammadi was sitting in a lounge chair, reading a newspaper and smoking a cigarette. Her hair was completely white, but well coiffed, the hand holding the cigarette was beautifully manicured and she was wearing a simple but elegant black linen caftan. She appeared to be a woman in her sixties who took great pains with her appearance.

She did not get up when they entered, and Edward rushed over to her and kissed her on the cheek. Then, moving aside, he introduced her to Alexandra.

"My dear," Mrs. Hammadi said in French and lifted her hand to her forehead in an absentminded fashion. "But I forgot, you do speak Arabic, don't you?" And without waiting for a reply, she continued in Arabic. "How nice of you to come and see me." Her smile was icy as her eyes swept over Alexandra. She made no effort to hide her displeasure.

"Won't you sit down," she said after a moment.

Alexandra felt a surge of anger as she seated herself opposite the woman.

Mrs. Hammadi continued, still eyeing Alexandra coldly. "You first met my children in Paris when you were on vacation, or something."

Alexandra nodded.

"And when you next came to Paris, you were looking for a job." She tried to smile. "And you found one as a maid, or an au pair or something? Am I correct?" The disdain was undisguised.

Alexandra felt her cheeks go red. "Yes, I did," she answered.

The maid walked in carrying a tray with tea and small pastries.

As soon as the maid was gone, Mrs. Hammadi started pouring the tea and continued her interrogation.

"You're not a Moslem, but Edward tells me you are going to convert."

Alexandra threw a look at Edward.

"Mother, I told you she is going to convert before we are married and that it will be before my baby is born."

Edward was discussing her as though she were not there, negotiating her identity as if it had nothing to do with her. She had accepted that fact, but hearing the words come from his mouth caused an uncontrollable anger to erupt in her.

"No, I'm not a Moslem, Mrs. Hammadi. And I do not intend to convert." She spoke the words slowly, looking directly at the older woman. The hate in Mrs. Hammadi's eyes made her look away. Mrs. Hammadi was talking down to her because she saw her as nothing but a lowly refugee. And who was Mrs. Hammadi? Alexandra's mind raced on furiously. Hadn't she once been a refugee herself? Alexandra had no idea where her wealth came from, but some Arab factions were benefiting from the Arab struggle. Jamie and his mother were obviously among them.

She was so engrossed in her thoughts that she was startled when a white angora cat jumped into her lap.

"What a beautiful cat," she exclaimed and looked up at Mrs. Hammadi. For a brief moment her features softened. "But then you are surrounded by beautiful things and I don't know why I'm surprised," Alexandra continued, encouraged by the crack in the icy facade and determined to turn the conversation away from her need to convert. "Solange told me what exquisite taste you have."

The mention of Solange caused Mrs. Hammadi to pale.

"Oh, please forgive me," Alexandra said, "I was so sorry to hear she died. And in such a cruel way." She could not understand what motivated her to say the last words.

"Yes, a heart attack at such a young age was most unfortunate."

"Heart attack?" Alexandra repeated, and she realized that Mrs. Hammadi had not been told the truth. "Oh, no. She was shot to death on a Paris street." She was shocked by what she was saying and could not decide whether it was anger at being humiliated by Mrs. Hammadi, or her rage at Edward for placing her in this position that made her do it. But the words were spoken almost as if another mind had taken over her mouth.

The older woman gasped and turned to her son. They stared at each other briefly and then she stood up and ran into the house. Alexandra looked up at Edward. His expression was identical to the one he had the day he broke the child's camera in Sidon. For a moment she thought he was going to strike her. Instead, he turned and ran after his mother.

Left alone, Alexandra felt strangely calm. The outburst had released something within her that had been bottled up for too long. She felt stronger than she had in a long time. The idea of converting was ludicrous. She may have forfeited her rights as an Israeli, but she was Jewish and no one was going to take that away from her. She would give birth to her child and if Edward was not willing to accept her for what she was, she would leave him. She was still young, she was capable. She would find a job in Beirut and make a life for herself and her child.

Without thinking she picked up the newspaper Mrs. Hammadi was reading. It was in Arabic and the headline was in big, bold red letters. She read it absently, her mind still married to thoughts of her future with her child. Suddenly the words of the accompanying news story came into focus.

"Our glorious forces have succeeded in destroying a major spy nest of Zionists on the Mediterranean shore. Our courageous frogmen went ashore before dawn and blew up what appeared to be a solitary, innocent-looking residence but was, in fact, an outpost used to gather information about our forces in southern Lebanon. The house was completely destroyed, killing all who were in it including the woman who ran the network. By coincidence, the woman proved to be a descendant of the infamous spies who in the First World War betrayed our Turkish Moslem brothers . . ."

The words blurred and Alexandra began to scream. The cries were deafening and she felt an excruciating pain in her stomach. She tried to get up. She wanted to run. She remembered nothing after that.

When she woke, she was in a hospital and Edward was leaning over her.

"We've got a beautiful baby boy," he whispered.

The idea of having given birth to a baby made her happy. But that thought was crowded out by another one, more urgent, more real. In her state of half-consciousness, it came to her slowly. Tanya. Tanya was dead, killed by terrorists. Her mind cleared. Who else might have been there? Deborah? Was Deborah dead? Uri? Rachel? Had the terrorists slaughtered her whole family? Frogmen. Edward was a frogman. While he might not have been involved in the raid on Tanya's house, as far as Alexandra was concerned, he was responsible for Tanya's death.

She turned her head to the wall, not wanting him to see her loathing and fear. She also knew that Abu Shara was a liar. Edward was a liar. Their whole movement was a lie.

# CHAPTER FIFTY-NINE

"URI, slow down," Bitti said sharply as the car raced along the highway, heading toward Bet Enav. "You're driving as if someone were chasing you."

Uri pressed his foot on the brake and brought the car down to a cruising speed.

"Sorry," he mumbled. "It's just that I would like to get there. You know how anxious Grandma gets when anyone is late."

"No, I don't know anything of the sort," Bitti said, eyeing him curiously. "You've been a bundle of nerves since early morning and totally unreasoanble. Like demanding Oren join us when he obviously didn't want to go with us. He's fifteen years old and I know he adores Deborah, but you can't force a child to join us for his great-grandmother's eighty-fifth birthday party."

"Why not?" Uri asked. "How many kids get to celebrate an occasion like this? It's an honor, not a burden."

"Is everyone else coming?" Ilan spoke up from the back seat, trying to defuse the argument between his parents.

"I suppose so. It is an event, an incredible event," Uri answered.

"Actually, your father is right." Bitti became conciliatory. Uri was behaving strangely, but he had been for several days and she was concerned. "Although Eli won't be there. Rachel called me yesterday. He had to report to his unit in Haifa and he dropped her and the kids off this morning. Benji and Ruth will obviously be there. Jack and Naomi have been there for several days." She stopped to think. "Daniel, Marian and the kids are driving up from Caesarea and Yariv and Leyanna are coming. It will be a real family reunion."

"I like Leyanna. She's a real beauty," Ilan said. "But I never thought Yariv would marry her."

"Why not?" Uri asked.

"Well, they're different in so many ways."

"Different or not, they're in love and they seem very happy," Bitti said quickly. "As a matter of fact, Leyanna is pregnant. Very early, but pregnant nevertheless."

"Are they married that long?" Uri asked.

"You're impossible, Uri." Bitti laughed. "They've been married for nearly a year."

"Will they go on living in Raphael's house or will they move to her father's settlement?" Ilan asked.

"I think they'll stay in Raphael's house. Tova is fine, but she's almost as old as Deborah, so it's good that Yariv and Leyanna live close by."

"Thank God for little favors," Ilan said. "That settlement of her father's is nothing but trouble."

"Are Leyanna's parents coming?" Uri asked.

"God, I hope not," Ilan said. "Since he's been living in that settlement, he and Jack just can't sit in the same room without getting into a fight. And frankly I agree with Jack all the way. We have no business settling in occupied territories."

"How often do I have to remind you that I wish you'd refer to those territories as disputed territories," Uri said through clenched teeth.

"Let's not start that," Bitti pleaded. "Not today."

"No, I insist that Ilan stop referring to that part of the country as occupied."

"Disputed or occupied, what difference does it make? I just don't see why the hell we have to build new settlements there. It causes so much hostility."

"I'll tell you what the difference is. Those territories were won in a war. They were in Jordanian hands from nineteen forty-eight. Then the Jordanians foolishly joined the Egyptians and Syrians in nineteen sixty-seven, although we warned them not to. They were sure they could push us into the sea and destroy us. Well, they lost that war and it became a disputed area. Now, if they want to discuss the situation with us, we'll gladly sit down and figure out what to do. It's mostly barren land, but today these settlements are flourishing and I assure you we would happily share our prosperity with any Arab who lives around there. So, if we could find someone who would be willing to talk to us, we could probably settle the dispute and there might be no reason for anyone to move."

"But the Arabs don't want us there."

"Ilan, the Arabs don't want us anywhere. And on the rare occasions when they give press releases to the world about how they love Jews, but not Zionists, I feel my skin crawl. Because their actions speak louder than words. Their acts of terrorism prove what they really think. The fact is that they don't want us even in the areas that the world has acknowledged belong to us."

"I'm aware of everything you're saying," Ilan said slowly. "But I can tell you that setting up settlements in their midst certainly doesn't help."

"So what are you suggesting?"

"I'd move out of there. Show good faith. Someone has to, if we're ever going to have peace."

"Peace is a negotiated compromise. As long as they don't acknowledge our existence and refuse to talk to us, we cannot simply walk away. The risks are too great." Uri said grimly. "But let me ask you. If we did take the risk and showed this good faith you're talking about and then they decided to attack us again, what would you do then?"

"We'd fight them, obviously."

"I see that as a prescription for another war and I'm not willing to risk your life and your children's lives needlessly."

"Supposing you let us decide on what our fate will be? You've done all you can and we're grateful, but obviously your methods aren't working anymore."

"Who is this *us?*" Uri asked.

"My generation."

"You're much too young to understand all the ramifications of the situation."

"How old were you when you decided on what was right for you?"

"I'm getting a headache," Bitti said. "Can't we forget politics for a few hours?"

"Done." Uri said.

"Will this party take long?" Ilan asked as the car swung into the main thoroughfare of Bet Enav and they started up the incline toward Deborah's house. "I wasn't going to say anything this morning, but I won't be staying very long. I've got to rejoin my unit this evening."

"Well, I think it's sweet of you to come, even for a couple of hours. As your father said, few young men get a chance to visit with their great-grandmothers, you know." Bitti reached over and pressed his hand affectionately.

"How is Grandma, anyway?"

"She's aged terribly," Uri sighed. "It sort of happened after Tanya's . . ." He paused and cleared his throat. "It's just that every time the family gets together, the missing members are missed more sorely. And it takes its toll on her."

"I guess no one gets used to having their children die before they do," Ilan said.

Uri was shaken by the statement. He stole a look at his older son in his rearview mirror. The boy was in uniform, doing his compulsory army duty. He was a good boy, bright, handsome and independent. He was artistic like Daniel. He played the guitar, wrote songs and wanted to be a writer. But now the peace-loving, antiwar young man would soon be fighting in Lebanon. Could he take losing Ilan?

The war was inevitable. Plans for it had been brewing for quite a while. Tanya's death in a senseless, vicious terrorist attack was, in a way, the turning point. After that, the terrorists became more aggressive and the shelling from

Lebanon had grown intolerable. Uri knew it was coming, was all for going into Lebanon and putting an end to those raids, once and for all. But he had not thought of Ilan when he asked for his opinion. He was thinking as the high-ranking Israeli officer he was, putting his country's safety ahead of personal considerations.

Well, at least this would not be a surprise attack. The whole country was aware that it was coming. He knew that Yariv was leaving to join his unit later in the day. That was why Ilan could only stay a short while, and that was why he was so tense. It could happen any time. He was put on alert and his whereabouts were known every minute of the day and night. His orders were to be no further away than a phone call and within one hour driving distance from his unit.

"I wish Oren had come with us," he said, almost to himself.

The house came into view. In spite of the bright June sun, it seemed to be shrouded in mourning. Uri suppressed a shudder as he swung the car into the driveway. Morbid thoughts were the last thing to bring his grandmother on this day.

Deborah stared aimlessly out of her bedroom window. She was eighty-five years old and she was very tired of living.

Time, everyone always said, healed all wounds. With the passage of time and the shedding of endless tears, the unbearable anguish and despair was slowly replaced by a gnawing emptiness. And then, as awareness of the living began to filter through, one was slowly drawn back to life and was re-infused with a sense of hope for the future. Time had done that for her in the past. This time, it did not happen. Time did not heal. Time made the pain bearable, made it possible to accept another day, but the sense of loss and the knowledge that the void would never be filled was as great now as it had been that morning, three years ago, when she was told that Tanya had been killed. She knew then that there was not enough time left to her to go through the long healing process and come to terms with the enormity of this latest tragedy.

"Why?" she whispered the word into the silent room. "Why?"

She had never questioned the death of any of the people whom she loved. Was it because Tanya's death was so senseless, so brutal?

The sound of children's laughter floated up from the garden. Were those sounds supposed to replace the void? Years back, they would have rejuvenated her, injected a sense of purpose into her soul. They would have forced her to put her pain aside and join the living. Today, the sounds were almost an irritant. The ghosts of the past refused to be drowned out.

She heard the door open and she turned to see Tova walk in. Tova placed a breakfast tray on the small table and the two women stared at each other silently. They did not need to communicate with words. Theirs was a closeness of mutual dependency, nurtured through a lifetime. Deborah stared at the door long after Tova was gone and marvelled at her stamina. Tova would be eighty on her next birthday, and Deborah remembered the young girl from Poland who had come to work for them. It was to be a temporary job. At the time, Deborah felt motherly toward her, hoped she would move on, get married, have a family. Now Tova was treating her like a daughter. Had Tova been cheated by staying with them? Deborah wondered. They had included her in their lives in every way. She shared their joy and sorrow, the good days and the bad days, but was that enough? It wasn't until Michael died that Deborah realized how lonely it must have been for Tova, especially when tragedy came. It struck her first when she knew Alexandra was lost to her. It hit more forcefully when Tanya was killed. Having family and friends helped. But when night fell and she was finally alone, without Michael, that was when the pain was unbearable. Tova had never had a Michael in her life.

Deborah turned back to the window.

Most everyone had arrived. Naomi and Jack were talking to Rachel's daughter, Gila, and Rachel's other little ones were romping about, laughing happily. She looked for Eli. He was nowhere around. Then she remembered. Rachel had told her that Eli was called to Haifa on urgent business. She shook her head. She was becoming forgetful and it bothered her. She looked over at Benji. He had Daniel's youngest boy on his lap and was watching the other three boys playing catch. Deborah heaved a deep sigh. Contrary to her hopes, Benji had grown old without ever growing up. He went from being Michael's son to being a doting grandfather of Daniel's children, since he had none of his own and was not likely to ever have any. He simply bypassed the responsibility of being a productive and independent man. He worked for her, taking care of her properties, but his life was completely taken up with Daniel's family. Briefly she looked at the children. They were healthy, lively boys, dressed in their Sabbath best. She looked for Ruth. She had misjudged her. After Benji's bankruptcy, she had taken charge and they had survived. It was she who forced Benji to sell the house to Deborah when no one else would buy it. Deborah intended to turn it into a convalescent home for wounded soldiers. Daniel spent many months there after he was blinded in the Yom Kippur War. It was there that he started playing the piano again, and Benji's ostentatious house finally came to serve a purpose.

Deborah looked for Daniel and Marian. He was sitting under a shaded tree, listening to his wife and smiling. The cane, resting beside him, was the only indication of his blindness. He had taken it well, never regretted coming to entertain the troops during the 1973 war. He had shown great strength through the years of surgery and had triumphed over his disability.

Deborah looked for Uri and Bitti. They had not yet arrived, but she was sure they would and she was about to turn away from the window when she caught sight of Yariv and Alexandra. She began to tremble when she realized the young woman was Yariv's wife, Leyanna. Deborah felt faint and leaned her head against the window pane. More and more the images of both Tanya and Alexandra were present in her mind. But the girl did look like Alexandra. *Alexandra.* Where was she? Tanya was dead. They had buried her in the Bet Enav cemetery. But no one knew anything about Alexandra. For all she knew, Alexandra could be dead and there was no one to mourn her. She put her hand to her eyes, trying to ease the pain brought on by the thought. She looked back at Yariv and Leyanna. He was in uniform and was leading Leyanna toward Daniel. They were followed by a man in uniform and a woman. For a minute Deborah wondered who they were. Then she remembered. Leyanna's parents. Yoram and Batel Azriel. A handsome couple in their early forties, he was tall, dark and self-assured and his wife, small, pretty, dressed in Oriental fashion, her statement of her Moroccan heritage. How pleased Yanosh and Tanya would have been at this union.

For the first time that morning, Deborah smiled. The dream was taking shape, after all.

At that moment she saw Uri drive up. She stood up and started toward the door. Tanya and Alexandra were gone, but now that Uri was there, the celebration could start.

The speeches, the gifts, the hugs and kisses were done with and Deborah, settled in a large rocking chair on the patio, felt tired.

She had felt strong when she first came down, but confrontation with the exuberance of the younger generation, made her all the more conscious of her physical and emotional frailty.

"Grandma?" Uri said softly.

She looked up and saw him standing with a tall young man in uniform. She realized it was Ilan. Or was it Oren? No, Oren had not come. More and more she'd been confusing people, especially when she was tired. In a way, all the younger ones were strangers to her. She recognized them, but she did have a hard time remembering their names. Those lapses were coming more often and they upset and embarrassed her.

"I've got to run, Grandma," Ilan leaned over and kissed her.

She watched him walk down the path. Bitti and Naomi accompanied him and Deborah saw them reach up and kiss him before he pushed the gate open. Even from a distance, Deborah could feel their concern. How often had she felt that way as she watched her loved ones walk toward their troubled destiny.

Rachel and Marian rounded up the children and wandered off with them. Their voices faded away and a peaceful air settled around her. The sound of Daniel playing the piano came through the open french doors and the remaining guests were sitting around, listening.

Uri threw himself on the floor beside her and took her hand.

"Did you enjoy your party?" he asked.

"Why is everyone in uniform" she asked, ignoring his question.

"Who?" Uri asked innocently.

"Except for you and Ilan, which I understand, why is Yariv? And why is Azriel? And Eli suddenly being called to Haifa on urgent business? He's a doctor and he's needed at home."

"Everyone is needed at home."

"Don't be smart with me, Uri," she said impatiently. "I'm an old woman, but I'm not a fool. Is there going to be another war?"

"We live in a constant state of alert," he answered evasively.

"Uri, something is going on and I wish you'd tell me what it is."

He looked around and then turned back to her.

"Yes, we're going to war again."

"Why?"

Why! That was not the question he expected from her. She was the one who always defended every decision made by the Israeli army.

"Because we've got to stop what's happening near the Lebanese border. The P.L.O. has taken control of the whole area and we've got to push them back, out of range of our homes. The Lebanese are equally unhappy with their situation and they promised to help us in this venture."

"Will it be a full-scale war?" She was as alert as she had been years back.

"It is a war meant to wipe out their enormous military arsenal and we're hoping to dismantle their whole infrastructure, which has become a real threat to us. The Arabs haven't given up the idea of throwing us into the sea. If anything they're more determined than ever to destroy us. We've got no choice."

"And you really believe this war will make the difference?" Deborah asked.

"Why are you being so skeptical?"

"Because I'm always afraid that there might be another motive."

"Our motives are always the same. We fight to make your generation's dream a reality we can live with."

"We dreamed and fought for a homeland. I tremble at the thought that we might get involved in fighting just for land."

"Good God, Grandma. Why would we want to take anything from Lebanon?" Uri asked angrily. "We're fighting the Arabs who want to destroy us and they're doing exactly what they did years back. Except that now they have Syrian missiles pointed at our northern settlements. That's a big difference from what you had to confront. Everything is different. The world is different. Wars are different. The pure dream that you had was replaced by harsh realities. There are different people fighting us. More dangerous. More determined. Far more cruel."

"They're the same people, with the same determination and the same cruelty. What I'm afraid of is that we will be forced to become like them in order to win." She sighed. "The dream is still there, and I don't want the purity to go out of it."

"Better a tarnished dream than no dream at all." Uri stood up, feeling helpless in the face of an old lady who was saying truths he could not cope with. He was a soldier and he knew his duty.

"A tarnished dream is a contradiction in terms," Deborah said, her voice rising in indignation. "To suggest that there can be a tarnished dream is like saying I had a wonderful nightmare." Her raised voice caused Daniel to stop playing and everyone turned their attention to them.

Uri looked from Jack to Naomi, to the Azriels, to Bitti and finally his eyes came to rest on Daniel. His brother had risen and was coming toward him. As he came closer, Uri put out his hand and Daniel caught it and held it.

"I trust you, Uri," Daniel gripped his hand firmly.

# CHAPTER
# SIXTY

T HE march through the southern part of Lebanon went smoothly. The Lebanese Christian forces as well as the civilians greeted the Israelis as saviors. Women and men cheered them on and youngsters threw flowers as they marched by. The Israeli air force suceeded in eliminating the deadly Syrian missiles, which were aimed at Israel, so that the possibility that Syria would join the fighting was also put to rest. The surrounding Arab countries were verbose in their condemnation, but did little in concrete terms to help their Arab brethren. Within days it appeared to Israel that their troops could withdraw to the line they had set as a goal when they first entered Lebanon, according to schedule.

But contrary to the agreement with the Lebanese army, the Lebanese forces did not take up the battle for their own land, thereby enabling the P.L.O. to withdraw to Beirut. It became obvious that the original Israeli aim of destroying the enemy's firepower wouldn't happen and the terrorists would have to have to be pursued to the capital of Lebanon.

Once on the outskirts of Beirut, the Israelis still hoped the newly elected Lebanese prime minister would take control of his army and live up to his commitments. The Israelis had done their share. The P.L.O. was trapped in a defined area in West Beirut and it was simply a matter of the Lebanese taking matters into their own hands. That hope was dashed when the young prime minister was assassinated, just days before his inauguration. It placed the Israelis in a dilemma and they were forced to continue the siege of West Beirut until a new leader in Lebanon could take over.

Uri, standing at the entranceway to his tent, stared down at the Beirut airport. It was a few miles away and he could see a huge sprawling slum beyond it known as Shatilla. He could not see it too clearly, but from a distance it looked like a larger version of the slums that had mushroomed in various parts of Israel, inhabited by Arab refugees. All efforts on the part of the Israeli government to clear those slums had met with resistance, since the P.L.O.

needed to perpetuate them as proof that the people living in them were in "occupied territories."

Uri felt helpless. If he could not explain the difference between *occupied* and *disputed* to his own son, why should an indifferent world understand? Thoughts of Ilan were replaced by Deborah's words. She was fearful that the invasion of Lebanon would turn into an attempt to acquire more land. What was she thinking now, after all this time? How could one explain to a civilian the broken promises of a presumed ally? That, he decided, had been the mistake. Israel had always fought alone. Depending on what appeared to be the most reliable partner was foolhardy.

"I don't understand the Lebanese." He turned back to his fellow officers. "Don't they want their land back? This country was once the gem of the Middle East and now it's lying in rubble, taken over by murderers and self-serving, slogan-wielding tyrants and the Lebanese just sit back waiting to be destroyed."

"The Christians in East Beirut don't seem to feel that," Lester, an American who had immigrated to Israel many years back, said. "They still go about their daily routine, walking through the bullets but leading a normal life. Their nightclubs are booming, the seashore is filled with elegant ladies, the hotels are packed." He smiled. "I was there the other day. They seem to think it will all work out."

"No, they don't," Adam snapped. A dark-haired young man who was part of the regular army, he spoke with authority. "They want us to do it for them. You see, the Lebanese are having a hard time defining who they are. They live like Europeans and they don't like to be referred to as Arabs, but they're too insecure to reject the latter label outright."

"Well, we're not going to do it for them. Although now that their president is dead, it will be even more difficult," Joseph spoke up. "I know I won't go into Beirut proper. That would be a disaster." Joseph, an older man, was a prominent lawyer in civilian life and he lacked the militaristic attitudes of Uri or Adam.

"Oh, yes, you will," Uri said firmly. "If we have to, we all will. It would be madness to have come this far, to have the P.L.O. cornered and just walk away. We started something and we'll have to finish it up. And we won't be doing it for the Lebanese, we'll be doing it for our security."

"The price will be very high," Joseph said. "It will cost many lives. Both of civilians and our own boys."

"Well, let's see what Colonel Sela comes up with." Uri knew Joseph was right and wanted to put an end to their speculations. "He's meeting with the late prime minister's men in Beirut and he'll try to persuade them to get involved, as promised."

A young soldier walked in and handed Uri a large envelope. Uri ripped it open and looked it over quickly. It was a report listing the arms the Israelis had confiscated since entering Lebanon.

"How could they?" he said in disgust. "To store such deadly equipment and explosives under the very houses their civilian populations live in. It's unheard of." He pushed the papers toward Adam. "No civilized people would believe it."

Adam scanned the papers briefly. "That's one of the reasons they do it." He handed the papers to Lester and Joseph. "But it's a fact. I saw it in Tyre, in Sidon and all along the way. And I hear that what they've got in West Beirut, stored in tunnels built under their refugee camps, is enough to blow up the whole Middle East, let alone Israel. But go explain to the world that when we appear to be bombing civilians, we're actually aiming to get rid of those arms."

"Why doesn't anyone take pictures of those stockpiles of arms?" Lester demanded angrily. Although he had lived in Israel for many years, he had never lost his conviction that good public relations was the best weapon. "Let the world know how barbaric the P.L.O. leadership really is. Show how the P.L.O. uses its own people as hostages and shields."

"Pictures of guns, bullets, missiles and all the other deadly weapons are meaningless beside a picture of a crying child, a wailing mother, a forlorn boy searching through rubble that was once his home," Adam answered.

"Well, thank God, we warned the civilians to get out before we entered Tyre and Sidon, so we avoided hurting many of them," Joseph said thoughtfully.

"Really?" Adam interjected sarcastically. "I assure you that no one took a picture of the warning leaflets we dropped." His sarcasm turned to bitterness. "The fact is that after nearly three months, the world is up in arms about our being here, including the Americans."

"What distresses me is that no one understands the size of the countries involved," Uri said angrily. "It takes most Americans longer to drive from their homes to their jobs every day, than it takes to drive from Haifa to Beirut."

"Especially if you consider traffic jams," Lester said with mock seriousness.

The sound of a jeep was heard lumbering up the hill and within minutes Colonel Sela appeared in the doorway. He looked haggard.

"It's hopeless," he announced, entering the tent.

Uri and his men looked at each other. Sela's meeting was crucial.

"Their dead leader was having a hard time deciding on going into West Beirut and finishing off the P.L.O. And with him gone, no one has the power or the nerve."

"What do we do now?" Uri asked.

"We might have to undertake the job ourselves. The P.L.O. is holed up in their tunnels, they're armed to the teeth with weapons, and they have lots of cameras to photograph our so-called brutality."

"It will be a massacre," Joseph whispered.

"The Lebanese know it and that's why they want us to do it," Colonel Sela said.

"I must confess I agree with Joseph," Adam said. "We've suffered casualties throughout this venture just to avoid killing civilians and now we're thinking of going into a civilian area and conquering it? This is Lebanon, not Israel."

"If we have to, we have to," Uri said angrily. "We went into this war with an aim. We've got to demolish the P.L.O., their weapons and that confounded infrastructure, once and for all. We've all seen what they've collected throughout the years and you can't believe they have all that stuff because they're planning on conquering the world. It's aimed at us and God damn it, we've got to destroy them before they destroy us."

"Well, we'll wait to hear from Jerusalem before we do anything," Sela said.

Uri was about to speak when Yariv walked in. He had not seen him since Deborah's birthday and for a second his heart leaped with joy. He started toward him, but stopped when he saw the expression on Yariv's face.

"Uri," Yariv said quietly. "Could I speak to you?"

Uri followed Yariv out.

"Ilan was killed yesterday." Yariv's voice was barely audible.

Uri threw his head back in despair while trying to stifle the cry that rose in his throat. Ilan, his beautiful, peaceful, kind boy, was gone and Uri felt his world had come to an end.

"Is there anything I can do?" Yariv asked.

"No," Uri answered. "I would like to be alone just for a while."

He watched the younger man walk away and he walked to the edge of the cliff, overlooking the airport. Slowly his eyes wandered toward the slum beyond it. How many young men like Ilan would be killed if they attacked that area?

Ilan was buried in the small cemetery outside Givat-Or. He was the first soldier from the village killed in war and the dates on his gravestone summed up the story of his young life.

ILAN STERN
DIED WHILE SERVING HIS COUNTRY
1964–1982

Uri drove away from Givat-Or, heading toward the intersection that would take him back to the Lebanese border. Reaching it, he came to a full stop and looked for oncoming traffic. It was early morning and the road was clear. He started to make a right turn when he changed his mind and turned left. He had to get to Bet Enav. He had to see Deborah. She was the only one he could talk to.

All his convictions, all his beliefs, all his training were a jumbled mass whirling around in his brain. None of it made any sense. His grandmother was the only one who would understand him at this tragic moment. Bitti, his mother, his father—everyone was in a state of shock and he could talk to none of them. Deborah was too weak to come up for the funeral, but somehow he was sure she would not only understand but would be able to help him sort out his confusion.

She was sitting in a hammock on her terrace, wrapped in a shawl, her thinning white hair pulled back, her face set with determination, hands resting in her lap. As he walked toward her, he felt she had been waiting for him.

He settled down beside her and she put her arm through his.

"I can't go back, Grandma," he said after a long silence. "I was given leave for the funeral and I'm expected back, but I can't do it."

"Why?" she asked without moving from him.

"I'll have to order my men to enter a heavily populated area where the P.L.O. hierarchy is entrenched. It's bound to be a total massacre and I can't bring myself to do it."

"Have you been ordered to go in?"

"Not yet. But it looks as though it can't be avoided and I'll have to give that order."

"Your men would follow you." It was a statement, not a question.

He nodded grimly.

"They trust you," she continued thoughtfully. "Daniel trusts you too."

"Maybe if he trusted me less, he wouldn't be blind," Uri said harshly.

"I don't think you can take credit or responsibility for what happened to Daniel. But your men—they're there waiting for you, aren't they?"

"Yes, they are."

She withdrew from him slowly. "And you came here instead of going to them?"

"I can't do it." He sat up and his voice grew firmer. "I thought you'd understand."

"I understand what you're saying. I might even feel as you do, but to desert your men in the middle of a battle?" She shook her head. "No. That I don't understand."

"Ilan's death is haunting me. It would make sense if I were killed. But he was a gentle boy who wanted peace. That's what he spoke about the last time we drove up here. Suddenly it's all so pointless. We bring a child into this world, teach him about democracy, freedom and the pursuit of peace and then, while trying to defend these goals, he's killed. It's makes no sense," he repeated, almost to himself.

"Tanya's death was senseless," Deborah spoke with difficulty. "Ilan died in a war, a war to help preserve what we have. That's different. But his death makes your going back all the more urgent." Her voice grew firmer. "We have children who dream of peace. Somewhere among those people we are fighting, among those killers and destroyers, there must be a boy, a young Ilan, who will stand up and announce, without fear, that he too wants peace."

Then, putting her arm through his, she leaned against him. "Uri, it's not easy for me to send you back there, you must know that. But you must go. I command you to go."

Uri could feel the tension the minute he walked into his tent. His men were sitting around and the expression on their faces were taut with apprehension. Yariv was sitting in a corner, staring into space.

"They entered Shatilla," Adam said when he saw Uri.

"Who?" Uri looked around. "Who entered?" His voice rose.

"The Lebanese who wanted to avenge their prime minister's assassination."

"Who gave them permission?"

"It's their country, Uri," Joseph said.

"Did Sela know they were going in?"

"They sent word that they were planning it. They said it was a mop-up operation to clear the area of the remaining P.L.O. forces."

"So what happened?" Uri found himself screaming.

"They mopped up all right, but they mopped up everything in sight," Yariv answered. "We hear it was a carnage."

"Let's go," Uri turned and ran from the tent. Everyone followed him.

Uri felt numb. He had seen death, had seen savage death. He had seen blood and dismembered bodies on battlefields. He had seen children with their eyes gouged out and pregnant women with bayonettes in their stomachs, but he had never seen what came into view when he started walking through the narrow alleyways of Shatilla. Yariv and Adam were beside him, the rest of his men were walking behind them, searching the area. No one spoke.

The massacre had taken place twenty-four hours earlier and the blood had already begun to cake on the shattered walls. The mud underfoot was red. Ambulances were trying to make their way through the rubble, nurses and doctors were running around trying to get to the wounded who were screaming with pain. Women and children were stumbling over the dead and wounded, searching for their homes, their relatives, looking for food. Seeing the Israelis, they fled into bombed-out ruins, screaming with terror.

"I don't believe this," Yariv finally spoke. "This can't be."

"Oh, but it is," Adam said. "They do it to each other all the time. It's a form of warfare. It's called revenge. They're known for their family feuds, which sometimes go back hundreds of years. And that's how they resolve them. I know, I come from Iraq. I saw it, over and over, as a little boy."

They walked slowly, bayonet drawn, each trying to digest the horror they were witnessing, when suddenly Uri felt Yariv grab his arm.

He swung around and looked at Yariv. The younger man was staring into a bombed-out doorway and Uri followed his gaze.

A woman was crouching on the floor, clutching a child.

"It's Alexandra," Yariv whispered.

She was dressed in black, her face was thin and drawn and covered with soot. A scarf covered her head. Yet Uri recognized her immediately.

"You'd better be careful," Adam called out, as Uri and Yariv started toward her. "She may have a gun under that dress."

Alexandra had seen the Israelis come down the street. She had waited for this moment since the day her son was born. She had fantasized running toward them, explaining who she was and being released from her captivity. But now she hesitated. Would they believe her? Or would she appear to be a frightened, demented Arab woman? That's what she had become in her own eyes, in the eyes of her neighbors, in Edward's eyes.

Sitting among the blood-splattered ruins with her child at her breast, she was paralyzed with fear. It was the same fear she had lived with since the birth of her son three years earlier.

Edward never forgave her for defying him. From the minute she arrived home after the birth, he became the man who crushed and killed everything that stood in his way. He named the boy Tayib without consulting her and saw to it that she was never alone with him. She was ignored, except as the wet nurse and then the nursemaid who cared for his son. When Edward was away, two guards stood outside their door and if she walked out, they followed, guns slung over the shoulders.

Edward was out when the massacre started. Alexandra could hear the women screaming, the children crying, the deafening bursts of gunfire, and she ran to the window. It was night and she could not make out who the attackers were, but she realized that her guards were not there.

Picking up her son, she ran out the back door toward the pine grove.

She had no idea how long she had been there, but when the sounds of horror abated, she walked slowly back to the camp, avoiding her house. That would be the first place Edward would look. She held her boy close to her, trying to protect him from the nightmare. He was so young and to her great sorrow, he had already witnessed too much brutality. Still, she prayed that somehow, someday, he would see a different world from the one Edward was offering him.

Tayib began to cry as she sat down in the doorway. It was late afternoon and she saw some soldiers turn into the street. Everyone fled in fear, leaving the area clear of civilians, but Alexandra realized they were Israelis. She noticed two soldiers start toward her and was wondering if she should talk to them, when she recognized Uri.

Relief and happiness quickly turned to fear. She had betrayed him. She had betrayed her people. How could she explain her actions to him, when she could no longer explain them to herself. Would Uri give her a chance to explain? Would he listen? Would he understand? Would he accept her back? Would he forgive her?

As these thoughts raced through her mind, she pulled the veil over her face and looked around to see if she could still get away. No one would understand. She had no right to expect them to understand, much less forgive.

Tayib, sensing her confusion, began to wail.

"It's all right, my precious," she whispered. "We'll be all right."

"Alexandra?" She heard Uri call her name.

She closed her eyes. The voice was that of her beloved cousin and he did not sound angry. Still, she dared not look up.

Uri leaned over and, putting his hand under her chin, he raised her face to his. Then, with great care, he removed the scarf.

His beautiful cousin had grown old. Her face was lined, her full, sensuous lips were dried and cracked, and her eyes, staring at him, were vacant.

"My poor Alexandra," he said, trying to keep the shock out of his voice.

Tayib's cries grew louder.

"Let me hold him," someone said, and Alexandra's eyes darted toward the person who spoke.

"Yariv," the young man said. "Alexandra, it's Yariv." As he spoke he reached over toward Tayib, who was now clinging to her frantically.

"He's our friend," she whispered to her son and, releasing him, she watched Yariv kneel down and gently stroke her boy's hair. For a minute the boy still clung to her and she realized that Edward, although he loved his son, never played with him, never stroked him, never kissed him, was never gentle with him. "He's our friend" she repeated and pushed him gently toward Yariv.

"What's his name?" Yariv asked, picking the child up in his arms.

"His father calls him Tayib. I call him Natanyahu." She tried to smile. "I felt he was my gift from God."

"I think we'd better get out of here," Uri said.

Alexandra stood up and looked around furtively. "Take the boy and walk ahead. I'll follow in a minute," she whispered.

"Don't you want to come with us?" Uri asked.

"Oh my God." She reached up and touched his face. "That's all I've dreamed about for . . ."

"You dirty Jewess," someone screamed.

Alexandra turned and saw Edward aiming a gun in her direction.

A burst of gunfire drowned out her cry as the bullets ripped through her and she sank to the ground.

The soldiers returned the fire and Edward fell over dead.

# CHAPTER
# SIXTY-ONE

D EBORAH scanned the empty beach. It was late September and as the sun
began to set, the heat of day was slowly being swept away by a breeze
coming down from Mount Carmel.

A peal of laughter made her look around. A red-headed girl was sitting close
to the water's edge, with a dark-haired boy beside her.

She squinted, trying to see their faces more clearly. Was it Naomi? She
dismissed the thought angrily. The girl was Gila and the boy was Natanyahu
and they were absorbed in building a sand castle.

Natanyahu. Yariv had told her that Alexandra considered the boy a gift
from God. To Deborah, he was a gift from Alexandra. Having him helped
diminish the pain of Alexandra's death. His arrival in her home had reignited
that old flame of hope that she was sure was gone from her forever.

She heard him laugh and her heart swelled with happiness. How resilient
he was, she thought. How quickly he adjusted to his new life. He had been
with them for only a month, but he seemed to have settled in and had become
part of their lives as though he'd been with them always.

She looked up at the mountains. She knew there were towns and farms and
highways that had been built over the years, but her failing sight saw none of
it. To her the mountains appeared as she remembered them all those years
back. Slowly her eyes wandered along the peaks and slopes and came to rest
on a green vineyard. Beyond it she saw a speck of a red-shingled roof nestling
in a valley. Then, closer to the shore, she saw two rows of palm trees and a
small house. She smiled. That would be Raphael's laboratory.

The present blended into the past.

She was fifteen and she was watching Raphael and Tamar ride away toward
the Crusaders' Castle and she was afraid. She forced herself to look in its
direction. It was partially hidden by the evening mist, and it was dark, formidable and gloomy.

She strained to see Tamar and Raphael. She could barely make them out.
They were a small speck on the horizon and she grew impatient. Then she saw

a swirl of sand rise up and she breathed a sigh of relief. They were on their way back. As they came closer, she realized there were four riders coming toward her. Two Arabs were galloping behind Raphael and Tamar. She wanted to cry out, warn her brother and sister of the danger, but no sound came.

"Yariv is coming." Natanyahu's voice broke into the vivid memory.

The dust began to settle, the horsemen disappeared and were replaced by a jeep racing along the shore line. It came to an abrupt stop and Yariv jumped out and rushed over to her.

"They're home, Grandma. Leyanna and the baby are home and they're waiting for you."

Deborah looked down at the tiny, blond infant lying in her cradle. Leyanna was standing beside Yariv, looking at her expectantly. The Azriels were watching her and she could feel Natanyahu's hand clutching hers.

"Would you name her, Grandma?" Yariv asked.

This infant was Tamar's great-great granddaughter. This little girl was the embodiment of the dream. This child was the proof that the eternity of Israel did not lie.

"Nili," she said slowly. "This little one is our Nili." Then, looking down at Natanyahu, she continued softly. "Touch your little cousin, Natanyahu."

He hid his face in her skirt.

"There's nothing to be afraid of," she said and, taking his hand in hers, she placed it gently on the baby's cheek. His fingers relaxed and with extraordinary gentleness, he traced the outline of fair, almost transparent skin of the newborn baby. Then looking up at her, he smiled.

"She's beautiful," he whispered.

Deborah felt her eyes mist. Her ancient, veined hand, was resting beside Natanyahu's young one, both touching Nili. She had lived to touch the future. She had lived to touch the dream.